PRINCESS IN THE MAKING

BY
MICHELLE CELMER

MILLS &
BOON

Published in Great Britain 2013
by Mills & Boon, an imprint of Harlequin (UK) Limited,
Eton House, 18-24 Paradise Road, Richmond, Surrey TW9 1SR

© Michelle Celmer 2012

ISBN: 978 0 263 90447 5
ebook ISBN: 978 1 472 00043 9

51-0113

Harlequin (UK) policy is to use papers that are natural, renewable and recyclable products and made from wood grown in sustainable forests. The logging and manufacturing processes conform to the legal environmental regulations of the country of origin.

Printed and bound in Spain
by Blackprint CPI, Barcelona

"I thought you wanted you a chance," he said.

But why the sudden change of heart? She couldn't escape the feeling that he was up to something. "Of course I do. You just didn't seem too thrilled with the idea."

"My father thinks it would be a good idea for us to get to know one another, and has asked me to be your companion in his absence. I'm to show you and your daughter a good time, keep you entertained."

Oh no, what had Gabriel done? She wanted Marcus to give her a chance, but not by force. That would only make him resent her more. Not to mention that she hadn't anticipated him being so...

Something.

Something that made her trip over her own feet and stumble over her words and do stupid things... like stare at his bare chest.

Dear Reader,

My office is currently under construction, so I'm sitting at my temporary desk (which today is my bed) wondering what I should write about. And feeling, unfortunately, quite uninspired. So I've decided to do another "About Michelle" letter.

Like everyone, I have quirks. Here are a few that my husband has so graciously pointed out for me...

If someone asks me a question, any question, and I don't know the answer, I have to look it up online. And I mean, that very second or it will drive me crazy. I honestly don't know how I managed all those years without Google, or maybe Google is to blame for my obsession. Who knows.

I'm impulsive. Once I make up my mind that I want to do or buy something, I want it *now*. And until I have it/ have done it, I'm obsessed. It's all I can think about. I will spend hours and hours online, searching articles and reviews, looking for the best deal. The internet is my enabler.

And last but not least, I have a *horrible* memory. Tell me your name, and five minutes later I will have forgotten it. I'll forget what I'm saying halfway through a sentence. I'll walk into a room to do something and completely forget why I'm there. I know there are nifty methods to improve memory, which I could probably look up on Google, but...

I'm sorry, what was I saying?

Michelle

Bestselling author **Michelle Celmer** lives in southeastern Michigan with her husband, their three children, two dogs and two cats. When she's not writing or busy being a mom, you can find her in the garden or curled up with a romance novel. And if you twist her arm really hard, you can usually persuade her into a day of power shopping

Michelle loves to hear from readers. Visit her website, www.michellecelmer.com, or write her at PO Box 300, Clawson, MI 48017, USA.

To Patti, who has been an invaluable source of
support through some rough times.

One

From a mile in the air, the coast of Varieo, with its crystal blue ocean and pristine sandy beaches, looked like paradise.

At twenty-four, Vanessa Reynolds had lived on more continents and in more cities than most people visited in a lifetime—typical story for an army brat—but she was hoping that this small principality on the Mediterranean coast would become her forever home.

"This is it, Mia," she whispered to her six-month-old daughter, who after spending the majority of the thirteen-hour flight alternating between fits of restless sleep and bouts of screaming bloody murder, had finally succumbed to sheer exhaustion and now slept peacefully in her car seat. The plane made its final descent to the private airstrip where they would be greeted by Gabriel, Vanessa's... it seemed silly and a little juvenile to call him her boyfriend, considering he was fifty-six. But he wasn't exactly her fiancé either. At least, not yet. When he asked her to marry him she hadn't said yes, but she hadn't said no either. That's what this visit would determine, if she wanted to marry a man who was not only thirty-two years her senior and lived halfway around the world, but a *king*.

She gazed out the window, and as the buildings below grew larger, nervous kinks knotted her insides.

Vanessa, what have you gotten yourself into this time?

That's what her father would probably say if she'd had the guts to tell him the truth about this visit. He would tell her that she was making another huge mistake. And, okay, so maybe she hadn't exactly had the best luck with men since...well, *puberty*. But this time it was different.

Her best friend Jessy had questioned her decision as well. "He seems nice now," she'd said as she sat on Vanessa's bed, watching her pack, "but what if you get there and he turns out to be an overbearing tyrant?"

"So I'll come home."

"What if he holds you hostage? What if he forces you to marry him against your will? I've heard horror stories. They treat women like second-class citizens."

"That's the other side of the Mediterranean. Varieo is on the European side."

Jessy frowned. "I don't care, I still don't like it."

It's not as if Vanessa didn't realize she was taking a chance. In the past this sort of thing had backfired miserably, but Gabriel was a real gentleman. He genuinely cared about her. He would never steal her car and leave her stranded at a diner in the middle of the Arizona desert. He wouldn't open a credit card in her name, max it out and decimate her good credit. He wouldn't pretend to like her just so he could talk her into writing his American history term paper then dump her for a cheerleader.

And he certainly would never knock her up then disappear and leave her and his unborn child to fend for themselves.

The private jet hit a pocket of turbulence and gave a violent lurch, jolting Mia awake. She blinked, her pink bottom lip began to tremble, then she let out an ear-piercing wail that only intensified the relentless throb in Vanessa's temples.

"Shh, baby, it's okay," Vanessa cooed, squeezing her chubby fist. "We're almost there."

The wheels of the plane touched down and Vanessa's heart climbed up into her throat. She was nervous and excited and relieved, and about a dozen other emotions too jumbled to sort out. Though they had chatted via Skype almost daily since Gabriel left Los Angeles, she hadn't been face-to-face with him in nearly a month. What if he took one look at her rumpled suit, smudged eyeliner and stringy, lifeless hair and sent her right back to the U.S.?

That's ridiculous, she assured herself as the plane bumped along the runway to the small, private terminal owned by the royal family. She had no illusions about how the first thing that had attracted Gabriel to her in the posh Los Angeles hotel where she worked as an international hospitality agent was her looks. Her beauty—as well as her experience living abroad—was what landed her the prestigious position at such a young age. It had been an asset and, at times, her Achilles' heel. But Gabriel didn't see her as arm dressing. They had become close friends. Confidants. He loved her, or so he claimed, and she had never known him to be anything but a man of his word.

There was just one slight problem. Though she respected him immensely and loved him as a friend, she couldn't say for certain if she was *in love* with him—a fact Gabriel was well aware of. Hence the purpose of this extended visit. He felt confident that with time—six weeks to be exact, since that was the longest leave she could take from work—Vanessa would grow to love him. He was sure that they would share a long and happy life together. And the sanctity of marriage was not something that Gabriel took lightly.

His first marriage had spanned three decades, and he claimed it would have lasted at least three more if cancer hadn't snatched his wife from him eight months ago.

Mia wailed again, fat tears spilling down her chubby, flushed cheeks. The second the plane rolled to a stop Vanessa turned on her cell phone and sent Jessy a brief text, so when she woke up she would know they had arrived safely. She then unhooked the straps of the plush, designer car seat Gabriel had provided and lifted her daughter out. She hugged Mia close to her chest, inhaling that sweet baby scent.

"We're here, Mia. Our new life starts right now."

According to her father, Vanessa had turned exercising poor judgment and making bad decisions into an art form, but things were different now. *She* was different, and she had her daughter to thank for that. Enduring eight months of pregnancy alone had been tough, and the idea of an infant counting on her for its every need had scared the crap out of her. There had been times when she wasn't sure she could do it, if she was prepared for the responsibility, but the instant she laid eyes on Mia, when the doctor placed her in Vanessa's arms after a grueling twenty-six hours of labor, she fell head over heels in love. For the first time in her life, Vanessa felt she finally had a purpose. Taking care of her daughter, giving her a good life, was now her number one priority.

What she wanted more than anything was for Mia to have a stable home with two parents, and marrying Gabriel would assure her daughter privileges and opportunities beyond Vanessa's wildest dreams. Wouldn't that be worth marrying a man who didn't exactly...well, *rev her engine?* Wasn't respect and friendship more important anyway?

Vanessa peered out the window just in time to see a limo pull around the building and park a few hundred feet from the plane.

Gabriel, she thought, with equal parts relief and excitement. He'd come to greet her, just as he'd promised.

The flight attendant appeared beside her seat, gesturing to the carry-on, overstuffed diaper bag and purse in a pile at Vanessa's feet. "Ms. Reynolds, can I help you with your things?"

"That would be fantastic," Vanessa told her, raising her voice above her daughter's wailing. She grabbed her purse and hiked it over her shoulder while the attendant grabbed the rest, and as Vanessa rose from her seat for the first time in several hours, her cramped legs screamed in protest. She wasn't one to lead an idle lifestyle. Her work at the hotel kept her on her feet eight to ten hours a day, and Mia kept her running during what little time they had to spend together. There were diaper changes and fixing bottles, shopping and laundry. On a good night she might manage a solid five hours of sleep. On a bad night, hardly any sleep at all.

When she met Gabriel she hadn't been out socially since Mia was born. Not that she hadn't been asked by countless men at the hotel—clients mostly—but she didn't believe in mixing business with pleasure, or giving the false impression that her *hospitality* extended to the bedroom. But when a king asked a girl out for drinks, especially one as handsome and charming as Gabriel, it was tough to say no. And here she was, a few months later, starting her life over. Again.

Maybe.

The pilot opened the plane door, letting in a rush of hot July air that carried with it the lingering scent of the ocean. He nodded sympathetically as Mia howled.

Vanessa stopped at the door and looked back to her seat. "Oh, shoot, I'm going to need the car seat for my daughter."

"I'll take care of it, ma'am," the pilot assured her, with a thick accent.

She thanked him and descended the steps to the tarmac, so relieved to be on steady ground she could have dropped to her knees and kissed it.

The late morning sun burned her scalp and stifling heat drifted up from the blacktop as the attendant led her toward the limo. As they approached, the driver stepped out and walked around to the back door. He reached for the handle, and the door swung open, and Vanessa's pulse picked up double time. Excitement buzzed through her as one expensive looking shoe—Italian, she was guessing—hit the pavement, and as its owner unfolded himself from the car she held her breath...then let it out in a whoosh of disappointment. This man had the same long, lean physique and chiseled features, the deep-set, expressive eyes, but he was *not* Gabriel.

Even if she hadn't done hours of research into the country's history, she would have known instinctively that the sinfully attractive man walking toward her was Prince Marcus Salvatora, Gabriel's son. He looked exactly like the photos she'd seen of him—darkly intense, and far too serious for a man of only twenty-eight. Dressed in gray slacks and a white silk shirt that showcased his olive complexion and crisp, wavy black hair, he looked more like a *GQ* cover model than a future leader.

She peered around him to the interior of the limo, hoping to see someone else inside, but it was empty. Gabriel had promised to meet her, but he hadn't come.

Tears of exhaustion and frustration burned her eyes. She *needed* Gabriel. He had a unique way of making her feel as though everything would be okay. She could only imagine what his son would think of her if she dissolved into tears right there on the tarmac.

Never show weakness. That's what her father had drilled into her for as long as Vanessa could remember. So she took a deep breath, squared her shoulders and greeted the prince with a confident smile, head bowed, as was the custom in his country.

"Miss Reynolds," he said, reaching out to shake her hand. She switched Mia, whose wails had dulled to a soft whimper, to her left hip to free up her right hand, which in the blazing heat was already warm and clammy.

"Your highness, it's a pleasure to finally meet you," she said. "I've heard so much about you."

Too many men had a mushy grip when it came to shaking a woman's hand, but Marcus clasped her hand firmly, confidently, his palm cool and dry despite the temperature, his dark eyes pinned on hers. It lasted so long, and he studied her so intensely, she began to wonder if he intended to challenge her to an arm wrestling match or a duel or something. She had to resist the urge to tug her hand free as perspiration rolled from under her hair and beneath the collar of her blouse, and when he finally did relinquish his grip, she experienced a strange buzzing sensation where his skin had touched hers.

It's the heat, she rationalized. And how did the prince appear so cool and collected when she was quickly becoming a soggy disaster?

"My father sends his apologies," he said in perfect English, with only a hint of an accent, his voice deep and velvety smooth and much like his father's. "He was called out of the country unexpectedly. A family matter."

Out of the *country?* Her heart sank. "Did he say when he would be back?"

"No, but he said he would be in touch."

How could he leave her to fend for herself in a palace full of strangers? Her throat squeezed tight and her eyes burned.

You are not going to cry, she scolded herself, biting the inside of her cheek to stem the flow of tears threatening to leak out. If she had enough diapers and formula to make the trip back to the U.S., she might have been tempted to hop back on the plane and fly home.

Mia wailed pitifully and Marcus's brow rose slightly.

"This is Mia, my daughter," she said.

Hearing her name, Mia lifted her head from Vanessa's shoulder and turned to look at Marcus, her blue eyes wide with curiosity, her wispy blond hair clinging to her tearstained cheeks. She didn't typically take well to strangers, so Vanessa braced herself for the wailing to start again, but instead, she flashed Marcus a wide, two-toothed grin that could melt the hardest of hearts. Maybe he looked enough like his father, whom Mia adored, that she instinctively trusted him.

As if it were infectious, Marcus couldn't seem to resist smiling back at her, and the subtle lift of his left brow, the softening of his features—and, oh gosh, he even had dimples—made Vanessa feel the kind of giddy pleasure a woman experienced when she was attracted to a man. Which, of course, both horrified and filled her with guilt. What kind of depraved woman felt physically attracted to her future son-in-law?

She must have been more tired and overwrought than she realized, because she clearly wasn't thinking straight.

Marcus returned his attention to her and the smile disappeared. He gestured to the limo, where the driver was securing Mia's car seat in the back. "Shall we go?"

She nodded, telling herself that everything would be okay. But as she slid into the cool interior of the car, she couldn't help wondering if this time she was in way over her head.

She was even worse than Marcus had imagined.

Sitting across from her in the limo, he watched his new rival, the woman who, in a few short weeks, had managed to bewitch his grieving father barely eight months after the queen's death.

At first, when his father gave him the news, Gabriel thought he had lost his mind. Not only because he had fallen for an American, but one so young, that he barely knew. But now, seeing her face-to-face, there was little question as to why the king was so taken with her. Her silky, honey-blond hair was a natural shade no stylist, no matter how skilled, could ever reproduce. She had the figure of a gentlemen's magazine pinup model and a face that would inspire the likes of da Vinci or Titian.

When she first stepped off the plane, doe-eyed and dazed, with a screaming infant clutched to her chest, his hope was that she was as empty-headed as the blonde beauties on some of those American reality shows, but then their eyes met, and he saw intelligence in their smoky gray depths. And a bit of desperation.

Though he hated himself for it, she looked so disheveled and exhausted, he couldn't help but feel a little sorry for her. But that didn't change the fact that she was the enemy.

The child whimpered in her car seat, then let out a wail so high-pitched his ears rang.

"It's okay, sweetheart," Miss Reynolds cooed, holding her baby's tiny clenched fist. Then she looked across the car to Marcus. "I'm so sorry. She's usually very sweet natured."

He had always been fond of children, though he much preferred them when they smiled. He would have children one day. As sole heir, it was his responsibility to carry on the Salvatora legacy.

But that could change, he reminded himself. With a pretty young wife his father could have more sons.

The idea of his father having children with a woman like her sat like a stone in his belly.

Miss Reynolds reached into one of the bags at her feet, pulled out a bottle with what looked to be juice in it and handed it to her daughter. The child popped it into her mouth and suckled for several seconds, then made a face and lobbed the bottle at the floor, where it hit Marcus's shoe.

"I'm so sorry," Miss Reynolds said again, as her daughter began to wail. The woman looked as if she wanted to cry, too.

He picked the bottle up and handed it to her.

She reached into the bag for a toy and tried distracting the baby with that, but after several seconds it too went airborne, this time hitting his leg. She tried a different toy with the same result.

"Sorry," she said.

He retrieved both toys and handed them back to her.

They sat for several minutes in awkward silence, then she said, "So, are you always this talkative?"

He had nothing to say to her, and besides, he would have to shout to be heard over the infant's screaming.

When he didn't reply, she went on nervously, "I can't tell you how much I've looked forward to coming here. And meeting you. Gabriel has told me so much about you. And so much about Varieo."

He did not share her enthusiasm, and he wouldn't pretend to be happy about this. Nor did he believe even for a second that she meant a word of what she said. It didn't take a genius to figure out why she was here, that she was after his father's vast wealth and social standing.

She tried the bottle again, and this time the baby took it. She suckled for a minute or two then her eyelids began to droop.

"She didn't sleep well on the flight," Miss Reynolds said, as though it mattered one way or another to him. "Plus, everything is unfamiliar. I imagine it will take some time for her to adjust to living in a new place."

"Her father had no objection to you moving his child to a different country?" he couldn't help asking.

"Her father left us when he found out I was pregnant. I haven't seen or heard from him since."

"You're divorced?"

She shook her head. "We were never married."

Marvelous. And just one more strike against her. Divorce was bad enough, but a child out of wedlock? What in heaven's name had his father been thinking? And did he honestly believe that Marcus would ever approve of someone like that, or welcome her into the family?

His distaste must have shown in his face, because Miss Reynolds looked him square in the eyes and said, "I'm not ashamed of my past, your highness. Though the circumstances may not have been ideal, Mia is the best thing that has ever happened to me. I have no regrets."

Not afraid to speak her mind, was she? Not necessarily an appropriate attribute for a future queen. Though he couldn't deny that his mother had been known to voice her own very potent opinions, and in doing so had been a role model for young women. But there was a fine line between being principled and being irresponsible. And the idea that this woman would even think that she could hold herself to the standards the queen had set, that she could replace her, made him sick to his stomach.

Marcus could only hope that his father would come to his senses before it was too late, before he did something ridiculous, like *marry* her. And as much as he would like to wash his hands of the situation that very instant, he had promised his father that he would see that she was settled in, and he was a man of his word. To Marcus, honor was not only a virtue, but an obligation. His mother had taught him that. Although even he had limits.

"Your past," he told Miss Reynolds, "is between you and my father."

"But you obviously have some strong opinions about it. Maybe you should try getting to know me before you pass judgment."

He leaned forward and locked eyes with her, so there was no question as to his sincerity. "I wouldn't waste my time."

She didn't even flinch. She held his gaze steadily, her smoky eyes filled with a fire that said she would not be intimidated, and he felt a twinge of…something. An emotion that seemed to settle somewhere between hatred and lust.

It was the lust part that drew him back, hit him like a humiliating slap in the face.

And Miss Reynolds had the audacity to *smile*. Which both infuriated and fascinated him.

"Okay," she said with a shrug of her slim shoulders. Did she not believe him, or was it that she just didn't care?

Either way, it didn't make a difference to him. He would tolerate her presence for his father's sake, but he would never accept her.

Feeling an unease to which he was not accustomed, he pulled out his cell phone, dismissing her. For the first time since losing the queen to cancer, his father seemed truly happy, and Marcus would never deny him that. And only because he believed it would never last.

With any luck his father would come to his senses and send her back from where she came before it was too late.

Two

This visit was going from bad to worse.

Vanessa sat beside her sleeping daughter, dread twisting her stomach into knots. Marcus, it would seem, had already made up his mind about her. He wasn't even going to give her a chance, and the idea of being alone with him until Gabriel returned made the knots tighten.

In hindsight, confronting him so directly probably hadn't been her best idea ever. She'd always had strong convictions, but she'd managed, for the most part, to keep them in check. But that smug look he'd flashed her, the arrogance that seemed to ooze from every pore, had raked across her frayed nerves like barbed wire. Before she could think better of it, her mouth was moving and words were spilling out.

She stole a glance at him, but he was still focused on his phone. On a scale of one to ten he was a solid fifteen in the looks department. Too bad he didn't have the personality to match.

Listen to yourself.

She gave her head a mental shake. She had known the man a total of ten minutes. Was she unfairly jumping to conclusions, judging him without all the facts? And in doing so, was she no better than him?

Yes, he was acting like a jerk, but maybe he had a good reason. If her own father announced his intention to marry a much younger woman whom Vanessa had never even met, she would be wary too. But if he were a filthy rich king to boot, she would definitely question the woman's motives. Marcus was probably just concerned for his father, as any responsible son should be. And she couldn't let herself forget that he'd lost his mother less than a year ago. Gabriel had intimated that Marcus had taken her death very hard. He was probably still hurting, and maybe thought she was trying to replace the queen, which could not be further from the truth.

Looking at it that way made her feel a little better.

But what if he disliked her so much that he tried to come between her and Gabriel? Did she want to go through life feeling like an intruder in her own home? Or would it never feel like home to her?

Was this just another huge mistake?

Her heart began to pound and she forced herself to take a deep breath and relax. She was getting way ahead of herself. She didn't even know for certain that she wanted to marry Gabriel. Wasn't that the whole point of this trip? She could still go home if things didn't work out. Six weeks was a long time, and a lot could happen between now and then. For now she wouldn't let herself worry about it, or let it dash her excitement. She was determined to make the best of this, and if it didn't work out, she could chalk it up to another interesting experience and valuable life lesson.

She smiled to herself, a feeling of peace settling over her, and gazed out the window as the limo wound its way through the charming coastal village of Bocas, where shops, boutiques and restaurants lined cobblestone streets crowded with tourists. As they pulled up the deep slope to the front gates of the palace, in the distance she could see the packed public beach and harbor where everything from sailboats and yachts to a full-size cruise ship were docked.

She'd read that the coastal tourist season stretched from April through November, and in the colder months the tourist trade moved inland, into the mountains, where snowboarding and skiing were the popular activities. According to Gabriel, much of the nation's economy relied on tourism, which had taken a financial hit the last couple of years.

The gates swung open as they approached and when the palace came into view, Vanessa's breath caught. It looked like an oasis with its Roman architecture, sprawling fountains, green rolling lawns and lush gardens.

Things were definitely starting to look up.

She turned to Marcus, who sat across from her looking impatient, as though he couldn't wait to be out of the car and rid of her.

"Your home is beautiful," she told him.

He glanced over at her. "Had you expected otherwise?"

Way to be on the defensive, dude. "What I meant was, the photos I've seen don't do it justice. Being here in person is really a thrill."

"I can only imagine," he said, with barely masked sarcasm.

Hell, who was she kidding, he didn't even *try* to mask it. He really wasn't going to cut her a break, was he?

She sighed inwardly as they pulled up to the expansive marble front steps bracketed by towering white columns. At eighty thousand square feet the palace was larger than the White House, yet only a fraction of the size of Buckingham Palace.

The instant the door opened, Marcus was out of the car, leaving it to the driver to help Vanessa with her things. She gathered Mia, who was still out cold, into her arms and followed after Marcus, who stood waiting for her just inside the massive, two-story high double doors.

The interior was just as magnificent as the exterior, with a massive, circular foyer decorated in creamy beiges with marble floors polished to a gleaming shine. A ginormous crystal chandelier hung in the center, sparkling like diamonds in the sunshine streaming through windows so tall they met the domed ceiling. Hugging both sides of the curved walls, grand staircases with wrought iron railings branched off to the right and the left and wound up to the second floor. In the center of it all sat a large, intricately carved marble table with an enormous arrangement of fresh cut exotic flowers, whose sweet fragrance scented the air. The impression was a mix of tradition and modern sophistication. Class and a bit of excess.

Only then, as Vanessa gazed around in wonder, did the reality of her situation truly sink in. Her head spun and her heart pounded. This amazing place could be her home. Mia could grow up here, have the best of everything, and even more important than that, a man who would accept her as his own daughter. That alone was like a dream come true.

She wanted to tell Marcus how beautiful his home was, and how honored she felt to be there, but knew it would probably earn her another snotty response, so she kept her mouth shut.

From the hallway that extended past the stairs, a line of

nearly a dozen palace employees filed into the foyer and Marcus introduced her. Celia, the head housekeeper, was a tall, stern-looking woman dressed in a starched gray uniform, her silver hair pulled back into a tight bun. Her three charges were similarly dressed, but younger and very plain looking. No makeup, no jewelry, identical bland expressions.

Vanessa smiled and nodded to each one in turn.

"This is Camille," Celia told her in English, in a flat tone that perfectly matched her dour expression, signaling for the youngest of the three to step forward. "She will be your personal maid for the duration of your stay."

Duration of her stay? Were they anticipating that she wouldn't be sticking around? Or more to the point, hoping she wouldn't?

"It's nice to meet you, Camille," she said with a smile, offering her hand.

Looking a little nervous, the young woman took it, her eyes turned downward, and with a thick accent said, "Ma'am."

The butler, George, wore tails and a starched, high collar. He was skin and bones with a slight slouch, and looked as though he was fast approaching the century mark…if he hadn't hit it already. His staff consisted of two similarly dressed assistants, both young and capable looking, plus a chef and baker, a man and a woman, dressed in white, and each looking as though they frequently tested the cuisine.

Marcus turned to George and gestured to the luggage the driver had set inside the door. Without a word the two younger men jumped into action.

A smartly dressed middle-aged woman stepped forward and introduced herself as Tabitha, the king's personal secretary.

"If there is anything you need, don't hesitate to ask,"

she said in perfect English, her expression blank. Then she gestured to the young woman standing beside her, who wore a uniform similar to those of the maids. "This is Karin, the nanny. She will take care of your daughter."

Vanessa was a little uncomfortable with the idea of a total stranger watching her baby, but she knew Gabriel would never expose Mia to someone he didn't trust implicitly.

"It's very nice to meet you," Vanessa said, resisting the urge to ask the young woman to list her credentials.

"Ma'am," she said, nodding politely.

"Please, call me Vanessa. In fact, I've never been one to stand on formality. Everyone should feel free to use my first name."

The request received no reaction whatsoever from the staff. No one even cracked a smile. Were they always so deadpan, or did they simply not like her? Had they decided, as Marcus had, that she wasn't to be trusted?

That would truly suck. And she would have to work extra hard to prove them wrong.

Marcus turned to her. "I'll show you to your quarters."

Without waiting for a reply, he swiveled and headed up the stairs to the left, at a pace so brisk she nearly had to jog to keep up with him.

Unlike the beige theme of the foyer, the second floor incorporated rich hues of red, orange and purple, which personally she never would have chosen, but it managed to look elegant without being too gaudy.

Marcus led her down a long, carpeted hall.

"So, is the staff always so cheerful?" she asked him.

"It's not enough that they'll cater to your every whim," Marcus said over his shoulder. "They have to be happy about it?"

With a boss who clearly didn't like her, why would they?

At the end of the hallway they turned right and he opened the first door on his left. Gabriel told her that she would be staying in the largest of the guest suites, but she hadn't anticipated just how large it would be. The presidential suite at the hotel where she worked paled in comparison. The main room was big and spacious with high ceilings and tall windows that bracketed a pair of paned French doors. The color scheme ran to muted shades of green and yellow.

There was a cozy sitting area with overstuffed, comfortable-looking furniture situated around a massive fireplace. There was also a dining alcove, and a functional desk flanked by built-in bookcases whose shelves were packed with hardback books and knickknacks.

"It's lovely," she told Marcus. "Yellow is my favorite color."

"The bedroom is that way." Marcus gestured toward the door at the far end of the suite.

She crossed the plush carpet to the bedroom and peeked inside, her breath catching. It was pure luxury with its white four-poster king-size bed, another fireplace and a huge, wall-mounted flat screen television. But she didn't see the crib Gabriel had promised.

The weight of her sleeping daughter was starting to make her arms ache, so she very gently laid Mia down in the center of the bed and stacked fluffy pillows all around her, in case she woke up and rolled over. She didn't even stir.

On her way back to the living area Vanessa peered inside the walk-in closet where her bags were waiting for her, and found that it was large enough to hold a dozen of her wardrobes. The bathroom, with its soaking tub and glass-enclosed shower, had every modern amenity known to man.

She stepped back into the living space to find Marcus standing by the door, arms crossed, checking his watch impatiently.

"There's no place for Mia to sleep," she told him, and at his blank expression added, "Gabriel said there would be a crib for her. She moves around a lot in her sleep, so putting her in a normal bed, especially one so high off the ground, is out of the question."

"There's a nursery down the hall."

There was an unspoken "duh" at the end of that sentence.

"Then I hope there's a baby monitor I can use. Otherwise, how will I hear her if she wakes in the middle of the night?" Though Mia slept through most nights, Vanessa was still accustomed to the random midnight diaper changes and feedings, and an occasional bad dream.

He looked puzzled. "That would be the responsibility of the *nanny*."

Right, the nanny. Vanessa had just assumed the nanny was there for the times when Mia needed a babysitter, not as a full-time caregiver. She wasn't sure how she felt about that. Vanessa worked such long hours, and was away from home often. Part of this trip was about spending more time with her daughter.

"And where does the nanny sleep?" she asked Marcus.

"Her bedroom is attached to the nursery," he said, in a tone that suggested she was asking stupid questions. In his world it was probably perfectly natural for the staff to take full responsibility for the children's care, but she didn't live in his world. Not even close. Surely he knew that, didn't he?

She would have to carefully consider whether or not she wanted the nanny to take over the nightly duties. She didn't want to be difficult, or insult Karin, who was probably more than capable, but when it came to Mia, Vanessa didn't fool around. If necessary, she would ask Marcus to move the crib into her bedroom, and if he had a problem with that, she would just sleep in the nursery until Gabriel returned. Hopefully it wouldn't be more than a few days.

"If there's nothing else you need," Marcus said, edging toward the door. He really couldn't wait to get away, could he? Well, she wasn't about to let him off the hook just yet.

"What if I do need something?" she asked. "How do I find someone?"

"There's a phone on the desk, and a list of extensions."

"How will I know who to call?"

He didn't roll his eyes, but she could see that he wanted to. "For a beverage or food, you call the kitchen. If you need clean towels or fresh linens, you would call the laundry...you get the point."

She did, although she didn't appreciate the sarcasm. "Suppose I need you. Is your number on there?"

"No, it isn't, and even if it were, I wouldn't be available."

"Never?"

A nerve in his jaw ticked. "In my father's absence, I have a duty to my country."

Why did he have to be so defensive? "Marcus," she said, in a voice that she hoped conveyed sincerity, "I understand how you must be feeling, but—"

"You have no *idea* how I'm feeling," he ground out, and the level of animosity in his tone drew her back a step. "My father asked me to get you settled in, and I've done that. Now, if there's nothing else."

Someone cleared their throat and they both looked over to see the nanny standing in the doorway.

"I'll leave you two to discuss the child's care," Marcus said, making a hasty escape, and any hope she'd had that they might be friends went out the door with him.

"Come in," she told Karin.

Looking a little nervous, the girl stepped inside. "Shall I take Mia so you can rest?"

She still wasn't sure about leaving Mia in a stranger's care, but she was exhausted, and she would have a hard time relaxing with Mia in bed with her. If Vanessa fell too deeply asleep, Mia could roll off and hurt herself. And the last thing she needed was Marcus thinking that not only was she a money-grubbing con artist, but a terrible mother as well.

"I really could use a nap," she told Karin, "but if she wakes up crying, I'd like you to bring her right to me. She's bound to be disoriented waking up in a strange place with someone she doesn't know."

"Of course, ma'am."

"Please, call me Vanessa."

Karin nodded, but looked uncomfortable with the idea.

"Mia is asleep on the bed. Why don't I carry her, so I can see where the nursery is, and you can bring her bag?"

Karin nodded again.

Not very talkative, was she?

Vanessa scooped up Mia, who was still sleeping deeply, and rolled her suitcase out to Karin, who led her two doors down and across the hall to the nursery. It was smaller than her own suite, with a play area and a sleeping area, and it was decorated gender-neutral. The walls were pale green, the furniture white and expensive-looking, and in the play area rows of shelves were packed with toys for children of every age. It was clearly a nursery designed for guests, and she supposed that if she did decide to stay, Mia would get her own nursery closer to Gabriel's bedroom.

The idea of sharing a bedroom with Gabriel, and a bed, made her stomach do a nervous little flip-flop.

Everything will work out.

She laid Mia in the crib and covered her with a light blanket, and the baby didn't even stir. The poor little thing was exhausted.

"Maybe I should unpack her things," she told Karin.

"I'll do it, ma'am."

Vanessa sighed. So it was still "ma'am"? That was something they would just have to work on. "Thank you."

She kissed the tips of her fingers, then gently pressed them to Mia's forehead. "Sleep well, sweet baby."

After reiterating that Karin was to come get her when Mia woke, she walked back to her suite. She pulled her cell phone out of her bag and checked for calls, but there were none. She dialed Gabriel's cell number, but it went straight to voice mail.

She glanced over at the sofa, thinking she would sleep there for an hour or so, but the bed, with its creamy silk comforter and big, fluffy pillows, called to her. Setting her phone on the bedside table, she lay back against the pillows, sinking into the softness of the comforter. She let her eyes drift closed, and when she opened them again, the room was dark.

Three

After leaving Miss Reynolds's suite, Marcus stopped by his office, where his assistant Cleo, short for Cleopatra—her parents were Egyptian and very eccentric—sat at her computer playing her afternoon game of solitaire.

"Any word from my father?" he asked.

Attention on the screen, she shook her head.

"I'm glad to see that you're using your time productively," he teased, as he often did when he caught her playing games.

And obviously she didn't take him seriously, because she didn't even blink, or look away from the cards on the screen. "Keeps the brain sharp."

She may have been pushing seventy, but no one could argue that she wasn't still sharp as a pin. She'd been with the royal family since the 1970s, and used to be his mother's secretary. Everyone expected she would retire after the queen's death, and enjoy what would be a very generous pension, but she hadn't been ready to stop working. She claimed it kept her young. And since her husband passed away two years ago, Marcus suspected she was lonely.

She finished the game and quit out of the software, a group photo of her eight grandchildren flashing on to her computer screen. She turned to Marcus and caught him in the middle of a yawn and frowned. "Tired?"

After a month-long battle with insomnia, he was always tired. And he wasn't in the mood for another lecture. "I'm sure I'll sleep like a baby when *she* is gone."

"She's that bad?"

He sat on the edge of her desk. "She's awful."

"And you know this after what, thirty minutes with her?"

"I knew after five. I knew the second she stepped off the plane."

She leaned forward in her chair, elbows on her desk, her white hair draped around a face that was young for her years, and with no help at all from a surgeon's knife. "Based on what?"

"She only wants his money."

Her brows rose. "She told you that?"

"She didn't have to. She's young, and beautiful, and a single mother. What else would she want from a man my father's age?"

"For the record, your highness, fifty-six is not that old."

"For her it is."

"Your father is an attractive and charming man. Who's to say that she didn't fall head over heels in love with him."

"In a few *weeks?*"

"I fell in love with my husband after our first date. Never underestimate the powers of physical attraction."

He cringed. The idea of his father and that woman… he didn't even want to think about it. Though he didn't doubt she had seduced him. That was the way her kind operated. He knew from experience, having been burned before. And his father, despite his staunch moral integrity, was vulnerable enough to fall under her spell.

"So, she's really that attractive?" Cleo asked.

Much as he wished he could say otherwise, there was no denying her beauty. "She is. But she had a child out of wedlock."

She gasped and slapped a hand to her chest. "Off with her head!"

He glared at her.

"You do remember what century this is? Women's rights and equality and all that."

"Yes, but *my* father? A man who lives by tradition. It's beneath him. He's lonely, missing my mother and not thinking straight."

"You don't give him much credit, do you? The king is a very intelligent man."

Yes, he was, and clearly not thinking with his brain. No one could convince Marcus that this situation was anything but temporary. And until she left, he would simply stay out of her way.

Vanessa bolted up in bed, heart racing, disoriented by the unfamiliar surroundings. Then, as her eyes adjusted to the dark and the room came into focus, she remembered where she was.

At first she thought that she'd slept late into the night, then realized that someone had shut the curtains. She grabbed her cell phone and checked the time, relieved to see that she had only slept for an hour and a half, and there were no missed calls from Gabriel.

She dialed his cell number, but like before it went straight to voice mail. She hung up and grabbed her laptop from her bag, hoping that maybe he'd sent her an email, but the network was password protected and she couldn't log on. She would have to ask someone for the password.

She closed the laptop and sighed. Since she hadn't heard a word from Karin, she could only assume Mia was still asleep, and without her daughter to take care of, Vanessa felt at a loss for what to do. Then she remembered all the bags in the closet waiting to be unpacked—basically her entire summer wardrobe—and figured she could kill time doing that.

She pushed herself up out of bed, her body still heavy with fatigue, and walked to the closet. But instead of finding packed suitcases, she discovered that her clothes had all been unpacked and put away. The maid must have been in while she was asleep, which was probably a regular thing around here, but she couldn't deny that it creeped her out a little. She didn't like the idea of someone else handling her things, but it was something she would just have to get used to, as she probably wouldn't be doing her own laundry.

She stripped out of her rumpled slacks and blouse and changed into yoga pants and a soft cotton top, wondering, when her stomach rumbled, what time she would be called for dinner. She grabbed her phone off the bed and walked out to the living room, where late afternoon sunshine flooded the windows and cut paths across the creamy carpet. She crossed the room and pulled open the French doors. A wall of heat sucked the breath from her lungs as she stepped out onto a balcony with wrought iron railings and exotic plants. It overlooked acres of rolling green grass and colorful flower beds, and directly below was the Olympic-size pool and cabana Gabriel had told her about. He put the pool in, he'd bragged, because Marcus had been a champion swimmer in high school and college, and to this day still swam regularly. Which would account for the impressively toned upper body.

But she definitely shouldn't be thinking about Marcus's upper body, or any other part of him.

Her cell phone rang and Gabriel's number flashed on the screen. Oh, thank God. Her heart lifted so swiftly it left her feeling dizzy.

She answered, and the sound of his voice was like a salve on her raw nerves. She conjured up a mental image of his face. His dark, gentle eyes, the curve of his smile, and realized just then how much she missed him.

"I'm so sorry I couldn't be there to greet you," he told her, speaking in his native language of Varlean, which was so similar to Italian they were practically interchangeable. And since she was fluent in the latter, learning the subtle differences had been simple for her.

"I miss you," she told him.

"I know, I'm sorry. How was your flight? How is Mia?"

"It was long, and Mia didn't sleep much, but she's napping now. I just slept for a while too."

"My plane left not twenty minutes before you were due to arrive."

"Your son said it was a family matter. I hope everything is okay."

"I wish I could say it was. It's my wife's half sister, Trina, in Italy. She was rushed to the hospital with an infection."

"Oh, Gabriel, I'm so sorry." He'd spoken often of his sister-in-law, and how she had stayed with him and his son for several weeks before and after the queen died. "I know you two are very close. I hope it's nothing too serious."

"She's being treated, but she's not out of danger. I hope you understand, but I just can't leave her. She's a widow, and childless. She has no one else. She was there for me and Marcus when we needed her. I feel obligated to stay."

"Of course you do. Family always comes first."

She heard him breathe a sigh of relief. "I knew you would understand. You're an extraordinary woman, Vanessa."

"Is there anything I can do? Any way I can help?"

"Just be patient with me. I wish I could invite you to stay with me, but..."

"She's your wife's sister. I'm guessing that would be awkward for everyone."

"I think it would."

"How long do you think you'll be?"

"Two weeks, maybe. I won't know for sure until we see how she's responding to the treatment."

Two weeks? Alone with Marcus? Was the universe playing some sort of cruel trick on her? Not that she imagined he would be chomping at the bit to spend quality time with her. With any luck he would keep to himself and she wouldn't have to actually see Marcus at all.

"I promise I'll be back as soon as I possibly can," Gabriel said. "Unless you prefer to fly home until I return."

Home to what? Her apartment was sublet for the next six weeks. She lived on a shoestring budget, and being on unpaid leave, she hadn't had the money for rent while she was gone. Gabriel had offered to pay, but she felt uncomfortable taking a handout from him. Despite what Marcus seemed to believe, the fact that Gabriel was very wealthy wasn't all that important to her. And until they were married—if that day ever came—she refused to let him spoil her. Not that he hadn't tried.

The wining and dining was one thing, but on their third date he bought her a pair of stunning diamond earrings to show his appreciation for her professional services at the hotel. She had refused to take them. She had drooled over a similar pair in the jewelry boutique at the hotel with a price tag that amounted to a year's salary.

Then there had been the lush flower arrangements that began arriving at her office every morning like clockwork after he'd flown back home, and the toys for Mia from local shops. She'd had to gently but firmly tell him, no more. There was no need to buy her affections.

"I'll wait for you," she told Gabriel. Even if she did have a place to go home to, the idea of making that miserably long flight two more times with Mia in tow was motivation enough to stay.

"I promise we'll chat daily. You brought your laptop?"

"Yes, but I can't get on the network. And I'll need plug adaptors since the outlets are different."

"Just ask Marcus. I've instructed him to get you anything that you need. He was there to greet you, wasn't he?"

"Yes, he was there."

"And he was respectful?"

She could tell Gabriel the truth, but what would that accomplish, other than to make Gabriel feel bad, and Marcus resent her even more. The last thing she wanted to do was cause a rift between father and son.

"He made me feel very welcome."

"I'm relieved. He took losing his mother very hard."

"And it's difficult for him to imagine you with someone new."

"Exactly. I'm proud of him for taking the change so well."

He wouldn't be proud if he knew how Marcus had really acted, but that would remain hers and Marcus's secret.

"Your room is satisfactory?"

"Beyond satisfactory, and the palace is amazing. I plan

to take Mia for a walk on the grounds tomorrow, and I can hardly wait to visit the village."

"I'm sure Marcus would be happy to take you. You should ask him."

When hell froze over, maybe. Besides, she would much rather go exploring on her own, just her and Mia.

"Maybe I will," she said, knowing she would do no such thing.

"I know that when you get to know one another, you'll become friends."

Somehow she doubted that. Even if she wanted to, Marcus clearly wanted nothing to do with her.

"I left a surprise for you," Gabriel said. "It's in the top drawer of the desk."

"What sort of surprise?" she asked, already heading in that direction.

"Well, it won't be a surprise if I tell you," he teased. "Look and see."

She was already opening the drawer. Inside was a credit card with her name on it. She picked it up and sighed. "Gabriel, I appreciate the gesture, but—"

"I know, I know. You're too proud to take anything from me. But I *want* to do this for you."

"I just don't feel comfortable spending your money. You're doing enough already."

"Suppose you see something in the village that you like? I know you have limited funds. I want you to have nice things."

"I have you, that's all I need."

"And that, my dear, is why you are such an amazing woman. And why I love you. Promise me you'll keep it with you, just in case. I don't care if it's five euros or five thousand. If you see something you really want, please buy it."

"I'll keep it handy," she said, dropping it back in the drawer, knowing she would never spend a penny.

"I've missed you, Vanessa. I'm eager to start our life together."

"If I stay," she reminded him, so he knew that nothing was set in stone yet.

"You will," he said, as confident and certain as the day he'd asked her to marry him. Then there was the sound of voices in the background. "Vanessa, I have to go. The doctor is here and I need to speak with him."

"Of course."

"We'll chat tomorrow, yes?"

"Yes."

"I love you, my sweet Vanessa."

"I love you, too," she said, then the call disconnected.

She sighed and set her phone on the desk, hoping there would come a day when she could say those words, and mean them the way that Gabriel did. That there would be a time when the sort of love she felt for him extended past friendship.

It wasn't that she didn't find him attractive. There was no doubt that he was an exceptionally good-looking man. Maybe his jaw wasn't as tight as it used to be, and there was gray at his temples, and he wasn't as fit as he'd been in his younger years, but those things didn't bother her. It was what was on the inside that counted. And her affection for him felt warm and comfortable. What was missing was that...*zing*.

Like the one you felt when you took Marcus's hand?

She shook away the thought. Yes, Marcus was an attractive man, too, plus he didn't have the sagging skin, graying hair and expanding waist. He also didn't have his father's sweet disposition and generous heart.

When Gabriel held her, when he'd brushed his lips

across her cheek, she felt respected and cherished and safe. And okay, maybe those things didn't make for steamy hot sex, but she knew from personal experience that sex could be highly overrated. What really mattered was respect, and friendship. That's what was left when the *zing* disappeared. And it always did.

Men like Marcus thrilled, then they bailed. Usually leaving a substantial mess in their wake. She could just imagine the string of broken hearts he'd caused. But Gabriel was dependable and trustworthy, and that's exactly what she was looking for in a man now. She'd had her thrills, now she wanted a mature, lasting relationship. Gabriel could give her that. That and so much more, if she was smart enough, and strong enough, to let him.

Four

Marcus was halfway through his second set of laps that evening, the burn in his muscles shaking off the stress that hung on his shoulders like an iron cloak, when he heard his cell phone start to ring. He swam to the side of the pool, hoisted himself up onto the deck and walked to the table where he'd left his phone, the hot tile scorching his feet. It was his father.

He almost didn't answer. He was sure his father would have spoken to Miss Reynolds by now, and she had probably regaled him with the story of Marcus's less than warm welcome. The first thing on her agenda would be to drive a wedge between him and his father, which the king would see through, of course. Maybe not right away, but eventually, and Marcus was happy to let her hang herself with her own rope. Even if that meant receiving an admonishment from his father now. So he took the call.

"Father, how is Aunt Trina?"

"Very sick, son," he said.

His heart sank. He just wasn't ready to say goodbye to yet another loved one. "What's the prognosis?"

"It will be touch and go for a while, but the doctors are hoping she'll make a full recovery."

He breathed a sigh of relief. No one should ever have to endure so much loss in the span of only eight months. "If there's anything you need, just say so."

"There is something, but first, son, I wanted to thank you, and tell you how proud I am of you. And ashamed of myself."

Proud of him? Maybe he hadn't spoken to Miss Reynolds after all. Or was it possible that he'd already seen though her scheme and had come to his senses? "What do you mean?"

"I know that accepting I've moved on, that I've fallen in love with someone new—especially someone so young—has been difficult for you. I was afraid that you might treat Vanessa...well, less than hospitably. But knowing that you've made her feel welcome...son, I'm sorry that I didn't trust you. I should have realized that you're a man of integrity."

What the hell had she told him exactly?

Marcus wasn't sure what to say, and his father's words, his misplaced faith, filled him with guilt. How would he feel if he knew the truth? And why had she lied to him? What sort of game was she playing? Or was it possible that she really did care about his father?

Of course she didn't. She was working some sort of angle, that was how her kind always operated.

"Isn't her daughter precious?" his father said, sounding absolutely smitten. Marcus couldn't recall him ever using the word *precious* in any context.

"She is," he agreed, though he'd seen her do nothing

but scream and sleep. "Is there anything pressing I should know about, business that needs tending?"

"There's no need to worry about that. I've decided to fly my staff here and set up a temporary office."

"That's really not necessary. I can handle matters while you're away."

"You know I would go out of my mind if I had nothing to do. This way I can work and still be with Trina."

That seemed like an awful lot of trouble for a short visit, unless it wasn't going to be short. "How long do you expect you'll be gone?"

"Well, I told Vanessa two weeks," he said. "But the truth is, it could be longer."

He had a sudden, sinking feeling. "How much longer?"

"Hopefully no more than three or four weeks."

A *month*. There was no question that Trina—*family*—should come first, but that seemed excessive. Especially since he had a guest. "A month is a long time to be away."

"And how long did Trina give up her life to stay with us when your mother was ill?"

She had stayed with them for several months in the final stages of his mother's illness, then another few weeks after the funeral. So he certainly couldn't fault his father for wanting to stay with her. "I'm sorry, I'm being selfish. Of course you should be there with her. As long as she needs you. Maybe I should join you."

"I need you at the palace. Since Tabitha will be with me, it will be up to you to see that Vanessa and Mia have anything they need."

"Of course." He could hardly wait.

"And I know this is a lot to ask, but I want you to keep them entertained."

Marcus hoped he didn't mean that the way it sounded. *"Entertained?"*

"Make them feel welcome. Take them sightseeing, show them a good time."

The idea had been to stay away from her as much as humanly possible, not be her tour guide. "Father—"

"I realize I'm asking a lot of you under the circumstances, and I know it will probably be a bit awkward at first, but it will give you and Vanessa a chance to get to know one another. She's truly a remarkable woman, son. I'm sure that once you get to know her you'll love her as much as I do."

Nothing his father could say would make Marcus want to spend time with that woman. And no amount of time that he spent with her would make him "love" her. "Father, I don't think—"

"Imagine how she and her daughter must feel, in a foreign country where they don't know a soul. And I feel terrible for putting her in that position. It took me weeks to convince her to come here. If she leaves, she may never agree to come back."

And that would be a bad thing?

Besides, Marcus didn't doubt for an instant that she had just been playing hard to get, stringing his father along, and now that she was here, he seriously doubted she had any intention of leaving, for any reason. But maybe in this case absence wouldn't make the heart grow fonder. Maybe it would give his father time to think about his relationship with Miss Reynolds and realize the mistake he was making.

Or maybe, instead of waiting for this to play out, Marcus could take a more proactive approach. Maybe he could persuade her to leave.

The thought brought a smile to his face.

"I'll do it," he told his father.

"I have your word?"

"Yes," he said, feeling better about the situation already. "You have my word."

"Thank you, son. You have no idea how much this means to me. And I don't want you to worry about anything else. Consider yourself on vacation until I return."

"Is there anyplace in particular you would like me to take her?"

"I'll email a list of the things she might enjoy doing."

"I'll watch for it," he said, feeling cheerful for the first time in weeks, since his father had come home acting like a lovesick teenager.

"She did mention a desire to tour the village," the king said.

That was as good a place to start as any. "Well then, we'll go first thing tomorrow."

"I can't tell you what a relief this is. And if ever you should require anything from me, you need only ask."

Send her back to the U.S., he wanted to say, but he would be taking care of that. After he was through with her, she would be *sprinting* for the plane. But the key with a woman like her was patience and subtlety.

He and his father hung up, and Marcus dropped his phone back on the table. He looked over at the pool, then up to the balcony of Miss Reynolds's room. He should give her the good news right away, so she would have time to prepare for tomorrow's outing. He toweled off then slipped his shirt, shorts and sandals on, combing his fingers through his wet hair as he headed upstairs. He half expected to hear her daughter howling as he approached her room, but the hallway was silent.

He knocked, and she must have been near the door because it opened almost immediately. She had changed into snug black cotton pants, a plain pink T-shirt, and her hair was pulled up in a ponytail. She looked even younger this way, and much more relaxed than she had when she stepped off the plane. It struck him again how attractive she really was. Without makeup she looked a little less exotic and vampy, but her features, the shape of her face, were exquisite.

He looked past her into the suite and saw that she had spread a blanket across the carpet in the middle of the room. Mia was in the center, balanced on her hands and knees, rocking back and forth, shaking her head from side to side, a bit like a deranged pendulum. Then she stopped, toppled over to the left, and rolled onto her back, looking dazed.

Was she having some sort of fit or seizure?

"Is she okay?" Marcus asked, wondering if he should call the physician.

Miss Reynolds smiled at her daughter. "She's fine."

"What was she doing?" Marcus asked.

"Crawling."

Crawling? "She doesn't seem to be getting very far."

"Not yet. The first step is learning to balance on her hands and knees."

She apparently had a long way to go to master that.

Mia squealed and rolled over onto her tummy, then pushed herself back up and resumed rocking. She seemed to be doing all right, until her arms gave out and she pitched forward. Marcus cringed as she fell face-first into the blanket, landing on her button nose. She lifted her head, looking stunned for a second, then she screwed up her face and started to cry.

When Miss Reynolds just stood there, Marcus asked, "Is she okay?"

"She's probably more frustrated than injured."

After several more seconds of Mia wailing, when she

did nothing to comfort the child, he said, "Aren't you going to pick her up?"

She shrugged. "If I picked her up every time she got discouraged, she'd never learn to try. She'll be fine in a second."

No sooner had she spoken the words than Mia's cries abruptly stopped, then she hoisted herself back up on her hands and knees, starting the process all over again. Rocking, falling over, wailing…

"Does she do this often?" he asked after watching her for several minutes.

She sighed, as if frustrated, but resigned. "Almost constantly for the past three days."

"Is that…normal?"

"For her it is. She's a very determined child. She'll keep doing something over and over until she gets it right. She gets that from my father, I think."

He could tell, from the deep affection in her eyes, the pride in her smile as she watched her daughter, that Miss Reynolds loved the little girl deeply. Which made her attempts to con his father all the more despicable.

"I'm sorry," she said, finally turning to him. "Was there something you wan…" She trailed off, blinking in surprise as she took in the sight of him, as if she just now noticed how he was dressed. Starting at his sandals, her eyes traveled up his bare legs and over his shorts, then they settled on the narrow strip of chest where the two sides of his shirt had pulled open. For several seconds she seemed transfixed, then she gave her head a little shake, and her eyes snapped up to his.

She blinked again, looking disoriented, and asked, "I'm sorry, what did you say?"

He began to wonder if maybe he'd been mistaken earlier, and she really was a brainless blonde. "I didn't say anything. But I believe you were about to ask me if there was something that I wanted."

Her cheeks blushed bright pink. "You're right, I was. Sorry. Was there? Something you wanted, I mean."

"If you have a moment, I'd like to have a word with you."

"Of course," she said, stepping back from the door and pulling it open, stumbling over her own foot. "Sorry. Would you like to come in?"

He stepped into the room, wondering if perhaps she'd been sampling the contents of the bar. "Are you all right?"

"I took a nap. I guess I'm not completely awake yet. Plus, I'm still on California time. It's barely seven a.m. in Los Angeles. Technically I was up most of the night."

That could explain it, he supposed, yet he couldn't help questioning her mental stability.

She closed the door and turned to him. "What did you want to talk about?"

"I want to know why you lied to my father."

She blinked in surprise, opened her mouth to speak, then shut it again. Then, as if gathering her patience, she took a deep breath, slowly blew it out, and asked, "Refresh my memory, what did I lie about?"

Did she honestly not know what he meant, or were there so many lies, she couldn't keep track? "You told my father that I made you feel welcome. We both know that isn't true."

She got an "oh *that*" look on her face. "What was I supposed to tell him? His son, who he loves and respects dearly, acted like a big jer—" She slapped a hand over her mouth, but it was pretty obvious what she'd been about to say.

Marcus had to clench his jaw to keep it from falling open. "Did you just call me a *jerk?*"

She shook her head, eyes wide. "No."

"Yes, you did. You called me a *big jerk*."

She hesitated, looking uneasy. "Maybe I did."

"Maybe?"

"Okay, I did. I told you, I'm half asleep. It just sort of… slipped out. And let's be honest, Marcus, you were acting like a jerk."

He was sure people said unfavorable things about him all the time, but no one, outside of his family, had ever dared insult him to his face. Twice. He should feel angry, or annoyed, yet all he felt was an odd amusement. "Are you *trying* to make me dislike you?"

"You already don't like me. At this point I doubt anything I say, or don't say, will change that. Which I think is kind of sad but…" She shrugged. "And for the record, I didn't *lie* to Gabriel. I just…fudged the truth a little."

"Why?"

"He has enough on his mind. He doesn't need to be worrying about me. Besides, I can fight my own battles."

If he didn't know better, he might believe that she really did care about his father. But he knew her type. He'd dated a dozen women just like her. She was only after one thing—his legacy—and like the others, he would make sure that she never got her hands on it.

"I would hardly call this a battle," he told her.

She folded her arms, emphasizing the fullness of her breasts. "You would if you were me."

Marcus had to make an effort to keep his eyes on her face. But even that was no hardship. She was exceptionally attractive and undeniably sexy. A beautiful woman with a black heart.

Her eyes wandered downward, to his chest, lingering there for several seconds, then as if realizing she was staring, she quickly looked away.

She didn't strike him as the type to be shy about the male physique. Or maybe it was just his that bothered her.

"Look," she said. "You don't like me, and that's fine. I can even understand why. It's disappointing that you aren't going to give me a chance, but, whatever. And if I'm being totally honest, I'm not so crazy about you either. So why don't we just agree to stay out of each other's way?"

"Miss Reynolds—"

"It's *Vanessa*. You could at least have the decency to use my first name."

"Vanessa," he said. "How would you feel if we called a truce?"

Five

A truce?

Vanessa studied Marcus's face, trying to determine if his words were sincere. Instead, all she could seem to concentrate on was his damp, slicked-back hair and the single wavy lock that had fallen across his forehead. She felt the strongest urge to brush it back with her fingers. And why couldn't she stop looking at that tantalizing strip of tanned, muscular, bare chest?

"Why would you do that?" she asked, forcing her attention above his neck. He folded his arms over his chest and she had to wonder if he'd seen her staring. Was she creeping him out? If she were him, she would probably be creeped out.

"I thought you wanted me to give you a chance," he said.

But why the sudden change of heart? A couple of hours ago he could barely stand to be in the same room with her. She couldn't escape the feeling that he was up to something. "Of course I do, you just didn't seem too thrilled with the idea."

"That was before I learned that for the next few weeks, we're going to be seeing a lot of each other."

She blinked. "What do you mean?"

"My father thinks it would be a good idea for us to get to know one another, and in his absence has asked me to be your companion. I'm to show you and your daughter a good time, keep you entertained."

Oh no, what had Gabriel done? She wanted Marcus to give her a chance, but not by force. That would only make him resent her more. Not to mention that she hadn't anticipated him being so...

Something.

Something that made her trip over her own feet and stumble over her words, and do stupid things like stare at his bare chest and insult him to his face.

"I don't need a companion," she told him. "Mia and I will be fine on our own."

"For your safety, you wouldn't be able to leave the palace without an escort."

"My safety?"

"There are certain criminal elements to consider."

Her heart skipped a beat. "What kind of criminal elements?"

"The kind who would love nothing more than to get their hands on the future queen. You would fetch quite the ransom."

She couldn't decide if he was telling the truth, or just trying to scare her. Kidnappings certainly weren't unheard of, but Varieo was such a quiet, peaceful country. No handguns, very little crime. Gabriel hadn't mentioned any potential threat or danger.

And why would he when he was trying to convince

her to marry him? There was a reason royalty had body-guards, right?

Wait a minute. Who even knew that she was here? It wasn't as if Gabriel would broadcast to the country that eight months after his wife's death he was bringing his new American girlfriend in for a visit.

Would he?

"The point is," Marcus said, "my father wanted you to have an escort, and that person is me."

"What about Tabitha?"

"She's flying to Italy to be with my father. He takes her everywhere. Some people have even thought..." He paused and shook his head. "Never mind."

Okay, now he *was* trying to mess with her.

But how well do you really know Gabriel, that annoy-ing voice of doubt interjected. He could have a dozen mis-tresses for all she knew. Just because he claimed to have been faithful to his wife didn't mean it was true. Maybe there was no sick sister-in-law. Maybe he was with another one of his girlfriends. Maybe there had been a schedul-ing conflict and he chose her over Vanessa. Maybe he—

Ugh! What are you doing?

She *trusted* Gabriel, and she hated that Marcus could shake her faith with one simple insinuation. And a ridicu-lous one at that. Maybe she hadn't known Gabriel long, but in that short time he had never been anything but honest and dependable. And until someone produced irrefutable evidence to the contrary, she was determined to trust him.

This wasn't another dumb mistake.

It wasn't Gabriel's fault that she'd had lousy luck with relationships, and it wasn't fair to judge him on her own bad experiences. If he wanted her to spend a couple of weeks getting to know his son, that's what she would do, even if she didn't exactly trust Marcus, and questioned his motives. She would just be herself, and hope that Marcus would put aside his doubts and accept her.

"I guess I'm stuck with you then," she told him.

Marcus frowned, looking as if she'd hurt his feelings. "If the idea of spending time with me is so offensive—"

"No! Of course not. That isn't what I meant." No matter what she said, it always seemed to be the wrong thing. "I really would like us to get acquainted, Marcus. I just don't want you to feel pressured, as if you have no choice. I can only imagine how awkward this is for you, and how heartbreaking it was to lose your mother. It sounds as if she was a remarkable woman, and I would never in a million years try to replace her, or even think that I could. I just want Gabriel to be happy. He deserves it. I think that would be much more likely to happen if you and I are friends. Or at the very least, not mortal enemies."

"I'm willing to concede that I may have rushed to judgment," he said. "And for the record, my father is not *forcing* me. I could have refused, but I know it's important to him."

It was no apology for his behavior earlier, but it was definitely a start. And she hoped he really meant it, that he didn't have ulterior motives for being nice to her. "In that case, I would be honored to have you as my escort."

"So, truce?" he said, stepping closer with an outstretched hand. And boy did he smell good. Some sort of spicy delicious scent that made her want to bury her face in his neck and take a big whiff.

No, she *definitely* didn't want to do that. And she didn't want to feel the zing of awareness when he clasped her hand, the tantalizing shiver as his thumb brushed across the top of her hand, or the residual buzz after he let go.

How could she zing for a man she didn't even like?

"My father will be sending me a list of activities he thinks you'll enjoy, and he's asked me to accompany you to the village tomorrow. If there's anything in particular you'd like to do, or someplace you would like to see, let me know and we'll work it into the schedule."

Honestly, she would be thrilled to just lie around by the pool and doze for a week, but she knew Gabriel wanted her to familiarize herself with the area, because how could she decide if she wanted to live somewhere if she didn't see it? "If there's anything I'll let you know."

"Be ready tomorrow at ten a.m."

"I will."

He nodded and walked out, closing the door behind him.

Vanessa sat on the floor beside her daughter, who had tired of rocking, and was now lying on her tummy gnawing contentedly on a teething ring.

The idea of spending so much time alone with Marcus made her uneasy, but she didn't seem to have much choice. To refuse would only hurt Gabriel's feelings, and make her look like the bad guy. At the very least, when the staff saw that Marcus was accepting her, they might warm up to her as well.

Vanessa's cell phone rang and she jumped up to grab it off the desk, hoping it was Gabriel.

It was her best friend Jessy.

"Hey! I just woke up and got your text," Jessy said, and Vanessa could picture her, sitting in bed in her pajamas, eyes puffy, her spiky red hair smashed flat from sleeping with the covers pulled over her head. "How was the flight?"

"A nightmare. Mia hardly slept." She smiled down at her daughter who was still gnawing and drooling all over the blanket. "But she seems to be adjusting pretty well now."

"Was Gabriel happy to see you?"

Vanessa hesitated. She didn't want to lie to Jessy, but she was afraid the truth would only add to her friend's doubts. But if she couldn't talk to her best friend, who could she talk to?

"There was a slight change of plans." She explained the situation with Gabriel's sister-in-law, and why he felt he had to be with her. "I know what you're probably thinking."

"Yes, I have reservations about you taking this trip, but I have to trust that you know what's best for you and Mia."

"Even if you don't agree?"

"I can't help but worry about you, and I absolutely hate the idea of you moving away. But ultimately, what I think doesn't matter."

To Vanessa it did. They had been inseparable since Vanessa moved to L.A. With her statuesque figure and exquisitely beautiful features—assets that, unlike Vanessa, she chose to cleverly downplay—Jessy understood what it was like to be labeled the "pretty" girl. She knew that, depending on the circumstances, it could be more of a liability than an asset. They also shared the same lousy taste in men, although Jessy was now in a relationship with Wayne, a pharmaceutical rep, who she thought might possibly be the *one*. He was attractive without being too handsome—since she'd found most of the really good-looking guys to be arrogant—he had a stable career, drove a nice car and lived in an oceanside condo. And aside from the fact that he had a slightly unstable and bitter ex-wife and a resentful teenaged daughter with self-cutting issues in Seattle, he was darn close to perfect.

Vanessa hoped that they had both found their forever man. God knows they had paid their dues.

"So, what will you do until Gabriel comes back?" Jessy asked, and Vanessa heard the whine of the coffee grinder in the background.

"His son has agreed to be my companion." Just the thought caused a funny little twinge in her stomach.

"Companion?"

"He'll take me sightseeing, keep me entertained."

"Is he as hot in person as he is in the photos you showed me?"

Unfortunately. "On a scale of one to ten, he's a solid fifteen."

"So, if things don't work out with Gabriel…" she teased.

"Did I mention that he's also a jerk? And he doesn't seem to like me very much. Not that I don't understand why." She picked a hunk of carpet fuzz from Mia's damp fingers before she could stuff it in her mouth. "Gabriel wants us to be friends. But I think I would settle for Marcus not hating my guts."

"Vanessa, you're one of the sweetest, kindest, most thoughtful people I've ever met. How could he not like you?"

The problem was, sometimes she was too nice and too sweet and too thoughtful. To the point that she let people walk all over her. And Marcus struck her as the sort of man who would take advantage of that.

Or maybe she was being paranoid.

"He's very…intense," she told Jessy. "When he steps into a room he's just so…*there*. It's a little intimidating."

"Well, he is a prince."

"And Gabriel is a king, but I've never felt anything but comfortable with him."

"Don't take this the wrong way, but maybe Gabriel, being older, is more like…a father figure."

"Jessy, my dad has been enough of a father figure to last a dozen lifetimes."

"And you've told me a million times how his criticism makes you feel like a failure."

She couldn't deny that, and Gabriel's lavish attention did make her feel special, but she wasn't looking for a substitute father. Quite the opposite in fact. In the past she always found herself attracted to men who wanted to control or dominate her. And the worst part was that she usually let them. This time she wanted a partner. An *equal*.

Maybe the main thing that bothered her about Marcus—besides the fact that he despised her—was that he seemed a bit too much like the sort of man she used to date.

"I don't trust Marcus," she told Jessy. "He made it clear the minute I stepped off the plane that he didn't like me, then a couple of hours later he was offering to take me sightseeing. He said he's doing it for his father, but I'm not sure I buy that. If he really wanted to please Gabriel, wouldn't he have been nice to me the second I stepped off the plane?"

"Do you think he's going to try to come between you and Gabriel?"

"At this point, I'm not sure what to think." The only thing she did know was that something about Marcus made her nervous, and she didn't like it, but she was more or less stuck with him until Gabriel returned.

"I have some good news of my own," Jessy said. "Wayne has invited me to Arkansas for a couple of days for his parents' fortieth anniversary party. He wants me to meet his family."

"You're going, right?"

"I'd love to. Do you realize how long it's been since I've met a man's family, since I've even wanted to? The thing is, they live in a remote area that doesn't have great cell coverage and I might be hard to get ahold of. I'm just a little worried that if you end up needing me—"

"Jessy, I'll be fine. Worst-case scenario, I can call my dad." Although things would have to be pretty awful for her to do that.

"Are you sure? I know you say everything is okay, but I still worry about you."

"Well, don't," she told Jessy. "I can handle Prince Marcus."

She just hoped that was true.

Six

Marcus was sure he had Vanessa pegged, but after spending a day with her in the village, he was beginning to wonder if his original assumptions about her were slightly, well…unreliable.

His first hint that something might be off was when he arrived at her door at 10 a.m. sharp, fully anticipating a fifteen- or twenty-minute wait while she finished getting ready. It was a game women liked to play. They seemed to believe it drew out the anticipation or gave them power, or some such nonsense, when in reality, it just annoyed him. But when Vanessa opened the door dressed in conservative cotton shorts, a sleeveless top, comfortable-looking sandals and a floppy straw hat, she was clearly ready to go, and with a camera hanging from a strap around her neck, a diaper bag slung over one shoulder and her daughter on her hip, she looked more like an American tourist than a gold digger angling for the position of queen.

His suspicions grew throughout the day while he witnessed her shopping habits—or lack thereof. Tabitha, with only the king's best interest at heart, had warned Marcus of the credit card his father had requested for Vanessa, and its outrageous credit limit. Therefore, Marcus requested his driver be at the ready in anticipation of armfuls of packages. But by midafternoon they had visited at least a dozen shops showcasing everything from souvenirs to designer clothing to fine jewelry, and though he'd watched her admire the fashions, and seen her gaze longingly at a pair of modestly priced, hand-crafted earrings, all she'd purchased was a T-shirt for her daughter, a postcard that she said she intended to send to her best friend in L.A. and a paperback romance novel—her one guilty pleasure, she'd explained with a wry smile. And she'd paid with cash. He had an even bigger surprise when he heard her speaking to a merchant and realized she spoke his language fluently.

"You never mentioned that you could speak Varien," he said, when they left the shop.

She just shrugged and said, "You never asked."

She was right. And everything about her puzzled him. She was worldly and well traveled, but there was a childlike delight and curiosity in her eyes with each new place she visited. She didn't just see the sights, but absorbed her surroundings like a sponge, the most trivial and mundane details—things he would otherwise overlook—snagging her interest. And she asked a million questions. Her excitement and enthusiasm were so contagious he actually began to see the village with a fresh pair of eyes. Even though they were tired and achy from lack of sleep.

She was intelligent, yet whimsical, and at times even a little flighty. Poised and graceful, yet adorably awkward, occasionally bumping into a store display or another shopper, or tripping on a threshold—or even her own feet.

Once, she was so rapt when admiring the architecture of a historical church, she actually walked right into a tourist who had paused abruptly in front of her to take a photo. But instead of looking annoyed, Vanessa simply laughed, apologized and complimented the woman on her shoes.

Vanessa also had an amusing habit of saying exactly what she was thinking, while she was thinking it, and oftentimes embarrassing herself or someone else in the process.

Though she was obviously many things—or at least wanted him to believe she was—if he had to choose a single word to describe her it would probably be... *quirky*.

Twenty-four hours ago he would have been content never to see her again. But now, as he sat across from her on a blanket in the shade of an olive tree near the dock, in the members-only park off the marina, watching her snack on sausage, cheese and crackers—which she didn't eat so much as inhale—with Mia on the blanket between them rocking back and forth, back and forth on her hands and knees, he was experiencing a disconcerting combination of perplexity, suspicion and fascination.

"I guess you were hungry," he said as she plucked the last cheese wedge from the plate and popped it in her mouth.

Most women would be embarrassed or even offended by such as observation, but she just shrugged.

"I'm borderline hypoglycemic, so I have to eat at least five or six times a day. But I was blessed with a fast metabolism, so I never gain weight. It's just one more reason for other women to hate me."

"Why would other women hate you?"

"Are you kidding? A woman who looks like I do, who can eat anything and not gain an ounce? Some people consider that an unforgivable crime, as though I have some sort of control over how pretty I am, or how my body processes nutrients. You have no idea how often as a teenager I wished I were more ordinary."

Acknowledging her own beauty should have made her come off as arrogant, but she said it with such disdain, so much self-loathing, he actually felt a little sorry for her.

"I thought all women wanted to be beautiful," he said.

"Most do, they just don't want *other* women to be beautiful too. They don't like competition. I was popular, so I had no real friends."

That made no sense. "How could you be popular if you had no friends?"

She took a sip of her bottled water than recapped it. "I'm sure you know the saying, keep your friends close and your enemies closer."

"And you were the enemy?"

"Pretty much. Those stereotypes you see in movies about popular girls aren't as exaggerated as you might think. They can be vicious."

Mia toppled over and wound up lying on her back against his leg. She smiled up at him and gurgled happily, and he couldn't help but smile back. He had the feeling she was destined to be as beautiful as her mother.

"So, if the popular girls were so terrible, why didn't you make friends who weren't popular?"

"Girls were intimidated by me. It took them a long time to get past my face to see what was on the inside. And just when they would begin to realize that I wasn't a snob, and I started to form attachments, my dad would uproot us again and I'd have to start over in a new school."

"You moved often?"

"At least once a year, usually more. My dad's in the army."

He had a difficult time picturing that. He'd imagined

her as being raised in an upscale suburban home, with a pampered, trophy wife mother and an executive father who spoiled her rotten. Apparently he'd been wrong about many things.

"How many different places have you lived?" he asked.

"Too many. The special weapons training he did meant moving a lot. Overseas we were based in Germany, Bulgaria, Israel, Japan and Italy, and domestically we lived in eight different states at eleven bases. All by the time I was seventeen. Deep down, I think all the moving was just his way of coping with my mom's death."

The fact that she, too, had lost her mother surprised him. "When did she die?"

"I was five. She had the flu of all things."

His mother's death, the unfairness of it, had left him under a cloud so dark and obliterating, he felt as if he would never be cheerful again. Yet Vanessa seemed to maintain a perpetually positive attitude and sunny disposition.

"She was only twenty-six," Vanessa said.

"That's very young."

"It was one of those fluke things. She just kept getting worse and worse, and by the time she went in for treatment, it had turned into pneumonia. My dad was away at the time, stationed in the Persian Gulf. I don't think he ever forgave himself for not being there."

At least Marcus had his mother for twenty-eight years. Not that it made losing her any easier. And though he knew it happened all the time, it still struck him as terribly unjust for a child to lose a parent so young, and from such a common and typically mild affliction.

"How about you?" she asked. "Where have you lived?"

"I've visited many places," Marcus said, "but I've never lived anywhere but the palace."

"Haven't you ever wanted to be independent? Out on your own?"

More times than he could possibly count. When people heard *royalty,* they assumed a life of grandeur and excess, but the responsibilities attached to the crown could be suffocating. When it came to everything he did, every decision he made, he had to first consider his title and how it would affect his standing with the people.

"My place is with my family," he told Vanessa. "It's what is expected of me."

Mia gurgled and swung her arms, vying for his attention, so he tickled her under the chin, which made her giggle.

"If I'd had to live with my dad all these years, I would be in a rubber room," Vanessa said, wearing a sour expression, which would seem to suggest animosity.

"You don't get along?"

"With my father, it's his way or the highway. Let's just say that he has a problem with decisions I've made."

"Which ones, if you don't mind my asking?"

She sighed. "Oh, pretty much all of them. It's kind of ironic if you think about it. There are people who dislike me because I'm too perfect, but in my dad's eyes I've never done a single thing right."

He couldn't help thinking that must have been an exaggeration. No parent could be that critical. "Surely he's pleased now that you're planning to marry a king."

"I could tell him I'm the new Mother Teresa and he'd find a way to write it off as a bad thing. Besides, I haven't told him. The only person who knows where I am is my best friend Jessy."

"Why keep it a secret?"

"I didn't want to say anything to anyone until I knew for sure that I really was going to marry Gabriel."

* * *

"What reason would you have not to marry him?" Marcus asked, and Vanessa hesitated. While she wanted to get to know Marcus better, she wasn't sure how she felt about discussing the private details of her relationship with his father. But at the same time, she hated to clam up now, as this outing was definitely going better than expected. And as she sat there on the rough wool blanket in the shade, the salty ocean air cooling her sunbaked skin, her daughter playing happily between them, she felt a deep sense of peace that she hadn't experienced in a very long time.

The first hour or so had been a bit like tiptoeing around in a minefield, her every move monitored, each word dissected for hidden meaning. But little by little she began to relax, and so did Marcus. The truth is, he was more like his father than she'd imagined. Sure, he was a bit intense at times, but he was very intelligent with a quick wit, and a wry sense of humor. And though it was obvious that he wasn't quite sure what to make of her—which wasn't unusual as she always seemed to fall somewhere outside of people's expectations—she had the feeling that maybe he was starting to like her. Or at the very least dislike her less. And he clearly adored Mia, who—the little flirt—hadn't taken her eyes off him for hours.

"Unless you'd rather not discuss it," Marcus said, his tone, and the glint of suspicion in his dark eyes, suggesting that she had something to hide.

She fidgeted with the corner of the blanket. Even though her relationship with Gabriel was none of his business, to not answer would look suspicious, but the truth might only validate his reservations about her. "My relationship with Gabriel is…complicated."

"How complicated could it be? You love him, don't you?"

There was a subtle accusation in his tone. Just when

she thought things were going really well, when she believed he was having a change of heart, he was back to the business of trying to discredit her, to expose her as a fraud. Well, maybe she should just give him what he wanted. It didn't seem as though it would make a difference at this point.

"I love him," she said. "I'm just not sure I'm *in* love with him."

"What's the difference?"

Did he honestly not know, or did he think she didn't? Or was he possibly just screwing with her? "Your father is an amazing human being. He's smart and he's kind and I respect him immensely. I love him as a friend, and I want him to be happy. I know that marrying me would make him happy, or at least he's told me it will. And of course I would love for Mia to have someone to call Daddy."

"But?" Marcus asked, leaning back on his arms, stretching his long legs out in front of him, as if he were settling in for a good story.

"But I want *me* to be happy, too. I deserve it."

"My father doesn't make you happy?"

"He does but…" She sighed. There was really no getting around this. "What are your feelings about intimacy before marriage?"

He didn't even hesitate. "It's immoral."

His answer took her aback. "Well, this is a first."

"What?"

"I've never met a twenty-eight-year-old virgin."

His brows slammed together. "I never said that I'm…"

He paused, realizing that he'd painted himself into a corner, and the look on his face was priceless.

"Oh, so what you're saying is, it's only immoral for your father to be intimate before marriage. For you it's fine?"

"My father is from a different generation. He thinks differently."

"Well, that's one thing you're right about. And it's a big part of my problem."

"What do you mean?"

"I believe two people should know whether or not they're sexually compatible before they jump into a marriage, because let's face it, sex is a very important part of a lasting relationship. Don't you agree?"

"I suppose it is."

"You suppose? Be honest. Would you marry a woman you'd never slept with?"

He hesitated, then said, "Probably not."

"Well, Gabriel is so traditional he won't even kiss me until we're officially engaged. And he considers sex before the wedding completely out of the question."

"You seriously want me to believe that you and my father have never…" He couldn't seem to make himself say the words, which she found kind of amusing.

"Is that really so surprising? You said yourself he's from a different generation. He didn't have sex with your mom until their wedding night, and even then he said it took a while to get all the gears moving smoothly."

Marcus winced.

"Sorry. TMI?"

"TMI?"

"Too much information?"

He nodded. "A bit."

"Honestly, I don't know why I'm telling you *any* of this, seeing as how it's really none of your business. And nothing I say is going to change the way you feel about me."

"So why are you telling me?"

"Maybe it's that I've gone through most of my life being

unfairly judged and I'm sick of it. I really shouldn't care if you like me or not, but for some stupid reason, I still do."

Marcus looked as if he wasn't sure what to believe. "I don't *dis*like you."

"But you don't trust me. Which is only fair, I guess, since I don't trust you either."

Seven

Instead of looking insulted, Marcus laughed, which completely confused Vanessa.

"You find that amusing?" she asked.

"What I find amusing is that you said it to my face. Do you ever have a thought that you *don't* express?"

"Sometimes." Like when she hadn't told him how his pale gray linen pants hugged his butt just right, and the white silk short sleeved shirt brought out the sun-bronzed tones of his skin. And she didn't mention how the dark shadow of stubble on his jaw made her want to reach up and touch his face. Or the curve of his mouth made her want to…well, never mind. "When I was a kid, every time I expressed an idea or a thought, my father shot it down. He had this way of making me feel inferior and stupid, and I'm *not* stupid. It just took a while to figure that out. And now I say what I feel, and I don't worry about what other people think, because most of them don't matter.

When it comes to my self-worth, the only opinion that really matters is my own. And though it took a long time to get here, I'm actually pretty happy with who I am. Sure, my life isn't perfect, and I still worry about making mistakes, but I know that I'm capable and smart, and if I do make a mistake, I'll learn from it."

"So what will you do?" he asked. "About my father, I mean. If he won't compromise his principles."

"I'm hoping that if we spend more time together, I'll just know that it's right."

"You said it yourself, you're a very beautiful woman, and my father seems to have very strong feelings for you. I'm quite certain that with little effort you could persuade him to compromise his principles."

Was he actually suggesting she *seduce* Gabriel? And why, when Marcus said she was beautiful, did it cause a little shiver of delight? She'd heard the same words so many times from so many men, they had lost their significance. Why was he so different? And why did she care *what* he thought of her?

And why on earth had she started this conversation in the first place?

"I would never do that," she told Marcus. "I respect him too much."

Mia began to fuss and Vanessa jumped on the opportunity to end this strange and frankly *inappropriate* chat. No matter what she did or said, or how she acted, the situation with Marcus just seemed to get weirder and weirder.

"I should get her back to the palace and down for a nap. And I could probably use one too." She was still on L.A. time, and despite being exhausted last night, she'd slept terribly.

He pushed himself to his feet. "Let's go."

Together they cleaned up the picnic, and to Vanessa's

surprise, Marcus lifted Mia up and held her while she folded the blanket. Even more surprising was how natural he appeared holding her, and how, when she reached to take her back, Mia clung to him and laid her head on his shoulder.

Little traitor, she thought, but she couldn't resist smiling. "I guess she wants you," she told Marcus, who looked as if he didn't mind at all.

They gathered the rest of their things and walked back to the limo waiting in the marina parking lot. They piled into the air-conditioned backseat, and she buckled Mia into her car seat. She expected that they would go straight back to the palace but instead, Marcus had the driver stop outside one of the shops they had visited earlier and went inside briefly. He came out several minutes later carrying a small bag that he slipped into his pants pocket before climbing back in the car, and though she was curious as to what was in it, she didn't ask, for fear of opening up yet another can of worms. He'd probably picked out a gift for his girlfriend. Because men who looked the way he did, and were filthy rich princes, always had a lady friend—if not two or three. And according to Gabriel, his son was never short on female companionship.

Mia fell asleep on the ride back, and when they pulled up to the front doors to the palace, before Vanessa had a chance, Marcus unhooked her from the car seat and plucked her out.

"I can carry her," she told him.

"I've got her," he said, and not only did he carry her all the way up to the nursery, he laid her in her crib and covered her up, the way a father would if Mia had one. And somewhere deep down a part of Vanessa ached for all the experiences her daughter had missed in her short life. Because she knew what it was like to lose a parent, to miss that connection. She hoped with all her heart that Gabriel could fill the void, that these months without a father hadn't left a permanent scar on Mia.

"She was really good today," he said, grinning down at Mia while she slept soundly.

"She's a pretty easygoing baby. You saw her at her very worst yesterday."

Vanessa let Karin know to listen for Mia so she could take a quick nap herself—thinking this nanny business was sort of nice after all—then Marcus walked her down the hall to her room. She stopped at the door and turned to him. "Thank you for taking me to the village today. I actually had a really good time."

One brow lifted a fraction. "And that surprises you?"

"Yeah, it does. I figured it could go either way."

The corners of his mouth crept up into a smile and those dimples dented his cheeks. Which made her heart go pitter-patter. He was too attractive for his own good. And hers.

"Too honest for you?" she asked him.

He shrugged. "I think I'm getting used to it."

Well, that was a start.

"My father would like me to take you to the history museum tomorrow," he said.

"Oh."

One brow rose. "Oh?"

"Well, I'm still pretty exhausted from the trip and I thought a day to just lie around by the pool might be nice. Mia loves playing in the water and I desperately need a tan. Back home I just never seem to have time to catch any sun. And you don't need to feel obligated to hang out with us. I'm sure you have things you need to do."

"You're sure?"

"I am."

"Then we can see the museum another day?"

She nodded. "That would be perfect."

He started to turn, then paused and said, "Oh, I almost forgot."

He pulled the bag from the shop out of his pocket and handed it to her. "This is for you."

Perplexed, she took it from him. "What is it?"

"Look and see."

She opened the bag and peered inside, her breath catching when she recognized the contents. "But...how did you know?"

"I saw you admiring them."

He didn't miss a thing, did he?

She pulled the earrings from the bag. They were hand-crafted with small emeralds set inside delicate silver swirls, and she'd fallen in love with them the instant she'd seen them in the shop, but at one hundred and fifty euros they had been way out of her budget.

"Marcus, they're lovely." She looked up at him. "I don't get it."

Hands hooked casually in his pants pockets, he shrugged. "If you had been there with my father, I don't doubt that he would have purchased them on the spot. It's what he would have wanted me to do."

She couldn't help but think that this meant something. Something significant. "I don't even know what to say. Thank you so much."

"What is it you Americans say? It's not a big deal?"

No, it was a *very* big deal.

It bothered her when Gabriel bought her things. It was as if he felt it necessary to buy her affections. But Marcus had no reason to buy her anything, other than the fact that he *wanted* to. It came from the heart. More so than any gift Gabriel had gotten her—or at least, that was the way she saw it.

Swallowing back tears of pure happiness—unsure of why it even mattered so much to her—she smiled and said, "I should go. Gabriel will be Skyping me soon."

"Of course. I'll see you tomorrow."

She watched him walk down the hall until he disappeared around the corner, then slipped into her room and shut the door behind her. Knowing how much it meant to Gabriel, she had really been hoping that she and Marcus could be friends. And now it seemed that particular wish might actually come true.

Marcus pushed off the edge of the pool for his final lap, his arms slicing through the water, heavy with fatigue due to the extra thirty minutes he'd spent in the pool pondering his earlier conversation with Vanessa. If what she said was true, and she and his father hadn't been intimate, what else could have possibly hooked him in? Her youth, and the promise of a fresh beginning, maybe?

Marcus's mother had confided once, a long time ago, that she and his father had hoped to have a large family, but due to complications from Marcus's birth—details she'd mercifully left out—more children became an impossibility. Maybe he saw this as his chance to start the family he always wanted but could never have. Because surely someone as adept at parenting as Vanessa would want more children.

Or maybe he saw what Marcus had seen today. A woman who was smart and funny and a little bizarre. And of course beautiful.

So much so that you had to buy her a present?

He reached the opposite end of the pool, debated stopping, then flipped over and pushed off one last time.

He really had no idea why he'd bought Vanessa the earrings. But as they were on their way back to the palace and he saw the shop, he heard himself asking the driver to stop, and before he knew what he was doing, he was inside, handing over his Visa card, and the clerk was bagging his purchase.

Maybe he and Vanessa had made some sort of...*connection*. But that wasn't even the point, because what he'd told her was true. If his father had seen her admiring the earrings he would have purchased them on the spot. Marcus did it to please his father and nothing more.

But the surprise on her face when she opened the bag and realized what was inside...

She looked so impressed and so grateful, he worried that she might burst into tears. That would have been really awful, because there was nothing worse than a woman in the throes of an emotional meltdown. And all for such a simple and inexpensive gift. If her only concern was wealth, wouldn't she have balked at anything but diamonds or precious gems? And if she were using his father, why would she admit that she wasn't in love with him? Why would she have discussed it at all?

Maybe, subconsciously, he'd seen it as some sort of test. One that she had passed with flying colors.

Marcus reached the opposite edge and hoisted himself up out of the water, slicking his hair back, annoyed that he was wasting any time debating this with himself.

He sighed and squinted at the sun, which hung close to the horizon, a reddish-orange globe against the darkening sky. The evening breeze cooled his wet skin. The fact of the matter was, though he didn't want to like Vanessa, he couldn't seem to help himself. He'd never met anyone quite like her.

From the table where he'd left it, his cell phone began to ring. Thinking it could be his father with an update about Aunt Trina, he pushed himself to his feet and grabbed the phone, but when he saw the number he cursed under his breath. He wasn't interested in anything his ex had to say, and after three weeks of avoiding her incessant phone calls and text messages, he would have expected that she'd gotten the point by now.

Apparently not. Leaving him to wonder what it was he'd seen in her in the first place. How could someone who had bewitched him so thoroughly now annoy him so completely?

Aggressive women had never really been Marcus's first choice in a potential mate. But sexy, sultry and with a body to die for, Carmela had pursued him with a determination that put other women to shame. She was everything he could have wanted in a wife, or so he believed, and because she came from a family of considerable wealth and power, he never once worried that she was after his money. Six months in he'd begun to think about engagement rings and wedding arrangements, only to discover that he'd been terribly wrong about her. And though the first week after the split had been difficult, he'd gradually begun to realize his feelings for her were based more on infatuation and lust than real love. His only explanation was that he'd been emotionally compromised by his mother's death. And the fact that she had taken advantage of that was, in his opinion, despicable. And unforgivable.

He shuddered to think what would have happened had he actually proposed, or God forbid *married* her. And he was disappointed in himself that he'd let it go as far as he had, that he'd been so blinded by her sexual prowess. And honestly, the actual sex wasn't that great. Physically, she gave him everything he could ask for and more, but emotionally their encounters had left him feeling…empty. Maybe it had been an unconscious need for a deeper connection that had kept him coming back for more, but now, looking back, he could hardly believe what a fool he'd been.

His text message alert chimed, and of course it was from her.

"Enough already," he ground out, turning on his heel and flinging his cell phone into the pool. Only when he looked up past the pool to the garden path did he realize that he had an audience.

Vanessa stood on the garden path watching Marcus's cell phone hit the surface of the water, then slowly sink down, until it was nothing but a murky shadow against the tile bottom.

"You know," she told Marcus, who clearly hadn't realized that she was standing there, "I have that same impulse nearly every day of my life. Although I usually imagine tossing it off the roof of the hotel, or under the wheels of a passing semi."

He sighed and raked a hand through his wet hair, the last remnants of evening sunshine casting a warm glow over his muscular arms and chest, his toned to perfection thighs. And though the Speedo covered the essentials, it was wet and clingy and awfully…well, revealing.

Ugh, what was she, *twelve?* It wasn't as if she hadn't seen a mostly naked man before. Or a completely naked one for that matter. Of course, none of them had been quite so…yummy.

Remember, this is your almost fiancé's son you're ogling. The thought filled her with guilt. Okay, maybe that was an exaggeration, but she did feel a mild twinge.

"That was childish of me," he said, looking as if he were disappointed in himself.

"But did it feel good?" she asked.

He hesitated, then a smile tilted the corners of his mouth. "Yeah, it did. And I needed a new one anyway."

"Then it's worth it."

"What are you doing out here?" He grabbed his towel from the table and began to dry himself. His arms, his pecs, the wall of his chest...

Oh boy. What she wouldn't give to be that towel right now.

Think son-in-law, Vanessa.

"Mia went down early, and I was feeling a little restless," she told him. "I thought I would take a walk."

"After all the walking we did today? You should be exhausted."

"I'm on my feet all day every day. Today was a cakewalk. Plus I'm trying to acclimate myself to the time change. If I go to bed too early I'll never adjust. And for the record, I am exhausted. I haven't slept well since I got here."

"Why not?" He draped the towel over the back of a chair, then took a seat, leaning casually back, with not a hint of shame. Not that he had anything to be ashamed of, and there was nothing more appealing than a man so comfortable in his own skin. Especially one who looked as good as he did.

"I keep waking up and listening for Mia, then I remember that she's down the hall. And of course I feel compelled to get up and go check on her. Then it's hard to get back to sleep. I thought a walk might relax me."

"Why don't you join me for a drink?" he said. "It might take the edge off."

She'd never been one to drink very often, and lately, with an infant in her care, she'd more or less stopped altogether. But now there was a nanny to take over if Vanessa needed her. Maybe it would be okay, just this once, to let her hair down a little.

And maybe Marcus would put some clothes on.

"Yeah, sure. I'd love one," she told him, and as if by magic, or probably ESP, the butler materialized from a set of French doors that led to…well, honestly, she wasn't sure where they led. She had gone out a side door to the garden, one patrolled by armed guards. She probably wouldn't have been able to find even that if Camille hadn't shown her the way. The palace had more twists and turns than a carnival fun house.

"What would you like?" Marcus asked.

"What do you have?"

"We have a fully stocked bar. George can make anything you desire."

She summoned a list of drinks that she used to enjoy, and told George, "How about…a vodka tonic with a twist of lime?"

George nodded, turned to Marcus, and in a voice as craggy and old as the man said, "Your highness?"

"The same for me. And could you please let Cleo know that I'll be needing a new phone, and a new number."

George nodded and limped off, looking as if every step took a great deal of effort.

Vanessa took a seat across from Marcus and when George was out of earshot asked, "How old is he?"

"I'm really not sure. Eighties, nineties. All I know is that he's been with the family since my father was a child."

"He looks as if he has a hard time getting around."

"He has rheumatoid arthritis. And though his staff does most of the real work these days, I assure you he's still quite capable, and has no desire to retire anytime soon. Honestly, I don't think he has anywhere else to go. As far as I'm aware, he's never been married. He has no children. We're his only family."

"That's kind of sad," Vanessa said, feeling a sudden burst of sympathy for the cranky old butler. She couldn't imagine being so alone in the world. Or maybe he didn't see it that way. Maybe his career, his attachments with the royal family and the other staff, were all the fulfillment he needed.

"If you'll excuse me a moment," Marcus said, rising from his seat. "I should probably go change before I catch a chill."

She had wanted him to put clothes on, but she couldn't deny being slightly disappointed. But the blistering heat of the afternoon did seem to be evaporating with the setting sun, and a cool breeze had taken its place.

While he was gone, Vanessa slipped her sandals off and walked over to the pool. She sat on the edge, dipping her feet in water warm enough to bathe in. She'd never been much of a swimmer—or into any sort of exercise, despite how many times her father had pushed her to try different sports and activities. She had the athletic prowess of a brick, and about as much grace. And firearms being his passion, he'd tried relentlessly to get her on the firing range. He'd gone as far as to get her a hunting rifle for her fourteenth birthday, but guns scared her half to death and she'd refused to even touch it. She'd often entertained the idea that he would have been much happier with a son, and had someone offered a trade, he'd have jumped at the chance.

As the last vestiges of daylight dissolved into the horizon and the garden and pool lights switched on, Vanessa noticed the shadow of Marcus's cell phone, wondering what—or *who*—had driven him to chuck it into the water. From what Gabriel had told her, Marcus was even-tempered and composed, so whatever it was must have really upset him.

She sighed, wondering what Gabriel was doing just then. Probably sitting at the hospital, where he spent the majority of his day. Trina was still very sick, but responding to the treatment, and the doctors were cautiously optimistic that she would make a full recovery. Though Vanessa felt selfish for even thinking it, she hoped that meant Gabriel would be home soon. She wanted to get her life back on track and plan her future, because at the moment she'd never felt more unsettled or restless. And it wasn't fair to Mia to keep her living in limbo, although to be honest she seemed no worse for wear.

"Your drink," Marcus said, and the sound of his voice made her jump.

She turned to find him dressed in khaki shorts and a pale silk, short sleeved shirt, that could have been gray or light blue. It was difficult to tell in the muted light.

"Sorry, didn't mean to startle you." He handed her one of the two glasses he was holding and sat next to her on the edge, slipping his bare feet into the water beside hers. He was so close, she could smell chlorine on his skin, and if she were to move her leg just an inch to the right, her thigh would touch his. For some reason the idea of actually doing it made her heart beat faster. Not that she ever would.

Eight

"I guess I was lost in thought," she said. "When I talked to Gabriel today he said that your aunt is responding to the treatment."

Marcus nodded, sipping his drink, then setting it on the tile beside him. "I spoke with him this afternoon. He said they're optimistic."

"I was kind of hoping that meant he would be home sooner. Which is pretty thoughtless, I know." She took a swallow of her drink and her eyes nearly crossed as it slid down her throat, instantly warming her insides. "Wow! That's strong."

"Would you care for something different?"

"No, I like it." She took another sip, but a smaller one this time. "It has kick, but the vodka is very…I don't know, smooth, I guess."

"George only stocks the best. And for the record, you're not thoughtless. I would say that you've been tremendously patient given the circumstances. Had it been me, considering my less than warm greeting, I probably would have turned around and gotten back on the plane."

"If it hadn't been for Mia, I might have. But another thirteen hours in the air would have done me in for sure."

Marcus was quiet for a minute, gazing at the water and the ripples their feet made on the surface. Then he mumbled something that sounded like a curse and shook his head.

"Is something wrong?" she asked him.

"Your proclivity toward brutal honesty must be rubbing off on me."

"What do you mean?"

"I probably shouldn't tell you this, and I would be breaking a confidence in doing so, but I feel as if you deserve the truth."

Vanessa's heart sank a little. "Why do I get the feeling I'm not going to like this?"

"My father told me that he would likely be three or four weeks. He didn't want you to know for fear that you wouldn't stay. It's why he wanted me to keep you entertained."

Her heart bottomed out. "But my visit will only be for six weeks. Which will leave us only two or three to get to know one another better."

What if that wasn't enough time?

Marcus shrugged. "So you'll stay longer."

Feeling hurt and betrayed, her nerves back on edge, Vanessa took another swallow of her drink. If Gabriel lied about this, what else was he lying about? "I can't stay longer. My leave from work is only six weeks. If I don't go back I'll get fired. Until I know for sure whether I'm staying here, I need that job. Otherwise I would have nothing to go back for. I have very little savings. Mia and I would essentially be on the streets."

"My father is a noble man," Marcus said. "Even if you decided not to marry him, he would never allow that to happen. He would see that you were taken care of."

"If he's so noble why would he lie to me in the first place?"

"He only did it because he cares for you."

It was a moot point because she would never take his charity. And even if she would, there was no guarantee that Gabriel would be so generous.

Marcus must have read her mind, because he added, "If he didn't see that you were taken care of, *I* would."

His words stunned her. "Why? As of this afternoon, you still believed that I'm using him."

"I guess you could say that I've had a change of heart."

"But, *why?*"

His laugh was rich and warm and seemed to come from deep within him. "You perplex me, Vanessa. You tell me that I should give you a chance, but when I do, you question my motives. Perhaps it's you who needs to give *me* a chance."

She had indeed said that. "You're right. I guess I'm just feeling very out of sorts right now." She touched his arm lightly, found it to be warm and solid under her palm. "I'm sorry."

He looked at her hand resting on his forearm, then up into her eyes, and said, "Apology accepted."

There was something in their sooty depths, some emotion that made her heart flip in her chest, and suddenly she felt warm all over.

It's just the vodka, she assured herself, easing her hand away and taking a deep swallow from her glass.

"Would you care for another?" Marcus asked.

She looked down and realized that her glass was empty, while his was still more than half full.

"I probably shouldn't," she said, feeling her muscles slacken with the warm glow of inebriation. It was the most relaxed she had felt in weeks. Would one more drink be such a bad thing? In light of what she'd just learned, didn't she deserve it? With Mia in the care of her nanny, what reason did Vanessa have to stop? "But what the hell, why not? It's not as if I have to drive home, right?"

Marcus gestured randomly and George must have been watching for it—which to her was slightly creepy—because moments later he appeared with a fresh drink. And either this one wasn't as strong, or the first had numbed her to the intensity of the vodka. Whatever the reason, she drank liberally.

"So, would I be overstepping my bounds to ask why you drowned your phone?" Vanessa said.

"A persistent ex-lover."

"I take it you dumped her."

"Yes, but only after I caught her in the backseat of the limo with my best friend."

"Ouch. Were they...you know..."

"Yes. Quite enthusiastically."

She winced. So he'd lost his mother, his girlfriend and his best friend. How sucky was that? "I'm sorry."

He slowly kicked his feet back and forth through the water, the side of his left foot brushing against her right one. She had to force herself not to jump in surprise.

"Each tried to pin it on the other. She's still trying to convince me that he lured her there under false pretenses, and once he had her in the car he more or less attacked her."

She let her foot drift slightly to the left, to see if it would happen again. "She cried rape?"

"More or less."

"What did your friend say?"

"That she lured him into the car, and she made the first move."

"Who do you believe?"

"Neither of them. In the thirty seconds or so that I was standing there in shock, she never once told him no, and she wasn't making any attempt to stop him. I think all the moaning they were both doing spoke for itself."

His foot bumped hers again, and a tiny thrill shot up from her foot and through her leg, settling in places that were completely inappropriate considering their relationship.

"Were you in love with her?" Vanessa asked him.

"I thought I was, but I realize now it was just lust."

"Sometimes it's hard to tell the two apart."

"Is that how it is with you and my father?"

What she felt for Gabriel was definitely not lust. "Not at all. Gabriel is a good friend, and I love and respect him for that. It's the lust part we need to work on."

Her candor seemed to surprise him. "And he knows you feel that way?"

"I've been completely honest with him. He's convinced that my feelings for him will grow. And I'm hoping he's right."

His foot brushed hers again, and this time she could swear it was intentional. Was he honestly playing footsies with her? And why was her heart beating so fast, her skin tingling with awareness? And why was she mentally willing him to touch her in other places too, but with his hands?

Because there is something seriously wrong with you, honey. But knowing that didn't stop her from leaning back on her arms and casually shifting her leg so her thigh brushed his.

Now this, what she was feeling right now, *this* was lust. And it was so wrong.

"I learned last week that her father's company is in financial crisis and on the verge of collapse," Marcus said, and it took Vanessa a second to realize that he was talking about his ex. "I guess she thought that an alliance with the royal family would have pulled him from the inevitable depths of bankruptcy."

"So you think she was using you?"

"It seems a safe assumption."

Well, that at least explained why he was so distrustful of Vanessa. He obviously looked at her and saw his ex. She shook her head in disgust and said, "What a bitch."

Marcus's eyes widened, and Vanessa slapped a hand across her mouth. Why couldn't she learn to hold her tongue? "Sorry, that was totally inappropriate of me."

Instead of looking angry, or put out, Marcus just laughed.

"No, it was more appropriate than you would imagine. And unfortunately she wasn't the first. But usually I'm better at spotting it. I think my mother's death left such a gaping hole, and I was so desperate to fill it I had blinders on."

"You want to hear something ironic? In my junior year of high school, I caught my boyfriend in the back of his car with my so-called friend."

His brow lifted. "Was it a limo?"

She laughed. "Hardly. It was piece of crap SUV."

"What did you do when you caught them?"

"Threw a brick through the back window."

He laughed. "Maybe that's what I should have done."

"I was really mad. I had just written his history term paper for him, and he got an A. I found out later from one of my 'friends' that he'd only dated me because I was smart, and in most of the same classes and willing to help him with his homework. I was stupid enough to do it for him. And let him copy off my tests. He played football, and if his grades dropped he would be kicked off the team. Pretty much everyone knew he was using me."

"And no one told you?"

"Suffice it to say they weren't my friends after that. My dad was reassigned a month later. It was one of the few times I was really relieved to be starting over."

"I hope you at least reported him to the headmaster," Marcus said.

"You have no idea how badly I wanted to go to our teachers and the principal and tell them what I'd been doing, that his work was really my work. Not only could I have gotten him kicked off the team, he would have been expelled."

"Why didn't you?"

"Because I would have been expelled too. And my father would have *killed* me. Not to mention that it was completely embarrassing. I should have known, with his reputation, he would never seriously date a girl who didn't put out unless he was after something else. Not that he didn't try to get in my pants every chance he got."

"You shouldn't blame yourself. You have a trusting nature. That's a good thing."

Not always. "Unfortunately, I seem to attract untrustworthy men. It's as if I have the word *gullible* stamped in invisible ink on my forehead, and only jerks can see it."

"Not all men use women."

"All the men I've known do."

"Surely not everyone has been that bad."

"Trust me, if there was a record for the world's worst luck with men, I would hold it. When Mia's dad walked out on me, I swore I would never let a man use me again. That I would never trust so blindly. But then I met Gabriel and he's just so…wonderful. And he treated me as if I were something special."

"That's because he thinks you are. From the minute he returned home he couldn't stop talking about you." He laid a hand on her arm, gave it a gentle squeeze, his dark eyes soft with compassion. "He's not using you, Vanessa."

Weird, but yesterday he was convinced she was using his father. When had everything gotten so turned around?

And why, as they had a heart-to-heart talk about his father—one that should have drawn her closer to Gabriel—could she only think about Marcus? Why did she keep imagining what it would be like to lay her hand on his muscular thigh, feel the crisp dark hair against her palm? Why did she keep looking at his mouth, and wondering how it would feel pressed against hers?

Maybe they both would have been better off if he kept acting like a jerk, because it was becoming painfully clear that Vanessa had developed a major crush. On the wrong man.

"Do you think someone can fall in love, real love, in a matter of two weeks?" Vanessa asked Marcus.

He could tell her that he believed falling in love so fast was nothing but a fairy tale, and that he thought his father was rebounding. What he felt for Vanessa was infatuation and nothing more, and he would realize that when he returned from Italy. Marcus knew if he told Vanessa that, she was confused and vulnerable enough that she might actually believe him. Which would discourage her, and fill her with self-doubt, and might ultimately make her leave. And wasn't that what he'd wanted?

But now, he couldn't make himself say the words.

Something had changed. He was instead telling her things that would make her want to stay, and for reasons that had nothing to do with his father's happiness, and everything to do with Marcus's fascination with her. She wasn't helping matters by encouraging him, by moving closer when he touched her, looking up at him with those expressive blue eyes. And did she have to smell so good? Most of the women he knew bathed themselves in cloying perfume, Carmela included, but Vanessa smelled of soap and shampoo. And he could smell that only because they were sitting so close to one another. *Too* close. If he had any hope of fighting these inappropriate feelings, he really needed to back off.

"I believe that when it comes to love, anything is possible," he told her, which wasn't a lie exactly. He just didn't believe it in this case. And the idea that she might be hurt again disturbed him more than he could have ever imagined possible. Maybe because he knew it was inevitable. He just hoped that when his father let her down, he did it gently. Or maybe after waiting for his father for so many weeks, she would grow frustrated and decide she didn't want to stay after all.

Now that Marcus had gotten to know her better, he wasn't any more sure of what to expect. He'd never met a woman more confusing or unpredictable. Yet in a strange way, he felt he could relate to her—understand her even—which made no sense at all.

But what baffled him most was how wrong he'd been about her, when he was so sure he'd had her pegged. He hadn't given his father nearly enough credit, had just assumed he was too vulnerable to make intelligent choices, and for that Marcus would always feel foolish.

George appeared at his side with two fresh drinks. Marcus took them and held one out to Vanessa. She looked in the glass she was still holding as if she were surprised to realize that it was empty.

"Oh, I really shouldn't," she said, but as he moved to give it back to George, added, "But it would be a shame to let the good stuff go to waste. No more after this though."

George shuffled off with their empty glasses, shaking his head in either amusement or exasperation, Marcus couldn't be sure which. None of the staff were sure what to think of her, and that was in large part Marcus's fault, as he'd made his feelings about her visit quite clear from the moment his father had broken the news. Now he knew that he'd unfairly judged her, and that was something he needed to rectify.

"Your dad said that when he met your mom it was love at first sight," she said. "And it was a big scandal because she wasn't a royal."

"Yes, my grandparents were very traditional. There was already a marriage arranged for him but he loved my mother. They threatened to disown him. He said it was the only time in his life that he rebelled against their wishes."

"That must have been difficult for your mom. To know that they hated her so much they would disown their own child."

"It wasn't her so much as the idea of her that they resented, but things improved after I was born. My father was an only child, so they were happy that she'd given my father a male heir."

"So your father wouldn't mind if you married a non-royal?"

"My parents have been very insistent my entire life that as sole heir it's imperative I also produce an heir, but they want me to marry for love."

"Like they did."

He nodded.

"What was your mom like?" she asked.

Just thinking of her brought a smile to his face. "Beautiful, loyal, outspoken—more so than some people thought a queen should be. She grew up in a middle-class family in Italy, so she had a deep respect for the common man. You actually remind me of her in a way."

She blinked in surprise. "*I* do?"

"She was brave and smart, and she wasn't afraid to speak her mind. Even if it got her into trouble sometimes. And she was a positive role model to young women."

"Brave?" she said, looking at him as though he'd completely lost his mind. "I'm constantly terrified that I'm doing the wrong thing, or making the wrong choice."

"But that doesn't stop you from *making* the choice, and that takes courage."

"Maybe, but I fail to see how I'm a role model to women. My life has been one bad move after another."

How could she not see it, not be proud of her accomplishments? "You're well traveled, intelligent, successful. You're an excellent mother, raising a child with no help. What young woman wouldn't look up to you?"

She bit her lip, and for a second he thought she might start crying. "That's probably the nicest thing anyone has ever said to me. Though I'm pretty sure that I don't deserve it. I'm a gigantic walking disaster waiting to happen."

"That's your father talking," he said.

"In part. But I can't deny that I've made some really dumb decisions in my life."

"Everybody does. How will you learn if you don't make occasional mistakes?"

"The problem is, I don't seem to be learning from mine."

Why couldn't she see what he did? Was she really so beaten down by her father's overinflated ideals that she had no self-confidence left? And what could he do to make her believe otherwise? How could he make her see how gifted and special and unique she really was? "You don't give yourself enough credit. If you weren't an extraordinary person, do you really think my father would have fallen so hard for you so fast?"

Nine

Their eyes met and Vanessa's were so filled with hope and vulnerability, Marcus had to resist the urge to pull her into his arms and hold her. His gaze dropped to her mouth, and her lips looked so plump and soft, he couldn't help but wonder how they would feel, how they would taste.

The sudden pull of lust in his groin caught him completely off guard, but he couldn't seem to look away.

Carmela and most other women he'd dated favored fitted, low-cut blouses and skintight jeans. They dressed to draw attention. In shorts and a T-shirt and with no makeup on her face, her pale hair cascading down in loose waves across her shoulders, Vanessa didn't look particularly sexy. Other than being exceptionally beautiful, she looked quite ordinary, yet he couldn't seem to keep his eyes off her.

Vanessa was the one to turn her head, but not before he saw a flash of guilt in her eyes, and he knew, whatever these improper feeling were, she was having them too.

Vanessa rubbed her arms. "It's getting chilly, huh?"

"Would you like to go inside?" he asked.

She shook her head, gazing up at the night sky. "Not yet."

"I could have George bring us something warm to drink."

"No, thank you."

They were both quiet for several minutes, but there was a question that had been nagging him since their conversation this afternoon in the park. "You said that you were afraid two or three weeks wouldn't be long enough to get to know my father better. I'm wondering, what guarantee did you have that four weeks would be? Or six?"

She shrugged. "There was no guarantee. But I had to at least try. For him. And for Mia."

"What about you?"

"For me, too," she said, avoiding his gaze.

Why did he get the feeling her own needs were pretty low on the priority scale? The way he saw it, either you were physically attracted to someone or you weren't. There was no gray area. And it seemed a bit selfish of his father to push her into something she clearly was unsure about.

She took a swallow of her drink, then blinked rapidly, setting her glass on the tile beside her. "You know, I think I've had enough. I feel a little woozy. And it's getting late. I should check on Mia."

It was odd, but although he'd had no intention of spending the evening with her, now he wasn't ready for it to end. All the more reason that it should. "Shall I walk you back to your room?"

"You might have to. I'm honestly not sure I could find it by myself."

"Tomorrow I'll have Cleo print a map for you." Two days ago it wouldn't have mattered to him, now he wanted her to feel comfortable in the palace. It was the least he could do.

He set his drink down and pulled himself to his feet, the night air cool against his wet skin, and extended a hand to help her. It felt so small and fragile, and it was a good thing he was holding on, because as he pulled her to her feet, she was so off balance she probably would have fallen into the pool.

"Are you okay?" he asked, pulling her away from the edge.

"Yeah." She blinked several times then gave her head a shake, as if to clear it, clutching his hand in a death grip. "Maybe I shouldn't have had that last drink."

"Would you like to sit back down?"

She took several seconds to get her bearings, then said, "I think I should probably just get to bed."

His first thought, depraved as it was, was "Why don't I join you." But, while he could think it, and perhaps even wish it a little, it was something he would never say out loud. And even more important, never do.

Could this be more embarrassing?

Feeling like an idiot, Vanessa clung to Marcus's arm as he led her across the patio. So much for letting her hair down a little.

"On top of everything else, now you probably think I have a drinking problem," she said.

Marcus grinned, his dimples forming dents in both cheeks, and she felt that delicious little zing. Did he have to be so...*adorable?*

"Maybe if you'd had ten drinks," he said, stopping by the table so she could grab her phone and they could both slip into their sandals. "But you only had three, and you didn't even finish the last one. I'm betting it has more to do with the jet lag."

"Jet lag can do that?"

"Sure. So can fatigue. Are you certain you can make it upstairs? I could carry you."

Yeah, because that wouldn't be completely humiliating. Besides, she liked holding on to his arm. And she couldn't help wondering what it would be like to touch him in other places. Not that she would ever try. She probably wouldn't be feeling this way at all if it weren't for the alcohol.

Well, okay, she probably would, but never in a million years would she act on it. Even though he thought she was smart and brave and successful. Plus, he'd left out beautiful. That was usually the first, and sometimes the only thing, that people noticed about her. Gabriel must have told her a million times. Remarkably, Marcus seemed to see past that.

"I think I can manage," she told him.

Clutching her cell phone in one hand and his forearm in the other, she wobbled slightly as he led her across the patio, but as they reached the French doors, she stopped. "Could we possibly walk around the side, through the garden?"

"What for?"

She chewed her lip, feeling like an irresponsible adolescent, which is probably how everyone else in the palace would see her as well. "I'm too embarrassed to have anyone see me this way. The entire staff already thinks I'm a horrible person. Now they're going to think I'm a lush, too."

"What does it matter what they think?"

"Please," she said, tugging him toward the garden path. "I feel so stupid."

"You shouldn't. But if it means that much to you, we'll go in the side entrance."

"Thank you."

Actually, now that she was on her feet, she felt steadier, but she kept holding on to his arm anyway. Just in case. Or just because it felt nice. He was tall and sturdy and reliable. And warm. He made her feel safe. She tried to recall if any man had made her feel that way before and drew a blank. Surely there must have been someone.

They headed down the path, around the back of the palace to the east side. At least, she was pretty sure it was east, or maybe it was west. Or north. Suddenly she felt all turned around. But whichever way it was, she remembered it from earlier, even though it was a lot darker now, despite the solar lights lining the path.

They were halfway around the building when Vanessa heard a sound on the flagstones behind them and wondered fleetingly if they were being followed. Being an L.A. resident, her first instinct was to immediately whip out her phone in case she needed to dial 911, which was how she realized her cell phone was no longer in her hand. The noise must have been her phone falling onto the path.

She let go of Marcus's arm and stopped, squinting to see in the dim light.

"What's wrong," he asked. "Are you going to be sick?"

She huffed indignantly. "I'm not *that* drunk. I dropped my phone."

"Where?"

"A few feet back, I think. I heard it hit the ground."

They backtracked, scouring the ground for several minutes, but it wasn't on or even near the path.

"Maybe it bounced into the flower bed," she said, crouching down to peer into the dense foliage, nearly falling on her butt in the process.

Marcus shook his head, looking grim. "If it did, we'll never find it at night."

"Call it!" Vanessa said, feeling rather impressed with herself for having such a brilliant idea in her compromised condition. "When we hear it ring, we'll know where it is."

"Right," he said hooking a thumb in the direction of the pool. "I'll go fish my phone out of the water and do that."

"Oh yeah, I forgot about that. Can't you borrow one?"

"Or we could look for your phone tomorrow."

"No!" Maybe he could blithely toss his electronic equipment away, but she worked for a living. Nor did she have a secretary to keep track of her life. "Besides the fact that it cost me a fortune, that phone is my life. It has my schedule and all my contacts and my music. What if it rains, or an animal gets it or something?"

He sighed loudly. "Wait here and I'll go get a phone."

She frowned. "By myself, in the dark?"

"I assure you the grounds are highly guarded and completely safe."

"What about that certain criminal element who would love to ransom the future queen?"

He smiled sheepishly. "Maybe that was a slight exaggeration. You'll be fine."

She'd expected as much. He'd been trying to drive her away, to make her *want* to leave. And as much as it annoyed her, she couldn't hold it against him. Not after all the nice things he'd said about her. Which she supposed was a big part of her problem. Someone said something nice about her and she went all gooey.

"You should stay in the general vicinity of where you lost it," Marcus warned her. "Or this could take all night."

"I'll stay right here," she said, flopping down on the path cross-legged to wait, the flagstone still warm from the afternoon sun.

Marcus grinned and shook his head. She watched as he backtracked from where they'd come, until he disappeared around a line of shrubs.

She sat there very still, listening to sounds of the night—crickets chirping and a mild breeze rustling the trees. And she swore, if she listened really hard, she could hear the faint hiss of the ocean, that if she breathed deep enough, she could smell the salty air. Or maybe it was just her imagination. Of all the different places her father had been stationed over the years, her favorite bases had been the ones near the water. And while she loved living close to the sea, the coast of California was exorbitantly expensive. Maybe someday. Maybe even here. The palace wasn't right on the water, but it was pretty darn close.

After a few minutes of waiting, her butt started to get sore, so she scooted off the flagstone path into the cool, prickly grass. Falling backward onto the spongy sod, she looked up at the sky. It was a crystal-clear night with a half moon, and even with the lights around the grounds, she could see about a million stars. In L.A. the only way to see the stars was to drive up to the mountains. She and Mia's dad used to do that. They would camp out in the bed of his truck, alternating between making love and watching the stars. She couldn't be sure, but she suspected that Mia may have actually been conceived in the bed of that truck. An unusual place to get pregnant, but nothing about her relationship with Paul had been typical. She used to think that was a good thing, and one of their strengths, because God knew those "normal" relationships she'd had were all a disaster. Until she came home to find a "Dear Vanessa" letter and realized she was wrong. Again. He hadn't even had the guts to tell her to her face that he wasn't ready for the responsibility of a child, and they were both better off without him.

So normal was bad, and eccentric was bad, which didn't leave much else. But royal, that was one she'd never tried, and never expected to have a chance to. Yet here she was. Lying on the palace lawn on a cool summer night under a sky cloaked with stars.

Which she had to admit wasn't very royal of her. She wondered if Gabriel's wife, or even Gabriel, had ever sprawled out on the grass and gazed up at the sky. Or skipped in the rain, catching drops on their tongues. Or snowflakes. Had Gabriel and Marcus ever bundled up and built a snowman together? Had they given it coal eyes and a carrot nose? Had they made snow angels or had snowball fights? And would she really be happy married to someone who didn't know how to relax and have fun, do something silly? Would Mia miss out on an important part of her childhood? Because *everyone* had to be silly every now and then.

Or was she worrying for nothing? Suffering from a typical case of insecurity? Was she creating problems where none really existed? Was she trying to sabotage a good thing because she was too afraid to take a chance?

So much for her being brave, huh?

She pondered that for a while, until she heard footsteps on the path, and glanced over to see Marcus walking toward her, looking puzzled. He stopped beside her, hands on his slim hips, and looked down. "You okay?"

She smiled and nodded. "It's a beautiful night. I'm looking at the stars."

He looked up at the sky, then back down at her. "Are you sure you didn't fall down?"

She swatted at him, but he darted out of the way, grinning.

"Could you join me?" she said. "Unless you're not allowed."

"Why wouldn't I be?"

"I thought maybe it wasn't royal enough."

"You know, you're not making a whole lot of sense."

"Do I ever?"

He laughed. "Good point."

And that apparently didn't matter, because he lay down beside her in the grass, so close their arms were touching. And she liked the way it felt. *A lot.* She liked being close to him, liked the warm fuzzy feeling coupled with that zing of awareness, and that urge to reach over and lace her fingers through his. It was exciting, and scary.

But of course she wouldn't do it, because even she wasn't that brave.

"You're right," he said, gazing up at the sky. "It is beautiful."

She looked over at him. "You think I'm weird, don't you."

"Not weird, exactly, but I can safely say that I've never met anyone like you."

"I don't know if I'm royalty material. I don't think I could give this up."

"Lying in the grass?"

She nodded.

"Who said you have to?"

"I guess I just don't know what's acceptable, and what isn't. I mean, if I marry Gabriel can I still build snowmen?"

"I don't see why not."

"Can I catch rain and snowflakes on my tongue?"

"You could try, I suppose."

"Can I walk in the sand in my bare feet, and make mud pies with Mia?"

"You know, we royals aren't so stuffy and uptight that we don't know how to have fun. We're just people. We lead relatively normal lives outside of the public eye."

But normal for him, and normal for her, were two very different things. "This all happened so abruptly. I guess I just don't know what to expect."

Marcus looked over at her. "You know that if you marry my father, you'll still be the same person you are right now. There's no magic potion or incantation that suddenly makes you royal. And there are no set rules." He paused then added, "Okay, I guess there are some rules. Certain protocol we have to follow. But you'll learn."

And Gabriel should have been the one explaining that to her, not Marcus. It was Gabriel she should have been getting to know, Gabriel she needed to bond with. Instead she was bonding with Marcus, and in a big way. She could feel it. She was comfortable with him, felt as if she could really be herself. Maybe because she wasn't worried about impressing him. Or maybe she was connecting in a small way. The truth was, everything had gotten so jumbled and confused, she wasn't sure how she felt about anything right now. And she was sure the drinks weren't helping.

Everything will be clearer tomorrow, she told herself. She would talk to Gabriel again, and remember how much she cared about him and missed him, and everything would go back to normal. She and Marcus would be friends, and she would stop having these irrational feelings.

"I've been thinking," Marcus said. "You should call your father and tell him where you are."

His suggestion—the fact that he'd even thought it—puzzled her. "So he can tell me that I'm making another stupid mistake? Why would I do that?"

"*Are* you making a mistake?"

If only she could answer that question, if she could hop a time machine and flash forward a year or so in the future, she would know how this would all play out. But that would be too easy. "I guess I won't know for sure until things go south."

He exhaled an exasperated sigh. "Okay, do you *think* you're making a mistake? Would you be here if you were sure this was going to end in disaster?"

She considered that, then said, "No, *I* don't think I'm making a mistake, because even if it doesn't work out, I got to visit a country I've never been to, and meet new people and experience new things. I got to stay in a palace and meet a prince. Even if he was kind of a doofus at first."

He smiled. "Then it doesn't matter what your father thinks. And I think that keeping this from him only makes it seem as though you have something to hide. If you really want him to respect you, and have confidence in your decisions, you've got to have faith in yourself first."

"Wow. That was incredibly insightful." And he was right. "You're speaking from experience, I assume."

"I'm the future leader of this country. It's vital I convey to the citizens that I'm confident in my abilities. It's the only way they'll trust me to lead them."

"Are you confident in your abilities?"

"Most of the time. There are days when the thought of that much responsibility scares the hell out of me. But part of being an effective leader means learning to delegate." He looked at her and grinned. "And always having someone else to pin the blame on when you screw up."

He was obviously joking, and his smile was such an adorable one, it made her want to reach out and touch his cheek. "You know, you have a really nice smile. You should do it more often."

He looked up at the stars. "I think this is probably the most I've smiled since we lost my mother."

"Really?"

"Life has been pretty dull since she died. She made everything fun and interesting. I guess that's another way that you remind me of her."

The warm fuzzy feeling his words gave her were swiftly replaced by an unsettling thought. If she was so much like Marcus's mom, could that be the reason Gabriel was so drawn to her? Did he see her as some sort of replacement for the original?

Second best?

That was silly. Of course he didn't.

And if it was so silly, why did she have a sudden sick, hollow feeling in the pit of her stomach?

Ten

Remember what you told Marcus, Vanessa reminded herself. *Even if this doesn't work out, it's not a mistake.* The thought actually made her feel a tiny bit better.

"Oh, by the way…" Marcus pulled a cell phone from his shorts pocket. "What's your number?"

She'd actually forgotten all about her phone. She told him the number and he dialed, and she felt it begin to rumble…in the front pocket of her shorts! "What the—"

She pulled it out, staring dumbfounded, and Marcus started to laugh. "But…I heard it fall."

"Whatever you heard, it obviously wasn't your phone."

"Oh, geez. I'm sorry."

"It's okay." He pushed himself to his feet and extended a hand to help her up. "Why don't we get you upstairs."

As stupid as she felt right now, she was having such a nice time talking to him that she hated to actually go to her room. But it was late, and he probably had more important things to do than to entertain her in the short amount of evening that remained. He'd already sacrificed most of his day for her.

She took his hand and he hiked her up, but as he pulled her to her feet her phone slipped from her hand and this time she actually did drop it. It landed in the grass between them. She and Marcus bent to pick it up at the exact same time, their heads colliding in the process. Hard.

They muttered a simultaneous "Ow."

She straightened and reached up to touch the impact point just above her left eye, wincing when her fingers brushed a tender spot. Great, now she could look forward to a hangover *and* a concussion. Could she make an even bigger ass of herself?

"You're hurt," he said, looking worried, which made her feel even stupider.

"I'm fine. It's just a little tender."

"Let me see," he insisted, gently cradling her cheek in his palm, turning her toward the light for a better look. With his other hand he brushed her hair aside, his fingertips grazing her forehead.

Her heart fell to the pit of her stomach, then lunged upward into her throat. *Oh my god.* If her legs had been a little wobbly before, her senses slightly compromised, that was *nothing* compared to the head-to-toe, limb-weakening, mind-altering, knock-me-off-my-feet rush of sensation she was experiencing now. His face was so close she could feel his breath whisper across her cheek, and the urge to reach up and run her hand across his stubbled chin was almost irresistible.

Her breath caught and she got a funny feeling in the pit of her stomach. Then his eyes dropped to hers and what she saw in them made her knees go weak.

He wanted her. *Really* wanted her.

Don't do it, Vanessa. Don't even think *about it.*

"Does it hurt?" he asked, but it came out as a raspy whisper.

The only thing hurting right now—other than her bruised pride—was her heart, for what she knew was about to happen. For the betrayal she would feel when she talked to Gabriel tomorrow. But even that wasn't enough to jar her back to reality. She invited the kiss, begged for it even, lifted her chin as he dipped his head, and when his lips brushed hers...

Perfection.

It was the kind of first kiss every girl dreamed of. Indescribable really. Every silly cliché and romantic platitude all rolled in one. And even though it had probably been inevitable, they simply could not let it happen again. To let it happen at all had been...well, there was no justification for it. To say it was a mistake was putting it mildly. But the problem was, it didn't *feel* like a mistake. She felt a bit as though this was the first smart thing, the first *right* thing, she had done in years.

Which is probably why she was *still* kissing him. Why her arms were around his neck, her fingers curled into his hair. And why she would have kept on kissing him if Marcus hadn't backed away and said, "I can't believe I just did that."

Which made her feel even worse.

She pressed a hand to her tingling lips. They were still damp, still tasted like him. Her heart was still pounding, her knees weak. He'd *wrecked* her.

Marcus looked sick with guilt. Very much, she imagined, how she probably looked. She had betrayed Gabriel. With his own *son*. What kind of depraved person was she?

A slap to the face couldn't have sobered her faster.

"It's not your fault. I let you," she said.

"Why did you?" he asked, and she could see in his eyes that he wanted some sort of answer as to why this was happening, why they were feeling this way.

"Because…" she began, then paused. She could diffuse the situation. She could tell him that she was just lonely, or he reminded her so much of Gabriel that she was confused. But it felt wrong to lie, and there was only one honest answer to give him. "Because I wanted you to."

He took a second to process that, looking as though he couldn't decide if it was a good or a bad thing, if he should feel relieved that it wasn't all his fault, or even more guilty. "If it was something I did—"

"It wasn't!" she assured him. "I mean, it was, but it was me too. It was both of us. We're obviously just, confused, or…*something*. And it would probably be best if we don't analyze it to death. I mean, what would be the point? It doesn't matter why we did it. We know that we shouldn't have, and even more important, we know that it can't happen again. Right?"

"Right."

"So that's that?"

He was quiet for several long seconds and she waited for his confirmation, because they really needed to put an end to this now.

But instead of agreeing with her, Marcus shook his head and said, "Maybe not."

Though it seemed impossible that a heart could both sink and lift at the same time, hers managed it. "Why not?"

"Because maybe if we figure out why we did it, I'll stop feeling like I want to do it again."

Marcus watched Vanessa struggle for what to say next, feeling a bit as though he were caught up in some racy evening television drama. This sort of thing didn't happen in real life. Not in civilized society anyway. Men did not have affairs with their fathers' female companions, and that was exactly what he thinking of doing.

What was *wrong* with him?

She'd admitted that she was not *in* love with his father, nor was she physically attracted to him. And Marcus truly believed they would never marry. But until Vanessa's relationship with his father was completely over, he had no right to lay a finger on her. Even then a relationship with her could potentially come between him and his father.

Not that he even *wanted* a relationship. After Carmela, he had vowed to practice the single life for a while. Like his father he was probably just rebounding, and this strange fascination was probably fleeting. He would be wise to remember that.

Like father, like son, right?

"Marcus—"

"No, you're right," he interrupted. "This was a mistake. I promise it won't happen again."

"Okay," she said, but he couldn't tell if she was relieved, or disappointed. Or if she even believed him. He wasn't sure if he believed himself.

They walked in silence up to her room, and she must have sobered up, because she was steadier now. When they reached her door she turned to him.

"I had a really good time tonight. I enjoyed our talk."

"So did I."

"And...well, thank you."

He wasn't quite sure what she was thanking him for, but he nodded anyway.

Without a backward glance, she stepped into her room and closed the door, and for a full minute Marcus just stood there, plagued with the sensation that nothing had been resolved, feeling the overpowering urge to knock on her door. The only problem was, he had no idea what he wanted to say to her.

That should have been the end of it, but something wasn't right. He just couldn't put his finger on what.

You're losing your mind, he thought with a bitter laugh, then he turned and walked down the hall. He pulled out the cell phone from his pocket, with the private number that not even Cleo knew about, and tapped on the outgoing calls icon. Vanessa's number popped up. Though he wasn't sure why he did it, he programmed the number into his address book, then stuck the phone back in his pocket.

Tomorrow would be better, he assured himself. Considering how stressful the past few months had been, and the fact that he'd been sleeping—on a good night—four or five restless hours, it was no wonder he wasn't thinking clearly. His physician had offered a prescription for sleeping pills, but Marcus was against taking medication unless absolutely necessary. The meditation that Cleo had suggested hadn't helped much either. There were times, especially in the evening, when he felt a bit as if he were walking around in a fog.

Tonight I'll sleep, he told himself, then things would be clearer in the morning. Instead, he laid in bed, tossing and turning, unable to keep his mind off Vanessa and the kiss that never should have happened. He drifted in and out of sleep, his dreams filled with hazy images that made no sense, but left him feeling edgy and restless.

Marcus dragged himself out of bed at 6 a.m. with thoughts and feelings just as jumbled as the day before. He showered, dressed and had breakfast, then he tried to concentrate on work for a while, but his mind kept wandering back to Vanessa and Mia. George had informed him that they went down to use the pool around eleven, and though he found himself wanting to join them, he knew it was a bad idea. Thinking that it might help to get away for the afternoon, he called a few acquaintances to see if anyone was free for lunch, but everyone was either busy or didn't answer their phone. Instead he ate his lunch from a tray in his suite while he read the newspaper, but after he was finished he went right back to feeling restless.

"Laps," he said to himself. Swimming laps always relieved stress. He didn't even know for sure that Vanessa was still down there. It was past one-thirty, so wouldn't Mia be due for a nap? Besides, maybe it was best to confront these feelings head-on, prove to himself that he was strong enough to resist this.

He dressed in his swimsuit, pulled on a shirt and headed down to the pool. He stepped out into the blistering afternoon heat to find that Vanessa was still there, in the water, her hair pulled back in a ponytail, not a stitch of makeup on her face. In that instant the emptiness melted away, replaced by a longing, a desire to be close to her that made it difficult to breathe. And all he could think was, *Marcus, you are in big trouble.*

Vanessa carried Mia around the shallow end of the pool, swishing her back and forth while Mia plunged her little fists into the water, giggling and squealing, delighting in the fact that she was splashing them both in the face. After what had turned out to be a long and restless night, all Vanessa really wanted to do was collapse in a lounge chair and doze the afternoon away. Thinking, of course, about anything but last night's kiss. Which she could do if she called Karin, but Mia was having so much fun, Vanessa hated to take her out of the water.

Deep down she knew it was a good thing that Marcus had decided not to join them today. Still, she couldn't deny the jerk of disappointment every time she looked over at the door and he didn't come through it. Maybe, like her, he just needed a day or two to cool down. Or maybe it had nothing to do with that, and he just had more important things to do. Either way, by lunchtime she had resigned herself to the fact that he wasn't going to show. Of course that still hadn't stopped her from looking over at the door every five minutes, just in case.

"I guess today we're on our own," she told Mia.

"You two look like you're having fun."

Vanessa nearly jumped out of her skin at the unexpected voice, and whipped around to see Marcus walking toward the pool, wearing nothing but a shirt and a little black Speedo.

Holy cow.

Her heart plunged to her knees, then shot back up into her throat, and she snapped her mouth shut before her jaw had a chance to drop open. Did the man not own a pair of swim trunks? The baggy variety that hung to the knee?

"Hi there!" she said, hoping she came across as friendly, without sounding too enthusiastic. Mia, on the other hand, heard his voice and practically dislocated her neck trying to turn and see him, and when she got a glimpse of him she let out a screech and batted at the water excitedly.

Marcus sat on the edge of the pool, dipping his feet in the water, putting his crotch exactly at eye level, and with his knees slightly spread, it was difficult not to stare.

"It's a hot one," he said, shading his eyes to look up at the clear blue sky.

It certainly was, and she wasn't referring to the weather. Maybe wishing he were in the pool with them had been a bad idea. Her gaze wandered to his mouth, which of course made her think about that kiss last night, and what they might have done if they kept kissing. If she invited him into her room.

Disaster, that's what would have happened. As it stood, the damage they had done wasn't irreparable. She could write it off as a serious lapse in judgment. Another kiss, and that may have been no longer the case.

Mia on the other hand had no shame. She practically jumped out of Vanessa's arms trying to reach him.

Vanessa laughed. "I think she wants you to come in."

He pushed off the edge and slid into the water, looking even better wet. But on the bright side, she didn't have to look at as much of him.

Mia reached for him and Marcus asked, "May I?"

"Of course," she said, handing Mia over.

He held her tightly to his bare chest, as if he were afraid he might drop her, and all Vanessa could think was, *you lucky kid.* But Mia wiggled in Marcus's arms, trying to get closer to the water.

"If you turn her around and hook your arm across her belly she can play in the water," Vanessa told Marcus, and the second he turned her, she began to splash and squeal.

"It's okay if the water gets in her eyes?" he asked, looking concerned.

"Are you kidding, she loves it. She does the same thing in the bathtub. You wouldn't believe the mess she makes. When she's all soapy it's a lot like trying to bathe a squid."

"She's pretty slippery without the soap too," Marcus said, but he was grinning.

"If you want to put her in her floating ring she likes to be pulled around the pool. The faster the better." Vanessa grabbed the ring from the side and Mia shrieked.

Marcus laughed. "Let's give it a try."

Vanessa held the ring still while Marcus maneuvered her inside, which, with all of her squirming, was a bit like wrestling a baby octopus. When she was securely seated, he tugged her across the pool, swimming backward into the deeper water, then he spun her in circles and Mia giggled and swung her arms, beside herself with joy. It warmed her heart, but also broke it a little, to see Mia so attached to him.

She backed up against the edge of the pool and just watched them.

"She really does like this," Marcus said, looking as if he was having just as much fun.

"She loves being in the water. I wish I had more time to take her swimming, but our complex back home doesn't have a pool. I could take her to the hotel, but if I dare show my face on my day off, I inevitably get wrangled into working."

"Maybe she'll be a champion swimmer someday," Marcus said.

"Gabriel told me you used to compete."

"I was working toward a spot on the Olympic team, which meant intense training. I swam at least fifteen to twenty thousand meters a day, plus weight training and jogging."

"Wow, that is intense."

"Yeah, and it began to interfere with my royal duties, so I had to give it up. Now it's just a good way to stay in shape."

It certainly was, she thought, admiring all the lean muscle in his arms and shoulders. "It's sad that you weren't able to follow your dream."

"I was disappointed, but not devastated. My life was just meant for different things."

"It must have been really amazing growing up with all this," she said, looking up at the palace.

"Well, it didn't suck," Marcus said with a grin, all dimples and white teeth.

Vanessa laughed. Sometimes it was easy to forget that

he was a future king. He just seemed so...ordinary. Gabriel, though just as approachable, had a more serious and formal manner. His confidence, his sense of self-worth, had been intoxicating, and a little thrilling. Even if he had doubts about his abilities as king he would never admit them. And though Marcus possessed that same air of conviction, he wasn't afraid or ashamed to show vulnerability, and there was something unbelievably sexy about that. Especially for a woman like her, who was constantly second-guessing herself.

"The truth is, I was away at boarding school for the better part of my childhood," Marcus said. "But I did come home for school breaks and summer vacations."

"I'm not sure if I could do that," Vanessa said.

"Go to boarding school?"

"Send my child away to be raised by someone else. It would break my heart."

"In my family it's just what was expected, I guess. It was the same for my father, and his father before him."

"But not your mother, right? She didn't mind letting you go?"

"I know she missed me, but as I said, that's just the way things were. She had her duties as queen, and I had mine."

Vanessa had a sudden heart-wrenching thought. "If I marry your father, would I have to send Mia away to boarding school?"

For several seconds he looked as if he wasn't sure how to answer, or if she could handle the truth.

"I can only assume that's what he would want," he finally said.

"And if I refused?"

"She's your child, Vanessa. You should raise her the way you see fit."

But if Gabriel were to adopt her, then Mia would be

both of theirs. Which he had already said would be an eventuality. Until just this moment, she had only imagined that as a good thing. Now she wasn't so sure. What if they had contrasting views about raising children? And suppose they had a baby together? Would she have even less control then?

"I guess that's just another thing we'll have to discuss when he gets back," she said, then for reasons she didn't fully understand, heard herself ask, "How would you feel about sending your children away to school?"

Why would she ask such a thing when his opinions about child-rearing had no bearing on her life in the least?

"I guess I've never really considered that," Marcus said. "I suppose it would be something I would have to discuss with my wife."

She couldn't help but wonder if he was just giving her the PC answer, or if he really meant it. And honestly, why did it matter?

Eleven

Vanessa heard her phone ringing from the chair where she'd set her things. Thinking that it might be Gabriel, she pushed herself up out of the pool and rushed to grab it, the intense afternoon heat drying her skin in the few seconds it took to reach it. Her heart sank when she saw her father's number on the display. She had played over in her mind about a million times what she would say to him when he finally called, yet she was still too chicken to answer. She let the call go to voice mail, waited until her alert chimed, then listened to the message.

"Hey Nessy, it's Daddy," he said and she cringed, in part because she was a grown woman and he still referred to himself as Daddy, and also because she absolutely hated being called Nessy. It made her sound as though she belonged in a Scottish loch. "I thought I might catch you before you left for work. I just called to tell you that my platoon reunion will be in Los Angeles next week so I'm flying in."

Oh, crap. She closed her eyes and sighed.

"The reunion is a week from Friday night and I want time to see my grandbaby, so I'll be taking a flight early Thursday morning."

He wasn't coming there to see Vanessa, just Mia. Ironic considering he'd barely acknowledged her existence until she was almost three months old. Before then he referred to her as Vanessa's *latest mistake.* Knowing how disappointed he would be, she hadn't even told him she was pregnant until it was no longer possible to hide it. And when she had, he'd responded in that same tired, disappointed tone, "Vanessa, when will you learn?"

"I'll call with my flight information when I get it," his message said. "You can swing by and pick me up from the airport. See you soon!"

He never asked, he only demanded. Suppose she'd had other plans? Or was it that he just didn't care? It wasn't unlike him to visit on a whim and expect her to drop everything and entertain him. She had to endure that same old look of disappointment when she didn't cater to his every whim. It had always been that way, even when she was a kid. God forbid if she didn't get the laundry washed and ironed and the dishes done, not to mention the vacuuming and the dusting and the grocery shopping. And of course she was expected to maintain straight As in school. He ran a tight ship, and she had been expected to fall in line. And he wondered why she lit out of there the day she graduated high school. Which was, of course, another mistake.

This time she wouldn't be there to disappoint him… which in itself would be a disappointment, she supposed. The truth is, no matter what she did, in his opinion it would never be the right thing.

She sighed and dropped the phone back onto the chair, then looked up, surprised to find Marcus and Mia floating near the edge watching her.

"Everything okay?" he asked.

She forced a smile. "Sure. Fine."

"You're lying," he said.

She went for an innocent look, but was pretty sure it came out looking more like a grimace. "Why would you think that?"

"Because you're chewing on your thumbnail, and people generally do that when they're nervous."

She looked down to find she'd chewed off the tip of her left thumbnail. Damn. He didn't miss a thing, did he? And the way he was looking up at her, she began to wonder if choosing her bikini over the conservative one-piece had been a bad idea. She felt so…exposed, yet at the same time, she *liked* that he was looking at her. She *wanted* him to.

Vanessa, that is just so wrong.

"It's fine if you don't want to talk about it," he said.

She sat on the edge of the pool, dipping her feet in the water. "My father just left a message. He's coming to Los Angeles to visit next week."

"Does that mean you'll be leaving?"

The old Vanessa may have. She would have been worried about disappointing him yet again. But she was twenty-four years old, damn it. It was time to cut the umbilical cord and live her life the way she wanted. But she was the new Vanessa now, and that Vanessa was confident and strong and no longer cared what her father thought.

She hoped so at least.

"I'm not leaving," she told Marcus. "I'm going to call him back and tell him that I won't be there, and we'll have to reschedule for another time."

"And when he asks where you are?"

That was the tricky part.

"I'll tell him the truth." Maybe.

You're strong, she reminded herself. *You are responsible for your own destiny and what he thinks doesn't matter.*

And if she told herself enough times, she just might start to believe it.

Marcus stood behind Vanessa while she examined an exhibit at the museum, thinking that of all the visitors he had escorted there over the years—and there had been many—she showed by far the most intense interest. She didn't just politely browse while looking bored out of her skull. She absorbed information, reading every sign and description carefully, as if she were dedicating it to memory.

"You do realize that there's no quiz when we get back to the palace," he teased, as she read the fine print on a display of artifacts from the Varieo civil war of 1899.

She smiled sheepishly. "I'm taking forever, I know, but I just love history. It was my favorite subject in school."

"I don't mind," he told her, and he honestly didn't. Just like he hadn't minded spending the afternoon at the pool with her and Mia the day before. And not because of that hot pink bikini she'd worn. Okay, not completely because of the bikini. He just…liked her.

"I just wish Mia would sit in her stroller," Vanessa said, hiking her daughter, who had been unusually fidgety and fussy all day, higher on her hip. "She desperately needs a nap." But every time Vanessa tried to strap her into the stroller Mia would begin to howl.

"Why don't you let me hold her for a while," he said, extending his arms. Mia lunged for him.

"Jeez, kid!" Laughing, Vanessa handed her over, and

when Mia instantly settled against his shoulder, said, "She sure does like you."

The feeling was mutual. He even sort of liked having a baby around the palace. Although the idea that this little person could become his stepsister was a strange one. Not that he believed it would ever really happen. But did that possibly mean he was ready to start a family of his own? Eight months ago he would have said absolutely not. But so much had changed since then. He felt as if he'd changed, and he knew for a fact that it had everything to do with Vanessa's visit.

They walked to the next display, where Vanessa seemed intent on memorizing the name of every battle and its respective date. He stood behind her to the left, watching her, memorizing the curve of her face, the delicate shell of her ear, wishing he could reach out and touch her. He felt that way all the time lately, and the impulse was getting more difficult to ignore. And he knew, by the way she looked at him, the way her face flushed when they were close, the way her breath caught when he took her hand to help her out of the car, she felt it too.

When she was finished, she turned to Marcus, looked at him and laughed.

"What are you? The baby whisperer?"

He looked down at Mia to find that she was sleeping soundly on his shoulder. "Well, you said she needed a nap."

"You could try sitting her in the stroller now."

"I don't mind holding her."

"Are you sure?"

"Why risk waking her," he said, but the truth was, he just liked holding her. And he'd been doing it a lot more often. Yesterday he'd carried her on his shoulders as they strolled down the stretch of private beach at the marina— Vanessa wearing that ridiculous floppy hat—and Mia delighted in tugging on handfuls of his hair. Later they sat on a blanket close to the shore and let Mia play in the sand and splash in the salty water. Those simple activities had made him feel happier, feel more *human*, than he had in ages.

With Mia asleep in his arms, they turned and walked toward the next section of the museum.

"You're really good with her," Vanessa said. "Are you around kids much?"

"I have a few friends with young children, but I don't see them very often."

"The friends, or the children?"

"Either, really. Since we lost my mother I haven't felt much like socializing. The only time I see people now is at formal events where I'm bound by duty to attend, and children, especially small ones, are not typically included on the guest list."

She gazed up at him, looking sad. "It sounds lonely."

"What does?"

"Your life. Everyone needs friends. Would your mother be happy if she knew how you've isolated yourself?"

"No, she wouldn't. But the only true friend I had betrayed me. Sometimes I think I'm better off alone."

"I could be your friend," she said. "And having experienced firsthand what it feels like to be betrayed by a friend, you can trust that I would never do that to you."

Despite everything he'd learned of her the past three days, the blunt statement still surprised him. And he couldn't help but wonder if that might be a bad idea, that if being her friend would only strengthen the physical attraction he felt growing nearly every time he looked at her, every time she opened her mouth and all that honesty spilled out. Which is why he shouldn't have said what he said next.

"In that case, would you care to join me for dinner on the veranda tonight?"

The invitation seemed to surprise her. "Um, yeah, I'd love to. What time?"

"How about eight?"

"Mia goes to bed right around then, so that would be perfect. And I assume you mean the veranda in the west wing, off the dining room?"

"That's the one. I see you've been studying your map."

"Since I'm going to be here a while either way, I should probably learn my way around." She glanced at her watch, frowned and said, "Wow, I didn't realize how late it is. Maybe we should think about getting back."

"I'm in no hurry if you want to stay."

"I really do need to get back," she said, looking uncomfortable. "Gabriel promised to Skype me at four today, so…"

So she obviously was looking forward to speaking to him. And was that jealousy he was feeling? He forced a smile and kept his tone nonchalant. "Well then, by all means, let's go."

You have no reason to be nervous, Vanessa told herself for the tenth time since she'd left her room and made her way to the veranda. They'd spent all day together and though it had been a little awkward at times, Marcus had been a perfect gentleman, and she was sure tonight would be no exception. He probably only invited her to dinner because he felt obligated to entertain her. Or maybe he really did want to be friends.

And what a sophomoric thing that had been to say to him, she thought, offering to be his friend. As if he probably didn't already have tons of people lining up to be his friend. What made her so special?

Or was that just her way of subtly telling him that's all they could ever be. Friends. And she was sure that with time, she would stop fantasizing about him taking her in his arms, kissing her, then tearing off her clothes and making passionate love to her. Tearing, because he wasn't the kind of man to take things slow. He would be hot and sexy and demanding and she would of course have multiple orgasms. At least, in her fantasy she did. The fantasy she had been playing over and over in her head since he'd kissed her.

Get a grip, Vanessa. You're only making this harder on yourself.

She found the dining room and stepped through the open doors onto the veranda at exactly seven fifty-nine. Taper candles burned in fresh floral centerpieces on a round bistro table set for two, and champagne chilled in an ice bucket beside it. Beyond the veranda, past lush, sweetly scented flower gardens, the setting sun was a stunning palette of brilliant red and orange streaking an indigo canvas sky. A mild breeze swept away the afternoon heat.

It was the ideal setting for a romantic dinner. But this was supposed to be a meal shared between friends. Wasn't it?

"I see you found it."

She spun around to find Marcus standing behind her. He stood leaning casually in the dining room doorway, hands tucked into the front pockets of his slacks, his white silk shirt a stark contrast to his deep olive skin and his jacket the exact same rich espresso shade as his eyes. His hair was combed back but one stubborn wavy lock caressed his forehead.

"Wow, you look really nice," she said, instantly wishing she could take the words back. This is a casual dinner between *friends,* she reminded herself. She shouldn't be chucking out personal compliments.

"You sound surprised," he said with a raised brow.

"No! Of course not. I just meant…" She realized Marcus was grinning. He was teasing her. She gestured to the sleeveless, coral-colored slip dress she was wearing. She had wanted to look nice, without appearing blatantly sexy, and this was the only dress she'd brought with her that seemed to fit the bill. It was simple, and shapeless without looking frumpy. "I wasn't really sure how formal to dress."

His eyes raked over her. Blatantly, and with no shame. "You look lovely."

He said it politely, but the hunger in his gaze, and the resulting tug of lust deep in her belly, was anything but polite. And as exposed as she felt just then, she might as well have been wearing a transparent negligee, or nothing at all. And the worst part was, she liked it. She liked the way she felt when he looked at her. Even though it was so very wrong.

He gestured to the table. "Shall we sit?"

She nodded, and he helped her into her chair, the backs of his fingers brushing her bare shoulders as he eased it to the table, and she actually shivered. Honest to goodness goose bumps broke out across her skin.

Oh my.

She'd read in stories about a man making a woman shiver just by touching her, but it had never actually happened to her. In fact, she thought the whole thing sounded sort of silly. Not so much anymore.

"Champagne?" Marcus asked.

Oh, that could be a really bad idea. The last thing she needed was something to compromise her senses. They were compromised enough already. But the bottle was open, and she hated to let good champagne—and noting the label, it was *good* champagne—go to waste.

"Just one glass," she heard herself say, knowing she would have to be careful not to let one glass become two and so on.

Marcus poured it himself, then took a seat across from her. He lifted his glass, pinned his eyes on her and said, "To my father."

There was some sort of message in his eyes, but for the life of her, she wasn't sure what it was. Was toasting his father his way of letting her know the boundaries they'd established were still firmly in place, or did it mean something else entirely?

She'd just as soon they didn't talk about Gabriel at all. And rather than analyze it to death, she lifted her own glass and said, "To Gabriel." Hoping that would be the end of it.

She took a tiny sip, then set her glass down, and before she could even begin to think of what to say next, one of the younger butlers appeared with a gleaming silver tray and served the soup. He even nodded cordially when she thanked him. Karin definitely seemed to be warming to her as well, and Vanessa's maid had actually smiled and said good morning when she came in to make the bed that morning. They weren't exactly rolling out the red carpet—more like flopping down the welcome mat—but it was progress.

The soup consisted of bite-sized dumplings swimming in some sort of rich beef broth. And it was delicious. But that didn't surprise her considering the food had been exemplary since she arrived.

"You spoke with my father today?" he asked.

Ugh, she really didn't want to do this, but she nodded. "This afternoon."

"He told you that my aunt is still in intensive care?"

"He said she had a bad night. That her fever spiked, and she may need surgery. It sounds as if he won't be home anytime soon." Despite what she had hoped.

"He told me she's still very ill," Marcus said, then his eyes lifted to hers. "He asked if I've been keeping you entertained."

Oh, he had definitely been doing that.

"He asked if I've been respectful."

Her heart skipped a beat. "You don't think he…"

"Suspects something?" Marcus said bluntly, then he shook his head. "No. I think he's still worried that I won't be nice to you."

Oh, he'd been "nice" all right. A little too nice, some might say.

"He said you seemed reluctant to talk about me."

The truth was, she hadn't known what to tell Gabriel. She worried that if she said too much, like mentioning the earrings, or their evening stroll, Gabriel might get suspicious. She didn't know what was considered proper, and what was pushing the boundaries, so she figured it was better not to say anything at all. "I didn't mean to be elusive, or give him the impression I felt unwelcome."

"I just don't want him to think that I've neglected my duty," Marcus said.

"Of course. I'll be sure to let him know that you've been a good host."

They both quietly ate their soup for several minutes, then Marcus asked, "Have you spoken with your father yet?"

She lowered her eyes to her bowl. "Uh, nope, not yet."

She took a taste of her soup and when she looked up, he was pinning her with one of those brow-tipped stares.

"I *will*," she said.

"The longer you wait, the harder it will be."

She set her spoon down, her belly suddenly knotted with nerves. She lifted her glass and took another sip. "I know. I just have to work up the nerve. I'll do it, I just...I need to wait until the time is right."

"Which will happen when?"

When he was at the airport waiting for her to pick him up, maybe. "I'll do it. Probably tomorrow. The problem is, whenever I have the time, it's the middle of the night there."

The brow rose higher.

She sighed. "Okay, that's a lie. I'm a big fat chicken. There, I said it."

One of the butlers appeared to clear their soup plates. While another served the salad, Vanessa's phone started to ring. Would it be funny—not ha-ha funny, but ironic funny—if that were him right now.

She pulled it out of her pocketbook and saw that it wasn't her father, but Karin. As crabby as Mia had been today, maybe she was having trouble getting her to settle.

"Mia woke with a fever, ma'am."

It wasn't unusual for Mia to run a low-grade fever when she was teething, and that would explain her foul mood. "Did you take her temperature?"

"Yes, ma'am. It's forty point five."

The number confused her for a second, then she realized Karin meant Celsius. She racked her brain to recall the conversion and came up with a frighteningly high number. Over one hundred and *four* degrees!

She felt the color drain from her face. Could that be right? And if it was, this was no case of teething. "I'll be right up."

Marcus must have seen the fear in her eyes, because he frowned and asked, "What's wrong?"

Vanessa was already out of her chair. "It's Mia. She has a fever. A high one."

Marcus shoved himself to his feet, pulled out his phone and dialed. "George, please get Dr. Stark on the line and tell him we need him immediately."

Twelve

Other than a mild cold in the spring, Mia had never really been sick a day in her life. Imagining the worst, Vanessa's heart pounded a mile a minute as she rushed up the stairs to her suite, Marcus trailing close behind. When she reached the nursery she flung the door open.

Karin had stripped Mia down to her diaper and was rocking her gently, patting her back. Mia's cheeks were bright red and her eyelids droopy, and Vanessa's heart sank even lower as she crossed the room to her. How, in a couple of hours' time, could she have gotten so sick?

"Hey, baby," Vanessa said, touching Mia's forehead. It was burning hot. "Did you give her anything?"

Karin shook her head. "No, ma'am. I called you the minute she woke up."

Vanessa took Mia from her. She was limp and listless. "In the bathroom there's a bottle of acetaminophen drops. Could you get it for me, please?"

Karin scurried off and Marcus, who stood by the door looking worried, asked, "Is there anything I can do?"

"Just get the doctor up here as fast as possible." She cradled Mia to her chest, her hands trembling she was so frightened.

Karin hurried back with the drops and Vanessa measured out the correct dose. Mia swallowed it without a fuss.

"I don't know what this could be. She's barely ever had a cold."

"I'm sure it's nothing serious. Probably just a virus."

"I wonder if I should put her in a cool bath to bring her temperature down."

"How high is it?"

"Over one hundred and four."

His brows flew up.

"Fahrenheit," she added, and his face relaxed.

"Why don't you wait and see what the doctor says?"

She checked the clock across the room. "How soon do you think he'll be here?"

"Quickly. He's on call 24/7."

"Is he a pediatrician?"

"A family practitioner, but I assure you he is more than qualified."

She didn't imagine the royal family would keep an unqualified physician on call.

"Why don't you sit down," Marcus said, gesturing to the rocker. "Children can sense when parents are upset."

He was right, she needed to pull it together. The way the baby lay limp in Vanessa's arms, whimpering pathetically, it was as if she didn't have the energy to cry. She sat in the chair, cradling Mia in her arms and rocked her gently. "I'm sorry to have interrupted dinner. You can go back down and finish."

He folded his arms. "I'm not going anywhere."

Though she was used to handling things on her own when it came to her daughter, she was grateful for his company. Sometimes she got tired of being alone.

Dr. Stark, a kind-faced older gentleman, arrived just a few minutes later carrying a black medical bag.

He shook her hand and asked in English, "How old is the child?"

"Six months."

"Healthy?"

"Usually, yes. The worst she's ever had was a mild cold. I don't know why she would have such a high fever."

"She's current on her vaccinations?"

She nodded.

"You flew here recently?"

"Five days ago."

He nodded, touching Mia's forehead. "You have records?"

She was confused for a second, then realized he meant medical records. "Yes, in my bedroom."

"I'd like to see them."

Marcus held out his arms. "I'll hold her while you get them."

She handed her to him and Mia went without a fuss.

She darted across the hall to her room, grabbed the file with Mia's medical and immunization records, then hurried back to the bedroom. Marcus was sitting in the rocking chair, cradling Mia against his shoulder. Karin stood by the door looking concerned.

"Here they are," she said, and the doctor took the folder from her.

He skimmed the file then set it aside. "You'll need to lay her down."

Marcus rose from the chair and set Mia down on the changing table with all the care and affection of a father, watching with concern as the doctor gave her a thorough exam, asking random questions. When he looked in her ears she started to fuss.

When he was finished, Vanessa asked, "Is it serious?"

"She'll be fine," he assured her, patting her arm. "As I suspected, it's just an ear infection."

Vanessa was so relieved she could have cried. She picked Mia up and held her tight. "How could she have gotten that?"

"It could have started as a virus. A round of antibiotics should clear it right up. The acetaminophen you gave her should bring the fever down."

It looked as if it already had started to work. Mia's cheeks weren't as red and her eyes seemed less droopy. "Could that be why she was so crabby during the flight here?"

"I doubt it. Some children are just sensitive to the cabin pressure. It could have been hurting her ears."

It broke her heart to think that all the time they'd been in the air, Mia had been in pain and Vanessa hadn't even known it. "What can I do to keep it from happening in the future?"

"I would keep her out of the air until the infection clears, then, when you fly home, try earplugs. It will help regulate the pressure."

If she went home, that is. She glanced over at Marcus, who was looking at her. Was he thinking the same thing?

"Right now the best thing for her is a good night's rest. I'll have the antibiotics delivered right away. Just follow the directions. Call if she hasn't improved by morning. Otherwise I'll check her again in two days."

"Thank you, Dr. Stark," she said, shaking his hand.

"Shall I put her back in her crib?" Karin asked Vanessa after he left.

Vanessa shook her head. "I'm going to take her to my room, so you can have the night off. Thanks for calling me so quickly."

Karin nodded and started to walk to her room, then she stopped, turned back and said, "She's a strong girl, she'll be fine in no time." Then she actually smiled.

When she was gone, Vanessa turned to Marcus. He'd removed his jacket and was leaning against the wall, arms crossed. "Thank you," she said.

He cocked his head slightly. "For what?"

"Getting the doctor here so fast. For just being here with me. I don't suppose you have a portable crib anywhere around here. She rolls so much that I get nervous keeping her in bed with me."

Marcus pulled out his phone. "I'm sure we have one."

The medicine arrived fifteen minutes later and Vanessa gave her a dose, and within half an hour a portable crib had been set up in her bedroom. Vanessa laid Mia, who had fallen asleep on her shoulder, inside and covered her with a light blanket. She gently touched Mia's forehead, relieved to find that her temperature had returned almost to normal.

She walked back out into the sitting room where Marcus waited. It was dark but for a lamp on the desk. He stood by the French doors, the curtain pulled back, gazing into the night. Her first instinct was to walk up to him, slide her arms around his waist and lay her head against his back. She imagined that they would stay that way for a while, then he would turn and take her in his arms, kiss her the way he did the other night.

But as much as she wanted to—ached for it even—she couldn't do it.

"She's in bed," she said, and Marcus turned to her, letting the curtain drop. "I think she's better already."

"That's good."

The phone on her desk began to ring and she crossed the room to pick it up. It was Gabriel. Thank goodness he couldn't see her face or surely he would recognize the guilt there for the thoughts she had just been having.

"George called," he said, sounding worried. "He told me that Mia is ill."

"She woke with a fever."

"The doctor was there?"

"He came right away. It's an ear infection. He put her on antibiotics."

"What can I do? Do you need me to come home? I can catch a flight first thing in the morning."

This was it. She could say yes, and get Gabriel back here and be done with this whole crazy thing with Marcus. Instead she heard herself saying, "In the time it would take you to get here, she'll probably be fine. Her fever is already down."

"Are you sure?"

"Trina needs you more than I do. Besides, Marcus is helping," she said, glancing his way.

His expression was unreadable.

"Call me if you need anything, day or night," Gabriel said.

"I will, I promise."

"I'll let you go so you can tend to her needs. I'll call you tomorrow."

"Okay."

"Good night, sweet Vanessa. I love you."

"I love you, too," she said, and she did. She loved him as a friend, so why did she feel like a fraud? And why did she feel so uncomfortable saying the words in front of Marcus?

Well, duh, of course she knew why.

She set the phone down and turned to Marcus. He stood

by the sofa, his arms folded across his chest. "Your father," she said, as if he needed an explanation.

"He offered to come home?" he asked.

She nodded.

"You told him no?"

She nodded again.

He started walking toward her. "Why? Isn't that what you wanted?"

"It was…I mean, it *is*. I just think…" The truth was, she was afraid. Afraid that Gabriel would come home, see her face and instantly know what she was feeling for Marcus. He trusted her, *loved* her, and she'd betrayed him. And she continued to betray him every time she had an inappropriate thought about his son, but she just couldn't seem to stop herself. Or maybe she didn't want to stop. "Maybe we need some time to sort this out before he comes back."

"Sort what out?"

"This. Us."

"I thought there was no us. That we were going to pretend like it never happened."

That had seemed like a good idea yesterday, but now she wasn't so sure she could do that. Not right away, anyhow. "We are. I just…need some time to think."

He stepped closer, his dark eyes serious and pinned to hers. Her stomach bottomed out and her heart started to beat faster.

"Please don't look at me like that."

"Like what?"

"Like you want to kiss me again."

"But I do."

Oh boy. Her knees felt squishy. "You know that would be a really bad idea."

"Yeah, it probably would."

"You really shouldn't."

"So tell me no."

He wanted *her* to be the responsible one? Seriously?

"Have you not heard a thing I've said this week?"

"Every word of it."

"Then you know that you really shouldn't trust me with a responsibility like that, considering my tendency to make bad decisions."

His grin warmed her from the inside out. "Right now, I'm sort of counting on it."

Thirteen

Thirteen

Vanessa reached up and cupped Marcus's cheek, running her thumb across that adorable dimple, something she'd wanted to do since the first time she'd seen him smile.

This was completely insane, what they were about to do, because she knew in her heart that this time it wouldn't just be a kiss. But with him standing right in front of her, gazing into her eyes with that hungry look, she just couldn't make herself stop him. And her last thought, as he lowered his head and leaned in, as she rose up to meet him halfway, was how wrong this was, and how absolutely wonderful.

Then he kissed her. But this time it was different, this kiss had a mutual urgency that said neither would be having a crisis of conscience. In a weird way it felt as if they had been working toward this moment since the minute she'd stepped off the plane. Like somewhere deep down she just knew it had been inevitable. It was difficult to imagine that at one time she hadn't even liked him. A big fat jerk, that's what she'd thought him to be. She'd been so wrong about him. About so many things.

"I want you Vanessa," he whispered against her lips. "I don't care if it's wrong."

She pulled back to look him in the eyes. How could she have known this beautiful man only five days when right now it felt like an eternity?

And right now their feelings were the only ones that mattered to her.

She shoved his jacket off his shoulders, down his arms, and it dropped to the floor. She ran her hands up the front of his shirt, over his muscular chest, the way she had wanted to since he stood in her doorway that day with his shirt unbuttoned. And he felt just as good as she knew he would.

Marcus groaned deep in his throat. Then, as if the last bit of his control snapped, he kissed her hard, lifting her off her feet and pinning her to the wall with the length of his body. She gasped against his lips, hooked her legs around his hips, curling her fingers into the meat of his arms. This was the Marcus she had fantasized about, the one who would sweep her off her feet and take her with reckless abandon, and everything inside her screamed, "Yes!"

Marcus set her on her feet and grabbed the hem of her dress, yanking it up over her head—as close to tearing as he could get without actually shredding the delicate silk fabric. When she stood there in nothing but a bra and panties, he stopped and just looked at her.

"You're amazing," he said.

Not beautiful, but amazing. Was it possible that he really did see more in her than just a pretty face? When she looked at Marcus she saw not royalty, not a prince, but a man who was charismatic and kind and funny. And maybe a little vulnerable too. A man who was looking back at her with the same deep affection. Could it be that her feelings for Gabriel were never meant to be more than friendship? That Marcus was the one she was destined to fall in love with? Because as much as she'd tried to fight it, she was definitely falling in love with him.

She took his hand and walked backward to the sofa, tugging him along with her. A part of her said that she should have been second-guessing herself, or feeling guilty—and a week ago, she probably would have—but as they undressed, kissing and touching each other, it just felt right.

When he was naked, she took a moment to just look at him. Physically he was just as perfect as he could possibly be, but she didn't really care about that. It was his mind that fascinated her most, who he was on the inside.

She lay back against the sofa, pulling him down with her, so he was cradled between her thighs. He grinned down at her, brushing her hair back from her face. "You know that this is completely crazy."

"I know. I take it you don't do crazy things?"

"Never."

"Me neither." She stroked the sides of his face, his neck, ran her hands across his shoulders. She just couldn't stop touching him. "Maybe that's why this feels so good. Maybe we both need a little crazy."

"That must be it." He leaned down to kiss her, but just as his lips brushed hers, he stopped, uttering a curse.

"If you're about to tell me we have to stop, I'm going to be very upset," she said.

"No, I just realized, I don't have protection with me."

"You *don't?* Aren't princes supposed to be prepared at all times?" She paused, frowning. "Or is that the scouts?"

"I wasn't exactly planning for this, you know."

"Really?"

He laughed. "Yes, really. But then you walked into the room wearing that dress…"

"*That* dress? Are you kidding me? It's like the least sexy thing I own. I wore it so I *wouldn't* tempt you."

"The truth is, you could have been wearing a paper sack and I would have wanted to rip it off you. It's you that I want, not your clothes."

It was thrilling to know he wanted her that much, that he would be attracted to her even at her worst.

"I'm going to have to run back to my room," he said, not sounding at all thrilled with the idea.

"I'm on birth control, so you don't have to."

"Are you sure?"

"I'm sure. And now that we have that settled, could we stop talking and get to the good stuff?"

He grinned. "I thought women liked to talk."

"Yes, but even we have our limits."

She didn't have to ask twice, and lying there with him, kissing and touching, felt completely natural. There was none of the usual first time fumbling or awkwardness. And any vestige of reservations, or hint of mixed feelings that may have remained evaporated the instant he thrust inside her. Everything else in the world, any cares or worries or feelings of indecision that were always there somewhere in the back of her mind, melted away. She knew from the instant he began to move inside her—slow and gentle at first, then harder and faster, until it got so out of control they tumbled off the couch onto the rug—that this was meant to be. He made her feel the way a woman was supposed to feel. Adored and desired and protected, and *strong*, as if no one or no thing could ever knock her back down.

And she felt heartbroken, all the way down to her soul,

because as much as she wanted Marcus, she couldn't have him, and she was terrified that no man would ever make her feel this way again.

"We're totally screwed, aren't we?" Vanessa asked Marcus, lying next to him naked on the floor beside the sofa, her breath just as raspy and uneven as his own, glowing from what had been for him some of the best sex of his entire life. Actually no, it had been *the* best.

Maybe it was the anticipation that had made it so exciting, or the forbidden nature of the relationship. Maybe it was that she had no hang-ups about her looks or insecurities about her body, or that she gave herself heart and soul and held nothing back. It could have been that unlike most women, whatever she took, she gave back tenfold.

Or maybe he just really liked her.

At this point, what difference did it make? Because she was right. They were screwed. How could he possibly explain this to his father? "Sorry, but I just slept with the woman you love, and I think I might be falling in love with her myself, but don't worry, you'll find someone else."

There was a code among men when it came to girlfriends and wives, and that was even more true among family. It was a line a man simply did not cross. But he had crossed it, and the worst part was that he couldn't seem to make himself feel guilty about it.

"My father can't ever know," he said.

She nodded. "I know. And I can't marry him now."

"I know." He felt bad about that, but maybe it was for the best. He believed that Vanessa came here with the very best of intentions, but she obviously didn't love his father the way a wife loves a husband. Maybe by stepping between them Marcus had done them both a favor. Vanessa was so sweet and kind, he could imagine her compromising her own happiness to make his father happy. Eventually though, they would have both been miserable. In essence, he had saved them from an inevitable failed marriage.

Or was he just trying to rationalize a situation that was completely irrational?

She reached down and laced her fingers through his. "It's not your fault that this happened, so please don't ever blame yourself."

He squeezed her hand. "It's no one's fault. Sometimes things just...happen. It doesn't have to make sense."

She looked over at him. "You know that no matter how we feel, you and I, we can't ever..."

"I know." And the thought caused an actual pain in his chest. A longing so deep he felt hollowed out and raw. He had little doubt that Vanessa was the one for him. She was his destiny, she *and* Mia, but he could never have them. Not if he ever hoped to have a civilized relationship with his father. It was as if the universe was playing a cruel trick on them. But in his world honor reigned supreme, and family always came first. His feelings, his happiness, were inconsequential.

It wasn't fair, but when was life ever?

"I need to call him and tell him," Vanessa said. "That it's over, I mean. I won't tell him about us."

The minute she ended her relationship with his father, she would have to leave. There would be no justifiable reason to stay. And the idea that this was it, that Marcus would never be with Vanessa again, that he had to give her up so soon, made his heart pound and adrenaline rush. He wasn't ready to let her go. Not yet.

"That's not the sort of thing that you should do over the phone, or through Skype," he told her. "Shouldn't you wait until he returns?"

Her brow furrowed into a frown. "It just doesn't seem

fair to let him think that everything is okay, then dump him the second he gets back. That just seems...cruel."

And this was the woman he'd been convinced was a devious gold digger. How could he have been so wrong? Because he was an idiot, or at least, he had been. And he would be again if he let her go now.

"Do you really think now is the right time?" he said, grasping for a reason, any reason, to get her to stay. "He's so upset over my aunt."

She blinked. "I guess I hadn't really thought about it that way. That would be pretty thoughtless. But I don't think I can wait until he comes back. That could be weeks still."

"Then at least wait until she's out of intensive care."

"I don't know..."

Oh, to hell with this. Here she was being honest and he was trying to manipulate her.

"The truth is, I don't care about my father's feelings. This is pure selfishness. Because the minute you tell him, it's over, and I just can't let you go yet." He pulled her close, cupped her face in his hands. "Stay with me, Vanessa. Just a few days more."

She looked conflicted, and sad. "You know we'll just be torturing ourselves."

"I don't care. I just want a little more time with you." Not wanted. *Needed.* And he had never needed anyone in his life.

"We would have to be discreet. No one can know. If Gabriel found out—"

"He won't. I promise."

She hesitated a moment, then smiled and touched his cheek. "Okay. A few more days."

He breathed a quiet sigh of relief. Was this wrong in more ways than he could count, and were they just delaying the inevitable? Of course. And did he care? Not really.

He'd spent his entire life making sacrifices, catering to the whims of others. This one time he was going to be selfish, take something for himself.

"But then I have to go," she said. "I have to get on with my life."

"I understand." Because he did too, as difficult as that was to imagine. But for now she was his, and he planned to make the most of what little time they had left together.

"You did what?" Jessy shrieked into the phone, so loud that Vanessa had to hold it away from her ear. "I don't talk to you for a couple of days and this happens?"

Vanessa cringed. Maybe telling Jessy that she'd slept with Marcus, several times now, hadn't been such a hot idea after all. But if she didn't tell *someone,* she felt as if she would burst.

"You realize I was kidding when I suggested he could be a viable second choice," Jessy said.

"I know. And it's not something I planned on happening."

"He didn't, you know…*force* you."

"God no! Of course not. What is your hang-up about the men in this country being brutes?"

"I'm just worried about you."

"Well, don't be. Marcus would never do that. He's one of the sweetest and kindest men I've ever met. It was one hundred percent mutual."

"But you've barely known him a week. You don't sleep with guys you've known a week. Hell, sometimes you make them wait *months.*"

"I know. And it's a wonder we held out as long as we did."

Jessy laughed. "Oh my God. Who are you and what have you done with my best friend?"

"I know, this isn't like me at all. And the weird thing is, if I could go back and do it differently, I wouldn't. I'm glad for what happened. And I'm glad I met him. It's changed me."

"In five days?"

"It sounds impossible, I know. I have a hard time believing it myself, but I just feel *different*. I feel…gosh, I don't know, like a better person, I guess."

Jessy laughed again. "You're sleeping with the son of the man you're supposed to marry, and you feel like a better person?"

It did sound weird when she said it like that. "It's hard to explain. And though I hate to admit it, I think what you said about Gabriel being a father figure was true. Nothing I do is good enough for my dad, and I guess in a way I transferred my feelings onto Gabriel. Deep down I knew that I didn't love him the way a wife should love a husband, that I never would. But he seemed to love me so much, and I didn't want to let him down. But then I met Marcus and something just…clicked. If it hadn't been for him, I may have made another terrible mistake."

"So you must really like him."

If only it were that simple. "That would be a major understatement."

Jessy was quiet for a second, then she said, "Are you saying that you *love* him? After *five* days?"

"Weird, huh?"

"How does he feel?"

She shrugged. "What does it matter?"

"It seems to me like it would matter an awful lot."

If only. "We can't be together. How do you think Gabriel would feel if I told him I was dumping him for his son? He might never forgive Marcus."

"You don't think Marcus would choose you over his father?"

"It doesn't matter because I would never ask him to. Nor would I want him to. Family and honor mean everything to Marcus. It's one of the things I love most about him."

"So, the thing you love most is what's keeping you apart."

"I guess so, yeah." And the thought of leaving, of giving him up, filled her belly with painful knots, and she knew that the longer she stayed the worse it would be when she left, yet here she still was. "This is making me sad. Let's talk about something else. How was your trip?"

"It was good," Jessy said, sounding surprised. "It was actually…fun."

"His family is nice?"

"Yeah. They're very small-town, if you know what I mean, and very traditional. Wayne and I had to sleep in separate rooms. They have this big old farmhouse with lots of land and though I've always been more of a city girl, it was really beautiful. Hot as hell though."

Vanessa smiled. "I'm really glad that it went well."

At least one of them was in a relationship that might actually work.

"I know you don't want to talk about it," Jessy said, "but can I just say one more thing about your affair with the prince?"

Vanessa sighed. "Okay."

"This is going to sound strange. But I'm proud of you."

It was Vanessa who laughed this time. "I slept with the son of the man I was planning to marry and you're *proud* of me?"

"You're always so hell-bent on making other people happy, but you did something selfish, something for yourself. That's a huge step for you."

"I guess I never thought of being selfish as a good thing."

"Sometimes it is."

"You know what the hardest part about leaving will be? Mia has become so attached to him, and he really seems to love her. I think he would be an awesome dad."

"You'll meet someone else, Vanessa. You'll fall in love again, I promise."

Vanessa wasn't so sure about that. In her entire life she'd never felt this way about anyone, she hadn't even known it was possible to love someone the way she loved Marcus. To need someone as much as she needed him, yet feel more free than she had in her life. And she just couldn't imagine it ever happening again. What if Marcus was it? What if he was her destiny? Was it also her destiny to let him go?

Fourteen

Vanessa woke to another message from her father, the third one that he had left in as many days, this one sounding more gruff and irritated than the last two.

"Nessy, why haven't you called me back? I called the hotel and they said you took a leave of absence. I want to know what's going on. Have you gotten yourself into trouble again?"

Of course that would be his first assumption, that she had done something wrong. What else would he think? She sighed, not so disappointed as she was resigned to the way things were. And a little sad that he always seemed to see the worst in her.

"Call me as soon as you get this," he demanded, and that's where the message ended. She dropped her phone on the bedside table and fell back against the pillows.

Beside her, Marcus stirred, waking slowly, the way he always did. Or at least, the last three mornings when they woke up together, he had. First he stretched, lengthening every inch of that long, lean body, then he yawned deeply, and finally he opened his eyes, saw her lying there next to him, and gave her a sleepy smile, his hair all rumpled and sexy. Creases from his pillow lined his cheek.

Watching this ritual had become her new favorite way to spend her morning. Even though what they were doing still filled her with guilt. She just couldn't seem to stay away.

"What time is it?" he asked in a voice still gravelly from sleep.

"Almost eight."

He rolled onto his back and laughed, the covers sliding down to expose his beautiful bare chest. "That makes last night the third night in a row that I slept over seven hours straight. Do you have any idea how long it's been since I got a decent night's sleep?"

"I'm that boring, huh?"

He grinned and pulled her on top of him, so she was straddling his thighs, his beard stubble rough against her chin as he kissed her. "More like you're wearing me out."

It had rained the past two days and Marcus had decided it would be best to spend them in the palace, in her suite. Wearing as little clothing as possible. They mostly just talked, and played with Mia, and when Mia took her naps, they spent the entire time making love. A few times Vanessa had even let Karin watch Mia for an extra hour or so, so they had a little more time together. And though it had been a week now, neither Vanessa nor Marcus had brought up the subject of her leaving, but it loomed between them, unspoken. A dark shadow and a constant element of shame that hung over what had been—other than Mia's birth—the best time of her life. She kept telling herself that when the time was right to leave, they would just know it. So far that time hadn't come, and deep down she wished it never would.

Marcus was it for her. He was the one, her *soul mate,* and of that she was one hundred and ten percent sure. For the first time in her life she had no doubts. She wasn't second-guessing herself, or worrying that she was making a mistake.

She wasn't exactly sure if he felt the same way. He seemed to, and he clearly didn't want her to leave, but did he love her? He hadn't actually said so. But to be fair, neither had she. At this point, what difference did it make? They were just words. Even if he did love her, his relationship with his father *had* to come first.

After that first time making love, she'd dreaded having to face Gabriel on Skype, sure that he would know the second he saw her face, but while she waited on her computer for over an hour, he'd been a no-show. She'd been more relieved than anything. He'd phoned the next day, apologizing, complaining of security issues, and said it might be better if they limited their calls to voice only. Which actually worked out pretty well for her. Already she could feel herself pulling away.

Their conversations were shorter now, and more superficial. And one day, when Marcus had taken them for a drive to see the royal family's mountain cabin—although to call the lavish vacation home a cabin was akin to calling the Louvre a cute little art gallery—she'd been out of cell range and had missed his call completely. She hadn't even remembered to check for a message. And though it was clearly her fault that they hadn't spoken, he had been the one to apologize the next day. He said he was swamped with work and tending to Trina, and he hadn't had a chance to call back.

She kept waiting for him to ask her if there was a problem, but if he had noticed any change in their relationship, he hadn't mentioned it yet. But Trina had been improving, and though she was still very weak, and Gabriel hadn't felt comfortable leaving her yet, it was only a matter of time.

And then of course she had her father to deal with.

"You look troubled," Marcus said, brushing her hair back and tucking it behind her ear.

He had an uncanny way of always knowing what she was thinking. "My dad called again."

He sighed. "That would explain it."

"He called the hotel and found out that I took a leave, so of course he's assuming that I'm in some sort of trouble. He demanded that I call him immediately."

"You should. You should have called him days ago."

"I know." She let out a sigh and draped herself across his warm, solid chest, pressing her ear to the center, to hear the thump of his heart beating.

"So do it now."

"I don't want to."

"Stop acting like a coward and just call him."

She sat up and looked down at him. "I'm acting like a coward because I *am* one."

"No, you aren't."

Yes, she was. When it came to dealing with her father anyway. "I'll call him tomorrow. I promise."

"You'll call him now," he said, dumping her off his lap and onto the mattress. Then he got up and walked to the bathroom, all naked and gorgeous, his tight behind looking so squeezable.

He stopped in the doorway, turned to her and grinned. "Now, I'm going to take a shower, and if you want to join me, you had better start dialing."

The door closed behind him, then she heard the shower switch on. Damn him. He knew how much she loved taking their morning shower together. He brought a change of clothes to her room every night so no one would see him the next morning wearing the same clothes from the night before. He also rolled around in his bed and mussed up the covers so it would look as if he'd slept there. It had to be obvious to pretty much everyone how much time they had been spending together, but if anyone suspected inappropriate behavior, they'd kept it to themselves.

Vanessa sighed and looked over at the bathroom door, then her phone. Well, here goes nothing.

She sat up, grabbed it and dialed her father's number before she chickened out. He answered on the first ring. "Nessy, where the hell have you been? I've been worried sick. Where's Mia? Is she okay?"

He'd been worried sick about both of them, or just Mia, she wondered. "Sorry, Dad, I would have called you sooner but I've actually been out of the country."

"Out of the country?" he barked, as if that were some unforgivable crime. "Why didn't you tell me? And where is my granddaughter?"

"She's with me."

"Where are you?" he said, sounding no less irate. She knew he was only acting this way because he was worried, and he hated not being in control of every situation every minute. If she gave him hourly reports of her activities he would be ecstatic. And usually when he spoke to her this way it made her feel about two inches tall. Right now, she just felt annoyed.

"I'm in Varieo, you know that little country near—"

"I *know* where it is. What in God's name are you doing there?"

"It's sort of…a work thing." Because she had met Gabriel at work, right?

"I thought you took a leave from the hotel. Or was that just a fancy way of saying they fired you?"

Of course he would think that.

Her annoyance multiplied by fifty. "No, I was not *fired*," she snapped.

"Do not take that tone with me, young lady," he barked back at her.

Young lady? Was she *five*?

In that instant something inside of her snapped and she'd had enough of being treated like an irresponsible child. And if standing up for herself meant disappointing him, so be it. "I'm twenty-four, Dad. I'll take whatever tone I damned well please. And for the record, I deserve the same respect that you demand from me. I am sick to death of you talking down to me, and always thinking the worst of me. And I'm finished with you making me feel as if anything I do is never good enough for you. I'm smart, and successful, and brave, and I have lots of friends and people who love me. So unless you can think of something positive to say to me, don't bother calling anymore."

She disconnected the call, and even though her heart was thumping, and her hands were trembling, she felt... good. In fact, she felt pretty freaking fantastic. Maybe Marcus was right. Maybe she really was brave. And though she didn't honestly believe this would change anything, at least now he knew how she felt.

Her phone began to ring and she jerked with surprise. It was her dad. She was tempted to let it go to voice mail, but she'd started this, and she needed to finish it.

Bracing herself for the inevitable shouting, she answered. "Hello."

"I'm sorry."

Her jaw actually dropped. "W-what?"

"I said I'm sorry," he repeated, and she'd never heard

him sound so humbled. She couldn't recall a single time he'd ever apologized for anything.

"And I'm sorry I raised my voice," she said, then realized that she had done nothing wrong. "Actually, no, I'm not sorry. You deserved it."

"You're right. I had no right to snap at you like that. But when I didn't hear from you, I was just afraid that something bad had happened to you."

"I'm fine. Mia is fine. And I'm sorry that I frightened you. We're here visiting a...friend."

"I didn't know you had any friends there."

"I met him at the hotel. He was a guest."

"He?"

"Yes, he. He's..." Oh what the hell, why not just tell him the truth? Since she didn't really care what he thought at this point anyway. "He's the king."

"The *king?*"

"Yes, and believe it or not, he wants to marry me."

"You're getting married? To a king?" He actually sounded excited. He was finally happy about something she had done, and now she had to burst his bubble. Figures.

"He wants me to marry him, but I'm not going to."

"Why not?"

"Because I'm in love with someone else."

"Another king," he joked.

"Um, no."

"Then who?"

If he was going to blow his top, this would be the time. "I'm in love with the prince. His son."

"Vanessa!"

She braced herself for the fireworks. For the shouting and the berating, but it never happened. She could practically feel the tension through the phone line, but he didn't make a sound. He must have been biting a hole right through his tongue. And could she blame him? Sometimes even she couldn't believe what they were doing.

"You okay, Dad?"

"Just…confused. When did all this happen? *How* did it happen?"

"Like I said, he was visiting the hotel and we became friends."

"The king or the prince?"

"The king, Gabriel, and he fell in love with me, but I only ever loved him as a friend. But he was convinced I would grow to love him if I got to know him better, so he invited me to stay at the palace, but then he was called away when I got here. He asked Marcus—he's the prince—to be my companion and we…well, we fell for each other. Hard."

"How old is this prince?"

"Um, twenty-eight, I think."

"And the king?"

"Fifty-six," she said, and she could practically hear him chomping down on his tongue again. "Which was part of the reason I wasn't sure about marrying him."

"I see," was all he said, but she knew he wanted to say more. He was going to need stitches by the end of this conversation. But she gave him credit for making the effort, and she wished she had confronted him years ago. Though he probably hadn't been ready to hear it before now. Or maybe she was the one who hadn't been ready for this. Maybe she needed to make changes first.

"So, I assume you'll be marrying the prince instead?" he said.

If only. "I won't be marrying anybody."

"But I thought you love him."

"I do love him, but I could never do that to Gabriel. He's a really good man, Dad, and he's been through so much heartache. He loves me, and I could never betray him that way. I feel horrible that it worked out this way, as if I've let him down. Not to mention that it would most likely ruin his relationship with his son. I couldn't do that to either of them. They need each other more than they need me."

He was quiet for several seconds, then he said, "Well, you've had a busy couple of weeks, haven't you?"

Though normally a comment like that would come off as bitter or condescending, now he just sounded surprised. She smiled, feeling both happy and sad, which seemed to be a regular thing for her lately. "You have no idea."

"So I guess I won't be seeing you Thursday."

"No, but we should be flying home soon. Maybe we can make a quick stop in Florida on our way."

"I'd like that." He paused and said, "So you really love this guy?"

"I really love him. Mia does too. She's grown so attached to him, and she loves being here in the palace."

"Are you sure you're doing the right thing? By leaving, I mean."

"There isn't anything else that I can do."

"Well, I'll keep my fingers crossed that you work it out somehow. And Nessy, I know I've been pretty hard on you, and maybe I don't say it often enough, but I am proud of you."

She'd waited an awfully long time to hear that, and as good as it felt, her entire self-worth no longer depended on it. "Thanks, Dad."

"It's admirable what you're doing. Sacrificing your own happiness for the king's feelings."

"I'm not doing it to be admirable."

"I know. That's why it is. Give me a call when you're coming home and I'll get the guest room ready."

"I will. I love you, Dad."

"I love you too, Nessy."

She hung up and set her phone on the table, thinking that was probably one of the nicest things her dad had ever said to her, and one of the most civilized conversations they had ever had.

"Now aren't you glad you called?"

She looked up to find Marcus standing naked in the bathroom doorway, towel-drying his hair. She wondered how much of that he'd heard. Had he heard her tell her father that she loved Marcus?

"I confronted him about the way he makes me feel, and instead of freaking out, he actually apologized."

"That took guts."

"Maybe I am brave after all. I'm not naive enough to think it will be smooth sailing from here. I'm sure he'll have relapses, because that's just who he is, and I'll have to stand firm. But at least it's a start."

He dropped the towel and walked toward the bed. And my goodness he looked hot. The man just oozed sex appeal. It boggled the mind that a woman would be unfaithful to him. His ex must have been out of her mind.

He yanked the covers away and climbed into bed, tugging her down onto her back, spreading her thighs with his knee and making himself comfortable between them.

"Thank you," she said, running her hand across his smooth, just shaved cheek. "Thank you for making me believe in myself."

"That wasn't me," he said, kissing her gently. His lips were soft and tasted like mint. "I just pointed out what was already there. You chose to see it."

And without him she might never have. She was a different person now. A better person. In part because of him.

"There's one more thing," he said, kissing her chin, her throat, the shell of her ear.

She closed her eyes and sighed. "Hmm?"

"For the record," he whispered, "I love you, too."

Fifteen

After a week of torrential rain the weather finally broke and though Marcus would have been more than happy to spend the day in Vanessa's suite again, sunny skies and mild temperatures lured them back out into the world. A calm sea made it the perfect day for water sports, and since Vanessa had never been on a personal watercraft, he figured it was time she learned.

They left Mia with Karin, who he thought looked relieved to have something to do. Many of the young parents he knew took full advantage of their nannies—especially the fathers, to the point that they'd never even changed a diaper—but Vanessa was very much a hands-on parent. He had the feeling Karin was bored more often than not. And because Mia was usually with them, they always took the limo on their outings, so today he decided they would take *his* baby for a spin.

"This looks really old," Vanessa said, as he opened the

passenger door, which for her was on the wrong side of the car.

"It's a 1965. It was my grandfather's. He was a huge Ian Fleming fan."

"Oh my God! Is this—"

"An Aston Martin DB5 Saloon," he said. "An exact replica of the car 007 drove."

She slipped inside, running her hand along the dash, as gently as a lover's caress. "It's amazing!"

He walked around and climbed in. He started the engine, which still purred as sweetly as the day they drove it off the line, put it in gear and steered the car through the open gates, and in the direction of the marina. "I've always loved this car. My grandfather and I used to sneak off on Sundays and drive out into the country for hours. He would tell me stories about his childhood. He was only nineteen when his father died, and he would tell me what it was like to be a king at such a young age. At the time, I just thought it sounded exciting to be so important and have everyone look up to you. Only as I got older and began to learn how much hard work was involved did I begin to realize what a huge responsibility it would be. I used to worry that my father would die and I would be king before I was ready."

"How old was your father when he became king?"

"Forty-three."

She was quiet for a minute, then she turned to him and said, "Let's not go to the marina. Let's take a drive in the country instead. Like you and your grandfather used to do."

"Really?"

"Yeah. I would love to see the places he took you."

"You wouldn't be bored?"

She reached over, took his hand, and smiled, "With you, never."

"Okay, let's go."

He couldn't recall ever getting in a car with a woman and just driving. In his experience they preferred constant stimulation and entertainment, and required lavish gifts and attention. In contrast, Vanessa seemed to relish the times they simply sat around and talked, or played with her daughter. And as far as gifts go, besides the earrings—which she wore every day—he'd bought nothing but the occasional meal or snack. She required little, demanded nothing, yet gave more of herself than he could ever ask. Before now, he hadn't even known women like her existed. That he once thought she had ulterior motives was ridiculous to him now.

"Can I ask you a question?" she said, and he nodded. "When did you stop thinking that I was after your dad's money?"

And she was apparently a mind reader. "It was when we went to the village and you didn't once use the credit card my father left for you."

Her mouth dropped open in surprise. "You knew about that?"

"His assistant told me. She was concerned."

"Gabriel insisted that I use it, but the truth is I haven't even taken it out of the drawer. It didn't seem right. He gave me lots of gifts, and I insisted he take them back."

"Well, if the credit card hadn't convinced me, your reaction to the earrings really drove the message home."

She reached up to finger the silver swirls dangling from her ears. "Why?"

"Because I've never seen a woman so thrilled over such an inexpensive gift."

"Value has nothing to do with it. It's the thought that counts. You bought them because you wanted to, because you knew that I liked them. You weren't trying to buy my affections or win me over. You bought the earrings because you're a sweet guy."

He glared at her. "I am not sweet."

She grinned. "Yes, you are. You're one of the sweetest, kindest men I've ever met." She paused, gave his hand a squeeze. "You know I have to go soon. I've probably stayed too long already. I feel like we're tempting fate, like someone is going to figure out what we're doing and it will get back to Gabriel. I don't want to hurt him."

Though it was irrational, he almost wished it would. He didn't want to hurt his father either, but it was getting more and more difficult to imagine letting her go. He wasn't even sure if he could. "What if he did find out? Maybe you wouldn't have to leave. Maybe we could explain to him. Make him understand."

She closed her eyes and sighed. "I can't, Marcus. I can't do that to him. Or to you. If our relationship came between the two of you I would never forgive myself."

"We don't know for certain that he would be upset."

She shot him a look.

"Okay, he probably would, but he could get over it. In fact, when he sees how much it means to me, I'm sure he will."

"But what if he doesn't? That isn't a chance I'm willing to take."

If she were anything like the women he'd dated in the past, this wouldn't be an issue. She wouldn't care who she hurt as long as she got what she wanted. Of course, then he wouldn't love her. And he knew that once she'd made up her mind, nothing would change it.

Her stubborn streak was one of her most frustrating yet endearing qualities. He liked that she continually challenged him. She kept him honest. And he loved her too much to risk losing her respect.

* * *

After a three-hour drive that they spent talking about their childhoods and families, then a stop in a small village for lunch, Marcus drove them back to the palace. He walked with her up to the nursery, only to discover that Mia had just gone down for a nap.

"Just call me when she wakes up," Vanessa told Karin, then she turned to Marcus and gave him the *look,* the one that said she had naughtiness on her mind. He followed her across the hall, but stopped her just outside her suite door.

"How about a change of pace?"

"What did you have in mind?" she asked, looking intrigued.

"Let's go to my room."

The smile slipped from her face. "Marcus…"

"But you've never even seen it."

"If someone sees us go in there—"

"The family wing is very private. And if you want, we won't do anything but talk. We can even leave the door open. We can pretend like I'm giving you a tour of the family wing."

She looked hesitant. "I don't know."

Despite the risk of being discovered by a passing employee, he took her hand. "We haven't got much time left. Give me the chance to share at least a small part of my life with you."

He could see her melting before his eyes. Finally she smiled and said, "Okay."

What he hadn't told was that just the other day Cleo had confronted him about all the time they had been spending together.

"Talk to my father," he'd told Cleo. "He's the one who wanted me to keep her entertained."

Her brows rose. "Entertained?"

"You *know* what I mean."

She flashed him a told-you-so smile. "I take it you're finding that she's not as terrible as you thought?"

"Not terrible at all," he'd told her, diffusing the situation entirely. Because if she believed the relationship was platonic, no one on the staff, except maybe George, would question it. But he still didn't dare tell Vanessa about the exchange. Especially now.

Under the ruse of tour guide, Marcus led Vanessa through the palace to the family wing, and the employees they did encounter only bowed politely, and showed not even a hint of suspicion. When they got to his suite, the hall was deserted. He opened the door and gestured her inside.

"Wow," she said, walking to the center of the living room and gazing around. He stood by the open door watching her take it all in. "It's huge. As big as an apartment. You even have a kitchen."

"I insisted. I figured, if I have to live here in the palace, I need a space of my own."

"I like it. It's very tasteful, and masculine without being too overpowering." She turned to him. "Comfortable."

"Thank you. And my designer thanks you."

"How many rooms?"

"Master suite, office, kitchen and living room."

She nodded slowly. "It's nice."

"I'm glad you like it."

She dropped her purse on the leather sofa and turned to him. "Maybe you should close the door."

"But I thought we agreed—"

"Close the door, Marcus." She was wearing that look again, so he closed it. "Lock it too."

He locked it, and crossed the room to where she was standing. "Changed your mind, did you?"

She slid her hands up his chest, started unfastening the

buttons on his shirt. "Maybe it's the element of danger, but the closer we got to your room, the more turned on I got." She rose up on her toes and kissed him, yanking his shirt from the waist of his slacks. "Or maybe, when we're alone, I just can't keep my hands off you."

The feeling was mutual.

"I know it's wrong, but I just can't stop myself. Doesn't that make me a terrible person?"

"If it does, I'm a terrible person, too. Which could very well mean we deserve each other."

She tugged his shirt off, but before she could get to work on his belt, he picked her up and hoisted her over his shoulder. She let out a screech of surprise, then laughed.

"Marcus, what are you doing!"

"Manhandling you," he said, carrying her to the bedroom and kicking the door open.

"Not that I mind, but why?"

He tossed her down onto the bed, on top of the duvet, then he reached under her dress, hooked his fingers in the waist of her panties and yanked them down. "Because I am not *sweet*."

She grinned up at him. "Well, I stand corrected."

Then she grabbed him by the shoulders, pulled him down on top of her and kissed him.

Every time he made love to her he thought it couldn't possibly get better, but she always managed to top herself. She was sexy and adventurous, and completely confident in her abilities as a lover, and *modest* was a word not even in her vocabulary. She seemed to instinctively know exactly what to do to drive him out of his mind, and she was so damned easy to please—she had a sensitive spot behind her knees that if stroked just right would set her off like a rocket.

She liked it slow and sensual, hard and fast, and she

even went a little kinky on him at times. If there were an ideal sexual mate for everyone, there was no doubt in his mind that she was his. And each time they made love that became more clear.

Maybe, he thought, as she unfastened his pants, it was less about skill, and more about the intense feelings of love and affection they shared. But then she slid her hand inside his boxers, wrapped it around his erection and slowly stroked him, and his thoughts became all hazy and muddled. She made it so easy to forget the world around him, to focus on her and her alone. And he wondered what it would be like this time, slow and tender or maybe hot and sweaty. Or would she get that mischievous twinkle in her eyes and do something that would make most women blush?

Vanessa pushed him over onto his back and climbed on top of him, then she yanked her dress up over her head and tossed it onto the floor. Hot and sweaty, he thought with a grin—his particular favorite—and as she thrust against him, impaling herself on his erection, she was so hot and tight and wet, he stopped thinking altogether. And as they reached their climax together, then collapsed in each other's arms, he told himself that there had to be some way to talk her into staying.

And at the same time, his conscience asked the question: To what end?

Sixteen

Somewhere in the back of Marcus's mind he heard pounding.

What the hell was that? he wondered, and what could he do to make it stop? Then he realized, it was his door. Someone was knocking on his bedroom door.

His eyes flew open, and he tried to sit up, but there was a warm body draped across his chest. He and Vanessa must have fallen asleep. He looked over at the clock, and realized that it was past suppertime. Oh hell. No doubt Mia was awake by now.

He shook Vanessa. "Wake up!"

Her eyes fluttered open and she gave him a sleepy smile. "Hey."

"We fell asleep. It's late."

She shot up in bed and squinted at the clock, then she uttered a very unladylike curse. "Where's my phone? Mia must be awake by now. Why didn't Karin call me?"

The pounding started again as they both jumped out of bed.

"Who is that?" Vanessa asked, frantically looking around, he assumed, for her purse.

He tugged his pants on. "Stay here. I'll go see."

He rushed out to the living room, unlocked the door and yanked it open. Cleo's hand was in the air, poised to knock again.

"There you are!" she said.

"I was…taking a nap," he said, raking a hand through his tousled hair. "I haven't been sleeping well."

"Well, we have a problem. Poor Karin is frantic. Mia woke from her nap an hour ago but she can't find Vanessa. She's not answering her phone and I can't find her anywhere in the palace. I thought perhaps you knew where I might find her."

Was that suspicion in her eyes? "She probably went for a walk," Marcus said. "Maybe she forgot her phone."

"If she left the palace, security would know about it."

He opened his mouth to reply and she added, "But just in case, I had them check the gardens and she isn't out there. It's as if she disappeared."

"Give me a minute to get dressed and I'll find her."

Behind him Marcus heard an "oof!" then a loud crash. He swung around to find Vanessa on the floor by the couch, wrapped in a bed sheet, wincing and cradling her left foot. Beside her lay the floor lamp that had been standing there. Then he heard a noise from the hall and whipped back around to find that in his haste he'd pushed the door open, and Cleo could see the entire sordid scenario.

"Miss Reynolds," Cleo said, her jaw rigid. "Would you please call Karin and let her know that you are in fact fine, and haven't been abducted by terrorists?"

"Yes, ma'am," Vanessa said, her voice trembling, her cheeks crimson with shame.

Cleo turned to Marcus and said tightly, "A word in private, your highness?"

"Are you okay?" he asked Vanessa, who looked utterly miserable, and she nodded. "I'll be right back."

He stepped out into the hall, pulling the door closed behind him, and the look Cleo gave him curdled his blood.

"You lied to me?"

"What was I supposed to do? Tell you the truth? I can see how well that's going over."

"Marcus, what were you thinking?"

Had it been anyone but her berating him this way, he would have dismissed them on the spot. But Cleo had earned this right through years of loyal service. She was more an extension of family than an employee.

"Cleo, believe me when I say, we didn't plan for this to happen. And if it's any consolation, she's not going to marry my father."

"I should hope not! Your father deserves better than a woman who would—"

"This was not her fault," he said sharply, because he absolutely drew the line at any disparaging remarks against Vanessa. She didn't deserve it. "I pursued her."

"Look, Marcus," she said, touching his arm. "I know you're upset over Carmela, and maybe this is your way of getting revenge, but would you risk your relationship with your father for a—a cheap *fling?*"

"No, but I would for the woman who I've fallen hopelessly in love with."

She pulled her hand back in surprise. "You love her?"

"She's everything I have ever imagined I could want in a woman, and a few things I didn't even know I wanted until I met her. And she loves me too, which, considering my track record with women, is pretty damned astonishing. And the irony of it all is that those things I admire most about her are the reason we can never be together."

"You can't?"

"She thinks our relationship will come between me and my father, and she absolutely refuses to let that happen."

"You know that she's right."

"Sometimes I think that I don't even care. But she does, and as much as I'd like to, I would never go against her wishes."

Cleo shook her head. "I don't know what to say. I'm just…I'm so sorry things have to be this way."

"I can count on you to keep this conversation private," he said.

"Of course, Marcus."

He leaned down and kissed her papery cheek. "Thanks."

He stepped back into his suite, leaving her in the hall looking unbelievably sad.

Vanessa was dressed and sitting on the couch, putting her sandals on, when Marcus stepped back into the room. And from his expression she couldn't tell what had happened. "Marcus, I am so sorry."

"It's okay."

"I left my phone in my purse on the couch, that's why I didn't hear Karin calling me. Then I tripped on that stupid lamp. And I didn't mean to fall asleep."

"I fell asleep too. I take it Mia is okay."

"Fine. I figured we would need to talk, so I asked Karin to feed Mia her dinner and get her into bed for me."

He sat down on the couch beside her. "There's nothing to talk about. It's no one's fault."

No, they had plenty to talk about. "Cleo looked so… disappointed."

He sighed. "Yeah, she's good at that. But I explained the entire situation and she understands."

"That's not good enough."

"Vanessa—"

"I can't do this anymore, Marcus."

"I'm not ready for you to go."

"We knew this was inevitable. We kept saying that eventually the day would come that I'd have to leave. And I honestly think that it's here."

He squeezed her hand, gave her a sad smile. "I can't lose you. Not yet."

She shook her head. "My mind is made up. But I want you to know that this has been the happiest couple of weeks in my life, and I will never, as long as I live, forget you."

"Say you'll leave tomorrow. That you'll give me one more night."

She touched his cheek. It was rough from afternoon stubble. "I'm sorry. I just can't."

He leaned in to kiss her, and someone knocked on his door again. Marcus muttered a curse.

"Marcus, it's Cleo!"

"Come in!" he called, sounding exasperated, and he didn't even let go of her hand.

She opened the door and poked her head in. "I'm sorry to bother you again, but I thought you might like to know that your father's limo just pulled up out front. He's home."

Vanessa and Marcus uttered the same curse, at the exact same time, and bolted up off the couch.

"We'll be right down," he told Cleo, and snatched his shirt off the floor. He tugged it on and fastened the buttons, tucking it into his slacks. She was pretty sure he wasn't wearing any underwear, not that it made a difference at this point. Her hands were shaking so hard she was just glad she was already dressed.

He raked his fingers through his hair and asked, "You ready for this?"

She had always thought she was; now she wasn't so sure. She swallowed hard, shook her head.

"Me neither." He pulled her against him and kissed her. Long and slow and deep. Their last kiss. And he definitely made it a good one. Then he pulled away and said, "We'd better go."

They rushed down the stairs, Vanessa's legs feeling like limp noodles. That would be a sure way out of this disastrous situation. Trip on the stairs, tumble down and break her neck when she hit the marble floor below. Talk about taking the easy way out. But she managed to stay on her feet.

The instant her sandal hit the marble floor the front door swung open and Gabriel walked through. He was dressed casually in khaki pants and a polo shirt. Though she had expected him to look tired and pale from splitting his time between working and sitting at Trina's bedside, instead he looked tan and well rested, as if he'd been on an extended vacation.

He saw the two of them there and smiled. "Marcus, Vanessa."

He walked over and gave his son a hug, then shook his hand firmly. Then he turned to Vanessa.

"My sweet Vanessa," he said, taking her hands and grasping them firmly. "It's so good to see you."

She would have expected a much more enthusiastic greeting from a man who supposedly loved her. Or could it have just been that he didn't feel comfortable showing her physical affection in front of his son? That made sense. Whatever the reason she was actually grateful. If he had pulled her into his arms and kissed her passionately, that would have been awkward. And seeing Gabriel and Marcus there together, side by side, she realized that while they were definitely built similarly, and had the same dark tones, in looks Marcus actually favored his mother.

"I talked to you yesterday but you didn't say you were coming home," she told Gabriel.

"I thought I would surprise you."

Oh, she was definitely surprised.

"You have a bit of sunburn," Gabriel said, touching her chin lightly. "You've been getting outdoors."

Actually, she hadn't been out in the sun for days, how could she—? Beard burn, she realized, from the last time Marcus kissed her. So she lied and said, "Yes, we were outside just today."

"Where is Mia?" he asked.

"Upstairs, having her dinner."

"Good, good," he said, and something about his demeanor was just slightly…off. As if he were nervous. And she had never seen him nervous. Strangely enough, now that he was here in front of her, any trace of nerves she'd had were gone. She just felt sad. And though she would always love and respect him as a friend, any desire she may have had to marry him was gone. In this case absence did not make the heart grow fonder. She was too busy falling in love with someone else. And she couldn't put this off any longer. She had to end it now.

"Gabriel," she said, forcing a smile. "Can we talk? Privately, I mean."

"Yes, yes, of course. Why don't we go up to your suite." He turned to Marcus, whose jaw was so tight it could have snapped like a twig. "Please excuse us, son. We'll catch up later. I have news."

Marcus nodded. He was jealous, Vanessa could see it in his eyes, but he stayed silent. What choice did he have?

As they walked up the stairs together, Gabriel didn't even hold her hand, and he made idle chitchat, much the way he had during their recent phone conversations. When they got to her suite, she held her breath, scared to death that he might suddenly take her in his arms and kiss her, because the idea of pushing him away, of having to be so cruel, broke her heart. But he made no attempt to touch her, and when he gestured toward the sofa and asked her to sit down, he didn't even sit beside her. He sat across from her in the wing back chair. And he was definitely nervous. Had someone told him that they suspected her and Marcus of something inappropriate? And if he asked her for the truth, what should she say? Could she lie to him?

Or what if...*oh God*, was he going to *propose?*

"Gabriel, before you say anything, there's something I really need to tell you."

He rubbed his palms together. "And there's something I need to tell you."

"I'll go first," she said.

"No, it would be better if I did."

Vanessa leaned forward slightly. "Actually, it would probably be better if I did."

"No, mine is pretty important," he said, looking slightly annoyed.

"Well, so is mine," she said, feeling a little annoyed herself.

"Vanessa—"

"Gabriel—"

Then they said in perfect unison, "I can't marry you."

Seventeen

Marcus watched Vanessa and his father walk up the stairs together thinking, *what is wrong with this picture*.

If his father was happy to see her, why hadn't he kissed her? Why wasn't he holding her hand? And why had he looked so…nervous? He never got nervous.

"Something is up," Cleo said behind him, and he turned to her.

"So it's not just me who noticed."

"As giddy in love as he was when he came back from America, I thought he would sweep her into his arms the instant he walked in the door, then promptly drop to one knee to propose."

"Are you thinking what I'm thinking?" Marcus asked.

"He doesn't want to marry her."

Marcus was already moving toward the stairs when Cleo grabbed his sleeve.

"This doesn't mean he won't be angry, Marcus, or feel betrayed."

No, it didn't, but every time Marcus imagined Vanessa leaving he got a pain in his chest so sharp, it was as if someone had reached into his chest, grabbed his heart and was squeezing the life from him. The thought of watching her and Mia get on a plane, of seeing it take them away from Varieo forever, filled him with a feeling of panic so intense it was difficult to draw a breath.

He shrugged. "I don't care, Cleo. I can't do it. I can't let her go."

Cleo let go of his sleeve, and smiled up at him. "So what are you waiting for?"

He charged up the stairs to the second floor and raced down the hall to her room. Not even bothering to knock, he flung the door open. Vanessa was seated on the sofa, his father in the chair across from her, and the sudden intrusion surprised them both.

"Marcus," Vanessa said. "What are you doing here?"

"I need to have a word with my father," he told her.

His father frowned. "Is something wrong, son?"

"Yes and no. I guess it just depends on how you look at it."

Vanessa rose to her feet, shaking her head. "Marcus, don't—"

"I *have* to, Vanessa."

"But—"

"I know." He shrugged helplessly. "But I have to."

She sat back down, as if she'd gotten tired of fighting it too, and whatever happened, she was willing to live with the consequences.

"Marcus, can this wait? I really need to talk to Vanessa."

"No, it can't. What I need to tell you must be said right now."

His father looked to Vanessa, who sat there silently. "All right," he said, sounding annoyed. "Talk."

Marcus took a deep breath and blew it out, hoping his father would at least try to understand. "Remember when you thanked me for agreeing to spend time with Vanessa, and said in return, if I ever needed anything, to just ask?"

He nodded. "I remember."

"Did you really mean it?"

"Of course I did. I'm a man of my word. You know that."

"Then I need you to do something for me."

"Anything, Marcus."

"Let Vanessa go."

He drew back slightly, blinking in confusion. "Let her go? But...I just did. I just now told her that I couldn't marry her."

"That's not good enough. I need you to *really* let her go, forget you ever wanted to marry her."

He frowned. "Marcus, what on earth are you talking about? Why would I do that?"

"So I can marry her."

His father's mouth actually dropped open.

"You told me that Vanessa is a remarkable woman, and said that once I got to know her, I would love her. Well, you were right. I do love her." He turned to Vanessa. "More than she could possibly imagine. Too much to ever let her leave."

She smiled, tears filling her eyes. "I love you, too, Marcus."

He turned back to his father, who sat there looking stunned. "You have to understand that we didn't mean for this to happen, and we did fight it. But we just..." He shrugged. "We just couldn't help it."

"You had an affair," his father said, as if to clarify.

"This was no affair," Marcus said. "We fell in love."

"So," his father said, turning to Vanessa, "this is why you couldn't marry me?"

"Yes. I'm so sorry. But like Marcus said, we didn't mean for this to happen. At first, he didn't even like me."

His father slowly nodded, as though he were letting it sink in, but oddly enough, he didn't look angry. Maybe the depth of their betrayal had left him temporarily numb.

"We had agreed not to say anything, to end it," Marcus told him. "She was going to do the honorable thing and leave. Neither of us could bear the thought of hurting you. But I need her. Her and Mia."

His father just sat there, eyes lowered, slowly shaking his head, rubbing his palms together. Marcus glanced over at Vanessa who looked both sad and relieved, and a little worried. He could relate. Telling his father the truth had been hard as hell, but he knew that living a lie would have been so much worse. It would have weighed on him the rest of his life.

"Would you please say something?" Marcus said. "Tell me what you're thinking."

His father finally looked over to him. "I find it ironic, I guess."

"Ironic how?"

"Because I have a secret, too."

"The reason you couldn't marry me?" Vanessa asked.

He nodded. "Because I'm engaged to someone else."

For a second Vanessa just sat there, looking dumbfounded, then she laughed.

"You think that's funny?" Marcus asked.

"Not funny ha-ha, but funny ironic. I guess because I

was so focused on Marcus, I didn't really see it. Suddenly everything makes sense."

Marcus was completely confused. "See *what?*"

"Why he stopped Skyping, why his calls were less frequent and increasingly impersonal. You were falling in love with her."

"It was difficult to look you in the eye," his father said, "to just hear your voice. I felt so guilty. I knew I had to end it but I didn't want to hurt you."

"I know exactly what you mean!" she said. "You have no idea how relieved I felt when you said we couldn't Skype anymore. I was so scared that the second you saw my face you would know what I was thinking."

Gabriel smiled. "Me, too."

"Excuse me," Marcus said, raising his hand. "Would someone like to tell me who is it that you were falling in love with?"

Vanessa looked at him like he was a moron, and right now, he sort of felt like one. "It's your Aunt Trina."

Marcus turned to his father, and could see by the look on his face that it was true. "You're engaged to *Trina?*"

He nodded. "Almost losing her opened my eyes to my feelings for her."

He and Aunt Trina had always been close, but Marcus honestly believed their relationship had been platonic.

"We didn't mean for it to happen," his father said. "But after spending so much time together, we just knew. I guess you can understand how that goes."

"When mother was still alive, did you and Trina...?"

"Marcus, *no!* Of course not. I loved your mother. I *still* love her. And until recently I never thought of Trina as anything but a friend. I'm still not sure what happened, what changed, I just know that it's right." He turned to Vanessa. "I was going to tell you this, and apologize pro-

fusely for dragging you and your daughter halfway around
the world, and for making promises I couldn't keep. It's
not that I don't care for you deeply. It's because of you
that I was able to open up my heart again. I was so lonely,
and unhappy, and then I met you and for the first time in
months I felt alive again. And hopeful. I wanted to hold on
to that feeling, but deep down I think I knew that it wasn't
going to last. I knew that we would never love each other
the way a wife and husband should."

"I wanted to love you that way," she said. "I wanted to
be that woman."

"You are that woman, Vanessa." He looked to Marcus
and smiled. "Just not for me."

"So, you're not angry?" Marcus asked.

"When I'm guilty of the same thing? You two love each
other. And you were going to forsake your feelings to protect mine."

"Well, that was the plan," Vanessa said, shooting Marcus a look, but she was smiling.

"Then how could I possibly be angry. Besides, I can't
imagine anyone else I would rather have as my daughter-
in-law. And at my age, I think I'd much prefer being a
grandfather to Mia than a father. I know men my age do
it all the time, but I'm just too old and set in my ways to
start over."

And Marcus felt as if his life was just beginning. As
if everything up until now had just been a rehearsal in
preparation for the real thing. It was so perfect that for an
instant he couldn't help wondering if they might still be
asleep in his bed and this whole thing was just a dream.

Marcus reached his hand out to Vanessa, and she
reached for him, and the instant their fingers touched he
knew this was very real. And very right.

"Father, could you give us a moment alone?" he asked.

He rose from the sofa, a smile on his face. "Take all the time you need."

The door had barely closed behind him and Vanessa was in his arms.

Vanessa buried her face against Marcus's chest, holding on tight, almost afraid to believe this was really happening. That it had worked out. That somehow, by breaking the rules and doing the *wrong* thing, she got exactly what she wanted.

"Is it real?" she asked him. "Could we be that lucky?"

He tightened his hold on her and she heard him sigh. "It sure feels real to me. But I don't think luck had anything to do with it."

She pulled back to look at him. "Why did you do it, Marcus? You risked so much."

"When I thought of you and Mia leaving...I just couldn't stand it. And when I saw the way he greeted you, I just had a feeling that something was wrong."

"He still could have been angry."

"I know. But that was a chance I had to take."

"For me?"

"Of course." He touched her cheek. "I love you, Vanessa."

He'd said it before, but until now, she hadn't allowed herself to really believe it. It would have been too painful when he let her down. But now, all that love, all those feelings she had been holding back, welled up inside her and she couldn't have held them back if her life depended on it. "I love you, Marcus. So much. I honestly didn't know it was possible to feel this happy."

"Well, get used to it," he said, kissing her gently. "Because if you'll have me, I'm going to spend the rest of my life making sure you stay that way."

"That's a long time."

"Vanessa, to truly express how much I love you, how much I *need* you, it would take an eternity."

She smiled. "Then I guess I'll just have to take your word for it."

"Does that mean you'll stay here with me, that you'll be my wife and make me the happiest man alive?"

In all the different places she had lived, Vanessa had never felt as if she truly belonged, but here, in Varieo with Marcus, she knew without a doubt that she was finally home.

"Yes," she told him, never feeling more sure about anything in her life. "I definitely will."

* * * * *

"Common sense tells me to walk away now," Emma whispered. **"You have a reputation for never going out with an employee."**

"I never have," Zach answered. "That doesn't mean I can't."

"That wasn't what I wanted to hear. I want this job."

"Don't quit on me," he replied, his voice raspy and quiet. A muscle worked in his jaw. "I'll double your salary."

"Double my salary?" she repeated, shaking her head.

"You don't need to pack and go. Don't walk out over a few casual kisses."

Exasperated and stung over his dismissal of kisses that had shaken her, she stared at him. "Those kisses weren't casual to my way of thinking," she whispered.

She stepped close, put her arm around his neck and placed her mouth on his, kissing him with all the heat and fury she felt over his dismissive attitude. In seconds, she broke off the kiss and looked up with satisfaction.

"I'd say your body's reaction isn't *casual*, either," she said, catching her breath.

Dear Reader,

Depending on circumstances, holidays can be painful or joyous, and *Midnight Under the Mistletoe* is about those opposing feelings.

For some, Christmas is a family celebration. It is a kaleidoscope of events and people, funny moments, happy ones, touching occasions, unpredictable occurrences and as the years go by, the holiday is laced with memories of loved ones and good times. This story, as well as one of the characters, reflects that view of Christmas. Also, the story is about the breaking away of the hardened shell of someone's hurt and loneliness acquired through too many disappointing childhood Christmases.

Watch handsome billionaire Texan Zach Delaney's life transform when Emma Hillman pours her love of Christmas into his life. His stunning secretary, who is a total opposite in personality and completely off-limits to him, becomes the biggest temptation of his life. What happens when a man who has always skipped Christmas falls in love with a woman who is the embodiment of the December celebration?

Thank you for selecting *Midnight Under the Mistletoe*.

Happy holidays to all!

Sara Orwig

MIDNIGHT UNDER
THE MISTLETOE

BY
SARA ORWIG

Published in Great Britain 2013
by Mills & Boon, an imprint of Harlequin (UK) Limited,
Eton House, 18-24 Paradise Road, Richmond, Surrey TW9 1SR

© Sara Orwig 2012

ISBN: 978 0 263 90447 5
ebook ISBN: 978 1 472 00044 6

51-0113

Harlequin (UK) policy is to use papers that are natural, renewable and recyclable products and made from wood grown in sustainable forests. The logging and manufacturing processes conform to the legal environmental regulations of the country of origin.

Printed and bound in Spain
by Blackprint CPI, Barcelona

Sara Orwig lives in Oklahoma. She has a patient husband who will take her on research trips anywhere from big cities to old forts. She is an avid collector of Western history books. With a master's degree in English, Sara has written historical romance, mainstream fiction and contemporary romance. Books are beloved treasures that take Sara to magical worlds, and she loves both reading and writing them.

With special thanks to
Stacy Boyd, Shana Smith and Maureen Walters.
May you have a blessed and joyous holiday.

One

Another secretary to interview.

Zach Delaney stood at the window of his west Texas ranch and watched the approaching car. This candidate was prompt. He had heard this one lived in Dallas, was single, only twenty-four, a homebody who insisted on weekends free to go home. She wanted a week off before Christmas and two days after Christmas. If she could do the work, it was all right with him. He didn't know her, but she had worked more than two years at his Dallas office, which held the corporate offices of his demolition company, his trucking company and the architectural firm he owned. She'd risen fast and was highly recommended.

As Zach watched the car approach the house, he thought about the other secretaries he'd interviewed and the conversation he'd had with his brother Will, who had stopped by an hour ago.

He remembered Will laughing. "I know you—you're probably about to go up in smoke from boredom."

"You've got that right. I feel as if I'm a prisoner and time seems to have stopped," Zach replied, raking his fingers through his thick, brown curls.

Will nodded. "Don't forget—you're supposed to stay off your feet and keep your foot elevated."

"I'm doing that most of the time. Believe me, I want my foot to get well."

Will smiled. "You should have just stayed in Dallas after Garrett's wedding earlier this month. You haven't been cooped up like this since you were five and had the mumps."

"Don't remind me."

"That was twenty-seven years ago. I don't know how you've made it this long in demolition without getting hurt."

"I've been lucky and careful, I guess."

"If you don't end up hiring today's interviewee, I'll send someone out to work for you. If I had known the difficulty you're having finding a competent secretary, I would have sent one before now."

"Thanks. One secretary lasted a few days before deciding the ranch was too isolated. Another talked incessantly," Zach grumbled, causing Will to laugh. His brother's brown eyes sparkled with amusement.

"One of those women hovered over me and told me what to do to take care of myself. Actually, Will, instead of hiring a secretary to help go through Dad's stuff, maybe we should just trash it all. Dad's been gone almost a year now and this stuff hasn't been touched. It's not important. The only value that stuff can have is sentimental. That makes it worthless as time passes."

"We don't know for sure there isn't something of value in those boxes," Will argued.

Zach nodded. "Knowing our father, he could have put some vital papers, money or something priceless in these boxes, just so someone *would* have to wade through them."

"You volunteered to go through his papers while you recuperate from your fall. You don't have to."

"I'll do it. The secretary will help go through all the letters and memorabilia while I also keep up with work. You became guardian for Caroline and you handled a lot of the dealings to bring our half sister into the family. Ryan's knee-deep in getting his new barn built while commuting back and forth to his business in Houston. Besides, I'm the one incapacitated with time on my hands. I'm it, for now. I don't know what got into Dad, keeping all this memorabilia. He would never have actually written a family history."

"Our father was not one you could figure. His actions were unfathomable except for making money. He probably intended to write a family history. In his old age I think he became nostalgic." Will headed toward the door and then paused. "You sure you don't want to join us for Thanksgiving? I'll send someone to get you," he added, and Zach was touched by Will's concern.

"Thanks, but no thanks. You enjoy Ava's family. Ryan leaves soon to spend Thanksgiving with the latest woman in his life—I can't keep up with which one this is. I'll be fine and enjoy myself all by myself."

"If you change your mind, let me know. Also, it's less than six weeks until Christmas. We're going to Colorado for the holiday. Do you want to come along? We'll be happy to have you join us."

"Thank you." Zach grinned. "I think I'll go to the house in Italy. It'll be beautiful there and you know I don't do Christmas."

"So who is the beautiful Italian lady? I'm sure there is one."

"Might be more than one." Zach smiled. "You hadn't been into Christmas much yourself until you got Caroline. Now you have to celebrate."

"Truthfully, with Caroline, it's been fun. Come with us and you'll see."

"I love little Caroline, but you go ahead. Doc told me to stay put and this is a better place than snowy mountains in Colorado."

"That's true, but we'd take care of you."

Zach shook his head. "Thanks, Will, for coming out."

"Let me know about the secretary. I'll get you one who's excellent."

"With Margo on maternity leave, I may have to find a new one permanently. I don't want to think about that."

Now, Zach shifted his foot and glared at it, recalling the moment the pile of rubble had given way and he had fallen, breaking an ankle, plus small bones, causing a sprain and getting one deep gash. Staying off his foot most of the time was hell. He didn't like working daily in an office, and the doctor told him he couldn't go back to working on site or travel much, but he could do some work at the ranch and stay off his foot as best he could.

Zach sighed as the car slowed in front of the house. Emma Hillman. She climbed out of her car and came up the walk.

Startled, he momentarily forgot her mission. A tall, wind-blown, leggy redhead, who would turn heads everywhere, was striding toward his front door. With looks like hers, she belonged on a model's catwalk or doing a commercial or in a bar, not striding purposefully toward his house in the hopes of doing secretarial chores. Even though she wore a tailored, dark green suit with an open black coat over it, she had a wild, attention-getting appearance.

The west Texas wind swept over her, catching more tendrils of long red hair and blowing them around her face. Immobilized, Zach stared. She didn't look like any secretary on his staff in any office he had. Nor did she resemble the home-body type to his way of thinking. All those recommendations she had—they must have been based on her looks. His spirits sank. He would have to ask Will to find him somebody else. He needed someone who would stay on the ranch during the week. This one was a declared homebody. Add that to her looks and he couldn't imagine it working out. He also couldn't imagine her being an efficient secretary, either. He would give Emma Hillman a lot of work and in less than two days, she would probably fold and run as her predecessor had.

When the bell rang, he could hear Nigel get the door. Zach hobbled back to the middle of the room to wait to meet her. Before he sent her packing, he might get her home phone number. Actually, even if she did work out here, when the temporary job ended she'd go back to the corporate office, so getting her phone number was only wishful thinking. She'd still be an employee. Even so, eagerness to meet her took the boredom out of the morning. This promised to be his most enjoyable moment since he arrived at the ranch.

Emma Hillman pushed a button and heard chimes. Her gaze swept over the large porch. The ranch was not at all what she had pictured in her mind. She had expected a rustic, sprawling house, not a mansion that bordered on palatial. When the door swung open, she faced a slender gray-haired man.

"Welcome, Miss Hillman?"

"Yes," she said, entering as he stepped back.

"I'm Nigel Smith. If you'll come with me, Mr. Delaney is waiting."

Following him, she glanced around the enormous entrance. Wood floors had a dark appearance with a treatment that gave them an antiqued quality and probably would not show boot marks or much of anything else.

She tried to finger-comb her hair and tuck tendrils back into the clips that held her hair on either side of her head. She had been warned about Zach Delaney—that he was difficult to please, curt, all business. Actually, he had conflicting descriptions—a charismatic hunk by some; others pronounced him a demanding ogre. She had been told too many times about her three predecessors who hadn't lasted more than a day or two.

She didn't care—it was a fabulous opportunity for another promotion in the company and the pay was terrific right at Christmastime. Even though she was going to miss being in Dallas with her family, she was determined to cooperate with Zach Delaney and be the secretary who got to stay.

Nigel led her through an open door into a large room with shelves of books on two walls, a huge fireplace on another and all glass on the fourth. In a hasty glance she barely saw any of her surroundings because her attention was ensnared by the tall man standing in the center of the room.

His prominent cheekbones and a firm jaw were transformed by a mass of dark brown curls and riveting blue eyes. A black knit shirt and tight jeans revealed muscles and a fit physique. Even standing quietly, he appeared commanding.

Dimly, she heard Nigel present her and she thanked him as he left, but her gaze was locked with the head of her company, Zach Delaney. Her breathing altered, her heart raced and her palms became damp. She felt flustered, drawn to him, unable to look away. For heartbeats, they gazed at each other while silence stretched.

With an effort she offered her hand. "I'm glad to meet you, Mr. Delaney," she said. Her voice was soft in her ears.

He stepped forward, his hand closing around hers, his warm fingers breaking the spell she had been temporarily enveloped in. "Welcome to the Delaney ranch. I'm happy to meet you, and it's Zach. We're going to work closely together. No 'Mr. Delaney.' And please have a seat." His voice was deep, warm and sexy, an entertainer's voice.

Feeling foolish, yet unable to control the physical reaction she was having to him, she sat in a leather chair. Another chair was close and he turned it to face her, sitting near her. "I've read your recommendations, which are excellent. If you want this job, you're to move here for the duration of the time you work for me—five, possibly six weeks total. Your weekends are free from one on Friday afternoon until Monday morning at nine o'clock."

"That's fine with me," she replied, thinking someone should have warned her about his appeal. He rarely was in the Dallas office and executive offices were on the top floor. She had never seen him or crossed paths with him before. She had no idea she would have such an intense reaction to meeting him.

"I expect this job to end around Christmas, when my foot heals. You can return to the Dallas office and I will be on my way back to the field."

"Fine," she replied, barely able to concentrate on what he was saying for getting lost in vivid blue eyes. His conversation might have been practical, all business, but the look in his eyes was not. Blue depths probed, examined and conveyed a sensual appraisal that shimmied warmly over her nerves. "As I mentioned in our phone call, I'd like to take that week before Christmas and two days afterward if the job hasn't ended."

"That's fine. As far as your duties, you're here to help with any correspondence or business matters I have and to help me sort through some family papers. My father intended to write a family history. He had old letters and family memorabilia that have been passed through generations, that sort of thing. I volunteered to go through all of it while I'm supposed to stay off my feet," Zach said, waving his hand toward the boxes of papers nearby.

"The memorabilia should be fascinating," she remarked.

"If your ancestors wrote these letters and sent them, how did they get possession of them again?"

"Good question. They wrote other relatives, sisters, brothers, and as far as I can see, everybody saved every word that was put on paper. There are letters in those boxes that aren't from Delaneys, but are written to a Delaney who saved it. You'd think one person would have tossed them. If the letter isn't from a Delaney, there is no reason to keep it."

"I imagine some were tossed. There were probably more since you had such prolific writers in your family."

"If I were the only Delaney of my generation, I would simply shred the papers this week because I think they're junk. Some of the letters date back to the 1800s."

Horrified at the thought of shredding old letters, she stared at him. "The 1800s? It should be spellbinding to read about your relatives," she blurted before she thought about how it might sound critical of her boss's attitude.

He smiled. "I suppose it's a good thing you feel that way because you'll be reading some of this stuff for me. Anyway, that in general is what I hired you to do. Does this sound acceptable?"

"Certainly. I'm looking forward to it."

"Great. Feel free to ask questions at any time. I'll have Nigel see about getting you moved in. You were asked to come prepared to move in. Is this what you did?"

"Yes. I was told to pack for the job because you might hire me and want me to stay."

"I'm getting desperate for a secretary. The salary should make up for some of the demands," he said and she merely nodded.

"Nigel is sort of jack-of-all-trades around the house. He acts as butler, assistant and a financial manager. You'll meet more of our staff, who have homes on the ranch."

"I wonder if I'll ever find my way around," she said as she glanced beyond him toward the hall.

"Nigel will give you a map of the house. We have an indoor pool and one outside. Feel free to swim after or before work hours. We have a gym, too."

"This is a modernized ranch home."

"This house has been remodeled many times. The family room was the actual original house, built in the 1800s. Anyway, my grandfather had an elevator installed, so I'm taking it temporarily. You're welcome to if you want."

"Thank you, I won't need the elevator," she replied with a smile. "I exercise each day, so stairs are good."

"Great. Do you think we can start work this morning in about an hour?"

"Certainly."

As he stood, she came to her feet and followed him to the door. He offered his hand. "Welcome to the Delaney ranch, Emma," he drawled in a mesmerizing voice that wrapped around her like a warm blanket. She shook hands again with him, an electric current flashing from the contact while she looked into the bluest eyes she had ever seen. Dark brown curly lashes framed his mesmerizing eyes.

"I hope you find your stay here worthwhile," he said, a dry, professional statement, but his tone of voice, with those blue eyes focused on her and her hand enveloped in his, made her think of sizzling kisses. Realizing how she was staring, she withdrew her hand and stepped back. He turned to walk into the hall to talk to Nigel, nodded at her, and in seconds she left with Nigel to see where she would stay.

The next hour was a whirlwind of getting unpacked enough to function through the day. To her surprise she had more than a room—it was a suite with a sitting area, a dream bedroom with a four-poster and fruitwood furniture. Dazzled by the lavish quarters, she looked at a bathroom as large as her apartment. The bath held a sunken tub, potted plants, mirrors, an adjoining dressing room plus a huge walk-in closet. She took pictures on her cell phone to send to her sisters. She could imagine how they would ooh and aah over where she was staying. Her paramount concern was how would she work constantly around Zach Delaney. She had heard rumors at the office about how appealing he was, but not from anyone who had actually worked for him. She had talked to one secretary who had spent two days with him and thought he was a monster, piling on work until it was impossible to get done what he demanded. Another secretary had complained about him being silent and abrupt during the day.

When she saw it was time to go back to meet with him, she smoothed her hair into a loose bun and left her room. Trying to familiarize herself with the mansion, she walked to the study where she had met Zach.

He sat behind a desk and stood the minute she appeared in the doorway. Once again, she tried to avoid staring. He looked muscled and fit except for his foot that was wrapped in a bandage and in an oversize health shoe. The unruly curls were a tangle around his face, softening his rugged features.

"Let's go to the office," he said, and she walked beside him down a wide hall filled with paintings, plants, side tables and chairs.

As they entered a large room, she drew a deep breath. It was a dream office with two large desks at opposite ends of the room. Shelves lined three walls and the remaining wall was glass with a view of a small pond and well tended grounds up to a white fence. Beyond the fence were stables, a corral and pasture. Through spacious windows, daylight spilled into the room. Fax machines, shredders, computers and electronic equipment filled each end of the office.

"That's my desk," he said, pointing to the larger one that was polished, ornately carved dark wood. Forming an L-shape with the desk, a table stood at one end. The table held two computers, one of which had dual oversize monitors. Another computer was centered on his desk. Two laptops and an iPad lay on the table.

The other desk was glass, looking far newer. File cabinets were built into one wall and not noticeable at first glance.

He sat behind his desk, motioning toward a leather chair facing him. She sat, crossing her legs, catching him looking at her legs when she glanced up. She inhaled sharply. She experienced an undercurrent of intense awareness and suspected he did as well. It was unexpected, definitely unwanted. Any hot attraction between them could put her job in jeopardy and this job was important to her. She was saving to go back to college and, ultimately, become qualified to teach. This was a temporary increase in pay she could use to achieve her dream.

"Since you and I and my staff are the only people here, you can dress casually. Jeans are fine."

She nodded. "Great."

"The glass desk will be yours. You'll find a stack of papers I've signed that need to be copied and put into the mail." He leaned back and stretched out his long legs.

She realized she was going to have a difficult time for a few days, focusing on what he was saying because she got lost looking at him.

"Hopefully you'll be able to read my handwriting. I have a document there for you to type for me to sign. Another stack holds filing. There's an in-box on the corner of my desk. When you finish anything, if it doesn't go in the mail or the file, place it in my in-box. If you have any questions, always feel free to ask. Take a break when you want and feel free to get what you want in the kitchen. Did Nigel show you where the kitchen is?"

"Yes, he showed me around briefly."

"Did you meet my very good cook?"

"Yes, I met Rosie."

"Good. You can start work each day at 8:00, quit at 4:00 or start at 9:00 and quit at 5:00. You're stuck here for lunch so we'll not add that to the time."

"I prefer 8:00," she said and he nodded.

"Any questions now?" he asked, giving her a direct look that made her pulse jump another notch.

"One—where do I take the mail?"

"There's a box on a shelf near your desk that is marked Mail and you put everything in there. One of the hands who works on the ranch will get the mail to take it down to the road to be picked up."

She nodded and headed over to her desk, feeling her back prickle because she suspected Zach's gaze was on her. She sat down and looked at the piles of work in front of her, remembering the angry statements from Brenna about Zach Delaney heaping mountains of work on her. It looked like a lot now—hopefully, by the end of the day, she would have made a big enough dent in the stacks to get to keep this job.

Still conscious of him across the room, Emma reached for a stack. As she began to read the first letter, she tried to keep from glancing his way. She pushed the stack aside and picked up a tablet with a bold handwriting. The writing to be typed looked the most time-consuming, so she started with it. In minutes she managed to put Zach out of her thoughts.

When she finished each task, she placed it in the proper pile. Standing, she gathered the work she had completed and put papers for Zach into his in-box. His back was turned as he worked at his computer and she looked at the thick hair curling on the back of his head.

She had not expected to be working in the same room with him. Also, she hadn't expected to work for someone who took her breath and set her pulse racing just by a glance from his sky-blue eyes.

With a deep sigh, she placed letters in the box for mail and then she started to file.

She looked across the room to see him setting papers in a pile. He picked up the letters in his in-box, glanced at her to catch her watching him again. She turned away to work on her computer, in seconds concentrating on what she was doing for the next half hour. She finished another stack and picked them up to take to his in-box and this time when she glanced his way, she met his gaze.

He seemed to be sitting and watching her. She picked up the papers and carried them to his desk, all the time aware of his steady observation.

As she started to put the letters into the box, he took them and riffled through them before looking at her. "You're a fast worker. And an accurate one."

"Thank you. I try to be."

"I figured with all the work I've piled on you this morning, you'd be out of here as fast as the others."

"I intend to stay," she said, amused, and realizing he might have been testing to see how she worked. She went back to her desk, again having that tingly feeling across her shoulders, certain he was watching her.

When she glanced at him, he had settled back to read. In seconds, he placed the letter in the stack beside him on his desk.

What kind of man did she work for? When she had gone to work at Z.A.D. Enterprises, she hadn't given much thought to the head of the business because she'd heard he was rarely in the Dallas office. The business comprised primarily of demolition, but also had a trucking company, an architectural firm and a concrete company. The international company had offices scattered worldwide and she heard Zachary Delaney traveled constantly from site to site, something she would detest. Other than that and the recent grumbling by Brenna, she knew little about him. Not one of the secretaries who had preceded her had said anything about his appeal, about his looks, about anything except he had proven difficult to work for. Maya, as well as Brenna, had thought he was unreceptive and uncommunicative. All had complained the workload was too heavy and she had to agree it was a lot, but it made time fly. On the other hand, around the office the word had always been that he was friendly. Perhaps part of his surly reputation with some secretaries was caused by his being injured and isolated on a ranch.

She returned to the stack, until she heard the scrape of a chair.

He stood and stretched, flexing muscles in his arms. When he glanced her way, she was embarrassed to be caught staring at him again.

"Want some lunch?" Without waiting for her answer, he motioned. "C'mon, we'll get something to eat. Rosie will have something fixed."

"Thank you," she said. "I still have letters, though."

"C'mon. You'll like Rosie's cooking and she'll be disappointed if you don't come eat. Those letters aren't urgent."

"Very well. You're the boss and I don't want to hurt her feelings." Glancing at her watch, Emma was surprised it was half past twelve. "I didn't realize the time."

"Time flies when you're having fun," he said, grinning at her. Creases appeared on either side of his mouth in an enticing smile that caused her to smile in return.

"So, Emma, tell me about yourself since we'll be working together for the next month or so."

Satisfaction flared because he must mean she would get to stay. "There's not much to tell. I've been at Z.A.D. for two years now. I have an apartment in Dallas and have two sisters and two brothers. My sisters, Sierra and Mary Kate, and Connor, my older brother, are married. Bobby and I are single. What about you?"

"I have two brothers, it was three, one is deceased. My older brother became guardian of our little niece, Caroline."

"That's sad. Is your niece's mother deceased, too?"

"No, her mother walked out when Caroline was a baby. She didn't want to be tied down with responsibilities, although she had a nanny and someone to cook and clean."

"I can't imagine," Emma said, staring at him.

He shrugged. "One more thing to sour me on marriage. My older brother felt the same way until this year. He just married in September."

"You don't want to get married and have a family?"

His mouth quirked in a crooked smile. "Not even remotely. The weeks I'm spending here recuperating are probably the longest I've stayed home in Texas in I don't know when. I'm a traveler."

"I've heard you work all over the world and I know Z.A.D. has offices worldwide. I have a vastly different life. I don't want to miss a weekend with my family."

"We're poles apart there," he remarked with a smile, directing her into a large kitchen with an adjoining dining room that held a table and chairs, a sofa, a fireplace, two wingback chairs and a bar.

"What's for lunch, Rosie? Something smells tempting," he said, raising a lid on a pot on the stove. A stocky woman in a uniform bustled around the kitchen. Her graying hair was in a bun and glasses perched on her turned-up nose.

"Chicken soup there and I have quesadillas or turkey melt sandwiches—your preference."

"How about soup, plus—" He paused and looked questioningly at Emma. "Either of the choices have any appeal?"

"Of course. Quesadillas, please."

"Good choice. Rosie's are special. Soup and quesadillas it is. We can help ourselves, Rosie."

Bowls and plates were on the counter. With that steady awareness of him at her side, Emma helped herself to a small bowl of soup, surprised when Zach set down his dishes and held her chair as she sat down. The gesture made their lunch together seem far less like boss and secretary eating together than a man and a woman on a date. Rosie appeared with a coffeepot, which Emma declined and Zach accepted.

When he sat, she said, "I'm sure everyone asks, what drew you to demolition?"

"A child's love of tearing something down, probably. I have an engineering degree and I almost went to architecture school. I have architects working for me so we build where we tear down. We build sometimes where nothing has stood. I find it fascinating work."

"I hear you go all over the world." She didn't add that she knew he was wealthy enough he would never have to work a day if he didn't want to.

The Delaney wealth was well publicized. She had never known anyone like him before. His love of travel was foreign to her. His disregard for family and marriage dismayed her even more than his apparent disregard for his family history. He had a lifestyle she could not imagine, but the head of the company was light-years from her clerical job, which provided an excellent way to save money to finish her college education.

"So, Zach, your favorite locale is where?" she asked as Rosie brought a platter with steaming quesadillas to set between them.

"There's too many to have a favorite. I love Paris, I love Torres del Paine, Iguazu Falls, the city of New York. They're all interesting. Where's your favorite?"

"Home with my family," she said, smiling at him, and he shook his head.

"Okay, I'll rephrase my question," he said. "Where's your favorite place outside of Texas?"

She lowered her fork. "I've never been outside of Texas."

One dark eyebrow arched as surprise flashed briefly in his blue eyes. "Never been outside of Texas," he repeated, studying her as if she had announced she had another set of ears beneath her red hair.

"No, I'm happy here."

"You might be missing something," he said, still scrutinizing her with open curiosity.

"I don't think so, therefore, that's really all that matters, right?" she asked, certain after today he would have satisfied his curiosity about her and lunch with the boss would cease.

"You're missing some wonderful places and you don't even know it."

She smiled at him again, thinking he might be missing some wonderful family companionship and didn't even know it. "As long as I'm content, it doesn't matter."

"So tell me about this family of yours and what they all do."

"My family lives near me in Dallas. Dad is an accountant and my mom is a secretary. My younger brother works part-time and is in school at the University of North Texas. I've taken classes to become a teacher. This semester I didn't enroll, but I hope to start back soon."

"How far along are you?"

"I have a little more than half the credits I need. Back to my family—in addition to my siblings, I have five small nieces and three nephews. We have assorted other relatives, grandparents, aunts and uncles, who live in the same general area."

"Big family."

"My siblings and I visit my parents on weekends," she said.

"So do my aunts and uncles. There are anywhere from twenty to thirty or forty of us when we all get together."

He paused as he started to drink his water, giving her a polite smile as if she said they spent every weekend at the park so they could play on the slides and swings.

"My family is definitely not that together," he said. "We go our separate ways. Dad's deceased and Mom disappeared from our lives when we were young."

"We have different lifestyles," she said, thinking this was a man she couldn't possibly ever be close to even if circumstances had been different. His world and hers were poles apart. Their families were so different—hers a huge part of her life, his nearly nonexistent, what with his father being deceased and his mother walking out years earlier. Those events had to influence him and make him the man he was today. This job would be brief and then she probably would never see him again. "The quesadilla is delicious," she said.

"I told you Rosie is a good cook. So, is there any special person in your life right now? I assume no one objected to you taking this job."

"Not at all and there's no special person at the moment. As long as I can go home for the weekends and holidays, I'm fine."

"I'm not sure I've been involved—friends or otherwise—with someone as tied into home and family."

"I'm your secretary—that's different from your women friends."

"We can be friends," he said, looking amused, and a tingle ran across her nerves. In tiny subtle ways he was changing their relationship from professional to personal, something she did not want. With every discovery about him, she saw what opposites they were. This was not a man who would ever fit into her world or her life other than on a physical level. She definitely did not fit into his.

Surprised that he was even interested, she had to wonder. She had never heard a word of gossip about him even remotely trying to have an outside relationship with an employee. Far from it—occasional remarks were made to new single women to forget about impressing the boss—if they even got to know him—except through efficient work.

"We can be friends to a degree in a professional manner," she said, wondering if she sounded prim.

"Emma, we're going to be under the same roof, working together for weeks. Relax. This isn't the office and it's not that formal. If I have something critical, a letter I just have to get out, an appointment that has to be made by a certain time, I'll tell you."

"Fair enough," she said, feeling as if their relationship just made another subtle shift. Or was it her imagination because she found him so physically attractive? "So you don't gather often with the family, you travel a lot—what else do you do?"

"Most of the time for the past few years my life has been tied up in my work. I have a yacht, but I'm seldom on it. I ski. I have a villa in Italy. I have a condo in New York, one in Chicago and I spend the most time between Paris and Chicago where we have offices. I like cities."

She placed her fork across her plate and stood. "That was a delicious lunch. If you'll excuse me, I should get back to the letters."

"Sit and relax, Emma. Those letters aren't urgent and they'll be there after lunch. I'm enjoying talking to you. There's no rush. And I suspect some tidbit will appear for dessert."

Surprised, she sat again. "I'm not in the habit of arguing with my supervisor. I don't think I can possibly eat dessert. This was more lunch than I usually have."

"Indulge yourself while you can," he said. Pushing his plate forward, he placed his arms on the table and leaned closer. "Emma, this is lunch. We're not at work. Forget the supervisor-secretary relationship, which doesn't have to exist 24/7. This is just two people having lunch together," he drawled in that husky voice that was soft as fur. Vivid blue eyes held her attention while his words poured over her and the moment shifted, holding a cozy intimacy. "Beautiful green eyes, great red hair—they sort of lend themselves to forgetting all about business," he said softly.

"We're about to cross a line we shouldn't cross," she whispered while her heart hammered.

"We crossed that line when you came in the door," he replied.

Two

Her heart thudded because his words changed their relationship. She realized her reply would set the standard. For a fleeting second, how tempted she was to flirt back, to give him a seductive reply that was on the tip of her tongue. For the moment, she wished he were someone else and not her boss.

Following the path of wisdom, practicality and caution, she smiled and chuckled, shaking her head and trying to diffuse the electrifying tension that had sprung between them. "I don't think so," she replied lightly. "We can't. I'm here for a secretarial job, which sets definite limits. I'm not crossing that line. If that's part of my work—then tell me now."

"Definitely not part of the job," he said, leaning back and studying her with a faint smile and amusement dancing in his blue eyes. "As rare for me as for you in an employer-employee situation. But we're not going to be able to shut it off that easily. As a matter of fact, I think the chemistry is in spite of both of us, not because of either of us wanting it to happen. That's a big difference and rather fascinating."

"We'll not pursue it," she persisted. Rosie appeared with a tray that held four choices of desserts. "What would you like, Miss Hillman?" she asked.

"Please just call me Emma," she said, looking at luscious desserts. She was no longer hungry, yet Rosie stood with a broad smile and Emma knew how her own mother liked for everyone to take some of her desserts, so she selected a small slice of chocolate cheesecake.

Zach took a monstrous concoction of vanilla ice cream and brownies topped with fudge sauce with a sprinkling of fresh raspberries.

"You must work out big-time to turn that into muscle," she observed and the moment the words were spoken, she wished she could take them back because she had just tossed the conversation back to the personal. "This is so much food. What does Rosie do with leftovers? Save them for dinner?" Emma interjected, trying to get the conversation on a different note as rapidly as possible.

He flashed a slight smile as he shook his head. "I work out and my injured foot has thrown me off schedule. As for the leftovers—there are a lot of people on this ranch. She'll pass them on after lunch and they'll be gone by midafternoon. You think all those hungry cowboys won't light into her cooking? They'll devour it."

She smiled, glad the moment had been diffused and they were back on a harmless topic. "This is delicious," she said as she ate a bite. She looked up to meet his steady gaze that fluttered her insides.

"She'll be glad to know you liked it. Rosie's been cooking for us since I was a little kid."

She smiled and they enjoyed their desserts, then she said, "Do you mind if I put a few family pictures on my desk?"

"Emma, within reason, put whatever you want on your desk or around your desk or in your room upstairs. I don't care what you do unless you want to paint something or make a permanent change."

"Of course not. Thanks. Now, if you'll excuse me, I think this time I will get back to work," she said, folding her napkin and standing. When she picked up her plate, he touched her wrist lightly.

"Leave the dishes or you'll get a Rosie lecture. She's in charge here and she wants to do things herself and her way," he said, releasing her wrist as he stood and walked around the table.

Smiling, she set her plate down. "I know how my mother and one of my sisters are. Sometimes they just want all of us out of the kitchen."

"You're so tied into your family. Are you going to be able to stay away from Dallas for the length of this job?"

"I gave that some serious thought, but this isn't permanent and far as I can see, this assignment is a great opportunity because it's a hike in pay, even temporarily, and I'm saving money to finish my education. And I did ask for the weekends off to go home."

"We both hope it works out. So far, so good. I'll admit, I didn't expect you to last the morning, because several before you didn't. I've been pleasantly surprised."

"Glad to hear I'm up to snuff. So far so good in working for you," she replied with a smile.

One dark eyebrow arched quizzically as he looked down at her. "You expected an ogre. Aah—let me guess—rumors from your predecessors."

Still smiling, she nodded. They entered the office and she left to return to the correspondence and filing. Within the hour she noticed he had stopped heaping work for her and she could see where she would catch up with all he had given her.

No matter how lost she got in the assignments, she couldn't shake her awareness of him. Carrying papers to his desk, she often met his gaze while he talked on the phone. Each time it was the same as a physical contact with a sizzle.

Common sense warned this job would not be as simple and straightforward as she had envisioned. When he talked on the phone, his voice was usually low enough that she couldn't hear much of what he was saying and she made no effort to try to hear. She caught snatches of words, enough to know he was discussing problems involving his work.

As she placed a letter in the box for mail, Zach got off his phone. "Emma, take a break. The afternoon is more than half gone."

"I'm fine."

"Take a break—walk around the place, go outside, go to the kitchen and get a snack—whatever you want to do. Don't argue or I'll come get you and we'll go for a stroll. As much as I can stroll right now."

She laughed. "What a threat," she said, placing mail in the box and hurrying out of the room as she received a grin from him. She hoped he didn't guess moments like that played havoc with her insides. How tempting to head back to work just to get him to spend the next few minutes with her.

She stood in the wide, empty hall and wondered what to do, finally going toward the kitchen to get a cup of tea. She suspected there was a very well-stocked pantry.

"Afternoon, Emma," Rosie greeted her.

"It smells wonderful in here."

"Roast for dinner. Can I get you something?"

"Yes, thank you. If possible, I'd like a cup of hot tea."

"Of course," Rosie replied. "Looks as if you might be the one who stays."

"I hope so."

Rosie chuckled. "Those others looked frazzled and unhappy from the first morning. I would have sent one packing faster than Zach did. Have a seat and I'll brew your tea—or if you want a breath of fresh air, go outside and I'll bring it to you."

"Thanks, Rosie."

"You can take it back to your desk if you want. Zach isn't particular about food in the office if you don't leave crumbs or make a big mess."

"I won't," Emma replied, smiling. "I'll wait outside," she added, stepping out onto the patio and strolling to the pool to look at the crystal water that was almost the same blue as Zach's eyes.

When she finished her tea, she went to her room to retrieve a small box of family pictures. She had already distributed some pictures in the bedroom. When instructed to arrive with her things packed she had brought what she really wanted with her. She stopped to look around again, still amazed at the size and beauty of where she would stay.

When she returned to her desk, Zach was on the phone and she had more work waiting. After placing her pictures on her desk and table, she focused on correspondence, so lost in concentration she was startled when Zach spoke to her.

"It's half past five. Just because the work is here in the house, you don't need to stay all hours. We'll close the office now. I eat a late dinner, but you can eat whenever you want—Rosie will be in the kitchen until eight. After that she'll have cold or easily heated choices on a chalkboard menu."

"Thanks," she said, wondering if she had eaten her last meal with the boss. If she had, it would be the wisest thing to happen. At the same time, she couldn't prevent her slight disappointment.

"You've done good work today, Emma. I hope you like the job."

She wanted to laugh and say that he sounded surprised. Instead, she merely nodded. "Thank you. I think this will be good."

He gave her a long look that killed the impersonal moments that had just passed. Once again her nerves tingled, invisible sparks danced in the air and she could feel heat rising. In spite of logic, she didn't want him to go.

Turning away, he walked out of the room without saying anything further. She stared at the empty doorway. The chemistry had not changed. He seemed to fight it as much as she, which was a relief and made the situation easier.

Zach continued to pile on a lot of work. While there wasn't as much as that first morning, letters to write, papers to proof, appointments to set, phone calls and various tasks streamed to her desk. Time passed swiftly as she worked diligently and kept up with what he sent to her. There were no more lunches together. Sometimes he worked straight through and then stopped about four. Sometimes he ate at his desk. He continued to make an effort to keep their relationship impersonal, which suited her completely. No matter how cool he was, there still was no way to stop that acute consciousness she had of him as an appealing male.

Thursday the work he gave her in the morning was done by noon. When she returned after lunch he sat by a large cardboard box filled with papers.

"Want to tackle some of the old letters and memorabilia?"

"Sure," she replied, watching him pull another chair near his. "That's a lot of letters."

"Many were written by my great-great-grandfather to his sister, his brother, later his wife. They were all saved and somehow ended up back with our family. Probably some relative didn't want them and another one took them."

"Zach, that's wonderful. I'd think you'd want to read each of these yourself."

"Hardly. They are letters from an old codger who settled out here and struggled to carve out a life on the plains. He was probably a tough old bird and about as lovable as a prickly porcupine. I think you are romanticizing him. Sit here beside me so whenever you have a question you can ask me. Want anything to drink before we start?"

"No, thank you, I'm fine." As she crossed the room, his gaze raked briefly over her, making every inch tingle. She became aware of the navy sweater and matching slacks she had pulled on this morning, her hair in a ponytail.

Catching a whiff of his enticing aftershave, she sat beside him.

"The big basket is for letters and papers that go to the shredder," he instructed. Sitting only inches from him, she was lost in his blue eyes and could barely focus on what he told her. She was even closer than she had been that first morning and it was distracting beyond measure.

"As far as I'm concerned, I think it would do the family a favor to shred all papers that don't contain pertinent information that would affect our lives today," he said. His voice deepened a notch and he slowed his speech. Was their proximity having an effect on him, too?

Lost in depths of blue, she was mesmerized. Her breath caught and held. He leaned a fraction closer. Her heart raced. With an effort she looked away, trying to get back to their normal relationship. Leaning away from him, she touched the yellowed envelopes in the large box as she tried to get back to his instructions.

"If there is anything about money, boundary rights, water rights, that sort of thing, then place the paper in the box marked Consider and I will read it. If you find maps, drawings, etc., then place them in Miscellaneous."

As what he had told her to do sank in, she frowned. She picked up a tattered, yellow envelope with flowing writing across the front. "This was in the 1800s. Look at the address on it. It's just a name and the county. You want to shred it?"

"If it doesn't have anything pertinent to the matters I listed—rights, boundaries, money. Something significant."

"The letter is significant if it has nothing like that in it. Isn't it written by one of your ancestors?"

"Probably my great-great-grandfather. Maybe further back than that by one generation."

"You can't shred it. It's wonderful to have all these letters from your ancestors and know what they were like," she said, staring at him and wondering how he could care so little about his own family history. "How can you feel that way about them?"

With a smile he shook his head. "It's past and over."

"You have an architectural firm, so you must like old buildings."

"Old buildings are more reliable than people. People change constantly and you can't always count on them. An old building—if it's built right—might last through centuries and you can definitely rely on it."

She stared at him, wondering who had let him down so badly that he would view people as unreliable. Had it started when his mother had walked out on the family? Three young boys. Emma shivered, unable to imagine a mother leaving her young sons. Maybe that was why Zach kept his feelings bottled up. "This is your tie to your past. And your ancestors were reliable or you wouldn't even be here now."

"Okay, so read through the letters. If they're not significant in the manner I've told you, toss them in this basket. Give me two or three of the most interesting and I'll read them and see if I can discover why I should keep them. I think when you get into it, you'll change your mind. I don't want to save letters that tell how the sod roof leaks or the butter churn broke or a wagon needs a new axle."

"I think all those things would be interesting." She tilted

her head to study him. "Family really isn't important to you, is it?"

Shaking his head again, he continued to smile. "Sure it is. I'm close with my brothers. That doesn't mean I want a bunch of old letters none of us will look at twice. They're musty, rotting and of no value." He leaned closer, so close she blinked and forgot the letters. He was only inches away and his mouth was inviting, conjuring up her curiosity about how he kissed.

"You're looking at me as if I just sprouted fangs."

She couldn't get her breath to answer him. His eyes narrowed a tiny fraction and his smile vanished. The look in his eyes changed, intensifying. Her pulse drummed, a steady rhythm that was loud in her ears. "I can't understand your attitude."

"Well, we're alike to a degree there—I can't understand yours," he said lightly. Again a thick silence fell and she couldn't think about letters or the subject of their conversation or even what he had just said. All she thought about was his mouth only a few inches from hers. Realizing the lust-charged moments were happening too often, she shifted and looked away, trying to catch her breath and get back on track.

She stood and stepped away, turning to glance back. "I'll get a pen and paper in case I need to take notes."

"I'll help sort some of these," he said, studying her with a smoldering look.

She wanted to thank him and tell him his help wasn't necessary. It definitely wasn't wanted. She needed to keep space between them. Big spaces. This wasn't a way to start a new assignment. She had no such attraction to men she worked with in Dallas, or anywhere else for that matter. Why was Zach Delaney so compelling?

It was certainly not because he was great fun or because they had so much in common. The only similarities they had were living in Texas at the same time in history and being connected in business to the same company. She had to get a grip on her reactions to him.

In every way he was not the man to be attracted to. Her boss, a world traveler, cared almost nothing for all the things that were important to her, family most of all.

Picking up a tablet, a pen and an empty wooden tray, she returned to her chair, pulling it slightly farther from his, but she couldn't move away because the basket and box to put the old documents in stood between them. She placed the wooden tray on the floor beside her chair.

When she opened the first envelope, a faint, musty odor emanated as she withdrew thin, yellowed pages covered in script. She read the letter from a man who wrote about frontier life, the "beeves" he had rounded up, and his plans to take them north to sell.

"Zach, if this is your great-great-grandfather, you should read this letter and see what kind of life he had," she said impulsively. "It's fascinating. He writes about a wagon train that came through and camped on his land. Is that this same ranch?"

"Same identical one," he remarked dryly, amusement in his expression.

"Listen—'their leader was Samuel Worthington,'" she read. "'Samuel asked if they could stay. He said they had traveled from Virginia and were going west. They had lost four people in their group. The four unfortunates drowned when they crossed a treacherous river after a rain. I gave them flour and beef so they had fresh supplies. Worry ran high about finding water in days to come so I drew Samuel a map of the land I know and showed him where to find water when they left my home. They have great expectations regarding their journey.'"

She lowered the letter to look at Zach. "I think that's wonderful. Don't you feel you know a little now about your great-

great-grandfather? He was kind and generous with those travelers. I would be so excited if these were letters written by my great-great-grandfather."

Zach smiled at her as if facing a bubbling child. "Okay. My great-great-grandfather was a nice guy who was good to people passing through. That knowledge really doesn't bring me closer because he lived years ago. It doesn't change the course of life. He was a rancher in the old days of the longhorns and he had a tough life. He worked hard and was successful and built on the land to pass that on to the next Delaney son. I don't need to wade through all his old letters about life on the plains in the early days."

She tilted her head to study Zach. She was both annoyed by his attitude and at the same time, mesmerized again by his enticing smile. "Do your brothers feel the way you do?"

"We haven't talked about it. I'll ask before I shred these. I would guess that Will might want them and Ryan will feel the same as I do."

She shook her head. "I can't understand your family. You must not have been close growing up."

He shrugged and shook his head. "When our mom walked out and divorced Dad, he sent us away to different boarding schools. I suppose he had some reason that seemed logical to him. We're close in some ways, but we were separated most of the time for a lot of years. It made a difference."

"That's truly dreadful."

He smiled again and her pulse fluttered. "Don't feel too sorry for us. Our father spent a lot of money on us."

"Money doesn't make up for some things."

"We could argue that one all night," he said, leaning back and placing his hands behind his head. The T-shirt stretched tautly across his broad shoulders and his muscles flexed. As he stretched out, she could not keep from taking one swift glance down the length of him. Feathers were holding a dance inside her. Everything quivered and lustful thoughts flashed in her mind. She realized silence was growing again and he watched her with a look of interest. Her mind raced for something, trying to think where the conversation had ended.

"Your great-great-grandfather—I wonder if any of you resemble him."

"You can see for yourself. In the last years of his life, someone painted his portrait. It hangs in the library." He put down his arms and leaned forward. "C'mon. I'll show you."

"You don't need to walk there now. I assume you're supposed to be staying off your foot."

"I can walk around," he said, getting the crutch. "I go to the doc next week and hope to get off this crutch. I'll still be in some kind of crazy medical shoe, but at least I may lose the crutch. C'mon. We'll go look at my old ancestor. I suspect he was a tough old bird. My dad was in his own way. I'm amazed he kept the letters. He didn't have a sentimental bone in his body until the last couple of years of his life. Or maybe since Caroline's birth. That little granddaughter changed him."

"That's family—little children wrap around your heart."

He gave her another big smile. "You're sentimental, Emma."

"I certainly am," she replied cheerfully.

He led the way into the library that held shelves of books from floor to ceiling. A huge portrait in a gilt frame hung above the fireplace and she looked at a stern-faced man with prominent cheekbones, straight gray hair, mustache and beard.

"I can't see that you look like him in any manner at all."

"No, I don't think so either." He gestured across the room. "Over there are portraits of my paternal grandfather and my dad."

She crossed the room. "You don't look like them either."

"If I have a resemblance to any forebears, it's my maternal grandfather. People say I look like him. I don't see it much myself except for the hair. No pictures of him here."

She returned to the fireplace to study the picture, thinking about the letter she had just read. "I'd think you'd want to read every letter in that box."

"I'm leaving that to you."

She turned to find him looking at her intently, a look that was hot and filled with desire, giving her heart palpitations. In spite of his injured foot, he looked strong and fit. Muscled arms, broad shoulders, flat belly. She stepped toward the door.

"We better go back and let me start reading them," she said, heading out of the room, aware that he fell into step beside her. "You said you have brothers. Do they have ranches around here or do all of you gather here?"

"Both. I'm not a rancher, so I've probably spent the least time here, but we were here plenty growing up. Plenty to suit me. I'm not a cowboy and not a rancher and my brothers can ride the horses. No, thanks. Will's ranch adjoins this one. Caroline loves it there, so they go quite often. Ryan's ranch is farther away. He's a cowboy through and through. Maybe it's because he spent too much time out here with Granddad."

"So will your brothers come here this week for Thanksgiving?" she asked, lost in thoughts about her own family's plans. She was taking a corn casserole and a dessert for everyone.

"No. Ryan's with a friend and Will and family are going to his home in Colorado."

"I can't imagine not being with family, but if you're with close friends or a close friend and family, that works," she said, glancing at him to see a grin. "You're staying out here alone, aren't you?" she blurted, aghast to think his brothers were going their own way and Zach had no plans. She started to invite him to her house, but she remembered that her predecessors had not lasted more than a few days at best

on this job. If she invited him and then he dismissed her, it
would be awkward.

"You're staring, Emma, and you have pity written all over
your face," he said. "A new experience in my adult life. I can't
remember anyone feeling sorry for me for any reason before."

Heat flushed her cheeks, and she forced a faint smile, hoping the pitying expression would vanish. They had stopped
walking and were gazing at each other. He placed a hand on
her shoulder lightly. The feathery touch with anyone else
would have been impersonal, but with Zach, it was startling.

"It's my choice," he said. "Stop worrying."

"Zach, you can come to our house," she said, changing
her mind about inviting him because it was sad to think of
him being alone. "My family would be happy to have you.
We've always invited friends who would have been alone
on Thanksgiving, so I know my family will welcome you."

His grin widened. "Thank you for the very nice invitation, but I rarely notice holidays and don't celebrate them."

"Is this a religious thing?" she asked.

"No. It's a 'my thing.' As I mentioned, my brothers and
I grew up in boarding schools, and sometimes we were left
there on holidays because our folks were in Europe or heaven
knows where," he explained. While he talked, she was acutely
conscious of his hand still lightly on her shoulder. His gaze
lowered to her lips and she could barely get her breath. It
took an effort to pay attention to what he was saying. "None
of us care much about holidays. Will is changing because of
Caroline and his wife, Ava. I'm usually not in the country
on Thanksgiving, but this year spending it alone here on the
ranch is what I choose to do. Thank you anyway for your invitation," he said, turning to walk again.

Still physically too aware of him at her side, she strolled
beside him. The hot attraction that obviously affected both of
them tainted this job. If she got to stay, could she keep their

relationship impersonal? She didn't think it would be much of a problem.

This loner, besides being her boss, was not the man to be attracted to. How could he possibly want to spend Thanksgiving alone? Even though he came from enormous wealth, he must have had a cold, lonely childhood. He seemed a solitary person who stayed out of the limelight and worked in distant places where he was unknown. She had seen pictures of his brother in the newspapers and in Texas magazines, but never Zach. He clearly kept a low profile.

As they entered the office, she parted with him and went to her desk to try to concentrate on work.

Over an hour later Zach received a phone call. She continued with her work, but by the time half an hour had passed and he had had three calls, she realized there must be a problem somewhere. He sat with his back to her, his feet propped up on a nearby computer table. The room was large enough that she couldn't hear exactly what he said. When she caught snatches of a few words, she guessed the language was German.

She worked until five to get everything done he had given her. He was still engrossed in phone calls when she shut off her computers and left the room. In her room, she spent over an hour reading and replying to emails from family and close friends before going to the kitchen for dinner.

Thinking of the loner in the office the entire time.

Lowering his feet Zach had swiveled in his chair and watched Emma leave the room, but his many phone calls had demanded his focus. Now, he glanced down at a letter on his desk she had typed. "I'll make the call at 8:00 in the morning your time and see if we can't get this worked out quickly," he said into the phone. "Right, Todd. I'll let you know. It's too late there to call anyone now." He replaced the receiver, glanced at his watch and sighed.

His cell phone indicated a call and he answered because it was Will.

"Can you talk now?" Will asked.

"Yes. We've had problems on a job and I've been on and off the phone for the past two hours."

"I've gotten a busy signal once. How's it going with the new secretary or is it too early to tell?"

Zach glanced again at the letter on the desk. "She's a good secretary. I don't think she'll last though. She's totally wound into her family in Dallas, which is several hours away from here, probably too far. They live, breathe, eat and stay together most of the time."

"Just say the word and I'll get someone else sent out."

"Not yet," Zach said, thinking about Emma's green eyes. "She's efficient. She's sentimental—you'd think these old letters were worth a million the way she views them. She can't keep from telling me I shouldn't shred them."

Will laughed. "Another one telling you what to do?"

"No, not like the first one. Emma's just so into families, she can't understand that I'm not treasuring every word from our ancestor. He was probably a tough old guy, even tougher than Dad. Why would I treasure every word he uttered?"

"You're a little more irreverent than most descendants would be. I'm a little curious about them, so I want to read a few and see what's in those boxes."

"You can have them, Will."

"No. You volunteered. You just need the right secretary to help you. Sounds to me as if you don't have a good fit yet and I should send someone."

"No. She's an excellent secretary. I've piled on the work and she's done it accurately and quickly. I don't want to dump her because she likes the box of old letters."

"True. At least she may really read them."

"Oh, she'll read them all right," Zach said, smiling as he remembered Emma poring over the one, her head bent. Her red hair held gold strands and a healthy shine. She had it pinned up, but strands spilled free and indicated long hair. Long hair and long legs.

"We'll leave in a few weeks for Colorado. If you change your mind and want to come along, or to spend Thanksgiving with us, let me know."

"Thanks, but I'm fine. My new secretary was a little shocked when she learned I'm spending the holiday alone. She invited me to join her family."

There was a moment's pause. "You two are getting to know each other."

"How can we avoid it? Remember, we work all day together and there are just the two of us here except when we see Rosie or Nigel."

"If you were Ryan, I'd ask if she's good-looking, but I've heard you talk too often about avoiding dating employees."

"You and I have agreed that's a complication no one needs in his life. I don't want any part of that kind of trouble," he said, thinking about her full lips and hearing a hollow sound to his words. "There's no need to bring emotions into the workplace—at least the kind of emotions that a relationship would create. Common sense says no way," he added, more to himself than Will.

"It worked with Ava."

"Yeah, but you hired her to work with Caroline—that was different from an office situation and you know it. It's not going to happen here. I get looks from her like I'm from another planet with my feelings about holidays, families and memorabilia."

Will laughed. "I can imagine that one. There are times

you get those looks from me. Ryan is the baby brother and he accepts whatever we do."

"Yeah. I do get those looks from you, but I don't know why because you're like me about sentiment. Or at least you were until Ava and Caroline. Especially Caroline. They've mellowed you until I hardly know you."

"You ought to try it sometime," Will answered lightly. "I'll talk to you before we leave for Colorado."

"Sure, Will. Thanks for the invitation. Tell Ava I said thanks." Zach ended the call and swung his chair around to look out the window without really seeing anything outside. Envisioning Emma, he wanted to be with her again. He had just blown the sensible course. He should have let Will send out another secretary, yet how could he get rid of Emma when her secretarial skills were excellent and she wanted the job? He couldn't send her back because of the steamy chemistry between them.

"Keep it strictly business," he whispered, lecturing himself. Stay away from her except when working. Don't share lunches or dinners or anything else outside of the office and work. Willpower. Resoluteness.

Thinking of the problems on the project in Maine, the buildings the company had bought and intended to replace with one large building, a parking garage and a landscaped area, he tossed down a pen and returned to thinking about Emma. He wanted to have dinner with her, but hadn't he just resolved to avoid her? He didn't want to get involved with an employee, especially a sentimental homebody who could barely leave her family and especially an employee living under the same roof with him. It could complicate his life beyond measure to have her expect some kind of commitment from him and to have rumors flying at the office. He didn't want tears and a scene when he told her goodbye. Thoughts of any of those things gave him chills.

She didn't look like a sentimental homebody, at least his idea of one. Her full red lips, the mass of red hair that was caught up on her head hinted at a wild, party-loving woman. The reactions she had to just a look from him implied a sensuous, responsive lover.

"Damn," he said aloud. Taking a deep breath, he yanked papers in front of him.

Wiping his brow, he leaned over his desk and tried to concentrate on tasks at hand. After two minutes he shoved aside papers and stood. He should send her away, get her out of his life, but the chemistry he wanted to avoid made it impossible to think about giving her up. No matter what he'd just told himself, he wanted to be with Emma—what could a dinner hurt?

With a glance at his watch, he saw he had probably already missed her and a hot dinner from Rosie. Annoyed he would have to eat alone, he headed to the kitchen, hoping Emma was still there.

His disappointment when she wasn't bothered him even more than her absence. Since when had he started to look forward to being with her so much?

Three

The evening was quiet and after dinner Emma stayed in her room. She had eaten alone, experiencing a mix of relief and disappointment that Zach hadn't appeared. It was wiser that he had not eaten with her. The less they socialized, the better, even though there was a part of her that wanted to see him.

On Friday, he appeared wrapped in business and he kept his distance. That afternoon, he told her to leave at one so she could get to Dallas ahead of the traffic.

"Thanks," she replied, smiling broadly. "I'll accept that offer." Shutting down her computer, she was on the road away from the ranch twenty minutes later. They had gotten through the first week, so she must have the job. They also had kept a distance between them. He had been professional, quiet, but there was no way she could feel she had imagined the chemistry simmering just below the surface. Any time they locked gazes, it flared to life, scalding, filled with temptation, an unmistakable attraction.

Now she could believe rumors she had always heard that

he never dated employees, never getting emotionally entangled with anyone on his staff, never even in the most casual way. She intended to keep that professional, remote relationship with him and this job would be a plus on her resume.

If she could just keep from dreaming about him at night—with a sigh, she concentrated on her driving and tried to stop thinking about Zach Delaney. Instead, she reflected on the fun she always had at home with the family and with her nieces and nephews.

Monday when she returned to work, she dressed in jeans, a T-shirt sprinkled with bling, and sneakers. Zach had said jeans were fine and that's what he had worn every workday. Even so, she felt slightly self-conscious when she entered the office.

He was already there and looked up, giving her a thorough glance.

"You said jeans are acceptable," she stated.

"Jeans are great," he said in a tone that conveyed a more personal response. "Yours look terrific," he added, confirming what she thought.

"Thank you," she answered, sitting behind her desk and starting to work.

"This afternoon I'm going to Dallas to see my doctor. Hopefully, I can toss this crutch when I come home."

"You can return to your traveling?"

"How I wish. No. He's already told me that I'll have to wear this and continue to stay off my foot except to get around the house. Still, it'll be an improvement."

"Sure," she replied.

He returned to whatever he had been doing and they worked quietly the rest of the morning. When she left for lunch, he stayed in the office. In the afternoon, she read more Delaney letters, occasionally glancing at the great-great-grandson, continuing to wonder how he could care so little about his history.

The next morning the crutch had disappeared. Zach remained professional and slightly remote. She noticed he hobbled around and kept his foot elevated when he was seated.

On Thursday afternoon she dug inside one of the open boxes of memorabilia and picked up a small box and opened it. Yellowed paper was inside and when she pushed the paper away, she gasped when she discovered a beautiful pocket watch.

"Zach, look at this," she said, turning to take the box to him. He stood by a file cabinet. Today his T-shirt was navy, tight and short-sleeved, revealing firm muscles and a lean, fit body. Dark curls fell on his forehead. As he came around his desk, she handed him the box. Their fingers brushed, sending ripples radiating from the contact.

"This is beautiful," she said. She looked up from the watch, meeting his gaze, ensnared, while tension increased between them. She could barely get her breath. It was obvious he felt something as he focused on her. His attention lowered to her mouth. Her lips parted, tingled while her imagination ran riot. How long before he kissed her?

"Zach," she whispered, intending to break the spell, but she forgot what she had been about to say. He shifted, a slight closing of the space between them. His hand barely touched her waist as he leaned closer. She couldn't keep from glancing at his mouth and then back into crystal blue that held flames of desire.

The air heated, enveloped her, and the moment his mouth touched hers, she closed her eyes. His lips were warm, firm, a dangerous temptation. Her insides knotted, dropping into free fall. Protests vanished before being spoken. Her breath was gone. His lips settled, opened her mouth.

His arm went around her waist tightly, holding her close against his hard body.

She spun away, carried on his kiss. A dream kiss, only it was real, intensifying longing, burning with the impression of a brand that would last. Her hands went to his arms, resting lightly on hard, sculpted muscles.

As his tongue probed and teased, her heart pounded. Passion swamped her caution. She wrapped her arm around his neck and kissed him in return. Standing on tiptoe, she poured herself into her kiss. His arm tightened and he leaned over her, kissing her hard and possessively, making her light-headed. She wound her fingers in his hair as she kissed him, barely aware he was tangling his hand in her own hair.

It was Zach Delaney she kissed wildly. The reminder was dim, but gradually stirred prudence. "Zach," she whispered, looking up at him. Her heart thudded because the look in his eyes scalded, sending its heat to burn her. His mouth was red from kisses, his eyes half closed. His expression held stormy hunger.

"Emma, you like this," he whispered, winding his hand in her hair behind her head, pulling her head closer again.

She wrapped both arms around his neck, holding him and kissing him back. Her heart raced as she gave vent again to desires that had smoldered since she met him.

Their breathing grew harsh while he slipped his hand down her back to her waist.

Again, she grasped at control and raised her head. "I wasn't going to do this."

"I've wanted to since the first minute I saw you," he declared in a rasp. His blue eyes darkened, a sensual, hot look that melted her and made her want to reach for him again.

Instead, she stepped away. "I came over here for a reason," she whispered, unable to get her voice. Her gaze was still locked with his and he looked as surprised as she felt.

His kisses had shaken her. Desire was a white-hot flame. She wanted him in a manner she had never experienced before and the attraction shook her even more than that first day she had met him.

"Zach, I should quit this job right now," she whispered. He gave her a startled look and she could feel her face flush.

"Over a few meaningless kisses?" he asked.

She didn't want to answer him. He stood there looking at her in that sharp manner he had while she struggled to get the right words.

"The kisses—" She paused. She didn't want to admit more to him, but he wanted an answer. "Kisses weren't like others. This was different. We have something—" She waved her hands helplessly.

He inhaled, drawing deeply, his chest expanding as longing flared again in his eyes.

"Common sense tells me to walk away now," she whispered. "You have a reputation for never going out with an employee."

"I never have," he answered. "That doesn't mean I can't."

"That wasn't what I wanted to hear. I want this job."

"We'll do something," he replied, his voice raspy and quiet. "Don't quit. We'll try to stick to work."

She shook her head, looking at his mouth and feeling her pulse speed as they talked. "I can't. I'm quitting. I don't think you need more notice than that. You can find a wonderful, efficient secretary soon enough."

"No," he replied, jamming his hands into his pockets while a muscle worked in his jaw. "I'll double your salary and you stay."

"Double my salary?" she repeated, shaking her head.

"You don't need to pack and go because we kissed. We're adults. If we kiss, it's not that big a deal. There's nothing between us—no history, no ties. If you don't want to get involved, we can both exercise control. With my offer, you'll earn twice as much. Don't walk out on that over a few casual kisses."

Exasperated and stung over his dismissal of kisses that had shaken her, she stared at him. "There's no relationship between us. There's not even any emotional bond. We're practically strangers. But those kisses weren't casual to my way of thinking," she whispered.

She stepped close, put her arm around his neck and placed her mouth on his, kissing him with all the heat and fury she felt over his dismissive attitude. After one second that probably was his surprise holding him immobile, his arm banded her waist and he returned her kiss. Fully. He pressed against her, his tongue going deep while she kissed him, trying to set him on fire. In seconds she broke off the kiss and looked up with satisfaction.

"I'd say your body's reaction isn't casual."

With his eyes darkened, his breathing was ragged. She had felt the hard throb of manhood against her and his heart pounding.

"Okay. Kisses damn well aren't casual, but I'm trying to get us back there," he said. A muscle worked in his jaw. When his attention focused on her mouth, she stepped back.

"Do you still want to double my salary—or do you want me to go?"

"I'll double your salary," he replied, grinding out the words.

"You'll double my salary to get me to continue as your secretary. You know I can't turn that down."

"I hope not. You're a good secretary," he answered in a more normal tone of voice.

Inhaling deeply, she promised herself she would exercise better control.

"Against good judgment, I'll stay. I can't say no. I need the money for my college plans."

"That's settled." They stared at each other until she realized what she was doing.

"I came over here for something," she said, feeling foolish, struggling against stepping into his arms again, yet determined to regain her composure. She looked around and spotted the small box on the corner of Zach's desk. She retrieved the box, clinging to it as if it were a lifeline.

"Look at this."

He was still gazing at her and his blue eyes had darkened again. His expression no longer appeared as impersonal. Her heart drummed while her lips tingled. The urge to reach for him tormented her. With a deep breath he looked down, picked up the watch and turned it in his hand.

"This is a find," he said, his voice deep, becoming hoarse, and she was certain the husky tone was not caused by the watch he held. "This watch is worth going through the box of stuff." Turning it in his hand, he studied the gold back. "These are my great-great-grandfather's initials," Zach said, extending it to her and she looked down, stepping closer to gaze at the watch, which she had already studied. "Warner Irwin Delaney," Zach read. "This we'll keep, thank you, Emma."

"It's a beautiful pocket watch. I'm glad you're keeping it. I'll research to find one like it to pinpoint how old it is. For the moment, I'll see what else I can find."

"I'll help for a while," he said. "The watch makes poking around in all the old stuff more interesting."

She returned to her chair, mindful of him pulling one up nearby. The awareness of him was sharp, intense and disturbed her concentration. She wanted to take a long look at him, but she didn't want to get caught studying him.

She tried to focus on a letter and realized her concentration was on Zach only. His kisses had been fantastic, setting her on fire in a blaze that still burned. She wanted more kisses, wanted to dance and flirt and make love—reactions that shocked her. Ones she had never experienced before in this manner. The men in her life had always been friends, family-oriented guys she had been comfortable with. Never anyone she had been very serious about either. Why did he hold such appeal for her?

She could barely think about the jump in salary for thinking about the man. Any other time in her life she would have been overjoyed at the increase in pay, but now it kept slipping her mind, replaced by thoughts about Zach.

The wise thing to do would be to pack and go no matter what salary he offered. She couldn't do it. The salary was important. College—and her classes on the internet—was expensive. This boost in salary filled a great need. Without thinking, she glanced at him. He was studying her openly and she felt her face flush as they looked into each other's eyes.

The glance had the same effect as a touch.

They worked in silence. As he methodically shoved aside letters, she realized he was looking for more things like the watch. She became absorbed in her reading.

"I feel as if I know part of your family," she said, folding a letter. "After the Civil War, Warner Delaney started building this ranch house. He brought his family out here. Earlier, he met a woman in Kansas City and is going to ask her to marry him."

"My great-great-grandmother? Her name was Tabitha, I think."

They heard a commotion in the hall and a tall man in Western boots, jeans, a navy sweater and a Stetson entered the room. He held the hand of a little black-haired girl who smiled broadly at Zach and then glanced shyly at Emma.

"Will. Caroline. How's my prettiest and favorite niece?" Zach asked, lifting her up and holding her to kiss her cheek.

She laughed and giggled as he set her on her feet. "Hey, Will. Where's Ava?"

"Stopped to talk to Rosie and leave Muffy with her. Muffy is a dog," he explained, glancing at Emma.

"Emma, this is my niece, Caroline, and my brother Will Delaney. Ah, here is Ava. Emma, meet Ava Delaney. This is Emma Hillman, my secretary."

As she shook hands with the adults, Emma gazed into warm welcoming green eyes of a sandy-haired blonde. Caroline, holding a small brown bear, could not stop smiling.

"C'mon, let's go into the family room where it's more comfortable and Caroline has things to play with while we talk," Zach suggested.

Will smiled. "We were on our way back from Dallas and stopped for a few minutes to see about you."

"Zach, all of you go ahead," Emma said. "I can stay in here. I don't want to intrude—"

"C'mon, Emma, or we'll all have to sit in here on these hard chairs," Zach said with a shake of his head.

"Please join us," Ava said. "Don't leave Caroline and me alone with these two."

Emma smiled and nodded, knowing Ava was teasing and it was nice that they would include her. Will was strikingly handsome without the ruggedness of Zach. She would not have picked them out of a crowd as brothers because Will's dark eyes were nothing like Zach's vivid blue ones. Their facial structure was as different as their hair.

"Well, the offer is still open for you to have Thanksgiving with us," Will said.

"Thanks. I'll still stay here. You know Rosie will cook a big turkey."

"You should join us, Zach," Ava said. "The snow will be beautiful and we'll have a great time."

"Thanks, Ava. I'll do fine here," he replied without glancing at Emma.

When they entered the family room, Emma mulled over his turning down the offer for Thanksgiving. How could he turn down Will and stay alone on the isolated ranch? She would never understand how Zach could possibly avoid being lonely and miserable. Was this all a carryover from childhood hurts, seeking isolation because it was a shield against times he had been left alone and deeply disappointed?

"So how are you doing with the memorabilia?" Will asked.

"I want to show you what Emma found in that box of old letters. I'll put it with anything else of value we find."

"I'll get it," Emma said. "You talk to your family." Before Zach could protest she hurried from the room. In minutes she returned to hand the box to Zach.

As she sat down, he took the watch and held it up. "Look at this."

"That looks like a fine watch and something nice to keep since it belonged to a Delaney ancestor," Will said. Zach carried it to show it to Ava and Caroline who crowded around them. Will got up to join them.

"If this isn't just like Dad," Zach said. "I'll bet he found the watch and stuck it back in with the letters to let us find it."

"I don't know. I had the feeling he had never gone through that stuff before," Will remarked.

"Maybe not. No telling what else I'll find. Or Emma will find."

"I hear you're the one reading the letters," Will said, smiling at her.

"Yes, most of them."

"She's far more interested and views them as sacred chunks of our family history and Texas history, but I don't have quite the same respect for them."

The men returned to their seats and Zach placed the watch in the box on a table.

Emma's mystification about Zach's solitary way of life grew as she listened to the brothers and realized they were close and enjoyed each other's company. And Zach was good with Caroline. When Caroline walked over to him, he lifted her to his lap and focused his attention on her.

Shortly she climbed down and went to get into Will's lap and turn his face so he looked at her. She whispered in his ear.

"Yes, we will right now," Will said, looking at Zach. "Caroline has some family news to tell you."

Caroline couldn't sit still and had a big smile. She climbed down and ran to Zach to stand at his knee. She gave another shy glance at Emma and Emma suddenly suspected she was interrupting a family moment. She wanted to leave them to themselves, but she was afraid that would be even more disruptive, so she sat quietly.

Caroline's big smile broadened. "Uncle Zach, I'm going to become a big sister."

"You are!" Zach looked over her head at his brother. "Congratulations!"

"It's early, but we told Caroline because we want to do some remodeling and build a nursery, not only in Dallas, but at my ranch here and in Colorado."

"That is great news, Caroline," Zach said. "Wow! You'll be a big sister and I'll be an uncle again."

She laughed and turned in a circle.

Zach crossed the room to hug Ava lightly. "Congratulations. That's wonderful."

"We think so," she said, her eyes sparkling. She looked radiant as she glanced at her husband and exchanged a look with him. They were obviously so much in love Emma felt slightly envious. Ava reached out to hug Caroline and Will picked her up, holding her while she wrapped her arm around his neck. "We're thrilled," Ava added.

"Congratulations to all of you," Emma said. "You have wonderful news." She looked at Caroline. "Caroline, you'll have lots of fun with your little brother or sister."

Caroline nodded and smiled.

"We're excited," Will said. "And we'll let you both go back to work. We need to get to the ranch. Caroline has been promised to get to ride her horse."

"It's been nice to meet you," Ava said to Emma. "We're glad you're working here. Zach needs help with all the old papers."

"Just keep him from shredding them," Will remarked dryly.

"I find them fascinating," Emma said. "I'm beginning to feel as if I knew Warner Delaney. It was so nice to meet all three of you and it was good of you to include me in your family moment."

"Do you think my unsentimental brother would care who he shares family news with?" Will remarked dryly, grinning at Zach.

As they left the room, Emma stayed back and returned to her desk. She didn't go back to work, but sat staring into space, thinking about Zach. What a waste of someone's life to take away the fabulous moments shared with family and friends. How could he turn down Ava's invitation to spend Thanksgiving with Will and his family? Instead, he would sit in isolation at home on the ranch—a sad choice.

She sat by the box to read a letter, finally concentrating on her work.

When Zach returned, her pulse jumped. He was off-limits, a danger to her peace of mind because her volatile reactions to him had not dwindled even a degree.

"I enjoyed meeting your family. They're great and that's fantastic news they shared."

"My brother amazes me. He'd been as opposed to marriage as any of us, yet he is so in love with Ava, it's ridiculous. And he's great with Caroline. None of us have ever been around children and to become her guardian was really tough for him."

"Well, from what little I saw, Caroline is a very happy little girl."

"Ava and Will have been terrific for her. Ava was the one who suggested Muffy, a little puff of a dog that brought Caroline out of her grief from losing her father more than anything or anybody else."

"Did I hear her call him 'Daddy Two'?"

He nodded. "We've gotten used to that. Will is her second dad since her blood father died and I think she wanted a mom and dad. You noticed she calls Ava Mom?"

"Yes, I did. They seem incredibly happy. How could you not want to be with them for Thanksgiving?"

"I'm my own company. I get along fine."

She shook her head. "Amazing," she said, reaching for another letter. "Do all of you get together for Christmas?"

He gave her a lazy smile and she guessed his answer. As shocked as she was over Thanksgiving, her surprise was greater this time. "You're spending Christmas here alone? You can't do that."

"Of course I can," he replied with laughter in his voice.

"I'd think all of you would gather here since this is the family ranch. Isn't this where you had Christmas celebrations when you were growing up?"

"Maybe twice when Granddad lived here. Never, after he was gone. My mother hated the ranch. Any ranch. If we celebrated together, it was in Dallas. After Mom walked, we didn't even come home for Christmas."

"Zach—"

His jaw firmed and an eyebrow arched. She realized she should stop talking about his personal life. She shrugged and turned away, going back to work without saying anything else. He did the same and she fought the urge to stare at him. How could he spend Christmas all alone? She couldn't imagine anyone doing that through choice.

They worked for the next hour and Zach stood, stretching again.

"Enough of this," he said. "Let's break. I'll go lift weights and do what I can do without involving my foot. We have treadmills or the track. Or an exercise bicycle. Nigel will be there because if any of us lift weights, he appears. He doesn't want us alone if we're working out with weights. That's a long-standing rule and he walks around the track, which is probably good for him. If you prefer, you can sit in the family room and have a lemonade or a cup of hot tea or anything else you want."

"Enough choices," she said, putting down a letter. "I'll change quickly and get on a treadmill. I'd rather sit on the terrace after work."

"Good enough. See you in the gym."

She left him, hurrying upstairs to change.

If only Zach felt about holidays the way Nigel felt about working out. That one shouldn't go it alone.

With Nigel walking on the indoor track, Zach hoisted a bar, lifting it high and lowering it slowly when he saw Emma enter the gym. He set the bar in place and wiped his forehead with a towel while watching her. She wore blue shorts and a blue T-shirt that revealed lush curves, a tiny waist and heart-stopping long legs.

She smiled and waved, going to a treadmill to start it.

He should have let her go back to Dallas. She was a great

secretary, as well as pure trouble. Their kisses were dynamite and the last kiss—when she wanted to prove their kisses couldn't be called casual—had ignited fires that still blazed. Her sudden kiss had shocked and electrified him. It had been a spunky, devil-may-care, I'll-show-you challenge that he would never have expected from her. If he could have burned to cinders from a kiss, he would have with that one. His reaction had definitely not been casual and she knew it. She had more than proven her point. She had driven it home with a wrecking ball.

She had a backbone and he suspected she was as strong-willed as he. Not his kind of woman in any manner except physically. She had been aghast over his plans for a solitary Christmas. He would bet the ranch he hadn't heard the last on that one. She would want to take him home with her for Christmas. The whole thing would be humorous and he could ignore it easily, except she was getting to him in a manner he hadn't thought possible. The hot kisses he had labeled "casual" blasted his peaceful life with constant fantasies about holding her and making love to her.

He wasn't concentrating well on his work. It took real effort to avoid eating lunch or dinner with her. He had offered this exercise time when he should have left the office, worked out with only Nigel and let her continue with her secretarial duties. Common sense said to either practice more self-control or get rid of her.

His lusty body just wanted to seduce her.

Frustrated, he returned to working out.

At one point he paused, glancing over to see Emma running on the treadmill. She was going at good clip, had an easy stride and looked as if she had done this before. She looked fit and tempting. The T-shirt clung, the blue darker where it was damp with perspiration. She had a sexy bounce as she ran and her long legs were as shapely as he had imagined.

With a groan, he returned to his weights. When he stopped, she had finished and had a towel around her neck as she stood talking to Nigel. He smiled, glancing at Zach who waved Nigel away as a signal he was leaving the gym. Since Zach was finished, Nigel headed for the door and, without a glance, Emma followed close behind.

Zach hung behind. He hobbled out of the gym, wanting his foot to heal so he could get back to normal. He went to shower, wrapping his foot in a plastic boot and keeping it out of the shower to avoid getting it wet.

He constantly thought about taking her out when his foot healed and taking her to bed even sooner. If he didn't want to complicate his life, that would not happen. She definitely would have her heart in an affair, something he had always avoided. In spite of what he knew he should refrain from doing, he could not keep from wanting to be with her and fantasizing about it.

Heat climbed, erotic images of Emma in his arms tormenting him. She was getting to him in ways no other woman ever had. So far, her resistance had been almost nil until he offered to double her salary. He suspected they both had acted impulsively. He couldn't bear the thought of losing his excellent secretary and to be truthful to himself, he just didn't want her to go out of his life yet. She hadn't been able to resist because she was trying to save money to finish her college courses. Had part of her wanted to stay because of the attraction?

Out of the shower, he decided not to go back to the office. He could work somewhere else in the house the rest of the day and keep space between them.

He ate dinner alone as he had most nights of his adult life. He had had affairs, but they had usually been brief, casual, on-and-off relationships. His job added to his solitary life. Tonight, he was restless, still drowning in thoughts of Emma. Finally, he had enough of his own company and went to look for her, hoping she had not shut herself in her room for the night.

But she had. He had to remember it was for the best.

Four

Monday, they returned to their regular work routine. Late that day local meteorologists began to warn of a large, early storm from the west predicted to reach Texas on Thursday or Friday. Each day they checked the weather, Emma surprised that Zach ate lunch and dinner with her, flirting, friendly and heightening desire with every encounter.

By Thursday, pictures were coming in from the west of all the snow. "We're ready for the storm, here at the ranch," Zach told Emma. "We have supplies of every sort and enough food for weeks. I think you're stuck, Emma, unless you want to take off work and head to Dallas this afternoon." They both listened as the TV weatherman showed a massive storm dumping twelve inches of snow in the mountains in New Mexico and blanketing Interstate 40, closing it down.

"Now they're predicting it'll come in here Friday," Zach repeated. "If you beat the storm home, you'll be stuck there, which is fine if you want to do that."

"I can miss one weekend at home," she said. "Actually, I

can go ahead and work and get more of the letters read and go through things."

"If you're sure. I've told Nigel and Rosie the same thing. Rosie's cooking up a storm herself, but if we get what they're predicting, neither of them will come in. I've told them to stay home."

"I'll stay here, Zach. I don't want to get caught in bad weather. From what they're predicting, it will come and go and be clear for me to go home for Thanksgiving next week."

"If you decide to stay, I'll pay you overtime."

"That isn't necessary. I'm happy to be out of the storm. Mom's already called worrying about me."

"Call her so she can stop worrying."

"Thanks, Zach."

"I wish I could take you out dancing Saturday night, but that's out because of the storm and my foot. We can have a steak dinner—I'll cook. We can have our own party here."

She laughed. "Sounds great, but you don't have to do that."

His blue eyes held a lusty darkness and his voice lowered. "I want to. Even though it might not be the wisest thing for either one of us, a cozy evening in front of a fire while it snows outside sounds fun. Now I can't wait for the first flakes to fall."

Shaking her head, she smiled at him while her insides fluttered. Saturday night with Zach would not be the same as working together in a spacious office. "In the meantime, let's go back to work," she said, pulling her chair close to the open box of letters.

She read more letters—some were by his great-grandfather, most by his great-great-grandfather, all of them mixed together. She had trays she would place them in according to generation. She had made trays labeled by dates, water rights, and "boundary disputes." She tried to sort them all the ways that would be helpful. If she had time before the job ended, she would put them in chronological order.

She had read five letters when she shoved her hand into the box to get more and felt a hard lump beneath the letters. She moved them carefully, placing them to one side in the box, and found two objects wrapped in cloth. "Zach, there are some things in this box. They're wrapped in rags." She carefully continued to remove letters as he crossed the room. He bent over to plunge his hand in.

"Zach, be careful with the letters."

"Ah, Emma, these letters are not priceless heirlooms."

"They may be to some of your family."

"I'll be damned," he said, grasping something wrapped in cloth and pulling it out of the box. He tossed away the rags. "This is a Colt. It's a beauty." He checked to see if it was loaded—it wasn't. "This is fantastic. You said there were two things."

He placed the Colt on an empty chair and turned to reach into the box to withdraw the other object wrapped in cloth.

"It's a rifle," he said, unwrapping strips of rags that had yellowed with age. Zach tossed them into a trash basket and held the rifle in his hands, checking to be certain it was not loaded. "It's a Henry. I'll say my ancestors knew their weapons. A Colt revolver and a Henry rifle." He raised it to aim toward the patio. "This is a find. Why would anyone stick these in with a bunch of letters? If I had been the only descendant, I would have pitched the boxes and never given them another thought."

"Well, aren't we all glad keeping the heirlooms was not left to you alone," she said sweetly and he grinned.

"The Henry was a repeating rifle that came out about the time the Civil War began. This is fabulous," he said, running his hand over it. "Now I can feel a tie with my ancestors with these two weapons. Ryan is going to love both of these. So will Will."

"You make it sound as if all of you are gun-toting cowboys, which I know is not the case. Far from it. You're a man of cities."

"I still love this. It's a beaut and Will and Ryan are going to love it. Garrett—he's a family friend—won't be so wound up over it, I don't think. He's the city person, which makes it funny that Dad willed this ranch to Garrett and not to any of his sons. It's also why Garrett is in no rush to claim it. This Henry is something."

She picked up an envelope. "If you'll excuse me, you can go drool over your guns while I read." She withdrew a letter. "Want me to read aloud?"

"I don't think so, thank you," he said, smiling. He picked up the revolver and carried a weapon in each hand back to place them on his desk. As soon as he sat, he called Will to tell him about the latest find.

They talked at length before he told Will goodbye and then called Ryan to tell him about the revolver and the rifle. She shook her head and bent over the latest letter, still thinking the letters were the real treasure.

It was an hour before he finished talking to both brothers. With his hands on his hips, he looked at the boxes. "Some of the boxes have objects of value. There's one more box. I wonder if each one will hold its own treasure. I'll start looking through this box," he said, sitting down and pulling a box close. He took out a bunch of letters and put them on the floor.

"These letters are not packed away in any apparent order," she said. "Put the letters in this box because it's almost empty now. You'll tear them up, dumping them out like that. I'll help you."

"The precious letters. I'll take more care," he said, and began to shift them to the box she had beside her. When his box was three-fourths empty, hers had been filled. He bent over his box and felt around. "I don't feel anything, except letters."

"Try reading a few," she suggested.

He frowned slightly and picked up a letter to skim over it. "Nothing," he said, tossing it into the discard box and taking another. After an hour, Zach was clearly tired of his fruitless search. "I can't find anything worth keeping."

"Maybe I *should* get in the car and go home now. It's sort of tempting fate to stay."

"You made a decision to stay. If you were going you should have left hours ago. You made your decision, so stick with it. If you leave now, you could get caught if the storm comes in early. You'd be in the snow in the dark. Not a good combination. Just stay."

Stay, she'd have to.

On Friday the storm arrived as predicted, the first big flakes falling late morning. Emma went to the window. "Zach, this is beautiful. I have to go outside to look." She left the office and went out the back to the patio to stand and watch huge flakes swirling and tumbling to earth. She stuck out her tongue, letting an icy flake melt in her mouth. She also held up her palm, watching for the briefest second as a beautiful flake hit her and then transformed into a drop of icy water.

In seconds she heard the door and glanced around to see Zach hurrying outside with a blanket tossed around his shoulders.

"I thought you might be cold," he said, shaking it so it was around her and over her head as well as covering him. With his arm around her shoulders, he held the blanket in place. Shivering, she pressed closer, relishing the cozy warmth of Zach beside her.

"Isn't this beautiful! I love the snow. It would be fun to have a white Christmas if it didn't keep people from their families."

"Your family will probably build snow forts and snowmen this weekend."

She smiled. "Our yard will be filled with snow sculptures, bunnies, snow dogs, forts, tons of snowballs, snowmen. Our local paper came out one year and took pictures. We have sleds and everyone will go sledding if they can."

"I guess in their own way, your family really enjoys life."

"In the best way possible, they enjoy life," she said, looking up at him. "Okay, I'm ready to go back in." She tossed the blanket over his shoulder and dashed for the back door, feeling her cascade of hair swing as she ran.

Inside she stomped her feet to get the snow off and wiped her shoes on the mat. Zach appeared and did the same, best he could with his still-injured foot. "Want coffee, tea or hot chocolate to take back to the office?"

"Sure, hot chocolate."

In minutes she had a mug and was at her desk, concentrating on work and trying to forget about Zach and how he had looked with big snowflakes in his thick brown hair and on his eyelashes.

"Emma," Zach interrupted her during the afternoon. "Look outside now."

She had been concentrating on work and forgotten the snow. The wind had picked up and when she glanced out, she gasped.

Snow was "falling" horizontally and the entire world was white. Everything in sight was buried in snow except the tall trees that were dark shadows as a blizzard raged.

"I didn't notice. Oh, my word. I'm glad I didn't get caught out in that." She walked to the window and heard him coming to join her. Once again he draped his arm lightly across her shoulders.

"Tomorrow night, we'll have our fancy steak dinners. Tonight it will be informal and cozy with Rosie's Texas chili and homemade tamales. We can curl up by the fire and watch a movie or play chess or whatever you want to do. I can think of a few other possibilities," he added in a huskier tone.

"Chess and a movie sound perfect. Forget the other possibilities. Stop flirting."

"We'll see what the evening brings," he said, caressing her arm lightly. "And at the moment, I can't resist flirting."

"Try," she said, taking a deep breath. She looked outside again, shivering just because the storm looked icy and hazardous. Once again she was thankful she wasn't traveling. "I'm glad Rosie and Nigel are off. No one should be out in this. What about your livestock?"

"That's who is out there fighting the elements and working—the cowboys who take care of that livestock at times like this. Just hope there's nothing unusual happening with any of the stock."

She nodded. "I'll go back to work. I've received a text from Mom and all my family is home now except those who work close and they'll be home soon. Some businesses have closed early."

"Our Dallas office closed two hours ago. I have a policy with my CEO and with the vice presidents—whoever is in charge when I'm away—I don't want anyone caught in this getting home. They've all had time to go home."

"That's nice, Zach," she said as she returned to her desk.

They worked until five when Zach stood and stretched. "Time to quit, Emma. Actually past time to stop."

"We're out of the storm and I don't mind continuing."

"I mind. Come on—knock off and we'll meet back down here for a drink and then dinner. Want to meet here at six?"

"Sure," she said, shutting down her computer while he turned and left the room. She closed up and went to her room to shower and change. Dressing in a bright red sweater and matching slacks, she brushed her hair and tied it behind her head with a scarf.

Eagerly, she went downstairs to search for him. She followed enticing smells to the kitchen and found Zach stirring a steaming pot. He put the lid back in place. The minute she saw him, she forgot dinner. He wore a bulky navy sweater that made his shoulders appear broader than ever, and faded jeans that emphasized his narrow hips and long legs. He was in the health shoe and his loafer. Tangled curls were in their usual disarray. Zach's eyes drifted slowly over her, an intense study that had the same results as a caress. Then his gaze locked with hers and her mouth went dry. She was held mesmerized while her heart became a drumbeat that she was certain he could hear. Captured by his look, she remained still while he stopped stirring and set aside the spoon to saunter toward her.

Her heart thudded as she tingled in a growing temptation. "Zach," she whispered, uncertain if she protested or invited because she wanted to do both.

He reached for her, drawing her to him to kiss her.

Her stomach lurched while longing blazed. His passionate kiss demanded her response. Trembling, she returned his kisses, her tongue stroking his and going deep, exploring and tasting. He smelled of mint and deep woods. His lean body was hard planes against her softness, building her excitement.

Zach reached beneath her sweater, sliding his hand up to flick free her bra and then cup her breast as his thumb stroked her. Pleasure fluttered over her nerves and tickled her insides while she clung tightly to him. Finally, she looked up at him.

"Zach, this is exactly what I intended to avoid."

"So did I," he whispered. "It's impossible. Just plain, downright impossible," he added before kissing her.

Moaning with pleasure again, she twisted against him. He was aroused, ready to love. He unfastened her slacks, pushing them off, and they tumbled around her ankles. Kicking off her shoes, she stepped out of them.

Tearing herself away from his kiss, she gasped. "Zach, we're crossing a line."

"I told you, we crossed that line the day you walked into my office for this job. This was inevitable."

"So ill matched and not what I want," she said, looking into eyes that had darkened to a cobalt blue. "A total disaster."

"You want this with all your being. You can't stop," he whispered. His mouth ended her argument. Knowing he was right, she wanted him and she wasn't inclined to stop. She kissed him even though she'd declared their lovemaking a disaster and meant every word.

With deliberation he held her away to look at her and she stepped out of her pooled slacks. He pulled free her red sweater and her unfastened lacy bra went with it. His seductive gaze inched slowly over her, made her pulse race.

"You're beautiful," he whispered, caressing her breasts. Pausing, he tossed away his sweater and she inhaled deeply at the sight of his chest that tapered to a flat washboard belly ridged with muscles.

His hands rested on her hips as his gaze dallied over her, taking in the sight with measured thoroughness. "You're gorgeous," he whispered hoarsely. "You take my breath."

She tingled beneath his sensual perusal. Wherever his gaze drifted, she reacted as if it were his fingers instead of eyes that trailed over her.

He untied her hair, pulling loose the delicate silk scarf, letting the free end slip down in a feathery whisper over her breast before he let go and the scarf fluttered away.

"Your hair is meant for a man's fingers. I've thought that since I saw you get out of your car the first day."

"Zach," she whispered, shaking with need as she reached to pull him close. He resisted, catching her hands, finishing his study. Caresses followed with his fingers touching where he had looked.

"Zach," she gasped, closing her eyes, trembling when she reached for him. He held her away, continuing his sweet torment. His feather strokes started at her throat, moving to her nape and down her back, up her side and then over her breasts, lingering, circling a taut point with his palm. She inhaled and moaned. "Zach," she protested, tugging on his waist because she wanted to press against him and kiss him, to caress him. "We shouldn't kiss."

"Neither of us wants to stop. You want this and I want you. We've been headed for this moment from the first. Ah, Emma," he whispered. His fingers slid over her belly, drawing light circles that tormented and heightened desire.

She throbbed with need. Hunger to love him built swiftly. His fingers slipped up the inside of her thigh and she gasped, spreading her legs. Then he caressed her intimately. Her heart pounded and her eyes flew open as she pulled him roughly to her and kissed him, pouring out her need.

With shaking fingers, she unfastened his belt and then his jeans, shoving them off.

"Your foot?"

"It's protected by the shoe. Ignore it." He yanked off his loafer and then his briefs followed.

She drew a deep breath at the sight of him.

His arms held her tightly. His rock-hard muscles pressed against her while his manhood thrust insistently. He picked her up to carry her in front of the fire, lowering her to an area rug. Flames warmed her side, but she barely noticed for looking into hungry blue eyes.

"You're beautiful." Kneeling, he showered kisses on her. She couldn't stop. Couldn't tell him no. A disaster was blowing in with the storm that raged outside. His hands strummed over her, building need. Her pulse thundered in her ears as she wrapped her arms around his neck, wanting to devour him.

As his hands stroked her, her hips arched to meet him. She wanted more, had to have his hands on her. He stretched out beside her, turning her into his arms while he kissed her and his hand stroked her thighs, moving between them to heighten her pleasure.

"Zach," she breathed, sitting up and leaning over him. She trailed her fingers over the hard muscles, tangling her hand in his chest hair, showering kisses on his shoulder and down over his chest to his belly, moving lower.

As she kissed and caressed him, Zach combed his fingers through her hair. In minutes he sat up to roll her over while he kissed her.

"Zach, I'm not protected," she whispered.

"I'll be right back," he whispered, his tongue trailing over the curve of her ear, stirring waves of sensation while his hand drifted down over her. He rolled away and stood, crossing to get something from the pocket of his jeans and return. He came down to hold her and kiss her, loving her until once again she thrashed beneath him.

Kneeling between her legs, he picked up a packet he had laid aside earlier. She drank in the sight of him while her heart thudded with longing. She had gone beyond the point of saying no, caught up in passion, wanting him.

Stroking his thighs, rough brown curls were an erotic sensation against her palms. He lowered himself, kissing her. His tongue went deep into her mouth, stroking her while she returned his kiss and clung to him. He eased into her, pausing, driving her to a desperate need as he thrust slowly.

Her pounding heart deafened her. Consumed by passion, she wanted him, longed to give herself to him. She had shut off thought earlier and was steeped in sensation, knowing only Zach's body and his loving.

She arched, moaning, crying out until his mouth covered hers again and his kiss muffled sounds she made.

Zach maintained control. Sweat beaded his brow as he continued to thrust slowly. Dimly, she was aware he held back to heighten her pleasure, a sensual torment that made her want more. Urgency tore at her. As she clung tightly to him, beneath her desire ran a current of awareness that she bonded with Zach during this snowy night. This would be a forever event, always in her memory, burning deeply into her life no matter what he felt.

She tossed wildly beneath him until his control vanished. Zach pumped frantically, thrusting deep, his hips moving swiftly.

She arched, stiffened and cried out, her hips moving while ecstasy burst over her, showering her with release.

He shuddered while she clung to him, moving with him, for once both of them, in this moment, well matched. Maybe the only such time. Rapture spread in every vein, running in streams of satisfaction. Sex was breathtaking, incredible, earthshaking in her world.

She could no longer turn back time or erase the occasion. Zach had just become a facet of her life. He could disappear tomorrow, but this night had happened.

"How did we get here?" she whispered, stroking damp curls off his forehead.

"We walked in here with our eyes open. We're where we both wanted to be. You can't deny that."

She kissed his shoulder lightly. "No, I can't," she said, smiling at him and winding her arms around his neck. To-night she had made him significant in her life, something she shouldn't have done.

"I think it's the perfect place to be," he said, combing long strands of her hair away from her face. "Snow outside, cozy and warm in here, you in my arms, wild lusty love. Totally gorgeous. Best sex ever. I couldn't ask for anything more."

"At the moment, I have to agree."

"For the first time, I'm glad I hurt my foot. Otherwise, our paths would have never crossed. If I had passed you in the Dallas office, I would have noticed you, but I wouldn't have gotten to know you. Not unless you had become my secretary there."

"Not likely. This Friday night hasn't gone according to plan."

"It definitely changed for the better," he whispered, showering kisses on her face and caressing her. "How about a hot tub together?"

"I think that's a great suggestion, but I thought you had to keep your foot out of water."

"I do. I've gotten very adept at hanging my foot out of the shower. I'm sure I can prop it on the edge of the tub."

"You can't hop into a tub," she said, laughing.

He laughed and stood, scooping her into his arms. "I'll carry you to a hot shower instead."

"No," she said, alarmed. "Zach, put me down. You'll hurt your foot."

"Nonsense. I carried you earlier and I didn't hear a protest. We'll do it this time the same way," he said, kissing her and ending her argument.

Carrying her to a bedroom with an adjoining shower, he set her down. He had to give up showering together. As soon as they returned to bed, he pulled her into his embrace to kiss her.

Past midnight Zach held her close. "Ready now for some of Rosie's chili?"

Emma stretched lazily, kissed his cheek and smiled at him. "I think I've lost my appetite."

"I've found mine. Let's go and when you smell it, you'll probably want some. Want a glass of wine or one of my margaritas first?"

"Seems like this is the way we started the evening," she said, wrapped in contentment. She suspected she had already complicated her life and she refused to worry about it on a wonderful night that had turned special. Tomorrow's worries would come soon enough.

"I think you're right."

He stepped out of bed, went to a closet and returned wearing a navy robe. He handed her a dark brown robe. "For you, although I definitely prefer you without it."

"No way, for dinner."

Zach placed his arm around her shoulders as they walked to the kitchen.

"The chili has cooked on low all evening, so it's ready," he said, getting out a covered dish. "I'll get our margaritas, build a fire and we'll eat when we're ready."

In minutes he had drinks mixed and logs stacked to get a fire blazing. He turned out the lights, leaving just firelight and the snowy view outside.

She walked to the window. "Zach, it looks even more beautiful than earlier today. Tomorrow morning we have to build a snowman if it's wet snow."

"Don't count on it. This is a cold night outside. It couldn't be hotter in here," he added in a husky voice.

She smiled at him. "When did you last build a snowman?"

"Probably when I was five. I don't remember exactly, but we did when we were little. A bunch of little boys—of course, we did."

She smiled and he walked to her, carrying their drinks.

"Here's to the very best night ever."

Surprised, she touched his glass with hers. "I'll drink to that and I agree," she said. She sipped the margarita and looked at the snow. "It's beautiful out there, but I'm ready to sit by the fire."

"In front of the fire is much cozier than here by cold windows."

Tossing a bunch of pillows from the sofa to the floor in front of the fire, he held out his arm. "Come here and enjoy the warmth."

She sat on the floor and he drew her back against him. "This is great, Zach."

He curled a lock of her hair in his fingers. "When do you plan to go back to college?"

"I'm saving money and this job helps. I hope to start again next September. I'll take night or Saturday classes or on the computer."

"You can't just take a year off to go back to college?"

"I like my job at your office. I hate to leave it."

"I can promise you it'll be there if you want to come back."

She smiled at him. "Thanks, but I probably need the income, too. I don't think I can save that much."

"Do you have to get presents for that enormous family of yours?"

"The adults draw names. We all give to Mom and Dad. Right now we don't draw names for the kids because there aren't that many and they're little, so they're easy, but I expect the year to come when they do draw kids' names. Our family is growing and two of us are still single."

He took her drink and placed it on the table. One look in his eyes and her pulse jumped while he drew her to him.

"Zach," she said with longing. Sliding her hands over his muscled shoulders, she wrapped her arms around him to kiss him as he pulled her down on the pillows.

Hours later Zach emerged from his bathroom and went to the kitchen. Emma wasn't there and the fire was dying

embers. The longer he had been with her, the more he had
wanted her. Now he felt insatiable. Lovemaking should have
cooled him. He had broken his own rules to avoid emotional
and physical entanglements with employees. With Emma, he
couldn't turn back time and now he didn't want to. Last night
had been fantastic, red-hot and unforgettable, making him
want her more than ever. He grew hot just thinking about her.
She excited him beyond measure and was unbearably sexy.
He hoped she didn't expect more than he could give because
she was sentimental, someone he never expected to become
involved with.

She was totally the type of woman he had always avoided
going out with. Always, until now. They were captives of circumstances that placed them in the same room, close proximity day and night. There were too many sparks between
them to avoid fire. When had he been unable to use more
control or maintain his cool resistance and good judgment?

"Here I am," she said, coming through the door.

"You changed," he said, looking at her jeans and thick blue
sweater. "You look great."

"I was just going to tell you that. And you also changed.
I like your black sweater. And your tight jeans," she said,
wriggling her hips.

"You'll never get dinner if you keep that up," he said, a
husky note creeping into his voice as his temperature jumped
just watching her twist her hips.

She held up a hand. "No, no. I get to eat."

"I know what I want."

"Let's try chili right now. If it isn't cooked beyond the
point of being edible."

"Not at all. Cooker on low, remember? Rosie left us sal-
ads in the fridge. I'll get them before I serve the chili. Want
a glass of wine or margarita first?"

She laughed. "I think we've done that before. We can't seem to get past it to dinner."

"It wasn't the drinks that interrupted. We'll try again. Do you want wine?"

"I'll take the margarita. Maybe this time, I'll actually drink one."

He left to mix her drink and she followed him to the bar.

"Before I forget," he said, "let me go get something that came in the mail earlier." He set down his bottle of beer and left to return with a large envelope. "Since you like family so much, here are pictures of our half sister's wedding to Garrett, our CFO and a longtime family friend. Bring your drink and we'll look at the pictures together."

She sat down on the sofa, and Zach sat beside her, removing a book of bound pictures from the envelope.

"Garrett has married Sophia, our half sister. We didn't know we had a half sister until the reading of Dad's will. You can imagine the shock, particularly to my mother. I thought we might have to call an ambulance and I'm not joking about it. She had no clue. No one could understand my dad. Not any of us, definitely not my mother. I don't think she even tried. Maybe Sophia's mother. He never married her, but he kept her in his life until the end."

"Sounds sad, Zach."

"Don't start feeling sorry for me over my dad. All of us wanted Sophia in the family. First, we really wanted her—that should please you. Second—Sophia, as well as all of us, stood to inherit a fortune from Dad if she became involved with the Delaney company. It was his way of forcing us to get her into the family. And forcing her to join us. Sophia was incredibly bitter over Dad and wanted no part of this family."

"Even though you were her half brothers?"

"That's where Garrett came in and you can see the results. We all like her and Garrett loves her."

Emma looked over the photographs. "She's beautiful and they both look radiantly happy."

"You're enough of a romantic to think that no matter what the picture shows."

Emma stuck her tongue out at him, making him grin.

He looked at her profile while she studied the pictures. Her skin was flawless, her lashes thick and had a slight curl. Locks of red hair spilled onto her shoulders. He set down his beer, took her drink from her hand and then placed it and the book of pictures on the table. He pulled her into his arms to kiss her.

Her mouth was soft, opening like the petals of a rose. Heat spilled in him, centering in his manhood. He couldn't get enough of her, relishing every luscious curve, her softness sending his temperature soaring. She wrapped her arms around him, kissing him in return, and he forgot dinner again.

Five

By Monday morning a bright sun made snow sparkle and icicles had a steady drip as ice and snow melted. When Emma went to the office she glanced out to see the snowman they had built Sunday afternoon. She had pictures of Zach clowning by the snowman.

Zach had run inside and returned with one of Rosie's aprons to put on the snowman. He removed the snowman's hat and placed sprigs of cedar for hair so he had a snow-woman. He posed for a picture with his arms around the snow-woman's waist and with Zach puckered to give the snow-woman a kiss.

Remembering, she smiled. They had turned the snow-woman back into a snowman because Zach said he needed to return Rosie's apron. She'd reminded him that *he* wore that very apron to cook their steaks Saturday nights, a point he'd conceded.

Monday was uneventful except she couldn't lose the constant awareness she had of Zach. She was getting too close to him, enjoying his company too much. The weekend had brought intimacy and an emotional bonding that she may have been the only one to experience. She thought about the job ending soon and not seeing Zach again, so the problem would resolve itself. In spite of the weekend, it seemed wiser to put the brakes on a relationship. How deeply did she want to get involved with him? They were totally different with different priorities and vastly different lifestyles. The weekend had been magical, but they were shut away into almost a dream world, isolated in the storm on the ranch. She should develop some resistance and keep from sinking deeper into growing close to him. At least she should try. The intimate weekend was over and she should avoid another if she could dredge up the willpower.

That evening she learned that he was having his dinner in the office. Disappointment was coupled with knowledge that she was better off not seeing him. As she filled her plate in the kitchen, she quizzed Rosie about how Zach spent his holidays and received the same version she'd heard from Zach.

"Christmas decorations are in the attic and haven't been touched in years because it's been so long since any of the family has been at the ranch at Christmas," Rosie said. "Nigel used to put them up in case the family came, but he stopped years ago because the Delaneys were rarely at the ranch in December. Actually, this house has been closed most of the time for the past ten years and the foreman runs the ranch."

Emma picked at her dinner, her focus on Rosie.

Peeling and cutting carrots, Rosie stood at the counter. "When Adam, Zach's eldest brother, was born, Mrs. Delaney was delighted and gave him her attention. He had a nanny and Nigel and I worked for them in the Dallas home. Back then, they had lots of help. By the time Will was born, Mrs. Delaney was losing interest. When Zach came along she wasn't happy and she told me herself—no more babies. They had their family."

"Rosie, that's awful," Emma said, thinking how every baby was so welcome in her family. Each birth was a huge celebration.

"That's the way she was. In those days she and Mr. Delaney were going their separate ways. When she got pregnant with Ryan, Mrs. Delaney had a screaming fit. She didn't want another child and she made that clear. She had lost interest in her boys."

"I can't imagine," Emma said, deep in thought about Zach.

"No. They were good boys. Adam was eight, Will was seven, Zach, five. She couldn't wait to get them out of the house and into boarding school. She sent Adam that year. Next year, Will went. Two years later, Zach went."

"That seems too young to send them away."

"Zach was never the same. He closed up and shut himself off. As a little fellow, he would hug me and climb into my lap. That all stopped. He was getting too big to get on my lap, but the hugs vanished. He was quieter, more remote."

"You and Nigel both seem to have a close relationship with him."

"Zach is nice to work for and I love him like another son, but he keeps his thoughts to himself. Any woman who thinks she'll come into his life and change him is in for a big disappointment."

"I can't imagine his solitary life," Emma said. "My family is like yours and we all gather together on holidays."

"Their mother just turned off the love, if she had ever really loved them. It hurt those boys. Maybe not Adam and Will so much because they were the oldest and had had more of her attention."

"I don't understand how she could do that."

"She's hardly ever laid eyes on Caroline who is her only

oldest grandchild, the daughter of Adam, who sadly passed away. She has no interest in the little girl. Caroline is showered with love by all those around her, so I don't think she's noticed or realized yet, but when she gets older, she will. Mrs. Delaney's interest is in herself. She doesn't come see them. Anyway, this is the first Christmas for a Delaney to be here on the ranch in years. I don't think Zach pays much attention to Christmas. He hasn't been home in years for a holiday celebration."

"I can't imagine that either. At Christmas, home is the only place I want to be."

"I agree," Rosie said, smiling broadly. "Open the pantry door."

Emma did and saw snapshots of children, babies, adults, teens.

"That's my family," Rosie said. "Zach has given me time off and I will be with my family for Christmas." She wiped her hands and came close to tell Emma the name and relationship of each person.

"That's wonderful, Rosie. I know you can't wait to see them."

"Most are in Fort Worth, but others are scattered across Texas. Dallas, San Antonio, Fredericksburg. I'll be off for three weeks."

"This will be a fun Christmas for you," Emma said, wondering if Zach would enjoy being alone as much as he said he did.

Later, while as she ran on the treadmill, Emma thought about all Rosie had said. Emma suspected Zach would not put up any Christmas decorations. She glanced at the ceiling, thinking about the room upstairs that led into the attic. Emma's jaw firmed. She would decorate for Zach. She wanted Christmas reminders in her room and on her desk, but while she was at it, she would decorate the house a little if she found the Christmas decorations.

Nigel was gone by six each evening. By now Rosie might have left. As soon as she finished on the treadmill and showered, Emma pulled on fresh jeans and a red T-shirt. In the attic it took only minutes to find containers, systematically marked Christmas and each box had an attached list of contents.

She carried a box to the office and placed decorations around her area. She glanced toward Zach's desk and debated, leaving it alone except for one small Christmas tree she placed to one side.

Wondering whether she would encounter Zach, she carried another box to the family room. In the attic she had spotted a beautiful white Christmas tree covered in transparent plastic and tomorrow she intended to ask Nigel to help her get it into the family room.

Maybe the decorations would get Zach into the holiday spirit.

In the family room she placed artificial greenery on the mantel and then placed sparkling balls, artificial frosted fruit. She set long red candles in a silver candelabra in the dining room, arranging them on the mantel. The scrape of a shoe made her turn toward the door as Zach entered.

He stopped to glance around. His black T-shirt and faded, tight jeans set her insides fluttering.

"What are you doing?" he asked.

"Decorating a bit for Christmas since the holiday approaches."

Zach's gaze met hers as he crossed the room. "I don't care about your room or your desk. Otherwise, don't put this stuff up in the house. Your intentions are nice, but this isn't what I hired you to do," he said, stopping only a few feet away.

"I'm not using work hours to do this," she said. "I thought you'd like it."

"No. I don't want the clutter. It's old stuff and doesn't conjure up warm memories. I'll get Nigel to see that it's cleared away."

"I can take it out," she said. "I didn't know it would be hurtful."

"It isn't hurtful," he said, with a slight harshness to his tone. "I just don't want it around and it's time-consuming to put up and take down. Besides, you shouldn't be lugging those heavy boxes out of the attic. The decorations are meaningless. These are old decorations that should be tossed."

"You don't think your family, Caroline in particular, might enjoy them?"

His eyes narrowed. "I'm having an argument over Christmas decorations. Caroline's house in Dallas and the house in Colorado will probably be decorated from top to bottom. She doesn't need more here."

"You don't think she'll see you as Scrooge?"

"No, she won't. I'll have presents for her and she's so excited over the baby, she won't care what's happening here. Caroline has reverted back to a very happy child, which is what she was before she lost her dad. These decorations won't matter to her. When she's older, she'll accept me the way I am. Maybe view me as her eccentric uncle."

"Very well," Emma said quietly.

"I'm fine about Christmas and the holiday isn't about decorations. Stop looking at me as if I've lost my fortune or some other disaster has befallen me."

"I don't think losing your fortune would be as disastrous as what you are losing. And I know Christmas isn't about decorations. You childhood doesn't have to carry over in the same way now."

"Stop worrying about me being alone," he said, smiling,

his voice growing lighter as he stepped closer and placed his hands on her shoulders. His blue eyes were as riveting as ever. Her heart thudded and longing for his kisses taunted her.

He glanced around and walked to the big box of decorations to rummage in it.

"What are you doing?"

"What you wanted. I'll observe one old Christmas custom. There are some decorations I want."

Smiling, wondering what he searched for, she stepped closer.

"Here's one," he said, pulling out a decorative hanging cage filled with sprigs of artificial mistletoe. "I'll put mistletoe up all over this part of the house. Let's see if we can follow one Christmas tradition," he added, his tone lowering another notch, strumming over her nerves. "You can help with this."

"I don't think that's such a great idea," she whispered.

"I think it's fantastic." He attached the ornament to the hook on the top of the door, then stood beneath it. "You want some Christmas traditions in my life. Well, here's one," he said, winding his arm around her waist to draw her closer as he leaned forward.

His mouth was warm, his lips firm on hers. She opened to him, melting against him while her unspoken protests crashed and burned.

Wrapping her arm around his narrow waist, she held him tightly. Her heart thudded and she could feel his heart pounding. Desire fanned heat as an inner storm built.

Her moan sounded distant. Longing strummed over every nerve. She had intended to avoid moments like this, stay coolly removed from anything personal with him. Instead, she was tumbling into fires that consumed her. Need became a throbbing ache, more demanding than before.

Their passionate kiss lengthened, became urgent. She wound her fingers in the tight curls at the back of his neck.

Time vanished and the world around them disappeared. Zach's kisses were all she wanted.

How could it seem so right to be in his arms? To kiss him? They were far too different in every way that counted for it to seem like the best place to be when he held her. His kisses had become essential to her, yet their lifestyles clashed. She held him tightly as if his kisses were as necessary to her as the air in the room.

One hand wound in her hair while he kissed her, his other hand caressing her nape.

Finally, she leaned away. "Zach, this isn't what I planned."

He raised his head, his blue eyes filled with hunger. He glanced overhead. "I'm surprised the mistletoe hasn't burst into flames. Now I'm glad you got out the Christmas box. Let me see if there's more mistletoe in there." His husky voice conveyed lust as much as the flames in his crystal eyes. He turned to rummage in the box again. "Here are three more bunches. I have just the places. Come help me hang these."

"I still don't think I should. Zach, we're sinking deeper into something we were going to avoid."

"You started this. You can't back out now. C'mon." He left the family room and headed for the office, stopping in the doorway to hand her two of the bunches. "This is perfect," he said, giving her a long look that shivered through her. "You wait while I get a hammer."

He disappeared into the hall. Common sense urged restraint. Now she wished she had left Christmas decorations alone. In minutes he was back. She watched him reach up to push a tack into the wood to hold a sprig of mistletoe tied with a red ribbon. He tapped it lightly with the hammer. She passed him, crossing the office to her desk. She wanted space between them.

She could hear him hanging the mistletoe, but she didn't want to watch. She straightened her desk and wondered if she could tell him to take the last sprig and go. She would put the box of decorations away when Zach wasn't around. She had never thought about mistletoe, never expected to even see him tonight.

She thought about the sharp tone in his voice when he had first spotted the Christmas decorations. Was he all bottled up over old hurts? When it came to interacting with other people, from what she had seen, Zach was warm and friendly. Were old hurts still keeping part of him locked away from sharing life with those closest to him?

After he hung the mistletoe, he turned to her as he stood beneath it. "Emma, come here a minute."

"Don't be ridiculous," she said, wanting to laugh, yet feeling her insides clinch over his invitation.

"Emma, come here," he coaxed in a velvet tone.

"Zach," she said, sauntering toward him while thinking about his past, "I'll come there if you'll go somewhere with me either this week or next."

"Deal," he said, clearly not giving that much thought.

With her pulse racing, she stopped inches away from him. He took her wrist to draw her to him. "Now we'll test this one," he said, framing her face with his hands as he placed his mouth on hers to kiss her again.

He tasted of mint while his aftershave held that hint of woods. She slipped her arms around his waist and kissed him. His arm banded her, pulling her close against him while he leaned over her and his kiss deepened.

When they paused, she took deep breaths, trying to get back to normal.

"We have a deal," she said. "Come home with me for the weekend and see what it's like to be with a family who wants to be together." She wanted him to see what a joy a loving family could be. Billionaire or not, she felt incredibly sorry for Zach, certain he was missing the best part of life and maybe with her family, he would see it. "When you see what you're missing, you'll want to start accepting your brothers' invitations to join them." Her last words tumbled out and she expected that curt tone and coolness he'd had earlier.

"You took advantage of me."

"Oh, please," she said in exasperation.

"Besides, I'm supposed to stay home to stay off my foot," he said. "I shouldn't be going anywhere for the weekend. That's the whole point of being stuck on the ranch." His voice held the husky rasp. His breathing was still ragged and his lips were red. His expression conveyed a blatant need that he made no effort to hide. Even though he argued, she suspected he was giving little thought to their deal.

"I'll drive and you can put your foot up in the car. At my folks' house, you can keep your foot elevated all the time you're there. We'll all wait on you. You'll have a good time."

"Emma, I don't want to go to my brothers' homes for holidays. Why would I go to your parents' when I don't know anyone except you?" he asked.

"Because you just agreed to do so."

He stared at her and she could feel a clash of wills and imagine the debate raging in his mind. "If I go home with you, won't your whole family think there's something serious between you and me?"

She smiled at him. "No. We all bring friends home a lot. Growing up, I'd say we often had at least one person eating with us who wasn't a family member."

"So how many men have you brought home?"

"None until now," she admitted. "It still doesn't mean anything other than you're my boss and I would like you to meet my family."

"Who takes her boss home to meet the family?" he asked and she was sure she blushed with embarrassment, but she wasn't giving up. Zach needed to see some real family life.

"As long as you're coming this weekend, you might as well come for Thanksgiving."

"Oh, hell, Emma, that's an extra two days."

"You said you would and you'll enjoy yourself and you can sit off in a room alone whenever you want and prop your foot up all you want."

"Dammit." He stared at her again with his jaw clamped shut and she was certain he would refuse. She felt silly for trying to get him to come. Her world-traveler billionaire boss was light-years away from her ordinary family.

"All right. If I'm going home with you for Thanksgiving, I get more than that one kiss," he said, pulling her back into his embrace and kissing her hard while he pulled her up against him. "A lot more," he added.

Startled, she was frozen with surprise for a few seconds and then her arms wrapped around his neck and she kissed him in return. His hand slipped down her back over her bottom, a long, slow caress, scalding even through the thick denim of her jeans.

His fingers traveled up again, slipping beneath her shirt, cupping her breast lightly, a faint touch causing streaks of pleasure. He pushed away the lacy bra, his warm fingers on her bare skin.

She moaned in delight, spreading her fingers wide and slipping her hand beneath his T-shirt to stroke his smooth, muscled back. Pleasure and need escalated swiftly.

Taking his wrist to hold his hand, she looked up. "Zach, we have to stop this for now. I can't—"

"Yes, you can" he said, showering kisses on her temple, her cheek, her throat. Protests faded into oblivion. She kissed and caressed him until he carried her to a bedroom where they made love for the next hour.

During the night she eased off the bed and slipped away from him, gathering her clothes as she went. She returned to her room, thankful for the space and the haven where she could be alone to think. In her own room, she fell into bed, her mind on Zach. Their lovemaking was binding her heart to him with chains that would hurt to break. Zach was becoming more important, more appealing and exciting. Was she tumbling headfirst, falling in love with him? A love that would never be returned. This past weekend, Zach had just become a bigger danger to her well-being and her heart. A weekend of love, three nights of passion, now another night. How long would it take her to get over what she already felt for him?

She fell asleep to dream about Zach and awoke early the next morning. Longing to go find him, kiss him awake and love again was strong. She slipped out of bed and looked at the clock, knowing she would follow a sensible course and get ready for a workday.

They both needed to step back and get things under control again. Just thinking about Zach, she wanted to be in his arms. Surprise lingered that she had asked him to go home with her and that he had accepted.

What had seemed a good idea at first, began to look like complication after complication. She had to let her family know. She thought about the family letters she had read and how little Zach cared and decided to hold him to his acceptance. She wanted him to see a family who relished being together and made the most of their moments. Maybe he would join his brothers more on holidays and participate with his own family.

Touching her lips lightly with her fingertips, she remembered his kisses. After Christmas she would return to her job in Dallas, and Zach would disappear from her life. She would be with him less than a month more. Despite her earlier worry, she *could* keep from falling in love with him because they had nothing between them except physical attraction. She didn't like his lifestyle, his attitude toward family, his disregard for all the things she loved so much. Maybe her heart was safe in spite of the attraction that was pure lust. She pulled out her phone to text her mother that company was coming. Company with an injured foot.

By Thanksgiving afternoon Zach wondered how he had gotten himself into this. Since he was twelve years old, he had been able to say no or get out of most things he didn't want to do unless it involved his father. Even with his father, by age twenty-one, he had become adept at escaping his father's plans for him.

He was in the center of a whirlwind. He had met four generations of Hillmans. They encompassed ages two to ninety-something. Brody, Emma's father, had made him feel welcome, as well as her mother, Camilla.

Zach tried to keep the names straight, learning her parents and siblings quickly. Connor, the married older brother, his wife, Lynne, Sierra, Emma's oldest sister, and Mary Kate, the youngest, both sisters married, Bobby, the younger brother. Zach mentally ran over the names of people seated around him while they ate the Thanksgiving turkey. He received curious glances from Connor and could feel Connor being the protective big brother even though they were far across the long table from each other.

The dining room table seated eighteen and other tables held more of the family with grandparents, aunts, uncles, nieces and nephews gathering together today.

Until the subject came up during the Thanksgiving feast, Emma had neglected to warn him that it was family tradition to decorate for Christmas after Thanksgiving dinner, which was eaten early in the afternoon. After dinner everybody under eighty years of age changed to jeans and T-shirts or sweatshirts. Also, the decorations didn't come out until the men had set up the Christmas trees in various rooms in the house, which they did while others cleared the tables.

Once trees and lights were up with an angel or a star at the top of each tree, the women and children took over with the decorations while the men decorated the porch.

As soon as Zach started to join the men, Emma took his arm to lightly tug him toward the living room. "You sit and elevate your foot. You can help the kids with the decorations. The little kids can't put the hooks on the balls and that sort of thing."

"Emma, I can do a few things outside."

"We need you in here and you know you should stay off your foot. The more you don't walk on it, the sooner you'll heal," she lectured, looking up at him with wide green eyes. His gaze lowered to her mouth and he longed to be alone with her and saw absolutely no hope until they left Dallas.

In minutes he began to help the little kids with ornaments while he sat with his foot resting on a footstool. Boxes of shiny trimmings were spread around him and on the table in front of him. Emma and her mother had a table over his propped-up foot to keep the kids from bumping his injury. The living room held what Emma had called the real Christmas tree. It was a huge live balsam pine that touched the ceiling. Spread around him were boxes of a family history of decorations with shiny ornaments mixed with clay and paper trimmings made by kids. Once Emma stopped beside him. "How are you doing?"

"You owe me," he said. "I intend to collect."

Her cheeks turned pink and he wondered what she was thinking. He remembered their lovemaking and wished with all his being he could be back at his ranch and alone with her. Instead, what seemed like a hundred people and kids were buzzing around him like busy bees. He had to admit she had a fun family and he'd had a good time through dinner. What he knew he would remember most, was when she had come down for Thanksgiving dinner. The whole family dressed for the occasion, which she had warned him about just before they had left the ranch.

He had been standing in the front hall and looked up as she came down the stairs. She wore an emerald green dress that came only to her knees and her red hair was caught up in a clip with locks falling free in the back. She looked stunning. The sight of her had taken his breath and he longed to be able to hold her and kiss her.

After a time Emma took away the table that sheltered his injured foot. "You're excused now to go watch football. They've finished decorating the porch and the guys turned on a game. We'll help the kids decorate and then clean up the Christmas tree mess. I'll take over your job."

"I don't mind doing this."

"Go watch football with the guys in the family room."

"You won't have to tell me again," he said, smiling at her and still wanting to kiss her. He stood and she slipped into his chair while he limped away.

During the second half of the game, his cell rang and he excused himself to answer Will's call.

"Happy Thanksgiving, Zach."

"Happy Thanksgiving to you and Ava and Caroline. Let me talk to Caroline," Zach said as he stepped farther into the hall so his conversation wouldn't interfere with everyone listening and watching football. He talked briefly to his niece and then Will came back on the line.

A touchdown was scored and the family members watching the game cheered and applauded.

"Where are you?" Will asked. "You sound as if you're at a game."

"I'm at Emma's house in Dallas," Zach admitted, certain there was too much background noise for him to convince

Will he was home alone at the ranch. He braced for what he knew was coming.

"You're where?" Will asked.

"You heard me. I sort of got finagled into this," he tried to say quietly.

"I can't hear you. You're at your secretary's house with her family?"

"That's right, Will. And I need to go. Happy Thanksgiving to you." As he ended the call, he was certain he had not heard the last from Will. Returning to his seat, he looked at the room filled with Hillman men and the older boys. This room held a huge white Christmas tree. Their attic had been filled to the brim with all the decorations that now covered the various trees in the house. With a deep sigh he settled to watch the game. The evening promised to be incredibly long, but he had to admit, the Hillmans had fun and obviously loved being together. To his surprise, he'd had a good time with them. They were nice people and her brothers were great to be around, actually making him miss seeing his own, which gave him a shock when he realized he was thinking about calling both of them, even though he'd just spoken to Will. He had to admit, Emma had been right about the weekend with her family versus his staying at the ranch by himself. He looked at her laughing at something her sister said to her. His insides knotted and he wanted badly to be alone with her and to hold her in his arms.

It took several hours to get the decorations up and the empty boxes put away. A sweeper was run. Finally the entire bunch of people settled in the family room, sitting on the floor, chairs, sofas. When the football game ended, Emma's sister, Mary Kate, sat at the piano to play Christmas carols and they all joined in singing. Emma came to sit beside him and to his amazement, the kids found him interesting, so they had squeezed onto the sofa beside Emma and him. Being crowded together suited him because he could put his arm around Emma's shoulders without it seeming a personal gesture. He had an arm around two of the little kids on the other side of him, but he enjoyed having Emma pressed against him.

To his surprise, he remembered the old songs he hadn't sung in years. Finally when they stopped singing, they began to pull coats out of closets.

"We're going outside because Dad turns on the Christmas lights, a tradition that means the Christmas season is officially kicking off at the Hillman house."

Zach laughed. "I don't know how I let you get me into this."

"I know exactly how," she said, giving him a sultry look, and his smile disappeared.

"Emma—" Smiling, she walked away and he watched her hips covered in tight jeans as she walked away from him to get her jacket.

The entire family and dogs gathered on the front lawn and waited for the light ceremony. In minutes the lights came on and it was bright as noontime. Zach stood next to Emma and applauded with the others when the lights sparked to life. "Emma, I've fallen into *Christmas Vacation*. This is the Griswold house," he said softly.

She laughed. "Except the lights all came on at the first try. Dad loves Christmas. Actually, we all do. It's wonderful."

The family stayed up talking until one when they began to say good-night. By the time Emma and her younger brother, Bobby, turned in, they had to lock up and switch off lights.

She had an apartment nearby, but she had told him she would stay at her parents' house. He hadn't known they wouldn't sleep at her place until they were almost to Dallas. A huge disappointment to him.

At her door, Zach placed his hand on the jamb to block

her way. He tugged on a lock of her hair to draw her closer and leaned forward to brush her lips with a light kiss. The instant his mouth touched her soft lips, his body reacted. He ached with wanting her. His arm tightened around her waist while he kissed her long and fervently. "I want you, Emma," he whispered.

The look in her eyes made his pulse pound. He inhaled deeply, fighting the urge to reach for her again. This wasn't the time or the place, so he told her good-night before going to the room given to him for his weekend visit.

He wanted to be alone with Emma now and couldn't wait to get back to the ranch, but the holiday had been a pleasant surprise.

By Saturday, the weather had warmed. The family sat at a long picnic table, made from five tables pushed together with Zach at one end, his foot propped on a wooden box. Emma's mother was to his right and Emma sat on his left. Her father was at the far end while various relatives lined both sides of the table. They sat in a sunny spot in a wooded park not far from Emma's parents' home.

It was easy to see where Emma got her looks. Her auburn-haired mother, Camilla, was a good-looking woman and appeared far younger than she had to be since she was the mother of Emma's older brother and older sisters. Brody Hillman, Emma's dad, had welcomed him, but Zach could feel the unspoken questions and saw the speculation in Brody's expression. Even more open about his curiosity was Emma's older brother, Connor. Connor studied Zach and Zach could feel disapproval simmering just beneath the surface. Connor had been friendly, but only in a perfunctory manner and Zach thought it was just a matter of time before Connor quizzed him about his relationship with Emma.

There had been enough curious looks from all of them to

remind him that Emma did not bring men home with her for the weekend. He had wished a hundred times over that he had not accepted her invitation, He would have to last until tomorrow afternoon when they would leave for his ranch.

"Zach," Emma said, "my nieces are so impressed with you. I told them you are a world traveler. They want to know the scariest trip you've had or scariest place you've been."

He smiled at a row of little girls staring at him expectantly and told about waking up with a huge snake in his tent, but that was not as scary as swimming and discovering a shark approaching him. By the time he got to that part, the boys had gathered around to listen. The girls sat quietly, their eyes opening wider, and he didn't want to scare them. "Those were scary moments. Then there was a time I was camped far from a town. My things kept disappearing. I thought someone who worked for me was taking them until I discovered it was a very sly monkey. We found the stash and I got back my things, except my golf cap. I left that for him and hoped I'd see him wearing it, but I never did."

As the girls laughed, he glanced at Emma to see her smiling while she watched her nieces.

He got out his phone. "I have pictures," he said, opening it and quickly finding his electronic scrapbook. He held out the phone and Emma had to join the kids to look. She gasped, maybe only slightly less than the little girls. She bent closer, looking at a massive snake that was held by four men.

"Zach, is it alive?" she asked.

"Yes, but it had been fed, so it wasn't moving much and everyone was safe."

She glanced at Zach, and he suspected he had just dropped a notch in her estimation of his lifestyle. He suspected she liked homebody types who spent their weekends playing with the kids versus someone who traveled and encountered wild snakes and ran some big risks.

After lunch, they cleaned up and when everything was put away, a tag football game was planned with everyone participating.

"You can be scorekeeper, Zach. We always have two or three scorekeepers, so no one person has to keep up with all of us," Brody said. "There's a lot of give and take to score-keeping for one of our family games. Usually we end up with about as many different scores as scorekeepers, so don't take any of this too seriously. You'll see."

Zach agreed to the task, sitting on the sidelines with his foot resting on a cooler. Brody's sister, Beth, joined him as scorekeeper along with Brody's mom, Grandma Kate. Emma's maternal grandmother, Grandma Nan, was on the field to play; she looked too young to be a grandmother. The oldest of the nieces and nephews was only six, so everyone played around the kids. As three-year-old Willie grabbed the ball and tried to run with it while the family cheered, Zach joined in, laughing at the child clutching the football as if it were a lifeline.

Zach glanced at Emma on the playing field. She had leaves in her hair. She had shed the bulky sweatshirt and wore a bright pink T-shirt with her jeans. She was watching him, laughing with him over the kids, and desire stabbed him. That electrifying tension flared to life, as unwanted and un-expected as it had been the first time she had walked into his home. He wished they were alone. Someone stepped between them and the tension eased, but it did not vanish.

The kids provided constant laughs with their antics and he saw why she liked to come home for the weekend. They were all happy with each other, having great fun. He had known fun with his brothers, but life had been tense if both his parents were present unless they were entertaining a house filled with their friends. Even then, it had never held this re-laxed closeness. He realized he was enjoying a whole family of people who loved each other and exhibited a joy in being together. He had this now with his brothers, but they seldom were all together and until Caroline, there had been no small children around.

He could see why Emma thought he was missing something and why she had hated to leave him alone. He looked at her parents, thinking how different they were from his own. The love they shared showed constantly even though they were across the field from each other, or at opposite ends of the long table earlier. He realized he had never seen that kind of warmth between his parents. He looked at Emma, laughing with a small niece. Maybe Emma was the wealthy one after all.

Breaking into his thoughts, he looked down into big brown eyes as a little boy walked up to him. "Did you give my team a point?"

He wasn't certain which child stood before him, guessing it was Jake. "Yes, I did give your team a very big point," he answered, amused that the little kid was checking on him.

The child nodded. "Thank you." He turned to his great-grandmother. "Did you give my team a point, Gran-Gran?"

"Yes, I did," she said, leaning forward to hug him. "You're playing a good game," she said.

"Thank you." Smiling broadly, he ran off, half skipped to his dad, who asked him a question, glancing over his head at Zach. The child told his dad something and his dad smiled at Zach and turned back to play.

Zach was unaccustomed to sitting out anything active. During the time-out, he motioned Emma over.

"I hate sitting on the sidelines. If three-year-old Willie can play, so can I."

"Zach, you have to stay off your foot."

"This shoe protects my foot. I am not accustomed to being a spectator. I'll stop if my foot hurts. It's only tag football."

"You'll be on my team then, so I can keep up with you."

"Don't hover. Your family will really think we have something going."

Zach got into the game, enjoying himself even though he knew he was being foolish and risking more injury, but he hated doing nothing except keeping score. He had never been one to sit on the sidelines and he didn't want to miss out now. He hobbled around and it was easy to keep up when they had geared down to a three-year-old level.

Before dinner they gathered wood to build a fire in a stone fireplace. When Zach started to help, Emma stopped him.

"This isn't a chore you have to do. Go sit and we'll get the wood."

"I'm not doing much," he said, brushing past her. Minutes later as he picked up a dead branch and turned, Connor blocked his way.

"Thought you were supposed to stay off your foot."

"A few branches and I'll quit. I still can't get accustomed to sitting around."

"Which is why Emma works on your ranch?"

"Right," Zach said. He could feel anger from Connor and see curiosity in his expression.

"You've been all over the world, so you're pretty sophisticated and experienced. Emma's not. Did she tell you she's never brought anyone home before?"

"We work together. I don't know what she's told the family, but I think I'm here because she feels sorry for me."

"Yeah. We heard you were alone. I just don't want to see my sister hurt."

"I wouldn't want her hurt either."

"Zach," Emma called, hurrying to join them. "Give those sticks to Connor and come sit. You shouldn't be on your foot. Just watch everyone."

All the time she talked, Zach looked at Connor who gazed

at him with a flat stare that held a silent warning. When Emma tugged on his arm to take the wood from him, Zach turned away.

"I think Connor was being a big brother and jumping to ridiculous ideas. Pay no attention to him," she said.

"Your older brother is a little difficult to ignore since he's five inches over six feet tall and probably weighs in at 250."

"Come on. They're getting the fire started and we'll cook dinner and then sit and sing and later, tell stories."

Amused, he went with her, hobbling along.

As they got dinner on the tables, Emma carried a hot dish and set it on the table, then turned to find Connor beside her.

"Emma." He glanced over her head and she realized they were the only two standing at the end of the long table. "Be careful. I don't want you to get hurt."

"I hope, Connor, you didn't threaten him. He's my boss."

"If that's all he is, that's fine. Guys like Zach Delaney do not marry into families like the Hillmans."

"I brought him home for the weekend because I didn't want him to spend Thanksgiving alone. We've always invited people who might be alone on holidays. I felt sorry for him. There's nothing more to it than that."

"It looks like more," Connor said, frowning.

"This is a temporary job that is on the verge of ending. When it does end, I'll never see him again. Most of the time he works abroad. There's nothing to be concerned about."

"I hope not. Take care of yourself."

She smiled. "I will. Stop worrying."

He jammed his hands into his pockets and walked away. She watched him and shook her head. Connor was forever the big brother.

As she got more dishes of food on the table, Mary Kate approached with more delicious looking food.

"Is Connor being big brother?" she asked.

"Ever so," Emma replied, rolling her eyes.

"Emma, *should* Connor be big brother?"

"No. I didn't want Zach to be alone over the holiday and he would have been. Anyone in this family would have invited him if they had been in my place."

"Are you sure?" Mary Kate asked, tilting her head to study her sister. "Here he comes." She moved away before Emma answered. She forgot her siblings. Zach approached and he was the only person she noticed.

After dinner they played a word game around a blazing campfire. When the sun went down the air cooled with a fall chill and the fire felt good. Emma sat close beside him and Zach longed to put his arm around her, but he did not give in to the impulse. It would look far too personal for a boss and secretary. The dancing red flames highlighted gold streaks in Emma's hair. She sat beside him playing a simple game where they sang and clapped and the little kids could play. Emma's dad sat with his arm around her mother while she clapped.

Zach continued to marvel at her family. Outside of old movies, he hadn't known families like this really existed. He completely understood why Emma treasured her weekends at home and her holidays. As a little kid he had hoped for this, but it had never happened with his own family or any that he visited and he finally had come to the conclusion such families did not exist, but Emma was proving him wrong.

Once as she sang, she glanced at him and smiled. More than ever, he wanted his arm around her or just to touch her, but he knew that wasn't a possibility now. If he wasn't careful, her family would have them engaged.

It was after ten when they began to break up. He helped clean until he was told to put his foot up. Finally he went with Emma back to her parents' house. Tonight, everyone was heading home except her younger brother, and Zach wanted to return to her apartment and be alone with her.

Instead, they sat up talking to Bobby until one in the morning. While Bobby and Emma talked about Bobby's school year, Zach looked at the Christmas tree. He had counted eight Christmas trees of various types and sizes that had been set up and decorated in the Hillman home.

Besides celebrating Thanksgiving, he was immersed in Christmas. The mantels in the family room and living room were covered in greenery and red bows. Decorations were everywhere he looked. No wonder she had tried to decorate the ranch a little. His attention shifted to Emma and his longing to be alone with her increased.

Finally, when Bobby went to bed half an hour later, Emma came to sit by him. He made room for her and she leaned against his chest, his arm around her and her feet beside his on the sofa.

"It's been fun, Emma. You have a great family."

"You really mean that?" she asked, twisting to look at him. She was in his arms, her face so close to his. "I love Thanksgiving," she said, turning and settling back against him. "I love Christmas. Look at the tree. It's beautiful and so many ornaments remind me of a special thing or person or time. I couldn't bear Christmas without a tree."

"I'm not as tied in to Christmas as you well know by now."

"You should get into the spirit and enjoy Christmas. If you did, you would never return to spending it the way you do now." She yawned and stretched. "I'm ready to turn in, Zach." She stood and he came to his feet. She walked to the tree and carefully lifted free a glass Santa to show to him. "This is my favorite."

He looked at the ornament and her delicate, warm hand. "I hope you have years of wonderful Christmases," he said quietly.

"I hope you do, too."

"This is turning into one so far."

"It's Thanksgiving and the start of the Christmas holiday. There's a month to go." She returned the Santa to the tree. "I love each ornament, Zach." He came to stand beside her and put his arm around her waist. "Look at our reflection," she said, touching a shiny green ball.

"I'm going to start carrying a sprig of mistletoe in my pocket," he said, turning her to him to kiss her.

His arm tightened around her waist and she slipped her arms around him, kissing him while her pulse drummed. She quivered while desire ignited. Finally, she raised her head. "We should go to bed."

"If only you would always say that at the ranch," he replied. He smiled and kept his arm around her waist to walk beside her as they headed toward the stairs.

"Night, Zach," she said and disappeared into the room where she slept. In his own room, he lay in bed with his hands behind his head, thinking about the day and the evening with her and her family. He couldn't imagine spending every weekend this way, but sometimes it would be fun. He still thought she was missing out on a wonderful world and when his foot was healed, he would try to show her some place exciting out of Texas since she had never even been beyond the boundaries of the Lone Star state. As soon as he thought of traveling with her, he knew it would never happen. When the job ended, she would go out of his life. She had been correct when she said they had vastly different lifestyles. Neither one was the right person for the other in even a casual way.

In spite of that knowledge, his common sense, caution and experience, he couldn't stop wanting her and he couldn't shake her out of his thoughts.

He finally drifted to sleep, still yearning to be alone with her.

After Sunday dinner, Zach and Emma left for the ranch. She drove again while he sat with his foot propped up across the backseat and resting on bags placed on the car floor.

"You have a nice family. I see why you value your weekends. Your family shows they enjoy being together."

"Thank you. You seemed to like being with your brother and his family."

"I do, but I don't think my brothers and I have the closeness your family does."

Emma could see Zach in the rearview mirror. "You can have that closeness. From what you've said, you're all congenial. Maybe you are alone so much because you keep up your guard, Zach. It might carry over from childhood and times you were alone. Life's different now. You don't have to keep everything all bottled up. You can enjoy your brothers and now there's a half sister. You and Will seem very close."

He sat in silence. She met his gaze when she glanced at him, but then she had to turn her attention back to the road. "You might be right," he said finally. "I've never looked at it that way. I was disappointed as a kid. So were they. We were dumped and couldn't even be home together some years. I don't know—maybe my feelings are a guard left from childhood hurts. As a little kid, I couldn't keep from resenting it."

"Well, the nice thing now is that you don't have to be alone," she said, smiling at him.

"Maybe you're right. I'll admit it's fun when my brothers are together. And now I enjoy having Caroline and Ava there, too. Your family certainly has a great time together."

"We do and in a crunch, we can count on each other too. I'm happy you came with me."

"I enjoyed the weekend. Neither of your brothers were thrilled. I got looks from them the whole time. If they intended to send me warnings, they succeeded."

"Pay no attention to them. You'll never see them again."

Zach smiled and looked at her as she glanced in the rear-view mirror at him. "I'm not invited back?"

Emma felt her cheeks flush. "Of course you are. When-ever you would like to go home with me. I just figured you wouldn't want to again. I sort of trapped you into this time."

He grinned. "I'm teasing you."

"Zach, would you like to come home with me for Christmas?" she asked sweetly. "We'll have the whole family and they would be delighted to have you."

"No, they wouldn't be delighted. Thank you for asking me. I'll stay home and give my foot a rest."

"They would be pleased to see you again, except perhaps Connor, but you can ignore him."

"Home on the ranch is where I belong."

When they stepped inside the empty ranch house, Zach dropped their bags and switched off alarms. As she picked up her bag, he turned to take it from her and set it back on the floor. He slipped his arm around her waist. "Now what I've waited all weekend to do," he said in a husky voice. "You do owe me."

Six

When his mouth covered hers, her heart lurched. Wrapping both arms around his neck, she pressed tightly against him. His mouth was warm, insistent, and she kissed him eagerly. She clung to him, returning his kiss while the air heated and her heartbeat thundered. How could he melt her in seconds? Why did he weave such a spell with her? She didn't care. All she wanted at the moment was to hold and kiss him. She felt as starved to make love as they had on the snowy weekend.

"Emma, I want you," he whispered.

Each kiss was more volatile than the last. At the moment she didn't care about caution and what was wise in dealing with him. All she wanted was to be in his arms and kissing him.

Still kissing her, he picked her up and carried her through the house to the family room. He sat on the sofa, cradling her on his lap. Her hands drifted over him while her heart raced. She was glad they were together. Running his fingers in her hair, he kissed her. Why did this seem necessary? Why did his loving seem so right and special? The questions were dim, vague speculation that was blown away by passion.

She combed her fingers through his thick curls and played her hand over his muscled chest.

His hand slipped beneath her T-shirt. His fingers were warm, his hand calloused and faintly abrasive against her skin, a sensual, rough texture that heightened feeling. In seconds he had pushed away her bra to caress her. Pleasure streaked from his slightest touch, fanning sexual hunger to a bigger flame. Emma sat up, her thick red hair falling on both sides of her face as she tugged his T-shirt free and pulled it over his head. His eyes darkened and he had her shirt whisked away in a flash.

Knowing she was pursuing a reckless course, but wanting him desperately, she sat astride him and leaned forward. They embraced each other to kiss, his sculpted, warm chest pressed against her with the mat of chest curls a tantalizing texture.

Desire raged while she struggled to dredge up control. Dimly, she thought about her fears of how hurt she would be when the job ended and she told Zach goodbye. The hard knowledge that when that time came, he would be gone permanently from her life was a cooling effect. And it hurt. Was she falling in love with him? Was she *already* in love?

She leaned away slightly to frame his face with her hands. "To my way of seeing, our continuing to make love is a road to disaster. I want to back up a little and think about what we're doing." As she talked, she shifted off Zach and stood in front of him. While he watched her, his fingers caressed her, dallying along her hip and down her thigh, causing her to pause. She inhaled sharply, closed her eyes and stood immobile while his hands created magic and made her want to go back to kisses and loving him.

After seconds or minutes, she didn't know, she grabbed his wrists and opened her eyes. "Zach, wait."

He stood, his arms wrapping around her. She ran her hands over his chest. "I want you, Emma. I want to make love to you all night."

"Part of me wants that. Part of me has enough sense to know that's a reckless course to follow. Getting involved with you isn't what I hired on to do. And that first day that's what you agreed to avoid. I don't want last weekend every night until this job is over. If we do, I'll never want to leave."

"I just know what we both want right now. Kisses don't have one thing to do with business or your job or mine. I wasn't even going to keep you that first day, but you proved to be such a damn good secretary, I did. Emma, I've spent the past four days wanting you. I've been with you, watching you, aching to hold and kiss you."

His words echoed her feelings. Constantly through the holiday, she had glanced at him, wanting to go somewhere they could be alone to kiss and love and lose themselves as they had the weekend before. At the same time, she knew the hopelessness of getting more deeply entangled with him.

"You and I are way too opposite to get closely involved. You might not care at all and that means nothing to you, but it means a lot to me. You saw my family. My lifestyle and background are totally different from yours. If we continue to make love now, it will mean certain things on an emotional level to me that lovemaking won't to you. We'll get more deeply involved with each other. I can't separate that from my deepest feelings."

Standing, he reached out to take her into his arms again. "We'll just kiss. You say when to stop."

"If we do this, Zach, you'll have my heart."

"Maybe you'll have mine," he whispered, showering kisses on her temple to her cheek and then on her mouth. He kissed her insistently, holding her close against him, ending her arguments. She wanted him and her hunger overcame the logic, her caution, her arguments. She held him, kissing him with fervor that grew. The weekend had been another chain binding her heart. She held him tightly. She couldn't stop now. Later, he picked her up, kissing her as he carried her to the closest bedroom to make love to her.

Near dawn she stirred and rolled over to look at Zach who lay sleeping beside her. She rose up, brushing a curl off his forehead. A dark stubble covered his jaw. He was muscled and fit except for his injury that would heal. With their loving and Zach going home with her, he became more appealing each day. It didn't matter. There was no way he could ever be the man for her. No matter what her heart wanted. They were far too opposite. Even if they both were wildly in love, there was no possibility she could ever accept his lifestyle. She had told him if they continued making love, it would mean more to her and it would hurt deeply when she had to break it off and leave. And should he want her to stay, or wanted to marry her, which was impossible with a man like Zach, she couldn't accept. Not with his nomadic lifestyle.

While he had been good about the weekend with her family, she suspected there was no likelihood he would ever settle. She hurt and the hurt would grow worse later, but they were mismatched and neither wanted change.

He had met her family now and knew enough about her that he should understand what she told him. She suspected this job would end soon because he had a doctor's appointment this week and she had noticed he was getting around far better each day.

She studied him, with his shadowy long lashes on his cheeks. As he slept, she took her time. Looking at his firm lips, she thought about their kisses. Unable to resist, she leaned closer to kiss him lightly. His arm banded her waist and his eyes opened lazily. He pulled her close to kiss her to make love. She stopped thinking and gave herself to feeling.

At nine o'clock, she sat up and reached across him to get his phone from a bedside table. "Zach, it's after nine. We have to—"

He kissed her and stopped her announcement. In minutes he raised his head. "We don't really have to do anything except stay here in bed."

"Oh, yes, we do," she said, stepping out of bed and tugging free the sheet to wrap around herself. "We need to get back to our business relationship. We're already deep enough in a personal one. It's time to slow this part down." He placed his hands behind his head, smiling and watching her.

"I'll see you in the office," she said, scurrying out of the room, praying she didn't encounter Nigel before she got away from Zach and got her clothes back on.

It was an hour before she had showered and dressed in fresh jeans, a blue cotton shirt and loafers. With an eagerness she couldn't curb, she went downstairs to the office to find Zach sitting behind his desk.

He smiled when she came in and stood to come around his desk. He looked sexy, more appealing than ever in fresh, tight jeans and a black sweater. The warmth in his eyes held her immobile, unable to look away, and her pulse drummed in her ear. Her breath caught as he closed the distance between them to take her into his arms and kiss her a long time.

"Good morning," he said in a deep voice that was like fur wrapping around her.

"Good morning," she whispered in return, aware she was in love with him to the extent she might not ever get over it. This was a man she absolutely had to get over. He would never be the man for her and she could never be the woman for him.

"We weren't going to do this in the office. Use some self-control," she teased, trying to make light of the moment and end it.

"Sure. For now," he replied, heading to his desk. As Zach circled his desk, she noticed that he no longer limped and she was certain he would be able to go back to his normal life very soon and would no longer need her. The thought of telling him goodbye hurt with a pain that ran deep. She had faced the truth that she was in love with him. Hurt was inevitable.

They both were busy and lunch was brief, but he ate with her and she was glad. She wanted to be with him and the clock was ticking. Their time together would end too soon. She wanted more than just dining with him, of course, but each time they made love, her heart was bound more tightly with his.

Zach sat with work in front of him, but he couldn't keep from continually watching Emma. She was filing, moving around from desk to file cabinet, paying no attention to him. The tight jeans molded her hips and long legs. Her hair was tied behind her head with a ribbon and through lunch he had wanted to reach over and untie it.

He should have told her goodbye when they got back last night and he should have eaten lunch on his own today. He thought about her brother; he had meant it when he had told Connor he didn't want to hurt Emma. He glanced at his desk calendar. He would go to the doctor tomorrow and he suspected he would be told he had recovered and could return to his usual activities, which meant her job would be over.

If someone had bet him everything he owned that he would go home with a secretary who was a homebody deluxe, he would have lost every cent he owned. All during the ride back in the car, he had longed to lean over the seat to kiss her. When they arrived home, their lovemaking was inevitable. He could not resist.

He thought of what she had said in the car about the way he was with his family. Was his solitary life because he didn't know how to open up with his brothers or risk his emotions again and get them trampled as he had when he was a child?

He was leaving the ranch and the country as soon as he could. He would probably spend Christmas in Italy. He thought about the fun she would have with her family and couldn't keep from comparing that with thoughts about him rattling around the house in Italy all alone. The Italian home didn't hold near the appeal it had a month earlier.

Thoughts of her heated him. He wanted her right now and he wanted her in his bed again tonight. What would it be like to marry Emma and have her in his bed each night? The question shocked him because it was the first time he had contemplated even a thought of marriage with any woman he was friends with. How emotionally entangled was he with Emma? She stirred responses and emotions in him no other woman ever had. But there was no way he could have a permanent relationship with her.

She made her choices and she knew the job would end soon and they would part and not see each other again. There was absolutely no future in seeing her after she returned to Dallas. This wasn't the woman for him. Except in bed. He couldn't get enough of her there. Just watching her and thinking about her, he was getting aroused.

Knowing he had to get his mind off her and cool down, he turned to pick up the weekend mail, trying to concentrate on business.

It was almost four when Zach's phone rang. Emma had closed her computer and it looked as if she were clearing her desk to get ready to go. Zach answered the phone to hear Will.

Zach turned to ice, swearing quietly, causing Emma to look at him. "I'll be there as fast as I can get there." He replaced the phone.

"Caroline's gone," he said, glancing at Emma as he punched a number on his cell phone while he came around his desk.

"Oh, no. How long ago?" Emma rushed to keep up with him. She hurried beside him. "What happened? What will you do?"

"Go look for her. You can stay or you can come with me." Zach broke off to talk to his foreman. "Carl, Zach. Caroline's dog ran off and she went after it. They don't know where she is. Organize the guys and get them to head over to Will's ranch to help look for her. I'm going now." He listened and then ended the call. He grabbed a jacket he kept in the back hallway. He tossed her one of his. "Take this if you're coming with me."

She yanked on the heavy jacket, half running to keep up with him.

"Will and Ava are in Dallas. They were going to the symphony," Zach explained as they hurried toward the eight-car garage. "They're flying back now."

"How did Caroline disappear?"

"Muffy got out and Caroline went after her. The nanny, Rosalyn, went after Caroline, but Rosalyn slipped and fell. They think she hit her head on a rock because she lost consciousness briefly. When she regained consciousness, Caroline was gone." He was tempted to tell Emma to stay at the ranch because he could go faster without her, but they probably would need everyone they could get to help search for Caroline. His insides were a knot thinking about the little girl wandering around on the ranch with night coming.

"Thank heavens the weather is warmer than last week," Emma said, half running to keep up with his long stride.

"Will already has a chopper in the air and he's calling Ryan. He'll notify the county sheriff after he talks to Ryan," Zach said. He was chilled with fear for Caroline and couldn't wait to get to Will's ranch to start searching. Hazards spun in his mind and he tried to not think about them. How long would it take Caroline to get to the highway? From what Will said, she must have been near the house when last seen. He'd think forty minutes to an hour at best before she could possibly reach the highway. He glanced at the sky. It probably would be dark in another two hours.

"Damn, there are some canyons and some woods on Will's land," he said. "She's just so little."

Climbing into a pickup, with Emma rushing into the passenger seat, Zach headed toward the highway pushing the truck as fast as he dared.

Emma called her mother, relaying the situation. "My family can at least say a few prayers," she explained to Zach. "How long has Caroline been gone?"

"Not long. The minute she regained consciousness, Rosalyn called Will on her cell, so it was just a brief time. The bad thing was Rosalyn had no idea which direction to go to look for Caroline."

"Surely she hasn't gone far from home. Maybe she'll find her way back soon."

"She'll be chasing that little dog," he said, explaining about how easily Caroline could find her way to the highway. "Little kids can go fast sometimes and they like to run."

"I think we'll find her. She hasn't had time to get far."

"We've got a creek that has a few deep spots. She swims, but it's cold and I don't know what she'd do if she panicked. We have rattlesnakes in abundance," he said, clamping his mouth closed. "At least it's winter and the snakes won't be the same problem as in summer," he said, aware he was thinking out loud. Caroline was too little, her life too sheltered, to have any idea how to take care of herself.

"Hope for the best, Zach," she said, looking every which

way out the windows. "I know she can't be this far out, but I can't keep from looking around."

He gritted his teeth. He couldn't understand Emma's hopeful tone as if finding Caroline had become a certainty. There had been only rare moments in his adult life he had felt terrified, but he did now. He never had to this extent.

The car left a cloud of dust in the graveled road as he sped along, sliding on curves, sending plumes of dust into the air. They reached the highway in record time and he was amazed his driving hadn't scared Emma. Feeling a grim foreboding, Zach pushed the truck to its limit, speeding on the flat road. He gripped the steering wheel until his knuckles hurt.

"When we get close to Will's land, especially in line with the house, should you slow to watch for her?"

"I'm going to the house to find out where Rosalyn last saw her. We have to find her before night falls. We have mountain lions, coyotes. She can't stay out alone tonight."

"She can't have gotten far," Emma said with a strong, positive tone. "We'll find her before dark. We'll split up to look," Emma said. "No point in staying together. Maybe Muffy will just go home."

"I don't think so," Zach replied, his nerves on edge and not helped by Emma's cheerful optimism. "That little dog isn't any more accustomed to being out on her own than Caroline is. Muffy won't know the way home. Damn, I've never felt so helpless."

"Have you ever been this panicked about yourself?"

He gave her a startled look. "That's entirely different."

"Have you ever been this concerned about another adult?"

"No. Adults are different. Caroline is vulnerable."

"You're going to help. There are lots of people to help in the search. I'm sure we'll find her."

"Emma, I don't know how you can be so certain we'll find her," he said, trying to avoid snapping at her. "All the odds are the other way." If he and Emma were opposites, it had never been more so than at this moment. He glanced at her and saw her watching the land spreading away from the county road.

"There are a lot of people to look for her and she hasn't been gone long," Emma replied.

She was right, but it was a huge ranch with too many hazards for a child. Caroline would be completely unpredictable because she had never been out alone before. He hurt for Will and Zach was terrified for Caroline, trying to avoid thinking about how afraid she must be.

They lapsed into another silence until Zach waved a hand. "We're less than a mile from the turn into Will's ranch."

A barb wire fence bounded the property and the land near the road was flat with mesquite scattered across it. "You can see a lot from here." Shortly, he spotted the gate ahead and beyond it a thick grove of trees. The road curved out of sight and two tall cottonwoods bordered the county road. "Let me out along here, Zach," Emma said.

"I don't think she's had time to get this far. I hope not."

"I'll start walking back toward the house. Maybe I'll meet her." She patted his arm. "Don't worry until you have to."

"How the hell can I not worry?" he snapped, knowing he was being sharp, but he was filled with worry and fear for Caroline and he couldn't understand or appreciate Emma's positive attitude.

"Let me out as soon as you turn off the highway please."

"Emma, I don't want to have to worry about you, too."

"Don't be ridiculous. I have my phone. Stop the car and I'll go on foot."

He slowed, turned and stopped.

"Be positive, Zach. We'll find her." She jumped out quickly and he drove away.

At least she had a phone and knew how to use it. He suspected Emma knew little more than Caroline about being out on her own on the ranch, but she was an adult and would be okay. She was insulated in her positive feelings while he had none. As he drove around a bend in the road, Emma disappeared from sight in his rearview mirror.

Emma stood still, her gaze searching the dark woods. It would be five soon and since it was winter, the daylight would fade quickly. Saying another prayer, she began to walk inside Will's fence, continuing on in the direction they had been headed before Zach turned onto the ranch drive. She had told him she would walk toward the house, but she wanted to look along the highway a bit first. The highway worried Zach and she could see why. She studied the darkness beneath the thick grove of trees as she went. Surely if a child and a dog were nearby, they would make noise.

"Caroline," Emma called, the cry sounding small, pointless in all the emptiness around her.

Emma walked briskly for ten minutes, following the wide curve of the road, listening for any sounds of a child and then she heard voices. The road still curved and whoever was talking was lost to sight, but it sounded like more than two people.

Emma jogged, following the road, and finally she saw a pickup ahead. It had pulled off the side of the road. Relief and joy swamped her because it was a couple standing and talking to Caroline. The child held a white dog in her arms.

"Caroline!" Emma lengthened her stride and ran, breathing deeply when she reached them.

"Caroline, everyone is looking for you," she said as she hugged the little girl lightly.

She looked expectantly at the couple standing watching. She offered her hand. "I'm Emma Hillman," she said.

"We're Pete and Hazel Tanner," a deeply tanned, white-haired man said. His wide-brimmed hat was pushed back on his head. "We saw the dog and stopped and in a few minutes the little girl came running into sight. She gave us a number to call and they are coming to get her."

"Thank you so much," Emma said. "I'll call her uncle and tell him in case he hasn't gone to the house." She turned slightly, calling Zach to tell him.

"I'm the one coming back to get her," Zach said. "When I drove up, they told me the Tanners had called. Thank goodness you're with them. I should be there in minutes."

"She's fine, Zach. And she has her dog with her. These nice people stopped to see about Muffy and then Caroline came along."

"Just wait and I'll get all of you. I won't be long."

"I'm sure you won't," she said smiling and thinking how fast he had driven. She called her mother to let her know Caroline was found safe.

Scratching Muffy's head while Caroline held her, she talked to the couple for a few minutes. She wanted a hand close to the dog in case Muffy decided to run again.

"Caroline told us her name and how her little dog ran away and she couldn't catch her. She said her nanny was probably looking for her," Mabel Tanner said.

"A lot of people are searching for Caroline," Emma stated, smiling at the girl.

Emma heard the car before she saw Zach and then she watched him pull onto the shoulder to park. He had a leash in his hand and hooked it on Muffy's collar after he had hugged Caroline. Picking up Caroline, he handed the end of the leash to Emma while he talked to the Tanners.

"Thanks beyond words for helping," he said, shaking hands with the couple and talking briefly to them. In minutes they climbed into their pickup while Zach held the door for Emma and Caroline. As Caroline buckled herself into the back, Zach buckled the leash in beside her. Caroline pulled Muffy onto her lap. Zach leaned in to brush a kiss on the top of Caroline's head. "You gave us a real scare," he said softly.

"I'm sorry." She smiled up at him, and he stepped back to close the door.

He slid behind the wheel and glanced at Emma. "After I talked to you and knew you were with Caroline, I called Will to tell him to go on to the symphony because everything is okay here. He's already landing. He said he wants to come home to hug Caroline."

"I can understand that," Emma answered. She turned in her seat to talk to Caroline.

"Caroline, did you have trouble finding Muffy?"

"No. I could see her, but she wouldn't come back to me. I had to run fast."

"I'll bet you did," Emma replied. "You ran a long, long way."

Caroline nodded her head. "She sat to wait for me and then she'd run. I think she wanted to play."

Emma had to laugh. "I'm sure she had great fun."

"Everyone was very worried about you and Muffy. I'm glad we found you and Muffy didn't cross the highway," Zach said.

"Mr. and Mrs. Tanner told me that they saw Muffy and stopped because they thought she was a lost dog. Then they saw me. When I told them I was alone, they called Daddy Two. I told them his phone number."

"That was the right thing to do," Zach said. "He'll be here soon."

Caroline's eyes narrowed. "Am I in trouble?"

"I don't think so," Zach said. "We'll just be glad to have you and Muffy home again. Rosalyn is very worried. We all were worried about where you were and if you were safe. You gave us all a big scare, Caroline," he said.

"I would have gone home, but I couldn't catch Muffy."

"Would you have known how to find home?" Zach asked her.

"I could have followed the fence. Except I got scared when I saw Muffy running toward the highway."

"I'll bet you were scared. How did Muffy get loose?"

"The back gate wasn't closed all the way. Someone had left it open and Muffy squeezed out."

"Well, we'll put a little sign on that gate to keep it closed," Zach said and Caroline smiled.

Caroline hugged Muffy who had stretched out to sleep. "Thank you for coming to get me, Uncle Zach."

"You're welcome," he said.

Soon they were home and as they approached the house, Rosalyn waited on the porch. Pulling her coat close around her, she came down the steps to greet them. With a bandage on her forehead, she looked pale and she walked slowly, carefully hanging to the rail.

"Rosalyn doesn't look so great," Zach said quietly.

They climbed out of the car, and Caroline ran to Rosalyn to hug her while Zach got Muffy out and held her until they were inside the fenced yard. He set the small dog on her feet to remove her leash.

Emma greeted Caroline's nanny and stood quietly while Zach talked to her about her fall. "You should get off your feet, Rosalyn."

"I will. I just had to come hug Caroline. She didn't know I fell. She thought I was probably coming behind her. I can't tell you how worried I've been. About as much as Mr. Will. I caught my foot on a root and I couldn't keep from falling. I hit something, and then I was just out. When I came to, Caroline was gone. I've never had such a scare," she said, looking at Caroline who was tossing a ball for Muffy.

"She's back with her dog so you mend. Take it easy and get well."

"I intend to," she said, smiling at him.

A car came up the drive and Will spilled out, hurrying around to open the door for Ava. They both rushed through the gate. The instant Caroline saw them, she threw out her arms and ran toward them.

Will picked her up to hug her and hold her out so she and Ava could hug.

"We'll go say hello and goodbye. Leave the family to themselves," Zach said.

Will turned to greet them, shaking Zack's hand. "Thanks for coming on the run and thanks, Emma, for finding her with the Tanners on the highway. They live over in the next county and we know each other to say hello. I couldn't believe Caroline made it to the highway in that time."

"We're all happy now," Zach said. "We'll leave you to talk to Caroline and Rosalyn. Night, sweetie," he added, kissing Caroline's cheek. Slipping a small, thin arm around his neck, she hugged him and Zach smiled at her.

He took Emma's arm to go to his car and in minutes they were on the road driving back to his ranch.

"I'm going home, kicking back and having a beer. Caroline looks so little and frail. That scared me. I still feel as if my insides are shivering." He glanced at her. "How did you keep so calm?"

"You were calm."

"I just had it all bottled up, but it's coming out now."

Emma was amazed, because Zach seemed so tough, and today, cool when he had taken charge to call his men and then get to Will's ranch quickly. He had traveled and worked in dangerous jobs all over the world where he'd had to keep his wits, yet now he was coming apart. She saw his hands had a tremor. "I don't know how you were calm," he repeated.

"Positive thinking and prayers, Zach. Expecting a happy outcome."

"You're the eternal optimist," he stated, shaking his head. "I've seen too much, Emma. Positive thinking and prayers can't guarantee happy endings."

"Neither can giving up hope and imagining all sorts of scary scenarios. Then if something happens, because of your imagination, you've suffered more than once. We're very different people."

"Amen to that one," he said. "There's the one thing we can agree about," he added and she smiled.

As soon as they were inside the house, Zach built a fire, got the wine she requested and a beer for himself. While he sipped, he stretched out on the floor. Firelight flickered over him and her breath caught. He looked virile, appealing. Broad shoulders, long legs, thick curls. She wanted to join him, but that was a path to deeper complications.

"How do people have kids and not have nervous breakdowns when they do something like Caroline just did?" he asked.

"You cope with it, just the way you and Will and Ava did. You do whatever you can," Emma said.

"I'll never understand how you could stay cheerful and optimistic that we would find her. I know the reason you gave me, but I still don't get it"

"We did find her," she reminded him, sitting near him to sip her drink. He removed it from her hands and drew her down into his arms to kiss her. "I just try to focus on the positive, Zach. And Caroline hadn't been gone long when everyone started looking for her."

"I keep thinking she had reached the highway and if the Tanners hadn't come along—"

"But they did come along, so don't think about the other possibilities," Emma said. He held her in his embrace as they were stretched on the floor together. She had been frightened for Caroline, but certain they would find her. Now to know

Caroline was safe and with Will, Emma felt as if they had been given the biggest Christmas gift early.

Desire, relief, joy all buoyed her and she wrapped her arms around Zach to kiss him hungrily. Instantly, his arm tightened around her waist and he pulled her closer. "I need you tonight, Emma," he said in a rasp. "This is an affirmation of life and all's right with our world," he said, his blue eyes darkening as he drew her closer.

Seven

Relief transformed into lust, and loving Zach *was* an affirmation of life.

Heat from the fire warmed her, but not as much as Zach's kisses that sent her temperature climbing.

Sex with him became paramount. To be alive, to be able to make love with Zach, to have loved ones safe—her emotions ran high and she threw herself into kissing him, tangling her fingers in his thick hair.

She thought Zach was caught in the same emotional whirlwind, relieved, celebrating life and that all was okay now because his kisses became more passionate as he concentrated totally on pleasuring her.

In seconds they loved with a desperate hunger. With ragged breathing, she kissed him while her fingers traced muscles and planes of his body. Wild abandon consumed her and when ⸱ were joined, they rocked together until she cried out his ⸱⸱ her thundering release.

⸱⸱ ⸱ve," she gasped, the word slipping out and

she hoped he hadn't heard her. Rapture enveloped her, a moment in time when they were in unison and meant something to each other. A moment she wanted to hold, yet would be as fleeting as the snowflake she had caught and watched disappear in her warm palm.

Afterwards, as they drifted back to reality, he held her close in his arms while he showered her face and shoulders with light kisses that made her feel adored.

She turned on her side to look at Zach, drawing her fingers along his jaw to feel the rough, dark stubble. "This isn't what I expected tonight. Yet it's a rejoicing of sorts."

"A definite celebration of life for me." He sighed and traced his fingers over her bare shoulder. "I hope next week is another occasion for cheer. I have a doctor's appointment and I have high hopes I can get back into a normal shoe."

"When you do we'll be through here. Zach, I still urge you to keep those letters. You don't know if Caroline will want them one day. If you destroy them, you can't get them back."

"I know you've scanned most of them into the computer, so now we have electronic copies."

"The original letters are far more important."

He smiled. "Emma, you're a hopeless romantic. You're talking about letters written over a hundred years ago."

"I feel as if I know that part of your family. They were brave, intelligent and your great-great-grandfather had a sense of humor. I've found touching letters by your great-great-grandmother, too. I think the letters are priceless. And the fact that the letters date from over a hundred yea___ ___ has value, Zach. The electronic copies hold *no* value___ ___ ___ are copies if the originals are destroyed."

"I think you're placing too high a value on___ the things we've found mixed in with th___ watch, the Colt revolver, the Henry rifle___ I can't believe someone put a Colt or a r___

"They put together what was important to them."

"No way are those letters as valuable as that Colt."

"Maybe not in dollars, but I think the letters are more valuable. The letters are a window into your ancestors' thoughts and dreams and lives."

He rose on an elbow to look at her. "We are polar opposites in every way. How can we possibly have this attraction that turns my insides out?"

"It does other things to you," she said, caressing him.

"You know what you're doing to me now," he said in a deep voice.

"Zach," she whispered, knowing the one part of their lives where they were totally compatible. "You're an incredibly sexy man," she added.

"That, darlin', is the pot calling the kettle black, as the old saying goes." His eyes darkened and his gaze shifted to her mouth as he leaned closer to kiss her.

She held him tightly while the endearment, his first, echoed in her mind and how she wished he had meant something by it. When it came to Zach, she couldn't hang on to that optimism she had everywhere else in her life.

Through the night they made love and slept in each other's arms. It was late morning before they dressed and ate. While Zach talked on the phone to Will, she sat at the kitchen table and gazed outside at the crystal blue swimming pool, the color reminding her of Zach's eyes. She thought about all she loved and admired about him—his generosity, his care for Caroline and his family, even if he didn't spend time with them, he obviously loved them. He was intelligent, talented, capable of running the businesses he owned and she had heard he started all of them, not his father. He was caring and fun, loving, obviously a risk-taker although that wasn't a part which appeal for her.

As soon as he told Will goodbye, she stood. "Zach, I'm going back to work. I can still get a lot done today."

Nodding his head, he stood as she left the room. Her back tingled and she was tempted to turn around to stay with him and postpone work, but there was no point and no future in spending a lot of time with him. After this job ended, she did not expect to see him again.

Each day the rest of the week she spent nearly all her time reading the letters. When she returned Sunday night after the weekend at home, she was certain this would be her last week to work for Zach. A new concern nagged her constantly—for the first time, her period was late. They had used protection, so she dismissed the likelihood of pregnancy, but she didn't know what was wrong. Tuesday morning she called to make an appointment to see her family doctor the following week when she would be at home in Dallas.

Later that day, forgetting time or her surroundings, she read a yellowed letter on crackling paper.

"Zach, do you have a moment? Listen to this letter," she said. "This one is from your great-grandfather when their first child, a son, was born. Was your grandfather the oldest son?"

"Yes, he was," Zach said, leaning back in his chair.

She bent over the paper spread on her knees, her hair falling forward around her face.

"My dear sister. Lenore gave me a son today. He is a fine, strong baby and I am pleased. He has my color eyes and his mother's light hair. He has a healthy cry. I am certain his cries can be heard at the creek.

"With her long hair down Lenore looks beautif'' ''s given me life's most precious gift. I feel humble, b is nothing as valuable that I can present to h have done what I hope will please her the m her I have ordered a piano for her.

"I wish I could give her fine satin gov

she would merely laugh if I told her my wish. Instead, I hope she likes her piano. It will be shipped to Saint Joseph, Missouri, on the train. I will send four of the boys with a wagon and a team to go to Missouri to pick up the piano. They must protect it from the elements, thieves and all hazards because they will have to cross more than one treacherous river. They have promised they can get the piano and bring it back here."

Pausing, she looked up as Zach crossed the room to her. "Surely, that letter means something to you."

Taking the letter from her fingers to drop it back into the box, he pulled her to her feet, putting his arm around her waist. "I still say you're a romantic."

"If you destroy these, I think you'll have regrets."

"That's impossible for me to imagine. Today I'm filled with positive moments because I expect a great prognosis when I go to the doctor this afternoon. I think he'll say I'm healed and can wear regular shoes. After Christmas I want to take you dancing."

Her heart felt squeezed. She was thrilled while at the same time, that was only postponing their final parting.

"We'll see when the time comes," she said, placing her hands on Zach's chest. She could feel his heart beneath her palms and wondered if his reaction to her was half as strong as how he affected her. His blue eyes darkened with desire, causing her heartbeat to quicken. "You may not be able to dance as soon as you think. What is more likely—you'll be half a world away by that time."

"I don't think that's why you aren't accepting, is it?"

"I don't see much future for us. I think when you fully recuperate, you'll be gone. You'll return to life as you've always lived it. You have to agree."

"I might hang around Texas for a while. There are things I do here. Wherever I am, I can fly home when I want to."

"'t know how you can even call one place home.

This is the family ranch, now Garrett's, not your home. You don't stay in your home in Dallas," she argued breathlessly, having to make an effort to concentrate on their conversation when all she could think about was being in his arms and wanting him.

He smiled at her. "I'll ask again." Sparks arced between them, the air crackling. Just as it had been between them that first encounter, she was caught and held in his steady gaze that made her even more breathless.

"Zach," she whispered, sliding her arms around his neck.

He kissed her. Tingles streaked across her nerves. Awareness intensified of every inch of him pressed so close. Holding him tightly, she refused to think about the future, the job ending, her saying goodbye to Zach. Each day she was more in love with him. The world, work, letters, her future, all ceased to exist in her thoughts that focused totally on him.

His kiss turned her insides to jelly, ignited fires, heat sizzling in her. She pressed against him more firmly, taking what she could while he was here in her arms because too soon he would be gone forever.

Finally, she gave a thought to their time and place.

"Zach, there are other people in the house now," she whispered, wondering if her protests fell on deaf ears.

He kissed her, silencing her conversation. When she felt him tug on her sweater, she grasped his wrists. Breathing hard, he looked at her as she shook her head.

"We're downstairs. Nigel and Rosie are here. Within the hour you should leave for your flight to Dallas to see your doctor. We have to stop loving now."

Combing long strands of hair from her face, Zach looked at her mouth. "You're beautiful. We'll come back to this moment tonight when I get home."

"We shouldn't," she whispered. "You need to get lunch now before you go."

"I know what I'd rather do."

She shook her head. "Lunch is on the schedule."

"Ok, come eat with me." She nodded, walking beside him, unable to resist. Through lunch he was charming, making her anxious for his return before he had even left the house.

While he was gone the house was quiet and she read, stopping occasionally to stretch, or pacing the room and reading as she walked.

Late afternoon shadows grew long and she added a log to the fire. It was winter and the days had grown shorter with a chill in the air. She heard his whistle before he appeared. When he came through the office door, he closed it behind him. Her heart thudded against her ribs. She took one look at him and knew her job was over.

Vitality radiated from him as if he had been energized while he was in Dallas. She didn't have to ask what the doctor had said. Zach crossed the room to pull her to her feet and kiss her heatedly

In minutes, clothes were tossed aside. The fire was glowing orange embers, giving the only light in the darkened room during early evening.

"Zach, we're downstairs and not alone in the house."

"The door is closed. No one will bother us," he whispered between kisses. "I want you, Emma." He kissed her before she could argue and she yielded, loving him back with a desperate urgency.

They moved to the rug in front of the fire. Heat warmed her side while Zach's body was hot against her own. He got a condom from a pocket and returned to kneel between her legs while he put it in place.

Orange sparks and embers highlighted the bulge of muscles and his thick manhood while the planes of his cheeks and flat stomach were shadows. Another memory to lock away in her mind and heart.

A log cracked and fell, sending a shower of sparks spiraling up the chimney. The sudden flash of red and orange dancing sparks illuminated Zach even more for a brief moment. He looked like a statue, power and desire enveloping him. She drew her fingers along his muscled thighs and heard him gasp for breath.

Lowering himself, he wrapped his arms around her to thrust slowly into her, filling her. He was hard, hot, moving with a tantalizing slowness as she arched beneath him.

"Zach," she whispered, wanting to confess her love, longing to hold him tightly and tell him she loved him with all her heart.

Their rhythm built, increasing need and tension, until release burst, spinning her into ecstasy, taking him with her seconds later.

She lost awareness of everything except Zach in their moment of perfect union. A physical bonding at the height of passion that carried with it an emotional bonding. Clinging to him with her long legs wrapped around him, she did not want to let go as if she could hold the moment and delay time itself. This man, so totally different from her, had become vital to her. Right now she couldn't face letting him go.

They slowed, calmed while she caught her breath. Her hands were light touches, caressing his shoulders and back while she drifted in paradise.

When he rolled over, taking her with him, he kissed her tenderly. There was still enough glow from embers to reflect on Zach and she touched his cheek lightly. "The doctor said your foot is healed, didn't he?"

"Yes, he did," Zach said, smiling. "I can toss this boot and wear my shoes. My own boots have to wait a while, but eventually, I can wear them."

"So my job ends this week. Christmas is coming and I wanted off anyway."

"I'll be gone for Christmas, but I'll come back afterwards and that's when I'm taking you out. I'd stay if you'd stay with me for a few weeks, but you'll want to be home for Christmas."

"Yes, I will," she said, hurting, even though she had known this time was approaching.

"I'll be in touch with you," he said. Glancing over his shoulder, he shifted away to stand and put another log on the fire. He returned to pull her close against him, warm body against warm body as he wrapped his legs with hers.

He combed her long hair away from her face with his fingers. Tingles followed each stroke and she could feel their hearts beating together.

"This is paradise, Emma."

How she longed to hear him say words of love. Common sense told her that would not happen, but wishes and dreams came with his strong arms holding her and his light kisses making her feel loved.

All were illusions that would disappear with the morning sun. For now she could pretend, wish, hope, give herself to fantasies that normally she wouldn't entertain for a minute.

She kissed him lightly in return.

The fire crackled and burned, causing dancing dark shadows and bathing Zach's body in orange.

"You're very quiet," he said.

"I'm savoring the moment."

"I'm savoring holding you close. Sometime tonight we'll get in a bed, but not yet."

Eventually, they gathered their clothing and each went to shower. They put away the dinner Rosie had cooked and made sandwiches to eat in front of the fire and sat and talked until Zach stood and took her hand.

"Let's go upstairs and I'll build a fire in my room. I can do stairs now with ease." He placed his arm across her shoulders as they climbed the stairs, leading her down the hall to his suite of rooms where he took her into his arms to kiss her.

Wednesday, she gave all her time to the letters. Zach's work had dwindled as Christmas approached, so since Thanksgiving she had devoted her time to trying to get through as many of the letters and memorabilia as she could.

She hoped someone else in the Delaney family wanted the letters because the few she had read to Zach and the ones he had read himself had not changed his feelings about them. He always sent them to the discard pile.

By Friday, the tension from being constantly around him—loving him, but not able to make him truly hers—was greater than ever. Today would change everything. Today she would return to Dallas, to her life before meeting Zach. Even though he had talked about seeing her after Christmas, she didn't expect to see Zach again.

Early that morning Rosie cooked while Emma ate breakfast. Halfway through breakfast, Emma felt sick and dashed to the bathroom. When she returned, she carried what was left of her breakfast back to the kitchen.

"Rosie, I can't eat any more. I felt sick and now food doesn't look good."

Rosie turned to study her while she dried her hands and took the dishes from Emma. "You were sick yesterday morning."

Emma looked at Rosie and met a speculative gaze. "My period is late," Emma said, confessing what had been worrying her each day. "I shouldn't be sick no matter what, but I am."

"Bless your heart," Rosie said, hugging Emma lightly. Emma stood immobile, stunned. Fear had blossomed earlier over a week ago. She had pushed away the nagging worry, telling herself it was her imagination. But it was too many days now for it to be her imagination. Two days in a row, she had been sick during breakfast and then it was gone.

"Rosie, I have two married sisters and a sister-in-law. They all have babies. I've seen both my sisters have morning sickness." Emma felt chilled and trembled. "Rosie, this wasn't in my plans."

"You don't know for certain, do you?"

"No. I'll get a pregnancy test this weekend when I go to Dallas. I already have a doctor's appointment for next week."

Rosie placed her hands on her hips while she faced Emma. "Then don't start worrying now. The stomach upset might be something you ate and your period could start tomorrow. How late are you?"

"A week now."

Emma rolled her eyes. "That's not enough to give you a worry. A few days is nothing. Wait a few weeks."

Emma nodded, but she was not reassured. "I'm extremely on time almost to the hour, so this is unique." Suddenly, to the depths, she was certain she was pregnant with Zach's baby. Her head swam and for an instant she felt light-headed. She reached out to grasp the kitchen counter to steady herself. Rosie's hand closed on her arm.

"Are you all right?"

Rosie's expression showed concern that threatened panic. "Rosie, promise me—please don't say anything yet until I know for sure."

"I would never. Don't give it another worry. That's not my business and I don't interfere in something like this. I'll not say anything." Rosie's brow furrowed and her eyes were filled with concern.

"I don't panic over things, but I feel panicky over this. I feel so out of control."

"Wait until you've seen a doctor and know absolutely," Rosie said, but her voice held only solicitude.

"This wasn't supposed to happen," Emma whispered, more to herself than Rosie.

"Some things are just out of our hands," Rosie declared. "Go back to your room and lie down if you need to." She took Emma's icy hand in her soft, warm hands, briefly and then released her. "You have a big, loving family. They'll take care of you and a little one."

A little one. Emma shook and clenched her hands. Rosie hadn't said a word about Zach being helpful. Was this going to be a huge shock—and an unpleasant one for him? Would it be a responsibility he didn't want? He had talked about how unprepared Will had been for Caroline. On the other hand, Zach seemed to truly care for Caroline and he had been a wreck when they couldn't find her. Of all men on earth— "I'm going to my room if he comes asking for me," she said, suddenly wanting to get behind closed doors and adjust to what was happening before she faced another person. "This is my last day. He doesn't need to know until I'm sure."

"I promise. You have your secret," Rosie said, nodding and going back to doing dishes.

Emma hurried out and raced out of sight, rushing to her room where she crossed the room to place her hands on her flat middle. "I can't be," she whispered.

In her dressing room she studied herself in the mirror, turning first one way and another. She had watched two sisters and a sister-in-law go through pregnancies. She looked in the mirror, running her hands over her flat stomach. There were no single mothers in her family.

Zach. How could she ever tell a man who wouldn't even spend Christmas with his family that he was about to become a father?

Eight

She was staring at her stomach in the dressing room of her suite when her stomach rolled and she ran for the bathroom. She was sick again and this time she knew it was partly with worry.

She thought of her brother, Connor. Connor was strong-willed, the take-charge oldest sibling, a total alpha male who would want to make Zach marry her. He wouldn't want to marry or he already would have talked about it. Zach would rebel and probably disappear to another country.

She shook again, chilled on the warm day. She ran a cold cloth over her face and went back to sit, knotting her fists and trying to think what to do, praying she was wrong.

She could leave, slip out without Zach even knowing and then say goodbye with a call from Dallas.

Too many things were so wrong. She had just tossed her future into uncertainty and chaos. Why had she ever stayed and worked for him? Why had she made love with him? Fallen in love with him when she had known it would be disastrous and hopeless? Why hadn't the protection worked?

The Dallas job would go, too. If she stayed there, word would get right back to him. *Just quit the company and go somewhere else,* she told herself. By the time she was ready to tell Zach, he would probably be halfway around the world, far from Texas and from her. Soon she would be only a memory to him.

Standing in front of the mirror, she inspected her figure. She could get through Christmas without anyone knowing. Common sense said to stop worrying until she was certain, but that was impossible. All her positive reactions to past upheavals were gone now. She couldn't hold the same cheerful certainty for herself and she needed to get a grip. This worry was not like her and there was a bright side. If she could just focus on the baby and try to avoid thinking about Zach. A total impossibility.

In her heart, there were no doubts. Because of their loving, she would become the mother of a Delaney. It seemed likely that Zach would help support his child, but that was all. A man whose heart was already given to traveling and his job would never be tied down by a family.

Feeling an ache of worry increasing, she rubbed her neck. Mary Kate was her closest sibling and she could tell her. The thought of Mary Kate's support lifted Emma's spirits slightly. Her sister would be a staunch ally and Emma was certain she could always count on her mother's acceptance. If she could just keep Connor from doing something wild like wanting to punch out Zach.

She remembered Will and Ava and Caroline and the love that shone between Will and Ava, plus their eagerness when they had announced a baby on the way. Emma hurt, her insides twisting into a knot while tears threatened. She wouldn't have that shared joy and love. This wasn't the way she had always dreamed about having a family. The love she had wished for was what she had witnessed between Will and Ava.

Emma wiped her eyes and got up, walking restlessly, wishing she could undo what had been done. She had no one to blame but herself. How she wished she could back up and relive her life.

Then Emma thought about the baby and put her hand protectively on her stomach. *Her* baby. Her family would be shocked, upset, angry, probably even with her, but when the baby arrived, they would all accept and love the tyke.

This baby would fit into her family and they would shower the baby and her with love. Her brothers would be dads for the baby. Her child would not come into the world unloved or unwanted.

She stretched on the bed, staring into space while her mind raced over problems and solutions.

The first hurdle was to get through today with Zach. She was already packed, ready to go home. How was she going to be able to tell Zach goodbye?

An hour later she went down to work. Zach sat stretched out, his feet on a window ledge while he talked on the phone. She sat at her desk, unable to work, looking at him and thinking about the future.

She could tell he was getting ready to end the call, so she returned to the box of letters where she had spent all of her time lately.

As she picked up a letter something rattled inside the envelope. Turning the envelope over, she shook it. A golden heart locket on a chain fell into her palm. Glittering brightly in the center of the heart was a brilliant green stone.

She withdrew the fragile letter and read, looking up to interrupt Zach. "Listen to this letter: '…this was my grandmother's locket with my great-grandmother's and my great-grandparents' pictures. I want you to have it because it should remain in the family to be passed to each generation.' This letter is signed by your great-grandfather, so this locket must be incredibly old if it belonged to his grandmother." Pausing, she put aside the letter. "Look at this beautiful locket. There are two tiny paintings inside with pictures, I suppose, of two more Delaneys, an even more distant generation." She carried the locket across the office to hand it to Zach.

Standing, he took the locket to turn it in his hand and inspect it.

Finally he looked up and held it out. "Emma, you take this. I want you to have it."

"Zach, I can't do that! You have a family and some of your relatives may want it. You should keep that jewelry. It's an heirloom and your great-grandfather wanted it to stay in the Delaney family."

"You said you feel as if you are part of the Delaneys when you read those old letters. I want you to have it as a bonus for your work and to give you a tangible memory of all this history you waded through. Here," he said, taking it from her and stepping behind her to fasten it around her neck.

"I really think you should keep this in your family," she said and then realized part of her would become part of his family. She placed her fist protectively against her stomach.

"I want you to have it," he insisted, taking her shoulders to turn her to face him as he judged how it looked on her. "It is pretty," he added, his voice deepening while it thickened with desire. He looked into her eyes. She met his blue ones, her heart beating faster. She wanted his strong arms around her. She wanted to hold him while she kissed him. As if he could read her thoughts, he drew her to him and placed his mouth on hers.

Her heart slammed against her ribs. Zach pulled her close, holding her tightly while he kissed her hard and possessively.

Her pounding heart should indicate her feelings as she

held him tightly in return. She let go all restraint, kissing him, her deepest love, the father of her baby. And she was certain she was pregnant. How she wished she didn't ever have to tell him.

"Zach," she said, on the verge of saying she would miss him. "Thank you for the necklace. Your brothers and your half sister may not be happy with you for giving away this heirloom."

"My brothers would definitely want you to have it. Sophia, I don't know. I want you to have it. Actually, I don't think I'm making you much of a gift except I suspect you think so."

She looked at the locket in her hand and got a knot in her throat as emotions choked her. "I do think so," she whispered, knowing it would go to a Delaney heir.

Zach put his finger beneath her chin to raise her face. Embarrassed because she couldn't hide her emotional reaction, she stood on tiptoe and kissed him quickly.

As their kiss became passionate, her emotions shifted. When she ended their kiss, they both were breathless and she suspected Zach had forgotten about her reaction to the locket.

"I'm going to miss you, Emma."

"You can still come spend Christmas with us," she said, certain of his answer.

He smiled. "Thanks, but I've already made arrangements. I'll be at an Italian villa I inherited. Dad always referred to it as his 'summer home.'"

His answer stung and made her leaving a reality. Yet it was for the best because now her emotions were on a rocky edge. They needed to part even though she felt as if her heart were breaking.

She placed her hand against his cheek. "I'll think about you on Christmas in your Italian villa."

"You are probably the one person in the entire world who

feels sorry for me spending Christmas that way," he said, smiling at her.

"I know what you're missing."

"We can both say that. You could come with me and let me show you that Italian villa and see how you like spending Christmas in Italy. Live a little, you have next Christmas with your family."

"Thank you, but I'll stay in Texas and you go to Italy. Zach, you get along with your family—your brothers and Caroline mean a lot to you. Realize what a treasure they are. Love and enjoy them. I think you shut yourself off in defense when you were hurt as a child. You have a wonderful family and your ancestors are fascinating. Don't sell them short. Try a Christmas with Will and family sometime, get Ryan, Sophia and Garrett there, too."

"You are a dreamer and a romantic," he said patiently. "I will enjoy my Italian villa immensely. It will be sunny, beautiful with no crowds, no schedules. You really should try it."

She shook her head. "Thank you. We'll each go where our hearts are, only I think yours is there out of an old habit more than because you really enjoy it."

"I suppose I never stopped to think about it."

She stepped away and glanced at her watch. "I need to get on the road now. The job has been wonderful." She tried to hold back tears as she stood on tiptoe to kiss him.

He held her tightly, kissing her fiercely. Finally, he paused. "You can stay this weekend if you want."

"I have plans in Dallas," she said, knowing it would be heartbreaking to spend the weekend and go through this last day again.

She stepped out of his embrace. It was time to go. She'd already said her goodbyes to Rosie and Nigel, and Nigel had already placed her things in her car.

Zach headed out with her, reaching around her to open the car door.

"You'll hear from me," he said.

"Maybe I'll see you at headquarters someday," she replied lightly, sliding behind the wheel. Closing the door, he stepped back and she started the car. As she waved and drove away, she glanced in the rearview mirror to see him standing in the drive, watching her.

She would tell her mother and sisters she had been invited to Zach's Italian villa. Connor didn't need to hear about it. An Italian villa sounded like paradise, but not at Christmas. That was definitely family time.

Family time. Worry and heartbreak stung. She couldn't keep from crying until she thought about the baby and making plans. How and when would she tell her family? She'd wait until after Christmas because she had no idea how they would receive the news.

Zach had seemed good with Caroline and interested in her. How would he be with his own child? He had told her how they had struggled to get Sophia into the family and how much they wanted to know her. Surely, if he wanted to know his half sister, he would want to know his child.

The first thing was to get a pregnancy test kit. If she wasn't pregnant, then all these worries would seem ridiculous.

Pregnant—it was a shock she couldn't absorb. It was so totally unexpected because they had always used protection. Something she had never thought would happen to her until after she was married. She had always looked forward to her own family, but in her mind, it had included a husband who was an active family man. A reassuring thought now was the knowledge she would never be alone raising this baby because her family would all participate. Clinging to that, she tried to ignore the steady hurt squeezing her heart.

Christmas with a baby on the way. Would she have to give

up college and her hope of teaching? Christmas had always been filled with magic for her, the best time of the year, and this Christmas would be so different. She would have to be responsible for someone else. It was an awesome task. She would get a present for her baby this week. And think of baby names. Her baby would not have the Delaney name. Another Hillman.

She missed Zach. As mismatched as they were, she liked being with him. He had been easy to work for. When she decided what and how she would tell him about the baby, she would get in touch with him. In the meantime, this break was as inevitable as it was necessary.

She fingered the locket around her neck. She thought it was a beautiful heirloom and she would take very good care of it. It would go into safekeeping for her baby soon.

She hoped Will prevailed on Zach to keep the letters. It would be sad to see them destroyed. Since she would be mother of a Delaney, if they decided to shred the letters, she intended to ask Zach for them.

She missed Zach badly and each mile between them increased her longing to be with him. She could have prolonged the separation, but there was no point and her emotions were on a raw edge. In a few hours she would be home and her family would keep her busy enough that the pain over parting with Zach should be alleviated.

By Monday, Zach missed Emma more than he had thought possible. He was planning to leave for Italy on Tuesday, but he had lost his enthusiasm for the trip. Should he do something else this Christmas? That was Emma's influence. He recalled times as a child that he had wanted to be with his family, but then he and his brothers had been left at their schools for the holidays. Eating at the home of an indifferent headmaster had never been fun and Zach began to count only on his own company. He would be happy in Italy once he was there.

Earlier that morning Will had called his brothers and Sophia, and the entire family was coming for lunch today to bring their Christmas presents to him, so he was having a little Christmas celebration with his family. Emma would have been relieved to hear it, but now she was wrapped up in her own family's activities. When he first was injured, Zach had given his secretary at headquarters a list of gifts to purchase for each member of his family. They'd been wrapped and delivered to the ranch.

Standing at the window, Zach looked at the dry, yellowed windswept landscape beyond the fenced yard. Why had life become empty without Emma? It had only been the weekend since she left, but it seemed eons ago. Common sense told him she was not the woman for him, not even in a casual way. He smiled at the thought. No relationship was casual to Emma. Not even the brief affair they had.

He paced the room restlessly. "Go to Italy," he advised aloud. "Pick up your life and forget her."

Memories flooded him of holding her, kissing her, making love to her. Of her laughter, her hands on him, her luminous green eyes studying him. Even the looks of pity she had given him came back to haunt him. Was he missing out on the best part of life as she had said? Was he letting that armor from childhood keep him from loving and being loved today?

Would he really want to be tied down with a family? Tied down with Emma? The last thought sounded like paradise.

Was he going to mope through Christmas? It was a time he had never given much thought to since he was grown.

He saw three limos coming up the drive so he left to open the front door.

Will, Ava and Caroline climbed out of the first limo. Ryan emerged from the second and Garrett and Sophia from the third limo. The drivers carried boxes filled with wrapped presents. Zach directed the drivers where to put the presents and then turned to greet everyone.

"Don't tell me all this stuff is for me," Zach said.

"Who else is here for us to give presents to? Although I do have one for Nigel and one for Rosie and I'll bet the rest do, too," Ryan said with a cocky grin. "You said you were giving Nigel and Rosie three weeks off."

"And I did. Come in," he said, picking up Caroline to give her a hug. He led them to the family room where the drivers had already placed boxes of presents.

A sofa beside a large wingback chair was piled high with Zach's presents for his brothers, Sophia and their families.

"You should have had Nigel bring down the Christmas tree," Will said.

"Don't you start that. Emma had decorations up and I got rid of them."

"You have turned into Scrooge," Will said.

"Hardly," Zach replied, waving his arm in the direction of the sofa with presents. "I believe I have a few presents for everyone."

"My apology," Will said, laughing. "Not entirely Scrooge. I do see mistletoe hanging over the door. That's a weird decoration to put up for a man living alone."

"Just drop it, Will," Zach said.

"Maybe I should have stopped by last week and met the secretary," Ryan said.

"Will a beer shut you two up?" Zach asked. "First, let me see about the drivers and get them settled with something to eat and drink. I'll be right back. When I do, we'll start this little family Christmas celebration that I suspect is totally for my benefit," Zach remarked dryly.

When he returned he asked them, "Eggnog, beer, wine, martini, margaritas, Scotch, an old-fashioned—none of you have to drive home and I have a full bar, so what do you prefer?" he said, going behind the bar to fill orders. In minutes he brought out snacks Rosie had left.

Ryan held up his bottle. "Merry Christmas to our newest family member, Sophia, to Ava and Caroline, to my big brothers, to Garrett who's been like a brother," he said, including Garrett as he always had.

They all held up bottles and echoed his toast.

"Now I'll propose a toast," Will said, "and a Christmas prayer of thanks for Caroline in our lives, for Sophia becoming part of our family and for Ava. The four of us have been blessed by them."

"Here, here and amen," Ryan said and they clinked bottles together again.

In a few minutes Ryan raised his bottle high again. "Here's to the two surviving bachelors in this group. Zach, my bro, I'm going to outlast you."

All three of the others protested at the same time. "Ryan, you're next," Garrett said. "No way is anyone getting Zach down the aisle."

"They can't get him to stay in one country long enough to fall in love," Will added, making Zach grin.

"Sorry, Ryan, but I'll win this one," he said, thinking about Emma.

They soon went to the kitchen where Zach got out ribs from a Dutch oven. All night he had cooked ribs and he had baked beans that had slowcooked for hours. He got a large bowl of Rosie's cold potato salad. He replenished beers and they all gathered around the big table to feast on the rib dinner. As he passed out the beers, he thought of Emma. If she could see him now, she would know he enjoyed his family. They just weren't together as often as hers.

"When are you leaving for Italy?" Will asked.

"Tomorrow. The weather prediction is good. So when is everyone else going?"

"We're leaving tomorrow morning for Colorado," Will replied. "Caroline is hyped over going and she is almost climbing the walls now," he said, smiling at her and Caroline giggled.

"Garrett, when do you leave?"

"We'll go to my folks' house Thursday. We're going out with Sophia's friends Friday night."

"Ryan, what about you?"

"I'm leaving to go back to Houston. I need to see if I still have a drilling business, I've been gone so long. Meg and I have parties Friday night, Saturday night and Sunday night. Meg's a party girl."

"Meg?" Zach asked. "Should I know who Meg is?"

"No. I can answer for him," Will said. "Meg is just the most recent." He grinned at Ryan. "You two are kids, still doing kid stuff," Will teased.

"May be kid stuff, but it's fun. At least I'm not so decrepit I have to sit around someone's home each of those nights," he teased.

"And Zach in Italy. Who is the latest beautiful lady?"

"I'll be alone at my villa, which is fine."

"Well, all of you should come to Colorado. This is going to be the best ever Christmas," he said, smiling at Ava and then at Caroline. "We have a Santa suit for Muffy that Caroline thinks Muffy loves to wear. We'll have worlds of fun and if anyone wants to come afterwards to ski and enjoy Colorado, you're invited. Except our invalid."

"Not an invalid any longer," Zach said. "Doc's given me a big okay and I can do whatever I want. We didn't discuss skiing."

"C'mon, Zach," Ryan said. "Garrett, you, too. Let's fly

up there after Christmas and ski. I'll come, Will, right after New Year's if you're staying that long."

"Sure. All of you come join us. You can bring anyone you want with you."

"I'll see how it goes in Italy," Zach said. "I doubt if I'll be back that soon."

"The bird has flown the coop again," Will teased. "You just can't stay put. We'll see you next summer."

"I'll pass this time, but thanks," Garrett said. "I'm building furniture and Sophia is painting."

"Still the workaholic," Ryan stated. "Some things never change."

They ate ribs until they had a platter filled with bones. When they finished, they all cleaned up and soon they returned to the family room to open gifts.

The first gift went to Caroline and her eyes sparkled as she unwrapped a box that held a new doll. She gave Zach a hug and he smiled at her. "Merry Christmas, sweetie," he said, wishing Emma was with him.

After the gifts were unwrapped and stacked neatly to go, Zach said he had something else for them.

He left and returned with a box holding the gold pocket watch, the Colt revolver and the Henry rifle. "My secretary and I have been through a lot of the memorabilia. I don't know why these things were buried under the letters. So far, we found these three items. Why doesn't each family take one. We can draw if you want to see who gets what, regarding this stuff."

"You ought to have something," Garrett said. "Leave me out. These are Delaney possessions and I'm not a Delaney."

"Sophia is," Zach said immediately. "There was a locket that I gave to my secretary. Sorry, I didn't wait to ask you, Sophia, when I gave Emma the necklace. She has pored over this stuff and enjoyed it. You'd think these people were related to her."

"That's fine, Zach," Sophia said. "Really. I don't need it and it's nice you gave it to her."

"Sophia, you participate," Zach said. "I'm staying out of it because all of you know I don't care about the letters and the ancestors and our past. It's history."

"Our parents weren't sentimental, and you're really a chip off the old block," Will said.

"Now that remark and comparison, I can do without." Zach scribbled out words on three pieces of paper and wadded each up. "We can draw or you can each say what you want and see if anyone else wants it. Or we can go in order of age."

"Hand us the papers and that will be that," Will said.

Zach held out his hand and in seconds Will picked up the Henry rifle, Ryan the Colt revolver and Sophia the pocket watch. "Okay. Is everyone happy with what you got?" Zach asked.

"Sure," Ryan said, rubbing his hand along the Colt. "This is excellent."

"I love this watch—more than I would the rifle or the revolver," Sophia said. "I would like one of the letters to put with it."

"Good choice. I like the watch," Garrett said, exchanging a smile with his wife.

"Go to the office and pick out whatever letters you want," Zach instructed. "We can divide them all three ways when someone finishes going through them."

"These things are treasures," Ryan said, continuing to turn the revolver in his hand.

"The Henry rifle is fantastic. I'm definitely happy," Will added.

It was late afternoon when Garrett stood. "We need to get home because we're flying back to Dallas."

Ryan stood and gathered his gifts. "I'll go, too. Soon I'll fly out for a tropical paradise, palm trees and warm breezes and a beautiful woman."

"Won't seem like Christmas," Will said. "Of course, you may not care. I'll bet you'll be ready for snow-covered mountains before New Year's."

"Probably will," Ryan replied cheerfully.

"You can bring your friend with you."

Ryan winked. "I think I'll come alone and see if I can find a new friend. See you in the summer, Zach, and thanks."

"You're welcome. I'll let your drivers know you're going."

Zach saw them out, then returned to join Will and Ava while Caroline played with her new doll. "Want one more beer? You don't have to go because they did."

"Sure, I'll have a beer. Is your foot hurting?"

"No. It's healed," Zach said, getting two beers from the bar.

"You don't look so great. Anything worrying you?"

"No. Maybe you're getting me mixed up with Ryan. He's the one who's always got a smile. Remember, I don't have his rosy outlook on life. This is my natural look all the time."

"I know that, but you aren't usually as quiet as today and you look as if something's on your mind besides Christmas and us."

"Actually, Christmas hasn't been on my mind, which I'm sure, surprises no one. "

"What do you think about the prospects for the Cowboys this next year?"

"Great," Will answered and the talk shifted to football and then moved to business while they told each other what the current projects were.

When Ava and Will finally stood to go, he paused. "Will you come back from Italy or just go to a job site?"

"Probably just go to a site. I'm through here, so I'm dumping the letters and memorabilia. It's up to you and Ryan now. Garrett, too, if you can rope him into it because of Sophia."

"I'll see. So you sent your secretary back to the Dallas office."

"Yes. We won't see each other again. She turned out to be efficient and good, Will. She's read a mountain of old letters."

"I don't want to shred them. She's right about a tie to our past."

"With time they'll disintegrate. She copied some of them carefully and put them in a scrapbook between clear acid-free sheets. She said that way we can make copies for family members who want them."

"I'm astounded they got through our parents without being destroyed. You know Mom wouldn't care at all about them. Dad didn't until the end of his life."

"Frankly, I can't work up a lot of interest."

Will chuckled. "So how did she get you to go home for Thanksgiving with her? Is there something going on here that I haven't been told?"

"Will, don't quiz your brother about his personal life," Ava said, smiling at Will. "Caroline and I will say goodbye. The ribs were delicious and thank you for the gifts. You know we'll all love everything."

"Merry Christmas, Ava," Zach said, walking her and Caroline outside. "Take care of him."

"Merry Christmas, Zach. I intend to," she answered and waited while he hugged Caroline before the two of them climbed into the limo to wait for Will.

"So how did your secretary get you to go home for Thanksgiving with her?" Will persisted.

"I think she's trying to rescue me. You can't imagine how sorry she feels for me and how much sympathy I get."

"Sympathy." The word burst from Will and he started laughing. "She feels sorry for you because you don't celebrate these holidays. Does she know how you live and how much money you spend whooping it up on holidays?"

Zach grinned as he shook his head.

"So she made you go home with her for Thanksgiving. Now what in the world incentive did she use to get you to do that?"

"Mind your own business, Will. And the best possible incentive of all."

"I never ever thought I'd see the day."

"You haven't seen it yet. Don't worry, there isn't anything serious between us and there won't be. She is one hundred percent a homebody. I'm almost one hundred percent traveler. That's not a good fit and we both know it."

"Yeah, right," Will said, smiling. "By the way, you didn't tell me that she's gorgeous. I know now why from the first you didn't want me to get someone else to work for you."

"She's an efficient secretary."

"With drop-dead looks. Well, merry Christmas," Will said, impulsively hugging his brother. Startled Zach hugged Will in return.

"I think Caroline and Ava are changing you," Zach said, stepping back. "It's a good change, Will. None of us wanted to turn out to be like Dad."

"Sure as hell not. He was as cold as ice until Caroline came along. She'll never know how she has affected this family."

"All for the better and you're good for her."

"I'm trying. Ava's the one."

"It's you, too. Don't sell yourself short," he said following Will to the limo door. The driver held it. "Merry Christmas, Will. Thanks for my presents."

Zach stepped back and watched as the driver closed the door and went around to get behind the wheel. He continued watching the limo go down the drive, but his thoughts were on Emma. Tomorrow he was scheduled to leave for a night in New York and then to Italy. Right now, he didn't feel inclined to leave Texas. This was home more than Italy. He was comfortable here. He had to admit, he was a lot closer here to Emma than he would be in Italy. If he just had to see her, he could in only a few hours' time. From Italy, it would be a real trek.

Jamming his hands into his pockets, he went back to the empty house. How could it seem so big and empty with Emma gone? What was she doing at this moment? Did she miss being with him?

Inside, he closed the front doors and heard the locks click in place. He stood in the entryway and debated whether to call her. It was pointless, so he went to the office, pausing beneath the mistletoe. He reached up to take down the decoration, turning it in his hands, remembering her kisses. Sex with Emma had been the best ever. Of all women, Emma was the only one who had created sparks the first moment they looked at each other. She definitely was the only one to include him in her family gatherings, the only one to make him rethink his past, the only one he had ever really missed.

With a sigh he tossed the mistletoe on a table. He didn't expect her to be back at the ranch ever.

He didn't want to go to New York tomorrow. He picked up his cell to tell his pilot they weren't going until later in the week. He didn't have to be anywhere at any specific time so there was no rush to leave Texas.

Tuesday afternoon he didn't feel any more inclined to leave for New York and Italy than he had on Monday. Even without Emma, he would rather be at the ranch than in an empty house in Italy. He didn't want to ruin his pilot's Christmas, just because he didn't care about his own, so he told his pilot he would stay in Texas until after the holiday. If he decided to go, he could catch a commercial flight. Or just go to New York and spend Christmas there.

Feeling glum, he reached for his phone to call Emma just to talk. How many times he had done that the past few days, and then decided he wouldn't call her?

He was restless and nothing interested him. Emma occupied his thoughts most of his waking hours.

Startling him, he received a call on his cell phone. Shaking his head, he was tempted to not answer when he saw it was from Will. Afraid it would be an emergency, he said hello.

"Zach, it's Will. Where are you? Italy or Texas?"

Zach swore and gritted his teeth. Will usually didn't call until Christmas day. "I'm still in Texas, but will go to Italy soon."

"I just thought you might still be in Texas. What's wrong?" Will asked.

"There's nothing wrong. Staying here is just easier."

"Right," Will said. "Could it be that you miss Emma? I imagine she invited you to spend Christmas with her family. You could, you know," Will said without giving Zach time to answer his question.

"I am not spending Christmas with Emma and sixty other Hillmans."

"So then pack and go to Italy. You'll forget her and get over her."

"Thanks. I plan to go to Italy. I'm just not in a rush," he said, thinking he wasn't going to get over Emma anytime soon.

"Well, I know it's a safe bet you haven't fallen in love, so I'll stop worrying about you. You can still fly up here if you want. Caroline will take your mind off Emma. Caroline is having a blissful time. Christmas is magical for her and she's turning it into magic for us."

"That's great, Will," Zach said with sincerity.

"Even Muffy is enjoying the snow. We have to clear paths

for her or she'll sink out of sight. Give some thought to join-ing us."

"Thanks. Bye, Will," Zach said and ended the call without giving Will a chance to prolong it.

Zach returned to staring at smoldering logs in his fireplace while Emma filled his thoughts. Did she miss him or was she immersed in family Christmas activities? He held up his phone, tempted to call her, finally giving in to the temptation.

At first he thought she wasn't going to answer, but then he heard her voice and his heart skipped beats.

"Zach, you're calling from Italy?"

"I haven't gone yet. I'm going to New York first," he said. "Ready for Christmas?"

"Hardly, but I will be soon. Something's always going on around here. People coming over or someone wanting me to do something or Mom needs help. I'm busier than ever. Have you heard from Will or Ryan?"

"Will today. They're having a great time," he said, long-ing to be with her. The phone call only made him miss her more and he felt ridiculous for calling. "I'll have to admit, the place seems empty with you gone."

There was a long silence. "I miss being there."

"No, you don't, really," he said, smiling, certain she didn't, but he hoped she missed him.

"I do miss you," she said solemnly in a quiet voice that made his heart lurch. He inhaled deeply, wanting her with him, in his arms now.

"Will you go out with me for New Year's Eve? I'll come home if you will."

There was another long pause and he held his breath. "Yes," she said. "The sensible part of me says no and I'm sure you feel the same."

"We'll have a good time," he said lightly, his heart racing with eagerness that he would see her again and go out with her. He settled back to talk, asking about her family, enjoying listening to her, glad for this tenuous connection that was still a link with her.

They talked for over an hour before Emma broke in. "Zach, my family is calling me. I promised I'd go shopping and they're waiting for me to join them."

"Sure. See you New Year's," he said.

The connection ended and he felt more alone than he had in years. He wanted Emma with him. How could she have taken such a place in his life that he couldn't get along without her now?

New Year's Eve seemed an eternity away. He stretched and walked around restlessly. He couldn't concentrate on work. He didn't want to go to Italy. He didn't want to join Will because all he would do was think about Emma.

He left to head for his gym while he stayed lost in thought about her.

Emma hurried out to join her sisters and mother to spend the afternoon shopping, but the entire time, she couldn't keep Zach out of mind. She was going out with him for New Year's Eve. Surprise had been her first reaction. She was astounded he wanted to pursue a relationship. She had debated only a moment with herself. Now that she was carrying his baby, everything had changed. Whether she or Zach liked it or not, she would be tied to him for years. Unless he totally rejected his child and she didn't think he would. Not when he seemed to care so much for his niece. She still couldn't accept having a casual relationship with him, but she would just have to see how he reacted and what he wanted.

The aching gloom that had enveloped her when she parted with him had lifted, leaving only worry over his reaction to her news. Excitement, joy over the prospect of an evening with him was tinged with concern over when and how to break the news to him about their baby. If he rejected this child, he would break her heart. Even though he had rejected her lifestyle and hadn't wanted her in his life permanently, this baby was more important now and life had changed.

By five in the afternoon, she was exhausted from shopping and wanted to go home and take a nap. She suspected her mother might be wearing down also, so she told Mary Kate she thought they should call it a day.

It was almost six before they actually unloaded the car and were settled back at home. Emma headed to her room, leaving her packages to get later. All she wanted to do was stretch out and get a quick snooze.

She hadn't been in bed five minutes when there was a knock on her door and Mary Kate appeared.

"Can I talk to you a minute?" she asked, stepping into the bedroom and closing the door. She shook her dark brown hair away from her face as she crossed the room. Her tan sweater emphasized gold flecks in her hazel eyes.

"Sure, come in. Does Mom need help with dinner?"

"No, she's lying down, too, and Sierra has gone home with her brood. So has Lynne to relieve Connor of watching their kids. They all promised to come back after a while." Mary Kate sat on the edge of the bed.

"You've got all the energy," Emma remarked.

"How are you feeling?"

"Tired. We did a lot of shopping and I guess the work I've been doing and the Christmas stuff has caught up with me. I'm sleepy."

"Sure. You were sick this morning when I came."

Emma sat up slightly. "Whatever it was, it passed."

"You know I'm here for you," Mary Kate said, her hazel eyes filled with concern and Emma took a deep breath.

"How did you know?" Emma asked, certain her sister had guessed she was pregnant.

Nine

Mary Kate shrugged. "I've been there," she said, tugging up the sleeves of her tan sweater.

Emma sat up. "You haven't been there as a single mom. Not in this family. MK," she said, reverting to the nickname, "I don't know what I'm going to do." she said. Tears threatened and she tried to get a grip on her emotions.

Mary Kate hugged her and Emma clung tightly to the sister who had stood by her through so many childhood scrapes.

As she released her sister, Emma wiped her eyes. "This was unplanned, unexpected and shouldn't have ever happened. I'm carrying Zach's baby."

"Zach Delaney. Boy, you picked one. That's what I was afraid of. Does he know?"

"No, not yet."

"Do you have any idea how he will react?"

"Not really. He seems crazy about his niece, but he's taken no responsibility for her. When her father was killed, Zach's older brother became guardian. Zach is solitary, a total loner and happy in that life. He rarely comes home. He works abroad, all over the world and loves what he does. He doesn't need the money. He travels to dangerous places and he likes it."

"I thought I heard you say he's in demolition."

"Yes. His company has other businesses, but that's the one he loves and takes an active part in. A big active part. That's how he hurt his foot. Somehow, I can't see him taking this well at all. He doesn't have serious relationships. I wonder if he goes out much because of his lifestyle. He keeps to himself and spends holidays alone, including Christmas."

"Christmas—alone? Through his own choice?"

"Yes."

Her sister's frown reflected her own feelings about Zach's view of holidays. "Wow. Well, even if he has nothing to do with you or the baby, you have a family who will be right with you."

"If Connor doesn't try to punch Zach."

Mary Kate laughed. "He won't. Connor grumbles, but he's too much like Dad to resort to fists unless someone else starts something. Do you think Zach will give you any financial support?"

"I'm guessing he will, but I don't know. If he doesn't offer, I'm not pursuing it. I'll manage and he paid me extravagantly for the job I just did, plus I have a good job with his company and money saved. I'll manage."

"I'm sure you will," Mary Kate said, shifting to a more comfortable seat on the side of the bed. "What about your education and a teaching job? That's what you've always wanted."

"I think that will have to be postponed," Emma said. "I'll use this money for the baby. Later on, I hope I can pick up where I left off, go back to college, get my degree and then teach."

"I hope Zach Delaney does what's right and gives you financial support. Marriage sounds like an unlikely event."

"It's impossible. He's totally solitary. MK, how will I tell Mom and Dad? It's Dad I'm worried about. I think this will break his heart. And I know—I should have thought of that before now."

"You're not getting a lecture from me. Dad's able to take news and he'll help you and so will Mom. I know it's hard to think about telling them, but don't worry about it. Just do it and get it over with."

"I'm waiting until after Christmas and you wait, too."

Mary Kate ran her fingers over her lips. "Absolutely. This is your deal to tell the family, not mine. I'm just here for you. And don't expect it to be long before Mom catches on. She's been through this five times."

"I know."

I better go see what the kiddos are doing. Bobby's watching them and he's as much a kid as they are. Holler if you want to talk again."

"Thanks, MK."

"Sure."

Emma settled back against pillows and watched her sister leave the room. She could count on MK. Actually, she could count on her whole family. It was just Zach who was an unknown factor.

She thought about New Year's Eve. That would be the time to break the news. As soon as Christmas had passed, she would tell the family.

She missed Zach. How long would she continue to miss him? Months, years, forever?

Christmas Eve morning, Zach sat at his desk trying to think about work and finding it impossible. Emma dominated his thoughts every waking hour. He hadn't gone to Italy and he still didn't want to go. He wouldn't do any more in Italy than he would on the ranch, so he just stayed. He felt closer to Emma here and the house reminded him of moments she had been there. How many times during the week had he pulled out his phone and started to call her?

He tossed his pen and rubbed the back of his neck. He wanted to see her and he was tired of trying to think about work and failing completely.

The phone rang and he saw the caller ID indicated Will, which was no surprise. Zach was tempted to avoid answering and the questions that would follow. Taking a deep breath, he picked up his phone to talk.

"Yes, Will, I'm here at the ranch. I decided to stay in Texas." He tried to put some cheer in his voice and realized he was failing.

"Are you sick?"

"No, I'm not."

"Is Rosie there?"

"No. You know I gave her and Nigel three weeks off. I'm okay. Merry Christmas. Let me talk to Caroline."

He talked briefly to his niece and she suddenly said goodbye and Will returned. "We're getting snow. How's the weather there?"

"I know you didn't call to get a weather report."

"No, I didn't. Just some small talk while I walked into another room and closed the door for privacy. Zach, if you're in love with Emma, do something about it. You might have to live life a little more on the ordinary side like the rest of us do."

Zach had to laugh. "And a merry Christmas to you, too, Dr. Phil. Stop giving me advice."

"Okay, but this is so unlike you. Do you want to fly up here today and spend tomorrow with us? I promise we're fun."

"I'm sure you're fun galore, but I'm happy here," he said,

giving some thought to Will's invitation. For the first time, he was slightly tempted, but he still preferred Texas where he was closer to Emma. "When have I not been happy alone?"

"Maybe since you met Emma Hillman. Well, you're a grown man and I won't give you advice, just an invitation. And a merry Christmas."

"Thanks, Will. Thanks for calling and for your invitation. I really mean it. Merry Christmas to you all."

As he hung up, Zach had to smile over his brother's ridiculous call. He paced restlessly and then stopped to look down at the largest box of memorabilia. He pulled up a chair and picked up a letter to read.

"All right, Emma. I'll try again to find something fascinating in my ancestors' lives."

He read two letters and tossed both in the discard box. He picked up another and saw it was his written by his great-great-grandfather during the second year of the Civil War.

"My dearest Tabitha:

"My love, we covered twenty miles today in the rain. It is dark and cold now and I write by firelight. I am glad we did not encounter any of our enemy because our ammunition and our supplies run low. I am fortunate to have both my rifle and my revolver, plus ammunition. Others are not so fortunate. This ghastly war between the States is tearing our country apart. My dearest, how I miss you! If I could just hold you against my heart. You and our son.

"This fighting is lonely and desperate. How I long to be with you this night and see your smile, that would be a Christmas treasure to me. Know that I send my love to you on this Christmas night. You and our little one are the most important part of my life and what I am fighting for. I dream of peace for our babe and his descendants and their offspring. How I wish I could see our son, this precious babe. My heart aches with wanting to be with you and my child on this night.

*Nothing else on this earth matters, but I fight to keep life se-
cure for the two of you."*

For the first time Zach felt a thread of kinship with this
ancestor from generations earlier. Feeling foolish for his
emotional reaction to the old letter, Zach continued to read.
*"I close my eyes and imagine you holding out your arms
and smiling at me. Someday, my love, we will be together
again. Know that I send my love to you and our son on this
Christmas night."* He could be saying those words to Emma.
Leaning back in his chair, Zach watched flames dance in the
fireplace. He missed Emma. He could imagine the ache in
his relative's life on a cold Christmas night away from his
young wife and a baby.

He picked up the letter to continue reading:

*"Know you are my life and you and our offspring have my
love always. I want this land to be safe for our son and his
sons. My family I hold dearest of everything on this earth. I
dream of when I can come home and we are together once
again. My love, how I long to hold you close to my heart. All
my love to you from your adoring husband, Warner Irwin
Delaney."*

Zach had a tightening in his chest and he placed the letter
in the discard box with the others without thinking about what
he was doing. As he finished reading, all his thoughts focused
on Emma and the letter. She would have been touched by it.

Was he missing out on life as she had said? Was he missing
the most treasured part—a woman's love and a family's love?

He had never really thought marriage could be happy and
filled with love until he had been with Emma's family, because he had never seen a loving family in his own home or
his oldest brother's or even in any of his friends. Garrett's
parents seemed the closest and Garrett had been happy growing up, but the Cantrells had not exhibited the warmth and
closeness the Hillmans had.

Will had not been married long enough for his marriage to count. Will was in euphoria and still steeped in his honeymoon. The Hillman seniors had been married for years and they were obviously in love. Zach had never thought of marrying or having a child—yet he loved Caroline and he barely saw her. How much more would he love one of his own that he saw often? Surely he would love his offspring deeply, and, if he ever had any, he intended to give them all the time and attention he possibly could.

Emma was a steadying influence, her calm faith in love, her cheer, her optimism—maybe he desperately needed that in his life. He needed her. It was still Christmas Eve morning. He reached for his phone and made arrangements to get the plane ready to fly to Dallas. He had to see Emma.

Christmas Eve at four in the afternoon Emma rushed back to her apartment. It was already getting dark outside with an overcast gray sky and a light snow predicted. Carrying an armload of packages, she hurried into her apartment building to be stopped by the doorman.

"Miss Hillman, you have a delivery."

Surprised, she waited while he disappeared into the office and returned with a red crystal vase that held several dozen red roses and stems of holly.

"That's for me?" she said, glancing at the packages filling her arms. "I'll come back to get it."

"I'll bring it up. I didn't want to leave it in the hall."

"Thank you." At her apartment she unlocked the door and stepped back to let him carry the bouquet inside and set it down.

"Merry Christmas, Miss Hillman. You have beautiful flowers."

"Thank you. Merry Christmas to you, Mr. Wilburton," she said, tipping him for carrying up her flowers.f

She dropped her packages and closed the door, hearing the lock click in place. The flowers had to be from Zach. She pulled out a card, looking at a familiar scrawling handwriting that she had seen so many times in the past few weeks.

"Merry Christmas, Emma. Zach." A pang rocked her. How she wished he were here! She missed him more each day and tried to avoid thinking about it if she could. With a glance at her watch, she realized she should get ready soon to join her family.

Hurrying to hang up her coat, she turned on her Christmas lights.

Lights sparkled on her tall green Douglas fir that held sparse ornaments, which she added to each Christmas. She had greenery and candles on her mantel, a wreath on her door and a dining room centerpiece of holly around the base of a large poinsettia that had been given to her by friends from her office.

This year she had added something new. She looked at the sprig of mistletoe she had hung above the doorway into the dining area. The mistletoe made her think of Zach and their mistletoe kisses. She wondered how he was enjoying his Italian villa. For all she knew, he might not be alone there.

Usually Christmas Eve filled her with anticipation and excitement, but this year she missed Zach and she could not keep from worrying about her baby and breaking the news to her family. In spite of her sister's reassurances, telling the family was going to be difficult, making her worry how they would take it. An even bigger concern was how Zach would accept the news.

She picked up all her packages to carry them to her bedroom and open them. She had been buying baby things because she was excited and wanted to get ready even if it was early. A bassinet stood by the window and she had a new rocking chair that had been delivered two days earlier. She began to open packages and finally had the new baby clothes laid out across her bed where she could look at them. They would all go into the wash, but she wanted to look at them first: the tiny onesies, tiny socks, little jumpers and bibs, rattles and a baby brush, plus small blankets.

She ran her fingers over the blankets. Even if Zach wanted to marry, which she knew he would not, she couldn't accept his lifestyle. He still wouldn't put family first. Travel and work would always take first place with him and fulfill the need for excitement in his life. It would never be family that would hold his interest. Sadness tinged her excitement over the baby. Sadness and worry about her baby's acceptance.

She showered to get ready to go to her parents' house for dinner and then a midnight service. Her new Christmas dress was a red crepe with a low V-neck and long sleeves. The skirt ended above her knees and she had matching high-heeled pumps. She caught her hair back on either side of her face and had clips with sprigs of holly attached. Last of all, she fastened the gold locket, stepping close to the mirror to look at it and rub the gold lightly with her finger as if she could conjure up Zach by doing so.

Startling her, her intercom buzzed. She answered to hear Mr. Wilburton.

"May I come back a moment? There's something else here."

"Sure, come up. I'll open the door," she answered, curious what he had. She gathered things to put into her purse until the bell rang. Wondering what he had forgotten, she hurried to the door to open it.

The first thing she saw was a huge stack of packages that hid the doorman.

"Come in," she said, wondering how Mr. Wilburton could have forgotten a mountain of gifts.

He turned slightly and she faced Zach. "Merry Christmas, Emma."

Stunned, she could only stare at him. "Zach? You're here? It's Christmas Eve. Where's Mr. Wilburton?"

Zach laughed. "These packages are getting heavy. Can I come in?"

Ten

"Come in," she said, her heart racing as she took presents off the top of his stack.

He rushed to her sofa to set them all down while she closed the door and trailed behind him. He was in a black topcoat over his suit. When he turned, she took one look in his eyes and she was in his arms. He had brought a rush of cold air in and his coat still was cold and smelled of the outside. As she slid her arms beneath his coat and jacket, he felt warm, holding her tightly against him while they kissed.

Her heart thudded with joy. Giddy to see him, laughter bubbled inside her. She was overwhelmed by surprise.

Desire raged, more than all else, and she pushed the topcoat away, hearing it fall to the floor. His suit jacket went with it. With shaking fingers, she unfastened the buttons to his snowy shirt. He held her away to look at her, taking in her red dress before he kissed her again.

Picking her up in his arms, Zach carried her to her bedroom while he kissed her. Emma clung to him, wrapped in his embrace and filled with longing. When he set her on her feet, she could feel his hands at the top of her zipper as he started to draw it down.

His hands grew still and he raised his head. "Is one of your sisters expecting?"

Startled, she looked up at him. "No, neither one." Zach looked beyond her at the bed and then his gaze went around the room and she realized why.

"Emma, that's a lot of baby clothes and a lot of baby things. More than you'd take to a shower."

His questioning gaze returned to her. Her heart drummed and her palms became damp. She hadn't expected Zach. All the most recent baby things were laid out. Her mouth went dry and she felt weak in the knees.

"I know only one way to tell you. I'm pregnant," she whispered.

"You're pregnant?" Sounding stunned, he stepped back to look at her. "You don't look it. You have all this ready for a baby. Are you sure? When are you due?"

"I've been to a doctor now. When I found out for certain, I couldn't wait to buy things. I know it's too early, Zach. I'm barely pregnant, but I'm excited. This isn't the way I was going to tell you, or this soon. I know you have your life and you're not the daddy type—"

"And you're not the single-mom type. I'm going to be a dad," he said and silence stretched between them. Suddenly his hands closed on her waist and he held her up while he gave a whoop.

"A dad! Emma, love," he said, setting her down and wrapping his arms around her to kiss her hard and long.

Shocked by his reaction, the last possible thing she had expected, she stood immobile for seconds until she caught her breath. Wrapping her arms around him, she held him tightly to kiss him back.

He stopped as abruptly as he started. "You're sure?"

"Absolutely. The doctor says yes. The pregnancy test was positive. My body is changing. Ask Rosie. And Mary Kate guessed."

"Rosie?" he said, looking stunned. "You knew then?"

"I suspected, but it was really early. Rosie did, too."

He laughed. "Emma, that's fabulous. We're going to be parents. My precious love, I came to ask you to marry me." He knelt on one knee and took her hand. "Emma Hillman, I love you and want you to be my wife. Will you marry me?"

"Zach, get up," she said, her smile fading because she hurt badly. He had just proposed, saying words she hadn't been able to avoid dreaming about, but there was only one answer. She looked up at him as he stood. "I love you and I'm thrilled and scared about the baby, but, Zach, we can't marry. Our lifestyles are poles apart. You wouldn't be happy. I wouldn't be happy with you gone all the time."

"Emma, we have to work this out," he said, framing her face with his hands. "I've been miserable without you. You've made me see a family can be happy and love each other. We'll work this out."

"I can't. You'll be gone and you do risky things. You won't be there to be a dad."

"Yes, I will," he said patiently. "And love isn't in one place or in a house. It's between two people. Your parents would have had the same love if your dad had traveled. You have to agree on that one."

"I guess they would have, but I don't want a dad who's gone all the time."

"I won't be. I can work more in the Dallas office and let others do the on-site requirements. For heaven's sake, I own the place. I don't have to go out and do hands-on work. I don't even have to work if I don't want to."

She didn't dare breathe as her whole being tingled and

hope flared. "You might not be happy with a desk job," she said, wondering if she dared accept his complete reversal of his lifestyle.

"I don't want to be away from you."

"You would do that?"

"Of course. Emma, you've made me open my heart and trust someone to return my love. Don't turn around and crush that now. I love you and I want to marry you. Besides that, it's been pure hell without you."

She trembled, wanting to believe him, scared to do so. "Rosie said you couldn't change."

"Well, there are some things Rosie doesn't know about me. She doesn't know I have fallen in love with the most wonderful woman in the world."

Unable to smile because of the moment for a life-changing decision, Emma stood looking into his eyes. They were both taking chances, but they loved each other and love was too precious to toss aside. As her decision came, she trembled. "Yes, I'll marry you," she answered, wrapping her arms around his neck to kiss him. Excitement and joy blossomed, enveloping her. Tears of happiness spilled down her cheeks.

"Don't cry. Not even happy tears," he said. "Darlin', this is too fabulous for even one tear. Marriage to you will be the most wonderful thing in my life. You're right, Emma. What counts in life is the people you love."

After a moment he raised his head. "How far along are you?"

"Just barely pregnant," she answered, smiling at him.

He looked beyond her at the bed covered in baby clothes. "Isn't this really premature?"

"It is, but I'm excited."

"And your family? They may not be happy with me, but when they hear we're getting married, they should be okay. Do you think?"

"They don't know. It's early, Zach. Mary Kate knows. She guessed and we're close so she asked me. No one else knows."

"Then don't tell them yet," he said. "Tonight let's announce we're getting married. Let's marry on Christmas." He smiled. "I don't want to wait any longer anyway."

"That's not possible, Zach. That's tomorrow."

"I know when Christmas is. Unless you have your heart set on a big wedding, we'll marry tomorrow with just your family. That's enough people to fill the church."

"What about your brothers and your half sister and her husband, whom you're close to?"

"Listen to me," he said. "We marry tomorrow. Then we're off on a honeymoon and I'll get you out of the state of Texas. First, the Italian villa and then Paris and back to New York, Niagra Falls and then home. How does that sound?"

"Impossible."

"No, it's not. We can get a church and just have the family and get married tomorrow afternoon. Then when we come back from a honeymoon we can have a big reception and invite everyone, including my family. We can announce the baby whenever you're ready."

Too thrilled to plan anything, she laughed. "It still sounds impossible. As a matter of fact, I have to be at my folks' home at six tonight. It's already after five."

"We have time to make some decisions. If you run late, you can call and tell them you're on your way."

"I go for the evening. We all eat there and then we go to midnight church service together. Will you go with me?"

He kissed her lightly on the forehead. "Of course, I'll go."

She smiled. "Why didn't you call me?" she asked, running her fingers over his shoulder.

"I should have, but I was going as fast as I could. I just decided to come this morning."

"You came from Italy?"

"No, I never did go to Italy," he said. "I missed you too much. Italy seemed empty and unappealing. My heart was here in Texas."

Her heart missed a beat as she gazed up at him. She combed her fingers through his thick hair. "I feel as if I haven't seen you for a long, long time."

"I know. That's the way I feel about you," he said. "I couldn't wait until New Year's Eve."

"I'm stunned," she said. "I thought you were in Italy. You said you were going."

"Italy lost its appeal and I kept putting it off until it seemed pointless to go. I've missed you," he said solemnly and another wave of happiness swamped her. She kissed him lightly on the lips.

"Zach, no one will marry us on such short notice, and not on Christmas."

"Sure they will," he replied. "Maybe you're not the optimist I thought you were. I think I can get our minister to do the ceremony. I'll call him unless you want to ask yours first."

"You get your minister. I can't imagine calling any minister on Christmas Eve and asking him to marry us on Christmas Day. That's wild, Zach," she said, dazed and unable to believe she was marrying him. "We don't have a license. We don't have what we need."

"I'll call my attorney and get him moving. He'll get it worked out. We can still marry in the church tomorrow."

"This is crazy. What'll I wear?"

"You'll look beautiful in whatever you wear and we can go from here to a dress shop and then to your parents' house. I know the perfect store and I'll see if they'll stay open until we get there."

She listened as he talked to his lawyer and her incredulity deepened. Everything seemed impossible. It was turning into a magical Christmas where the impossible became possible. Mrs. Zachary Delaney. Was she rushing headlong into disaster or into paradise? Right now, she viewed it as paradise. Zach had already made astounding changes in his life.

He called a store and talked briefly. "Grab what you need," he said to Emma. "They were just about to close, but she'll wait. You can find something you like there."

"What store?"

He told her the name of an exclusive shop that was far beyond her budget and she had never crossed the threshold even to look there.

"Zach, are you certain? We're really rushing into this and you just blithely said you'd change your whole way of living."

"I sure did. That's how much I love you. Wait a minute." He rummaged through the mound of presents he had brought with him and returned swiftly to hand her a gift in a small box wrapped in green foil paper with a red ribbon and sprigs of artificial mistletoe in the bow.

"It's too pretty to open."

"Open it. What's inside may be prettier."

She opened it with shaking fingers and he caught her hand. "You're shaking."

She looked up. "I'm thrilled and happy and so in love. And my whole life is changing before my eyes. I'm scared."

He hugged her. "I love you, Emma," he said quietly and firmly in his deep voice. "Truly love you with all my heart and want to make you happy. You think I want to be off blowing up some building when I can be home in bed with you every night?"

She laughed while tears stung her eyes. He tilted her face up. "Don't cry, love. I love you and I don't want to ever hurt you."

"Tears of joy, Zach," she whispered, wiping her eyes. She opened the box and a dazzling diamond glittered in the light. "Zach, it's magnificent," she gasped.

He removed the ring and placed it on her finger. "Emma, will you marry me?" he asked again.

"Yes, Zach," she said and kissed him.

In seconds he released her. "We better run."

"Let me think. You've got me so rattled. I'm supposed to be taking something to my parents. It's a chocolate cheesecake from the fridge. Let me get it."

She hurried to the kitchen and returned to the living room where she stopped to look at her sofa. "Zach, what are all these presents?"

"They're your Christmas presents from me. I had the ones for your family sent out to your parents' house."

"How'd you know you'd even be invited?"

He grinned. "C'mon. Someone's holding open a store for us."

She shook her head as she pulled on her coat. He carried the chocolate cheesecake that was in a plastic container.

He had a limo waiting and she climbed into the back. The limo gave her pause, a sobering moment, because it brought back how much Zach was worth. "Zach, you are part of the Delaney fortune that has been well publicized. I don't see a bodyguard."

"I have one at times. He's not with us now because our driver can cover if needed, but Will's the one in the limelight. I'm not in papers and haven't been in the country lately. Ryan could pass for any cowboy in west Texas. He's not in papers a lot either. Besides that, Ryan's a tough cowboy and he looks like the type to be packing. If I were going after a Delaney, I'd put Ryan at the bottom of the list. Ryan and I are both low-key and I don't feel threatened."

"I'm thinking about your baby."

"Don't worry about it. I'll have all the security you and I both feel we need. A baby is different. We'll have plenty of security."

She realized her life was changing drastically as she looked at her fiancé whom she loved with all her being. She pulled out her cell phone. "I want to call and let Mom and Dad know you're coming with me. Then it won't be a surprise when you walk in."

"Good idea. My presents should have arrived."

In minutes she put away her phone. "They'll be glad to see you. And they did get your presents. How in the world did you know what to buy? And how many to buy for?"

"Someone told me how many were eating Thanksgiving dinner. How many adults and how many kids. They're sort of generic presents. Electronic games for the kids, baskets of fruit for the adults."

She laughed. "Zach, our house will be buried under baskets of fruit."

He grinned and hugged her. Emma held out her hand to look at her ring. "This is the most gorgeous, giant ring I have ever seen."

"I'm glad you like it." He placed his arm around her. "Emma, I read some of the family letters. I got a touching one that you'll have to read. I saw what you were talking about. Somehow with that one letter, I actually did feel a tie to my great-great-grandfather."

"I'm glad, Zach," she said with another increase in her happiness. "I was going to ask for any of the letters you decided to shred because I'll be the mother of a Delaney. And this little Delaney is going to grow up with a love and appreciation of family."

"The mother of a Delaney, my baby's mother," he said. "That sounds wonderful to me. You've given me the best possible Christmas gift I've ever received," he whispered and pulled her close to kiss her. Pausing, he framed her face with his hands. "Emma, you've made up for all those miserable Christmases I had as kid. Will told me once to hang on, that our lives would get better."

"Zach, that makes me hurt for all three of you. But that's all in the past. You'll have so much family stirring around you on holidays, you may miss your solitude."

"No, I won't. Not as long as I have you," he said and kissed her again.

When the limo parked, Zach climbed out to help Emma. "You get whatever you want in here. I'm buying it for you, so don't even ask a price."

The second dress they brought out, a white raw silk with thin straps and a short jacket, was the one. The skirt was slim and came to mid-calf. She liked it immediately and in minutes she said that was the one she wanted. She didn't want Zach to see it until their wedding, so when she came out of the dressing room once again in her Christmas dress, his eyebrows arched.

"What's this?"

"I've picked the dress I want and you're not to see it until tomorrow."

"You've set a record for the fastest woman shopper I've ever seen. I'm falling in love all over again."

She laughed, but she wondered how many women he had taken shopping. In minutes they parked at her parents' house.

"This has to be the most decorated block in all of the state of Texas," Zach said, stepping into bright lights from her parents' decorations.

"Dad started this and then our neighbors began to get into the spirit."

"Thank heaven I'll be able to afford to have someone do ours for us," he said, eyeing her roof. As they walked to the front door, she felt butterflies in her stomach. "Zach, I feel jittery about tonight and having a wedding so fast tomorrow."

"Your family will accept what you want to do," he said.

"Would you rather take your time, marry later and have a big wedding?"

She thought a moment. "No, this is exciting and I think marrying tomorrow is a great idea. We're rushing into this—something I never thought I'd do."

"We're getting married tomorrow—something I never thought *I'd* do," he said with a broad smile and she laughed.

"Let's break the news. Get ready for a hullabaloo," she warned and opened the front door.

"You're right there."

As they walked inside, her dad came forward to greet them. Emma grasped her father's arm. "Dad, get Mom to come here. It's important."

With a glance at Zach, Brody turned to send a granddaughter on the errand and in seconds Emma's mother walked up to greet them and welcome Zach. Family members trailed after her, gathering around them.

"Mom, Dad, before someone notices and asks—Zach has asked me to marry him and I've accepted," she said, holding out her hand to show her engagement ring.

Instantly her mother hugged her while her dad shook hands with Zach and in seconds the whole family huddled around while Emma showed them her engagement ring.

From that moment on she felt as if she were in a dream. She spent an hour on phone calls, making arrangements that she couldn't believe were happening so quickly. She went through dinner in a daze and felt that way afterwards. Constantly, she was aware of Zach, even if he stood across the room. When they drove to church all the kids piled into the limo with them.

"Your life will change drastically," Emma reminded him.

"It already has," he remarked, eyeing the kids surrounding him.

Through the midnight Christmas service Zach sat close beside her. Finally they told everyone good-night and left.

"Emma, you've never even seen my home. Not any of them. Let's go back to my house tonight and I'll take you home as early in the morning as you want."

"All right. Is this where I'm going to live?"

"That's up to you. If you want a new place, I don't care. I got the Dallas place because it's comfortable and a good investment. If you want something else, fine."

"I hope you're always this agreeable."

He smiled. "I'll try. I want to call Ryan and Will. I should call Garrett, too. I want you to meet Ryan and Garrett and Sophia when we get back. I don't expect any of them to come home tomorrow. When we get back from our honeymoon, we can repeat our vows in a big church wedding if you want."

She shook her head. "I'm happy. Let's just have the reception and invite everyone. That'll be a party for all."

His limo entered an exclusive gated suburban area with a gatekeeper. As they wound through the neighborhood, through pines and oaks, she glimpsed twinkling lights indicating homes. Finally they went through another tall iron gate with a gatekeeper who waved.

"I guess I didn't need to worry so much about security."

"I have security. The family ranch is more open, but we had security around the perimeter of the yard and motion lights outside, with someone watching the grounds at night. You just didn't notice."

"You didn't tell me that," she said.

He shrugged. "I didn't expect you to leave in the dead of night without me knowing about it."

In minutes she could see lights through trees on a mansion and when it came into full view, her breath caught. "This is home?" she asked. "It's a resort hotel."

"No, it's not and we can move if you want. You'll see. It's comfortable inside."

"I can imagine," she said, unable to grasp that after tomorrow this would be her home. One of her homes.

"I feel like Cinderella," she whispered.

"And I feel like the luckiest man on earth," he said. "I called ahead and told them we were coming."

"Zach, I'm just now seeing your Dallas home. This reinforces that we barely know each other."

"I know what I want," he replied solemnly. "It's you, Emma, with all my heart. This is a house, maybe big and fancy, but it's just a house I have because of those ancestors you've been reading about and feeling so close to. You know my history, my family, my secrets, my work, me. We know each other. I know your family, your very open book growing up in a happy, loving family. Maybe you're right and you're the wealthier of the two of us," he said with a smile. "We know each other well enough. Our love will cover the rest and discovery sounds wonderful."

She hugged and kissed him briefly and then turned to look at the house. "I'm overwhelmed."

"You'll get used to the place. Nigel will work here when we return from our honeymoon. Rosie sort of goes from family to family."

They stepped out of the limo at the side of the mansion. At the door he unlocked it, picked her up and carried her inside. Setting her on her feet, he turned off the alarm.

"Now the quick tour. When we return from our honeymoon, you can have the full tour of the place."

Dazzled, she felt in a dream once again. They walked through an enormous kitchen with rich, dark wood hiding appliances, granite countertops, a smooth stone floor that held small area rugs. The adjoining informal eating area was as large as the kitchen.

Zach took her hand. "This way. You can look as we go and I'll show you around better later."

They climbed winding stairs and walked down a wide hall that held a strip of thick beige carpet down the center. Zach's bedroom was an enormous suite and the moment she stepped inside, she barely glimpsed polished oak floors, elegant fruitwood furniture and a wide-screen built into a wall.

"Come here. I called this afternoon and told my staff to put this up. Next year I'm sure we'll be as decorated as Rockefeller Center." He led her to a doorway between the sitting room and his bedroom with a massive four-poster king bed. Mistletoe hung in the doorway overhead and Zach stopped beneath it.

"I love you and I can't wait to marry you. In my heart we're already husband and wife," he said.

Her heart thudded with happiness as she hugged him while she kissed him beneath the mistletoe.

Epilogue

"Zach, I still feel like this isn't really happening to me," she said, thinking that was the way she had felt most of the time when they had been in Europe on their honeymoon. She looked at herself in the mirror, her gaze going beyond her image to Zach's. He looked incredibly handsome in his navy suit.

"My love is real, Emma," he said, brushing a kiss and his warm breath on her nape.

"All those wonderful cities and the charming small towns in France, Switzerland, Germany and Italy. They were beautiful and the people were welcoming. The places and buildings were breathtaking, so beautiful. Ah, Zach, I saw them all because of you. I will treasure the memories we have of this trip forever. It was wonderful to go and now it's grand to be home."

"The next long trip will be in this country. I want to show you special places in the U.S."

She smiled. "I'm nervous about meeting Ryan tonight."

Zach laughed. "Of all people on this earth, don't be nervous over Ryan. He's as down to earth as any man can get. He would have flown in to meet you earlier this week when we returned, but he had a bull-riding show in Wyoming or Montana. I don't remember where. Don't be nervous about any of them. Sophia is almost as new to the family as you are. I think you two will become good friends."

"Do you still want to tell my family the news about the baby when we go for Sunday dinner tomorrow?" she asked.

"Yes, unless you want to tell them tonight. We'll tell them and my family and anyone else you want to let know."

"Rosie, even though she guessed, and Nigel."

"Sure. All my staff will be told. I want everyone watching out for you."

She laughed. "Don't make it sound as if I'm an invalid. Let's tell them tomorrow."

"I love you, sweet wife," he whispered and kissed her.

She kissed him passionately, in seconds forgetting the evening until he reached for the zipper of her dress.

"Zach, we have a wedding reception to attend," she said, wriggling away from him and smiling.

"So we do, but I'd rather make love."

"Later," she said.

"Can't wait," he replied. "I'm ready and I'll wait downstairs. You look absolutely gorgeous."

"So do you, Zach," she said, her heart beating with happiness.

An hour later she stood in a country club ballroom talking to Sophia and Ava when she saw Zach and his brother approach. Ryan was tall, handsome, dressed in a black suit and wearing black Western boots.

"Finally you'll meet my brother Ryan. Ryan, meet Emma, my bride."

Ryan hugged her and kissed her cheek. "Welcome to the Delaney family," he said.

"Thank you," she answered. "All of you have made me feel welcome."

Zach clasped his brother on the shoulder. "Ladies, congratulate a champion bull rider. He just won again."

Ryan grinned as he received congratulations and Emma marveled again that the Delaneys resembled each other except for Zach. She couldn't see any similarities in his looks and theirs.

She saw Will and Garrett approaching and their circle enlarged. Will draped his arm around Ava's shoulders. "Caroline is playing with your nieces and nephews and your sister Mary Kate is with them," he said. "I told her to call my cell if I need to come get her."

"Caroline will be fine and Mary Kate loves being with the kids."

The band commenced another song and Ryan turned to Emma. "May I have this dance? If I want to get to know you, we have to get away from this crowd."

She laughed and went with him the short distance to join the dancers.

"You've worked a miracle with my brother," Ryan said. "Will and I are delighted. Sophia hasn't been in this family long enough to know how much he'd changed."

"I love Zach and I want him to be happy."

"He is. You're good for him. Will and I wouldn't have thought it was possible to get him to settle down even a little. You have a great family. I've met most of them. I told all of them to bring their kids out to my ranch and let them ride. We have gentle horses. I think Connor is going to take me up first and bring his boys."

"I'm sure they'll love it. That's nice."

He spun her around and she glanced at Zach, already wanting the reception to be over and to be alone with him again.

When the dance ended, the group had broken up and Zach waited. "You've spent enough time with her, so goodbye, Ryan," Zach said, taking her hand.

"Thanks for the dance. I don't know how he talked you into marrying him," he teased. "Try to put up with him."

She laughed. "I think I can put up with him. It was nice to meet you, Ryan."

Zach led her to the dance floor to take her into his arms. "I'm ready for this to be over now."

"So am I," she said, gazing into his blue eyes that were as fascinating as the first day she met him. "I love you so," she whispered.

He pulled her close to wrap his arms around her and she danced slowly with him while her happiness bubbled. Her wonderful husband and their baby on the way—joy overflowed and she squeezed him. "Zach, this is paradise," she whispered, and he smiled at her, his eyes filled with warmth and love.

* * * * *

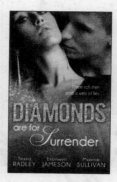

The World of Mills & Boon®

There's a Mills & Boon® series that's perfect for you. We publish ten series and, with new titles every month, you never have to wait long for your favourite to come along.

Blaze®

Scorching hot, sexy reads
4 new stories every month

By Request

Relive the romance with the best of the best
9 new stories every month

Cherish™

Romance to melt the heart every time
12 new stories every month

Desire™

Passionate and dramatic love stories
8 new stories every month

GOING DOWN

Also by Kate Thompson and published by
Bantam Books

IT MEANS MISCHIEF
MORE MISCHIEF

GOING
DOWN

Kate Thompson

BANTAM BOOKS

LONDON · NEW YORK · TORONTO · SYDNEY · AUCKLAND

GOING DOWN
A Bantam Book: 0553 812998

First publication in Great Britain

PRINTING HISTORY

Bantam Books edition published 2001

3 5 7 9 10 8 6 4 2

Copyright © Kate Thompson 2001

Set in 11/13pt Baskerville by
Phoenix Typesetting, Ilkley, West Yorkshire

Bantam Books are published by Transworld Publishers,
61–63 Uxbridge Road, London W5 5SA,
a division of The Random House Group Ltd,
in Australia by Random House Australia (Pty) Ltd,
20 Alfred Street, Milsons Point, Sydney, NSW 2061, Australia,
in New Zealand by Random House New Zealand Ltd,
18 Poland Road, Glenfield, Auckland 10, New Zealand
and in South Africa by Random House (Pty) Ltd,
Endulini, 5a Jubilee Road, Parktown 2193, South Africa.

Reproduced, printed and bound in Great Britain by
Cox & Wyman Ltd, Reading, Berks.

Acknowledgements

Thanks are due to the following: the staff in Oceantec Adventures in Dun Laoghaire, whose patience was monumental. I will leave it to the dive gods there to speculate about the resemblance to persons living or dead – but because gods are omniscient, they should *know* that the scars, shaven heads, dreadlocks, charisma, breathtaking physiques, sex appeal etc that I make reference to are the stuff of pure fiction. Aren't they? Dan, Declan, Enda, Mick, Tommy, Willy (and Tiernan of Scubadive West) – you were all inspirational! Kathy Brickell – thank you for holding my hand on my night dive. Jan Lee in Lady G'Diver, Jamaica, for the training dives. Moynihan-Russell Recording Studios for allowing me to annoy them for research purposes, and especially Orla O'Kelly in said studio for the brilliant excuses for having lunch. Sandra O'Sullivan for her invaluable musical savvy. Robert Dogget and the bar staff of the Trocadero for the cocktail recipe. The lovely, obliging staff at Leopardstown racecourse. Hugh Morton, expert in trivia. Michael Opperman, my tipster. Laura Philips of the Clarence Hotel. Susannah Godman and Sadie Mayne for always saying the right things, and Lucy Bennett for finding the right face – again! Eileen Cleary for keeping me sane. Marian and Cathy for the support system. Francesca Liversidge and Sarah Lutyens for being so wise. My husband, Malcolm, for instigating the diving, for encouraging me to do the advanced course and for just being so completely amazing. My daughter, Clara, for being such a fearless waterbaby, and to whom this book is dedicated.

For Clara

Chapter One

Endorphins! Those were exactly what she needed!

Ella Nesbit was sitting on the white Formica counter of the small coffee room, swinging her legs and waiting for the coffee to perk. She had filched a magazine from the selection she had fanned out on the glass-topped table in reception earlier, and was idly leafing through the pages. There was a feature in the health section about these things called endorphins that supposedly triggered a chemical reaction in your brain to produce a natural high. Apparently these endorphins kicked in when you were feeling good about yourself and enjoying life – like when you were eating chocolate, or when you'd finished a workout in the gym. The chocolate thing she could understand, the gym thing she couldn't. *'Endorphins are also generated by great sex,'* she read. *'And every time you laugh spontaneously, you experience an endorphin rush.'* No wonder she was feeling so bloody sorry for herself lately. Not only had she not had great sex – she hadn't had *any* sex for months. And she couldn't remember the last time she'd laughed spontaneously.

The coffee was done. She poured herself a mug, wandered back out into the reception area of the recording studio where she worked, and tossed the magazine onto the table. The calendar needed changing. She hadn't done it for ages. Now here was an ideal opportunity to experiment with endorphins! There were at least five Gary Larson cartoons waiting to be torn off. She studied the first one. *Nul points* for endorphins. It was the same with the second. And the third, and the fourth, and the fifth. Either the *meister* cartoonist had lost his touch, or she had become terminally challenged in the humour department. What scared her most was that she was starting to feel an increasing empathy with Larson's losers. One of her recent favourites showed a bunch of sad individuals mooching around in a hell so hellish the demons even served up cold coffee. It was strange. On last year's calendar she'd identified herself more readily with his smiley, doolally cartoon characters.

She dumped the cartoons in the wastepaper basket, and was just about to pick up the phone to confirm the availability of a voice-over artist for later that afternoon, when it rang.

'Nesbit & Noonan, good morning!' she said in her best receptionist's voice. She actually wasn't a receptionist, she was a sound engineer, but since Hattie the real receptionist had run off with a Scottish radio producer, she'd been roped in to man the desk. She hated it, but she hadn't much choice. Her Uncle Patrick – who was the Nesbit part of

10

Nesbit & Noonan – had taken a trainee sound engineer on board a couple of months ago, and he was running a tight ship. Until Patrick could afford to fork out a salary for a new receptionist, Ella was doing him a favour by standing in. And she owed him more than just one favour. Her uncle was her mentor, her friend, her port in a storm. For most of her life he had acted *in loco parentis* when one or both of Ella's parents were in globe-trotting mode – which was more often than not. The walls of the spare bedroom in the house he shared with his two teenage sons and his wife Claudia were still covered in her embarrassing Bros posters, and she sometimes found herself automatically scribbling in her uncle's address instead of her own on any forms she had to fill in. She loved him fiercely, and Patrick in turn doted on her, treating her like the daughter he'd never had. Patrick had booked conjurers for her birthday parties when she was little, he had bawled out Ms Ní Bhriain, her Irish language teacher, for undermining Ella's confidence at school, and he had organized orthodontia when her teeth started to grow skew-whiff. He had picked her up from teenage discos, assessed her boyfriends with a hypercritical eye, steered her ever so subtly away from the jail-bait look that some of her schoolfriends adopted, and nursed her through her first head-exploding, gut-heaving, I-will-never-drink-again-as-long-as-I-live-hangover. Ella suspected that he had done the Daddy stuff miles better than Declan, her own father, ever could have. Declan would have let her kick up her heels and run wild – in fact, the more sand she sent flying in the face of convention, the more he would have sat back and looked on admiringly.

It was Patrick's voice now on the other end of the phone.

'Hi, toots. How's the day shaping up?'

'Busy. The Complete Works have cancelled, but Reflex and PBCF&C have booked sessions.'

'Can we fit them both in?'

'Just about. It's going to be a tight squeeze.'

'I'll pick up extra Danish on the way. I'd have been there earlier, but the traffic on the canal is—'

'Bumper to bumper.'

'Got it in one. Is Julian there yet?' Julian Bollard was the new trainee.

'No. He's late. Again.' She couldn't resist the dig, but her uncle didn't seem to notice.

'Put him on the PBCF&C gig, will you? I want to see how he copes under pressure. That gobshite of a client's going to be there today. This will be Julian's litmus test in the diplomacy department.'

Hah! Ella wanted to laugh. If she was currently challenged in the humour department, then Julian bloody Bollard was most definitely challenged in the diplomacy department – at least when it came to her. From the moment they first met they just hadn't hit it off – and when Ella tried to analyse the reasons *why* they hadn't hit it off, she didn't much like what she learned about herself. Because deep down she suspected that her mistrust of the new trainee was motivated by nothing more complicated than professional jealousy. Julian was gaining a bit of a reputation as an engineering wizard, and she was fed up with people finishing off their phone calls to the studio with the words: 'By the way – will you make sure Julian's on the session?' Ella was feeling very scared that she might find herself behind the reception desk for longer than she liked.

'OK. Will do. By the way, Patrick, both studios are booked over lunchtime. I'll be running out for sandwiches again.'

'Can't you send out for them?'

'No. That delivery service is crap. They keep getting the orders wrong.'

'Hell. I'm sorry about all this gofering lark, toots. I know you're fed up with it.'

Ella picked up a pen and started doodling on the desk diary. 'When am I going to be allowed back on the technical side of things, Patrick? People treat me with more respect when I'm wearing my engineer's cap. I'm just not receptionist material.'

'I've had no complaints. And you know what a huge favour you're doing by saving me a salary. When the new studio's up and running and we've all that new hi-tech equipment installed you'll have a ball, but until then I just have to keep costs to a minimum. And think what's down the line in just a few more months. Three studios, four sound engineers, and a *brand new receptionist.* I promise.'

Ella sighed. *A few more months . . .* If she didn't love her uncle so much she'd be hurling abuse at him.

But he was right. Although the studio he was having built in the disused garage at the rear of the building was costing him a fortune, it promised to be a technological dream, and she was dying to play with all the latest state-of-the-art toys.

'Patience is a virtue,' Patrick reminded her.

'"*And virtue has its own reward but no sale at the box office*,"' she trotted out automatically.

'Where did I hear that before?'

'Francesca used to say it all the time. It's a quote from Mae West.'

'God, yes! How could I forget?' She could hear the smile in Patrick's voice. 'What was that other Mae West gem she used to chant like a mantra?'

'Um. Let me think . . . Oh yes – "Living well is the best revenge." Except I think that's Scott Fitzgerald.' One of Ella's earliest childhood memories had been of Francesca, her mother, confiding in her girlfriends at some bohemian soirée shortly after her less than amicable split from Ella's father. She'd had a spliff in her elegant right hand, a champagne flute in her elegant left, her Pre-Raphaelite hair had been floating around her like a cloud, and her smoky, kohl-rimmed eyes had flashed fire as she spat the word 'revenge' over and over again. 'I got a postcard from her the other day, by the way. From Gstaad.'

'I didn't know Francesca was into skiing?'

'She's not. But Giorgio is. She's just gone along for the off-piste stuff.'

'There's a bad joke there somewhere,' remarked

14

Patrick. 'But it's too early in the day for my grey cells to figure it out.' An electronic bleep sounded. 'Ah. Incoming call, sweetheart. I'd better take it. See you later.'

'Later.' Ella put down the phone and picked up her coffee. It was cold.

A thud on the floor of the lobby off the reception area announced the arrival of the mail. She wandered through, scooped up the pile of envelopes and sat down at the desk to sort through it. Bills, mostly, and invoices. There was a boring-looking manila envelope marked for the attention of her uncle: a Jiffy bag for Jack, his partner. A trade magazine. A postcard from Hattie in Scotland with one sentence on the back: 'Sorry to leave you in the lurch.' Hah! thought Ella. A circular. A letter for – hey! A letter for her! She hardly ever got letters at work.

'NOTIFICATION: TO CERTIFIED BEN-EFICIARY!' yelled the highlighted copy on the vibrant orange envelope. 'You have in your hands the chance of winning £250,000! Open immediately to find out how!' There was more. Through the cellophane window on the envelope she could make out the words: '. . . procedures are in place to declare Miss Ellen Nesbitt of 14 Lower Winston Street, Dublin 2, Rep of Ireland, the winner of £250,000. Please reply promptly for full prize chances.'

They couldn't even get her name right! She curled her lip at the envelope and dropped it into

15

the wastepaper basket alongside the Larson cartoons. *You have in your hands the chance of winning £250,000!* What kind of a sucker did they take her for?

'Morning.' Jack Noonan came through the door, swinging his motorbike helmet.

'Oh – hi, Jack.'

'Coffee made?' he asked.

'Mm-hm. Help yourself.' She smiled at him as he hung his helmet on the hat stand. You couldn't not smile at Jack. He was a ringer for Pierce Brosnan, and had an identical glint in his eye. He'd been her uncle's right-hand man for the past ten years, and he'd been responsible for her technical training. She'd always secretly fancied him, but she knew it wasn't reciprocated. She just wasn't his type – he was into high-achieving, ball-breaking, post-feminist-type dames (you should have seen them when he was finished with them – you couldn't help but feel sorry for them), and she also knew that Jack would never, ever dream of laying a hand on his partner's niece. He poured himself a cup of coffee and looked over her shoulder at the desk diary. She felt the hair on the back of her neck stand to attention. 'What time's the first session?'

'Nine-thirty. There are two gigs booked.'

'Who's in the main studio?'

'Reflex.'

'Oh, good. I'll do that one. That Angie's a foxy bitch.' Jack smiled at her raised eyebrow. 'Gotta

16

allow us boys a little political incorrectness from time to time.'

Ella shrugged. 'I wouldn't have thought she was your type.'

'Oh? What *is* my type, Ella?'

Not me, anyway, she thought, but: 'I dunno,' she said. 'It's just that Angie's a bit ditzy, if you know what I mean?' Oh, God – was she sounding petulant here? 'Don't get me wrong, I don't mean that in a bitchy way – it's just that she's more . . . well . . .' she realized just in time that she was just about to say 'fun', and stopped herself. 'More – *frivolous* than the kind of woman you usually have strung on your arm, anyway.'

'I'm maturing, Ella. I've got to that enlightened stage in life where a man suddenly realizes he'd much rather talk dirty than talk sense.'

'Oh! Maybe there's hope for me after all!' Ella sent him a ravishing smile.

'You talk dirty, little El? I don't think so. I've known you since the rudest word you knew was "bum", remember.'

'I've learned a lot ruder words since then, Jack.'

'No! What bounder was responsible for your miseducation, Ms Nesbit?'

'You.'

'*Touché*. Don't let on to your uncle. He'd have my guts for garters.'

Jack tipped her nose with his forefinger. Kiss me, you big eejit! thought Ella. But of course she didn't say it. Instead she yawned and started doodling again. 'It's going to be a long day,' she said. 'There's a load of clients due in. I really hate the way those bastards have been treating me like a girly since I've been stuck behind this desk. I keep feeling that I should be filing my nails and saying things like "Mr Nesbit will see you now" into intercoms. And wearing fluffy jumpers.'

Ella wasn't a fluffy jumper type, but she made a bit more of an effort with her appearance when she was doing the desk. Today she was wearing a boat-necked sweater in olive-green cotton, a cream cotton stretch skirt, and heels to make her look taller. She was only five feet two, and she hated having to look up at people all the time. She'd tied back her long, red-setter-coloured hair in a scrunchy and put on tiny silver earrings and a little discreet makeup. At least her hair was long enough to tie back now. She'd tried a Sinead O'Connor crop once, and had spent years regretting it. An enemy in school had told her she looked like a tennis ball with lips. Because her mouth was big and lop-sided she always outlined it with lip pencil now to try and redress the balance, and because she considered her eyebrows to be her best feature she always smoothed them with a smidgen of Vaseline.

'*When* am I going to be allowed to do my proper job again, Jack?' she said. She suddenly realized that the doodle she'd been scribbling on the desk diary was a skull and crossbones.

'When the new studio's finished, that's when.' Jack sat on the edge of the desk and narrowed his eyes at her. 'Anyway, I quite like treating you like a girly for a change, and your ass looks great in that skirt. You might come up to the office and take dictation later, Miss Nesbit.'

The phone rang. Ella stuck her tongue out at him and picked up the receiver. 'Nesbit & Noonan, good morning!' she said into the phone. 'Yes. Yes? *Yes!* No. Not today, thank you!' She put the phone down. 'A telesales rep,' she said.

'You handled that call beautifully, Ella. You might want to start making a few cock-ups, otherwise Patrick will keep you behind the desk indefinitely.'

'Oh, Jack – I just want my proper job back. It's not fair. Patrick's taking advantage of my dynastic loyalty. If he's not careful I just might run off to Scotland with a married radio producer. I can understand now why Hattie did it.' The phone rang again. 'Oh piss off,' she said, picking it up. Then: 'Nesbit & Noonan, good morning!'

She could hear Jack's low laugh as he loped up the stairs that led to the main studio, and left her to it.

*　　*　　*

Patrick and Julian arrived together. She could see them talking and laughing as Julian padlocked his bicycle to the railings outside the studio. When he'd finished Julian unzipped his jacket and stretched so that his horrible six-pack was displayed to its full advantage, and then he 'casually' flexed his biceps a couple of times. Julian was big into fitness and he rode a state-of-the-art cycle, even when it was raining. But all the hours he devoted to circuit training and weights and Nautilus couldn't disguise the fact that he was quintessentially a nerd.

'Hi, toots,' said Patrick as he came through the door. 'Julian was just telling me about his father's new car. He's invested in a Lotus Elan that will make my little coupé look pedestrian.'

This was yet another reason to hate him – Julian Bollard was *rich*. Or rather, his daddy was, and his rich daddy had contacts. Unfortunately, one of these contacts had turned out to be Jack Noonan, and that's how Julian had ended up working here. Ella had hoped that maybe Julian would get bored with being a sound engineer, the way he'd got bored with all the other groovy professions he'd dabbled in – photography, film production, journalism, acting (someone had told her he'd actually only ever been an extra). But so far he showed no sign of flagging.

'Hi, Ella.' Julian smiled at her with his thin lips, and then he raised one of his black Noel Gallagher eyebrows. 'Great skirt.'

Ella pretended not to have heard. She opened the desk diary and started punching in numbers on the phone. 'Good morning! May I speak to Monica, please? Ella Nesbit here. Thank you.'

Jingly music kicked in as she was put on hold.

'What's the best way of producing a premix and a final mix, Patrick?' she heard Julian ask.

'Mix your premix first,' Ella said authoritatively, pressing the 'on' switch on her computer. 'Load it back into the Audiofile and then play out your mix.'

'Oh?' said Julian, looking at her in a vaguely patronizing way. 'Can't you mix your premix into the Audiofile, and then play out your mix and your premix simultaneously? That would save all that loading time.'

'You're right, Julian,' said Patrick. 'That would do it in half the time.'

Fuck, fuck, fuck, thought Ella. He was outstripping her already. She'd been doing things according to established principle for ages now, while Julian had obviously been accessing all the new software. She'd need to do some hard work if she wanted to keep up. Ella was fed up with watching the new trainee scooting up and down the studio floor on his wheely chair, tweaking and mixing and humming along to the playout. She sat colouring in her skull and crossbones as she waited for her call to be put through, trying not to listen to the conversation the two men were having. Julian sounded so know-it-all she felt sick. 'Blah, blah, blah,' she heard. 'Blah, blah and blah.'

Ella had been working for Nesbit & Noonan for nearly three years now. She'd kind of drifted into the recording business. She'd had problems finding work the year after she'd graduated from music college, and Patrick had taken her on as a part-time receptionist. In those days she'd spent five mornings a week behind the desk, five afternoons a week practising her violin, and occasional evenings as a deputy player with various orchestras. But there were no permanent positions available – apart from one in a Baroque chamber orchestra which would have required her to dress up in a wig and period costume, and she just couldn't hack that idea. So in the end she'd returned her violin to its case, put the case in the back of her wardrobe, and asked her uncle for a proper job. After a year's apprenticeship, she'd qualified.

She no longer entertained ambitions of becoming a professional musician, although that didn't stop her fantasizing about it. It was in her blood, after all. Her paternal grandfather had been the Stradivarius of Irish fiddle makers, producing the most sought-after instruments in the country until the day his liver had packed in; and her father, Declan, was a star on the trad scene, travelling the world with a highly respected and successful band. Her mother, Francesca, had been a violinist with the National Symphony Orchestra before she'd given it up and run away to Tuscany with an Italian tenor. Francesca had sounded only mildly regretful when Ella had made the long-distance phone call telling her she was giving up the violin. 'Oh, well. I'm sure it's the right decision for you, darling,' she'd said reassuringly. And then Ella had heard the sound of the receiver being covered, and her mother's muffled voice saying: 'Open another bottle, *mio caro*. This one's corked.'

She'd waited until her father had come back from tour before telling him. For some reason she'd wanted to tell him to his face. After opening the glossy Fifth Avenue department store bags he'd brought back for her (he did this every time he went away, and Ella knew it was his way of assuaging his guilt at being such a crap father) and admiring the Gucci watch and the Ralph Lauren sunglasses and the Prada handbag, she'd poured him a large Jameson, and calmly informed him of her career choice. Declan had gone ballistic. He'd shouted, gone bright red in the face, and practically frothed at the mouth. 'Look what happened to Patrick!' he'd fulminated. '*He* could have been a contender, but he hadn't the guts! He opted for the safe option. Running a fucking *recording* studio, for Christ's sake!' He'd made the words 'recording studio' sound tackier than 'cat house'. 'Your uncle wouldn't recognize a fiddle now if it came flying at him and took a chunk out of his arse!' Patrick had played once upon a time – played brilliantly, according to Declan – but he had given it up when the recording business proved more lucrative.

When Declan had finally run out of steam on that unforgettably explosive occasion, he had looked at Ella for a long time in silence, and then, registering her stony face and determinedly set chin, he had turned on his heel and walked out the door. She hadn't heard from him again until a week later, when a massive bouquet from Interflora had arrived on her step with SORRY FOR SHOUTING AT YOU printed in block capitals on the card. And that had been the last time her father had ever referred to Ella's non-starter of a career as a violinist. Or to her new-found career as a sound engineer.

All in all, Ella had enjoyed working in her uncle's studio until she'd been shunted behind the reception desk full time. The recording business was buzzy and sociable, and although sound engineering was a mostly male preserve, she liked being one of the boys. She'd always preferred boys to girls. Most of the pupils at her all-girls boarding school had been consummate practitioners in the art of bitchcraft – and she knew that the rarefied world of the orchestra was inhabited by divas with agendas – so she felt more comfortable behind an Audiofile. But occasionally she thought about all those years she'd devoted to the study of music, and couldn't help feeling a little gutted.

Now she looked over at Julian again. He was standing nursing a mug of coffee, sucking up to her uncle. He may have gained a reputation for being a bit of a wunderkind, but Ella knew he was a dilettante at heart, with no real appreciation for – or understanding of – music. This wasn't a major disadvantage, since Nesbit & Noonan specialized mainly in commercial work, and very little music was recorded there. But as far as she was concerned, the only thing Julian Bollard had going for him was his technical savvy. This madly impressed the clients who sat in on recording sessions, but it cut no ice with her. Ella might not be as fluent in technospeak as he was, but intuition was her trump card. She could run her eye over a script, gauge to the nearest nanosecond what the running time would be, and establish immediately whether it needed a pacy or a leisurely read. She knew which voices could safely launch a thousand products, and which ones would have listeners lunging for the 'off' switch on their radios. She established instant rapport with agency creatives and with voice-over artistes because she spoke the same language they did, and because she laughed a lot. Or had done until recently.

The jingly 'on hold' music coming through the receiver was giving her a headache. Ella put the phone down, pressed redial, and scribbled black hair and a big nose on the skull to make it look more like a living person. It just ended up looking like Julian.

* * *

Later that day there was an unexpected lull between sessions. Ella unclingfilmed her salad sandwich and sat down on the big leather couch in the reception area to eat it. She was browsing through the *Evening Herald* when foxy Angie, the copywriter from Reflex, came downstairs.

'Finished?' asked Ella, looking up from the paper.

'No. I just want to take a breather. There's some problem with the DAT. It's going to take a while to get it sorted.' Angie flung herself down on the couch beside Ella, yawned and stretched. 'Anything in the paper?'

'A feature on how to be an "it" girl.'

'Ow. Sad. Anything else earth-shattering?'

'A competition to win a holiday for two in Jamaica.'

'Jamaica? Wow! Give us a look.'

Angie leaned forward, tucking a stray strand of glossy silver-blond hair behind her ear, and Ella slid the newspaper sideways to give her a better view. The competition was being run by a food consortium that was promoting a new line of fruit juice called Pirate's Punch. The punch was a blend of tropical juices like mango and pineapple and guava, and the advertising campaign featured a bunch of parrots dressed up as pirates with cutlasses hanging off their belts, bandannas on their heads and eye-patches over their eyes. They were brandishing musical instruments. One had maracas, one a squeezebox and one a trumpet. The one with its beak open was obviously the singer.

'Jesus,' said Angie, looking horrified. 'I wonder what agency was responsible for this piece of shit. Why on earth are they all playing instruments?'

'They do in the telly ad. The parrots play the jingle.'

'How does the melody go?'

'I don't know. I always zap it off when it comes on.'

'I'm not surprised. What a *mélange*! I pity the poor schmuck who got stuck with this account.' She ran her eyes along the copy. 'Let's see – what do you have to do to win the holiday? "Simply answer the following questions blah, blah, blah"' she read. '"And then dream up a name for our band of piratical parrots! It can be as zany as you like – in fact, the zanier the better! And if you're our lucky winner, you could be winging your way to your warmest winter wonderland ever. In the luxurious Salamander Cove resort, Port Antonio, Jamaica!"'

'As zany as you like?' repeated Ella. 'How about Schopenhauer and the Thundering Intellects?'

Angie laughed. 'Excellent. Or Jean-Paul Sartre and the Existentialists?'

'The Exceptionally Sad Dickheads?'

'Yes! Or zanier still – The Plumed Prats!'

'The Feathered Farts?' Ella was laughing too.

'Yes – yes! That's it!' Angie reached for a pen and entered the words 'The Feathered Farts' in the space left blank for suggestions. Then she said: 'Whose name shall we put?'

Ella didn't hesitate. She took the pen from Angie and wrote in block capitals: 'Julian Bollard, c/o Nesbit & Noonan, 14 Lower Winston Street, Dublin 2.'

*   *   *

She was closing down the computer when Jack came through reception, yawning and looking at his watch. 'Holy schomoly – it's half-past six already. That was a day and a half. Patrick gone home?'

'Yep.'

'You closing up now?'

'No. Julian wants to stay on and mess about with sound effects. I'll let him lock up.'

'Dedication, enthusiasm, eagerness to learn – that boy will go far.'

Ella shot him a basilisk look.

'C'mon, sweetie, lighten up. You'll be back at the control panel before the end of the year.'

'But it's only October now!'

'Well, let's look at it in terms of positive thinking. How about this? Next month's one of the shorter ones. Only thirty days.' Jack shouldered on his jacket and reached for his helmet. 'Come on. Let me buy you a drink. A pint of Guinness will put the roses back in those pallid cheeks of yours.'

'All right. I'd love a pint. But let's not go to Daly's – it'll be crowded with media types, and I've a headache looming. Can't we go somewhere a bit quieter for a change?' She got up and fetched her coat from the hat stand.

Jack made an apologetic face. 'Sorry. Daly's it has to be.'

'Why?'

'Angie's going to be there. I kind of made an arrangement to meet her. Nothing definite, but it would be bad form not to show.'

She turned to him, trying to keep disappointment

28

out of her eyes. 'Cor blimey, O'Reilly. Could this be the start of something beautiful?'

He shrugged as he held the door open for her. There was a blaring car alarm going off on the other side of the street. 'I don't really know. She dropped what might have been a kind of hint during the session earlier.'

'Oh?'

'Of course there may be nothing meaningful about it, but she said she'd just split up with her significant other.' He raised his eyebrows at Ella as they hit the footpath and took a left turn in the direction of the pub.

Ella stuffed her hands in her coat pockets and considered the situation. For some reason the notion of Jack and Angie hooking up together didn't afford her the same stabbingly jealous pain as some of his past liaisons had. Most of her boss's previous women had been worldly and sophisticated – real Bond girl types – and they'd taken pains to keep Ella at arm's length. She suspected that they were jealous of her easygoing relationship with Jack, and she often fantasized about wiping the floor with them. *Sorry, Tamara/Saskia/Magda. Jack and I won't be inviting you to the wedding. We've decided on a small affair on a beach somewhere exotic . . .* But she'd always got on well with Angie. It would at least make a nice change not to be condescended to by a girlfriend of Jack Noonan's. 'So. You reckon she's available? Actually, I think she kind of likes you too, Jack. She always gives herself a quick spray

29

with Gaultier before she goes into a session with you.'

'Does she really?'

'Mm.' Hell. Maybe she should have kept shtum about that. 'I can't say I blame her. You're a very attractive bloke, you know.' A drop landed on her cheek, and she wiped it away. 'Uh-oh. It's starting to rain.'

'You're a doll for saying that.'

Jack slung an arm round Ella's shoulders, and she tried not to tense.

'What? For saying that it's starting to rain?'

'No. For reminding me that I'm not unattractive. I'll be hitting forty soon, and I could do with all the female reassurance I can get. And something tells me Angie is no walkover. I'm going to have to work at this one.' He stopped suddenly and gave her a speculative look. 'Hell, Ella. Look at yourself and then answer me this. Why is there no significant other in *your* life right now? There hasn't been anyone in the picture for ages, has there?'

'No.'

'But you used to have bevies of boyfriends baying after you like – like *beagles*.'

She gave him a cynical look. '*Bevies* is something of an exaggeration, Jack. I had a string of botched relationships, that's all. They were all gobshites.'

'All of them?'

'Every last one. I've had egotists, bullies, misers, sadists, manic depressives. I even went out with someone who didn't find *Father Ted* funny. It's made me fussy about men. I'm waiting for Mr Right to come along.'

'Define Mr Right for me. I suppose he has to be tall, dark and handsome?'

Like you, thought Ella. 'Preferably. But there's a more important prerequisite than that.'

'Let me guess. He has to have a sense of humour.'

'Hey! How did you know?'

'That's what all the girls say. They say that the best way to get a woman into bed is to make her laugh. Can't say it's ever worked for me. They all run a mile at my jokes.'

'I've got a good one for you,' said Ella. 'Knock, knock.'

'Who's there?'

'The Interrupting Cow.'

'The Interrupt—'

'*Moo!*'

Jack gave a gratifying laugh before giving her a ruminative look. 'You might have a long wait for this Mr Right, you know, darlin'. Remember what it says in the song.' A flurry of raindrops fell just as the green man on the pedestrian lights opposite turned to red. Ella made to dodge through the traffic, but Jack tightened his grip on her shoulder. 'Hey! Not so fast, sweetie.'

'Sorry.' She hopped back onto the pavement. 'What does it say in the song?'

'A good man is hard to find.'

No he's not! she thought. *Sometimes he's right under your nose, and he just doesn't realize it!* But she didn't

31

say it. Instead she said: 'And vice versa.'

Jack laughed and cuffed her lightly on the head. 'What would you know about that?'

'Jack. I'm not still Patrick's baby niece, you know. You may not have noticed, but I grew up some time ago.'

'I'd noticed,' he said. 'It would have been pretty difficult not to.'

Ella sent him a coquettish look from under her eyelashes, and was surprised not to receive the usual bantering-Jack look back. Instead there was something so new and so disturbing about the way he was looking at her that she berated herself for automatically sliding into their well-worn we're-such-good-mates-we-can-even-play-at-flirting routine.

Oh God. Change tack, Ella! Quick, quick – *change tack*! In nanoseconds the coquettish look was history, and she was casting around in a panic for a more appropriate, grown-up response to the sudden sexual tension that had sprung up between them. Poor Ella couldn't know it, but she had simply succeeded in making herself look incredibly vulnerable. Suddenly, awkwardly, Jack removed his arm from her shoulders, gave a little, unconvincing cough, and focused his gaze on the horizon somewhere to his right.

There was a long silence while mutual confusion reigned.

'Anyway – how will you know him when he eventually shows up?' said Jack, finally turning

32

back to her. 'Your Mr Right.' He had resumed the expression he habitually wore when talking to her – that amused, slightly indulgent expression that had 'avuncular' written all over it. There was no trace left of the stranger who'd locked eyes with her barely one minute earlier.

Ella forced back her disappointment. More than anything she wanted to meet that stranger again. 'Well,' she said, making sure her voice was light and her smile chipper. 'He'll announce himself, of course, in time-honoured *coup de foudre* fashion—'

'*Coup de* what?'

'A *coup de foudre*, dummy, is French for "love at first sight". You know – like a bolt from the blue.'

Jack gave her a sceptical look. 'Life ain't that simple, little El.'

'Isn't it? Oh, look. The green man.' Ella skittered across the road towards Daly's on light feet, but with a heart that weighed a ton. An image of beautiful Angie had come into her head, and she couldn't stop thinking of her sitting in the pub, waiting for Jack. As he opened the door of the pub, a wave of heat, noise, alcohol fumes and cigarette smoke billowed out.

'Oh God, Jack,' said Ella suddenly. 'I'm sorry. I'm not going to be able to hack it after all. I think I'll just head on home. It's a night for staying in and watching something mindless on the telly.'

'Are you sure? It's not like you to be anti-social. Come in for one.'

'No, no, no. You know there's no such thing.'

Over by the counter Angie had caught Jack's eye and was waving at him.

Ella gave Jack's hand a quick squeeze. 'See you tomorrow.' Before he could twist her arm further, she slid back out through the door.

A bus was at the bus stop – the last passenger in the queue just boarding. She ran towards it, waving, but the driver ignored her and pulled away from the kerb. Shit. There wouldn't be another one for ages, and if she was going to organize something to eat and do her laundry before visiting the video shop, she'd need to get going. She set off up the road at a brisk pace just as the first drops of really heavy rain began to fall.

*　　*　　*

The next day was Friday. Ella was the first to arrive at work, as usual. She thought longingly of the days before she'd been tethered to the reception desk, when she'd had an extra half-hour in bed.

Julian had obviously worked on until quite late last night. There was an empty can of Diet Lilt on the coffee table, and the remains of a pizza in its cardboard box. He might have had the decency to dump it in the bin, she thought crossly, as she started to clear away the detritus. Yesterday's *Evening Herald* was there amongst the mess, still folded open at the page with the Pirate's Punch competition, and she felt a sudden flush of alarm. What if Julian had spotted his name on the competition entry? She picked up the paper and looked at it blankly. Where the entry form had been was a rectangle of nothingness. It had been torn out.

The door opened, and Ella let the newspaper drop as if it had burned her. Thankfully, it wasn't Julian. 'Oh – hi, Jack!' she said, sounding effusive with relief.

'Why are you looking like a little criminal?' he asked, eyeing her curiously.

Ella lowered her tone even though there wasn't anyone there to overhear her. 'I know this sounds bananas, Jack, but I did something a bit juvenile yesterday, and I'm scared that Julian might have found out about it.'

'You're talking about something juvenile pertaining to Julian? Some sort of practical joke, I take it?'

She nodded. 'Yes. And you know he has no sense of humour. He won't see the funny side of it.'

'OK. What have you done to exacerbate the already precarious nature of your professional relationship?'

She filled him in, and when she'd finished, Jack smiled. 'You don't have to worry that Julian saw it, sweetheart. He couldn't have. Angie sent it off.'

'What?'

'She thought it was an excellent jape. She loved the idea of all these unfortunate competition judges sitting around reading banal suggestions for names

35

for those miserable parrots. She said the idea of someone opening an envelope and seeing "The Feathered Farts" instead of the usual predictable stuff like "The Piratical Parrots" or "The Merry Midshipmen" made her want to crease up, so she couldn't resist sending it. She's going to put something even ruder on today's entry form.'

'Oh, hell, Jack – I didn't just put Julian's name on the form. I put the Nesbit & Noonan address as well! What if word gets back to the copywriter responsible? It could be one of our clients!'

'So?'

'They'll think we're sending them up.'

'They deserve it for coming up with such an appalling campaign.' Jack gave her an amused look. 'Hell. Look at it this way. Maybe Julian'll win. After all, they wanted zany and the Feathered Farts is as zany as it gets. And if he does win, he'll just be extremely grateful to you for a free holiday in Jamaica. Oh, hi – Julian.'

'Hi, Julian!' Ella flashed him a guilty smile as he came through the door. He was looking nerdier than ever in a waterproof suit with bicycle clips round his ankles. She moved to the bin and dropped his pizza box into it.

'Here's the post,' he said, dumping a sheaf of envelopes on the desk and reaching for the diary. 'How many sessions have we lined up for today?'

'We're busy again,' said Ella. 'I don't mind covering for you if you want to take a lunch break,' she added hopefully.

'That's not possible, Ella,' said Jack. 'I'll answer the phone any time I have free so that you can do a sandwich run, but I can't lose Julian today. He has his own set-up on the Audiofile. It would take you too long to change it to your settings in the time booked.'

Ella thought she could detect smugness in the expression on Julian's face, and she hated him more than ever. Git! When she finally got off that desk she would show him a thing or two about sound engineering! She turned her attention to the post that he'd dumped in front of her. A grey envelope with urgent yellow and black type on the front caught her eye. 'Six Sweepstakes numbers allocated exclusively to Mrs Alan Nesbit' she read. With a sinking heart she tore open the envelope and took out a glossy A4 document. 'As an eligible Irish finalist you could be holding a number that is already worth over 1.6 MILLION DOLLARS! Plus this beautiful condiment set could be yours FREE with our very best wishes if you send away for our mouth-watering recipe book . . .'

How on earth had she got on a mailing list for prize draws? She looked at the picture of the condiment set. Who in their right mind could describe it as beautiful? What kind of people were they aiming at? The irresistible offer went into the bin alongside the envelope that had arrived for her in the afternoon post yesterday, exhorting her to *act immediately* because it was her *last chance* to win a *million yes a million lovely smackers* . . .

37

*　　*　　*

Over the course of the next few days junk mail streamed through the letterbox of Nesbit & Noonan. All the petitioners offered mind-boggling incentives to potential subscribers. As well as draws and competitions with millions of pounds of prize money on offer, there were other inducements. Ella was offered a free Photo Frame cum Alarm Clock, a home breadmaker, a solar watch, a wall clock that marked the hours with birdsong, a beautiful rose bush SPECIALLY for HER, and a Majestic Garden Arch.

One morning she received a letter that was – amazingly – correctly addressed to her in her grandmother's perfect italic script. She slit open the envelope and took out a card with a photograph on the front of a fluffy blue-eyed kitten poking out of a satin slipper. It had a miniature top hat on, and it was wearing a pink bow. Hang about, thought Ella. This was emphatically *not* Leonie's style. Leonie usually sent the most beautiful cards – reproductions of Matisse or Picasso or Miró. This card was more like a Jeff Koons aberration.

'Darling Ella', she read. 'A card to say thank you for my birthday flowers. Tacky, isn't it! What sad geezer dreamed up the idea of sticking a kitten in a shoe! I was thinking of writing to the ISPCA about it until I remembered that I used to stick Ronan in my slipper when he was a kitten, but at least I never made him wear a ribbon or a top hat. By the way

38

have you won anything yet? With very much love from your doting ~*!# Leonie. XXX'

Leonie hated the word 'grandmother', and always refrained from using it when she could. Hence the ~*!#.

Ella skimmed through the note again. *Have you won anything yet*... Now the competition entries and draws for smart cars and lump sums of money and dream holidays made sense. Her grandmother must have put her on some junk mailing list. Oh God. Leonie had lost it. She was obviously doting in more ways than one. But then, Ella supposed, Leonie had always behaved erratically. She had married Ella's paternal grandfather – a fervent Irish republican – to spite her father, who'd been a colonel in the British army. The marriage had lasted just long enough for her to produce Patrick and Declan in rapid succession, and then Leonie had scarpered, abandoning her husband for a career on the stage. She had been a great beauty, and had done a mean line in celebrity consorts until she decided to give up men and espouse environmental causes instead. She'd dumped her last lover two years ago, and claimed to have been celibate since.

Ella stuck the blue-eyed kitten up on the pinboard behind her desk, and then picked up the phone and punched in her grandmother's number. The answering machine picked up. *This is a recorded message*, heard Ella. *Do not under any circumstances vote for Jim Moran at the next by-election. He is a complete shyster. He has done bugger all about the noise pollution in the Liberties, he connived on the planning permission for that hideous high rise office block, and he also completely ignored my letters concerning recycling. I repeat. Do not vote for Smiling Jim Moran.* Then: *Beeeep* went the answering machine.

'Leonie?' said Ella. 'If you're there will you pick up the phone? Pick up the phone, Leonie.'

There was a beat, and then she heard her grand-mother's voice. 'Oh, hello, darling. I'm glad it's only you. I thought it might be that awful Mrs Hardiman from down the road reminding me about her coffee morning. How are things?'

Ella got straight to the point. 'Leonie – have you put me on some kind of mailing list?'

'Oh, yes! Didn't I tell you? Brilliant prizes, aren't they?'

'Leonie – you would not believe the kind of stuff I've been offered. You thought that kitten in a shoe was tacky? How's this for tacky? Personalized writing paper with your photograph on it? A stuffed lamb that plays "Jesus Loves Me"? A garden lamp in the shape of a gnome?'

'Oh – ignore all that crap, Ella. Just go for the big stuff. You know – the cars, the holidays, the cash, the—'

'Leonie – I'm not going to win *anything*. If you think Jim Moran is a shyster, those people who manipulate you into forking out pounds and pounds for their cruddy products are shysters twenty times over. It's a mug's game.'

40

'All right, darling,' said Leonie with equanimity. 'Just fling them in the bin if you're not interested.'

'Leonie – you're the one who's concerned about recycling.'

'You're right.' A pause while her grandmother digested this. 'I shall demand that your name is taken off every single mailing list.' Leonie was starting to sound animated. 'In fact – this could be my new pet project. Putting an end to mindless junk mail. Maybe I should give Jim Moran another chance. Yes. I'll do that. I'll write to him and see if he rises to the challenge.'

'What made you put me on a mailing list anyway?'

'Because you seemed so out-of-sorts the last time I talked to you. I thought the idea of winning something might cheer you up.'

Ella smiled at her grandmother down the phone. 'You are sweet,' she said. 'Why did you give them my work address?'

'Because you told me some of your mail had gone missing. I suspect it's that man who lives next door to you. He's intercepting it somehow. His moustache is too thin and his eyes are too close together.'

'He's running for the by-election,' said Ella.

'Well, that explains everything,' said Leonie.

*   *   *

'Nesbit & Noonan, good morning!' said Ella into the phone later that morning, trying hard

41

to remember to use receptionist's exclamation marks.

'Hello,' came the unfamiliar voice at the other end of the line. 'Could I speak to Miss Ellen Nisbit, please?' He pronounced the name with a precision she found offensive.

'This is Ella Nesbit speaking,' she replied flatly.

'Ah – hello, Miss Nisbit.' The voice was irritatingly cheerful. 'I have some news for you that I think you'll find extremely exciting.'

Oh God, thought Ella. Leonie had obviously given her phone number to some telesales rep. 'I'm sorry, I'm not interested,' she said, hoping the geezer wasn't going to be persistent.

'Oh ho – I think you will be,' said the caller. 'When I tell you the news I have for you, I think you'll be more than interested.'

Hell. He *was* going to be persistent. And the fact that he had actually said 'Oh ho' made it a matter of urgency to get rid of him. She was just about to come out with her firm but polite 'Not today, thank you' when one word made her stop in her tracks.

'Jamaica!' said the voice. 'How does Jamaica sound to you? Two weeks with a lucky girlfriend – or boyfriend, ha ha – in the Salamander Cove resort?'

Salamander Cove? That was the name of the resort in that competition in the *Evening Herald*. 'Sorry,' she said. 'Who is this? Is this some kind of practical joke?'

'Ha ha ha! You think you're dreaming, don't you, Ellen? Well, it's a dream come true – or maybe I should say a dream holiday come true!!!' She knew that he'd invested the end of the sentence with at least three exclamation marks. 'My name is Manus McNulty, of Toptree Foods Ltd. You entered our competition recently to win a holiday in Jamaica, and you won – with your wonderful suggestion for a name for our trademark parrots.'

Oh God. How could 'The Feathered Farts' have won? Could it be that they really really *did* want zany, as they'd said in the ad? Not possible. 'The Feathered Farts' wasn't even zany, it was just infantile. Anyway, if it had won, they'd be phoning Julian, not her. 'You – er – you don't mean "The Feathered Farts", do you?' she enquired tentatively.

'Come again?'

'"The Feathered Farts"? Was that the name that won?'

The voice down the other end of the phone sounded confused. 'I'm sorry. I don't know what you're talking about. You're sure you're Ellen Nisbit, aren't you? Of Nisbit & Noonane, 14 Lower Winston Street, Dublin 2?'

She wasn't sure of anything right now. But: 'Yes, yes. That's me,' she said.

'Well, your entry has no – er – feathered farts on it. The name you put down was "The Polly Rogers". That was the name the judges thought bang on for our band of pirate parrots.'

43

Oh God, she thought. Things were suddenly starting to make sense. 'Of course,' she said. 'How stupid of me. It was "The Polly Rogers", not "The Feathered Farts". I was – er – thinking of something else.'

'Well,' said Manus McNulty. 'When would it suit you to take your holiday?'

* * *

As soon as she put the phone down she picked it up again and punched in her grandmother's number.

'Oh, hello, darling,' said Leonie. 'How lovely to hear from you again so soon. Let me just put this stethoscope in the right place.'

Ella didn't ask.

'S-C-O-P-E,' Leonie enunciated carefully. 'There we are. The *Irish Times* crossword isn't getting any easier. Now. What can I do for you?'

'Leonie?' said Ella. 'Do "The Polly Rogers" mean anything to you?'

'The Polly Rogers? No, darling – I can't say they do. Oh – wait a minute. Wasn't Polly MacPherson married to somebody called Roger?'

'No, no, Leonie,' said Ella patiently. 'I'm talking about a competition. Did you put my name on a competition entry form recently?'

'Oh, yes.' Leonie's tone was careless. 'I've been doing that for weeks now, as well as those prize draws. I rather hoped you might win that set of

44

Hugh Grant videos and invite me round to watch them one night. I keep missing *Four Weddings* every time it's on the television. I've drafted a brilliant letter, by the way, telling all those purveyors of tack to remove your name from their junk mailing lists with immediate effect. I told them Jim Moran would be down on them like a ton of bricks if they didn't. That should make them sit up and take note, eh?'

'Have you taken that defamatory message about him off your answering machine?'

'Yes, yes. Smiling Jim has got a reprieve. Stop that, Ronan. Ronan's eating the geranium. Stop it, you evil cat!' There followed a pause full of muttered expletives before her grandmother spoke again. 'Sorry about that,' she said, breathlessly. 'I think he's addicted to that geranium. Now – tell me. *Did* you win those videos?'

'No, Leonie. I didn't win any videos. I won a holiday.'

'Oh, excellent! Where to?'

'Jamaica.'

'Jamaica! How exotic! Now – which competition was that? You have to be reminded of things like that when you get to my age.'

'The one where you had to make up a name for that band of parrots dressed up as pirates.'

'Oh, God yes. Now I remember. Horrific creatures, aren't they, those parrots? I zap them off the television every time they come on. What name did I call them?'

'You called them the Polly Rogers.'

'The Polly Rogers! An appropriately *ghastly* name, don't you think? I was actually tempted to call them something like The DTs but I restrained myself. "My beautiful Ella needs a holiday", I thought to myself. "And she's not going to get one if I give in to the temptation to write down something smart." So I came up with "The Polly Rogers" instead. That's the sort of thing they're looking for, isn't it? Oh listen – Ronan's purring.'

A noise like a sewing machine came down the phone as her grandmother stuck the receiver next to the cat. After a minute of listening to Ronan purr, Leonie came back on again. 'So, the jolly old Polly Rogers won, did they? Good for them. I wonder did "Grant My Wish" get anywhere?'

'Grant My Wish?' echoed Ella, perplexed.

'Yes. That's what I put down for the Hugh Grant video competition.'

'If it didn't win, it should have.'

'Better than the Polly Rogers anyway. I can't believe they bought that!' Leonie gave a scornful laugh, and then resumed. 'So – Ella, my darling – you'll be jet-setting off to Jamaica soon! You lucky, lucky girl. I've always wanted to do the Caribbean. How sad to think I never will. That's the grimmest thing about getting to my age. You start eliminating things from the list of "Things I've Always Wanted to Do" and "Places I've Always Wanted to Visit". I finally got round to scratching off "Snorkelling on a Coral Reef" last week.'

'I think you should put it on again,' suggested her granddaughter with a smile.

'Really, darling? Why's that?'

'You're coming with me,' said Ella.

Chapter Two

Friday evening in Daly's was always the busiest of the week. When she swung through the door with Jack at around six o'clock the place was heaving with media types, but this evening Ella didn't mind. She was feeling sociable again, and so full of gratitude to Toptree Foods that she very nearly ordered a Pirate's Punch when Jack asked her what she wanted to drink. Word had got round that Ella had won a holiday for two in Jamaica, and as she made her way towards the corner table that her uncle always took pains to commandeer on Friday nights, the regulars were speculating vociferously about what lucky man she might be taking with her. One extremely attractive (married) actor generously volunteered to accompany her if she was stuck. 'Who *are* you taking then, Ella?' he asked when she turned him down. She raised her eyebrows at him and gave him an enigmatic smile. 'C'mon – who is it?' persisted the actor. 'One of your groovy musician friends, I suppose?'

'No,' she said. 'I'm taking my grandmother.'

'E*lla*!' groaned the actor. 'You're taking your

grandmother to a romantic tropical paradise! What a waste!'

'I'll call you if she gets cold feet,' said Ella. 'But it ain't likely. Leonie's hot to trot.'

Her uncle was sitting in his usual corner, a pint already in front of him.

'Hi, Patrick!' she said, plonking herself down beside him and giving him a kiss on the cheek. She'd picked up a brochure from a travel agent's after leaving work, and she pulled it out of her backpack now and started leafing through the glossy pages. 'Look!' Her voice was sing-songy with delight. 'That's where I'm going! Palm trees! White sand! Cocktails on the beach!' She spread the brochure out on the table in front of him.

Patrick shook his head in disbelief. 'I can't believe you're bringing Leonie, Ella.'

'Why can't you believe it?'

He indicated a blue-sky, blue-sea photograph in which two smiling thong-clad babes were prominent. 'Can you imagine my mother sitting on that beach? You haven't given this very much thought, have you?'

'I couldn't not take her, Patrick,' she replied reasonably. 'She was the one who won the competition, after all. And she's not a prude, if that's what you're worried about. She told me that she used to go skinny-dipping in the Mediterranean when she was my age.'

'It's not that I'm worried about,' said Patrick. 'It's

just that she's getting dottier by the day. I'm not sure you could handle her on your own – especially on the other side of the Atlantic. What did she say when you invited her along?'

'She told me to get real.'

'Get real? She used those actual words?'

'Yes. She told me to get real and bring a friend my own age. She was absolutely adamant about it until I told her that I wouldn't go at all if she didn't come. Then when she knew there was no way round it, she started getting excited. She rang me back later to tell me she'd been in touch with some scuba diving outfit in Portdelvin.'

'Jesus!' said her uncle. 'Leonie can't go scuba diving. At her age she'd have problems learning how to snorkel.'

'Don't worry, Patrick. She was checking it out for me. Apparently you can start learning here and complete the training anywhere in the world.'

'That sounds like a bloody good idea.' Jack had rolled up. He set two pints down on the table and sat down on Ella's left – close, but not close enough for physical contact. The banquette was narrow. Ella resisted the temptation to shift to her left, congratulating herself on her self-restraint. God! What a sad bitch she was, mooning over this man! 'That time I went to Australia I cursed myself for not having done a course in scuba beforehand,' he continued. 'Leonie's dead right, you know. You *should* investigate having lessons.'

'You really think so?' Until that afternoon Ella

50

had never even entertained the idea of taking up scuba diving, but now she could see it made sense. Diving in the Caribbean would be like diving in Paradise.

'I absolutely think so. I'll never forget the afternoon I saw a dive boat coming back from the Great Barrier Reef, full of people comparing stories about what they'd seen underwater. They were high on it – euphoric. It's one of my biggest regrets ever that I travelled halfway across the planet, but let a whole new world go unexplored.'

'A new world?'

'The world under the waves.'

The world under the waves . . . It sounded so romantic! She'd seen a diver on a *National Geographic* programme once, feeding fish in the Tropics. She pictured herself swimming through Caribbean water, picking up shells and surrounded by flocks – no, shoals – of multi-coloured fish, looking slinky and svelte and streamlined in her scuba suit, and with her hair drifting around her like the Little Mermaid's. Hell. She'd have to do it.

'OK,' she said. 'I'll book a course first thing on Monday.'

'When are you off?' asked Patrick. 'To Jamaica?'

'Whenever I like,' she said breezily. 'Or rather – whenever suits you. Around the beginning of December might be good. Things will be easing off by then.' Hooray! she thought. He and Jack would have to think seriously about finding a receptionist now.

Her uncle looked pensive. 'We'll have to think seriously about finding a receptionist now,' he said.

*   *   *

The following Monday, along with an envelope that exhorted her to: 'HURRY! We're giving away a Philips Mini Hi-Fi System to each of the first 50 replies drawn', and another which was obviously meant to set her heart racing with excitement at its 'URGENT' invitation to enter a prize draw which could win her £100,000, there was a third envelope addressed to her. It contained a brochure with the portmanteau word 'ActivMarine' emblazoned on the front across a picture of a diver silhouetted against an underwater background of aquamarine blue. A spotty blue and yellow fish hovered in the foreground, and a whole shower of little stripy ones were surging over a reef below. There was a stream of silver bubbles emerging from the diver's mouth, which was clamped around a rubber tube. Leonie must have given the scuba outfit her address.

Ella opened the brochure and perused the contents. Inside was a list of the diving courses available. There were beginners' open water courses and advanced open water courses. There were wreck diving courses and night diving courses, rescue diving courses and Blue Shark diving courses. There were dive weekends away in the West of Ireland, and dive holidays in more exotic locations. Barbados, the Red Sea, Thailand.

There were photographs of people looking happy and windswept on dive boats, and pictures of people gliding effortlessly through deep blue water. It looked enormously seductive.

A colour-coded calendar showed her when the next beginners' classes were starting. This Wednesday, at 7 p.m. Every week for six weeks! It seemed a ridiculously long time to learn how to float around underwater sucking air in through a tube. She had a friend who'd gone scuba diving in Australia once, and she hadn't had any training at all. The geezer who'd taken her down had done all the necessary fiddling round with tubes and gauges and whatever, and she'd just trailed along behind him, holding onto his hand. Still. It would be nice to be independent instead of being a mere water baby. To have some diving education. Her friend had tried to pick up a shell at one point, and her guide had practically given her a Chinese burn in his efforts to prevent her. Admittedly she'd found out afterwards that that particular species of cone shell had a highly venomous barb. If she trained she'd learn about all that jazz. She might even invest in an underwater camera. It would be a lot more interesting to bring home wonderful photographs of coral reefs and exotic fish and divers rather than the usual run-of-the-mill 'Me on the beach. Me sipping a cocktail. Me diving into the pool' holiday shots.

'Morning,' said Jack, coming through the door. Today he was wearing his motorbike leathers and looking more like Pierce Brosnan than ever. 'What's that you've got?' he asked, glancing at the brochure as he pulled the zip on his jacket all the way down and peeled it off. Ow, thought Ella. 'More offers of millions of pounds?'

'No,' replied Ella. 'It's a scuba diving brochure.'

'Let's have a look,' said Jack, sitting down on the reception desk and leaning in to her, as was his habit every morning when he arrived at work. He whistled through his teeth as he scanned the glossy pages. 'Oh, yes, Ella! You've gotta do it. Wow. I can just picture you emerging from the water with a dagger on your hip like Ursula Andress in *Dr No*.'

'Ursula Andress I ain't,' said Ella.

'Well – I'll concede that you're not as well endowed. Still. It's a seriously glamorous sport. Sure as hell beats golf for sex appeal. Go on. Give them a ring now and book yourself in.'

'It's a six-week course, Jack.'

'It'll be worth it. Go on, Miss Intrepid. Didn't you do a parachute jump once? This has got to be less scary.'

'OK.' Ella took the brochure from him and gave him a challenging look. 'I'll bring you back a shark's tooth necklace,' she said as she punched in the number. 'One that I'll make from teeth plucked from the jaws of death by my own fair hands.'

'Way to go, Ella. You'll make Lara Croft look like Goldilocks.'

The phone rang for ages. Then, finally: 'ActivMarine, good morning,' she heard. Whoever

54

had picked up the phone had forgotten the mandatory exclamation marks. It was a man's voice.

'Oh – good morning!' said Ella in her brightest receptionist's tones. 'I'm ringing to enquire about diving lessons. Can you tell me something about the beginners' course, please?'

'Sure. There's one starting this Wednesday at seven o'clock.'

The accent was Galway. Quite attractive, she thought. She decided it might be worth giving him her full warm receptionist's treatment, and she replied with a smile. 'Yes. I saw that from your brochure. It's an hour-long class, is it?'

'No. We do two hours of academic work between seven and nine, and then two hours of practical pool work. You'll be out of the pool by eleven o'clock.'

'Eleven o'clock!' Ella was horrified. 'But that's four hours!' She made a rapid calculation. 'Four hours a week for six weeks – that's twenty-four hours altogether!' She looked up at Jack and opened her mouth in a silent scream.

'There's not a lot wrong with your mental arithmetic. Can't you spare the time?'

'Well – yes, I can. I just didn't realize there was so much work involved.'

'You're training to be a certified open water diver. It's not like taking night classes in flower arranging.'

Ella narrowed her eyes at his tone. Who did he think she was? Some bored dilettante who'd been flicking casually through the *Guide to Evening Classes*? 'I understand I can complete the course abroad?' she said, adopting a rather more distant tone. There was obviously no point in wasting friendly exclamation marks or warm smiles on this individual.

'That's right. You can do your certifying dives at any affiliated dive outfit in the world.'

'Oh? Does that mean I could do four weeks' training here and two in Jamaica?'

'You're off to Jamaica, lucky lady?'

'Yes.'

'Well, I'm afraid it doesn't work like that. You do your twenty-four hours here, and then you sit a written exam. You then have to demonstrate that you've mastered the skills you've been taught.'

'In a pool?'

'No. In open water, in four separate dives. You can choose to do them here – in which case you'll be already certified when you hit Jamaica – or we'll refer you on and you can perform your qualifying dives once you're there.'

Oh God. It all sounded horribly complicated. She was beginning to wish she'd never hit on this learning to dive idea. 'Where do you do the open water dives?' she asked, suspecting she wasn't going to like the answer very much.

'Sheep's Head Bay, near Portdelvin.'

'But it's nearly winter!'

That irritating smile was in his voice again. 'You'd be amazed how hot you can get in a wetsuit, even in the Irish Sea, even in the month of November.'

'Actually, we're in October.'

'If you manage to get through the six weeks of training, it'll be November when you do your dives.'

If you manage to get through the six weeks of training! He'd obviously got her totally wrong! Ella Nesbit was no wimp. She was one of the lads – able to equalize, compress and mix with the best of them. *And* she drank pints. 'OK,' she said with authority. 'Book me in for the course starting this Wednesday.'

'Sure. What's your name?'

'Ella Nesbit.'

'All right, Ella Nesbit.' Wow. He'd actually got her name right. 'You're down. You might like to come out to us beforehand to pick up your manual.'

'My manual?' Ella made another face at Jack. He was earwigging shamelessly, and was obviously highly amused.

'Your dive manual. It goes over the course step by step, and it'll give you a taste of what's in store. It's a good idea to have read the first chapter before you come to class.'

The first chapter! Phooey. She wasn't going to go all the way out to Portdelvin to pick up a poxy manual. He probably thought she had the IQ of an idiot, and wouldn't be able to understand a word of her lesson without having laboriously read the whole thing through in advance. She'd never been one for swotting – she'd winged every exam she'd ever taken. She could pick up whatever she needed to know in the classroom.

'Um. No. I think I'll pass on that,' she said.

'That's your lookout.' This was obviously not the 'very helpful and charming' individual Leonie had spoken to when she'd made her enquiries. 'We'll see you on Wednesday, then, Ella Nesbit. The class starts at seven o'clock sharp.'

'I'll be there at five minutes to,' she told him, and then – just as she was about to put the phone down she said: 'Oh – by the way! How much does it cost?'

'Three hundred and ninety-five pounds.'

'Oh!' She was so taken aback at the amount that she found herself trying to cover her confusion. 'A snip!' she said in a jokey voice. 'Thanks for your help!'

Ella put the receiver down with a heavy hand, and – she realized to her dismay – a heavy heart as well. What in God's name was she letting herself in for? An opportunity to indulge in a relaxing rec-reational sport, or the prospect of forking out £395 for boot camp? The person she had spoken to was obviously some despotic Pol Pot type. And it sounded as if he was totally challenged in the humour department, which wouldn't help matters. The word 'fun' had featured a lot in their glossy brochure. She wondered if she should draw it to the attention of the trades description people.

'Having second thoughts?' Jack raised an eyebrow at her pensive expression.

'No,' said Ella. 'It just costs a lot of money.'

'What costs a lot of money?' Patrick had swung through the door with a flurry and shake of his wet umbrella.

'Ella's just enrolled on her scuba diving course.'

'Oh? When do you start?'

'Wednesday. I'd better get in touch with Toptree Foods and find out about booking the dates for the holiday today. I should just about have time to get all my training out of the way before I go.'

'Are you still thinking about disappearing in December?'

'Yeah.' Ella dragged the desk diary towards her and drew a big smiley face on the page marking the first Monday of December. 'That's my optimum date. Is that cool with you, Patrick?'

'That's cool. The Christmas rush will be just about over by then.'

'You'll miss a lot of agency parties, Ella,' cautioned Jack.

She shrugged. 'I won't miss the hangovers.'

Patrick picked up the scuba brochure. 'They mention the word "fun" a lot in here,' he remarked, as he flicked through the pages.

'Well, if they're all going to be like that geezer who answered the phone it's not going to be a barrel of laughs. Twenty-four hours of training, Patrick! Two hours a week desk work, followed by two hours in a pool! And an exam, and you have to get through four dives in the Irish Sea.' She shuddered and then reconsidered. 'No. I'll go for the referral option. I'm not diving in Sheep's Head bloody Bay. I'll definitely do those dives in Jamaica.'

'Aw, come on, Scubagirl. Give us a laugh, why don't you?' said Jack. 'I'll sit on the beach in my sheepskin jacket with a hip flask and a picnic and cheer you on.'

'A hip flask sounds like a very good idea,' said Ella. 'Maybe you should drive me out and then whisk me off to the Harbour Bar for copious hot whiskies afterwards.'

'Talking about transport – how are you going to manage the long haul out to Portdelvin every Wednesday?' asked Patrick.

'I'll get the DART.'

'What? And DART it home again after spending two hours shivering your ass off in a pool? C'mon, Ella – get real. I'll lend you the car.'

Patrick occasionally lent her his car if her need was greater than his. It was very handy – she had friends out in Wicklow whom she would probably never have managed to see at all if it hadn't been for him. And she loved driving it – it was a seriously smart little two-seater Merc convertible.

'Every Wednesday, Patrick? I can't expect you to do that.'

'It's not a problem, Ella. You can drop me off on your way, and leave the car back when you're through. And it's a way of saying thank you for being such a sweetheart and bringing Leonie to Jamaica with you. She hasn't had a foreign holiday for years, and I was starting to feel guilty about it. I was even toying with the idea of inviting her to come to France with us next summer.' Patrick and his wife Claudia owned a small villa in the Midi.

'But that would be disastrous! Claudia would go demented!' Leonie and her daughter-in-law did *not* get on. In fact, they couldn't even bear to be in the same room.

'I know. That's why I really owe you, Ella.'

'Well, thanks, Patrick! I feel awful now for all that moaning I've been doing about being the receptionist. I promise you won't hear another peep out of me between now and December. It'll be like Home, Home on the Range in here.'

'Home, Home on the Range?' repeated Jack.

'Where Seldom is Heard a Discouraging Word,' explained Ella.

'And the Sky is not Cloudy All Day.' Julian came in, and Ella's smile faded. She snuck a look at her watch. It was bang on nine-thirty. He was on time. 'It's cloudy out there, though, I can tell you. Some amateur weatherman said on the radio this morning that we're going to have the worst winter in a decade.' He was wearing his waterproof suit, and there was a drip on the end of his bony nose.

'Well, if that's the case, Ella, you're one lucky baggage.' Jack got to his feet and performed that lovely lazy stretch he did so well. The fact that he was so completely unselfconscious about how well he did it made it even lovelier.

'What's so lucky about the worst winter in a

61

decade?' asked Julian, divesting himself of his bicycle clips.

'Ella's not going to be here,' explained Jack. 'Well, for two weeks of it, anyway. She's heading off to go scuba diving in the Caribbean.'

It was the first Julian had heard of it. 'Oh? When?'

'The beginning of December, with a bit of luck.' Ella tried not to look smug. 'I've won a holiday to Jamaica.'

'Oh. Great.' Julian gave her his thin-lipped excuse for a smile. 'I didn't know you were into scuba.'

'I'm not. Well, not until now, that is. I'm taking a six-week course before I go.'

'Where?'

'ActivMarine, in Portdelvin.'

'Ah. Yeah.' Julian nodded his head in an irritatingly knowledgeable way. 'That's the outfit I trained with.'

'*You* did?' She couldn't prevent her jaw from dropping a little.

'Yeah. I did my advanced open water training with ActivMarine last year.'

Oh shit. She couldn't bear it. Not only was Julian a certified open water diver, he was an *advanced* open water diver! She thought she might get sick. Why was life so unfair? Now she'd have to sit through hours of him droning on about scuba diving as well as showing off in the studio.

'They're a great bunch of lads out there.' Julian did something with his chin that she supposed was meant to look manly. 'Know their stuff. You'll be in good hands, Ella.' He put his bicycle clips in the pocket of his waterproof suit and hung it on the hat stand. It looked like a dripping bat. 'Scuba's tough, but it's fun. I've had some great experiences in tropical water, but there's some excellent diving off the West Coast of Ireland. In fact, I might head west for a dive weekend over the Christmas break,' he added, nodding his head again, this time in a nauseatingly contemplative way.

'Christmas? In the worst winter of the decade?' said Jack. 'Won't the water freeze your bollocks off?'

'Not when you're wearing a dry-suit,' said Julian. 'Mine's a customized state-of-the-art compressed neoprene. Keeps me warm and bone-dry.'

'I wouldn't have thought the visibility would be much good in December, either,' remarked Patrick.

'Well, it depends on conditions. It can be murky, sometimes. But even in poor visibility you can encounter marine life. Wrasse, for instance.' Wrasse? Ella had read somewhere that 'rass' was Jamaican patois for arse. Was Julian trying to put her off? 'And pollock. And I saw a shark down in Killary once. Yeah. You can see some amazing stuff off the West Coast. Tubeworms are totally astonishing.'

Thank you for sharing that with me, Julian, thought Ella. So. Scuba diving was fun, was it? Freezing water, crap visibility, nerds like Julian floundering around in murk, wrasse and pollocks, for Jesus' sake, and *tubeworms* – yeuch – and, and – sharks and Pol bleeding Pot types like the one she'd spoken to on the phone earlier . . .

'You'll have fun, Ella,' said Julian. The f-word again! 'If you get through the training, that is.'

She bloody well would.

Chapter Three

The following Wednesday evening, Ella slid into
the driver's seat of her uncle's cherry red Merc
feeling quite chuffed with herself. Here she was in
a groovy car, heading off to learn all about one of
the sexiest hobbies in the world! Recreational
diving! She slid the seat forward, adjusted the rearview mirror and changed the channel on the car
radio. Time Saver Traffic told her that there'd been
an accident on the coast road, and that traffic was
backed up as far as Booterstown. Uh-oh. Maybe she
should have got the DART after all.

Progress was slow. She'd allowed herself an hour
to get to Portdelvin, but she now realized it wasn't
going to be enough. Well. It wouldn't matter if she
was a few minutes late, would it? Pol Pot had said
seven sharp, but nothing in Ireland ever started on
time. The Irish were a laid-back race – that was part
of their charm, after all. Visitors to the country were
always commenting on how refreshingly easygoing
the Celtic nature was.

Forty minutes later, looking round her at the
other motorists stuck in commuter belt hell, she
saw high-achieving, stressed-out Celtic tiger types

snarling with road rage behind the wheels of their Beamers and Mercs. Somewhere along the line the sleepy-village mentality of the average Irish person had been given either a shot in the arm or a kick up the arse. Even she was starting to whimper a little with mild road annoyance, despite the lazy jazz she'd put on the CD player to conjure a mellow vibe. By the time she reached Portdelvin it was seven o'clock on the dot. Shit. She hoped that Pol Pot wouldn't remind her that she said she'd be there at five minutes to. She cruised along the seafront, looking for ActivMarine. When she hit the little harbour, she knew she'd gone too far. She turned the car, drove back the way she'd come, and looked some more. Finally she stopped a passing dog-walker. 'Excuse me?' she said. 'Would you happen to know where ActivMarine is?'

'The scuba-diving place?' said the man. 'Yes. It's right there.' He indicated a shop front two doors down. She wasn't surprised she'd missed it. The joint looked shut.

'Thanks,' she said. 'Enjoy your walk.'

A parking space was what she needed next. Again she drove up and down the seafront, starting to feel a little panicky. It was ten past seven now. At last she saw someone pull out and she swooped down on the vacant space, thanking God for her uncle's power-steering. She grabbed her bag, zapped the locks and ran down the road, cursing her girly heels. Her receptionist's garb of the day was the stretch cotton skirt that Jack had said made her ass look great, teamed with a plain black FCUK top. When she got to the dive shop she rang the bell. After a minute or two spent peering through the window at the dim interior lined with rails of scuba suits and serried ranks of tanks, she rang again and eventually saw a door opening at the back of the shop. A shaven-headed man in his twenties approached and looked at her questioningly, and by pointing to the door and to her watch and spreading her palms apologetically she managed to convey that she was there for the class. A bunch of keys was produced, and the door unlocked. 'Sorry I'm late,' she said as she teetered through. 'The traffic was a bitch. I'm Ella Nesbit – I'm starting your open water course this evening.'

'No problem. You haven't missed much – they've just been filling in forms. You can do yours later.' He smiled at her and held out his hand. She noticed that a long scar zigzagged along the back of his wrist. 'My name's PJ Farrell.' Was this Pol Pot? She thought not. Pol Pot would have given out to her for being late, and this geezer had lovely crinkly eyes and an easygoing manner.

'Are you an instructor?' asked Ella, shaking his hand. She hoped he was.

'Yeah. I'm not doing any of the academic stuff with you, but I'll be helping out in the pool later. Come on through.'

She followed him through the door at the back of the shop, along a corridor whose walls were hung with framed photographs of underwater scenes featuring divers and reefs and exotic fish, and into a fluorescently lit room where a dozen or so individuals were sitting at rows of desks. They were all male, with the exception of one sporty-looking woman in an olive-green tracksuit.

A tall bloke was standing at the top of the classroom writing on a blackboard. Long blond dreadlocks snaked down his back beyond his shoulder blades. He turned when Ella came through the door, and then referred to a clipboard. 'Ella Nesbit,' he said, raising an eyebrow at her. He didn't bother with a question mark, and she was reminded of the way he hadn't bothered with exclamation marks either, that time she'd talked to him on the phone. He looked at his watch in an irritatingly meaningful way. This had to be Pol Pot. Somehow she'd imagined him as looking very different. More of a sergeant-major type. The last thing she'd have predicted would have been dreadlocks. He even had quite good bone structure – apart from a broken nose.

'We've a full quota now,' said PJ Farrell.

Pol Pot nodded, and motioned her to a seat. The only ones free were at the very front of the class, and she felt a bit stupid as she high-heeled her way to the top of the room and slid out of her coat and into a chair. She'd immediately registered that everyone else in the room was dressed in jeans and sweaters and sensible-looking shoes, and she could feel their eyes taking in her girly gear.

'Here's a form to fill in,' he said, handing it to her.

She noticed a diagonal scar running from the edge of his jaw to his cheekbone. It terminated just below the outer corner of his left eye. Ella decided she was going to do an inventory of scars. If scars were a feature on every single instructor's anatomy she might have serious second thoughts about taking up recreational diving as a hobby. 'It's to verify that you're in good physical nick,' he added, as she opened the questionnaire.

'I am,' she said.

'Oh?' His look of amused enquiry invited elaboration, and she felt herself colour. Infuriating git! He was *smirking* at her!

'I had an assessment done at my gym recently,' she explained in brisk tones, taking a pen out of her bag.

'You still need to fill it in. No cheating.'

No cheating! Where was she – at a night class or in kindergarten? She scanned the checklist of questions on the form and mentally crossed them all off. No, she didn't suffer from obesity; no, she didn't suffer from a collapsed lung; no, she didn't have a history of drug or alcohol abuse, blah blah blah. The list went on and on.

Only one of the conditions made her think twice. Claustrophobia. She had suffered from it as a child, but she hadn't had an attack for ages – which was just as well, because one of the recording booths she was required to work in was pretty poky.

Pol Pot leaned back in his seat, splayed out long, combat-clad legs, and addressed the class. 'OK.

Hands up who hasn't read the first chapter of the manual you were issued with?'

Ella looked round. Not one person in the room had raised their hand.

Pol Pot resumed. 'Everyone's done their homework? Good. It's important that you familiarize yourself with the relevant chapter before coming to class because—'

'Excuse me?' said Ella. 'I don't have a manual.'

He narrowed his eyes at her and she found herself going pink again. 'So, Ella,' he said. 'You're at a disadvantage. Please come prepared next week because I don't want to have to waste time doing remedial work.' Remedial work! Ex*cuse* me? 'It's not fair on the rest of the group.'

Oh. The old guilt trip tactic never failed with her. 'Of course,' she said quickly. 'I'll do two lots of homework next week. I don't want to run the risk of ending up in detention.' It was a pathetic joke, and possibly ill-timed, but Pol Pot acknowledged it with what could best be described as a perfunctory smile.

'We don't do detention here. We're more into traditional maritime forms of punishment.'

Ella didn't want to ask, but somebody else in the classroom did. 'Hey! Whips and manacles are considered forms of *punishment*?' came a male voice.

'Only if you're a deeply unimaginative individual,' said Pol Pot, raising an amused eyebrow. 'I might have known you'd suss that one, Richie.'

Ella turned round. Pol Pot had directed the remark at a good-looking geezer who she gauged was somewhere in his early twenties. He had eyes the colour of blue denim, an open, extremely engaging expression, and he was sitting back in his chair with his feet up on the one in front of him. Timberlands, noticed Ella. She also noticed the rather sexy way his brown hair flopped over his forehead and the jacket in a truly appalling shade of green he was wearing. He smiled at her, and she smiled back before returning her attention to Pol Pot.

'Here's your crew pack.' He passed her a blue nylon folder. 'Happy reading, Ella.'

Ella opened the folder. There was a logbook in it, and some Filofaxy pages and a plastic card with DIVE TABLE printed at the top. It was so busy with figures that it looked as if a spider had been tap-dancing across it. She took out her manual. There were the usual seductive pictures on the cover of rainbow-coloured fish and aquamarine scenery and graceful divers. Flicking through the introduction she saw that the 'fun' word featured heavily, alongside similar nouns such as 'excitement' and 'adventure' and 'new friends'.

But the pages further on told a different story. They were dense with text and diagrams and photographs of divers doing complicated stuff with equipment. As she leafed through the book, her heart plummeted. There were sections on contaminated air and nitrogen narcosis and decompression

sickness. There was advice on problem management such as Running Out of Air, Near Drowning
and Entanglement. Where was the fun and excitement in all that? she wondered. Although nitrogen
narcosis sounded cool. Apparently it induced feelings of euphoria.

'OK,' said Pol Pot. 'Let's get going.' He reached
behind him and turned a dimmer switch, then
aimed a remote control device at a television
monitor. 'We'll start by watching a video. It's pretty
seductive stuff – a lot of it shot off reefs in the
Tropics. Diving in Irish waters is more – challenging.'

'Module One,' Ella read on the screen. 'The
Principles of Buoyancy . . .'

* * *

The video contained a lot of footage of people on
beaches fiddling about with scuba equipment.
They all smiled a lot, to show what fun they were
having as they strapped huge tanks onto each
other and gave each other high-fives and waddled
around sideways on flippers. Except they weren't
called flippers, the soothing mid-Atlantic voice-
over told her. They were called fins. Ella tried hard
to concentrate, but by the end of the video she still
wasn't sure what a BCD was and what SPG stood
for, or what blind bit of difference there was
between a J-valve and a K-valve.

When the credits finally started to roll, Pol Pot
turned the monitor off and then went over every-

thing they'd just watched on the screen. By the time the two hours was up, Ella's mind was reeling. The only thing that really had made sense to her in Module One was the bit about always having a buddy at hand as a support system. She hoped it wasn't considered mandatory to high-five each other, as well.

'Does everyone have transport?' enquired Pol Pot at the end of the class. 'The pool's a couple of miles away. Hands up anyone who needs a lift.'

A couple of hands were raised.

'And hands up who's prepared to give lifts?'

Ella stuck her left hand up. Her right was busy filling in answers about her fitness level on her questionnaire.

'OK – Gerry, you go with Stephen. Have I got the names right? Good. And Richie, you go with Ella.'

Ella turned round to face the bloke with the great smile and the vile green jacket.

'Hi,' she said. 'You're Richie?'

'That's right.'

'I'm Ella Nesbit.'

'Ellen, or Ella as in Ella Fitzgerald?'

'You got it right second time.' She returned her attention to her form. She'd got as far as the question about claustrophobia. Should she answer yes or no? Fuck it, she thought, scribbling in 'no'. It was highly unlikely her childhood condition would recur now she was halfway through her twenties. She quickly filled in 'no' to all the other questions, and then she got to her feet, slid her manual into its blue folder, and zipped it up. Everyone else was doing the same, in that pseudo-absorbed way that people do when they need some business to cover their awkwardness at not knowing anyone. At the top of the class Pol Pot was leafing through the forms that had been filled in earlier. 'Excuse me, P—' said Ella. 'I mean, excuse me. Please. Here's mine.' She handed it to him and he ran his eyes down her filled-in form.

'Well, Ella,' he said. 'You were right. You *are* in good physical nick.' Ella made to move away, but he reached out a hand to stop her. His hand against the white skin of her wrist was as brown, hard and rough as the pad of an animal's paw. 'Hang on,' he said. 'You missed a bit. I need your signature here.'

As Ella rummaged in her bag for her pen, Pol Pot yawned and stretched. The fabric of his T-shirt rode up, and Ella immediately slid her eyes away from the tanned expanse of skin that was exposed. Stop stretching, she thought crossly. Jack Noonan's the only man in the world who's allowed to stretch like that. She quickly signed the form, and made to back off again.

'I like the way you loop your L's,' he remarked.

'What?'

'Your L's,' he said, indicating the form. 'You've a great signature.'

'Oh. Thanks.' She tried a smile out on him, but he wasn't looking at her any more. He was yawning again. Ella turned away before he could ease himself into another stretch.

The class had started to file out of the door and back through the shop. Ella followed them past a group of people who were talking in the arcane language of scuba. Seasoned divers, obviously, to judge by the scars.

Outside, PJ and some helpers were just finishing loading equipment into a white van with ActivMarine emblazoned on it in blue. 'I'd appreciate it if you could all help unload once we get to the pool,' said PJ. 'Does everyone know the way?'

'I don't,' said Ella.

'I do,' said Richie. 'I'll direct you. Where's your car?'

'This way.' Ella indicated where she'd parked, and she and Richie set off down the road. The rest of the class climbed into various vehicles and started their engines, and Ella got her car keys out of her bag and zapped the locks on Patrick's Merc.

'Wow. Class car,' said Richie.

'It's not mine. It's my uncle's,' she explained with alacrity. She didn't want this bloke to think she was some super-cool rich bitch with a Merc for a runabout. As she slid into the driver's seat, the dive van lumbered past with Pol Pot at the wheel. PJ was in the passenger seat. 'What's the name of the geezer who lectured us?' she asked, putting the car into gear and moving away from the kerb.

'That's Ferdia MacDiarmada,' said Richie.

'Bit of a crosspatch, isn't he? Kind of gives the lie

75

to all that guff in the book about scuba diving being fun.'

'He's just a bit depressed at the moment. His dog died last week.'

Ella looked surprised. 'And he felt he had to share this news with the entire *class*?'

'Jesus, no.'

'So how come you know his dog died, then?'

'He's my cousin.'

'Oh.' She bit her lip. 'Sorry for bad-mouthing him.'

'No problem,' said Richie. He turned to her and smiled. 'I won't tell him what you said if you promise to give me a lift to the pool after class every week.'

'OK,' she said, smiling back as she put the car into fourth. 'It's a deal.' She turned on the CD player. The jazz she'd been listening to on the way out oozed through the speakers, and she quickly switched back to 98FM. Slow jazz was way too sexy to be playing for a mere acquaintance. 'What did you think of the class this evening?' asked Ella. 'Could you make sense of all that stuff?'

'Pretty well,' Richie admitted. 'I took Ferdia's advice and did my homework.'

'I felt like a bit of a dilettante,' confessed Ella. 'He obviously thinks I am, anyway.'

'Ferdia? Why? Just because you hadn't read the first chapter?' Richie shook his head. 'Nah. His bark is worse than his bite, you know. But be warned. He doesn't suffer fools gladly.'

'I'll swot all week, then.' She furrowed her brow.

'Hell – I'll need to. I got completely mixed up with all those technical terms. Why can't they just call a regulator "the breathing thingy" or a BCD "the blowy-up floaty jacket". And what's an SPG when it's at home? I find all that acronym stuff really confusing.'

'It gets worse,' said Richie. 'I've heard Ferdia come out with shit like "OK, then we had to lose the DV and the BCD and get the ABS on to the RIB for CPR ASAP."'

'Jesus!' Ella laughed. 'It's just as well PJ wasn't involved in that particular scenario.'

'He was. And to add to the confusion, another of the divers was called TP.'

'Well. It looks like I'm going to have to learn a foreign language as well as everything else.'

'It'll be worth it.'

'So everyone keeps telling me. I just thought it would be more straightforward.'

'Can't you handle technical stuff?'

'On the contrary,' she said, with a small degree of hauteur. 'I'm a sound engineer by profession. But that's a very different kind of technology.'

'A sound engineer? Wow. Do you work with any famous bands?'

'No,' she admitted. 'Sorry to disappoint you. The studio I work in specializes mainly in ads. We do some film and television stuff too.'

'So you get to work with famous actors?'

She smiled and shrugged. 'Sometimes. What do you do, Richie?'

'I'm a student. With a bit of luck I'll be graduating in marine archaeology in a couple of years.'

'Cool!'

'Not as cool as sound engineering. What made you decide to get into that?'

'I had the most important qualification for the job.'

'Oh? What's that?'

'A good ear,' said Ella.

Richie looked quizzically at her. 'It's funny,' he said. 'To look at you, the last thing I could imagine you doing would be engineering of any kind.'

'Oh? What could you imagine me being?' If he said 'receptionist' she'd stop the car and boot him out.

'I dunno really. Something classier, I suppose.'

'Classy! Me! Get off! I stagger through life making mistakes all over the place.'

'I can relate to that. I made the huge mistake of buying this jacket today. I hate it.'

'Then why did you buy it?'

'It seemed like a good idea at the time – the colour didn't look so acid in the shop. And it had been marked down three times in a sale.'

'I'm not surprised. It's really horrible.' They smiled at each other and an idea struck her. 'Hey! Will you be my buddy, Richie, in the pool sessions?'

'With pleasure, Ella,' he replied urbanely.

The archway they finally drove through was hung with a sign that read *Rosemount Leisure Centre* in wavy aquamarine lettering. Ella pulled up alongside the ActivMarine van and killed her lights. People were already unloading equipment from the back of the van.

'Time to heave-ho,' said Ella to Richie as they joined the queue. She dragged out a tank and staggered sideways on her high heels. 'Holy shomoly – this weighs a ton!'

'Take it easy,' warned Ferdia, who was passing down the gear. 'You don't want to strain your back. Take this instead.' He handed her a box full of masks.

'No, no, I'm fine with this,' said Ella, stung by the implication that she was a wimp. She struggled through the door of the leisure centre after the other divers, noticing that the one other girl on the course was handling her tank with comparative ease.

They changed, then assembled by the poolside, and were divided into groups of four. Ella was teamed with Richie and Jan – the sporty-looking girl – and a middle-aged man called Dan. Crinkly-eyed PJ was their instructor. It took ages to assemble the equipment, and Ella felt utterly ridiculous when she was finally kitted out. The length of the fins strapped onto her feet meant that she could only shuffle backwards or sideways, and entering the water was an exercise so humiliating it might have been devised by someone with a grudge against recreational divers. Her tank got stuck on the side of the pool, and she dangled for a while, unable to move either up or down. At least it was smiling PJ who extricated her from her predicament, not grim-faced Ferdia. She'd seen him barking instructions at some unfortunate assistant earlier.

The water was cooler than tepid. Her group of four lurched around in the shallow end for a while, watching PJ demonstrating the skills they'd be required to learn. Down at the other end of the pool, the other members of the class had already disappeared under the water, learning fast. She was obviously in the duffers' group.

'Some buddy you are,' she remarked as Richie went bobbing off in the direction of the deep end.

'I can't help it,' he said, laughing over his shoulder. 'I've no control over where I'm going. I feel like an inflatable beach toy.'

She realized what he meant as soon as she pressed the inflator button on her BCD and found herself colliding into Dan, feeling very foolish. 'Sorry,' she said, as she bounced off his chest.

'That's all right,' he said to the back of her head as she took off in the opposite direction. The only one who didn't seem to have a problem controlling her manoeuvres was Jan.

'OK,' said PJ, when they'd all somehow managed to reunite. 'Regulators in your mouths, take a few breaths, then deflate your BCDs and you'll find out what it's like to breathe underwater for the first time.'

They did as they were told, and as Ella felt the water creep up her face and over her head she felt a *frisson* of excitement. Endorphins at last! She found herself smiling as she inhaled once – a long, slow breath – and then again and again. She had gills!

She might have had gills, but the thermoplastic fins she'd strapped to her feet weren't much help to her in her new incarnation as mermaid. When they eventually got round to exploring the deep end of the pool she felt as if she was free-falling in slow motion. Her uncoordinated movements on the surface were positively balletic compared to her underwater manoeuvres.

But at least she wasn't the only one who was finding it impossible to manage. Divers were drifting surreally all around her. It was hard to make out who was who behind the masks, but it was easy to distinguish the masters from the pupils. The instructors, kitted out in neoprene suits, swam around effortlessly, like elegant aquatic shepherds tending their flock. At one stage she noticed Ferdia glide past, his blond dreadlocks rendering him instantly identifiable. The way they drifted around his head reminded her of a film she'd seen as a child, which had starred a palomino pony. In slow-motion sequences of the horse galloping, its tail had looked just the way Ferdia's ponytail did now, streaming out behind in feathery tendrils. He glanced briefly at her as he passed. Mortified by her own clumsiness she looked away, only to see Dan's head sticking out from between her splayed legs. The expression on his face under the mask was one of such profound apology that Ella wanted to laugh.

But when she did, water trickled into her mouth through the gap she'd made between her lips and the regulator. She began to cough.

'Are you OK?' PJ signalled to her, raising his eyebrows into question marks and making a circle with his thumb and forefinger.

'I'm OK,' she signalled back, before realizing that she wasn't. She scrabbled back up to the surface and took her regulator out of her mouth so that she could cough freely. PJ joined her.

'Are you all right?'

'Yeah. I'm all right now,' she insisted after she'd recovered herself. 'I've just realized that it's probably not a very good idea to laugh underwater.'

'Oh, yes it is,' said PJ. 'In fact, I can guarantee you'll be doing a lot of it.' He smiled at the sceptical look she gave him. 'I mean it,' he said. 'Ready to go back down?'

'Yeah,' said Ella, taking a deep breath. 'I'm ready. But I still don't believe you about the laughing bit.'

As they descended, she caught sight of Ferdia and one of the other instructors sharing a private joke in sign language on the other side of the deep end. They were laughing their asses off.

* * *

'How did you get on?' asked Julian the following morning after he'd divested himself of his cycling gear.

'Fine,' returned Ella airily. She wasn't going to tell him that she'd floundered around like a drunken mermaid and nearly choked to death.

The aftermath of the training session had been a bit grim. Her duffers' group was the last one out of the pool, and they'd had to dismantle their equipment before they could get dressed. The changing rooms were very end-of-dayish, and she wished she'd remembered to bring flip-flops. She was certain she was going to end up with athlete's foot. Verrucas, too, probably, knowing her luck.

'Who did your academic stuff with you?'

'Ferdia.'

'Sound bloke, Ferdia. We go way back – I was at school with him. Who took you for the pool work?'

'PJ.'

'Hey! PJ!'

Oh shut *up*, Julian, she thought.

'It's fun, isn't it?' he said, sitting on her desk the way Jack did. She thought it a bit over-familiar of him.

'Yeah,' said Ella, wishing she was a better actress.

'Not very glamorous, though. Especially when you end up with a bad case of diver's face.'

'What's diver's face?'

'Well, the deeper you dive, the more pressure there is on your sinuses. When you get back up to the surface and take off your mask you find your face is covered in snot.'

Jesus! She'd looked in the changing-room mirror last night, and while there'd been no sign of snot, the mask had left a vivid red mark across her forehead and along her cheekbones. Her face had looked like the muzzle of some badly drawn cartoon animal. 'Thank you for sharing that with me, Julian,' she said, crisply, sorting through mail.

He smirked. 'It's only fair to let you know what you're in for. Did you go for a drink with the boys afterwards?'

'No. I was tired.' PJ had mentioned that the divemasters usually gravitated to the leisure centre club after the training session, and that their neophytes were welcome to join them there, but Ella had been too self-conscious about how idiotic she looked with her cartoon face to take him up on the invitation.

'You should. You get to learn a lot from those boys just by talking to them. Tell them I said hey next time you're out there, will you?'

'Sure.' She bloody wouldn't. The last thing she wanted was to be associated with a nerd like Julian Bollard. *Hi, PJ! Julian Bollard says 'hey'!* Oh, no.

He stood up and stretched, and Ella got the impression that he was trying to look like Jack when he performed his gloriously languid morning stretch. 'Right,' he remarked, looking at his watch. 'It's time to hit the Audiofile.' He helped himself to the latest copy of *Pro Sound News* that was fanned out with all the usual suspects on the coffee table, and set off up the stairs. 'See you later, toots,' he said, as he disappeared from view.

Toots! How fucking dare he! Ella swigged back her coffee, and set the mug down on the table with

84

a bang. She picked up the phone and pressed the button for the upstairs studio. 'Julian?' she said in her frostiest tone. 'I'd just like you to know that my uncle is the only person in the world who gets away with calling me "toots".' She put the phone down before he could reply. Then she reached down and pulled her dive manual out of her bag. There was a half-hour lull before the next session. She flicked through until she found the relevant page, and then she steeled herself. 'Module Two', she read.

*　　*　　*

Over the course of the following weeks Ella studied hard. By reading each module in advance of the actual class, she got a better grasp of the academic side of things, and she was glad to see that she never scored less than 90 per cent in the written tests they had to take.

The pool work was a different matter, though. She found it gruelling, and every Thursday morning she'd wake up with bruised and aching limbs. It was all right for blokes like PJ and Ferdia and all those divemaster types. They were big and hulking or tough and wiry, and they strode around the poolside swinging heavy tanks of pressurized air as if they were as lightweight as carrier bags from Marks and Sparks' lingerie department.

Out of the water, Ella was about as graceful as a beached walrus. She just couldn't get used to feeling so clumsy. Underwater, things were improving a bit because she was learning more about controlling her buoyancy, but on land she felt ridiculous. She would trudge along the side of the pool with Richie, laden with tank and weight-belt, and muttering imprecations.

'I hate this hobby,' she found herself saying one evening.

'Why don't you give up then?' he asked.

'Because I don't give up easily,' she returned.

'Time for your Giant Stride, Ella,' pronounced PJ, and she tried to ignore Richie's snigger.

She dreaded having to do her Giant Stride. It had to be the single least elegant physical manoeuvre she'd ever performed in her life. It involved shuffling sideways to the very edge of the pool and then stepping out into mid-air in the goose-step style favoured by the Gestapo, clutching your mask to your face. Richie had doubled up with laughter when he'd first seen her do it.

But every week she improved, and every week she learned a new skill. She learned how to flood and clear her mask underwater, she learned how to buddy-breathe and she learned how to communicate in sign language. She also learned how to laugh underwater without running the risk of drowning, and she and Richie spent a lot of time communicating in a rather juvenile makey-uppy sign language when PJ was busy testing Jan and Dan's skills.

They were still the duffer group, she was sad to admit. When she looked at the other groups she could see that they were all miles ahead in the skills they were mastering, and every week she and Richie and Jan and Dan were the last ones out of the pool. It was really Dan's fault, she reckoned, that they were lagging so far behind. He never did his homework, and she'd seen him cheating in the weekly test, riffling through his manual when he thought no-one was looking.

On the fifth Wednesday of the course Richie took her off for a drink with 'the boys' – as Julian had called them. Ella had loosened the strap on her mask at the start of the session, and she was relieved to see that there was no cartoon character's muzzle on her face when she looked in the mirror, and no snot either.

Richie was waiting for her when she emerged from the changing room, her heels echoing on the tiled floor. It was bitterly cold outside, and they legged it fast across the car park to the club.

'What'll you have?' asked Ella.

'I'll get it,' said Richie. 'As a reward for giving me all those lifts.'

'I won't hear of it,' said Ella. 'You're an impoverished student. I'm on an income.'

'A good one?' asked Richie.

'I wish.'

'But one that means you can swan off to Jamaica?'

'I *won* that holiday, Richie, remember?' She'd filled him in on the holiday thing a couple of weeks ago, when she'd given him his lift to the leisure centre. 'Or rather, my grandmother did.

Now, go and find somewhere for us to sit.'

She ordered two pints. At the other end of the bar Ferdia was ordering drinks too. Ella avoided his eyes. She paid for the pints and took them over to the table where Richie was sitting. She was happy to see that PJ was there too.

'I hear you're off to Jamaica,' said PJ, when she'd settled herself down between him and Richie. 'When are you going?'

'Beginning of December,' said Ella. 'I'm going to do all my training dives when I get there.'

PJ gave her a look of appraisal with his wonderful crinkly eyes. 'You might think about doing at least one dive while you're here, Ella. That means there won't be such pressure on you while you're on holiday, and you can do more dives in Jamaica for the sheer pleasure of it.'

'But that means I'd have to dive in Sheep's Head Bay! It'll be freezing!'

'You'll be wearing a wetsuit,' he pointed out. 'And it's a good idea to get a dive out of the way here before you go off diving in tropical waters. If you can master a dive in the Irish Sea in the month of November you can master a dive anywhere in the world.'

Ella laughed.

'I mean it,' said PJ.

'I believe you. I'm laughing at the idea of me swanning around the world on dive holidays like something out of Condé Nast's *Traveller*.'

'You don't have to do it the Condé Nast way.

Lots of people work up to instructor or divemaster status and work the dive sites.'

'That would be a brilliant way to see the world,' said Richie. 'Better than sitting on your arse having servants bring you iced Pimm's like those *Traveller* readers.'

'I feel sick every time I open that magazine,' said Ella with a heavy sigh. 'Who can *afford* those kind of holidays?'

'You'd be amazed. The Celtic tiger and his wife bugger off on them all the time.'

PJ gestured to Ferdia, who was standing in the middle of the floor with two pints in his hands, looking around him. 'Over here, Ferdia!' The other instructor clocked him and started to move towards their table. 'Not all dive holidays are unaffordable, you know Ella,' he resumed. 'We organize packages a couple of times a year. And we have brilliant dive weekends away in Lissamore in the west of Ireland every month.'

'Is the diving there really that good?'

'Yeah. Some of the best in the world.'

'How's that?'

'There's spectacular scenery – you would not believe some of the walls and cliffs out there – and there's no pollution.'

'Yet,' said Ferdia, putting a pint in front of PJ and sitting down beside him.

'I'd love to go on one of those dive weekends,' said Richie.

'Then you should think about doing an advanced

course,' said PJ, 'and go for the dry-suit speciality option. Dry-suits take some getting used to, but they're kinda mandatory for Irish diving.'

'Why?' asked Ella.

'Because they do what they say. They keep you bone dry, and you don't get as cold. You can stay down longer in a dry-suit.'

'I'm going to do a wreck diver speciality course some time,' said Richie. 'I'm dying to dive a wreck.'

Ferdia was lounging back in a seat across from Richie, nursing a pint and looking ruminative. He looked up at his cousin's words. 'You won't be specializing in anything if you carry on messing about the way you have been, Rich,' he remarked. 'I've noticed that your group's lagging behind. It'll be your own fault if you don't pass your exam.'

'No it won't. It'll be Duffer Dan's fault,' argued Richie.

'Duffer Dan?' queried PJ. 'Who on earth is Duffer Dan?'

Ella tried not to laugh.

'That's what Ella calls the middle-aged geezer who's holding us up.'

Ella gave Richie a dig in the ribs. 'That's not fair,' she hissed at him. 'I called *myself* a duffer. You were the one who came up with "Duffer Dan."'

'See what I mean?' said Ferdia, leaning back further in his chair and surveying the pair of them as they tried not to giggle. 'You're a pair of messers. I saw you tonight, clowning around and making daft gestures at each other instead of concentrating on what PJ was demonstrating.'

'We only did that when he was working with Jan and d-Dan,' said Richie. He and Ella burst out sniggering again, and kept their heads averted.

'It's a good idea to watch your divemaster all the time, even when he's concentrating on other individuals in the group,' said PJ equably. 'That's the best way to learn.'

'That's right,' concurred Ferdia. 'You want to show your instructor a little more respect. What he teaches you could save your life one day.' He took a swig of his pint and the pair of them sobered instantly.

'OK,' said Richie humbly. He turned to PJ. 'Sorry, PJ. I promise to stop messing in the pool. Maybe Ella and I should swap groups.'

She saw PJ and Ferdia exchange glances, and she knew that they were thinking the same thing. Oh, no! she thought. Her dive buddy's juvenile sense of humour was the only thing about Wednesday evenings that was keeping her sane.

'That's probably not a bad idea,' said PJ. 'You'll catch up faster if you stop distracting each other.'

Ferdia said nothing. He just raised an eyebrow and shot Richie a sceptical look. 'Well? Are you going to wise up a bit?'

'Yeah, yeah.' Another sceptical look from his cousin. 'I'm determined to qualify, you know, Ferdia!' protested Richie. 'I'm going to dive the

Lusitania one day. Maybe I'll even get to dive god status, like you.'

'Then you are going to have to work your ass off, Rich.'

'I damn well will,' said Richie, with feeling. 'I'm going to do as many courses as I can afford. I'll end up getting hooked, I suppose. Like you did.'

Ferdia smiled. It was such a rare a sight that it took Ella a bit by surprise. 'That's right,' he said. 'The first time I went down I never wanted to come up again.' He looked at Ella suddenly. 'You're a lucky woman to be heading off to Jamaica to dive. I spent three months diving the reefs there once.'

Ella was surprised. 'Three months on holiday?'

He gave her a pitying look. 'No,' he said. 'Working for a dive outfit.'

Of course. How stupid of her.

'Whereabouts are you going?' asked PJ.

'Salamander Cove, on the north-east coast. Near Port Antonio.'

'I know it,' said Ferdia. 'It's a classy joint.'

'Is that where you worked?'

'I helped out from time to time. Desirée had a reciprocal arrangement with the resort that employed me. She used to call on us if she was stuck.'

'Desirée?'

'She runs the outfit. She's some lady. If you're very lucky she might take you down herself.'

Ella said nothing. She'd actually prefer to go down with some gorgeous dive god type like PJ. She snuck a look at him from under her lashes, and was pleased to see he was looking back.

'Ella's thinking about doing her first qualifying dive off Sheep's Head,' said PJ, smiling at her. 'So that she can get a taste of what it's like to dive in less than perfect conditions.'

Ferdia cocked his head to one side. 'Thinking about it? People who think about it never do it.'

That decided her. 'I *am* going to do it,' she said.

PJ gave her another smile – of approval this time – and she felt the same small thrill of smugness she used to get when her teacher at prep school told her she'd come top of the class. It hadn't happened that often. A girl called Shetty Deepak had usually come top. She had never forgotten the name.

*   *   *

A little later she said good night to Richie and the rest of them and went to get the car. The leisure centre car park was a bit scary. There was nothing parked there now apart from the dive van, and the place wasn't particularly well lit. As she took the key from her bag and went to zap the locks, she froze suddenly. Something had whimpered. She stood motionless for a moment, listening. A low whining noise was coming from beneath the dive van, which was parked in a dark corner under a tree. Ella moved cautiously towards it, and then she got down on her hunkers and peered under the van. A black-and-white collie dog was looking back at her with a fearful expression on its intelligent face.

'Hello, boy,' said Ella gently, stretching out a tentative hand, ready to withdraw it at once if the dog growled. It didn't. It licked its muzzle and then it leaned towards her, sniffing cautiously. Its breath was warm on her cold fingers. 'Come here, boy,' said Ella. 'C'mon. I'm not going to hurt you.' Slowly the dog advanced towards her, keeping its belly low against the ground and moving in that way that dogs do who have been beaten regularly. It was painfully thin. Ella remained crouching on her hunkers. 'Hello, darling,' she said, as her hand made contact with the dog's ear. 'What are you doing here? Why aren't you at home? It's a horrible night to be stuck outside in a car park.' She rubbed the fur of the dog's ear, and as she did so, she saw its tail begin a tentative movement. 'There, now!' said Ella. 'Good boy!'

'It's a bitch.' A voice came from just behind and above her, and she turned, startled. Ferdia was silhouetted against the navy-blue sky, looking down at her. From her crouched viewpoint he looked even taller than usual.

'Jesus – you gave me a fright!' she said, nearly losing her balance on her heels. The hand that had been stroking the dog's ear had flown to her throat in alarm.

'Sorry,' he said, not sounding sorry at all. He lowered himself to his hunkers beside her and looked at the collie. 'Hello, beautiful,' he murmured. The dog responded by moving her tail more vigorously and raising a paw. Ferdia took it

94

and then he sucked in his breath. 'Ow. Who did that to you, darling?' he asked. For the first time Ella was aware of a gaping wound running from just above the dog's right front paw to the very top of its skinny leg. Ferdia ran a hand along the animal's flank, assessing her physical condition. Her eyes took on a dazed look. It was as if she'd never been caressed before. 'You've been starved, too, haven't you, sweetheart?' He examined her some more, and then sucked in his breath again. 'Jesus, hell. Oh, darling, you need to be seen by a vet. This is urgent.'

'Oh, God – is it really? You'll never get a vet to come out at this hour of the night.' Ella had wrapped her arms around herself, and was hopping from foot to foot to try and stay warm.

'I will,' said Ferdia. 'I've a mate who's a vet, and he owes me a favour.'

'Oh?'

'Yeah. He had to put my dog down for me last month.'

Oh, hell. 'I'm sorry,' she said, getting to her feet.

'Don't be. She had a massive tumour. It was a mercy killing.' He stood up, unlocked the back of the dive van and pulled out a worn woollen blanket. 'Here, sweetheart,' he said to the dog. 'You're coming with me.' He kneeled down and wrapped the dog in the blanket, then picked her up very carefully and laid her in the back of the van. Ella was so used to seeing Ferdia barking orders and striding along the poolside like a conquistador marshalling his forces that it came as something of a surprise to see him suddenly behaving like Saint Francis of Assisi. The dog was looking up at him with liquid brown eyes. The expression on her face as he closed the door verged on worship. It reminded Ella of the expression on the dog's face in a painting she'd seen once of *The Adoration of the Magi.*

Ferdia stood back from the van and looked down at Ella. 'That's your car, isn't it?' he asked, nodding his head at Patrick's shiny little Merc.

'Yes,' she said. She didn't bother explaining that it wasn't her car. She didn't think he'd be interested.

'I'd park it outside on the road next week, if I were you. There's a lot of vandalism in this car park after the pool closes. They always go for the posh ones.'

'Thanks for the advice. Good night, and good luck with the vet.' She shimmied across the car park, zapped the locks and slid into the driver's seat, kicking off her heels as she always did when she drove. Across from her, Ferdia was climbing into the van. 'See you next week,' she called, before closing the door.

'Yeah,' he remarked absently. 'Good night, Ella.'

Wow. He'd actually remembered her name.

Chapter Four

The following Wednesday was their final session in the pool. Ella had got a headache from trying to work out dive tables on the dive planner earlier, and she was cross because she and Richie had been split up. 'It's for your own good,' she'd been told, which made her feel more than ever like a badly behaved schoolgirl. Richie stayed with PJ's group, Ella was banished to Ferdia's.

The group descended at the deep end of the pool, and Ferdia began his demonstration of how to take a scuba unit off underwater. Ella couldn't imagine ever wanting to do this in a real-life scenario, but she'd been told it might be necessary if her unit ever became entangled in weed. The instructor went through the manoeuvre effortlessly, step by step, and after the demonstration he turned to Ella. 'You,' he signalled with an authoritative index finger, indicating that she follow his example. She undid her waistband with relative ease, and snapped the release catch on her shoulder straps. She then extracted first her left arm and then her right from her BCD. To her embarrassment, as she slid the BCD away from her right shoulder, the strap of her swimsuit came with it, and when she looked down she saw that her right breast was fully exposed. There was nothing she could do – she needed both hands to keep hold of her unit. Well, the geezers in her new group were pretty damn lucky, she thought resignedly, having a nice flash of tit to keep up their morale.

She couldn't see the hand that made contact with her upper arm because her peripheral vision was restricted by her mask, but she felt someone drawing the strap back up until it was securely in place on her shoulder once more. She turned to find herself looking directly into Ferdia's vigilant eyes. She was glad that he'd had enough cop-on to come to her aid. Another man might not have had the nerve to touch her, and might just have pretended nothing had happened.

Now she had to put the damn unit on again. But the incident with her swimsuit had seriously messed up her concentration. She tried to struggle back into her BCD, without success. Again Ferdia came to her assistance. He held the unit out for her, and she finally managed to twist herself into the jacket and refasten the belt around her waist. The shoulder straps had to be adjusted next. She'd always had trouble with them – even above water. They needed to be given a sharp tug downward in order to tighten them fully. She pulled and pulled, but the bloody things wouldn't budge. Her buoyancy was banjaxed now, as well as everything else. She added a quick blast of air to her BCD, and suddenly she was ascending rapidly.

Ferdia was beside her again. He turned her to face him, and then pulled her down till she was on a level with him. Ella felt absurdly small and absurdly inept as she was dragged back down through the water, but worst of all she felt absurdly passive, like a rag doll. As the instructor vented the air from her BCD she was aware that the upper part of his leg had wedged between her own awkwardly splayed limbs. She almost choked in surprise. She shifted her hips in an effort to put some distance between them, but only succeeded in gliding further along his leg.

Oh! She was totally unprepared for the sensation of the black neoprene-clad thigh as her crotch slid against it. It was quite electrifyingly erotic. She felt charged by a thrill so shockingly intense that she had to resist a sudden overwhelming impulse to pull herself closer. She struggled a little to disentangle their limbs, and then gave up. She was back in limp rag doll mode as he took hold of the rings on her shoulder straps and jerked hard. Again her pelvis was rammed into his thigh, but he was oblivious, concentrating as he was on adjusting her BCD. Once it was snug, Ferdia's hands moved down to her waist. He inserted an expert finger between her belt and her belly to ensure that the clasp on her belt was as secure as the shoulder straps now were.

Ella could feel her breath coming fast, and she made an effort to control it. But the bubbles soaring upwards were a giveaway. Her instructor looked at her curiously, signalling to her to take it easy. *Breathe slowly*, he gestured with an eloquent hand, and as she tried hard to concentrate on her breathing she found herself wanting to laugh out loud at the sheer ludicrousness of the situation. How totally bizarre! Here she was, drifting around underwater, half naked, being manhandled by someone she barely knew . . .

You really wouldn't want to have any hang-ups about intimate physical contact in this sport, she thought, as he finally finished checking her straps to his satisfaction. Then he resumed eye contact and asked if she was OK. Yes, she signalled back, she was OK. But when he turned his focus on the next novice she was aware that she was actually extremely confused.

The next novice was gazing lustfully at Ella, and she wondered how much he could read in her face under the mask. Then she heard a muffled rapping noise, and realized that Ferdia had taken his diving knife from the sheath on his thigh, and was striking it against his tank to attract attention. *You*, he signalled to his pupil, jabbing his finger at him. The guilty-looking novice immediately diverted his gaze and started to take off his unit. She was glad to see that he was almost as inept as she'd been, and that she wasn't the only one in the group who needed the assistance of the divemaster this evening.

Later she adjourned to the leisure centre social

club with Richie. 'How did you get on?' she asked, taking hold of a hank of damp hair and shaking it dry. She was glad she wouldn't have to do any more sessions in the pool. The chlorine wasn't doing anything for the condition of her hair, and she suspected that the blond streaks in Ferdia's dreadlocks were due more to the effects of chemically treated water than to hours spent bumming around on beaches.

'OK,' he said. 'I'd a few problems getting into my unit at the surface.'

Ella could relate to that. She'd spent more minutes than she'd have liked bobbing around with her tank between her legs, while Ferdia had held her steady. 'Hey! That manoeuvre could save your life one day,' she intoned solemnly, mimicking the instructor's Galway accent. Then she made a little grimace of apology. 'Oops. Sorry to take the piss out of your venerable cousin.'

Richie smiled. 'He's in much better form these days, as a matter of fact. He's found a dog to replace the one who died.'

'Oh?' Ella wondered if the dog was the one she'd come across last week.

It was. Minutes later the door swung open and PJ and Ferdia strolled through. The black and white collie was at Ferdia's heels. The instructors ambled up to the bar and the dog sat patiently while the barman pulled their pints. The animal looked a million dollars compared to the waif she'd been a week ago. She had gained some weight – although

101

she was still very thin – and her coat was noticeably glossier. Her right front leg and her tail had been bandaged, and she wore a collar of red leather. She was gazing up at her new master with a totally lovesick expression.

PJ and Ferdia picked up their pints and moved over to sit at a table by the door. Ella felt a bit miffed that they hadn't gravitated towards their table. She loved the way PJ smiled at her from underneath his eyebrows.

'Will you have another?' asked Richie, draining his pint.

'No,' she said, doing likewise. 'I'm driving, remember? I've got to make tracks.' She shrugged into her coat and slung her bag over her shoulder.

'Enjoy swotting up on Module Five during the week,' said Richie as he moved in the direction of the bar.

'I will damn well have to swot. If anything's going to mess up the exam for me next week, it'll be those hellish dive tables. See you, Richie.'

She made her way across the room trying to remember what she'd learned this evening about surface intervals and bottom time.

'Final exam next week, Ella,' PJ remarked with a smile as she passed by his table.

'Thanks for reminding me.' She stopped, and smiled back at him.

'You won't have any problems.' She was mildly surprised that the encouraging words came from Ferdia, and that *he* was actually bestowing a smile on her, too! 'Your academic work's fine.'

'Oh! Thanks!' And then: 'Um. I see you've adopted the dog we found,' she remarked, mainly to disguise her surprise at Ferdia being nice to her.

'Yeah. She's a lady.'

'What have you called her?'

'Perdita.'

'Perfect. That's Latin for "lost one".'

He sent her an amused look. 'Smart girl.'

'Hi, Perdita,' she said, stooping down and caressing the dog's ears. Her tail gave a gratifying thump against the floor. 'Hi, gorgeous! You look a lot better than you did the last time we met.'

'That's because her master's been stuffing her with prime fillet steak,' remarked PJ. 'She's going to get spoilt rotten if you're not careful, Ferdia.'

'Not a chance. It's just to fatten her up a bit. No more gourmet meals for you once the scales hit twenty kilos or thereabouts, you gorgeous girl.'

Ella looked up at him and he smiled again, and she suddenly remembered how her breast had been exposed earlier that evening. She found herself going pink, and then pinker still as she recalled the impulse she'd had to grind herself into him when he'd pulled down on the shoulder straps of her BCD.

To cover her embarrassment she delved into her bag and produced her Filofax. It was a rather smart pigskin one her father had brought back for her after his last American tour. She could feel Ferdia's eyes on her as she leafed through it. 'Is the weekend after next still pencilled in for the open water dives?' she asked PJ. She'd put her name down for two dives that weekend. One wasn't mandatory – it was just a skin dive without scuba – but she'd been advised to do it anyway because it would familiarize her with the suiting-up procedure.

'Yeah. It seems to suit everyone.'

'What time?' she asked, pen poised over the page. There was a big party marked in for that Saturday night. Patrick was throwing a bash for Jack's fortieth birthday.

'Nine o'clock on Saturday morning. Same again Sunday. That's when the tide's at optimum height. You'll need to get out here at eight, though, to allow time for briefing and suiting up.'

Eight o'clock on a freezing cold November morning! And it *would* have to be a morning after the night before! Hell's bells. Why was she *doing* this to herself? And then: Oh God, oh God, she thought in a panic – would Patrick be an angel and let her have the car for that weekend? The idea of trailing hungover through early-morning DART stations filled her with dread.

'OK,' she said, trying to sound keen as she scribbled in the relevant space in her diary. Then she closed the book and snapped the popper. 'Well – see you next Wednesday.'

'Yeah,' said PJ. 'By the way, Ella – if you want to do a pool session after your exam there'll be a master available to take care of you. Some trainees like to hone the skills one last time before performing their open water dives.'

'Oh.' She'd hoped she wouldn't have to do any more pool work, but she could see the sense of this. 'Well. I'll think about it.' Ferdia caught her eye and smiled, and she remembered what he'd said last week. *People who think about it never do it.* 'It's probably a good idea,' she conceded. 'I could do with another go at taking my mask off underwater. I found that a bit spooky.'

'You might want to practise taking your BCD off underwater, too,' said Ferdia. 'That didn't go as smoothly as it might have.'

Ella thought of her exposed breast again, and his thigh between hers, and she couldn't meet his eye. She was saved by the arrival of Richie with a fresh pint. 'Still here?' he asked unnecessarily.

'No, no – I'm off now. *A bientôt.*' *A bientôt?* Where had that come from? Shit. She'd a feeling that that little sally into French would strike 'the boys' as being madly pretentious. Before she could blush again she turned towards the door, painfully aware of the three pairs of male eyes that were scrutinizing her retreating rear.

* * *

Ella studied hard that week, and passed her exam with no problems. She fouled up on only three of the fifty questions on the paper, and that was because she hadn't read them properly. She'd even worked out how to use the dive tables.

As the class trailed out of the room, she asked Richie if he was going to the pool to practise. 'Nah,' he said. 'Can't be bothered. I'm going to the club to celebrate never having to read that fucking manual again.'

She asked Sporty Jan and Duffer Dan if they were going. Jan couldn't and Dan wouldn't. He should, if he has any sense, thought Ella. He needs all the practice he can get. She'd spotted him cheating in the exam, frantically flicking through Module Five.

As far as she could ascertain, the only person going to the pool was the bloke who'd sent her lecherous looks underwater last week. She didn't fancy the idea of practising buddy-breathing with him, so she decided to go for the club option with Richie.

Ferdia was already there, ordering a pint at the bar, but there was no sign of PJ.

'He's gone off to the Red Sea,' said Ferdia when she asked. 'For two weeks of dive heaven.'

They took their pints over to the table by the door, where Richie was tethering Perdita to a chair.

'Well, Ferdia?' said Richie, when he'd finished showering the dog with compliments. 'What's your verdict? Are Ella and I divemaster material?'

'Could be,' was Ferdia's measured response. 'You both did OK tonight. Should've taken the opportunity to do some extra pool work, though.'

Ella knew this was directed more at her than at Richie. 'I'm not divemaster material,' she admitted.

'You'd be surprised.' Ferdia gave her an appraising look. 'You might get hooked. You may even decide to do the advanced course after you've qualified.'

'What's involved?'

'There are a number of options. Navigation, night and deep dives are the toughest. We go to a flooded quarry near Blackwater. A place known as the Blackpits.'

The idea of navigating a flooded quarry at night was about as appealing to Ella as getting into a bath of cold sick blindfolded. 'Pass,' she said in a jokey voice. 'I'll stick to the Caribbean.'

'I thought you'd say that,' said Ferdia.

There was something faintly patronizing about his tone. Jesus Christ – would he ever lighten up? She hadn't meant it seriously, for heaven's sake! She wished PJ hadn't taken his infectious smile and crinkly eyes off to the Red Sea. An uneasy thought struck her suddenly. 'Who's supervising the dives this weekend?' she asked. She hoped she wasn't going to be landed with Ferdia.

'Whoever's least hungover. Diving and hangovers don't go together. Throwing up underwater is possible, but it's not something I'd recommend.' He looked at Ella, and she thought there was something of a challenge in his eyes, as if he was assessing how squeamish she might be.

Richie gave his cousin a sceptical look. 'Come on, Ferdia. I've known you to dive on mornings after you've been on complete benders.'

'That's my prerogative. I'm a master instructor, remember? You're only a trainee.'

'Hey! I heard a good one this evening.' Richie gave Ferdia a shrewd look. 'What's the difference between God and a master scuba instructor?'

'Tell me. What *is* the difference between God and a master scuba instructor?'

'God doesn't think he's a master scuba instructor,' returned Richie.

'Very droll.' Ferdia took a swig of Guinness. But his eyes above the rim of his pint were smiling.

Ella wasn't much liking all this stuff she'd just heard about diving and hangovers. She'd have to take it easy at Jack's birthday party on Saturday night. She should be taking things a bit easier, anyway. She'd been spending too many evenings in the pub after work, having her arm twisted by the reprobate Pierce Brosnan lookalike. She looked at her watch. 'Time I was off,' she said.

Richie gave her a pleading look. 'Don't go yet,' he said. 'Have another drink to celebrate passing your exam.'

She gave her watch a second glance, and then relented. 'All right then. But I'd better stick to Ballygowan.'

Richie stood up and headed towards the bar, leaving Ella stuck with Ferdia. She racked her brains for something to say, and then gave up. She knew that he thought they had about as much in common as Barbie and Action Man. She wouldn't waste her breath.

'Are you going to Jamaica with a boyfriend, Ella?' he asked politely after a beat or two of silence.

'No, I'm going with – a girlfriend,' she said. She didn't want to tell him she was going with her granny who'd won a holiday from Toptree Foods. It sounded so naff.

'You'll have a blast. It's a beautiful country.' He gave her that look of assessment again, that slightly superior look he was so good at. 'Of course, you may decide not to bother exploring. When you stay in a resort as luxurious as Salamander Cove the temptation is to stay put, lounge around, eat too much and drink too much.'

'And dive,' put in Ella, stung by the implication that she had no sense of adventure. She tried to think of more adventurous things to do. 'I might hire a car and explore the island. I'd like to visit Montego Bay, and I definitely want to do the Blue Mountains. And go rafting.' With her *granny*?

'I'd think twice about hiring a car if I were you. You'd be unlikely to get something as nifty as that little Merc you're used to running, and it'd actually be a better idea to opt for something a lot heavier. The roads are worse than they are here, and Jamaicans are even lousier drivers than the Irish. The best thing for you to do would be to hire a taxi for the day. Sometimes the driver will act as a minder for you.'

'A minder?'

'Yeah. Two white women on their own can be vulnerable. You'll have cameras, money-belts, credit cards. Most Jamaicans are desperately poor. The temptation can sometimes be too much. I got mugged once.'

She found herself looking at the scar on his cheekbone.

'No,' he said. 'That's not how I got that scar. That one's from an accident I had on a reef. The scars I got from being mugged are lower down. They slashed me here.' He briefly indicated an area low down on his hip, but she didn't allow herself to look.

'There was more than one?'

'There were three.'

'Jesus. You're lucky to be alive.'

He looked down at his pint, and then back at her. There was something lacklustre about the expression around his eyes. '*They're* lucky to be alive,' he said. 'I didn't want to hurt them, Ella. They were desperate, they were poor and they were punks. Something just possessed me.'

'You sent them packing? On your own?' Bruce Willis eat your heart out.

'Yeah. I was so consumed with rage that I scared the shit out of them. I'd had a bad day and I was mean drunk. I'd just found out my girl had been cheating on me, and to make matters worse it was my birthday. They just happened to choose the wrong man on the wrong day.'

Wow. How breathtakingly macho. She looked down at her nails. She wouldn't give him the pleasure of looking impressed. But she knew she had to say *some*thing.

'Did you end up in hospital?' she asked.

'Only as far as Outpatients. That was the worst thing about the whole unpleasant incident.'

'Oh? Are Jamaican hospitals that bad?'

'No. I just hate getting injections,' said Ferdia MacDiarmada. 'Needles scare the shit out of me.'

* * *

The next morning, Thursday, Julian rang in sick. His adenoids were at him. They were at him again on Friday.

The studios were booked back-to-back and mayhem ruled. Ella spent the last two days of the week running between the reception desk and the sound desk trying to wear her receptionist's cap and her sound engineer's cap simultaneously. Inevitably, one of them kept slipping off, and she was delighted when Claudia was roped in to man reception on Friday afternoon. In spite of the extra pair of hands, they ended up working right through until nine o'clock on Friday, when they'd finally hit the pub. That evening Ella fell into bed absolutely knackered and more than a little pissed.

She woke on Saturday morning with a smile on her face, having just emerged from a gloriously erotic dream about Jack. They'd been indulging in incredibly streamlined sex underwater, and Jack had been swathing her in some kind of black satiny stuff just before she woke. Ella stretched and rolled over onto her tummy, and her smile became even

111

broader as she action-replayed further details of the dream in soft focus in her mind's eye, pausing occasionally to freeze the frame. Then she allowed her mind to wander back to the night they'd walked together through the rain to Daly's, and the way he'd looked at her then with eyes that had positively glowered with sexual attraction. He hadn't looked at her that way since – not once. Maybe it was time to make him look at her that way again? Hell. It was worth a try. There was no woman in his life at the moment, and because Reflex hadn't booked a session for weeks, there'd been no distractions in the form of foxy Angie.

She finally reached out a hand for the alarm clock. It read half-past nine. The dream receded abruptly, and real life came swilling back into her brain. Fuck. She should at this precise moment be performing her skin dive in the Irish Sea. Ella let her head fall back on the pillow and turned her face to the window. It was drizzling with rain outside. That made it even worse. There was no way Ferdia would believe that she hadn't just wimped out on a rainy day. Sleeping in was such a pathetically unimaginative excuse.

Cursing herself, she flung back the duvet and shambled into the kitchen to put the kettle on. Her dive manual was lying open on the table at the page that outlined the skin-dive performance requirements. 'A skin dive isn't required for certification,' she read again. She chewed her lip and thought. She'd be all right. It just meant that she'd be at a slight disadvantage tomorrow when it came to the suiting-up procedure, that's all. And suiting up couldn't be *that* demanding, could it? She looked at the manual. OK. So she'd blown it today, but she was damned if she'd blow it tomorrow. She'd just have to make sure to stay sober tonight at Jack's party.

The thought of Jack reminded her of her dream. Before the black satiny stuff had materialized, she'd been wearing something really weird in the dream. No, she hadn't. She hadn't been wearing anything at all. But there had been something on her body. *What?* It came back to her with blinding clarity. She'd had delicately curved tattoos on either side of her spine in the shape of the arabesques that are carved into the surface of a violin. Oh! How beautiful! Like Man Ray's *Violin d'Ingres* . . . Jack had been playing her like a violin in the dream! She re-ran more footage. His elegant fingers had certainly known how to build through a crescendo to a climax – he'd hit the right notes unerringly. Except his fingers hadn't been that elegant, had they? They'd been kind of calloused . . .

As she tried to remember what melody he'd been playing, she thought of how she'd played every single day up until the decisive date three years ago when she'd consigned the instrument to the back of her wardrobe, and given up on her dreams of playing professionally. Ella was suddenly overcome with an intense, nostalgic yearning. This happened to her occasionally, and when it did she

113

took her violin out of its case and tuned it. It wasn't what you'd call serious practice – more messing around. Sometimes she'd get pissed off by how many mistakes she made, and she'd return the instrument to the wardrobe after only minutes of playing.

She fetched a pile of sheet music from her bookshelf, walked thoughtfully back into her bedroom and retrieved the case from the bottom shelf. She ran the square of silk that she kept in the case over the polished wood of the violin, and then she tuned it, tautened the bow, rubbed the horsehair with a little rosin and tucked the instrument under her chin.

Bruch was on the top of the pile of scores. It was strange to hear the notes fill the room. She bit her lip, frowning in concentration. She was rusty, but not so rusty that she didn't still sound OK. She played tentatively at first, then with increasing confidence, swaying along with the music as it spilled out of the instrument, unable to resist the physical compulsion to move. Beethoven next. The slow movement from the Seventh. Holy shomoly, she thought, as she drew the bow across the strings, ignoring the few bum notes that tumbled out – she'd forgotten how sexy it was! This was music to seduce by! She let the bow drop a little way into the allegretto. It felt silly playing a symphonic piece all by herself.

The third book of sheet music was Irish. The music her father had taught her. She swung into a little virtuoso improvisation of grace notes as a kind of preamble to the main treat. Then, just as she was about to launch into 'Pull the Knife and Stick it Again', the phone rang.

She came to with a start. The electronic jangle struck a harsh, discordant note in the aftermath of the thrillingly rich music that had filled the room moments before.

Setting her violin down carefully on the bed, she picked up the receiver.

'Ella?' she heard. 'Hi – it's Angie from Reflex. Listen – I'm sorry for disturbing you at home, but I'm in a bit of a tizzy. The thing is – I ran into Jack in Fitzer's restaurant late last night, and he invited me to the party Patrick's throwing for him this evening. The quandary for me is that I forgot to ask whether it's formal or casual. What do you think I should wear?'

*　　*　　*

Tom Jones's cover version of 'Sex Bomb' was blasting over the speakers. Ella was scanning the party to see if Angie had arrived, and sipping at the first of the two glasses of champagne she was going to allow herself that evening. Ferdia's advice about diving with a hangover had sunk in. As she hummed along to 'Sex Bomb' she couldn't prevent her eyes from sliding towards Jack. He was looking like Pierce Brosnan might in a scene from *The Thomas Crown Affair*.

Suddenly Patrick's hand was on her shoulder. 'D'you mind if I give you some avuncular advice, toots?'

'Sure.' She swung round to face her uncle. 'Fire ahead.'

'Stop wasting your time hankering after Jack.'

Ella had just taken a gulp of champagne. She nearly spat it out. 'What? What are you talking about?'

'Come on, Ella. You know what I'm talking about.'

She knew there was no point in pretending otherwise. She'd always been crap at dissembling. 'How – how on earth did you guess, Patrick?'

'I've known you since you were a baby. I can read you like a book.'

'Oh! Oh, hell, Patrick! This is *embarrassing*!' She knew that her face had gone scarlet.

Patrick was twisting his glass round and round in his hand. 'Look. This isn't easy for me either, sweetheart. But I just can't let you carry on blindly trotting down the wrong road. Let it drop, Ella.'

She bit her lip and looked away from him, down at the carpet. When she raised her eyes it was to find Jack in her direct line of vision. Oh, no! He was giving her his wonderful smile! Instantly she diverted her attention to her uncle without returning Jack's smile.

'I know why you *think* you want Jack Noonan,' persisted Patrick, 'but he's not right for you, believe me. Think about it. Jack is practically *family*. It's time you stopped looking for the daddy you never had. Oh, hell.' Patrick had stopped twisting his glass and reached for his cigarettes instead. There was a pause while he lit one and inhaled deeply. Then: 'I'm sorry to be so blunt, sweetheart. Really I am. I've never been good at straight-talking.'

He sounded so miserable that Ella jumped in with alacrity. 'No, no. No. It's OK, Patrick. Honestly. You're right – you're *absolutely* right to tell me what you think. I'm just – I'm just feeling a bit mortified now.' She took another hefty swig of champagne, and another.

There was something else she needed to know. 'I haven't – I haven't made too much of an eejit of myself, have I? Have people been sniggering at me behind my back?'

Now it was Patrick's turn to jump in with re-assurance. 'No, no. No-one else would have a clue. Not even Jack. But if you'd ever – well, you know . . .'

'You mean if I'd ever made overtures?'

'Yes. I'm not saying you would, but if you *had* – well – it would put him in a very awkward situation. You know – what with being your boss and all that. Because I suspect he might find it difficult enough to resist . . . I mean, you're a very – well – attractive young woman, and—'

Patrick was clearly so uncomfortable with the situation now that Ella couldn't let him struggle on any more. 'It's OK, Patrick. I know what you're trying to say. Please don't worry. I promise I won't do anything stupid to compromise you or—'

'Patrick! Ella! Hi!' It was Angie from Reflex, looking foxier than ever.

'Angie!' A little flurry of kisses followed.

'Did you just get here?' asked Patrick.

'About ten minutes ago. And I must say I am im*pressed*. Perrier Jouet is my very favourite champagne.' She drained the remains in her flute.

'Then let me get you another one. Ella? Another glass of champagne?'

Ella considered. 'Actually – d'you know what I'd love, Patrick? I'd love a shot of tequila.'

Patrick sent her a look that was half warning, half apology as he disappeared in the direction of the kitchen.

'Fab dress, Ella,' remarked Angie.

Ella had worn her sexiest little slip dress to the party. There'd been no way she was going to give up without a fight. But with Angie looking sensational in gold lamé, there was simply no contest. 'Thanks. But look who's talking. Is that a Galliano, by any chance?'

'Mm. I decided to push the boat out tonight.' Angie slid her a confidential smile. 'Shall I let you into a secret? I'm crazy about your boss.' She reached for a bowl of cashew nuts and casually fired one into her mouth.

So am I, Ella wanted to say. But she didn't. Instead she found herself saying 'And he's crazy about you'. She didn't even kick herself for saying it. There was no point.

Angie's champagne arrived. Ditto Ella's tequila. She knocked the shot back in one and then stood watching miserably as Angie wove her way through the party to where Jack stood watching Angie. Their body language said it all. They were going to end up in bed together tonight.

Patrick looked at the expression on Ella's face. 'I'm sorry, toots,' he said.

'No problem, Patrick.' Ella executed a little, stoical salute for her uncle's benefit, and then she made her way into the kitchen to locate the bottle.

The last thing she had any recollection of doing that night was booking an alarm call for seven o'clock, just before she hit the futon in Patrick's spare room. She'd managed to kick off her shoes and pull off her stockings, but she was still wearing her best Agent Provocateur underwear and her sexy little slip dress. She didn't dream of anything.

* * *

The phone by the bed woke her, and she knocked the receiver to the floor. She lay there with her eyes clamped shut for ages, anticipating with dread the pain that was going to kick in when she opened them. Was it going to be that blinding kind of Sabatier-sharp pain, or the dull thudding kind? She couldn't decide which was the worst.

It was the dull thudding kind. She edged her way out from under the duvet and sat on the edge of the futon for a minute or two with her head in her hands. Then she got up and tiptoed into the bathroom, anxious not to wake Claudia and Patrick and her two sleeping cousins. There was a packet of Solpadeine propped up on the basin, with a Post-It from Patrick stuck on the side. 'Take this before you take the car,' she read. 'If you trash it you're in big trouble. Good luck with your dive, love P. XXX.' She splashed her face with water and scrubbed her teeth with the toothbrush Claudia had given her the night before. Her tongue, too. God, she was thirsty!

In the kitchen she drank two pints of water, made strong coffee, and looked glumly round at the post-party mess. Claudia and Patrick and the boys would have their work cut out for them today. But if she had to choose between clearing up party detritus and diving off Sheep's Head, she knew which one she'd rather do.

She'd left herself very little time to get out to Portdelvin, she realized. Only thirty minutes. But at this hour on a Sunday morning the roads would be clear. Unfortunately there was no time to go home and get changed. She rolled on her stockings and slid her feet into her high mules. She was going to look utterly ridiculous arriving at the dive outfit decked out in satin and tat, but she didn't care. She was hungover and she had a broken heart and she was going to have to get into the Irish Sea. As she shrugged into her fake leopardskin coat she found herself thinking that life really couldn't get much worse.

Outside the sunlight was blinding – that cold,

crisp end-of-November sunlight. She shielded her eyes with her hand as she rummaged in her bag for the Ralph Lauren sunglasses that had been a present from her father, and then she got behind the wheel of Patrick's Merc, kicked off her shoes, took a deep breath, and started the ignition.

The journey out took her twenty-five minutes, and she got to the dive shop at exactly eight o'clock. The dive van was just pulling up alongside the kerb outside. The driver's door opened and Ferdia got out, followed by Perdita. Ella swung her legs out of the Merc and stood on the footpath in her stocking feet, swaying a little in the dazzling sunlight. She was glad of her dark glasses. It meant that Ferdia couldn't see how bloodshot her eyes were.

'Hi,' she managed, sliding on her shoes and trying to sound bright. The 'hi' came out as a croak. She seemed to remember having smoked a cigarette last night.

Ferdia took in the fur coat slung round her shoulders, her tight, silk-embroidered frock with the maribou feather trim, and her Agent Provocateur enhanced cleavage. He let his eyes run down her glossy-stockinged legs to her feet in their baby-blue mules, and then up again to her black lensed, gold framed shades. Then he flung back his head and laughed.

'Jesus! What a girl!' he said.

She could tell it wasn't meant in any complimentary sense. There was too much disparaging emphasis on the word 'girl'.

121

She didn't need any more grief in her life. 'Oh, fuck off, Ferdia,' she said. Then she turned on her high heel and strode into the dive shop. Except her tight dress meant that she couldn't 'stride'. She actually *minced* into the dive shop, followed by her incredulously smiling instructor and his devoted dog.

The trainees were assembled in the classroom for their briefing. A chorus of wolf whistles and appreciative catcalls greeted her entrance. Ella walked up to the top of the room and executed a perfect curtsy before sitting down in the front row where Richie was sprawled open-mouthed. 'What the *fuck* are you wearing?' he asked.

'I was at a party last night,' she said. 'I didn't have time to go home and get changed.'

'Well, all I can say is, he was a jammy bastard, whoever he was.'

She felt rather than saw the sideways look Ferdia gave her as he moved to the top of the class to start the briefing. Her skirt had ridden up, exposing the lacy trim on her stocking-top. Ella crossed her legs ostentatiously, took off her sunglasses and flashed him a dazzling smile. She'd give him *girly*, but she'd bloody well prove him wrong. She, Ella Nesbit, was one of the lads. Always was, always would be. Hangover notwithstanding, she was damn well going to do that dive today.

After the briefing, Sporty Jan and Ella got themselves kitted out with wetsuits and gloves and bootees and suited up in the ladies' changing room.

Because she had no swimsuit to get into, Ella was obliged to put the wetsuit on over her sexy underwear. Sporty Jan pretended not to be looking, but Ella could tell that she was slightly nonplussed. The other woman was at an advantage, having already done the skin dive the day before. She did expert things like spray the cuffs and ankles of her suit with silicone before putting it on, and when she'd finished she gave Ella a hand. It took forever to get the gear on. The neoprene felt clammy against her naked flesh, and when she slid her bare feet into the bootees she thought she might get sick. It reminded her of the time she'd got out of the car and stepped on a slug.

'Are you sure you're OK?' asked Jan, looking at her curiously.

'Sure,' croaked Ella, dead enthusiastically.

They fetched their fins and masks from the rental area and then waddled back along the corridors. The divers were all congregated in the shop, looking like Michelin Men in their thick neoprene suits. Only the masters looked good, in professional, stylish black and neon suits. The poor trainees had to make do with more proletarian designs.

'How do we get down to the shore?' asked Ella. 'It's too far to walk.' She'd presumed there'd be some kind of bus to take them to where they were to perform their dives.

'You take your cars,' said Ferdia.

'I've got to drive in *this*?' said Ella, astonished.

'You got it, Ella. Unless you want to put your leopardskin coat on over your suit to disguise it. You might try wearing your sunglasses as well in case anyone recognizes you.'

Richie sniggered.

'Ha ha, Ferdia,' said Ella.

* * *

The drive took them five minutes, and by the end of it Ella and Richie were creased up with laughter. They'd folded down the soft-top, and passers-by stopped and gaped in open amazement at seeing two people in wetsuits bowling along in a Mercedes. Ella had put her film-star sunglasses on for a lark, and was waving her neoprene-gloved hand in the manner of Her Majesty Queen Elizabeth of England. She had got to that stage of hungoverness that makes the sufferer behave in a very giddy, juvenile fashion, and when she and Richie got out of the car, they were laughing so hard they were hanging on to each other.

'OK,' said Ferdia when he caught a load of them. 'You two are definitely not diving together. You and Dan can be buddies, Ella. Richie, you team up with Jan.'

Richie and Ella stole guilty looks at each other and nearly giggled, but when Ferdia said: 'Do you really want to dive the *Lusitania*, Richie? Do you really want to dive that reef, Ella?' they wised up a bit.

Ferdia appointed himself dive leader to her and Dan, and Ella wished harder than ever that smiley PJ wasn't away in Dive Heaven on the Red Sea. When the water trickled its way into Ella's suit and snaked down her spine she squealed – but Ferdia had been right when he'd told her it was easy to get hot in the Irish Sea, even in the month of November, because the sea-water soon reached body temperature. In fact, when they had donned their tanks and weight-belts back on shore, Ella had been perspiring with exertion.

They performed the entry into the water walking backwards, over rough terrain strewn with treacherous boulders. She and Dan clung to each other for support, and Ella was relieved beyond words when they eventually hit water deep enough to float in. Her hangover was really starting to kick in now.

When they'd finned out far enough, Ferdia dropped a line with a weight attached, and they went through the pre-dive signalling ritual. Ella copied her instructor's fluent sign language with clumsy fingers, not really sure of what she was doing. Then she groped for the deflator button on her BCD, pressed it hard, took her last surface breath – and she was going down. She took a few shallow, nervous breaths, and then she did something stupid. She looked down. She couldn't see the bottom. She looked at Ferdia. Though he couldn't have been more than a metre away, the water was so murky that she could barely make out his features under the mask. Beside her, Dan was descending with relentless determination. She looked up. She couldn't see the surface. This was her idea of hell.

In a panic, she bit down hard on the rubber of her breathing apparatus. Water began to trickle through into her mouth. It tasted of salt. She was used to chlorine. This fazed her even more. She waved wildly to attract Ferdia's attention, and then, forgetting everything she'd been taught in her twenty-four hours of training, she scrambled madly to the surface. Her instructor was beside her in an instant, and then Dan's head appeared. He looked mildly quizzical under his mask.

Ferdia took his regulator out of his mouth. 'Calm down,' he said. 'Calm yourself.' He waited, studying her with concern until her rapid, shallow breathing gradually became more measured. 'OK. What's the problem?'

'I couldn't see,' said Ella. 'You said it was shallow, but I couldn't see the bottom and I couldn't see up to the surface, and I just got completely disorientated.'

'A kind of claustrophobia?'

'I guess.' She'd been hit with a touch of nausea, too, but she didn't want to tell him that. She knew the nausea was hangover-induced, and although he'd plainly guessed she was hungover, she didn't want to admit it.

'Do you want to go down again, or do you want to abort the dive?'

She was calmer now. She thought hard. She

couldn't abort the dive! She couldn't wimp out. She remembered the expression on Ferdia's face when he'd called her a *girl*, and she took a deep breath.

'Let's go again,' she said.

'OK. And if you want to come back up, Ella, remember what you learned. Slowly Ascend From Every Dive.' She registered the capital letters and nodded. Ferdia reinserted his regulator, and they repeated the procedure.

Again, Ella panicked. Slowly Ascend From Every Dive, she thought uselessly as she frantically kicked her way back up, Ferdia and Dan following at a less frenetic pace.

She wanted to cry. Beside her Dan was looking vaguely puzzled by all the fuss. 'Come on, Ella,' he said encouragingly. 'It's great down there. Remember what the manual says? When we finish demonstrating our skills we can tour underwater for "pleasure and experience". You don't want to miss out on that, do you?'

'No,' she said in a small voice. The idea of touring underwater for pleasure and experience was actually anathema to her at this stage, but she was determined to do it. 'I'll try one more time.'

'Are you sure?' asked Ferdia carefully. 'Don't feel under pressure, Ella. Not if you're not feeling happy about it.'

'I'm sure. If I can't hack it this time I'll abort,' she said.

'I was watching you,' he said. 'You're tensing up your jaw muscles. Relax your lips. Keep them firmly wrapped round your regulator, but don't bite down, OK? The most important thing is to stay relaxed.'

Third time not so lucky. Ella was so disorientated when she bolted for the surface this time that she wasn't sure whether she was heading upwards or downwards.

'I'm sorry,' she said when she got her breath back. 'I can't do it. I'm going to have to abort the dive. I'm really sorry, Ferdia. Dan.'

'That's all right,' said Dan mildly.

'D'you mind waiting here for me while I take Ella back to the shore?' asked Ferdia.

'Not at all,' said Dan. He gave her a big smile. 'Take care, Ella. Have a good holiday.'

Ella thought she hated herself more at that moment than at any other time in her life. How dare she make fun of him and call him Duffer Dan when she was the one who was the Duffer and the Wimp and the Big Girl's Blouse all rolled into one? Under the mask she could feel tears of humiliation start to come. 'Thanks, Dan,' she said. 'Good luck.'

She and Ferdia finned back to shore leaving Dan bobbing imperturbably alongside the float. They swam in silence for a while. Then Ferdia spoke. 'Hangover?'

'Yes,' she admitted. 'You can say "told you so" if you like.'

'I never say "told you so". It's a really pointless thing to say to anyone.'

Ella bit her lip. 'God! I'm so crap!'

'Hey. Stop beating yourself up. Once you get to Jamaica things will pan out. The visibility there is phenomenal. You won't have a problem with orientation.'

They'd reached the shallows, and Ferdia helped her out of her BCD. As she was relieved of the weight of the tank she gave an audible sigh.

He looked down at her and smiled. 'You really are tiny, aren't you? No wonder you find it difficult.'

'What do you mean?'

'I know it's not a terribly politically correct thing to say, but there's a very obvious design fault in women. You compensate for it by being cleverer and by living longer and by being more dextrous than men, but you just don't have the same physical strength. Next time you dive, Ella, celebrate the fact that you're different, and do the clever thing. Take advantage of some sucker's superior strength and ask for help if you can't manage your equipment. I know we encourage you to handle your gear yourself, but in Jamaica you can tip the boatman to do it for you. I used to feel so sorry for you when I saw you staggering down the poolside, determined at all costs to be one of the lads.'

Ella was staring at him in astonishment. This was the last thing she expected someone like Ferdia to come out with.

'But I hate being perceived as a girly sort of girl!' she blurted.

Ferdia laughed. 'I'm surprised you can say that after the way you showed up here this morning.

You cut some girly swank then. Even I had to compliment you on it.'

'That was supposed to be a *compliment*?'

'When I called you a girl? Absolutely.'

'Oh,' said Ella, feeling really silly now. 'I thought you were making fun of me.'

He shook his head, still smiling down at her. Then: 'I'd better get back to Dan,' he said, looking over his shoulder.

'Oh, God,' she said. 'What's poor Dan going to write in his logbook about his first ever dive? "Abandoned by buddy?"' She sighed again. 'I don't think I'll hang about for the debriefing, Ferdia, if you don't mind. I feel too embarrassed at being the only one not to have done the dive, and Richie will take the piss bigtime.' She also didn't much like the idea of sitting in the classroom in her party frock sans underwear – subjected to the ultimate debriefing. She'd have to leave the tiny sodden items off or she'd freeze to death. 'Say goodbye to Rich for me, will you?'

'Sure I will.'

She paused and looked thoughtful for a moment. 'It's funny – I'll probably never see him again. Or you, for that matter. Bye, Ferdia. Thanks for everything.' She actually meant it.

'Don't say bye. Say *sayonara*. This time next year you might be doing your Underwater Hunter course.'

'Hah!'

'Be sure to send Desirée my love. And enjoy Jamaica.'

'Desirée?'

'Remember I told you about her? She runs the dive outfit at Salamander Cove.' He allowed himself a small, nostalgic smile. 'My favourite dive goddess in the world.'

'I'll do that.' She smiled at him, then turned and headed for the car, feeling water uncomfortably slooshing round in her wetsuit. She'd have to put newspaper down on Patrick's leather upholstery to prevent it from getting watermarked. She could hear Ferdia whistling something as he made his way back into the sea. For a moment she couldn't place the melody, although it was incredibly familiar. Then the whistling stopped mid bar.

'Ella?' he called after her. 'Can I say something else politically incorrect?'

She looked back. He was hip deep in water. 'Sure,' she said. 'I never was a stickler for political correctness.'

'I loved the stockings,' he said. Then he turned, laughing, and struck out for the float bobbing around in the Irish Sea where Duffer Dan was still waiting patiently for him.

She watched him go, and then she realized what it was he'd been whistling. It had been from Beethoven's Seventh. The slow movement.

Chapter Five

Ella spent the next week organizing clothes to take with her on holiday. It felt weird to be looking out little bikinis and sunhats and sandals and sarongs when the skies outside her window were leaden. It felt weird to walk into Boots and fill her wire basket with suntan lotion and calamine lotion and aftersun lotion when everyone else was filling theirs with cold remedies and vitamin C. And it felt weirder still to emerge from the taxi at Dublin airport in nothing warmer than a cardigan when the wind-chill factor was sharp as a spiv's suit.

In Heathrow she and Leonie stood in a queue of other summer-clad individuals at the Air Jamaica desk. There were a lot of stressed-out, bewildered-looking travellers milling about, but Ella wasn't one of them. She loved the buzz of airports. She'd negotiated them since she was tiny: a young flyer in the charge of jolly air stewardesses, flying out to visit her father wherever he might be on tour, or heading off to the sun to spend holidays with her mother. Now she and Leonie were playing a favourite airport game – looking around and speculating about the people travelling with them. Ella loved doing this, watching complete strangers and making up stories about them. The couple who couldn't keep their hands off each other were obviously honeymooners, the smiling black couple were emigrants returning home after years of soulless London living, the man with the Rolex and the designer shades was a drug dealer. Leonie decided that the leather-clad youth checking into first class was a member of a boy band.

'I'm seriously pissed off that they had nothing left in first class.' A peevish female had just joined the queue behind them. Ella resisted the impulse to turn round and have a good look.

'You were lucky to get anything at all at such short notice.' A man's voice. 'Now. Have you taken your Becalm tablets?'

'Yes. I took two already today.'

'Maybe you're immune to them now. They don't seem to be helping much these days, do they?'

'Nothing could help me with the amount of stress I've had to put up with recently. I sincerely hope this holiday works. I'll probably only just have begun to unwind by the time I have to come home again.'

'It's ideal for you, darling. A holiday where you can just chill and lie on the beach and read.'

'I won't get much reading done for pleasure. I've all those scripts to get through, remember?'

A sigh. 'I wish you'd taken my advice and left them behind. You need a complete escape. Try to read only the ones that need immediate attention.

Put the others on the back boiler until you get home. You'll end up having a total breakdown if you don't ease up.'

'I'll have to read the one that Juliet Rathbone-Lyon sent. She wants an answer ASAP or the deal's off.'

Ella was fascinated. She was earwigging so hard that the muscles in her ears had actually gone taut.

Beside her Leonie kicked her hand luggage. 'Oh dammit,' she said. 'I forgot to pack my St John's Wort. Did you know, Ella, that it's meant to be an excellent preventative cure for – what's that disease called? Anyway, I've been taking it religiously since – what on earth's the matter with you?'

Ella was making frantic facial signals to Leonie to shut up. She beetled her brows at her, and rolled her eyes backward to indicate that Leonie should join her in eavesdropping on the couple behind. She'd obviously got quite good at sign language since she'd taken up scuba diving because her grandmother quickly registered what Ella was trying to convey.

'I'm just so sorry I can't come with you,' the male voice was saying. Ella was convinced that his tone had an insincere tinge to it.

'Yes. What a shame you decided to do that bloody panto. It's not as if we need the money.'

'I've always wanted to do pantomime. You know that, Soph.'

Ella couldn't stand it any more. She turned to her left on the pretext of studying the flight monitor, and swivelled her eyes as unobtrusively as possible. A very beautiful blonde woman was standing next to a trolley piled high with expensive-looking luggage. She was wearing a pale pink linen suit and a pair of sunglasses so dark she had to be somebody famous. In fact, Ella was pretty certain she'd seen her somewhere before. Her peripheral vision took in the male half of the duo. Tall, dark and impossibly handsome. A perfect pantomime prince. Ella tore her eyes away from him and returned her attention to the pink linen woman, who had removed her sunglasses and laid her head on his shoulder in a cuddly, proprietorial fashion when she'd seen Ella eyeballing her man.

'Oh, Ben! Oh, God – I'm going to miss you so *much*! Do you realize that we've never been apart for as much as a week since we first met?' The tetchy tone had been replaced by one of heart-searing anguish. Was she imagining it, or was the woman putting on a performance for Ella's benefit? 'And now we're going to be separated for a whole *fortnight* – with an entire *ocean* between us! Thank *God* for mobile phones – you will remember to carry yours with you at all times, darling, won't you?'

'I can hardly carry my phone on stage with me, Sophie,' he pointed out reasonably.

'Don't be facile, darling. You know what I mean. I just need to know that I can contact you any time the agony of separation gets too unbearable.' Ella predicted that it would end in tears. She was right. Out of the corner of her eye she could see the woman called Sophie starting to dig about in her handbag. 'Oh! Oh! Why does life have to be so *stress*ful? I can't even find my *hanky*!'

'Here you are darling,' said Ben. 'I have one here.'

'Oh! Oh, no! I don't think I can bear it!'

'There, there. What is it, Soph?'

'It smells of you! The handkerchief! Oh *God*. Why am I going off on this hateful odyssey all by myself?' She blew her nose. 'I expect the resort will be full of odious Germans.'

'Well, at least you won't have to talk to anyone. When they ask for your autograph you can just smile sweetly and sign and say "Ich spreche kein Deutsch."'

'What does that mean?'

'It means "I don't speak German."'

'A very useful phrase to know. "Ich spreche kein Deutsch." Write it down for me, sweetheart, will you?'

There was a hiatus, and then the Sophie person spoke again. 'Guess what I'm going to do, Benny?'

'What, sweetheart?'

'I'm going to take this hanky with me and sleep with it on my pillow every night.'

'Oh, darling. That's so typical of you. What a totally sweet Sophie thing to do.'

'Will you do the same?'

He sounded uncertain. 'Sleep with one of your handkerchiefs?'

'No, no, darling. Maybe something a little more

136

intimate?' There came a sound of whispering, followed by a girlish giggle.

Ella and Leonie exchanged glances and smirked. This was brilliant! Ella hoped that this Sophie woman would sit near her on the plane. She'd be better entertainment than the inflight movie.

*　　*　　*

In fact, she *was* the inflight entertainment. She was Sophie Burke, best supporting actress Oscar nominee and winner of a BAFTA. Also the star of the inflight movie, a weepy romantic drama that Ella had had absolutely no interest in seeing when it had been released a month or two previously.

To her delight, Sophie was seated just across the aisle and a little forward from her, so Ella and Leonie could observe her while remaining unobserved. When the opening titles of the movie began unfurling on the screen in swirly purple lettering, Sophie had given a little theatrical gasp and immediately lunged for her handbag. She'd extracted her black glasses and fitted them to her face, and then she'd bent her head forward so that her profile was obscured by a curtain of silver-blond hair. The disguise immediately attracted attention, and a little murmur of interest started up among those passengers who hadn't already recognized her. When the movie ended, a respectful round of applause pittered around the plane, and Sophie got to her feet, removed her sunglasses so that her fans could gaze upon her beautiful but emotional face, and made a little bow. 'Thank you. Thank you so much,' she murmured, before resuming her seat and putting her glasses back on.

*   *   *

They stepped off the plane to be shrouded in air as warm and soft as a pashmina. The airport was buzzing. Hers and Leonie's and Sophie Burke's and the honeymooners' and the drug dealer's were the only white faces going through immigration. Sophie Burke, with her straight platinum hair and porcelain skin, looked especially out of place, and attracted a lot of looks, especially from the men, who were quite openly appreciative.

The Jamaican people were stunning. The women didn't walk – they swayed. They sashayed. The men were loose-limbed, graceful as gazelles. It was obvious that they'd descended from a breeding stock of princes and warriors, with their proud bearing and their exceptional bone structure. This must be what angels look like, thought Ella, gazing around at the most beautiful race on earth.

Outside on the tarmac Jamaicans milled around Ella and Leonie as they hovered helplessly, looking out for the coach that was to take them to Salamander Cove. They saw the honeymooners get into a minibus that had HUMMINGBIRD HOTEL printed on a cardboard sign in the windscreen. The drug dealer was swooped upon by a stretch limo.

Across the concourse Sophie Burke stood beside her mountain of luggage, looking lost. Leonie and Ella exchanged glances.

'D'you think she's going to Salamander Cove?' asked Leonie.

'She could be,' said Ella looking across the tarmac to where the film star shimmered with film star-ishness. 'Should we ask?'

'Do,' said Leonie. 'Lucky for you if she is. It'll be nice for you to have someone of around your own age to play with.' She responded to Ella's sideways look with a disingenuous smile.

Ella approached Sophie with a tentative 'Excuse me?'

The actress gave a little sigh, and produced a Mont Blanc pen from her handbag.

'You wouldn't happen to be going to Salamander Cove Villas, would you?' asked Ella.

The look of resigned condescension in Sophie Burke's green eyes turned to relief. 'Oh, yes! Are you?'

'Yes, I am. Or rather, *we* are. I'm travelling with my grandmother.' Ella indicated Leonie who was smiling at a small Jamaican child.

'Oh, I'm so glad there's someone else in the same predicament! What are we to *do*? They told me there'd be a coach waiting at the airport.'

'That's what they told us, too. I expect the Jamaicans are as laid back about things as the Irish.'

A spark of interest ignited in Sophie's eyes. 'You're Irish?' she said. 'Of course, I should have known from the accent. I'm Irish, too, although I've been living in London for the past few years.' Ella had read somewhere that Sophie Burke was Dublin born and bred, but there was absolutely nothing about her accent to indicate that this was so. It was polished mid-Atlantic. 'Nice to meet you.' Sophie extended a perfectly manicured hand. 'My name's Sophie Burke.'

'Yes. I know. Congratulations on your performance on the plane this evening.' Sophie couldn't know that it wasn't her screen performance Ella was referring to.

'Oh, thank you!' The actress gave a coy little shrug. 'And you are . . . ?'

'Ella Nesbit.' A pause ensued – the kind of pause that happens when people are thrown together and don't know what to do next. 'Well,' said Ella. 'I wonder what's the best thing to do. Maybe I should—'

'Yo! White ladies!' Ella turned to see a gangling black man bearing down on them. He was wearing loose pyjama-type trousers, a baggy Hawaiian shirt and a crocheted tam-o-shanter. He flashed an enormous smile at them, showing off great gaps in his mouth where teeth had once been. 'You going to Salamander Cove Villas?'

Ella nodded. 'That's right.' She looked at Sophie. Sophie was staring at the black man, incredulity scrawled all over her face.

'I yo' chauffeur. You wait here. My bus done

140

been impounded. I come back, I pick you up when they give me my bus back.'

'Oh. OK. How long is that likely to be?' asked Ella politely.

'I come back soon.' He gave them another wide smile, and then he turned and started to walk away.

'Excuse me,' said Sophie peremptorily to his retreating back. He paused, looked over his shoulder, and walked slowly back to them. 'How long is the journey to Salamander Cove?'

'Oh – 'bout two hours.'

'Two hours!' Sophie was plainly horrified.

'But it's only about sixty miles on the map,' observed Ella.

The black man nodded sagely. 'We go slow. We go Jamaican time.' Then he threw back his head and laughed. 'You in Jamaica now, lady. You take things easy. No white man time here. No problems in Jamaica.' Then he shambled off and was swallowed up in the maw of the heaving throng.

'Oh, my God!' exclaimed the actress. 'That's our chau*ffeur*?' Sophie Burke set herself down on her pile of luggage as delicately as if she was a piece of Sèvres porcelain. And started to cry.

*   *   *

The journey actually took three hours. Four, by the time the driver's bus had been liberated from the pound.

When Sophie had got a load of the transport she was expected to travel in she started to whimper. No luxury air-conditioned coach pulled up on the airport concourse. This was a vehicle that might best be described as 'basic'. The suspension wasn't that hot, either. Not surprising, thought Ella, given the condition of the roads. They were worse than the worst Irish boreen she'd ever driven down. At times the driver had to slow to a crawl to negotiate potholes. At other times he careered around hairpin bends at a speed so reckless that Sophie started to hyperventilate. He pumped his horn frequently at other drivers, sometimes belligerently, sometimes as a greeting, shouting 'Yo, man!' and 'Yo, brudder!' at fellow taxi drivers out of his open window. On one occasion he stopped and had a conversation in almost unintelligible patois with another man. 'He my friend,' he threw over his shoulders to his passengers. 'He taxi driver too.'

The friend squinted in through the open window and grinned when he saw the women. 'Nice girl passengers,' he said, grabbing hold of his crotch and gesturing graphically.

Sophie looked away immediately. 'They're all obviously out of their brains on pot,' she hissed at Ella.

They passed through townships brilliant with early Christmas decorations. The coloured fairy-lights which festooned the little houses looked like sequinned spider's webs. Thumping reggae blasted out at them through massive speakers set up at intervals along the streets, and Leonie, who was wide awake, nodded her head in time to the music as they passed from one street party to the next, smiling out of the window at the locals and provoking periodic shouts of 'Yo! Whitey!' She found this so amusing that she was disappointed when they didn't shout it.

'Dear God,' moaned Sophie, clutching her head. 'Do they never sleep?'

By the time they reached Salamander Cove Villas the film star was slumped against her leather luggage, and her linen suit, once crisp, looked almost as limp with exhaustion as she did. Her complexion had lost its delicate pallor, and her face now looked as if someone had powdered it with grey chalk dust for a joke.

They pulled up under the *porte-cochère* in front of a pair of cerulean-blue louvred doors. Bougainvillaea trailed over the pale pink stucco that fronted the building. The airy reception area was tiled in terracotta, with arched windows over-looking a plaza.

Ella went to the desk where a big, rotund Jamaican man smilingly invited her to check in. A smiling bell-hop took their luggage, and a smiling housekeeper told them that, although the restaurant and bar were now closed, they would find refreshments waiting for them in their villa. They all *smiled*! And although she was knackered, Ella couldn't help smiling back.

Sophie staggered past them, announcing that

there was no way she was checking in at this hour. 'Just show me directly to my villa,' she demanded, pronouncing it 'veelya'. 'I'll check in tomorrow. I'm so exhausted after that hellish journey that I couldn't even manage to sign my own name.' That was surprising, thought Ella. She'd signed autographs like a polished automaton on the plane earlier.

Ella and Leonie followed the bell-hop down a wide, winding flight of stone steps and across the floodlit plaza. A tinny bell in a miniature clock tower chimed midnight as they walked into Paradise.

Above them Orion hung at a lower angle than usual in a midnight-blue velvet sky. Ella couldn't remember the last time she'd seen it. You'd count yourself lucky to find even one star in the night sky back at home in Dublin. The bell-hop led them along a path flanked by villas with balconies, villas with verandas and villas with roof gardens. Tree frogs and crickets serenaded them as they descended more steps alongside a miniature waterfall. She could hear the sea now. They rounded a bend in the path and found themselves on a grassy esplanade. Beyond a low wall that bordered a turquoise-blue swimming pool, waves danced and beckoned to her.

Their villa was a stone's throw away from the pool and maybe two stones' throw away from a small but perfectly formed white sand beach. There were two bedrooms, a bathroom and a well-equipped little kitchen off a central sitting room.

The furnishings were quietly sumptuous, and Ella couldn't wait to fall into the king-sized bed with its filmy mosquito net. She'd cherished a fantasy about sleeping under a mosquito net since seeing some madly romantic film set in the Tropics when she was ten years old.

The bell-hop told them that breakfast was served in the beach restaurant from seven-thirty onwards. They tipped him in Jamaican dollars and he smiled and wished them an enjoyable stay in his beautiful country. Jah-may-kah. He pronounced the syllables slowly, as if enjoying the feel of them on his tongue. Then he turned and loped slowly away back up the path.

Ella and Leonie looked at each other, smiling incredulously, and then they hugged each other. 'Oh, Leonie!' said Ella. 'You totally clever thing!'

'Aren't I just?' said Leonie, with a feline smile. 'Now – where's the minibar? I'm dying for a drink.'

Ella located the minibar in a carved wooden cupboard. 'There's champagne!' she said. 'Two snipes. Shall we crack them?'

'Absolutely,' replied Leonie.

Ella popped the corks, and filled their glasses.

'I want to propose a toast,' Leonie said, raising hers solemnly.

'To whom?'

'To the Polly Rogers of course, darling,' said her grandmother, laughing.

* * *

The first thing Ella did when she woke the next morning was make a beeline for the pool. It was early, and there was no-one about apart from a beach attendant raking the sand, and a gardener wandering between ranks of bright flowerbeds. She dived and splashed and performed somersaults, and then she floated on her back and watched buzzards lazily cruising the periwinkle-blue Jamaican skies. By the time she climbed out of the pool some twenty minutes later, a life-guard was ascending his lookout post, a platoon of pink-frocked, white-aproned chambermaids were peeling off into villas, and an army of Germans was marching towards the beach with heaps of towels.

Leonie was sitting on the step of the veranda painting her toenails when Ella returned to their villa.

'We'd better get a move on,' she told her grand-mother, as she towelled her hair. 'The Germans really do do that thing with the towels.'

'Just wait till I finish the top coat,' said Leonie, sticking out the tip of her tongue as she concen-trated on painting her pinkie cherry red. 'Guess what was the first thing I saw when I opened my bedroom curtains this morning?'

'What?'

'A hummingbird. It was hovering at eye level right outside my window, sipping nectar from a hibiscus blossom.'

'Wow! We really are in the Garden of Eden, aren't we?' Ella leaned over the wooden rail of the veranda and breathed in the scent of a pink hibiscus flower. It was growing alongside a ginger lily which was growing alongside a bird of paradise flower which was growing alongside something even more exotic, with dangling red blossoms.

'There! Finished,' said Leonie, putting the top back on her nail varnish. 'Let's get ready to strut our stuff. Are you going to breakfast in your swimming costume?'

'I'll put a sarong on over it.'

They walked barefoot to the restaurant on the beach. It was thatched with palm leaves. A coconut palm grew through a ceiling festooned with vines, and glossy black birds hopped cheekily in and out of the open windows, scavenging for leftovers.

There was a dish laden with fruit at the breakfast counter. Until now, Ella had only ever eaten mango that tasted of some vaguely unpleasant oil, and watermelon that tasted of water. This fruit was *fragrant*. As well as mango and watermelon, there were guava and papaya and pineapple. There were freshly baked croissants, there was fried plantain, there was a spinachy-looking dish called callaloo, there was kedgeree. A smiling chef prepared an omelette for Leonie, and a smiling waiter poured Blue Mountain coffee for Ella.

They'd decided to do nothing on their first day. 'Let's just chill,' said Leonie. She had splurged out on an expensive swimming costume, and she looked sensational in her flower-splashed sarong, cartwheel sunhat and shades. When they strolled onto the beach a little later they made an impact, but Ella suspected that the appreciative looks were focused more on her glamorous grandmother than on her.

'When are you going to check out the dive outfit?' asked Leonie as she removed towels from two sun-loungers and made herself comfortable.

'I don't know. I'm not really sure I want to dive ever again after that grim fiasco in Sheep's Head Bay.'

'Oh, you must, Ella! You can't miss out on the opportunity of diving in the Caribbean! It's a once-in-a-lifetime experience!'

'Yes, I know,' said Ella, ruefully. 'But I think I've lost my nerve.'

'Well, just mention that to the instructor! They probably have to reassure nervous divers every single day. You won't be the first one, darling, you can depend upon that.'

'I suppose you're right.'

Ella looked over at the dive outfit. It was housed in a timber-built shack further down the beach. She came to a sudden decision. 'I'll book a dive now,' she said, getting off her sun-lounger. 'If I procrastinate I'll never do it.'

She walked across hot sand and stood by the counter of the dive shop, drumming on it with nervy fingers while she waited for someone to show up. There were stickers plastered over the walls. 'Happiness is Being In over your Head,' she read on one. 'Remember when Sex was Safe and Diving was Dangerous?' on another. And finally: 'Dive Deep, Dive Hard. Fear Nothing.'

She was studying this last sticker, uncertain of what response it produced in her, when a voice came from behind her. 'Dive deep, dive hard. Fear nothing,' she heard. 'The first rule of diving.'

'I thought it was "Never hold your breath"?' Ella turned to confront the person who'd spoken, and her breath was snatched away. She thanked God she was wearing shades, because they hid the expression in her eyes that she was quite unable to disguise. It was one of naked stupefaction.

He was the most beautiful man she had ever seen in her life. He stood more than six feet. He was ebony. His dreadlocks gave him the air of a Pharaoh, and his eyes invited you to dive right in. He was smiling, showing teeth white as pearls set in the most kissable mouth she had ever laid eyes on, and he carried himself like an insouciant prince.

'You know your scuba,' he said. 'You wanna book a dive?'

'Please,' said Ella. 'Are you an instructor?'

'No,' he said.

Ella hoped disappointment didn't register too obviously on her face.

'I don't dive.' Disappointment number two.

'You wanna talk to my woman.' Ow! Disappointment number *three*.

The terrestrial god moved to the door of the dive outfit. 'Desirée!' he called. 'There's a lady here wants to go divin'.'

The woman who emerged from the dive shop could have been any age from her late twenties to her early forties. She wasn't much taller than Ella, but she had a neat, lean, almost wiry physique. Her face had the high cheekbones, full mouth and slanting eyes of a Buddha, and she radiated chutzpah. She moved towards the Rasta, who laid a relaxed arm across her shoulders, and they both gave Ella the kind of smile that would be impossible not to return.

'You certified, honey?' The woman had a sweet, low voice.

'Not yet. I'm on referral from Dublin, in Ireland.'

'Ireland!' The woman's eyes gleamed with interest. 'I had an instructor from Dublin, Ireland work here for me once.'

'I think I know who you're talking about,' said Ella. 'You're Desirée, right?'

'That's my name.'

'So you're talking about Ferdia MacDiarmada? I trained with him.'

Desirée's smile became even broader. 'Hey! Ain't *no* instructor I trusted more than that Ferdia. How is my main man?'

'He's doing fine.'

Desirée nodded. 'Yeah. Him a fine t'ing. When you go back to Ireland you tell him that. Anytime he want to come back to Jamaica, he come to Desirée. Desirée find him work anytime.' She strolled across to the counter and picked up a desk diary. 'Now, honey. How many training dives you need to do?'

'All of them.'

'And when you wanna do them?'

'Um.' Oh God. Did she really *want* to do them? 'Whenever *you* want,' she said.

Desirée scanned the pages of the diary, humming a melody under her breath, while Ella chewed her lip. She suddenly realized that she was being observed, and she looked round to find the eyes of the beautiful Rastafarian on her. He was leaning against the jamb of the door, hands resting low on lean hips like a gunslinger. 'What's your problem?' he asked.

Ella was baffled. 'My problem?'

'Yeah, man. You have a problem. I see it in your face.'

Desirée glanced up at him and then turned to Ella. 'What is it, honey?'

'I'm scared,' confessed Ella. 'I wimped out of my first dive in the Irish Sea.'

'Oh? Why did you do that?'

'I felt a bit claustrophobic. I had a kind of panic attack.'

'What was the visibility?'

'Two metres.'

Desirée threw back her head and laughed. 'Two metres! Oh, look, girl – here you can see for twenty, thirty, forty metres no problem! You won't have no problem with claustrophobia!'

'Are you sure? Are we going to be going down very deep?' God! How she *hated* herself for being a wimp!

Desirée looked at her appraisingly. 'What's your name, honey?'

'Ella Nesbit.'

'OK, Ella Nesbit. This is what I am going to suggest to you. I am going to hand-rear you. I am going to finish the job my friend Ferdia started, and this is how I am going to do it. I will take you round to the Blue Lagoon, OK? There the water is very calm, very still – not choppy like the sea out there today. We go in off the dive boat there, OK?' Her laid-back Jamaican accent sounded wonderfully reassuring. 'We stay on the bottom for as long as it takes you to get comfortable. We maintain eye contact at all times. I won't take my eyes off you until I sense you are a happy girl, OK? Then I take you by the hand and we explore a little. Cruise around.'

Ella considered. There was something about this woman that inspired absolute trust. She remembered how Ferdia had told her that she'd be damn lucky if she got to train with Desirée. She nodded her head. 'OK,' she said. 'This sounds good.'

'That's what I like to hear. I think this girl has guts. But if at any time you feel nervous, even a little, you just signal to me and we'll go up. How are you fixed tomorrow morning?'

'I'm free as a bird.'

'OK. Show up around ten-thirty, Ella Nesbit, and

I will take you down. And when you go back to Ireland you tell our friend Ferdia that you were hand-trained by Desirée.'

Ella smiled at her. 'I'll do that. Thanks a lot, Desirée. I'll see you in the morning.' As she turned away, she made eye contact once again with the beautiful Rasta. 'Goodbye – ?' she said.

'Raphael,' he said, bestowing a beatific smile on her. Ella remembered how she had compared the Jamaican people to angels when she'd arrived in Kingston. This man didn't just *look* like an angel! He even had the name of one.

'Goodbye, Raphael.' She walked back across the beach to rejoin Leonie, with a song singing in her heart. It was the song Desirée had been humming, and Ella suddenly knew what it was. It was: 'Don't worry. Be happy.'

As she drew nearer the stretch of beach where she'd left Leonie, she became aware that someone had commandeered her sun-lounger. There was a man sitting next to her grandmother, and they were laughing away together as if they'd known each other for years. Ella gave Leonie a questioning look.

'Hello, darling. Let me introduce you,' she said. 'This is Dieter Bleibtreu. He and his son-in-law were responsible for hogging the sun-loungers. He's apologized for it, so we're friends now. Dieter, this is my granddaughter, Ella Nesbit.'

Dieter Bleibtreu rose to his feet and executed a little bow. '*Enchanté*. It is a pleasure to meet two so charming ladies on my first day here.'

153

You wouldn't have thought it was his first day. He was tanned to a dark honey colour, which made his blue eyes look bluer and his white hair whiter. He had an urbane manner, he wasn't in bad shape for a man whom Ella guessed to be somewhere in his sixties – and he was rich. Ella could tell by the gold Rolex. Trust her grandmother to find a man like this on the first day of her holiday!

'Let me get you something to drink,' he offered. 'It is a little early in the day for champagne, but perhaps you would care for a fruit punch?'

'It's never too early in the day for champagne,' said Leonie. 'It's the only alcoholic drink one's allowed to drink at any time of the day. Thank you. I'd love a glass.'

Dieter Bleibtreu smiled. 'Ella? Champagne?'

'No thanks, Dieter. I'll stick to punch.' She wasn't going to start knocking back alcohol at this hour of the morning. She didn't want to end up with a hang-over tomorrow in the Blue Lagoon with Desirée.

Dieter headed off in the direction of the bar, and Ella sat down beside Leonie. 'Honestly! You are incorrigible! I leave you alone for ten minutes, and when I come back you've picked up a complete stranger. What am I going to do with you?'

Leonie looked smug. 'He's rather gorgeous, isn't he? He's a divorcee, and he's here on holiday with his daughter and her family. They have the poshest villa in the joint, with their own private swimming pool. He's invited me for cocktails later.' She looked over at Dieter, who was leaning on the bar, and sent him her wonderful smile. Then she turned back to Ella. 'How did you get on? Does that woman you were talking to run the dive shop?'

'Yup. Her name's Desirée, and she is the Man. Or rather, the Woman.'

'So who was the man? He was pretty damn sexy. Is he a diver?'

'No. He's also a strictly no-go area. He and Desirée are an item.'

'So when are you diving?'

'Tomorrow. Desirée's taking me down.'

'Good girl!' said Leonie approvingly. 'That's the spirit. Never give up too easily. Oh, look. There's that film star person.'

Sophie Burke was walking across the grassy esplanade. She was wearing a thong, a skimpy sun top, high-heeled gold sandals and a sunhat with the widest brim Ella had ever seen. There was gold at her ankle, her wrist, her throat and her earlobes, and a diamond sparkled in her belly-button. Men gaped, and women looked away. Sophie kicked off her shoes, doffed her hat with a flourish of her left hand and her shades with a flourish of her right, and swept back her shiny platinum hair. Then she removed her sun top and dived into the pool.

'Goodness,' said Leonie. 'She's got amazing bazookas. Do you think they're real?'

Sophie swam one lap, and then rose up like Aphrodite at the other end, lifting both hands to push back her wet hair from her forehead and looking around with a Bambi-ish blink for a sun-lounger.

A blond youth obliged the starlet immediately, jumping to his feet and indicating that she could use his lounger before hurling himself into the pool to cool off. Sophie settled down on the lounger, produced a tube of suncream from a beach bag, and began to unscrew the lid. This time everyone on the beach looked away.

Dieter returned with drinks on a tray.

'Thank you, Dieter,' said Leonie, raising her glass of champagne at him. 'Here's to happy holidays.'

*   *   *

Some time later Ella got bored listening to her grandmother and Dieter flirting, and decided to go to her villa to fetch something to read. As she passed by the pool, she heard her name being called.

'Ella! Hi!' Sophie Burke was waving at her.

Ella veered reluctantly round the pool to where Sophie was reclining. 'Hi,' she said. 'How's your jet lag?'

'Pretty awful, really. I had a massage in the beauty parlour earlier to perk me up. What do you think of the resort?'

'It's heavenly, isn't it?'

'So-so. I've seen better. And there are so many *Germans.* The masseuse told me that 90 per cent of the residents at any given time are German. Shall I give you some advice? Just say: "Ich spreche kein Deutsch". That'll put them off trying to harass you.'

Ella couldn't imagine being harassed by any of

the people she'd seen so far. And Dieter had turned out to be perfectly charming, with a nice line in irony. If only her grandmother would stop monopolizing him. Ella had barely been able to get a word in edgeways.

'It's lucky for us, isn't it, that we met up at the airport? Otherwise we might never have run into a single other English-speaking person. Oh – look. That sun-lounger's free. Grab it, quickly, before anyone else can.'

Sophie flung a towel across the next-door lounger, and Ella found herself sitting down beside her.

'Here,' said Sophie sweetly. 'Would you like to have a look at my *Harper's*? You might do my back for me first though. I need to use a total block because my skin's so fair. And having a tan is so deeply untrendy, don't you think? I mean, look at all these Germans. Their skin's like leather. And did you know that the highest proportion of skin cancer . . .'

Uh-oh, thought Ella. If she wasn't careful, life on this holiday could turn out to be more of a bitch than a beach . . .

Chapter Six

The following morning saw Ella on board a boat beating its way towards the Blue Lagoon, looking svelte and sexy in Lycra at last. No horrible slugskin neoprene necessary in Dive Holiday Heaven! She sat in the stern with her hair streeling out behind her like a scarf and her skin all aglow from the sun and the sea wind. The sad thing was there was no-one to look svelte and sexy for. There was just her and Desirée and the boatman on board.

She'd discovered that Salamander Cove Villas wasn't exactly bursting at the seams with people her age. It seemed to cater for an affluent, upmarket clientele, and most of the residents were dripping with gold and sagging with middle-aged spread. This was emphatically *not* a swinging singles holiday resort. How ironic that her sixty-something grandmother had managed to embark on a whirl-wind flirtation with a gorgeous German, while her young and not screamingly unattractive grand-daughter hadn't hooked up with anyone! Pah – she didn't really care. Since Jack and Angie had become an item she'd lost interest in men.

She disengaged a strand of hair from the zip of her exposure suit, and turned her thoughts to a more immediate consideration. Her dive. Desirée had told her that she wouldn't test Ella on her dive skills today. She just wanted her pupil to get comfortable in the underwater environment. She had radiated reassurance, but Ella was still feeling antsy. Was she going to wimp out again? Had all those lessons been a complete waste of time and money? Would those twenty-four hours of struggling with dive tables and J-valves and ton-weight tanks have been better off spent doing something else? Studying *Pro Sound News* to keep up with Julian? Practising her violin?

The dive boat rounded a headland, and there, suddenly, was the Blue Lagoon, surrounded by high escarpments covered in verdant forest. It was every bit as beautiful as the photographs in her guidebook, but the photographs hadn't done justice to the colour of the water. It was of a blue-green so smooth and dense that when Ella dipped her fingers in the water she half expected them to come out dripping with colour like thick gloss paint.

The boat chugged to a halt, and Desirée leaned forward. 'OK, Ella. How are you feeling?'

Ella's heart started to beat a little tattoo. 'Fine,' she lied.

'We'll do a backward roll into the water. Let me go first – and remember to signal to me that you're OK the minute you surface.'

Ella donned mask and fins, inflated her BCD, and, feeling like a condemned prisoner, stuck her regulator in her mouth.

Desirée performed an elegant backward roll, and surfaced. 'Go, Ella!' she urged.

She leaned back and the weight of the tank pulled her over. The warm water churned round her in an explosion of bubbles and refracted silvery light, and then she was at the surface, floating calmly amidst the wavelets she'd made, signalling to Desirée that she was OK.

'Hey!' Desirée gave her a great, broad grin, and Ella found herself smiling back. 'Not a lot wrong with your backward roll, girl! You ready to go down?'

'I think so, yeah. That was cool!'

'OK. Let's take it real easy, Ella. Remember to breathe slowly.'

Ella pressed her deflator valve. Very slowly, she felt the Blue Lagoon close over her head. She looked down. The bottom was only a few metres away. It was sandy, strewn with pebbles. She looked up. She could see sunlight dancing on the surface. A shoal of tiny, jewel-coloured fish went by, and she laughed. She looked at Desirée and made the OK signal with thumb and forefinger. Then she signalled that she wanted to go back up.

'What's the problem?' asked Desirée when they were buoyant on the surface. 'Ain't you comfortable, honey?'

'Oh, hell – yes! I just wanted to say – can I do the skills today?'

Desirée laughed. 'Hey! She's hooked!'

'Oh, Desirée – it's blissful down there! I saw fish!'

'Blissful? Phooey. There ain't much to see in the Blue Hole. You ain't seen nothing yet, Jacqueline Cousteau. Just wait till you dive a reef.'

Ella laughed again. She had stuck her regulator back in her mouth and was rapidly going through the pre-dive signalling sequence.

'Hey! Not so fast, honey!' Desirée was laughing too. 'You gotta wait for your old lady!'

* * *

She spent the next three days performing her training dives in open sea. After each of the tests, she and Desirée would tour the reefs together. They glided over caverns and precipices so vertiginous that Ella kept catching her breath, and had to remind herself of the first rule of scuba diving. *Never* hold your breath. She spiralled slowly downwards, feeling weightless and wonderful and – well – *watery*.

The reef was a revelation. She had never seen such extraordinary beauty. She saw shoals of spotty fish, stripy fish and neon fish. She bought a book on fishes of the Caribbean so that she could identify the creatures. She saw shy hamlets, indigo hamlets, butter hamlets. She saw fairy brasslets, flamefish, cardinalfish and trumpetfish. She saw angelfish and cherubfish and neon blue parrotfish kissing. She saw an aptly named rock beauty poised provocatively in her boudoir like an Amsterdam whore, wearing the prettiest makeup. A yellow base, blue lipstick to accentuate her pout, and blue eyeshadow to emphasize her *beaux yeux*.

The reef itself was like an underwater tapestry. It was as if someone had draped the most luxurious cashmere shawl they could find over the seabed and scattered it with soft cushions of coral. She could picture mer-princesses reclining on them. Some were embroidered in gold thread, some had been spangled with sequins, some gleamed with mother-of-pearl buttons, others with tortoiseshell. The fabrics were chenille and velvet and angora; the hues were purple, amber, red ochre, saffron, rose, moss green. Lainey Keogh would have been in seventh heaven!

The architect that had been employed to design the mer-kingdom had been a visionary. There were castles, turreted and castellated, there were gorgeous palaces, there were magnificent garden urns and mazes and statuary. The beauty of her surroundings made Ella feel like an alien intruding on the habitat of a superior species, but she thanked her lucky stars that she was a privileged alien, able to feast her eyes on all this sub-aquatic sumptuousness.

And it moved! Little shrubs decorated like Christmas trees swayed to the rhythm of the ebb and flow, and intricate lace fans undulated along-side silken fronds and ostrich-feather plumes and tendrils of mermaids' hair. The mer-princesses had plainly abandoned their kingdom at the first sign of human invasion, and they'd abandoned it in a hurry, knocking over jewel boxes and spilling gems onto the rich carpet. They'd been having a party. There were coral cups and exquisitely-wrought goblets strewn around. She'd seen goblets like that once in an expensive craft shop in Temple Bar. Temple Bar! How far away that place seemed now, and how pedestrian!

'Let's look for starfish,' Desirée suggested one day, writing on her underwater slate. They searched under rocks on the seabed for the creatures, and Ella thought how bananas it was that underwater she could heft around weighty-looking rocks with ease, while on the surface she could barely manage her own tank. Desirée found the first starfish, and passed it to Ella, who watched the delicate creature glide across her palm with laugh-out-loud delight. She had found her gills at last, and was so reluctant to return to the real world that she wanted to swim away and hide in the reef every time Desirée made the signal to ascend.

She had a problem once only. As part of her training she was required to take her mask off underwater, and put it back on again. Without a mask it was impossible to see anything with any degree of clarity, and she found herself disorientated again. Her breathing was verging on hyperventilation when she struggled, panicking, to the surface with Desirée following. It was an action replay of the dive she'd performed in Sheep's Head Bay. Desirée calmed her, then they descended and tried again. Again Ella panicked and bolted for the surface. 'I'll try it one more time,' she said. 'But if I can't hack it, I'm aborting the dive.' It would break her heart if she had to abort. She knew that if she did, she would never certify, and she would never be able to dive again. She'd be like an addict denied a drug.

'Do it, honey,' said Desirée, 'and I will ask Otis to invent a cocktail specially for you.'

'What? Who's Otis?'

'Otis is the head barman in Salamander Cove Villas. He dreams up special cocktails for special people. So some evening before you go, you and I are going to celebrate, Ella. With a cocktail named after you. All right?'

'That's a lovely idea, Desirée,' said Ella, giving a self-deprecatory shrug as she strapped her mask back on. 'But you could hardly call me special.'

'Anyone who overcomes a fear is special, Ella. You did it in the Blue Lagoon. You can do it again. Now. Tell me when you're ready to go down again.'

Ella stuck her regulator in her mouth, took a couple of deep breaths and forced herself to relax. She looked at Desirée, registered the reassurance in her eyes, and then made the OK signal. This time when she hit the bottom the mask was off, on again, and cleared of water before she could allow herself to think about what she was doing. Dive deep, dive hard, she thought. Fear nothing. Desirée clapped her hands and then scribbled something on her slate. *I can tell you are a fighter!* read Ella, and she laughed. She laughed with relief and pride and pure euphoria. She remembered what PJ had said all those weeks ago on her very first training session. He'd told her she'd be doing a lot of laughing underwater. He'd been right.

Later, back on dry land, Desirée signed her logbook for her, and stamped it.

'Congratulations,' she said, handing it over to Ella and giving her a big kiss on the cheek. 'You are now a certified open water diver, Ella Nesbit. And you've earned that cocktail.'

'Wow,' said Ella. 'It's hard to believe. I honestly thought I'd never do it.'

'You're persistent. That's how you did it.'

'Yeah,' said Ella, with a rueful laugh. 'That's how I lost my last boyfriend. He told me I was a stubborn bitch.'

Desirée smiled. '"You don't give up easily" is a nicer way of putting it.'

*　　*　　*

Later that afternoon she took her logbook down to the poolside so she could enter her dive. PJ had told her how important it was to keep a log, but she was getting lazy and her descriptions were becoming less and less detailed. She had just finished scribbling in 'Marine life: the usual stunning suspects' when a shadow fell across the page. She looked up to see Sophie Burke. 'Hi,' said the actress, commencing her daily striptease ritual.

'Oh – hi.'

Sophie discarded her sarong as if it was the seventh veil in the dance, and then stretched out on the sun-lounger beside Ella. You could almost hear the collective male groan. 'Diving again, were you?' she asked, sliding what looked like a film script out of her beach bag.

'Mm.'

'All that salt water won't do your skin any favours, Ella. Look how chapped your hands are compared to mine.'

Ella looked down at her hands. Sophie was right. They were dry and chafed, and she'd broken a couple of nails while assembling her gear. 'I'll worry about that when I get home,' she said. 'Anyway – I think I'll only dive on alternate days from now on. Now my training's out of the way I can take some time out to explore the island.'

'Drop by my villa later. I'll let you have some hand cream.'

'Thanks.' Ella reached for her Lonely Planet guide. 'D'you fancy hiring a cab and heading off somewhere tomorrow, Sophie? I'd hate to stay cooped up in this resort for the entire duration of the holiday, and Leonie wouldn't be able for the more strenuous stuff.'

166

Sophie looked suspicious. 'What did you have in mind?'

'Well, there's masses to do.' Ella leafed through the pages. 'We could go hiking, or rafting or canoeing. Or bicycling in the Blue Mountains – and I think I saw paragliding mentioned somewhere . . .' She trailed off as she registered the blank expression on Sophie's face. It was obvious she was wasting her breath.

'Paragliding? Eeyoo. I don't *think* so.'

'Well, maybe we could opt for something more cultural, then? There's a walking tour of Port Antonio. We could visit the craft market afterwards.'

'Ella?' Sophie swiped her sunglasses away from her face and looked at Ella with a pitying expression. 'I didn't come here for an *adventure* holiday. I came here to escape from the stresses and strains of my career. Because I am very much in demand as an actress, my life is fraught with responsibilities and decision making. Which script?' She held up a spiral-bound volume and started fanning herself with it. 'Which agent? Which charity? Even here I cannot escape. I sign dozens of autographs every day. I do not resent it, because I have a duty to my public. But sometimes it seems to me that there is nowhere on this planet where I can bask in blissful anonymity. This –' she indicated the pool, the beach, the kaleidoscopic gardens with an expansive gesture '– is as good as it gets. But still I feel eyes staring at me from behind all those dark glasses.'

Ella looked perplexed. What had she done to invite this discourse? Sophie sounded as if she was rehearsing lines from the film script she was wielding. 'I only suggested that we maybe hire a taxi and—'

'Ella.' Sophie placed a perfectly manicured index finger on her glossy lips. 'I am here to *chill*. I am here to relax by the pool, have massages and facials, maybe take a modicum of exercise in the gym or play a little tennis. I am under doctor's orders to take it easy. I cannot be hurtling through mountains on a bicycle, or slashing my way through rain forests. I have no intention of venturing into the ghettos of Port Antonio and running the risk of being mugged or raped. *Capisci?*'

The actress bestowed a patronizing smile on Ella, and Ella shrugged. 'OK. I just think it's an awful waste to travel all the way to another country and not see any of the local colour, that's all.' It had been stupid of her to try and interest Sophie in an excursion. She might have known that the starlet's interest in this tropical island paradise wouldn't extend beyond the parameters of their exclusive resort. She looked down at the picture of a smiling Rasta in her Lonely Planet. Hell's bells. She *couldn't* spend all her time in Jamaica surrounded by European faces! Maybe she could cajole Leonie into visiting some of the sights with her? But she knew now that paragliding and cycling would be out of the question.

Sophie had cast aside her film script with a dismissive 'pah!' and had started to leaf through *OK!* magazine instead. Ella was now beginning to bitterly regret the charitable impulse that had made her take pity on the actress at the airport. She wished she'd had the good sense to pretend that she was German.

'Oh, look!' said Sophie with a pleased smile. 'Hasn't Jodie Kidd got enormous! She's put on at least half a stone since I last saw her. At the BAFTAs, I think it was.' She turned another page. 'Eeyoo. I don't think much of the Spring collections, do you?' – flashing a glossy photograph at Ella and resuming her commentary without waiting for a response. 'That dirndl shape is *sooo* unflattering, isn't it? Even I couldn't carry it off. Oh look – somebody else I know!' She looked at Ella, plainly waiting to be asked Who?

'Who?' obliged Ella dully.

'Rory McDonagh. I knew him before he became a Hollywood big shot, you know.'

'Oh?' Ella perked up a bit. Rory McDonagh was an actor she'd always liked. There was something of the maverick about him. 'What's he like?'

'Well, he's quite a private individual, so there's not a lot to tell.'

'He married that actress who used to be in that soap opera that was axed, didn't he? What was the name of that soap?'

'*Ardmore Grove.* I was in that as well, you know.'
Sophie sounded vexed that Ella hadn't remembered. 'And yes, Rory did marry that actress. Her
name was Deirdre O'Dare.' She looked pensive for
a minute and then she said: 'Poor Deirdre. She
didn't have any success at all as an actress after she
left the "soap", as you call it. I prefer to use the term
"urban drama."' She gave Ella a sweet smile, and
then continued: 'Not like me. My career went into
the ascendant when *I* left. Now Deirdre's having
babies! Ha ha ha! What a joke. She once said she'd
never settle down.'

'I wouldn't mind settling down and making
babies with someone like Rory McDonagh.'

'He's not that good in bed, actually,' said Sophie,
and then her eyes went very wide and her hands
shot to her mouth. 'Oh! How indiscreet of me!
Forget I ever said that, Ella, will you?' She turned
imploring eyes on Ella.

'Sure,' said Ella. She really wasn't interested in
Sophie Burke's sex life.

But Sophie obviously was, because she continued
to fill Ella in, keeping her eyes demurely downcast.
'It was before I met Ben, of course. When I met Ben
he just swept me off my feet, and I had to let Rory
down. It was awful. He begged me to stay, but Ben
and I just had this incredible instant rapport – do
you know what I mean? It was – quite simply – love
at first sight.'

'Mm.'

'Then poor Rory went off and married Deirdre

on the rebound,' concluded Sophie happily. Suddenly she gave a little scream. 'Oh my God!' she said, clapping her hands to her mouth.

'What is it?' asked Ella.

'It's Eva Lavery!'

'The film star? In *OK!* magazine?'

'No. In real life – over there! Look!' Sophie had sat bolt upright, and was pointing to a blonde woman and a dark-haired man, who were strolling along the path that bordered the lawn. 'Oh my God! Eva! Eva!' Sophie grabbed her sarong, got up and teetered across the esplanade on her high heels, clutching her enormous sunhat to her head, and practically pratfalling in her desperation to reach Eva Lavery and her companion. The heads of all the men on the poolside turned to follow her progress, eyes glued to her jiggling breasts as she ineffectually attempted to wrap the sarong around her.

The couple stopped and turned towards Sophie, and Ella could see them exchange glances as the actress bore down upon them. They stood stoically while she showered them with air-kisses and then regaled them with a non-stop torrent of words, all the time gesticulating theatrically. Ella resisted the impulse to applaud. She felt as if she was watching a one-woman show.

She studied Eva as Sophie prattled on. Eva Lavery in her late forties was more beautiful than most women are in their prime. Ella had seen the actress in loads of films, but she looked different off screen. On screen she was a chameleon, famous for being able to change her look for each movie she made. Today her golden skin was devoid of makeup, her blond hair was piled messily on her head and her feet were bare. She was wearing tiny silver earrings and a very simply-cut long cotton dress splashed with flowers. The only thing remotely film-starrish about her were her sunglasses.

After about two minutes of chat, Sophie allowed her victims to beat a retreat, and then she tottered back across the grass, and collapsed onto her sun-lounger. 'Isn't that the most amazing coincidence!' she gasped. 'That was Eva Lavery, the film star and David Lawless her husband, the famous director! Gorgeous, isn't he? I've known them for the longest time, ever since I turned professional! The first show I ever did was for David Lawless – it was *A Midsummer Night's Dream* in the Phoenix theatre – Rory MacDonagh was in it as well!'

Ella murmured something polite, but Sophie wasn't listening.

'Goodness! How *wonderful* to have run into them!' Sophie's exclamation marks were even more irritating than usual. 'They're staying around the corner, in a villa near the Blue Lagoon. David's here to discuss some project he's working on with a famous producer – I'm not allowed to say who – that's top secret!' Sophie turned a radiant smile on Ella, as if she was bestowing on her the most magnificent gift on the face of the planet. 'Would you like to meet Eva?' she asked, magnanimously. 'I'm joining her at the bar for a drink.'

Actually, Ella would, quite. She really admired Eva Lavery's work. 'That would be nice,' she said.

They meandered down to the bar on the beach. At least, Ella meandered. Sophie made a beeline towards where Eva was sitting on a stool sipping Planter's Punch. Her husband was at an umbrella-topped table on the terrace, engrossed in conversation with some dripping-with-gold type.

'Ella Nesbit – this is Eva Lavery. Eva, Ella,' pronounced Sophie when she joined them.

'Hello, Ella,' said Eva in honey tones. 'Pleased to meet you.' She actually made the clichéd greeting sound genuine.

'Likewise,' said Ella. 'I'm a fan. I loved your last movie – I went to see it twice.'

'Well, thanks!'

'My friends will be dead jealous when I get back to Dublin and tell them that I stayed in a joint frequented by celebrities!'

'Hey! You're from Dublin? I thought I recognized the accent.'

Ella smiled. 'It's a giveaway, isn't it?'

'Mine isn't,' said Sophie, in polished mid-Atlantic.

Ella noticed the corner of Eva's mouth twitch, and decided she was going to like this woman.

'Let's see,' resumed Eva in a speculative voice. 'Your accent's somewhere south of the Liffey – but not as far south as Dun Laoghaire.'

173

'Right first time. I'm from Portobello.'

'Hey! I used to live there! In Pleasants Street.'

'Then I lived just around the corner from you. In Grantham Street.'

'Hang about. Grantham Street? Wasn't there another Nesbit there? I seem to remember that Declan Nesbit from Celtic Note had a house in Grantham Street.'

Ella laughed. 'He still does, but he's hardly ever there. He's my dad.'

'No shit!' Eva threw back her head and crowed. She had one of the most full-bodied laughs Ella had ever heard. 'Dear God, but it's a small world!'

'What d'you mean?' asked Sophie.

Eva's expression changed suddenly. She wore the look of a guilty pussycat. 'Oh, it's just I – er – knew him, back in the early eighties some time . . .' Her voice had a rather contrived vagueness about it.

Ella smiled. 'You knew my dad?'

'Um. Yeah.'

Ella's smile grew broader. She suspected from the way Eva was demurring that they'd had an affair. Her father had gone through the eighties and early nineties having a string of affairs with gorgeous women all over the world, before he'd settled down with his current wife, an Alaskan Innuit. 'Did you – um – know him well?'

'Mm. Afraid so.' Eva smiled back, acknowledging that further prevarication was pointless. 'He was pretty bloody irresistible, your dad. I imagine he still is.'

'He is,' conceded Ella. 'But he's on the straight and narrow now. In fact, he's going to present me with a baby brother or sister early next year.'

'Wow. And we were of the generation who thought we would never settle down.' Eva leaned over and shook Ella's hand. 'Well, neighbour,' she said. 'What'll you have to drink?'

'I'll have what you're having, thank you.'

'Sophie?'

'I'll just have a mineral water, thanks.' Sophie sounded virtuous. 'How long are you staying, by the way?' she asked as Eva signalled to the barman.

'We're flying out late tomorrow night.'

'Oh, no! What a shame!' An expression of devastation ravished Sophie's beautiful face. 'We could have hung out together, Eva. Visited a few beaches. *Discovered* Jamaica.'

Ella's jaw dropped.

'I've done loads of jaunts since I've been here,' said Eva. 'I discovered a wonderful guide. He knows everything there is to know about the island.'

'Look – if you're leaving tomorrow, why don't you have dinner with us tonight?' suggested Sophie. 'The Pavilion restaurant here is wonderful.'

Ella's jaw hit the deck. Sophie had done nothing but moan about how mediocre the Salamander Cove cuisine was since they'd arrived.

'No thanks, Sophie,' said Eva. 'We're going out

175

to dinner this evening. We've arranged to meet someone in the Blue Lagoon restaurant at eight o'clock.'

'Oh.' Sophie couldn't hide her disappointment. She let a little hiatus dangle in the conversation, waiting for Eva to suggest that she join her and David for dinner at the Blue Lagoon, but no such invitation materialized.

Then: 'How about meeting up tomorrow?' suggested Eva. 'David's got an appointment to see some backer. He'll be stuck in discussion for hours, and I'll die of boredom if I have to hang around that villa all day. I'd love to visit Navy Island.'

Ella cheered inwardly. At last she had a chance to escape from the luxury compound! 'Yes! I'm on for that!' she said.

'Navy Island?' said Sophie. 'Where's that?'

'Just off the coast at Port Antonio. You take the ferry. There are beaches, and some lovely walks, apparently. A good reef, too, for snorkelling. And you can visit Errol Flynn's mansion.'

'I don't have a snorkel,' said Sophie. 'But I'd love to see the mansion.'

'OK. It's a date.' Over on the terrace Ella could see David Lawless getting to his feet and shaking hands with his colleague. Eva waved at him, and then slid off her barstool. 'Say I pick you up here at around ten o'clock tomorrow morning?'

'Ten's cool. Thanks, Eva,' said Ella.

The actress started to walk across the sand towards her husband, and then she paused. 'Oh – by the way,' she called back to them. 'Remember to wear sensible shoes.'

'Sensible *shoes*?' said Sophie Burke.

Chapter Seven

The next morning Ella and Sophie waited in reception for Eva to arrive. Sophie seemed to have more outfits than Barbie. Today she was wearing a kind of Jemima Khan flowing white embroidered tunic and the most sensible shoes she had: a pair of barely there flat Jimmy Choo sandals with criss-cross leather thongs. Ella had filled a backpack with the usual day tripper's paraphernalia and was wearing gingham shorts and a T-shirt over her bikini.

'Are you going to swim off the island?' asked Sophie.

'Sure. There are three good beaches, according to the Lonely Planet guide.'

'I hate swimming in the sea,' said Sophie. 'I only ever swim in pools.'

Ella was swotting up about Navy Island in the Lonely Planet. 'It says here that one of them's a nudist beach.'

'Really?' said Sophie, brightening. 'Maybe we should go there. It would be nice to go home with an all-over tan.'

'I thought you said you didn't want to get a tan?' said Ella.

178

Sophie looked vague. 'Oh – I wouldn't mind just a touch of colour, you know. It lets people know you've been away somewhere exotic.'

Ella suspected that Sophie was rather more intent on showing off the amazing physical symmetry that had all the male residents of Salamader Cove agog every time she unknotted her sarong.

'Miz Nesbit? Miz Burke?' A low voice came from behind her.

Ella turned round and gave a little 'oh!' of surprise. There, standing at the reception desk, was Raphael, Desirée's partner. She hadn't seen him since her first day in the resort.

'Raphael! Hi!' she said.

He gave her his wonderful smile. 'Glad to see you again, Ella.'

'Hey! Glad to see you, also!'

'I'm driving you today. I'm Miz Lavery's guide.' He leaned against the desk, pushing back his heavy dreadlocks, and for the first time Ella noticed the sickle moon of a scar etched in silver on his cheekbone. It did nothing to diminish his beauty. 'Desirée tells me you got certified?'

'Yeah. I'm a total convert.'

'I knew she'd see you right. My old lady's the best teacher in the business.' Raphael turned his attention to Sophie. 'Are you Miz Burke?'

'That's right. Is the car out front?'

He gave Sophie a look of narrow-eyed assessment, and then he gave a slow nod. 'Yes, ma'am.'

There was nothing remotely servile about the 'ma'am'. 'Follow me.'

A gleaming Lexus was waiting under the *porte-cochère*. Eva was sitting in the leather-upholstered front seat, looking like the cat that got the cream. 'Isn't he *gorgeous*?' she mouthed at Ella as she slid into the back seat, and Ella gave an appreciative smile back.

'Nice car,' said Sophie. 'It'll make a change from that bloody awful bus that brought us here.'

Today Eva was wearing baggy cotton trousers, flip-flops, a T-shirt and sunglasses. There were diamonds cascading from her earlobes. Sophie's gimlet eyes assessed them at once.

'Eva?' she said. 'I'm not sure it's a good idea to wear real diamonds into Port Antonio.'

'Goodness, Sophie – you're absolutely right. How inconsiderate of me to flaunt my good fortune in the face of poverty.' She unhooked the diamonds and flung them into glove compartment.

'I was thinking more along the lines of being a target for mugging,' said Sophie, fastening her seatbelt as the car took off down the driveway. 'But, er – do you think the glove compartment's a safe place for them?'

'Right again.' Eva retrieved the jewels and handed them to Raphael. 'Will you look after them for me?' she said. The look on Sophie's face when she saw Eva pass her driver a small fortune in diamonds was so appalled it was comical.

'No problem,' said Raphael, sliding the earrings into his pocket.

Ella took the opportunity to study him further as he drove. His eyes slanted upwards at the corner, his cheekbones were razorshell sharp, and when he laughed – which was frequently – he showed the tip of a tongue like red satin. Eva flirted shamelessly with him, and the appalled look on Sophie's face intensified.

When Eva turned to them and said, 'Wonderful country, isn't it?' Ella felt guilty. She'd been so transfixed by the vision that was Raphael that she'd barely clocked the scenery.

Jamaica was dazzling. She found it hard to believe that there were only forty shades of green in the spectrum – this place was greener than Ireland on St Patrick's Day. They drove through countryside dense with trees dripping moss and looped with vines. They passed coconut groves and orderly plantations of broad-leaved banana trees. They passed colonial-style palatial homes like giant wedding cakes, and small villa-style houses so neat and dainty they looked as if they were prinking themselves in proud testament to pernickety house-keeping. They passed garages that looked like relics from the fifties, with pump attendants gyrating to blasting reggae on the forecourts, and stalls selling everything from jerk pork to frocks to raffia baskets.

Some of the townships they drove through were more rundown than others. There were shacks so wretched it was difficult to imagine how people lived in them. These were patchwork houses of haphazard construction, with roofs of corrugated iron. Goats bleated and chickens scratched around in the dusty growth by the side of the road. Most of the shacks were painted in vibrant colours – cerulean blue or hibiscus-blossom pink – and decorated with jewel-like patterns, but much of the paintwork was washed out and peeling, and Ella was appalled to find herself contemplating how picturesque poverty could be.

Port Antonio was crammed with people and bicycles and parping beat-up cars, and when they emerged from the car in the ferry car park Sophie was the instant target for appreciative remarks and graphic gestures. Luckily there was a ferry waiting, because the remarks were becoming more and more voluble, with lots of references to 'rasses' and 'battys', and Sophie was looking more and more tight-lipped.

'They're not abusing you, Sophie,' said Eva mildly as they boarded the ferry. 'They're complimenting you. They think you've got a great ass.'

'Pardon me, Eva, but I don't consider being called a "yum-yum tart" much of a compliment,' said Sophie, bristling.

The ferry ride was short. Ella took out her camera and snapped views. Then she snapped Eva and Sophie and the ferryman, and finally she snapped Raphael. 'Do you mind?' she asked, and he shook his head slowly and gave her that heart-stopping smile again. She actually found herself blushing as she smiled back. There was something about his eyes – something *unfathomable*. It felt as if he was looking into her soul.

On the island, he left them on the jetty and went into the waterfront hotel to check out the refreshment situation. There was no-one else around.

Ella sat down on the grass and watched him go. He had the familiar Jamaican gait she found so attractive, but for the first time she noticed that he walked with a barely perceptible limp. 'What a beautiful man he is!' she observed.

'Mm. Isn't he devastating?' Eva produced a bunch of bananas from her bag and handed them round. Sophie shook her head. She had divested herself of her Jemima Khan robe, and was spreading out a towel so that she could sunbathe. Ella noticed that she kept her top on. She'd obviously received enough compliments for one day. 'I'm genetically predisposed to fancy the pants off attractive men,' resumed Eva. 'David's forever telling me off for flirting with the riggers on location. Flirting is as far as it goes, I hasten to add. I have all the man I need at home.'

'I can't say I'm really into dreadlocks,' said Sophie. 'I always imagine they must be alive with all kinds of unpleasant creatures. And he's spoken for, anyway. I saw him wrapped around a rather strange-looking woman yesterday.'

'That's Desirée, his missus,' said Eva. 'She's a real dynamo. We had both of them round for dinner the other evening.'

'Did you?' said Ella. 'I know her. She's my dive instructor.'

'Hey! You dive?'

'Yeah,' said Ella, feeling inordinately proud to be able to answer in the affirmative at last.

'Oh, wow!' breathed Eva. 'You totally lucky thing! I've always wanted to scuba dive, but I've never done it.'

'Ow, that sun's hot.' Ella peeled off her shorts and T-shirt and took a bottle of water out of her bag. She took a long swig, and then passed the bottle to Eva.

Eva peered at her through her dark glasses. 'Ooh. Look at all your lovely freckles!'

'The sun brings them out. I hate them,' said Ella. 'I was called Freckle Face at school.'

'It's funny the way some people hate having them, isn't it? It's a bit like people with curly hair envying people with straight hair, and vice versa. I used to paint freckles all across my nose and cheekbones when I was a teenager.' She screwed the lid back on the bottle of water and handed it back to Ella. 'How long have you been scuba diving?'

'I only just certified. You should give it a go, Eva. It's amazing.'

'I tried to once, but I failed my medical. Like Raphael, I'm not allowed to dive, on doctor's orders.'

'Oh?' Sophie's eyes gleamed as if she'd just found a gold nugget. 'Why's that?'

'None of your business,' returned Eva amiably.

'Raphael failed his scuba medical?' Ella was

surprised. He seemed such a prime specimen of physical rude health.

'No. But he's been precluded from diving ever since he got the bends. It's a pretty tragic story.'

'The bends? Hell. It must have been a really bad case if he can't dive any more?'

'It was. According to Desirée he underwent months of treatment before the doctors put the final kibosh on his career.'

'He was a pro?'

'Yes. Top level.'

'A master instructor?' That explained the scar. 'Wow. And he doesn't dive at all now?'

'Absolutely not. He won't ever dive again.' Eva carefully wrapped her banana skin in a paper bag and then lobbed it into her beach bag. 'Desirée told me he was completely, utterly floored when he heard the news.'

'Oh, God – how awful!' said Ella. 'How did the accident happen?'

'I'm not sure. During some deep dive, I think. He wasn't at fault, though. The outfit responsible forked out a lot in compensation.'

'Still. It's terribly sad that he won't ever dive again.'

'Yes, it *is* sad. He turned his back on diving completely after that, apparently. He even left the running of the shop – which he had originally been responsible for setting up – to Desirée.'

'But he didn't have to do that! Couldn't he have carried on working as an instructor in the classroom? There's loads of academic stuff involved in scuba.'

'Think about it, Ella. If you were as passionate about something as Raphael was about diving, how would you feel if you could only sit back and watch from the sidelines?'

'Oh – I agree absolutely!' said Sophie earnestly. 'If I had to stop acting, I'd never set foot in a theatre again!'

Ella looked pensive. 'So. What made him decide to become a guide?' she asked.

'He'd earned a living through learning all there was to learn about his underwater habitat. So when his career as a diver was scuppered, he decided to earn a living through learning all there was to learn about his terrestrial habitat. He knows Jamaica inside out.'

'He can't earn that good a living as a guide,' sniffed Sophie.

'You saw the car.'

'The Lexus?'

'Yes.'

'It's his?' Sophie looked sceptical.

'Yes. He didn't want to be dependent on anyone else for work. So when his compensation money came through, he sank a load of it in the car.'

'It's funny,' said Ella. 'He's obviously been through the emotional mill, but you wouldn't think so to look at him. There's something incredibly – *serene* about him.'

'The spirit of Jah shines out of his eyes. He's a Rastafarian, after all.'

'Pity about the dreadlocks. But, yes,' Sophie conceded, 'he does have lovely eyes. Kind of soulful.'

'I'd have soulful eyes too if I lived in the most laid-back marijuana-producing country in the world.' Eva took a tube of suncream out of her bag and shimmied out of her trousers and T-shirt. Underneath she wore a plain black bikini. 'Be a doll and do my back, Ella, will you?'

'Sure.' The actress was still in pretty good nick for a woman her age, thought Ella, as she drizzled cream down her spine.

Sophie was sending them sideways looks. 'Have you managed to get in a workout since you've been here, Eva?' she asked.

Eva looked blank. 'A workout? You mean a gym kind of workout?'

'Mm-hm.'

'Good God, no. That's my idea of hell.'

'How do you manage to stay in shape, then?'

'Lots of rampant sex, of course, darling. Do you want me to do you, Ella?'

'Please.'

Eva took the tube from her, and started on Ella's back. 'What's the tattoo?' she asked. Ella had had a bar of music tattooed onto her shoulder blade in her first year in college, and had regretted it ever since.

'It's – um – the first bar of Beethoven's Seventh,' she said. 'The slow movement.'

'One of my favourite pieces.' Eva slapped the last of the cream onto Ella's back. 'D'you need some, Sophie?'

'No thanks. I plastered myself with factor 30 before I left the villa.'

Eva lay back on the jetty and looked up at the sky. There was a vapour trail wisping across it. 'Hell. I wish I could stay here for ever, and not have to take that flight back to real life tonight,' she said.

'What's real life got in store for you?' asked Ella.

'A film première, unfortunately.'

'Oh? Which one?' asked Sophie.

Ella kicked off her espadrilles and sat down on the edge of the jetty, eating the banana Eva had given her and kicking up little spatters of water with her toes. What did real life have in store for *her* when it was time to re-enter? Nothing as exciting as a film première, that was for sure. But at least she'd be off the Nesbit & Noonan reception desk. Beside her, Sophie prattled on in film talk, which was punctuated by the occasional 'mm' or half-hearted 'really' from Eva. It was getting hotter. Gradually a drowsy silence descended.

'*Mesdames.*' Ella blinked and looked up. Raphael was standing on the path that led from the jetty to the hotel. His back was to the sun, giving his dreadlocks the appearance of a burnished nimbus. 'I have arranged for beer to be brought to you on the beach in around one hour.' Angel Raphael.

'*Beer?*' said Sophie, as if she'd never heard of the stuff. 'Haven't you any white wine? I'd really prefer a chilled Chablis.'

'Oh come on, Sophie,' said Eva. 'This isn't a chilled-Chablis-on-the-beach kind of place. Let's go for the Red Stripe option.'

'Oh, OK,' said Sophie, a touch ungraciously. 'When in Rome and all that jazz rules, I suppose.' She looked around her. 'Whereabouts on the island is Errol Flynn's mansion, by the way?' she asked.

'That's Errol Flynn's house,' said Raphael, nodding his head at the timberbuilt hotel. 'You gonna eat there later.'

'Sorry?' said Sophie. 'Did you say *that* was Errol Flynn's *mansion*?'

'Sure. One of them. That man owned a lot of property on Jamaica.'

'Ee-*yoo*,' said Sophie contemptuously. 'Call that a mansion? You'd think he might have built something a bit more luxurious than *that* kip.'

Raphael just smiled at her. Then he turned his attention to Eva. 'OK. I tell you the best way.' He pointed to a track that led along the tree-dense coast. 'You go there. That path takes you right round the island.'

'Aren't you coming?' Ella remembered what she'd been told about white women on their own being vulnerable.

He looked at her with toasted almond eyes. 'You safe here, Ella. Ain't no-one on this island I don't know. And you are the first visitors here today. You

189

will be taken good care of. There will be someone waiting on the beach for you with beer and coconuts.'

'But *you're* our guide!' protested Sophie.

'Lady. I have a friend here who works in the hotel. I ain't seen him for a long time. I will stay here, talk with my friend, then I will bring you back to the resort when you are ready.'

'It's cool,' said Eva, in response to Sophie's mutinous look. 'Raphael and I talked about this earlier. We're perfectly safe, and there's no point in him wasting his time trailing round the island after us if he's got something better to do.'

'It's a small island,' said Raphael. 'You gonna end up on a beach on the west side, near here. Or maybe you want to go to nudist beach?'

'Good God, no,' said Eva, pulling on her trousers. 'Are you out of your mind – at my age? I'm not into strutting my stark naked saggy stuff in front of a load of nubile young things.'

Raphael looked her up and down and laughed. 'You look in pretty good shape to me, Eva,' he said.

'Thank you, darling.' Eva gave him her wickedest smile and slung her beach bag over her shoulder. 'We'll see you back here later. You'll join us for something to eat?'

'Sure.'

Sophie was still looking doubtful. 'I'm still not convinced we'll be all right on our own,' she said.

'Trust me,' said Raphael. And then he turned and strolled back into the hotel.

Ella shucked into her shorts and Sophie swathed herself in Jemima Khan, and they set off up the path Raphael had indicated, with Sophie bringing up the rear. She looked like something from a fashion shoot in her flowing white garb, which kept getting caught on foliage, and she was soon 'tching' noisily. 'Have you noticed,' she said, 'that this path is getting muckier and muckier? The hem of my garment is bogging with mud, and my Jimmy Choos are going to be ruined.'

'Jimmy Choos? I told you to wear sensible shoes,' Eva reminded her.

'These *are* sensible. They're the only ones I have that don't have heels.'

'Take 'em off,' suggested Ella.

'And have this swamp oozing between my toes? No thanks,' said Sophie.

'Actually, that sounds good,' said Eva. 'I love the idea of mud oozing between my toes.' She kicked off her flip-flops and hooked her finger through the straps. 'Ooh – *wow!*' she said. 'It's heavenly.'

Ella took off her espadrilles and wriggled her toes. 'Hey! So it is! Oh – go on, Sophie – have a go.'

'Are you out of your mind?' said Sophie. 'That mud is probably crawling with poisonous insects.'

The path got narrower and narrower the higher they went – and Sophie had been right about one thing. It was getting muckier, too. They were ankle deep now, and at times it was like negotiating a swamp. Ella and Eva had to keep waiting for Sophie to pick her way round on any dry bits she could find, which were becoming increasingly scarce. At one stage Eva fell on her arse. Ella went to help her up, and felt a flash of panic when the actress bent double, but a peal of laughter reassured her that Eva was doubled up with laughter, not agony.

'Oh, God, look at my bum!'

'Oh – Eva, that's awful,' said Sophie. 'What label are your trousers?'

'I dunno. I think I got them in Hennes,' said Eva indifferently.

They'd reached the top of a hill, and rhythmic seashore sounds drifted up to them. It was a steep descent all the way from now on.

'Oops,' said Eva. 'It's going to be tough doing this without suffering another pratfall.'

They inched their way down the slope, Sophie making occasional whimpering noises that featured the words 'Jimmy Choo' quite a lot. Suddenly she slipped backwards. Immediately she lunged forward to compensate, and without any warning whatsoever the lunge suddenly turned into a run, and Sophie was off, like an albino bat out of hell. Away she sped down the hill at full pelt, sending showers of mud spattering all over her white robe, obviously unable to stop or slow down. Ella and Eva stood and looked on in open-mouthed astonishment as Sophie hurtled downwards, her feet running away with her so fast that they became a blur of movement. Her arms were flailing, and her dress billowed out behind her like a parachute.

'The flight of the snowy egret,' remarked Ella,

and all at once the two women were laughing, clutching each other for balance. They couldn't prevent a loud hoot escaping when Sophie finally slipped and tobogganed onto the clearing below flat on her rear end. Gradually her trajectory slowed to a halt.

Ella and Eva sobered suddenly. Sophie's descent had been punctuated with 'oh-oh-ohs' of alarm, but nothing prepared them for the scream of terror that came reverberating back up the hill.

The pair descended rapidly, squelching as they went. When they emerged from the forest they found her sitting on the ground, frozen in an attitude of abject terror. 'What is it, Sophie?' asked Eva.

Sophie raised a trembling hand and pointed to something behind them. Ella turned to see a tall Rasta standing there. He had a machete in one hand and a stout stick in the other. 'Oh my God!' said Sophie in a croaky voice, clutching her throat. 'Oh my God!'

The Rasta looked perplexed. 'Everyt'ing irie?' he said, mildly. Then he grinned and indicated his machete. 'Hey! You ladies want coconut? I ready for you thirsty white ladies with coconuts.' He rattled the stick among the high branches of a nearby palm tree and a shower of coconuts descended. Then he slashed one open with the machete and handed it to Eva.

'Cool! Thanks!' said Eva, lifting the coconut to her lips and drinking long and thirstily.

'Good for drinking after long walk.' The Rasta

repeated the process for Ella and Sophie.

'No, thank you,' said Sophie, looking as if she'd just been offered a poisoned chalice. Her eyes wandered warily to the machete in his hand.

'Hey, lady! You no trust me?' said the Rasta. He laughed. 'Why you white lady not trust we Rastafarians? We gotta trust in one another, man. Trust and respect, they go hand in hand.'

He turned to Ella and proffered a high-five, which she automatically found herself returning. It was the first time she'd ever performed a high-five without feeling utterly ridiculous. How amazing, she thought as he went through the ritual with Eva, to land on a verdant island and be offered coconut milk to drink!

'How much?' asked Eva.

'Two hundred Jamaican dollar.'

'OK,' said Eva, dipping into her bag.

The Rasta looked shocked. 'Hey, lady – you don' wan higgle wit me?'

'Higgle, hell,' said Eva. 'I am a rich woman. If I get an opportunity to spread some of my money around, I'm glad to do it.'

The Rasta shook his head and laughed. 'You some lady,' he said. 'You damn bad higgler. But you damn pretty.' He took Eva's hand and shook it. 'Respect,' he added, as she handed over a wad of dollars. Then he gave her one last appreciative grin and loped off down the path.

'Ow!' Ella and Eva turned back to Sophie, who was now looking like a bedraggled snowy egret that

194

had been swept off course. 'What is it? Quickly, someone. On the back of my neck! Quick! Get it off! Get it *off*!'

Ella plucked a leaf away from where it had got caught in the hair on the nape of Sophie's neck. 'It's OK, Sophie,' she said. 'It's only a leaf.'

'You should have seen the look on your face when you spotted our friend, Sophie,' said Eva, draining her coconut. 'It was priceless. I should have taken a picture.'

'How was I supposed to know he was only felling coconuts?' replied Sophie indignantly. 'He looked like he'd just walked out of *The Blair* bloody *Witch Project* standing there with his machete and his cudgel. Oh *shit*!' This was said with great feeling.

'What's wrong now?'

'I broke a fingernail trying to grab onto passing branches.'

'Well, thank God there's a beauty parlour in the resort!'

'Too right,' agreed Sophie earnestly. Hell's bells! This woman had the worst case of irony deficiency Ella had ever encountered.

*   *   *

It would have been a perfect day, if it hadn't been for Sophie. She turned her nose up at the beer that was waiting for them when they hit the beach, she refused to swim, and she also refused to talk with the Rastas who were hanging there, convinced that their friendliness concealed sinister ulterior motives. Instead she plugged herself into Andrew Lloyd Webber on her CD player.

Some hours later, as they sat waiting for Raphael to join them in the restaurant of the waterfront hotel, Sophie announced that that was the last time she intended leaving the luxurious confines of Salamander Cove. 'I'm sorry,' she said. 'I just don't enjoy wading through swamps and being attacked by sandflies and mosquitoes. I came on holiday to enjoy being pampered a little, and that's the way it's going to be from now on.'

'What'll I do?' said Ella morosely, when Sophie was in the loo. 'I've no-one to explore Jamaica with. Although, come to think of it, Sophie's so completely uptight she's actually *worse* than no-one.'

'Mm. That coconut-felling Rasta was dead right, you know. There's not enough trust in the world. If Sophie trusted people more she might learn to relax a bit.' Eva stretched. 'Ow. I'm going to have very stiff muscles after that hike.'

'Maybe it wasn't such a good idea: going for a trek through a rain forest on the same day as you're flying.'

'What do you mean?'

'Well – trying to get comfortable in those sardine-can seats isn't going to be easy.'

'Oh – I'll sleep like a log, darling. That's the best thing about being able to afford first-class travel.'

Ella laughed. 'Of course you're going first class!

'How daft of me even to imagine you in economy! Oh, Eva – I will miss you, you know. It's been fun today. I wish I'd run into you earlier in the holiday. We could have gone on loads of jaunts.'

'What about your grandmother? Couldn't you get her to go places with you? She sounds like a pretty laid-back individual.'

'Since she discovered Dieter and his villa, she's not too keen on leaving the resort either. I can't say I blame her. They're so into each other that I'm starting to feel like a total gooseberry.'

The waiter arrived with their beers, and they moved to a table on the balcony overlooking the jetty. 'Oh, look,' said Eva. 'There's Raphael.'

She pointed to where Raphael was sitting on the small jetty that protruded into the bay. He sat cross-legged, very straight and very still, gazing out to sea.

'How beautiful he is, and how utterly serene,' remarked Eva in an admiring voice. 'I must get a photograph.' She rummaged in her bag, then upended it. A lot of junk spewed out, including a dog-eared *Rough Guide to Jamaica*, but no camera materialized. 'Shit,' said Eva. 'I must have left it on the beach. Lend me yours, Ella, will you? And be sure to send me a copy.'

As Eva snapped happily away, Sophie returned from the loo. 'Why's Eva using your camera?" she asked.

'She left hers on the beach,' said Ella. 'We'll have to go back for it.'

Sophie gave her an incredulous look. 'There's no point in doing *that*, Ella. One of those Rastas will have claimed it by now.'

On the jetty, Raphael had been joined by one of the youths from the beach. They exchanged a few words, and then Raphael turned and looked up at the hotel, shading his eyes against the sun. He located Eva on the balcony, and pointed at her. The two men high-fived each other, and then the newcomer turned and headed in the direction of the hotel. Eva's camera case was hanging from his shoulder.

'Hey! Thanks!' Eva leaned over the balcony and shouted down at him. 'You've saved me a journey back to the beach!'

'No problem!' returned the youth.

Sophie sat down stiffly and picked up a menu.

'What's everyone having?' asked Eva, doing the same.

'Oh, God,' said Sophie. 'More jerk food. My heart sinks every time I walk into the restaurant in the resort and look at the specials advertised on the blackboard. Jerk pork, jerk chicken, jerk beef. I can't wait to get home to some decent fresh fish.'

'Don't worry, Sophie,' said Ella in a jokey voice. 'Maybe we'll walk into the restaurant tonight to find the words Jerk Off on the blackboard.'

'Very funny, Ella,' said Sophie, shooting an unamused look at Eva, who had burst into paroxysms of laughter.

On the jetty below, Raphael had finished his

contemplation of the sea, and was strolling towards the hotel. He raised a hand at them in salute. There was something beneficent about the gesture.

'Hey, Ella!' exclaimed Eva. 'I know who you can explore Jamaica with! How stupid of me not to have thought of it earlier!'

'Who?' asked Ella.

'Hire Raphael, of course.'

* * *

And that's exactly what she did. For the rest of the holiday she alternated between one day exploring with Raphael, and the next diving with Desirée. By the end of the holiday she wasn't sure which of the two terrains she preferred – the world under the waves, or the world above. But she *was* sure about one thing. She had fallen head over heels in love with the island.

Chapter Eight

Every single time Raphael took her out, she had a blast. They did all the things she'd hoped to do, and more. He took her to a reggae bar, he took her body surfing on Long Beach, and he even took her to his cousin's birthday party. His aunt and uncle lived in a shantytown shack on a dirt road beyond the ghettos of Port Antonio, and although Raphael's cousin was only ten, it had been one of the most kicking parties she'd ever been to. She'd spent the whole night dancing to pounding reggae. She'd danced with children and with women and with old men who moved like demons. She'd been plied with birthday cake and sweets and ganja, and had flirted bigtime with the birthday girl's teenage brother. Hers had been the only white face there.

On the second-last day of her holiday, Raphael came to pick her up as usual.

'Where are we going today?' she asked, climbing into the front seat beside him.

'Reach Falls,' he said, sliding a cassette into the player. Mellow Marley thrummed out. 'And then I will take you to a beach that no tourist knows about. There is a good reef there.' He put the car into gear, raised a hand in farewell to the doorman, and they took off down the drive, scattering peacocks as they went.

Ella checked her bag. 'Shit. I left my snorkel in the villa,' she said. 'D'you mind going back for it?'

'Have you your mask?'

'Yes.'

'Then it's cool. You can borrow my snorkel. I seldom use it.'

Oh God. Ella remembered what Eva had told her about Raphael contracting the bends. She wondered if it even prevented him from snorkelling.

'I can dive without a snorkel,' he said. 'I got gills.'

Eva laughed. 'What?'

'I can hold my breath a long, long time.'

'Like how long?' asked Ella.

'Like three, four minutes.'

She opened her eyes very wide. 'Wow. You *do* have gills,' she remarked.

'I used to do a lot of free-diving. Still do, sometimes.'

'Free-dive? What's that?'

'Diving without scuba.'

It was the first time he had ever referred to his career as a diver. 'You must miss it tremendously, Raphael, do you?'

He turned his golden eyes on her. 'I have learned to accept what I must accept. When you have a gift you are grateful and full of praise. Jah gave me my gift. Jah gave me my gills. But Jah has the right to take away that gift also. I will not question that right.'

They were passing through one of the more run-down townships now. Advertisements for Craven A cigarettes and Guinness, Red Stripe beer and over-proof rum were plastered on shop fronts with names so uncool they were cool. DR MUFFY'S NATURAL VITAMINS AND HERBS, SHAGGY'S PLACE, KOOL KAT KORNER and SIR PLUGGY'S JERK SHOP. WELCOME TO KATHY'S LITTLE BAR AND GROCERY, she read outside a shack that was festooned with bunches of exotic fruits. A woman wearing a pink taffeta dress straight out of the fifties and clutching a matching purse was waiting by a bus stop with two equally prinked little girls. They were obviously on their way to somewhere special. The woman stood tall and erect, and gazed at Ella with solemn eyes in a proud face as she glided by in the passenger seat of the Lexus, feeling shameful and inadequate. These people existed at subsistence level, struggling to put food on their tables. Raphael, with his business, was one of the luckier ones. But even in the face of crippling poverty these people managed to behave with more dignity than almost any other race on earth.

They swept past a timber church painted in blue and white, and crowned with a red corrugated iron roof. 'The Grace and Truth Temple,' she read out loud. 'Your churches have such beautiful names, Raphael! My local church is called St Sepulchre. No wonder I'm a heathen.'

'Grace and truth. That's what it's all about, man. Grace and truth. Peace. Unity. And love.' She realized he was looking at her again. *One love*, she heard, as a new Marley track slid over the speakers. 'One love,' he echoed. 'Do you know what that means, Ella?'

She smiled and gave a little shrug. 'One love? I suppose it means true love, doesn't it?'

'It can mean that, yeah. But for Jamaicans it also means "Unity". When we part with someone, that is what we tell them. One love.'

* * *

The graffiti in the dingy café at Reach Falls read 'Peace, Love, Unity – Strengthens'.

Ella was the only white person there. She hadn't felt self-conscious about this at Raphael's cousin's party, but now she did – especially when she stripped down to her bikini. Jamaican women hanging out on the rocks by the waterfall eyed her with suspicion, while the men's eyes were full of carnality they didn't bother to conceal. As she passed a group of geezers swigging Red Stripe, she heard a chorus of muttered patois. Raphael said something in patois back. His was the kind of tone you don't mess with, and the geezers shuffled a bit, and looked at her more furtively.

'I take you upriver,' said Raphael, obviously sensing her discomfort. 'There will be fewer people up there.' He took her backpack from her and they set off, away from the curious eyes that regarded her without friendliness and made her seethe with discomfort.

They made their way past the rushing waterfall that cascaded down over the rocks like a dense bridal veil, and waded upriver for about half a mile in crystal-clear water that was only ankle deep in some places, and deep enough for swimming in others. In those places where the water ran deep, Raphael carried her backpack on his head, in the way she'd observed Jamaicans walking on the roads carry bundles. There was no-one else around, and Ella started to feel more relaxed. It was utterly silent, apart from the gurgling of water and the occasional burst of unfamiliar birdsong from some exotic species of bird. The forest on either side was full of fauna and exotic flora, like something out of a Rousseau painting. There were fabulous insects, and dragonflies and beetles, and shrubs that were so thick with yellow butterflies they looked as if they were covered in fluttering blossoms. She was wandering through a terrestrial Paradise. But after twenty or more minutes of perfect tranquillity, Ella gradually became aware of men's voices drifting upstream. Soon she spotted three shapes in her peripheral vision. They were distinctly masculine shapes, and they were moving purposefully towards them.

With a flash of fear she realized that they were the men who'd muttered and laughed about her earlier. As they gained on her and Raphael, Ella started to feel very panicky indeed. If these men were after what she suspected they were after, one bloke on his own wasn't going to stop them. She could tell that Raphael was aware of the maleficent vibe, because as soon as the men got too close for comfort, he stopped.

'Go on upriver,' he instructed Ella. 'I gonna talk to these boys. These boys are makin' you nervous, Ella, and if you are feelin' nervous then I am not doin' my job right. You go up to the first deep pool you find, and you have a little swim around. Relax. I will follow you up when I done finish dealin' with these facety boys.'

'Are you sure?' asked Ella uncertainly. She knew the fear on her face was graphic.

'Trust me,' said Raphael. 'I will teach these boys respect.'

Ella turned and continued on shaky legs, trying to resist the temptation to look back. She stumbled occasionally on the pink and gold rocks that were strewn over the river-bed, and at one point found herself wading through a chest-deep fissure where the current ran so strong it was almost impossible to negotiate, but eventually she reached a calm green pool.

Now she allowed herself to look back. Raphael was standing thigh deep in the river. The men he was talking to were all bare-chested, and the water hit them around their midriffs. As Ella watched, one of them moved towards the bank. He turned in her direction and then he pulled his penis out of his swimming trunks and proceeded to urinate into the water, watching her as he did so. She turned away immediately. When she looked back again, very covertly, two of the men were heading off back down the river, and Raphael and the most powerful-looking of the three were exchanging an unsmiling high-five. Then the burly individual turned and followed his cronies back the way they'd come.

Silhouetted against the sparkling water Raphael watched them go, one hand on his hip. She remembered how he'd reminded her of a gunslinger the first time she'd met him. Now his stance had even more of an insouciant arrogance about it. Gunslinger, warrior prince, guardian angel – he was all of these. Finally he turned and made his way up to where Ella was floating in the pellucid water. He stood looking down at her, and she found it difficult to read the expression on his face because his back was to the sun. 'You OK?' he asked.

'Yeah.' She pushed her wet hair back from her face. 'What did you say to them that made them back off?'

'I made them see sweet reason, Ella. Those boys are wolves, but I know how to talk to wolves. I understand their language. How-ev-er,' he drawled the word, extending it into a kind of growl: 'maybe it is a good time to get out of here. I know a short cut that will take us back up to the road. Come with me. I am going to take you to the prettiest beach you ever saw.' He held out his hand and pulled her, dripping, from the water.

*   *   *

On their drive to the beach, they passed the same woman still waiting at the bus stop, still standing tall in her Sunday best. Ella wanted to weep for her, and Raphael told her not to.

'What good are your tears to her?'

She was about to suggest that she could offer money instead, but some wise instinct advised her against it. That would be possibly the ultimate sign of disrespect – the ultimate slur on her dignity: to be offered money she hadn't earned.

It wasn't a long drive. Ella sat up front with Raphael and helped him smoke a spliff. By the time they reached the beach she had a totally blissed-out smile on her face. There was no-one else there. This beach belonged exclusively to them, and it was Bounty Bar perfect. She and Raphael gazed out over talcum powder sand towards the sea. Golden, golden sand, thought Ella. Blue, blue sea. She remembered the blue-sky blue-sea picture in the holiday brochure she'd looked at all those weeks ago, and how she'd fantasized about being in that picture. The reality was even more fantastic.

The water was inviting them in with seductive whispery splashes.

'Let's swim,' said Raphael.

Ella took her last deep drag of pungent smoke, opened the door and floated out of the car. Quite suddenly they were chest deep in water that shimmered in dinky little wavelets to where it met the baby blue blanket of the sky. She had no idea how they'd got there.

'Are you some kind of a pooka?' she asked, laughing.

'A pooka? What do you mean by pooka?'

'A pooka's a kind of Irish genie. It wouldn't surprise me if you *were* one. This place is magic.'

They swam out about thirty metres until they reached the shallow reef. Then Raphael took Ella's hand and they dived. She could not believe how shockingly pale her hand was in his. The tan she had acquired since arriving in Jamaica seemed to have been washed away. She felt like a phantom, feather light and whiter than white. He turned to her underwater and gave her his blissful smile, and she smiled back, incredulity written all over her face.

His claim to have gills wasn't an arrogant one. Ella would let go of his hand any time she needed to surface for air, but he remained underwater for what seemed to her to be an eternity. Occasionally he would disappear from sight, and then she would look down and see him patrolling the reef like some sleek aquatic beast, or she'd look up and see him swimming above her, hands casually clasped together like a guardian angel at prayer, dreadlocks haloed round his head. At one point he took up an anemone from the seabed and split it. Myriad jewel-like fish came to feed on the flesh, and Ella clapped her hands and smiled too broadly. She found herself at the surface again, spitting water out of her snorkel.

Raphael surfaced beside her. 'Time to go,' he said, and the switch behind her smile clicked off. 'It gets dark fast, remember?'

Reluctantly she swam back to shore. She didn't want to go. This was the second-last evening of her holiday!

'Why so sad, Ella?' asked Raphael, when they hit the beach.

'I'm dreading going back.'

'You don't want to leave our country?'

'No. I don't. It's just so beautiful.'

'Yeah, man. That is what all the visitors say. Most of them say that they will return some day, and some of them do. A Dutch girl has come to live on the beach where I live. She is the only white person living there, but she has the soul of a Rastafarian. She gave up a good livelihood in Holland to come and live with us.'

'Where do you live, Raphael?'

'Me and Desirée's got a house on Hummingbird Beach, just round the headland from Salamander Cove.'

'On the Blue Lagoon side?'

He laughed. 'What! You think we live in one of those white palaces? On the other side, Ella. On the Rasta side.'

In the car, Bob Marley accompanied them all the way back to the resort. Raphael pulled up under the *porte-cochère* and killed the engine.

'Where you want to go tomorrow, Ella?' he said. 'Or you gonna dive tomorrow?'

'I can't leave the resort again, Raphael,' said Ella, feeling gutted. 'Dieter – my grandmother's friend – is going back to Germany tomorrow. I can't abandon her.' What had started as a mild flirtation between the two sexagenarians had developed into something a lot more meaningful, and Ella suspected that Leonie was going to be feeling very bereft on the last day of her holiday.

She rooted in her bag for the money she owed Raphael, and in return he handed her a slender spliff. 'Keep it for later,' he said. 'When you are looking at the moon on the bay. That's what I do most nights. I sit on the headland down from my house. Smoke a spliff and watch the moon.'

'Thanks,' she said, pocketing it.

When she looked back at him he was watching her with an infinitely wise expression in his slanting, golden eyes. 'Remember, Ella, what I told you earlier. Be grateful for what you have. Be grateful, and full of praise.'

For some reason the words made the hair rise on the back of her neck. 'I will,' she whispered. Then, impulsively, she leaned forward and kissed his cheek. 'I won't see you again, Raphael. It's a really horrible thought. You and Desirée made this holiday incredibly special for me. Thank you, both. For everything.'

'Why you say you won't see me again? Maybe you come back one day, like my Dutch friend.'

'Maybe.' She tried a smile, but couldn't manage

it. Feeling really choked now, she slid out of the car and turned to wave at him.

Raphael sent her his blissful, blissed-out smile, and saluted her with a relaxed hand. 'One love,' he said. And then he was gone.

Chapter Nine

The following morning they saw Dieter and his family off on the coach that was to take them to Kingston airport. Dieter was the last passenger to board.

Leonie stapled a brave smile onto her face. 'Goodbye, my darling Dieter,' she said. 'It's so amazing that we found each other!'

'Don't say goodbye, Leonie,' said Dieter, looking down at her with tender eyes. 'Say *Auf Wiedersehen.* Till we meet again.'

Ella had never felt more like a gooseberry in her life. She stood slightly to one side of the star-crossed lovers, pretending to be fascinated by a buzzard that was circling overhead. On the coach, Dieter's family were obviously feeling equally embarrassed. They too were studiously ignoring their father, while the rest of the passengers were gawping shamelessly. The love story between the two sixty-somethings had engendered a lot of interest among the guests in Salamander Cove, to the extent that it had become a kind of running soap opera, and now everyone was anxious to see how it was going to end. Ella snuck a surreptitious glance at the pair.

Yikes! Now they were kissing! Oh God – it really was too much. Her uncle had been right – she should never have asked Leonie to come on holiday with her. She was a complete liability.

Eventually the coach driver pumped his horn, and Dieter freed Leonie from his embrace and boarded, lobbing endearments over his shoulder as he went. 'Auf Wiedersehen, mein Schatz, mein schöner Liebling, mein Herz, meine—' Thankfully, the doors cut him off before he could come out with any more.

Ella and Leonie stood and waved as the coach sailed down the driveway, and then Ella turned to her grandmother. 'Honestly, Leonie,' she began, 'don't you think it's a bit—' And then she shut her mouth like a trap. Leonie was crying.

*   *   *

'There, there, Leonie.' Ella handed her another wad of tissues. They were sitting side by side on the couch in their villa. 'Blow your nose and have another swig of champagne. That'll do you more good than anything.'

'Oh, Ella – I'm sorry.' Her grandmother's tears had dried up but she was still a bit sniffly. 'It's just *awful*. If I'd known I was going to fall in love I would never have come on this holiday.'

'Don't say that, Leonie! I think it's brilliant that you had a holiday romance.'

'But at my age! It's too absurd for words!'

213

'No, it's not. I'm madly jealous, you know.'

'Oh, darling – it's not fair! You're young and gorgeous. You should be the one being wined and dined and having glorious sex.'

Ella's jaw dropped. 'Glorious *sex*?'

'Yes.' Leonie gave her a look of mild reproach. 'Just because I'm fifty-nine doesn't mean I can't still enjoy it, Ella.'

Leonie had shaved a few more years off her age, but it wasn't that that surprised Ella. She'd just never thought of her grandmother as being sexually active.

'Was it *really* glorious?' she ventured cautiously.

'Yes. I'm not sure whether the fact that I haven't indulged for a while made it glorious, or whether it was all down to Dieter. He was terribly special.' Leonie looked as if she was about to burst into tears again, and then she took a deep breath, blew her nose and shook her head, as if to shake off the glooms that were threatening to overcome her. 'Now,' she said with decision, chucking the damp wodge of tissue into the wastepaper basket. 'I must shut up crowing on about how splendid my sex life is, and concentrate on yours instead. How come you didn't fancy anyone in the resort, Ella? You could have lifted a little finger and any number of men would have come running. I've seen the way they look at you.'

'There was only one man I found attractive, Leonie. And he wasn't available.'

'Let me guess. That Rasta you told me about?'

214

'Right first time.'

'Was he a dish?'

'You don't really call good-looking men dishes any more, Leonie.'

'Oh? What do you call them? I'd hate to think I was too terminally unhip.'

'Well, you call them "babe". Or "dude".'

'I prefer "dude". Dieter's a dude, isn't he?'

Ella smiled at her. 'Absolutely.'

'So this Rasta was also a dude?'

'Yeah. But it wasn't just that. We had a great rapport. And he had the most trustworthy eyes of any man I've ever met.'

'I imagine the ganja helped.'

Ella shot her grandmother a look. '*Leonie*! What makes you think I smoked ganja?'

'Don't look so injured, Ella. It doesn't suit you to protest too much. Of course you smoked ganja. *My* generation invented sex, drugs and rock 'n' roll, remember? And no self-respecting granddaughter of mine would come all the way to Jamaica and not get potted.'

Ella laughed. 'Oh, all right then. Yes. We indulged.'

'Good weed?' asked Leonie, with a kind of knowledgeable insouciance.

'Yes. Excellent. Hey!' She remembered Raphael's present to her. 'I have a reefer he gave me. We might smoke it later?'

'You keep it all to yourself, darling. It's so long since I had a blast that I'd get completely out of it

215

and wind up embarrassing you bigtime. I'll stick to champagne.' She swigged back the rest of the champagne in her glass and looked at her watch. 'Holy shomoly! Is that the time? I can't believe that I wasted so much of my last day in Paradise boo-hooing. And you have a dive booked, Ella, haven't you? You'd better hurry if you're not going to miss it.'

'Oh – I'd written that off. I'm not going swanning off around coral reefs when you're so miserable. I'm going to stay here and feed you champagne until your broken heart has mended a bit.'

'Don't be daft, darling. Go and enjoy the last day of your holiday.'

'But what will you do?'

'Read.' Leonie reached for a magazine on the coffee table and started to leaf through it. 'There's a competition in here for a holiday in Thailand, and it's a cinch. "Answer the following questions. What colour is your hair?"'

'What?' said Ella.

'I'm kidding. But it's nearly as facile. "How many years are in a millennium? How many nights did Scheherazade regale the Sultan with stories? A regular Hollywood beanfeast is the Night of the – how many – Stars?"'

'What's the tie-breaker?'

'"I use Matt Miller's Thousand Island Dressing because – dot dot dot".'

'How many words?'

'A thousand. Only joking, darling. Hah! I crack

216

myself up. Twelve, actually. Now. Run along and do your dive.'

'Are you sure you'll be all right, Leonie?'

'Absolutely.' Leonie looked at her with eyes in which only a trace of misery remained. 'And doing this asinine competition will take my mind off Dieter.'

*　　*　　*

After her dive, as Ella stripped off her exposure suit and rinsed down her gear she realized that this was the last time she'd dive for the foreseeable future – unless she won the lottery, or Leonie won her Thailand competition. She said as much to Desirée.

'No chance, sweetheart,' said the dive mistress. 'You are hooked now. Ain't nothing going to stop you diving again. I know people like you who work their asses off all year just so's they can get the money together to come back here and dive for two weeks. Anyhow, you can always carry on diving in Ireland.'

Ella's mind went back to Sheep's Head Bay, and she shuddered.

Desirée registered the grimace. 'Come on, Jacqueline Cousteau! Where's your fighting spirit? That Ferdia – he told me that your country has some incredible diving. I always did threaten that I would come visit him there, just to check it out. Sloosh out your BCD now, sweetheart,' she said, handing Ella the hose before disappearing back into the dive shop. 'And don't forget I promised you that drink.'

'It's me who should be buying *you* a drink, Desirée, after all you've done for me.'

'No, no, Ella. The cocktail is on the house. I've even thought up the perfect name for it.'

'Oh? What?'

'You'll find out later. But I'll give you a clue. All those special cocktails are named after fish.'

'Oh? Just don't call me a wrasse, OK?'

Desirée laughed. 'You got a sweet rass, honey! Will I see you in the bar on the beach later? How does nine o'clock sound?'

'I'll be there,' said Ella.

* * *

Later that evening she and Leonie were sitting together on the veranda, sharing a final celebratory bottle of champagne. They were showered and scented, and dressed for dinner in the kind of casual-formal clothes required for dining in the Pagoda restaurant. Leonie was wearing something long and fluid in silk, and Ella had on one of her mother's cast-offs – a loose white dress by Ghost. Tree frogs were serenading them, a blue dusk was descending, and the gentle rhythm of mento was drifting up from the beach, where the resident band was playing. It had rained earlier, and the earthy smell of wet grass mingled with the scent of expensive cigar smoke from the villa next door. The

218

mood was bitter-sweet; redolent of nostalgia and a kind of regret.

'Well,' sighed Leonie, raising her glass. 'Here's to the last evening of our dream holiday.'

'Here's to our next one,' said Ella. 'In Thailand. Did you come up with any ideas for that Thousand Island Dressing competition?'

'Nothing madly inspired, I'm afraid,' said Leonie. 'I was torn between "I use Matt Miller's Thousand Island Dressing because *it's so much classier to dress up than dress down*," or the rather more pragmatic "I use Matt Miller's Thousand Island Dressing because *it's cheaper than Paul Newman's.*"'

'Mm.' Ella considered. 'In this case I don't think honesty's the best policy. Not if we want to win that holiday.'

'How about this?' A man's voice came from the adjoining veranda. A rich, velvety, German-accented voice. 'I *don't* use Matt Miller's Thousand Island Dressing because it is cheap and nasty, and if I accept my wealthy consort's proposal of marriage I can go to Thailand any time I damn well please.'

'Dieter!' Leonie had gone very white, and her hands had flown to her face. 'Dieter!' she exclaimed again, jumping to her feet and parting the branches of the hibiscus bush that separated the two verandas.

There he was, lounging back on a cane chair with a cigar between his fingers and with his long legs elegantly crossed. 'Do you ladies mind if I join you?' he enquired politely, getting to his feet in a leisurely fashion, and setting the cigar down in an ashtray.

'Dieter!' said Leonie again.

'The very same.' His tone was urbane as he stepped off his veranda and on to theirs.

'Dieter!' It was Ella's turn to address him. 'What on earth are you doing here?'

'I'm here to ask for your grandmother's hand in marriage, *Fräulein*. Do you think she'll have me?'

There was a beat of shocked silence. Ella looked from Dieter to her grandmother, and then back again. Dieter's face was smiling and handsome, Leonie's was ghost-white. She had sunk back down on her chair, and was gazing at Dieter with an expression of such profound shock that Ella felt a sudden rush of concern for her. 'Leonie!' she exclaimed, dropping to her knees and taking her grandmother's hand in hers. 'Are you all right?'

Leonie nodded, mutely. A tear rolled down her cheek. Dieter got down on one knee on the other side of the cane chair, and gently wiped away the tear with his thumb. Then he took a box from his inside jacket pocket and held it out to his *inamorata*. 'Will you marry me, Leonie?' he said.

Leonie nodded again. 'Yes,' she said in a voice so tiny it was barely audible. 'Yes please, Dieter. I would love to marry you.' She leaned forward and kissed him very gently on the lips.

Ella knew she was *de trop*. 'Um,' she said, casting around for an exit line. Then: 'Champagne!' she

220

pronounced in ringing tones. 'Let me fetch you a glass, Dieter.' She escaped inside and loitered there a while to give the lovers a chance to do whatever lovers did in situations like this. Oh God. Patrick was going to *murder* her when she went back to Dublin. He'd told her to keep Leonie under strict surveillance, and now her granny had gone off and got herself proposed to by someone she'd known for only a fortnight!

Dieter was sitting next to Leonie when Ella re-emerged with the champagne flute. Their hands were joined on the table between them, and they were gazing at one another with supremely foolish expressions on their faces. There was an exquisite diamond on Leonie's ring finger.

'Thank you, Ella,' said Dieter, when she set the glass down on the table. He poured, raised his glass, and then said solemnly: 'To true love.'

'To true love,' chorused Leonie and Ella, smiling at each other. Then Leonie added: 'And to the Polly Rogers.'

'The Polly Rogers?' echoed Dieter.

'Yes. That was the name I dreamed up for the Toptree Foods competition. Without them, Dieter, you and I would never have met.'

'What a truly horrible thought,' said Dieter, with an expressive shudder.

'When did you decide to turn round and come back?' asked Leonie.

'At the airport,' he said. 'I realized in a blinding flash that I simply couldn't live without you.'

221

They spent the next ten minutes listening to the tale of his *crise de coeur*. He had spent the journey to Kingston agonizing over how he might get to see Leonie again. At the airport he'd abandoned his astonished family on the tarmac, climbed into a cab, and instructed the driver to take him back to Salamander Cove, stopping off in Kingston to buy the ring and some basic items of clothing. All his luggage was on the plane, heading for Berlin.

'You mad, impetuous fool,' said Leonie, taking his head between her hands and covering his face with kisses. 'I am not worthy of you, you utterly amazing man.'

Oh God. Now her granny was talking Mills-and-Boon-speak. It was obvious that the lovebirds needed some time to themselves. Ella rose to her feet and glanced at her watch. The fingers of her right hand curled around the joint Raphael had given her. She'd transferred it earlier from the pocket of her backpack to the pocket of her dress, anticipating that she might like a little blast on her last evening in the greatest ganja-producing country in the world. 'I think I'll have a stroll before dinner,' she said. 'I'll see you two in the Pagoda in half an hour or so?' The radiant couple smiled at her, and then turned and smiled at each other.

Ella wandered off in the direction of the beach, passing halfway there to light up the spliff. The band was playing that sexy, lazy, rhythmic mento, and people were dancing. She veered to her left, towards the sea wall. Swinging her legs over it, she sat there and looked out to sea, listening to the wavelets match their rhythm to the mento, watching darkness fall.

By the time she'd finished the spliff, the stars above her head were more beautiful than the most beautiful diamond necklace ever sold by Tiffany's, the ambient song of the tree frogs was more melodic than Beethoven's Seventh, and the light breeze on her neck was the most erotic sensation she'd ever experienced. The band on the beach had taken a break, but Ella was still clicking her fingers to the rhythm that had crept into her head and lodged itself there. She made a mental note to herself to buy some mento when she got back to Ireland. Then she chucked the roach into the sea below, and stretched luxuriously before turning round to head in the direction of the restaurant.

Suddenly she remembered something. She looked towards the bulky mass of the headland that was silhouetted against the dark sky to her right, and stood quite motionless, waiting. There! For a split second she saw a tiny dot of red light glowing against the blackness of the rocky outcrop . . . But when she looked harder there was nothing. Her eyes were playing tricks on her. She pressed the cool pads of her fingers against her closed lids momentarily, then opened her eyes and looked again. And then she saw the pinpoint of red light shine again, briefly, and she knew immediately what it was. It was the glowing end of Raphael's ganja spliff.

She remembered the way he had sat cross-legged on the jetty on Navy Island, the time Eva had photographed him, gazing out to sea with serene eyes. Now she pictured him sitting loose-limbed and relaxed on his stone headland, contemplating the Caribbean. Her pooka. Her guardian angel, Raphael. She blew a kiss into the air, hoping that the wind would take it to him, and stood with her eyes closed and the warm breeze lifting her hair, waiting for the kiss to be returned. The breath that grazed her cheek moments later was so palpable that she was surprised when she opened her eyes to find nobody there.

Ella drifted across the grass to the path that led past the Pagoda restaurant with a dreamy smile on her face. Dieter and Leonie were sitting at a table on the long veranda, with a bottle of champagne in a cooler between them. She floated up the steps, and Dieter rose to his feet and pulled out a chair for her. 'What's on the menu tonight, Leonie?' asked Ella, sitting down and sending them both seraphic smiles. She picked up the printed sheet and squinted at it. The words formed themselves into the prettiest hieroglyphics she'd ever seen.

'The jerk prawns are excellent,' said Dieter. 'Here. Have a taste.' He peeled a prawn, stabbed it with his fork and passed it to her.

'Mm. Oh, my God, you're right,' agreed Ella. She thought she'd never tasted anything quite so delicious. 'Definitely prawns for me.'

'And champagne.' Dieter took the proffered flute

from the waiter and filled it. Ella took a sip and sneezed as the fizz went up her nose. The sneeze was so brilliant she laughed. Then she looked round the room with soft-focus eyes, taking in the exotic décor, the elaborate trelliswork of the veranda, the backdrop of midnight blue velvet beyond the open windows, the flowers and candles on each table, the low murmur of the other diners, the ceiling fans swishing currents of air, the rich vibrato of the solo violin that was playing . . .

'Oh!' Ella was overcome with nostalgia. 'My favourite Brahms!'

'Did you know, Dieter,' said Leonie, 'that my granddaughter is an exceptionally talented violinist?'

'No, I did not know that,' said Dieter, turning interested eyes on Ella. 'Did you train?'

'For years,' sighed Ella, turning yearning eyes on the elegant dark woman playing the violin on the other side of the room. 'And years. I adored it. But I couldn't get a job. So I renounced the first true love I ever had.' She gave another great sigh and then turned her attention abruptly back to the table as her prawns were set in front of her. 'God – I'm ravenous,' she said, falling upon her plate.

She was glad that she'd chosen finger food. It meant that she didn't have to worry too much about her manners. When she'd finished her prawns, she dabbled around in the finger bowl and then wiped each digit fastidiously to get rid of any traces of oil. It didn't work. Her fingers actually felt oilier every time she dipped them in the scented water, and the smell of prawns was becoming more and more intense. 'Excuse me, please,' she said, getting up from the table. 'I think I need something a bit more heavy-duty to shift this prawny smell off my fingers.'

In the loo she spent at least five minutes with her hands under the tap. What on earth was the scent of the soap she was using? It had the most glorious perfume she'd ever smelt. Musky. Slightly masculine, with top notes of . . . vanilla. She wanted it as a memento. Every time she smelt it, it would remind her of Jamaica, just like Proust's madeleine reminded him of – whatever it was that it reminded him of. She stuffed a cake of soap in her pocket, dried her hands on a soft-as-swansdown towel, and went back to the table.

The dark violinist was standing next to Dieter, talking with him and smiling.

'Ah – here she is!' announced Dieter with satisfaction as Ella joined them. 'Ella – this is Diandra. She has very kindly volunteered to let you take a turn on her violin. Will you oblige us, please, by playing something for us?'

'What?' Ella's eyes were huge with astonishment. 'I can't. I – it's ages since I've played. I'm completely out of practice and – No no no.' She shook her head violently.

'Oh, do play, darling. Please?' cajoled Leonie. 'I'd love to hear you. It must be three years since I last heard you play a note.'

Diandra was holding her violin and bow out to Ella with an encouraging expression on her face. Around her the faces of the other diners were all looking at her expectantly. 'Please do,' echoed Diandra. 'The gentleman has offered me a generous fee for the loan of my instrument.'

Oh, God. There was no getting out of it now. What had Eva Lavery said that day on Navy Island? *If I get an opportunity to spread some of my money around, I'm glad to do it* . . . The image of the woman waiting for the bus with her two children came back to her, her dignity in the face of poverty, and Ella's aborted impulse to give her money. She couldn't deny this woman the opportunity to earn a little more . . .

Ella bit her lip. 'Thank you, Diandra,' she said. 'I'd consider it an honour.'

She took the violin and tucked it under her chin, adjusting the angle until she felt comfortable with it. Then she raised the bow and drew it experimentally across the strings. Though inferior to her own, the instrument hadn't a bad tone. A little flurry of scales came next. An adjustment to the tension, with a 'May I?' to Diandra before screwing one of the pegs a fraction tighter.

Then Ella took a deep breath, centred herself, and launched into 'Erin Shore'. The first notes were gentle – almost tentative – as she familiarized herself with the instrument. Then, as her confidence increased and she drew the bow more vigorously across the strings, the plangent strains swelled, filling the room and filling her heart. Ella shut her eyes, smiled, and gave herself up to the music.

When she finished, the applause took her by surprise. It was a long, long time since she'd played in public. She opened her eyes and registered the smiling, appreciative faces around her, and felt colour sweep into her face as she bowed her head in acknowledgement. Diandra was clapping too, and joining in with the calls for an encore. Wow! Ella was blown away. She laughed out loud. She'd played stoned before, but never in front of an audience.

She paused for a beat or two before raising the bow again, casting around for what to play next. Something livelier would be good. She'd show them that Irish music could be sexy – less laid back than mento or reggae, but a serious contender in the world raunchiness stakes. Which piece, though? There were so many to choose from 'The Clare Jig?' 'The Hag's Purse?' 'Pull the Knife and Stick it Again?' No. She hadn't played that for ages – she'd make too many mistakes.

'Toss the Feathers!' That was the one! She tapped her foot – one, two – before launching into the jig with a flourish. Yes! The notes soared out of the violin in a stream of indescribably beautiful colours. Emerald green, hot pink, lapis lazuli . . . They hung quivering in the air like exotic insects. Looking around, she could tell by the way that people were moving in their chairs – swaying, drumming their fingers on tabletops, tapping their feet in time to her playing – that they were aching to dance. It was the greatest compliment she could have got – apart from the cheers that rang out when she finished. The audience whistled and clapped their hands high in the air and stamped their feet. The applause only subsided when she finally returned Diandra's violin to her and sat back down, feeling breathless. 'Thanks a lot,' she said to the other violinist. 'I'm really glad Dieter approached you. I haven't played in public in a long time, and it's kind of reassuring to know I can still just about hack it.'

The dark girl smiled back at her and gave that wonderful slow, Jamaican nod of the head. 'You can hack it for sure,' she said. 'No problem.' Then Diandra moved gracefully back across the room and took up her position on the little podium where the resident musicians played. 'I dunno how I gonna match that!' she remarked, with a laugh. But the sweet strains of Debussy were soon floating through the room, and once again Ella was swamped with nostalgia.

'Oh, Ella,' said her grandmother with a rueful smile. 'You really shouldn't be recording sounds for a living.'

'Oh?' said Ella, perplexed. 'What should I be doing, then?'

'You should be making them, of course, darling.'

*　　*　　*

After dinner, Ella remembered that she'd arranged to meet Desirée at the bar on the beach. Her instructor was there already, talking to the barman.

'Desirée! Hi!' Ella danced up to the bar and perched on a stool beside her.

'Hey! How's my Siamese Fighter!'

'Siamese Fighter?'

'It's a beautiful little fish. A feisty little fish. And it's the name of the cocktail Otis has made for you. I thought it right for my fighting girl. Tell Ella what's in it, Otis.'

The barman was expertly juggling ingredients. 'I mix Bombay gin with pink grapefruit juice. Then I squeeze in the juice of one blood orange, and rim it to the top with vodka.' He gave her a big smile and handed her the colourful concoction with a flourish. 'Here you go. My congratulations on adding a new cocktail to the list, Miz Siamese Fighter.' The glasses were set ceremoniously on the counter in front of them.

'Wow! I feel so chuffed,' said Ella, 'to have a cocktail named after me. It's like having a star named after you, isn't it? Or a rose.' She lifted her glass. 'Cheers.'

'Here's to you, Siamese Fighter,' said Desirée. 'And here's to a long and happy diving career.'

Ella took a sip. 'Wow,' she said. 'That packs some punch!' She'd better take it easy. She was already woozy from champagne and wine and that excellent weed of Raphael's. She ran her eyes down the expansive cocktail list. 'Will it ever get listed here?'

'Sure. Otis gets a new list printed up every season.' Desirée indicated a name halfway down the list. 'Look. There's your friend Ferdia.'

'Leopard Shark,' said Ella. 'Why did you call him that?'

'Because he's streamlined and sexy.'

'And dangerous?'

'Hell, no. Those leopard sharks are big pussycats. You get close enough to one, you can pet him.'

I think not, thought Ella. 'Um. Who's that beneath him? Rock Beauty?'

'That was his girl at the time. Miss Jamaica.'

'Oh.' Ferdia and Miss *Jamaica*? 'And – er – are you here somewhere too, Desirée?'

'Sure honey. That's me there.' She pointed to Starfish. 'Ferdia chose the name for me.'

Ella smiled. 'He chose well,' she said.

'Excuse me?' An American accent came from behind them. 'I wanna congratulate you on your playing earlier. That was some virtuoso performance.'

'What? Oh – you mean my fiddle playing? Well, thanks very much indeed.' Ella raised her glass at the middle-aged geezer who'd rolled up at the bar.

'Are you a professional?' he asked.

'No. I just play for fun, really.'

'Well. I was seriously impressed. I have a bar? – an Irish bar? – in Manhattan? If you're ever in New York give me a call. We have sessions there every night of the week. You'd be more than welcome, and I'd be glad to let you have work as a resident player.' He slid his wallet out of his pocket and handed her a card.

231

'Well. Thank you.' Ella glanced down at it, registered the name Bob O'Mahony, and then pocketed it. 'I'm really very flattered, Bob.'

'You're welcome,' said Bob O'Mahony. 'You're a very gifted young lady.' And he shook hands with her before moving off down the beach.

'What was all that about?' asked Desirée.

'Oh. I played a couple of tunes in the restaurant earlier. Diandra lent me her fiddle.'

'Yeah? You must be *good* honey! It's a real Irish thing, isn't it? The fiddle? Doesn't everybody over there play it?'

'Well, not so much nowadays. But once upon a time every household in the country would have had a fiddle – just like every township here has those massive speakers, blasting out reggae. The Jamaicans and the Irish have loads in common when you scratch the surface. Music, green countryside, bad roads . . .'

'Desirée!' A passing woman called to her. 'I'm not going to be able to make that dive tomorrow after all. Can we make it the day after?'

'No problem, honey.'

'Thanks!'

Desirée turned back to Ella. 'Ferdia tried to teach that Miss Jamaica, but she couldn't master it.'

What! Why was Desirée harking back to Miss Jamaica again? For some reason Ella didn't want to hear about Ferdia and Miss Jamaica. She decided to change the subject.

'Is Raphael on the cocktail list, Desirée?' she asked, opening it again.

'He sure is, honey. He's right at the top. Look there.' She indicated the first name on the list with a calloused forefinger. It was Angel Fish.

Ella nodded. 'That's perfect!' she said.

'I know,' said Desirée. 'I'm a very lucky woman.'

Chapter Ten

Ella was mildly surprised to find Dieter shaving in the bathroom of their villa the following morning, and had to remind herself that he was going to be part of her family. The three of them breakfasted together, and packed, and went to wait for the airport coach in the lobby.

Sophie was already there, sitting in a hilly landscape designed by Louis Vuitton, wearing the pink linen suit she'd worn on the flight over. Thankfully the coach that arrived to drive them to Kingston was so state-of-the-art that not even Sophie could find anything to complain about. Hell's bells! Imagine being such a sad individual that moaning was your favourite hobby, thought Ella, as she observed the actress looking around trying to find fault with something. And then she remembered how down in the dumps she herself had been before heading off for her Jamaican idyll, and she wondered if she'd be back down in those dumps by the time she got home to Dublin.

Dieter and Leonie re-enacted the farewell episode from their real-life soap opera at Kingston airport, although this time there were no tears from

Leonie. After Dieter's flight to Berlin was called and the lovebirds had exchanged final kisses, Ella and her grandmother wandered around the duty-free shops to kill time and escape from Sophie. Most incongruously, 'Frosty the Snowman' was playing over the airport speakers as the Jamaican sun blazed down on the tarmac outside. It was just as bonkers, Ella thought, that her grandmother should be going home with such an outrageously romantic tale to tell, while she, Ella didn't have so much as a romantic anecdote.

They said goodbye to Sophie at Heathrow. Practically the first thing the actress did upon arrival was to switch on her mobile phone. 'Thank God I'm in range again,' she said, fingers flying across the keypad faster than a concert pianist's. 'Tch. Engaged.' She made a little face, then turned to Ella. 'Give me your phone number. The next time I'm in Dublin I'll give you a bell and we can meet up somewhere hip for coffee.'

Ella hoped she didn't blanch too visibly, but Sophie was absorbed in locating the electronic organizer she kept in her handbag.

'OK?' she resumed, finger poised over the gadget. Ella was on the verge of obliging when someone in the arrivals hall called out Sophie's name. The actress dropped the organizer back into her bag as if it had given her an electric shock. 'Ben!' she shrieked, propelling herself and her luggage trolley into his arms. 'Oh, thank God! I've had the most appalling time. You would not believe—'

Leonie and Ella slid a look at each other and sidled in the direction of Flight Connections. They needn't have bothered sidling. As far as Sophie Burke was concerned, Ella and her grandmother were no longer part of her universe.

When they arrived in Dublin airport, festive songs were jingling around all over the place. 'Go, Frosty, go!' trilled Leonie as they looked about for Patrick, who was to meet them.

The place was milling with expats returning for Christmas, all hugging and kissing their family and friends and gabbling delightedly. Bah! Humbug! thought Ella, hating herself for being sour. She couldn't remember ever having had a Christmas when all the members of her family had been present. Every Christmas at least one family member cried off, either because they couldn't tolerate the icy vibe between her mother and father, or because they'd had a better offer elsewhere. If she wasn't flying out of the country to visit one or other of her parents, Ella generally Christmased with her uncle and Claudia and her cousins; but the last couple of Christmases had been spent with her musician friends in Wicklow. She hadn't a clue what she was going to do this year. Before she could think Bah! Humbug! again, she stapled a big smile on her face, determined to make an effort. 'There's Patrick now!' she said brightly to her grandmother.

Leonie made a beeline in his direction. 'Oh darling,' she breathed when they drew level with him. 'You'll never guess what's happened!'

Patrick took in Ella's averted eyes. 'I've a feeling I'd hate to even hazard a guess,' he said, giving his niece a dark look as he commandeered the luggage trolley. 'But I'll try. Let's see. You met the man of your dreams and you're getting married?'

'Right first time, clever clogs!' Leonie gave a tinkling little laugh. Then: 'Oh – I love this bit!' she said with a rather alarming enthusiasm. And she continued to sing along to 'Frosty the Snowman' with blithe brio.

Ella stole a look at her uncle's face. 'Merry Christmas, Patrick,' she said.

*   *   *

The subject of Leonie's forthcoming nuptials were deftly skirted round on the drive back to Dublin. Ella could tell that Patrick was reluctant to make any comment until he'd grilled her about it. He left her off at her gaff first, telling her in an ominous voice that he'd talk to her later, and then he and Leonie went to pick up Ronan the cat from the posh kennels he'd been staying in for the past fortnight.

At around six o'clock, Ella poured a hefty glass of red wine and braced herself to phone her uncle.

'What in *God's* name made Leonie decide to get married?' was the first thing he said.

'Oh, Patrick – don't be angry. Dieter's gorgeous, really he is. He's an absolute gentleman. You mustn't have no worries about him and Leonie.' The double negative had just slipped out. She prayed she wouldn't start speaking in a Jamaican accent as well.

The bummer about having a musician's ear meant that she always ended up talking in the accent of the region she'd most recently visited. She was sure everyone thought she was madly pretentious the time she'd been to New York, because she kept lapsing into *Friends*-speak when she came home.

'Of course I have worries – she's my mother. You worry about *your* mother, don't you?'

Ella considered. 'Um – no,' she said, matter-of-factly. 'Francesca's really happy. She's got her gorgeous villa and her lover and her collection of paintings. Why would I worry?'

'I can't understand this family's predilection for getting involved with glamorous foreigners,' said Patrick in a voice groaning with incomprehension. 'Your mother bolts with an Italian, your father shacks up with an Alaskan Innuit, and now your grandmother's running off with a German. I suppose you'll tell me next that you've fallen in love with a Jamaican.'

'I *wish*,' said Ella. 'My love life's still emphatically a no man's land. Anyway, Patrick – you married a glamorous Swiss model, so you're hardly one to talk.'

'Well, at least Claudia has Irish connections.' Patrick sounded defensive. 'We know nothing about this man who's knocked Leonie for six.'

'You've *got* to let her do it, Patrick. It's what she wants more than anything. I think it's wonderful that she should find romance at this stage of her life. She didn't even have to do the personal column thing or go on *Blind Date* to do it.'

Patrick sucked in his breath. 'Jesus. I suppose you're right. I wouldn't have put it past her to have volunteered herself as a guinea-pig to Cilla.' Ella could tell he was thawing a bit. Leonie's unexpected *affaire de coeur* was at least preferable to the idea of her conducting a holiday romance on a television show. 'How are they going to keep in touch, by the way?' he resumed, as if trying to pick as many holes as he could in this bizarre scenario. 'Her phone bill's going to be astronomical.'

'They'll do it by e-mail.'

'Don't be daft, Ella! Leonie's a complete techno-phobe! She doesn't even have access to a computer!'

'Dieter's offered to buy her one, and supply her with tuition.'

There was a fractional pause while Patrick digested this information. His voice when he replied sounded resigned. 'So. When are we going to meet this munificent Dieter?'

'Not for a while. He can't take any time off before the summer, so Leonie'll be jetting off to Berlin on a regular basis. Before you know it she'll have acquired Frequent Flyer status. Dieter's coming over in July. It'll be his first trip to Ireland.'

'And that's when the wedding will be? In July?'

'No. They're delaying that until November, when the rainy season's over.'

'What rainy season? It's always bloody raining in Ireland.'

Ella took a swift swig of wine before answering. 'They're not getting married in Ireland, Patrick. They're getting married in the Grace and Truth Temple.'

'The Grace and Truth Temple? Where in hell's name is that?'

'Jamaica. Near Port Antonio. At least, that's what they're hoping to do. They'll be happy enough to have the wedding on the beach if they can't organize a church ceremony.'

'Holy shit,' said Patrick.

*   *   *

By the time Christmas arrived, everyone had grown to accept the fact that Leonie and Dieter were perfectly serious about getting married. Patrick and Claudia decided to 'do' Christmas, and Declan, Ella's father, flew in from the States to be with them for a few days. He'd left his gorgeous Alaskan girlfriend behind because she was too heavily pregnant to fly. Ella's mother had phoned just before Christmas to say she was sorry she couldn't be there, but a long-lost daughter of her lover had arrived on their doorstep quite out of the blue, and she felt it was only fair to stay on as a kind of surrogate mother for the child. 'The child' was, it transpired, older than Ella. Ella had received this latest news with unfazed equanimity. Nothing her family could do had the power to surprise her any more.

It was a hectic, buzzy week. On Christmas Eve Declan and Ella snuck away from the drinks party Claudia and Patrick were hosting to try and grab some time to themselves. Ella had expected the local pub to be heaving, but in fact it was surprisingly quiet, and they even managed to get the snug to themselves.

She'd brought her holiday photographs to show to her father. There were lots of smiling shots of Dieter and Desirée among them, but for some reason hardly any of her shots of Raphael had come out. There were only two that were halfway decent, and they'd both been taken by someone else. One was the picture that Eva had taken of him in the pose she would always associate with him – sitting on the jetty at Navy Island, so absolutely at one with everything around him; the other had been taken on the evening of his little cousin's birthday party. She and Raphael were looking into the camera with beatific, slightly stoned smiles.

'I recognize that smile,' said her father indulgently. 'Good weed?'

'*Very* good weed.'

'So. Jamaica rocks?'

'Jamaica rocks.' Ella gave him an oblique look. 'You know I met an old friend of yours there?'

'Who?'

'Da-dah!' She produced a photograph of Eva on board the Navy Island ferry. Her hair was whipping around her face, she was laughing, and although you couldn't read the expression in her eyes behind the black, black lenses of her sunglasses, you knew that it was wicked.

'Eva Lavery?' Declan gave an incredulous smile. 'Wow. There's a real blast from the past. How is she?'

'She was great. If it hadn't been for her, I don't think I'd ever have set foot outside the resort. I'd have been stuck inside with all the other pampered prisoners.'

Her father's smile had gone from incredulous to nostalgic. 'She always had an adventurous spirit, that girl. And a charm that was irresistible.'

'That's what she said about you.' Ella smiled at him. 'She said *you* were irresistible.'

Declan raised a sceptical eyebrow. 'That was a long time ago, sweetheart.'

'I dunno. You're still pretty charming.' She laughed. 'Eva remembers you as having long blond hair like a Viking.'

'Hah! She'd get a shock if she saw me now, wouldn't she? A balding middle-aged git.' He handed back the photograph. 'She's hardly changed at all.'

'You're not a balding middle-aged git, Declan. You're a charming balding middle-aged git.' She drained her pint and set the empty glass down on the table. 'Your round, pater.'

Declan went up to the bar and came back with two more pints of Guinness and two packets of peanuts. They sat in companionable silence for a while, and then came the question Ella had been expecting – the question he always asked her when he came back on his visits. 'How's your form these days?' he said.

She looked a bit guarded. 'D'you mean my musical form or my mental form?'

'Both. Try running the musical bit by me first.'

Ella poured a small pile of peanuts into the palm of her hand and started to eat them one by one. 'Well. It's not brilliant, I'm afraid.' She was realistic enough to know that the euphoria she'd experienced the evening she'd played in Jamaica was down to the excellent ganja in the spliff that Raphael had rolled for her. Her rendition of 'Erin Shore' and 'Toss the Feathers' had been mediocre at best, and the rapturous response of the diners in the Pagoda restaurant had been merely polite. It was amazing how easily you could fool yourself into believing you were a ringer for Sharon Corr when stoned.

'I'd really love to hear you play, Ella,' continued her father. 'It's ages since I last did.'

No you wouldn't, she thought. I sound like shit. But she didn't want to admit that to Declan. He was so *proud* that she'd inherited his talent! So instead she just said: 'I'm a bit rusty, Dad. I don't have much time to practise.'

'You've *got* to practise, Ella.' Her father turned

uncharacteristically solemn eyes on her. 'You have a God-given gift. You can't let it go.'

She looked down at the photograph of Raphael that was still lying on the table, and remembered what he'd said to her on the last day she'd spent with him. *When you have a gift you are grateful and full of praise. Jah gave me my gift. But Jah has the right to take away that gift also. Be grateful for what you have, Ella. Be grateful, and full of praise . . .*

Ella slumped in her seat. She didn't want to be having this conversation. 'I'll never be a professional like you. You know that.'

'You still dream about it though, don't you?'

'Of course I do, Dad. But those kind of dreams don't come true.'

'On the contrary, Ella. Dreams can come true if you pursue them hard enough and want them badly enough.' He gave her a penetrating look. 'But that's beside the point. Think of the pleasure you get playing for yourself. Think of the pleasure you can give your friends and family. Sakatook loves it when I play. She says it's the best aphrodisiac there is. You know she thought I was a pretty nondescript kind of a guy when we first met in a bar in Chicago? It wasn't until I invited her along to a gig that she got the hots for me bigtime. Having mastery of an instrument is very sexy, Ella.'

Ella laughed. 'I can just imagine producing my fiddle the next time I fancy someone and sending him big seductive looks as I woo him with Weber.'

Her father gave her a pitying glance. 'Not Weber,

Ella. You know yourself who the sexy guys are.'

'The Irish guys?'

'For sure, yeah. But classical is sexy, too. I used to get really turned on when I watched your mother play. Those boys knew what they were doing, all right. Think of Bach. Think of Bruch. Think of Beethoven.'

She nodded. 'Let me guess. The Seventh?'

'The Seventh, for sure. Bloody critics have been falling over each other since it was first written to read an agenda into that piece. Bollocks to all that theorizing.' Declan threw a handful of peanuts into his mouth and chewed vigorously. Then he gave Ella a look of assessment. 'What do *you* think was in his head while he was writing it?'

'That's easy,' she said. 'It's all about sex.'

'That's right! It's all about sex! It's a musical tribute to the best ride Beethoven ever had.'

Ella smiled at her father. 'Does Sakatook like it?'

'She adores it,' said Declan, returning her smile. He took a hefty swig of his pint and then leaned back in his chair. 'So. Tell me about *your* love life, darlin'.'

'Will not,' said Ella, giving him a supercilious look.

'Why not? You've never been particularly coy about it before.'

'It's not because I'm coy, Dad. It's because there's bugger all to tell.'

Declan winced. 'Oh, baby,' he said. 'I *am* sorry.'

'Don't be sorry, Dad. I'd hate to think that I was

one of those sad singletons whose entire *raison d'être* is whether or not they've got a partner. I'm just not interested in the one-night thing, and I like to think I'm choosy about who I'm going to wind up with. I've had it up to here with gobshites.' She looked contemplative. 'And for some reason all the men I've ever been really interested in have turned out to be involved with someone else. Maybe my subconscious is trying to tell me something.'

'Like what?'

'Like I'm not ready for a relationship yet.'

'That wouldn't surprise me. You come from a long line of broken relationships, Ella. You need to be sure that whoever you end up with really is Mr Right.'

She remembered how she'd said as much to Jack once, before he'd hooked up with Angie. She sometimes wondered if she shouldn't have put up more of a fight where Jack was concerned, but then she thought of what her uncle had said to her on the night of that fateful birthday party, and she knew that he'd been right to discourage her. She sighed, and took another swig from her pint.

'I'm sorry,' said Declan.

'For what?'

'For being such crap parents. Francesca and I really messed up, didn't we?'

Ella laughed. 'Don't beat yourself up, Dad. I got so used to the fireworks after a while that I started to think that conventional families were the weird ones. You know, daddies who worked from nine to five and played golf at the weekends; mummies

246

who looked after the kids and did coffee mornings. I mean – *that's* spooky. And don't think I didn't inherit some good things from you.'

'Well, at least you got your looks from your mother. What did you get from me?'

She raised her eyebrows at him. 'A taste for Guinness, of course.'

*   *   *

Her father disappeared back to the States a couple of days after Christmas. He had some big Irish-American gig in Boston to get ready for – a ceilidh to celebrate the New Year. As well as the presents he'd given her for Christmas – expensive, last-minute designer-label purchases he'd obviously picked up in the duty-free on the way over – he'd left behind a package which contained a rake of CDs. Most of them were recordings of his own band's traditional Irish stuff, but he'd included a handful of classical CDs too. *Have a listen to refresh your memory*, read the accompanying note. *And have fun trying to decide which is the sexiest. Then practise playing them for yourself. With love from your prodigal Dad. XXX.* The penultimate sentence had been underlined. Twice.

*   *   *

Ella spent New Year's Eve at a party given by the creative director of Reflex Advertising. When midnight came she was rather taken aback to be inundated with numerous men – and a couple of women – trying to snog her. Somewhat to her chagrin, she resisted all comers without any difficulty. She'd have quite liked to have found at least one of the snoggees worth making a bit of an effort for.

Across the room Jack and Angie were locked in an embrace that wouldn't have looked out of place in a Bond movie. Bloody hell, thought Ella, grabbing a glass of wine from a passing waiter and turning her back on them, only to find herself face to face with the Christmas tree, which was covered in little papier mâché cupids. Cupid! Pah! He was a complete and utter bastard, and Aphrodite was the biggest bitch who ever walked the planet. She glowered at the cupids for a bit, and then gave a sigh of resignation. She wished she didn't like Angie so much. She hadn't even felt the impulse to indulge in the sabotage fantasies she usually devised about Jack's girlfriends this time round. She wasn't very proud to admit it even to herself, but sometimes the sabotage fantasies had really helped. There had been something enormously satisfying in running footage across her mind's eye of her and Jack shopping for lingerie together while Tamara/Saskia/Magda looked on. *Oh – hi, Tamara/Saskia/Magda! Fancy running into you here in the lingerie department of Brown Thomas! Tell me – what do you think of this teddy? Frankly, I always find the poppers on the crotch a little on the uncomfortable side, but ripping them apart just drives Jack wild . . .*

The volume had been turned up on that awful Slade song about wishing it could be Christmas every day, and a load of drunken people had started jumping up and down and punching the air. Ella had just about made up her mind to get out of there when she heard her name being called. It was Rebecca, a girl she'd been pally with during her time at music college. She was shouldering her way towards her through the pogo-ing revellers.

'Ella! How's it going?' she shouted, when she reached her. 'I haven't seen you in ages!'

'Rebecca! Hi!' Ella shouted back.

Rebecca kissed her on the cheek. 'How've you *mumble*?' she said. 'I meant to *mumble* ages ago, but I've been *mumble mumble mumble* . . .'

Ella squinted at her, trying to lip-read, and then she gave up and laid a hand on the other girl's arm. 'Let's go into another room,' she suggested in stentorian tones.

'What?' said Rebecca, with a blank expression.

Ella pointed towards a door to the right. 'It's – quieter – in – there. We'll – be – able – to – hear – each – other.'

They squeezed through the crowded sitting room into the adjoining study, and sat down on the floor in the corner where no-one could trip over them.

'Well, Beck! How are things?' asked Ella, glad to be able to use her normal voice at last.

'Good, good,' said Rebecca, sliding a spliff out of her breast pocket and lighting up. 'On the social side of things, anyway.' A cloud of smoke escaped her lips in a perfect O. 'If you're talking career-wise, on the other hand, it's more *comme-çi, comme-ça.*' She made a wavy motion with her fingers.

'Oh? What are you up to? Anything interesting?'

Rebecca made an apologetic face. 'I'm working for a computer firm.'

'A *computer* firm? *You?*' Rebecca had been one of the most highly regarded students in college. 'Wow. That's a turn-up for the books!'

'Yeah.' Rebecca shrugged, and drew on the joint again. 'Hell. It's the money thing, Ella. I couldn't afford a career as a violinist. I managed to pick up some work with a chamber orchestra in London for a while, but the money was rubbish. When it got to the stage where I was so poor I was actually contemplating selling my fiddle, I knew it was time to get a real-life job. There's stupid money to be made in computers.'

Ella nodded. She could relate to that. How many other casualties had there been from her year? she wondered. She had an image of a legion of injured musicians, dropping out of their musical careers like flies. 'Do you enjoy it?' she asked, curiously.

'Not much. But I keep myself sane by gigging a couple of evenings a week.'

'Oh? Where?'

'O'Brien's.'

Ella knew O'Brien's. It was a small pub in

Rathmines that held regular sessions. There was a good buzz there, but Ella hadn't been near the place for a couple of years. It was more convenient to hang out in Daly's.

'You should drop by some time,' suggested Rebecca.

'I might do that.'

'And bring your fiddle. Join in the session.'

'I haven't played for ages, Becky. I'm very out of practice.'

Becky passed her the joint. 'So? Start practising.'

*　　*　　*

And she did. She spent the next two months practising and practising and practising – until she was satisfied that her confidence was re-established beyond the shadow of a doubt. And then one evening in early March she dropped into O'Brien's with her fiddle, and had a blast. The band played until well after the official closing time, and she established such good rapport with the other musicians that they paid her the ultimate compliment for a fiddler. They asked her back.

January had gone fast, February faster. But March flew. Ella had never been busier. She ran between her day job and her evening sessions, buoyed up by endorphins.

In April there was an unanticipated lull. Bookings in Nesbit & Noonan took a dive, and O'Brien's changed hands. It was bought by a

London consortium who announced that they were going to turn it into a theme pub. The musicians abandoned the joint like rats fleeing a sinking ship. They made desultory noises about investigating a music option elsewhere, but nothing materialized, and Ella suddenly found herself with her evenings free again. It was the first time for ages that she had no idea what to do with herself.

'Do competitions,' said Leonie when Ella rang her to get the latest update on the Dieter saga.

'Won anything recently?' asked Ella, idly hoping that Leonie might have netted another holiday somewhere exotic.

''Fraid not,' said Leonie. 'I spend all my time e-mailing Dieter these days. It's amazing. On my 56 kps modem I can now send text *and* graphic files in a matter of seconds, *and* get a reply back in as many again.'

Holy shomoly. Leonie sounded like a bad voice-over for an IT commercial. 'Is he still coming over in July?' asked Ella, after listening to five minutes of Leonie's technospeak.

'Oh, yes. We're going to have such fun, Ella! I'll be able to pay him back for all the wonderful places he's taken me to on my visits to Berlin. We're going to dine in the Shelbourne and the Merrion and the Clarence—'

'Leonie, I hate to alarm you, but I think you'll find that the Clarence has changed quite a lot since you were there last.'

'Well, of course it has, darling. It's U2's hotel

now, not the hang-out of some dandruffy priests up from the provinces looking for illicit sex. I'm dying to see how Bono and the boys have done it up. And I'm going to take him to the races. Dieter, that is – not Bono. You'll come too, of course, won't you? I'm going to book a table at Leopardstown so we can drink champagne and eat strawberries all afternoon – and have a flutter too, of course. Oh sorry, darling – gotta go. Call waiting is beeping at me. It might be him.'

'Bye, Leonie.'

'Oh, by the way – have a look at today's *Evening Herald*. There's a big competition you might want to enter. The prize is a romantic trip for two to Paris. Bye, darling.'

Ella put the phone down feeling glum. She had no intention of entering the competition. Even if she did win, who would she take with her on a romantic trip to Paris? Bloody no-one.

She heaved a big sigh and returned her attention to the chore she'd been doing before she'd phoned her grandmother. It was a task she'd been putting off doing for months – sorting out her bureau. Her bureau was a repository for everything and anything – brochures, bills, mail that she should have answered ages ago, instruction manuals on everything from her mobile phone to her coffee machine. As she stuffed an application form for life insurance into a binbag, her eyes fell on yet another brochure sticking out from under an unpaid parking ticket with the reg of Patrick's Merc listed on it. Shit. She'd better pay that, she thought, as she put it on top of her 'to keep' pile.

The brochure she'd spotted had a picture of a diver silhouetted against an underwater background of aquamarine blue. A spotty blue and yellow fish hovered in the foreground, and a whole shower of little stripy ones were surging over a reef below. There was a stream of silver bubbles emerging from the diver's mouth, which was clamped round a – she'd called it a 'rubber tube' when she'd first seen that photograph. Now she knew it was a regulator. She opened the brochure and ran her eyes down the text. *Fun, adventure, excitement . . .* she read. *New friends, weekends away, blah blah blah . . .*

She was just about to bin it when an image swam up before her mind's eye, of the first time she'd performed that backward roll off Desirée's dive boat in the Blue Lagoon. The aquamarine fizz as she tumbled through the water, the rush of adrenalin, the first long breaths of cool, compressed air . . . And then she remembered the endorphins it had produced in her the next time she'd done it, and the next and the next, and suddenly she had an overwhelming urge to do it again.

She reached for the phone and punched in the number printed on the brochure. 'Hello?' she said when the phone was picked up at the other end. 'This is Ella Nesbit. I'd like to book a dive.'

*   *   *

The following Thursday evening she drove out to Portdelvin in the little fourth-hand Renault she'd recently purchased. It wasn't anywhere near as gorgeous to handle as Patrick's sleek Merc, of course, but it was nice to have her own set of wheels at last.

It was such a glorious spring evening that she opened the windows. As she drove along the coast road a flotilla of yachts appeared around the headland like a scattering of paper-white butterflies. A light breeze was up, waves were dancing – sunlight bouncing off them – puffy clouds were scudding in the bright blue overhead, and she had Mozart's Fortieth on the cassette player. All in all, it was one of those special April evenings that reminds you that winter does come to an end, and that life can be pretty damn special.

She congratulated herself on a nifty bit of parking on the seafront, and got her gear out of the boot. As she slammed it shut, she heard a familiar voice call her name. She turned, wind whipping strands of hair across her face.

'Richie! Hi!' She skipped across to where he was lounging outside the dive shop, and, standing on tiptoe, kissed him on the cheek. She noticed that he coloured slightly.

'How's it going, my small dive buddy and cohort?' he said, giving her an awkward little punch on the shoulder. 'It seems ages since I last saw you. How was Jamaica?'

'Brilliant. I got certified!'

'Well done, Ella.' He saluted her. 'I can see you inexorably climbing towards divemaster status.'

She made a face. 'Pah! Some hope. What about you? I suppose you're an advanced diver now, with all kinds of specialities under your weight-belt?'

'Sadly, not.' He sat down on the low wall that fronted the dive shop, stretching out long legs.

'Oh?' Ella perched beside him. 'I thought you were going to go straight into advanced training when you finished the first course?'

'So did I. I had to put it off.'

'But why, Richie? You were dead keen.'

'I broke my foot just after I got certified.'

'Ow. How?'

He looked sheepish. 'I slipped on a copy of *Penthouse* and fell down the stairs.'

'What?' She couldn't not laugh. 'I don't believe you!'

'Strange, but true. This will be my first dive since.'

'And this is my first one since Jamaica. Funny we should have picked the same evening!'

'Not really. Ferdia told me you'd booked yourself in, and I thought it would be cool if we could be buddies again.'

'If Ferdia allows us,' she said.

'He's not going to be here. PJ's the dive leader this evening.'

'Oh? Well then, we'll definitely buddy up.' She wondered where Ferdia was, but didn't want to ask.

256

'Ferdia's supervising a Rescue Diver course in Lissamore.'

'Oh.'

'Anyway, I thought it would be a good idea to get a dive in before I do my advanced stuff. I'm starting the course next week. Why don't you sign up for it?'

'Me? Hah! What's the point?'

'You learn dry-suit diving. I'm damn sure the next time I dive in Irish waters I'm going to want to wear a dry-suit. And you'd be certified for deeper dives. The deeper you dive, the more you see.'

She remembered the reef in Jamaica with its mysterious chasms, and how she'd yearned to explore them further.

'And of course, there's the fun aspect,' Richie reminded her. 'And the adventure and the excitement and all those new friends. *And* the riveting reading material. Da-dah!' With a theatrical flourish he produced a book from his sports bag. It bore the legend *Advanced Training for Open Water Divers*.

Ella made a cross with her fingers as if warding off a vampire. 'Agh! Do you have to go through the whole manual?'

'No. Only the relevant chapters.'

She took the manual from him and started to flick through it. 'Oh look! There's a chapter on spooky night diving. Yikes! Get a load of the illustration.' She indicated a picture of a couple of divers with big, round, scared-looking eyes.

The dive van was rounding the corner. It drew

up alongside them and PJ got out. He looked sick-makingly fit and sporty, and Ella felt inadequate. 'Hey, you two,' he said. 'Are you both diving tonight?'

Ella noticed that a single magpie had landed on a fence across the road. 'If I can hack it,' she said, blowing the bird a kiss. 'I might wimp out again. How's visibility?'

'Not bad. Four, five metres.'

Another magpie joined the one on the fence, and Ella breathed a little easier. 'Four, five metres,' she repeated. 'I'll give it a lash.' She remembered what Desirée had written on her underwater slate when she'd done her qualifying dive in Jamaica. *I can tell you are a fighter* . . . I will do it, she said to herself. I *will* do it.

PJ looked at his watch. 'We'd better get our act together,' he said. 'We don't want it getting dark while we're out there.'

Richie and Ella got up and followed him through into the shop. There was a selection of T-shirts on display on the wall behind the counter. One of them had a picture of a ferocious-looking eel on the front, and bore the legend: GO WHERE OTHERS FEAR TO TREAD. Thanks for that, thought Ella. How very reassuring.

'So you're all certified?' remarked PJ over his shoulder, as he headed towards the rental area where the gear was stored. He riffled among the wetsuits hanging on a rail and handed one over. 'You're a 36, aren't you, Ella?'

'Yeah. And a size three boot, please.'

PJ laughed. 'It's like kitting out one of my niece's Polly Pockets,' he said, running his hand along the shelf where the hideous neoprene bootees were lined up. 'Here you go.' He handed the boots over, and gave her a challenging look. 'Did you know there's an advanced course starting next week, Ella? Why don't you see how you get on tonight, and then make up your mind as to whether you'd be interested in doing it? You might surprise yourself.'

* * *

She did surprise herself. The visibility was adequate, and she didn't get spooked. Of course, there was no comparison to Caribbean waters, but she went down with a different set of expectations. There was no point in being disappointed that there were no jewel-like fish to feed, or fabulous reefs to visit, or Technicolor vistas to feast her eyes on – this underwater terrain was remarkable in its own way, with a restrained, sepia-tinted, rather grainy beauty. Visuals aside, it was the sensation of absolute tranquillity that enraptured in this silent, slow-mo environment. Real life with its humdrum minutiae couldn't touch her down here. She had found the ultimate escape route from the mundane.

At one point she found herself swimming over another buddy team below. Their air bubbles came gliding up to her through the water like silver spheres, and Ella wondered what it would be like to dive stoned. As she watched the great gleaming globes of air travel up past her towards the surface she found herself gazing in wonder at them, and realized that what she was experiencing really didn't need any drug-induced enhancement. She was on a natural high.

All the other divers that evening were men. Some of them did the usual macho things like haw and spit unapologetically once back on the dive boat; swap stories about the wrecks and the depths they'd dived, and indulge in other ostentatious displays of machismo. But the rather sweet thing, Ella thought, was that while diving was for the most part still a male preserve, the motivation behind it revealed a curiously feminine aspect. Other traditionally male sports were thrill-dominated, like rally driving or motorbike racing, or else they were boring, like cricket or golf. These men were going through a quintessentially macho ritual – suiting up, handling tons of backbreaking equipment with apparent insouciance, sporting fearsome-looking knives and enormous torches and compasses and dive computers and hi-tech cameras – all this so that they could spend an hour underwater teasing crabs, tickling sea anemones and starfish, exploring kelp forests – and in spellbinding slow motion. All that relentless *maleness* was really camouflage for what was actually a rather girly sport.

On the way back to harbour Ella found that she couldn't stop smiling. To the west the sun was setting, turning the water an unreal shade of bubblegum pink. To the east, a full moon was rising like a celestial pumpkin. The sky was hazy now, washed with pale cloud, and she was unable to distinguish any demarcation line between sky and sea. The boat bumped fast over the water, and her hair streeled out behind her. She turned shining eyes on Richie. 'I'm going to do it,' she said.

'Do what?'

'The advanced course.'

Richie grinned at her. 'That's my girl,' he said.

*　　*　　*

Their first class was in underwater navigation. Oops, thought Ella, whose sense of direction was seriously dodgy. PJ told them that with the aid of a compass and their own natural navigational ability they'd soon be able to navigate for themselves. What if you don't *have* any natural navigational ability? Ella wanted to ask, but didn't. Now that she was doing advanced stuff she supposed she'd better try and put a rein on her juvenile sense of humour.

But it wasn't easy. The class had to practise navigating on the promenade before getting into the water, and they all looked like barking loons as they adopted the required position for compass-reading, with one arm thrust straight ahead and the other hand grasping the opposite elbow. 'I – am – a – dalek,' intoned Richie as he trundled along in a northerly direction. 'Search – and – exterminate.'

261

'It's meant to be "search and recover", Rich,' Ella reminded him.

'Oh, all right then.' Richie put on his dalek voice again. 'Search – and – recover. Search – and – recover. What are you searching for, sweetiepie?'

'Doubloons, of course, darling. What about you?'

'Um. I hadn't really thought about it. How about my *raison d'être*?'

'Oh.' Ella considered. 'I'm not really sure I want to search for my *raison d' être*. What if it turned out to be non-existent, like in a Beckett play? Oh shit – I'm meant to be heading west now, aren't I? One, two, three, four paces. And – turn.'

'Six paces, Ella. We're doing expanding squares now.'

'Oh hell,' she said. 'Why did I ever let you talk me into doing this, Rich?'

'Because I'm a dangerous, silver-tongued bastard, of course,' he replied, flashing her a smile. 'And you can't resist me.'

'Oh yeah,' said Ella. 'I forgot.'

After the navigation dive came a deep dive. ('It'll be dark. If you get disoriented, just hug yourself to double-check you're still alive,' said PJ reassuringly, 'and make sure your bubbles are still going in an upwards direction.' Thanks, PJ, thought Ella.) Then there was a dry-suit dive, a search and recovery dive, and finally a boat dive. Ella spent an entire weekend clambering in and out of the quarry known as the Blackpits in County Wexford. The weather wasn't great, but she didn't mind that the water temperature was only 10 degrees now that she was in a dry-suit. When she first emerged from the latex-sealed garment she was amazed to find that she was indeed bone dry – just like James Bond when he unzipped his dry-suit to reveal a tux. OK, so she wasn't wearing anything as glam as a tux – just a cosy fleecy thing like a babygro called a 'woolly bear' – but she was snug as a bug in it. That, for her, was the biggest plus of the advanced course. Now that she knew she would never have to peel off a wetsuit again she had a real incentive to investigate diving in the cold Atlantic. She and Richie had signed up for one of the dive weekends away in the West. That's where Ferdia was now, Richie had told her. Supervising trainee open water divers.

The dive Ella had most fun with was the search and recovery dive. You had to locate an object underwater, attach a line to it and send it to the surface by filling an air bag with compressed air. She'd finally mastered the art of underwater navigation, and she couldn't help feeling chuffed with herself when her newly acquired compass skills led her straight to the lead weight that PJ had deposited on the bottom for her to find. It was really just like being in the Boy Scouts, she thought, as she deftly twisted the nylon rope into two half-hitches.

Except Boy Scouts weren't allowed to go drinking after their pow-wows or whatever they were called. Once this group of ten students and five masters had completed their briefs and packed up their gear for the day, they would head straight to the local pub. Most of the students were knackered and bruised and stiff-muscled after all the exertion, but once through the pub door, second-wind syndrome invariably set in. Ella found that what the manual had predicted was coming true. She was having fun, she was buoyed up by a sense of adventure, and she was making new friends.

Chapter Eleven

One sunny Monday morning developers moved into the building next door to Nesbit & Noonan. It had recently been sold to a firm of accountants. Uh-oh, thought Ella when she saw a skip parked outside. Patrick made no reference to it when he arrived in, but the expression on his face was more eloquent than words. This was going to cause problems, and possibly major ones.

Halfway into her first session of the day, the hammering began. She was working on a television commercial for a cosmetics company who were launching a new range of body lotions. The visuals were stunning, the backing track was silky, the voice she was recording sexy and persuasive. 'For satin-smooth skin,' read the voice-over artist (Bang! A mighty crash came from next door) 'soft as rain-kissed petals' (Bang! Another – even higher on the Richter scale) 'sweeter-smelling than summer in Provence . . .' (Bang!) The voice-over artist hesitated fractionally and then continued. You could hear the uncertainty in her voice. 'That starts to work from the moment you smooth it on in the morning . . .' (Bang again!)

This was useless. There was no point in continuing. 'OK,' said Ella. 'Sorry to stop you there, Lauren. We'll just have to wait until the banging stops.'

'What on earth's going on next door?' asked the agency copywriter who was sitting in on the recording of the commercial.

'They're renovating the building.'

'Oh.' The copywriter frowned. 'That's going to make life very awkward for you lot, isn't it?'

Ella knew it was a potential headache, but she couldn't have word getting around advertising agencies that future recording sessions in Nesbit & Noonan could be problematic. She tried to sound careless. 'Nah. Shouldn't be a problem. I've known this to happen to other studios. Generally speaking the builders are very understanding, and will stop working when you let them know you're about to record. I'm sure Patrick will talk nicely to them. And if they don't want to play ball, we can always threaten them with legal action.' Ella knew she was bluffing. Legal action was something of an empty threat. It could take a year for the case to be heard, and by that time the building work would have finished and the developers would have scarpered. She paused, and cocked an ear. There was a reassuring silence. 'Good. Seems like they've finished. OK, Lauren? Ready to have another go?'

'Sure.' The actress's warm voice came over the speakers.

'Go ahead, then. In your own time.'

They heard Lauren clear her throat and take a deep breath. 'For satin-smooth skin,' she began again (Bang!) 'that feels soft as rain-kissed petals—' (Bang! Bang! Bang!) 'Oh, for Christ's sake!' The actress gave a rather exasperated laugh. 'There's no point in me going on with this, is there?'

'Take five, Lauren. I'll phone up to Patrick now, ask him to check out the situation next door. He'll have things sorted in no time.'

Ten minutes later the banging was as relentless as ever, and the copywriter was 'tching' irritably. She turned to Ella. 'Honestly – this is bananas!' she said. 'You guys are going to have to get something done about this, Ella, and the sooner the better. I'm not prepared to run into another hour of studio time. I've to be somewhere else at eleven.' She gave her watch a fractious glance.

Uh-oh, thought Ella for the second time that day. Things were not looking good.

*　　*　　*

And they got worse. The entire interior of the building next door was disembowelled with painful slowness, its guts dumped unceremoniously in the skip outside. Many skips were filled over the course of the next few weeks. The builders were so noisy and disruptive and so cavalier in their attitude that eventually legal action had to be threatened. Patrick consulted his solicitor and was told that he could sue for loss of income incurred if regular clients had taken their business elsewhere – as they had done, in their droves. The threat of legal action had the effect of making the developers a little more compliant, but there were still inevitably occasions when a session was disrupted by the sharp whine of an angle grinder or the dull vibrato of a drill. Ella developed a perpetual headache, and took to dropping paracetamol. She felt knackered after work every day, sometimes going straight to bed when she got home. The last straw came when the geezer in the house next door to hers started to do home improvements. The noise of drilling pervaded her entire life. She was incensed enough to write to her local political representative – smiling Jim Moran – to ask what he intended doing about the level of noise pollution in Dublin city, but because there was currently no election to curry votes for, she never received any reply to her letter. Neither, unsurprisingly, did Leonie.

One Thursday she staggered out of the studio and made straight for the refuge of her little artisan house in the Liberties, praying that the DIY merchant wouldn't be wielding his drill this evening. The display on her answering machine indicated that there were four messages. Ella poured herself a huge glass of red wine, grabbed a packet of Kettle chips, curled up on her couch and pressed play. No, she didn't want to talk to her friend Tom the trombonist whose message informed her that he was deliriously in love and was coming out of the closet at last. No, she didn't want to talk to her other friend Iseult, who wanted to know if she was going clubbing over the weekend. No, she didn't want details of a new insurance plan. The fourth message was from Richie. 'Hello, my little dive buddy. How's it going? Give me a buzz when you get this. And never forget – Begin With Review And Friend.'

It was the ridiculous mnemonic that divers use to check that their buddy's safely kitted up. Ella laughed for the first time that week. She thought for a minute, and then reached for her Filofax and accessed Richie's number. 'Begin With Review And Friend yourself,' she said when he picked up.

'Ella! Are you all set?'

'All set for what?'

'For our dive weekend away, of course. Don't tell me you've forgotten. We're meant to be going to Lissamore.'

Ella bit her lip. 'Oh, hell, Richie. I'd completely forgotten.'

'But you *are* still coming?'

Oh God. She really just wanted to take it easy this weekend. The idea of kitting up and plodding around weighed down by pounds and pounds and *pounds* of equipment held no allure whatever for her.

'Oh, Richie. I have had the week from hell. I've been working under the most godawful circumstances. I really don't think I could hack it. I'm sorry.' She heaved a big sigh.

The sigh obviously sounded heartfelt, because:

'Look, Ella, it's not important,' he put in with alacrity. 'No problem at all.' But she could tell he was trying hard not to sound disappointed. 'I'll see if there's someone else I can buddy up with. I'll ring Ferdia and ask him who else is going. He's organizing this weekend.'

Ella thought hard. She knew it was highly unlikely that Richie would find another buddy at this late stage in the proceedings. It was Thursday evening – they were scheduled to head west in less than twenty-four hours. And for some reason she was goaded by the idea that Ferdia would more than likely assume that she'd wimped out again if she didn't show.

'No, no, Richie,' she said with decision. 'It's OK. I'll go.'

'Look, Ella – you mustn't do it just on my account. If you're not feeling up to it—'

'I'm not feeling up to it right now, but I'll be fine by tomorrow. I've an easy enough day.' There were very few gigs booked. Business was not booming at Nesbit & Noonan.

'Are you sure?'

'Absolutely.' She injected her voice with as much enthusiasm as she could. 'In fact, I can't think of a better way of recovering from the week in hell than by escaping to twenty-five metres.'

'So! We're sorted!'

He sounded so relieved she was glad she'd changed her mind. 'Where'll we meet up?' she asked.

'Wherever suits you.'

'Um. Let's see. Why don't you come by the studio around five? I should be finished before then. My last session's at four, and it's a dawdle.' As long as the fucking drills don't start up, she thought grimly.

'What constitutes a dawdle in the recording world?'

'A producer who wants out of there ASAP after a stressful week. The lure of the pub on Friday is the biggest incentive I know to get the job done fast.'

'OK. I'll get to you by five at the latest.'

'Excellent. We could be in Lissamore by around nine o'clock if the traffic isn't too hellish.'

There was a slight pause at the other end of the phone. 'Hang on a sec, Ella. I know you're mad about that little Renault, but will it get us all the way down to Lissamore? It's a long journey, and the roads after we hit Galway are shite.'

'Ah. You're right.' She'd ask Patrick to lend her the car if he didn't need it himself. He owed her a favour, what with the hard time she'd been having from advertising executives and copywriters about the construction work over the past few weeks. 'Don't worry, Rich. I'm pretty sure I can get my hands on the Merc.'

'Way to go! We'll do this weekend in style, Ella!'

He sounded so pleased that she found herself smiling in spite of herself when she put down the phone. She swigged back her wine, then got up from the couch and wandered into her bedroom, looking out stuff to pack for the weekend. She located her mask and her snorkel and her dive manual in case she needed to revise anything. She stuffed underwear into an overnight bag, along with tracksuit bottoms, T-shirts, jeans and Timberlands. Her suede jacket. It was a Ralph Lauren jacket that had cost her a bomb four years ago, even at its reduced sale price, but she had ripped one of the pockets and had had to demote it to the scruffier section of her wardrobe. She filled a washbag with basics, then added a tube of tinted moisturizer. A waterproof mascara. Lip gloss. Her Chanel 19. Concealer for the horrible zit on her chin. That was the bloody builders' fault, she thought bitterly, peering into the mirror. She only ever got spots when she was run down, and during the last few weeks she'd been run into the ground. She plucked away one or two stray hairs from her eyebrows with tweezers, and reminded herself to add her eyebrow brush and a tub of Vaseline to the contents of her bag. Then she looked more closely at her reflection. The bags and dark circles under her eyes, the pallor and the blotches on her skin sent her flying straight off to bed. She badly needed her beauty sleep.

* * *

Patrick did lend her the car. 'Make the most of it,' he told her. 'It's probably the last time you'll ever drive it.'

'Oh? How come?'

'It's too damn expensive to run. I'm in the market for a new car that will cover a mile on a teardrop of petrol.'

'Shame,' replied Ella. 'But mere budgetary constraints have never stopped you buying groovy cars before, Patrick.'

'I never had *real* budgetary constraints before, toots.'

Ella shot him a questioning look, but he just put a finger to his lips. 'I don't want to talk about it, OK?'

'OK.' She put a lid on her curiosity. She knew better than to ask her uncle questions he wasn't prepared to elaborate on. But somewhere in her subconscious a tiny warning bell started to go off. She knew something was up.

When she finished her final session of the day she went through to reception to find Richie chatting to Julian.

'You never told me you worked with someone who was into diving,' said Richie.

'Oh. Hi.' Ella looked at Julian and then she looked back at Richie. 'You two have met, have you?' she asked without enthusiasm.

'Yeah. We've been dive-talking since I spotted the snorkel sticking out of Richie's bag,' said Julian.

'Julian's doing the deep diver speciality course the same weekend I am, Ella. We thought we might buddy up together.'

Ella tried not to look too aghast at the idea of Julian poaching her dive buddy. She made an attempt to change the subject. 'How can you afford to go on a speciality weekend so soon after forking out for this one?' she asked.

'I've got a part-time job doing telesales. I've discovered I'm kinda good at it,' he added, sounding rather perplexed.

Ella wasn't surprised. Richie had a knack of making friends quickly. He'd done it with her, and now, much to her chagrin, he'd obviously gone and done it with Julian. She wished she'd had the nous to warn him off in advance, and then she copped herself on. What business was it of hers who Richie chose to be friendly with? It wasn't as if she had exclusive rights to him, after all. But part of her couldn't help feeling extremely miffed that Julian had now started hijacking her friends. It was bad enough having to work with him.

'Why didn't you *tell* me you were going diving this weekend, Ella?' he asked now in an aggrieved tone, sitting up on the reception desk and swinging his legs. 'You should have done. We could've all three of us gone down in my car.'

'What do you mean?'

'I'm heading down to Lissamore myself. I haven't done a dive weekend for months, so I rang ActivMarine on an impulse yesterday. I was lucky to get a place. They were fully booked, but someone had dropped out at the last moment.'

Oh no! Her weekend was ruined!

'Why *don't* we travel down together?' suggested Richie. 'It would save on petrol money.'

'No!'

Two pairs of eyes turned to Ella. 'Why not?' asked Richie reasonably. 'It makes sense to me.'

'I er – I'd rather have my own transport. I get antsy if I'm somewhere and I have to rely on other people for lifts.'

'Well, maybe I should travel down with you, then,' said Julian.

'No!'

'Why not?'

'Because I'm taking Patrick's car, not the Renault. The Merc's only a two-seater.'

Julian shrugged. 'Oh well. A missed opportunity. Next time you're going diving, Rich –' Rich! How dare he! '– give me a buzz. I'd be glad to give you a lift and buddy up with you.'

Ella looked at her watch. 'Come on, Richie. We'd better head if we're going to try and avoid the worst of the traffic. What a shame you've another session, Julian.'

'No worries. It's a nice gig. Some ISDN with Gabriel Byrne. That guy's a gent.'

'Gabriel Byrne?' exclaimed Richie. 'Holy shomoly! Maybe we could hang about for a bit, Ella? My sister would love his autograph.'

'I'll get it for you another time,' said Ella, shooshing Richie towards the door.

'I'll get it for you this afternoon, if you like,' offered Julian. 'No problem.'

'Hey! Thanks, Julian. I'll be able to bribe my sister to introduce me to all her foxiest friends for that. Nice one! See you later.'

'Yeah. I'll catch up with you in Sweeney's.'

'Sweeney's?'

'The pub next door to where we'll be staying. It's where all the boys go after a day's diving.'

The boys! 'What about the girls?' asked Ella sweetly.

'Oh, they're welcome too,' said Julian with a laugh. 'But I think you'll find that they're outnumbered. You might find that you're very popular all of a sudden, Ella.' He gave her a big wink. 'Even dogs are popular on dive weekends.' *Jesus!* 'That's not to say you're a dog, Ella, or anything like one,' he added hastily, on seeing the look that crossed her face.

Ella swung her bag up over her shoulder and legged it through the door. Fuck, fuck, fuck, she thought as she zapped the locks on the Merc that was parked just outside. Julian Bollard was becoming the bane of her life.

'He seems like a nice bloke,' remarked Richie, sliding into the passenger seat.

Ella made a noncommittal sound as she slid the car into gear. She would have loved to tell Richie the truth, but she knew it wasn't fair to poison his mind against Julian just because *she* had a problem with him. In fact, she supposed, when she allowed herself to think about it, the only person who *did* seem to have a problem with Julian was her. She had just never allowed herself to overcome the rivalry that had sprung up between them from the very first day they had met.

* * *

At half-past nine that evening they pulled up outside Sweeney's pub. It was a typical country pub with no pretensions whatsoever. The furnishings were basic, there was worn lino on the floor, and the place looked as if it hadn't had a facelift since the sixties. A fire was burning even though the evening was mild, and there were posters advertising traditional music sessions on the wall.

The place was Friday night crowded, mostly with locals. Looking around, Ella recognized some faces from her ActivMarine course, and was glad to see Sporty Jan's among them. At least there was *one* other girl on this dive weekend. She sat down beside Jan on the end of the vinyl banquette and made small talk until Richie arrived with her pint. She learned that Jan had done her advanced course immediately after Christmas, and had notched up an impressive number of dives. She also learned that Duffer Dan had gone into orbit, and was now aiming for master diver status. How weirdly misleading first impressions were, she thought. She would never have believed that Duffer Dan would make it through even the preliminary course.

As the evening wore on, more diver types

arrived, and a serious party element started to manifest itself. Ella was standing by the bar trying to attract the barman's attention when she had that peculiar sensation you feel when you know instinctively that someone is looking at you. 'How's it going, Ella?' came a voice from behind. She turned round to find Ferdia MacDiarmada standing there. 'I saw your car outside,' he said. 'Are you down for the weekend?'

She nodded. 'Yeah. I got hooked.' She hadn't seen him for six months. He was taller than she remembered, his dreadlocks were blonder, the jagged silver line of the scar on his cheekbone was more marked in contrast to his tanned skin. He'd obviously been away somewhere in the sun.

'So you certified in Jamaica?' he asked.

'Yes.'

'I knew the Caribbean would suit you.'

There was a hiatus while Ella flailed around for something to say. 'Desirée sends her love, by the way.'

Ferdia smiled. 'She's a class act, isn't she? Did she go down with you?'

'Yes. When I told her I'd trained with you she said she would finish the job for you.'

His smile grew broader. 'I'd better drop her a line to say thank you. You're a privileged girl, Ella Nesbit. Desirée doesn't usually have much truck with trainees. She's too busy running the joint.' There was another slightly awkward pause, and then Ferdia said: 'Is this your first time to dive in Irish waters?'

'No. I did the Blackpits.'

'No shit.' He gave her an interested look, which took her off guard. 'You did the advanced course? When?'

'Um – oh, when was it? About three weeks ago.'

'I'm impressed. How was the visibility?'

'Two metres.'

'Well. Sheep's Head Bay will be a cakewalk for you now. Congratulations.'

'Thanks.' She could feel herself going a bit pink. It was time to lob another shot into the conversational vacuum that was spreading uncomfortably between them. 'How's Perdita?' she was inspired to ask.

'Doing well. She's had her first litter.'

'Oh! How old are the pups?'

'Four weeks. Do you want one?'

She shook her head. 'I couldn't. I've no garden. It's a shame. I haven't had a dog since I was little.'

'What kind had you?'

'A shih-tzu.' Ella actually hadn't much liked the dog. It had been overbred and highly strung. She'd always preferred the mongrel next door who looked like Just William's dog. She was just about to explain how they'd been bequeathed the shih-tzu by a neighbour who'd emigrated to Australia, when she heard her name being called.

'Ella! Hi! I just got here.' Julian was shouldering

his way towards her through the crowd. 'God – that was the drive from hell. I got a flat – can you believe it? – just outside Galway. Boy, am I glad to be here at last! I badly need a drink. Anyway, how are *you*, toots? Sorry, sorry – I know you hate being called toots! Maybe I should call you "buddy" instead.' He leaned over and kissed her on the cheek.

Ella was too totally gobsmacked to say anything.

'Let me get you a drink,' said Julian. Then: 'Hey! Ferdia! I haven't seen you in a while. How's it going, man!' Julian looked as if he was going to give Ferdia a high five, but then obviously thought better of it.

'Fine. And you?'

'Cool. Yeah, yeah. Ella can testify to that, can't you, Ella?'

Ella looked blank. What had happened to Julian? He'd transmogrified suddenly into some kind of wannabe blokey dive type.

'Any good dives lately, Ferdia?'

'Yeah. The Red Sea.' Ella noticed that Ferdia's eyes were starting to scan the crowd, as if looking for an escape route.

'Hey! That *Thistlegorm* wreck! Wow. Something else, yeah?' He made a clicking noise with his tongue against the side of his cheek. 'And did you manage to dive the reef at Gebr El Bint?'

Ferdia gave a vague nod.

'Cool, isn't it? Yeah – I got some of my best dives ever there. I'll never forget—'

'Sorry – excuse me, Julian, but PJ's just come in. I need to go over tomorrow's briefs with him. I'll talk to you later.'

And Ferdia disappeared through the crowd.

'Keep blowing bubbles, man!' Julian nodded at his departing back, and did that thing with his chin that Ella hated so much. 'Sound bloke,' he said. He turned to Ella and winked. 'Hope you're not feeling too outnumbered, Ella. I told you there'd be a lot more men than women on this weekend, didn't I? You must be glad you've got me to look after you. Hey – bartender! A bottle of Coors Light! By the neck!!'

Ella looked over to where Richie was roaring his head off in response to some joke of Duffer Dan's. Jan was having an animated conversation with a very sexy-looking divemaster. Ferdia was nowhere to be seen. And then she spotted him over by the door. A stunning-looking woman had just come in, and was greeting Ferdia like someone long lost to her.

'Let's join the gang, Ella,' said Julian. 'We can just squeeze into that corner by the fire if Dan shifts up. You know Dan? Let me tell you about him. He only started diving last October, and already he's got over forty dives notched up. That man is heading towards master scuba diver, no problem. He's doing the rescue diver course next week, and immediately after that he intends to—'

Julian had taken her by the arm and was steering

her towards the corner of the room. She didn't hear any more of what he was saying because she was too busy desperately trying to work out an escape plan.

* * *

It didn't work. She spent the rest of the evening miserably sandwiched between Julian and the wall. The wall was marginally more interesting, but even more interesting than the wall was the woman who had hijacked Ferdia. She was at least ten years older than him, and elegant in that very *county* way. Her jumper was of butter-coloured cashmere, she was wearing soft suede jeans that shrieked 'expensive', and her glossy chignon could have been styled by Nicky Clarke. She looked a bit like a younger Sophia Loren, smoked Sobranie cigarettes and touched Ferdia on the arm a lot.

As the pub became crowded, Ella's view of the pair was obscured more and more. Two extremely overweight farmers had positioned themselves directly in front of her and she could no longer indulge her voyeuristic tendencies unless she craned uncoolly to one side. When Julian started to drone on to someone about his dives on the Great Barrier Reef yet *again*, she returned her attention to the wall. Finally she announced that she was heading for bed, using the long drive as an excuse for being a party pooper.

'See you for breakfast at eight-thirty, Ella,' said Julian. 'Be sure to eat a hearty one. It's not a good idea to dive on an empty stomach.'

Oh, shut *up*, Julian, she thought as she headed towards Richie to say good night.

'Ella! How art thou, my beloved buddy!' said Richie when he saw her. He got to his feet a bit unsteadily, and wrapped his arms around her. 'Why are you abandoning me so soon? Stay for another.'

'I won't. I'm knackered, Richie. If I don't get a decent night's sleep I might have to wimp out of the dive tomorrow. Remember what happened that time in Sheep's Head Bay.'

'But that was a hangover, not mere tiredness.'

'That was a *colossal* hangover, and if I stay on here drinking I'll run the risk of yet another one. Good night, Rich.'

'I can't let you walk to the hotel on your own. Allow me to escort you.'

'Richie – I'll be fine! It's just across the road!'

He looked dubious but was distracted by the arrival of Duffer Dan. 'There you go, Richie,' said Dan, setting a pint down in front of him.

'Thanks, Dan.' He turned back to Ella. 'Well. If you're sure, Ella?'

'Of course I'm sure, silly. See you in the morning.'

'Well. Good night, then, gorgeous.' Richie leaned down and gave her a big kiss on the cheek.

She took her leave of Jan and Dan and PJ, and left the pub. She noticed, as she headed towards the door, that the two fat farmers who'd obscured her view earlier were now sitting in the place previously occupied by Ferdia and his friend.

Chapter Twelve

The hotel was an old-fashioned place, comfortable, but not remotely luxurious. Ella's room had two single beds, no bathroom, and a shelf with an assortment of books. She ran her eyes along the spines. There was a volume on fly-fishing, a selection of writing by Myles na Gopaleen, the ubiquitous *Men are from Mars, Women are from Venus*. Some paperback romances. She chose one at random. *Passion's Monument*, she read on the cover. *A Tale of Romance, Desire and Lust*. The picture on the front was of a man stripped to his waist with big bulging muscles on him, clutching to his bare chest a fragile-looking chick with long flowing hair. The book fell open at what was obviously a very thoroughly read page.

'Hah!' he laughed, showing his white teeth. 'You little spitfire! You don't want to make it too easy for me, do you?' He jammed his bronzed thigh between her legs and forced them apart. She felt the powerful muscles rub against her pleasure kernel, and in spite of herself felt a shameful stirring there in her most secret place. 'No,' she murmured, drawing the delicately embroidered strap of her gown back up over

her shoulder. 'Please – no.' He raised a hand, and,
before she could prevent him, he had wrenched the
flimsy fabric asunder. He pulled aside the satin of
her bodice and put his mouth to the creamy skin
of her breast. She felt her nipples blossom into
miniature rosebuds under his tongue, and then she––

'You bastard.'

It was a woman's voice, raised in anger, and it
came from the room next to hers. She heard a man's
response, but it was pitched so low it was difficult to
make out what he was saying. It went on for quite
a long time. Ella could make out the occasional
isolated phrase – 'going away', 'can't commit',
'please stop beating yourself up, Philippa –'

The woman's voice came again, tearfully this
time. 'This is the last time I'm going to allow you to
make love to me. I mean it. I just can't *handle* the
deceit any more.' As she spoke her voice got quieter
and more reasonable, and it became more and
more difficult to hear what she was saying. When
Ella realized that she was actually straining to hear,
she copped herself on at once.

There was silence for a while, and then came a
long sigh of pleasure.

Eavesdropping on a row was one thing, but Ella
was damn sure she wasn't going to eavesdrop on
her neighbours' lovemaking. She'd escape to the
bathroom and leave them to it. Quickly she
stripped off her clothes and got into her robe. It was
a rather gorgeous creation that her father had

brought back for her from a tour in Japan – a kimono in rich pink silk, handpainted with lotus flowers. It was far too special to be wearing on a dive weekend in a not-very-groovy provincial hotel, but she'd spilled the contents of an entire cafetière all over herself that morning, and the towelling robe she usually wore was now soaking in her bath at home. She grabbed her washbag, a couple of hotel towels and an apple, and tucked her dive manual under her arm. Suddenly she had second thoughts.

She chucked the manual back into her overnight bag and tucked the steamy paperback under her arm instead, then headed down the corridor to the bathroom. As she kicked the door shut behind her, the paperback slipped to the floor. She picked it up and was instantly arrested by what she read. *You bastard. This is the last time I'm going to allow you to make love to me. I mean it, Dashiel.* Hey! She'd just heard those very words articulated in the bedroom next to hers! Truth *was* stranger than fiction!

Ella turned on the taps and sat on the edge of the bath, running her eyes over the pages. The words 'pleasure kernel' featured a lot, and when she fast-forwarded to the end of the book, she found that it *wasn't* the last time the heroine allowed Dashiel to make love to her. In fact, he 'took' her on numerous more occasions, and in numerous lo-cations – in a box at the opera, in the conservatory of his mansion, on a massive leather couch in his gentleman's club (she'd disguised herself as a serving boy). God! Were women *really* that much of a walkover when it came to great sex? She couldn't remember.

She turned off the taps and got into the bath. She'd been sensible enough to bring Badedas with her – after the last dive weekend she'd been stiff for days – and she soaked for a long time, scanning the paperback romance for more sex scenes. It was risible stuff, but undeniably steamy – full of thrusting, throbbing and 'damp softness'. 'Damp' was such an unattractive word, she thought, casting around for some alternatives. Moist? Yuck – no! That was just as bad. Squelchy? Oh – *gross*! All the synonyms she could think of for women's sexual arousal were horrible.

She flicked on through the pages. The adjectives used for the men bordered on the aggressive: they were all hard and lean and craggy. The women were all soft and supple and yielding. Out of curiosity, she took a disinterested look down at her own naked body. It was . . . Well. She supposed it *was* soft. And kind of supple. And her breasts were . . . creamy. The novelette was pretty damn accurate after all, she thought, as she reached for the soap and ran it over her breasts, noticing that her nipples actually did look a bit like miniature pink rosebuds . . .

Suddenly the door opened and Ferdia MacDiarmada walked in wearing nothing but a towel around his waist. Ella's mouth fell open with shock, and she slid under the Badedas foam like an electric eel. Water swilled into her mouth and she surfaced again, spluttering like a drowning person. Ferdia instantly turned round, his eyes going automatically to her miniature pink rosebuds before being wrenched upwards. Ella crossed her arms over her breasts, made an inarticulate noise of indignation, and tried to conceal her face with the book.

'Ella. Oh, shit – I'm sorry. I should have knocked.' He spread his hands apologetically and backed out of the room before she could say a word.

Across the room she could see herself reflected in the steamy mirror. Her face was bright purple, her mouth was a big round O, and the title of the book screamed at her from the mirror in swirly neon letters nearly as purple as her cheeks. *Passion's Monument,* she read again. *A Tale of Romance, Desire and Lust* . . . It might as well have read: *Passion's Monument. A Tale Told by an Idiot.* Or: *Passion's Monument. A Tale for Sad Singletons with the IQ of Pond Life* . . . Oh fuck. How completely, how *utterly* humiliating.

Ella hurled the book across the room. If the pages had been contaminated with radioactivity she couldn't have hurled it harder. Then she dragged herself out of the bath, wrapped herself in her robe and tiptoed back to her bedroom. In the room next door the couple were still making love. It wasn't loud, huffing and puffing, moaning and groaning kind of lovemaking, but she could tell they were still at it by a kind of gentle susurration that emanated from the room.

She looked crossly at her travel alarm. Jesus – she'd been in the bath for nearly an hour – you'd think they'd have run out of steam by now. Ella got into bed, set her alarm for eight o'clock, turned off the light and shut her eyes. It was no good. Knackered as she was, she just couldn't sleep. The faint murmurings and sighs and low, low laughs from the next door room sharpened the knife edge of her consciousness, keeping longed-for sleep at bay. The minutes dragged on. What was she to do? She'd be like a dog's dinner in the morning if she didn't get to sleep soon.

Suddenly the activity level next door accelerated. Ella could tell from the urgency of her breathing that the female half of the partnership was approaching orgasm. There was a crescendo of little moans, then one loud shuddering sigh, and then a cry of pure pleasure that seemed to go on for ever, followed by a euphoric: 'Oh *God* that was good!'

Wow. Lucky lady, thought Ella. She turned over in bed and made herself comfortable again, thanking God that the bonking couple had stopped at last. The silence was a blissful relief. She had descended to the very verge of oblivion when something brought her back. There was movement in the room next door, followed by a murmur. Followed by a sigh. Followed by a low, low laugh.

Excuse me? she felt like saying. *You said something*

earlier about that being the last time you'd ever allow him to make love to you? This wasn't funny. Either the woman was insatiable, or she had an indefatigable lover, or both. Not only was Ella cross now, she was also very jealous. As the sighs from next door increased in volume, she was seized with rage. She flung back her duvet, knelt on the bed and banged on the wall with a furious fist. The sounds stopped. There was one more low, throaty laugh, and then silence fell at last.

Thank God for that, thought Ella, falling on the mattress and then falling fast asleep.

* * *

Next door's alarm went off at the same time as hers. She slid out of bed, slung on her silk kimono and shambled doorwards. As she stepped into the corridor someone emerged from the adjacent room. It was Ferdia. Again he was naked apart from the towel around his waist. It was too late for her to dive back into her room. They looked at each other with rather aghast expressions. Then Ella averted her eyes and Ferdia said: 'Morning, Madam Butterfly. Off to the opera?'

She tried to look scathing while still keeping her eyes averted.

'Sorry, that was a cheap gag. I'll let you get through the bathroom first. See you at breakfast.'

Ella gave a gracious nod in his direction and proceeded down the passageway with what she hoped was elegant insouciance. In fact, her progress was more of a kind of reined-in scamper.

'By the way,' he called after her when she reached the door, 'the latch does work. You just have to make sure you shoot it all the way home.'

*   *   *

Downstairs in the breakfast room, PJ and Ferdia and the other instructors were sitting around a table working out buddy groups. There was no sign of the nymphomaniac Philippa. Ella slunk past them, sat down beside Sporty Jan and helped herself to cornflakes. There seemed to be rather a dearth of divers. One by one they skulked in, some looking rather the worse for wear. 'You missed a great session last night, Ella,' said Sporty Jan.

'Oh? What time did it go on until?'

'I dunno. I left while the going was good, at around half-past midnight. Your buddy was still there with a rake of pints in front of him.'

'Richie?'

'Yeah. You might want to give him a wake-up call.'

'I will.' Ella put in an order for scrambled eggs and sausages and rashers, then drained her coffee and ran upstairs to Richie's room. PJ had told her he was in Room 27, which was on the other side of the room she'd seen Ferdia coming out of earlier. She wondered, as she tapped on his bedroom door, if Richie too had been kept awake by all that nocturnal activity.

'Rich? Richie!' She knocked harder. 'Hey, Rich,' she called through the keyhole. 'It's time to get up.'

'Uh.'

'Time to get up, Richie!'

'What? Oh. Oh, fuck.' She heard stumbling noises, and then Richie was at the door. He was still fully dressed in the clothes he'd been wearing yesterday.

Ella looked at him in dismay. His hair was sticking up like a brush, his eyes were Basset-hound bloodshot, and his face was as pale as death. He might as well have had a sign hanging around his neck saying: 'This boy will not be going diving today.'

'Richie.'

'Ella. Hi.'

'Go back to bed.'

'No no. No. What time's it? Are we ready to go diving? Um. Oh God.'

'Go back to bed, Richie.'

'What? No, no. I'm fine. Really I am. I'm just a bit, you know . . .'

'Hungover?'

'Mm. Yeah. A bit.' He was having some trouble focusing his eyes.

'Jesus, Rich. You're not just a bit hungover. You're still pissed. There's no way you can dive today.'

'But, Ella, I can't let you down. Look – just give me five minutes. A bit of breakfast and I'll be—' His hand flew to his mouth and he turned a shade which Ella couldn't identify. It was somewhere between jaundiced yellow and poisonous green. 'Oh fuck,' he said. 'I think I'm going to—' He suddenly shut the door in Ella's face and she could hear him stumbling across the room again.

'Throw up,' she finished for him.

There came the sound of violent retching, and then Ella heard him say in a very small voice: 'It's OK, Ella – I made the wash-hand basin.'

'All right, Rich. Go back to bed and take it easy. I'll find another buddy, no problem.'

She trailed back down the stairs and into the breakfast room, almost walking straight into Ferdia. Oh God, oh God. How could she ever bring herself to look him in the face again? She looked into his face. It was the bravest thing she had ever done. 'Richie's not well,' she said.

'You mean Richie's hungover,' he said.

She nodded. 'What'll I do about a buddy?' she asked.

'It's OK. There were a few casualties last night. Richie wasn't the only one. We can re-jig the buddy teams and make sure nobody's left out. Leave it with me.'

Ella meandered across the room to her place beside Jan. The waitress had just set her breakfast in front of her. 'Sorry – that's not mine,' said Jan. 'I ordered boiled eggs, not poached.'

'Oh. It must be for this gentleman, so.' The waitress turned to the table behind Ella's chair.

'Yes – that's mine all right,' said Julian. 'Morning, Ella. How did you sleep?'

Ferdia was passing the table. Their eyes met, and the air between suddenly crackled with – with what? In her case the moment was charged with the purest embarrassment. *How did she sleep?* He knew very well how she'd slept – or rather, not slept. She could tell that he, too, was clearly thinking back to the peremptory way she'd banged on the wall to interrupt his *coitus* last night. However, she wasn't at all convinced that he was embarrassed by it. She was sure she saw his mouth curve in a barely perceptible smile after they'd broken eye contact.

'Um. I slept OK,' she said, pouring herself more coffee, and bracing herself for a further bombardment of dive savvy from behind. Luckily, Julian had found a novice to bore. 'Residual nitrogen . . .' she heard. 'Narcosis . . . decompression limits . . .' Drone, drone, drone . . .

Ella's breakfast arrived and she ate as much of it as she could, although she didn't have much of an appetite. Julian put away all of his, as did Sporty Jan. Before they got up from the table, Ferdia rose to his feet.

'I just want to run the new buddy teams by you. Some of the group are a bit under the weather this morning—'

'Under the weather? Under the influence, you mean, Ferdia! Ha ha ha!' went Julian.

Ferdia gave him a wan smile in return. 'You and Ella will be buddying up, Julian. Dan – you and Frank are a team. Jan, you're diving with . . .'

Ella didn't hear any more. She felt like Roy Scheider that time the camera zooms in on him when he first spots the shark in *Jaws*. Like an automaton, she turned to her new dive buddy, her face a mask of rigidity.

'Well, Ella,' said Julian, jocularly raising his teacup to her. 'Here's to the start of beautiful buddydom.'

*   *   *

He was the buddy from hell. He was a complete martinet underwater, bossing her around and refusing to let her take any initiative whatsoever. Instead of chilling and taking time out to explore their surroundings in a laid-back, leisurely manner, he insisted on swimming off like a NATO sub-marine, ploughing through forests of kelp without once stopping to investigate what intriguing creatures might inhabit this seascape. He navigated with ruthless efficiency, heading north, south, east and west like a male version of Lara Croft on speed. Any time Ella tried to slow down the proceedings he would hover directly in her line of vision with his arms folded and an expression of terminal boredom on his face under the mask.

He also kept making denigratory remarks in sign language about her buoyancy control. She still hadn't quite mastered dry-suit buoyancy, and every time he criticized her technique or demonstrated to her exactly how she should be venting air, she would find herself ascending uncontrollably, and in total confusion. *I'm up here, you idiot*, she felt like shouting to him the third time she disappeared, while he searched around for her ineffectually below. When he eventually found her, he actually had the temerity to practically manhandle her back down to the bottom.

When they finally surfaced, Julian was smirking. 'Well, Ella,' he said, as they inflated their jackets, 'you've still got a lot to learn about buoyancy control, haven't you? Maybe you should re-read that module in the manual. You see, what you're doing wrong is—'

Ella didn't want to hear any more. She put her snorkel in her mouth, stuck her face in the water, and started finning back to shore. Once there, she began taking off her gear.

'You should wait for me,' shouted Julian. He was floundering around in the shallows trying to pull off his fins. 'We should be helping each other to doff our equipment according to the buddy system.'

'Oh fuck off back to hell, Julian. Some buddy you were.' Ella dropped her weight-belt on the slipway, and pulled at the releases on her jacket.

'Oh! Excuse *me*, Ms Nesbit. I was only trying to help.' She was glad to see that he was continuing to flounder ineffectually.

'I'll help you out of that.' Ferdia was coming

down the slipway towards her. 'How was your dive?'

'Bloody awful,' she said, anger making her forthright. 'My buoyancy control was non-existent – and there's another thing.' She lowered her voice. 'Please, please, Ferdia – let me have another buddy this afternoon. I can't hack Julian.'

'I thought you'd be well matched.' Ferdia hefted the tank off her back and set it down beside her weight-belt. Relieved of all those excess pounds, she felt as if she was levitating. She looked up at him. Because he was further than her up the slipway, he appeared taller than ever.

'What on earth made you think that?' she asked.

'You're obviously very good friends.'

'What?'

'Well – that's the impression I got in the pub last night.'

'We're colleagues, that's all.' How could he think that she and Julian had *anything* in common? He'd obviously totally misjudged her. 'We work in the same studio.'

'So you're in the élite world of recording as well?'

Something about the amused tone in his voice made her bridle. There's bugger all élite about it, macho man, she wanted to say, but didn't. She needed to keep him on her side. 'Yeah,' she replied. 'You see, that's one of the reasons I don't think it's a good idea for me and Julian to be buddies. We work in such close proximity that we know each other too well. I think it's probably a good idea if we take a break from each other this weekend.'

Ferdia pondered. 'OK. Leave it with me.'

Julian was staggering up the slipway. 'Hey, man!' He tried to give Ferdia a high-five and then changed it into a kind of salute when he realized it wasn't going to be reciprocated. 'Great dive.'

'Speak for yourself,' muttered Ella. Under the tight-fitting neoprene hood Julian's face looked like a squashed bun. Realizing that hers probably did too, she hastily pulled her hood off.

'I understand Ella had some problems with her bouyancy,' remarked Ferdia.

'Yeah. She was all over the place, man!' Julian laughed, and started to do an impersonation of her flailing around underwater. Ella was not remotely amused. She also wished he'd stop saying 'man'. As far as she was concerned, the only people who could get away with high-fiving and saying 'man' were black.

'Look,' said Ferdia. 'I'm going to propose a change to the buddy teams. Ella could obviously do with some more tuition, so I'll go down with her this afternoon. You can buddy up with Alex, Julian.'

'Alex? Hey! When did he arrive?'

'Just this morning. He was too late for the first dive.'

'OK,' said Julian. 'That's cool with me. At least I won't have to keep worrying about where Ella's taken off to every five minutes.' And he started his flailing piss-take again.

'Ha ha, Julian.' Ella stomped off up the slipway in search of her sandwiches.

She spent the interval between dives sitting in the car going over the dry-suit chapter in her manual. Within minutes it had sent her to sleep and she drifted off into a dream that started off innocuously enough but became increasingly erotic. Now she was being clasped against some man's muscular torso, and her hair was streaming out behind her in the wind. She could feel her nipples rubbing against his bare chest, but she didn't have a clue who he was, and she didn't have the nerve to look up at his face. A name suddenly came into her mind. 'Dashiel?' she said tentatively, but when she finally plucked up the courage to look at him she found that it wasn't Dashiel, the hero of *Passion's Monument*, it was—

Someone was tapping on the driver's window.

'Ferdia?' she hazarded, groggily emerging from her dream.

'Yeah. Ready to get wet?'

'What?' The dive manual slithered to the floor.

'We're diving together this afternoon, remember?'

'Oh. Oh, yes. Right.' She stepped out of the Mercedes, feeling a bit ridiculous in her woolly bear. Ferdia had his dry-suit only half on so that he wouldn't overheat, the arms knotted loosely around his hips. He looked like something from a sword and sorcery flick. A thick, heavy-duty zip ran from hip to hip across his pelvis. She'd never seen a suit like it before.

'I've been searching for a suit with a fly opening for ages,' he said, when he saw her looking. 'They're difficult to find and they don't come cheap, but it's a real relief when you're doing repetitive dives not to have to get in and out of a suit every time you need to take a leak.'

'What about us girls?' asked Ella, stepping into the legs of her much less glamorous membrane garment.

'Yet another design fault,' he said, laughing down at her.

*   *   *

This dive was a revelation. She had never dreamed that Irish waters contained such wonderful stuff! Once Ferdia had successfully taught her how to manage her buoyancy, she was able to look around at leisure and see for herself all the exotica she'd missed during the earlier disastrous dive with Julian. The marine life wasn't as abundant as it had been in Jamaica, but what she saw was just as awe-inspiring. She remembered how she'd compared the Jamaican reefs to something by Lainey Keogh. That had been her Spring collection: this was her Autumn one. The terrain looked as if it had been scattered with gold dust. There were tattooed crabs, there were starfish ranging from the size of a dinner plate to the size of her smallest fingernail all tangled up in skeins of silk, there were jellyfish, translucent, and ethereal – and so sensuous to touch! He led her through pink algae like giant swansdown powder puffs, and Ella was reminded of her Caribbean mermaids. If the reefs she explored off that far-away tropical island had been the mer-queen's banqueting hall, then this was her boudoir!

She'd sneered at Julian when he'd used OTT adjectives like 'amazing' and 'astonishing' to describe tubeworms. Now she had to admit that he'd been right. The word 'tubeworm' itself was a totally off-putting misnomer. They should be called sea jewels, she thought, or sea fairies – something that did their dazzling beauty justice. Each individual home was a miniature angel's trumpet, while their colonies were the kind of confections you'd see in the window of a prize-winning florist's. Some of the worms had laid claim to an old rubber tyre, transforming it into a stunningly gorgeous iridescent wreath. Ella laughed out loud when a flick of Ferdia's finger sent the muppet-haired worms diving back into their shells, and laughed even more when she tried it for herself. It was just like seeing the lights on a Christmas tree going on and off she thought, as she swam around flicking her fingers at them like a crazed witch casting spells.

But what made her laugh more than anything were the scallops. When prodded by Ferdia they took off up into the water, snapping their shells open and shut over and over again like furious

302

animated false teeth, until they finally settled down on the seabed once more.

When she was able to stop laughing, she became aware that Ferdia was touching her lightly on the arm. She turned to him, and he pointed across a marine valley. On the other side, about ten metres away from them, she could just make out a dozen or so great, streamlined shapes. She turned back to him with alarm scrawled all over her face. He knew by her expression that she was asking if the creatures were sharks. He shook his head. Then he drew a smile across his face with his left index finger, and moved his right hand in an undulating, rhythmic fashion, the way a dolphin swims through the water.

Dolphins! Oh – heaven! *Dolphins!* Ella wanted to cry with happiness. She had never experienced such euphoria in her life as she did now, watching the school's graceful progress into the blue beyond. To judge by their comparative sizes there were about eight adults and three calves. Come back! Come back! she wailed inwardly. Surely they could sense the yearning that was emanating from her like ectoplasm? But the svelte outlines slowly disappeared into the distance like a receding dream.

She turned back to Ferdia, wonder in her eyes. He smiled and spread his hands in an attitude of regret, then indicated that she should follow him.

As they descended into a valley carpeted with billions upon billions of brittlefish – starfish whose filmy limbs floated around them like fronds – Ella realized that they'd gone quite deep. Her gauge read twenty-seven metres. She also saw that she'd used up rather a lot of air with all that laughing and oohing and aahing. She showed Ferdia the level on her gauge, and gave him a questioning look. He responded by signalling: *It's cool, relax. Everything's OK* with his right hand, and then: *Let's get ready to go up* with his left.

Wait, she told him. The legs of her suit had become filled with excess air, and she needed to perform the trick that would help her dump the stuff, otherwise she would make a thoroughly undignified and hazardous feet-first ascent. She tucked herself into a ball and quickly rolled over on to her back, feeling the air rush to the exhaust valve on her arm. Her legs dropped back on a level with the rest of her body, and she couldn't help feeling chuffed with herself for having executed the manoeuvre with such dexterity.

OK, she signalled, readying herself to fin upwards. Nothing happened. Maybe she was carrying too much weight? She depressed the inflator valve on the front of her suit a couple of times to give her buoyancy a boost, and tried harder, concentrating on using her thigh muscles to get her ascent going. It was no good. Something was holding her back. She descended a little, pushed herself off the bottom and made another effort to ascend – again without success.

Ella was no longer feeling chuffed with herself. Claustrophobia threatened, and she was starting to feel scared now. She signalled to Ferdia that she had a problem. As soon as he saw the expression on her face he signed to her to stop moving. *Take it easy*, he motioned with a hand. *Stay calm, everything's cool. Breathe slowly.* She tried to do as he advised, but she could hear her breath coming and going in a rush, very shakily. Ferdia checked the air level on her gauge again, and she saw his brow furrow a little under his mask. When he next looked at her, however, there was nothing but reassurance in his demeanour, nothing whatsoever to indicate that he was concerned. *Trust me*, said his eyes.

He moved round behind her, and in her peripheral vision she could see him withdraw his knife from the scabbard on his thigh. For a split second she felt a surge of pure blind panic. What the fuck was going on? Oh God oh God – she was in some grotesque nightmare, and she just wanted *out* of there! Ella lunged for her inflator valve with her left hand, and for the release on her weight-belt with her right. In a flash Ferdia had pre-empted her, grabbing both her hands with his free one before she could dump her weights. *No!* he signalled in no uncertain terms. *Trust me!* He hovered there, holding her wrists together, looking directly into her eyes, forcing her to think. She remembered the rule that was iterated on every single page of the dive manual that dealt with potential emergencies. Stay calm. *Stay calm.* What she had been about to do had been an act of lunacy. If she'd dumped her weight-belt she would have gone into a runaway

305

ascent straight to the surface, possibly rupturing her lungs in the process, and running a real risk of contracting the bends.

Ferdia waited until he was sure she was calmer, and then pointed to some fine lines of nylon that were undulating upwards. With an articulate hand he mimed a cutting motion, studying her expression closely to make sure she understood what he was going to do. He pointed to her tank and then showed her the knife again.

Oh God. She was entangled in fishing line. It must have happened when she'd done her backward roll. Jesus. Here they were, down deep, consuming air four times faster than they would on the surface, and Ferdia was going to have to waste precious minutes cutting her free of the nylon that had wound itself insidiously around her life support system. She showed him her gauge again. It was perilously low. In response, he showed her his own, letting her know that if they needed to share air, he had enough to spare. He had at least twice as much remaining as she did. How could that be? And then she remembered that, because he was the more experienced diver, he automatically conserved air by always, always breathing slowly.

OK. She'd do the same. She made a huge effort to control her breathing. Stay calm, she told herself. Breathe easy and stay calm. Ferdia had moved around behind her again and was working methodically at cutting away the fishing line. She fought hard against the impulse to try and help him by

306

attempting to wriggle free of the tenacious stuff. She knew that if she did that she ran the risk of making the entanglement even worse. So she just hung there in the water like a puppet, quite inert, trying to breathe evenly.

Ferdia's hands moved to her shoulders. He angled her around to face him and looked intently into her eyes. Was she OK? Yes, she signalled back. She was OK. He showed her the knife again, formed his thumb and forefinger into an eloquent O, and then stowed the blade back in its scabbard. She was free!

The relief she felt drenched her, and she took a long, shuddery gasp of air, realizing as she did so that breathing was becoming more difficult. Again Ferdia could tell by her face that something was wrong. *What's the problem?* he asked with his eyes. She responded with the 'out of air' signal, and Ferdia reached for her gauge. Then he took hold of his spare regulator and indicated that she was to ditch her own and insert the one he was holding out to her. *Trust me?* he asked, and Ella responded with the OK sign. Oh God. She wasn't sure if she *was* OK. She hadn't performed this exercise in sharing air since her training dives in Jamaica. Her hand was shaking as she took her own regulator out of her mouth, dumped it and then reached for Ferdia's spare. For a split second she felt terrifyingly vulnerable. Here she was, twenty-seven metres under, reaching out to the only person on the face of the planet who could help her. She grabbed the regulator, stuck it in her mouth, registered the taste of salt water, purged it, coughed a little into it, and then started to take great gulping breaths. After a few dodgy seconds, she settled down.

OK? his fingers asked her.

OK, replied Ella's.

Shall we go up? This time he signed with his thumb.

She found herself nodding her head. 'Yes please,' she said into her regulator in a very small voice.

Ferdia extended his forearm to her, and for a second Ella wondered what he was doing, offering her an arm as if he were escorting her into dinner . . . Of course! They would have to ascend in tandem, maintaining physical contact until they hit the surface, using the Roman handclasp.

It seemed to take for ever. She kept her eyes glued to Ferdia's; he only let his drop from hers when it was essential to consult his pressure gauge for their ascent rate. Five metres away from the surface he indicated that they had to perform the requisite safety stop for three minutes. Did she feel confident enough to do it? Was she settled? Would she rather go straight on up? Ella knew how important the safety stop was after deep dives, and she found herself automatically giving the OK signal, before realizing that yes, in fact, she *was* perfectly calm now. Her breathing was no longer ragged: it was slow and measured. She could hear it in her head – the rythmical in and out of it. Ferdia had a firm hold on her and his eyes were eloquent with reassurance. He looked at his watch, and then back at her. Two minutes, he signalled. Oh God. One minute. She started counting her breaths. This had to be the longest sixty seconds of her life.

Then at last came the longed-for signal to surface. They finned in tandem, up through the filtered rays of the tantalizing sunlight that was shimmering on the surface. Once they broke through the water Ferdia immediately inflated his jacket, and then he put his mouth to the valve on her BCD and blew into it, steadily, rhythmically. It took only three breaths to make her positively buoyant. 'OK?' he asked, regarding her closely. His eyes were narrowed against the sun and fringed with spiky lashes, and two drops of water were glistening on his earlobes like diamonds.

'OK,' she mumbled. She wanted to kiss him. This man had saved her life. She took the spare regulator out of her mouth. 'You saved my life,' she said.

'Save your breath,' he returned – a tad ungraciously, she thought. 'We've a fair way to swim. Stick your snorkel in your mouth and we'll fin back to shore.'

By the time they made the shore she was exhausted. Ferdia helped her off with her fins and tank and weight-belt and she flopped down on her back on the slipway.

'Thank you,' she said, when she could breathe again.

'No problem,' he said, shrugging out of his BCD and depositing it tank-side down on the ridged concrete. Then he started pulling off his black neoprene gloves, looking down at her with speculative eyes. 'Well. You learned two new facts of life this afternoon, Ella, my girl.'

'Yeah? What did I learn?'

'You learned to keep calm under pressure. And you learned that there's nothing like a near-death experience to give you an appetite. I am fucking starving after that one, I can tell you. I will demolish my bacon and cabbage this evening.'

Ella gave a shaky laugh. 'I don't know about the keeping calm under pressure bit. I got seriously spooked down there. I bet you were tempted to just stick that knife in me and leg it.'

He smiled. 'And leave you to the sharks? I'm too well-mannered to do that.' He pushed his damp dreadlocks back from his face, and then he stretched. The way he did it was easily as sexy as the way Jack stretched. In fact, she decided, it was sexier. 'It's a real plus that you managed that safety stop, Ella. It's like overcoming a psychological hurdle. You'll find that it'll do wonders for your confidence.'

'Well,' she said, pulling off her hood and shaking out her hair. 'I suppose that manual is pretty accurate when they talk about the adventure of scuba diving. I'm not sure about the fun element, though.'

He raised an eyebrow at her. 'Come on. You had a ball down there. You were like a little girl with a toy shop all to herself.'

She thought about it for a minute. Then: 'Yes,' she admitted. 'I suppose I was.' She sat up suddenly, wreathed in smiles. 'Those dolphins! Oh man! I got such a blast!' She realized that she was talking a bit like Julian did when he went into 'I am a super-cool dive god' mode, and she told herself to shut up. 'Have you ever dived with dolphins, Ferdia?'

'Oh, yeah. And with seals, too. They've an amazing sense of humour. They love to play games.'

'Oh!' She wanted to do that! She wanted to play underwater with dolphins and seals. Dolphins were the best endorphins she'd ever had. 'Maybe we'll see them again tomorrow?'

'With a bit of luck I might see them again tonight.'

'How come?'

'I've a night dive scheduled.'

For some reason she felt absurdly disappointed. 'Does that mean you won't be going to the pub?'

He gave her a scathing look. 'Damn right I'll be going to the pub. I'll just hit it a bit later than you guys, that's all. Do you really think I could stay away after what you put me through this afternoon?'

She realized as he smiled down at her that he was focusing on her mouth, and she automatically found herself parting her lips a little.

But he didn't kiss her. He just put out a finger and lightly indicated the area between her nose and

311

mouth. 'You might want to do something about that,' he said.

'About what?'

'You have diver's face.' And then he turned and strode up the slipway, swinging his tank by the valve.

Chapter Thirteen

When they got back to the hotel, Ella nabbed the bathroom. She had a quick shower, washed her hair and scrubbed her teeth. Back in her bedroom she lashed on body lotion and inspected her face in the mirror. Thank God her skin wasn't as blotchy as it had been, but the spot on her chin was still in evidence. She coloured it in with concealer, and then she stuck on some mascara, telling herself that if she was going to be going diving on a regular basis it might be advisable to invest in an eyelash tint from time to time. She combed Vaseline through her eyebrows, slicked a little gloss over her lips, and sprayed herself with Chanel 19.

On her way to the dining room she passed Ferdia, who was emerging from the bathroom with that ubiquitous towel around his waist. His hair was wet, and Ella found herself wondering how often dreadlocks needed washing. He smelt gloriously clean. Musky, masculine, with top notes of . . . vanilla. Ella was reminded of the soap she'd nicked in Jamaica.

'Oh, hi!' she said, trying to sound dead casual. It wasn't easy.

'Hi,' he said. 'I was just about to knock on your bedroom door.'

'Oh?' Oh God! Why? 'Why?' She hoped she didn't sound too disingenuous.

'I found this in the bathroom.' He held up a book. It was fucking fucking *Passion's Monument*. Oh *no*! 'It *is* yours, isn't it?' he asked. 'I couldn't help noticing that you were reading it in the bath last night.'

'Oh – yes. Well, it's not mine really, actually. It's um – the hotel's. I found it in my room.'

'I noticed that you were dozing under your dive manual this afternoon.' He smiled and started flicking through the pages. 'You certainly wouldn't have dropped off if you'd been reading this. This stuff's steamy enough to rouse the dead.' He ran his eyes down one of the pages and shook his head. 'Page sixty-nine's a real eye-opener. Must try it some time.' He handed her the book, raised an eyebrow at her, smiled and strolled off down the corridor. 'See you at dinner, vixen,' he threw over his shoulder.

Vixen? What was he on about? Ella staggered back into her room to jettison the odious book. Before she returned it to the shelf, however, she decided she had time before dinner to have a quick look at page sixty-nine. Dashiel and Victoria were at it again, this time starkers in a lake.

'Oh,' she gasped as his hands moved to her two firm, well separated breasts. She raised her loins to him, unable to resist the overwhelming desire to rub

314

her pleasure kernel against his muscular thighs.

'Hah!' he spat. 'This time we'll do it my way!'

She gasped. 'Which way is that?' she queried. 'You would not wish to harm me, Dashiel?'

'I harm you, vixen? Nay. My aim is merely to pleasure you.' He flipped her over and before she could gasp again he thrust—

Ella suddenly became aware that someone was tapping on the wall.

'Ella?' It was Ferdia's voice. 'Have you got to the bit where he flips her over yet?'

Ella felt her face flare up. 'D'you know something, Ferdia?' she said. 'I'm not very sure about you.'

'That's OK, vixen. You're not the only one.' She heard him laugh in the next-door room, and then he started humming something. A sudden image of him flashed across her mind's eye, standing naked mere feet away from her on the other side of the wall, towelling dry his dreadlocks. She had tried not to look at his physique too much earlier when he'd accosted her outside the bathroom, but it had been difficult not to. He had a wonderful, toned, muscular body – but he wasn't off-puttingly muscly the way some blokes were. Those kind of blokes kept in shape by working out: her gym was full of narcissistic types who didn't impress her at all with their pathetic posing and the way they ostentatiously clanked the weight-lifting equipment.

She doubted if Ferdia even knew what the inside

of a gym looked like. She reckoned it was sheer physical hard graft that kept him in prime nick, the way construction workers often were. There was something incredibly sexy about a guy who could look so good without working at it the way most other people had to. She knew she'd get flabby if she didn't exercise regularly. Hey! Maybe if she kept on diving she wouldn't need to go to the torture chamber that was her gym. Yet another incentive to carry on with her new hobby!

It wasn't the only incentive. She now knew with gobsmacking clarity that she fancied the arse off Ferdia, and would welcome any chance she could grab to see him again – even if it meant diving in that vile quarry. When had it happened, she wondered? There'd certainly been no *coup de foudre* to announce it. Had it kicked in today, maybe, when he'd saved her life? Or had the first seed been planted last night in bed, when she'd been subjected to the unmistakable evidence of his talent for 'pleasuring' women? Or had it been that time in Sheep's Head Bay when he'd told her that he loved her stockings and then wandered away whistling Beethoven's Seventh? No. Something told her that it went back earlier still. Something told her that she'd actually fancied him from that first night in the classroom when he'd told her that he loved the way she looped her L's, and that her infatuation had kicked in irreversibly when she'd witnessed his handling of the poor stray bitch he'd adopted. Something told her that she and Perdita had become smitten simultaneously. But while Perdita had made no secret of the fact, Ella had been in denial for months.

What was she to *do*? She sat down on the bed and chewed her lip, then got up again and checked out her eyebrows, plucking away a few hairs to make them look slantier. She started to think tactically. In the mirror her eyes went narrow with concentration. In the room next door, Ferdia was still humming.

Absent-mindedly Ella started to plait a hank of hair. She was reasonably certain that the stunning-looking woman who'd accosted the instructor in the pub last night was Philippa, the one who'd been at the receiving end of all the 'pleasuring' that had gone on later. Hah! If that was the case, then she, Ella, wasn't even a contender. That woman had been incredibly sexy. Elegant, too. Way too classy for a country pub. Hell's bells! Life was so bloody *unfair*! First there'd been Jack with his string of sophisticates, and now Ferdia with what was obviously a similar preference. What *was* it about classy women? How did you get to *be* classy?

Hang on. She started to drum her fingers lightly on the edge of the dressing table. This was interesting. After all, didn't she have a few classy trappings? Ferdia couldn't know that Patrick's nifty little Merc didn't belong to her. He imagined – like most people – that the recording business was glamorous. He assumed she had the kind of lifestyle that permitted her to go jet-setting off to Jamaica for dive holidays. He even thought she was the kind of dame that swanned around in silk kimonos in preference to more pedestrian high street shop dressing gowns. And Richie had told her the first time he met her that *he* thought she was a classy chick . . .

Maybe she could do it! Maybe she *could* do class . . . She looked at herself in the mirror and adopted the bored expression favoured by catwalk models. It looked stupid. Then she twisted her plait into a chignon like posh Philippa's. Nah . . . Nice try, but no cigar. She ran her fingers through her hair and shook it out. There was nothing much she could do about the way she looked, she decided, or even about the way she behaved. She was no actress. But she'd been handed some very convenient props on a plate. The posh car, the expensive holiday, the 'groovy' job just might have gone a little way towards establishing her somewhere in his consciousness as a gal with style and taste. She took a last look in the mirror. Her eyebrows looked lovely. Hell – it was a long shot. But it was a shot worth aiming for.

Suddenly she noticed the tacky paperback where it lay open on the dressing table, and a wave of despair washed over her. What gal with style and taste would read books like *Passion's* bloody *Monument*? Hah! What was she *doing*, pretending to be somebody she wasn't? She was crap at bluffing: it had always been her Achilles' heel in poker games. And this game involved a whole new set of rules: this game was dangerous because it involved playing with fire. Ella suspected she could get very badly burned. And then she remembered the way she'd felt when she'd watched Ferdia stretch earlier in the day on the slipway after he'd saved her life, when she'd wanted – really, really wanted – him to kiss her . . .

She took a deep breath, opened the door and walked down the stairs towards the dining room, preparing to light the fuse.

*   *   *

At dinner she sized up the seating arrangements. A long table had been set with a dozen or so places. She wasn't the first one there, but she was early enough to take her pick. One place still had unclaimed chairs on either side, so she sat down there.

She ordered seafood chowder to start, and a glass of wine, and was just about to ask what the catch of the day was when Julian walked into the dining room, followed by Ferdia, the *real* catch of the day. She stiffened, willing Julian to sit at the opposite end of the table, and willing Ferdia to sit down beside her. She sent him a smile that she hoped was inviting. Good. He'd seen her. Oh, wow – amazing! He was heading in her direction.

'The catch of the day is hake,' said the waitress.

'Sounds good,' said Julian, pulling out the chair beside her. He sat down and rubbed his hands together. 'I've one hell of an appetite. Always have after a day spent thirty metres under. How did you get on, Ella? Got a grip on your buoyancy control yet?' And he did that stupid jokey imitation of her for the third time that day.

Across the room she could see Ferdia registering Julian's presence beside her. He paused fractionally, obviously reviewing his seating plan, and then he turned and joined PJ at another table. Ella felt full of murderous rage. She wanted to grab a knife off the table and stick it in Julian's heart.

Instead: 'Hake would be lovely,' she said to the waitress. 'And maybe you could bring a banana for the ape who's just sat down beside me.'

'Hey! Lighten up, Ella,' said Julian, with an irritating laugh. 'Everyone else thinks my take-off of you is brilliant. I had people in stitches over it earlier. Someone even captured it on camera for posterity. It'll go down a bomb at the ActivMarine Christmas party.'

'At which you, no doubt, Julian, will be the life and soul,' returned Ella frostily.

'God – what's got into you? I thought, being a new girl, you'd have been grateful to me for joining you and not leaving you sitting there all by yourself like Ms Norma No Friends.'

Richie wandered into the dining room, looking a little green around the gills, but nowhere near as wretched as he'd looked that morning. 'Hello, ex-buddy,' he said, sliding into the chair on her left. 'How did things go for you today?'

'Good,' she said, ignoring Julian's smirk. 'It's a

shame you missed it. There's some amazing stuff down there.'

'I'll give it a lash tomorrow.'

'How are you feeling now, Rich?'

'Um. Better. Well, better enough to have something to eat, anyway.' He took a look at the menu. 'Chowder. Oh, Jesus, no.'

'I've ordered it, I'm afraid.'

'That's all right, if you don't mind me not looking at you while you eat it. I'll go for the consommé, I think. And the grilled chicken.'

'Fancy sharing some wine with me, Richie?' asked Julian. 'It's not much of a wine list, but there's a vaguely decent Chablis there.'

'Oh, God, no. Thanks, Julian – but no. I'm never touching alcohol again as long as I live.'

'There'll be a session in Sweeney's later,' said Julian. 'You can't miss out on that.'

'I'll go, for sure, but I'll stick to Ballygowan.'

'A session?' asked Ella. 'A musical session?'

'Yep.'

'Who's playing?'

'Nobody special,' said Julian. 'Just a shower of locals. They congregate there every Saturday night with fiddles and tin whistles and uilleann pipes.'

'Oh God. Uilleann pipes. I'm not sure my head could hack all that droning,' remarked Richie.

'Trad wouldn't be the same without the pipes, Richie,' Ella informed him.

'I know, I know. You can call me a philistine again if you like.'

321

'Did I call you a philistine once?'

'Yeah – that time I told you I was fed up with listening to all that classical shite you play in the car.'

She gave him a pitying look. 'I suppose you listen to nothing but house?'

'Hey! I'm not that sad. No – I like trad, and I don't mind the pipes when they're there as an accompaniment, but *solo* piping! I don't understand how anyone can enjoy that stuff.'

'How can you say that, Rich! You should take a listen to Paddy Moloney or Liam O'Flynn. Or Davy Spillane. They're amazing players!'

'How come you know all this, Ella?' he asked curiously. 'You never really struck me as the kind of gal who'd be into trad.'

'Ella's big into all kinds of music,' said Julian. 'She even plays. Or used to. Didn't you, Ella?'

'Yeah. I'm a musician *manqué*,' said Ella, shooting her colleague a resentful look. She didn't like being reminded of the fact.

'No shit. What instrument?'

'The violin.'

Just then Ella's chowder was set in front of her. Richie took one look, turned green, and clapped his hand over his mouth. 'Oh fuck,' he said, getting rapidly to his feet. 'Excuse me. I need to get out of here . . .' He turned and stumbled out of the dining room.

On the other side of the room, Ferdia looked up as his cousin fled past him. Then he rose from the table and ambled over to where Ella was sitting.

'Do you often have such an emetic effect on people?' he asked.

'Emetic?' This sounded good. Like a cross between 'kinetic' and 'electric'. She dimpled up at him.

Julian sniggered. 'Don't know what it means, do you? Emetic means to make someone get sick.'

'Of course I know what it means,' she lied. 'And for your information, Ferdia, it wasn't me who made Richie want to throw up. It was the unfortunate appearance of the chowder. Which –' she took an experimental taste '– is actually very good indeed.'

Ferdia sat down on the seat vacated by Richie. 'How is he?' he asked.

'In much better shape than he was this morning,' said Ella. 'But obviously still a bit queasy.'

'Will he be able to dive tomorrow, do you think?'

'If he's as good as his word and doesn't touch any alcohol tonight,' said Julian.

'Good. That takes care of all the buddy teams for tomorrow, then. Julian – you'll be diving with Alex again.'

Thank you, Ferdia, thank you! Ella wanted to say. Instead she said: 'And I'll be diving with you again, will I?'

'No. Now that Richie's OK you'll be diving with him.'

'Oh,' she said dully. She hoped he couldn't hear the disappointment in her voice. 'Have you a training group to supervise tomorrow?'

'No. I won't be around. Something's come up, and I need to get back to Dublin.'

No! Oh, no! He couldn't go! Not when she'd just realized she wanted him so desperately! Hell's teeth! What was she going to *do*?

'Are you heading back tonight?' asked Julian.

'No. I've a night dive to do, and I don't want to drive back in the dark. I'll hang around for the session in Sweeney's, and head off at the crack of dawn.'

At least he'd be around later. Nothing in the world could keep her away from that session this evening!

'I don't envy you your early start, after a session,' said Julian. 'Must be something urgent.'

'It is. I got a call to say that Perdita's sick. She's not able to feed her pups and she's very distressed.'

Ella's eyebrows furrowed. 'Oh no! How awful!'

'Yeah. She hates me going away. I don't know how she'll cope when I disappear for good.'

'Where are you off to, man?' She hardly heard Julian's question. She was too busy registering what Ferdia had just said. *Disappear for good . . .*

'I'm heading off around the world. Jamaica first.'

'Hey! Working the dive outfits?'

'If they'll have me.'

'You know they'll have you, Ferdia. With your credentials? You could work anywhere in the world you want.'

The waitress set an open bottle of Chablis in front

324

of Julian. 'It's customary to open it at the table,' he said.

'Sorry, sir.' The waitress shrugged and ambled off.

Julian heaved a heavy sigh. 'I suppose that's the provinces for you,' he said. 'Full of peasants. Knock back that plonk, Ella, and have some of this.' He poured himself a glassful. 'Ferdia? Will you join us for a glass?'

'No thanks. I've a dive to do.' He stood up from the table. 'Catch you later.'

'Yes,' said Ella automatically. 'See you in Sweeney's.'

He paused. 'You do know there's a session on there this evening?'

'Yes.' Something about his tone puzzled her. 'Why do you ask?'

'I just wouldn't have thought it was your scene, that's all. Enjoy your Chablis.' And he walked back to the table where the waitress was setting a plate piled with bacon and cabbage in front of his empty chair.

'Top bloke,' observed Julian, after a beat.

'Yeah.'

'Fancy him, do you?'

She looked Julian directly in the face. 'No,' she said, with emphasis. 'As if it's any business of yours.'

'I find that surprising, somehow. All the chicks seem to fall for him. Especially the bored married ones with wealthy husbands. Never underestimate the appeal of a bit of rough, Ella.' He stretched ostentatiously in his chair.

Aagh! So that was why Julian was going around talking in cool language and being blokeish! He was trying to impress! But *who* was he trying to impress? She and Jan were the only women diving this weekend. Maybe he had the hots for Jan? She doubted it, somehow. She didn't think she'd seen them exchange more than two words. Oh God. Could it be – was it possible that Julian Bollard had the hots for *her*? No, no – life couldn't be that grotesque . . .

Beside her he was droning on. God – if Richie thought the uilleann pipes were bad, he wanted to get a load of Julian in full flight. 'Yeah – I've seen some very classy broads indeed make idiots of themselves over Ferdia. You saw the one that was in the pub last night? She's married to local landed gentry. She's on the society page of *Individual* magazine every other month. But every time there's a dive weekend scheduled here in Lissamore she turns up and slums it in Sweeney's just so she can join Ferdia in bed later.'

So she was right! Ferdia MacDiarmada had a thing about class ass.

'I suppose it's a bit like being a rock star and being surrounded by groupies all the time.' Julian suddenly couldn't keep the resentment out of his voice. He was so obviously seething with jealousy that Ella intuited that the only reason he tried so hard to be chummy with Ferdia was to enhance his own credibility. Maybe he thought that some of the instructor's sex appeal would rub off on him if he high-fived him often enough.

She looked over to where Ferdia was sitting laughing with PJ, and started to do some more strategic thinking. So. He would be gone in the morning. He had a dive tonight. That gave her very little time to put her campaign into action. She'd just have to make sure she bumped into him in Sweeney's. That would be difficult if there was a session on. She knew from experience that men tended to get so wrapped up in the sexiness of the music and the whole session vibe that lovemaking was – paradoxically – sometimes the last thing on their minds. Hell's bells. If she wanted to end up in Ferdia MacDiarmada's bed tonight she was going to have to be very, very clever. Imagining what could be in store for her if she played her cards right provoked that half-enjoyable, half-unsettling feeling that the anticipation of good sex always gave her – that feeling as if a small animal somewhere in the pit of her stomach was curling itself up into a ball.

'You're looking very pensive, Ella,' remarked Julian. 'What are you thinking about?'

'Nitrogen narcosis,' she said.

*　　*　　*

Ella kept her fingers crossed that posh Philippa wouldn't be in the pub. She cased the joint as soon as she got through the door, and was glad to see that there was no sign of her. Maybe she was off at a hunt ball somewhere, or at a nobby dinner party. Ella pictured her sipping sherry, chatting to some chinless type, all the time pining for her bit of rough. She looked around to see if there were any other likely fillies who might be in competition with her for the attention of Ferdia, but she couldn't spot any contenders. There was an ostentatiously foxy girl sitting up at the bar wearing a belly top, but she was way too vulgar for his tastes.

Ella tried to take it easy on the Guinness, but it was hard because Richie kept putting pints in front of her. He tried to stick to water, but got bored with it very early on, and started experimenting with soft drinks. He even tried a Pirate's Punch. 'Sweet Jesus Christ!' he said, pushing the glass to the other side of the bar. 'This stuff is undiluted shite! It nearly made me throw up again.'

'I will hear no evil talked about Pirate's Punch,' said Ella. 'They paid for me to have the best holiday of my life.'

There was a palpable sense of anticipation in the crowd, as there always was in pubs on session nights. The place was even more jammed than it had been yesterday, and Ella was far too hot in her Ralph Lauren suede jacket. She slung it over the back of her chair, feeling quite glad that she could now show off the sexy little T-shirt she was wearing underneath.

She caught Richie looking. She wasn't wearing a

328

bra, and she knew that her miniature pink rosebuds must be pretty prominent. She'd got so used to her easy friendship with Richie that she'd almost forgotten that he was as susceptible as any man to the red-blooded male thing, and she remembered that she'd read somewhere that there was no such thing as a 100 per cent platonic relationship between a man and a woman.

'Will you – um – go back, do you think?' he said. 'To – um – to Jamaica?' Ella got the impression that he was trying too hard to make small talk.

'I hope to. My grandmother's getting married there in the autumn, and her affianced has offered to fly the family over for the wedding.'

The musicians were warming up now, and the atmosphere was tense with reined-in excitement.

'Jamaica's Ferdia's first stop.'

Of course it was! Maybe he *wasn't* about to disappear from her life for ever! Maybe there'd be a chance of running into him there . . . She knew she was clutching at straws, but at least she had *something* to be optimistic about. 'Oh, yeah,' she said, trying to sound casual. 'He mentioned something about travelling round the world. When's he off?'

'End of July.'

The crowd settled and a hush descended as a single tin whistle piped out the first notes of the evening. Ella recognized the tune immediately. It was 'Wallop the Spot', a rousing jig.

'How long's he going for?' Ella lowered her voice. It was considered very unclued-in to indulge in prolonged or loud chat during a session.

'Kinda indefinitely.' Richie had lowered his voice correspondingly.

'And he's guaranteed work in any dive outfit in the world?' The bodhrán joined the whistle, drumming out the heartbeat of the tune.

'Well, work's never guaranteed anywhere. But Ferdia shouldn't have much of a problem. He's one hell of a pro. And he's one of the luckier bastards who can afford to take it easy until the right job comes along.'

'Oh?' Ella was perplexed. 'Why do you say that?'

'He's a man of some means. He's selling his horse.' A fiddle – no, *two* fiddles took up the air. The decibel level of the music soared.

'His house?'

'No. His *horse*.'

'What?'

'He has a *mumble mumble mumble*.'

'A *what*?'

'*Mumble* beautiful thoroughbred. He's *mumble* to sell it. *Mumble* load of money. *Mumble mumble* thousands. *Mumble* surprised you hadn't heard. Everybody in *mumble* talking about the mega *mumble* farewell party he's *mumble* to throw.'

Richie had leaned in to her and was speaking directly into her ear, but it didn't make any difference. The uilleann pipes had blared in. There was no more point in trying to talk.

'*Mumble* clever bloke,' she heard vaguely. 'One

mumble mumble.' Or was it 'won *mumble mumble*'?

'What's the name of the horse?' She made one last-ditch attempt to worm a nugget of information out of him, wondering why she was asking such an irrelevant question when there were millions more important ones she wanted to ask.

He squinted at her, with blank enquiry in his eyes. He obviously hadn't heard her. There was no point in repeating the question. It was a stupid one, anyway. But Richie must have guessed correctly what she'd asked him. His answer coincided with a pause in the music. 'Black Jack,' he enunciated loudly, and then made a cringy face as people around them shot cross looks at him. He turned back to her, drawing an index finger across his mouth to indicate that he'd better zip his lip, then turned his attention to the remaining bars of 'Wallop the Spot'.

She was so flummoxed by what she'd just heard that she could barely concentrate on the session. She smiled vaguely and tapped her foot automatically, but her mind was awhirl, trying to make sense of what Richie had said. Ferdia owned a thoroughbred horse. It was worth thousands of pounds. He was a man of means. Of enough means, apparently, to be able to afford to bugger off around the world without having to bother too much about how he was going to subsidize himself.

Now things started to pan out! So Ferdia really *was* part of a jet set! Now his dalliance with Posh

Philippa made sense! A woman like her wouldn't 'slum it' with a 'bit of rough', as Julian had so charmingly put it.

Hell's bells! This was some revelation! Ella felt a bit like Jane must have done when she'd discovered that Tarzan, King of the Jungle was actually the Earl of Greystoke, or like Cathy in *Wuthering Heights* when Heathcliff reinvented himself as a man of wealth and taste, or like the heroine of *Passion's Monument* when she found that Dashiel (whom she had initially mistaken for a lowly groom) was in fact the heir to a shipping fortune . . .

Ella realized that she was watching the door now, more than she was watching the musicians. Although the playing was top-class, this was the worst session she'd ever had to sit through. She just sat there stewing, waiting for the door to the pub to open and for Ferdia to come through.

The band took their first break of the evening. A respectful path was being cleared through the crowd for the thirsty musicians, and just as a pint of Guinness was being put into the fiddle player's hand by the barman, Ferdia materialized beside him, as if by magic. She noticed that the foxy lady at the bar prinked visibly. Ella gazed at her dive god with parted lips and dewy eyes, unaware that Richie was looking at her sideways.

'Oh Christ,' he said. 'Not you as well.'

'What do you mean?' she asked, colouring slightly.

'It's called Dive God syndrome. And you've got it for my cousin.'

'No I haven't,' she replied, sounding snappier than she meant to, and regretting it immediately. She should just have admitted the truth, and then asked Richie all the questions about his intriguing cousin that she wanted to know the answers to.

Richie gave her a sceptical look, and she looked away. 'Well, if you're not suffering from Dive God syndrome,' he said, sounding resigned, 'you're definitely suffering from dehydration by now. You finished that pint ages ago. Let me get you another.'

Common sense told her that she'd had enough Guinness, and that she should follow Richie's example and remain teetotal for the rest of the evening, but now that Ferdia was finally here, she felt the need for a little more Dutch courage. 'Thanks, Richie,' she said, as he got to his feet and began to struggle his way up to the bar.

As soon as he was gone, she returned her attention to Ferdia. The fiddle player had greeted him with great gusto, slapping him on the back and smiling broadly. Ella supposed that all the ActivMarine instructors were familiar faces in Sweeney's. According to Richie they'd been coming here for years. She sat there rigidly, hands clasped in her lap, preparing herself to send him her best smile when he finally turned round, but he just carried on talking to his fiddler friend, and kept his back squarely to her. Then the pair of them picked up their pints and headed over to the other side of the room where the musicians were reconvening.

Stop it at once, she told herself briskly, as sick disappointment threatened. You are not to go all moony and pathetic with love, Ella Nesbit. You are a fighter. Desirée told you so. You will do your very best to hook Ferdia this evening, and if your very best doesn't work, then you will just have to try a lot harder.

She tried to think rationally. He hadn't seen her, after all. If he'd seen her, he might have come over and joined her, especially since the repellent Julian wasn't hanging around her like a miasma any more. Richie was heading towards her now, a pint of Guinness in one hand and a Coke in the other. He had just set the pint down when an extraordinary thing happened. The fiddler who'd greeted Ferdia handed him a fiddle and a bow with an air of casual camaraderie. Ferdia took the instrument from him, rose to his feet, ran an experimental bow across the strings and began deftly to tune up. Then, with a slow, sexy slur of an introduction, he launched into 'Tom Ward's Downfall'.

Ella sat there with her mouth hanging open. She simply could not believe what she was seeing. Ferdia MacDiarmada was *good*!

The initial long, teasing way he'd stroked the instrument with his bow accelerated almost immediately into more conventional jig time. The fingers of his left hand flew up and down the board of the instrument as fast as the wings of the hummingbirds she'd seen in Salamander Cove. His right hand manipulated the bow with assurance, the short light strokes coaxing a flurry of notes from the belly of the fiddle. The bodhrán joined him now, setting feet tapping involuntarily, then the whistle, another fiddle, the pipes – and they were off!

The crowd was in rollicking form – punctuating the rhythm of the jig with whoops and yells of enthusiasm and encouragement. Bodies swayed in time to the music: hands were clapping, heads nodding, fingers beating time on tabletops. Faces – most of them red with Guinness and heat and excitement – were smiling, foreheads were sweating, camaraderie mixed with the fug in the air. The music gained momentum, racing towards the finale. And now the spoons were in there, frantically stirring the frenzied crescendo that announced the final phrases.

After Ferdia's bow had slid across the string, producing that last, long note, there was a momentary silence. Then the crowd whooped again, and showed their appreciation with claps and cheers and whistles. The applause was well deserved. And hard-earned, thought Ella, noticing the sweat on Ferdia's forehead and the stains that were spreading under his arms.

The audience finally settled down, and Ella turned to Richie to voice her astonishment that this man was a master fiddler as well as a master diver. What a dark horse he was proving to be! But Richie was no longer there. She searched the room with her eyes until she saw him standing in the opposite corner, talking to his cousin. She felt washed with a kind of rapturous agony when Ferdia turned and looked directly at her with interested eyes, then beckoned her over. Ella rose and wove her way between the tables, drawn across the room as if there was a compass in her heart and Ferdia was north.

'Richie told me you play,' he said, when she drew level with him.

'I do.'

'Trad or classical?' enquired Ferdia.

'A bit of both.'

'Play a tune with us, then.' Ferdia indicated a fiddle case on the shabby vinyl banquette next to him. It was obviously a spare kept in reserve for any visiting players.

'What are you going to play next?'

Ferdia consulted with the geezer who'd handed him the fiddle earlier. '"Toss the Feathers,"' he said. 'Do you know it?'

This was perfect!

'Yes,' she said.

'Well,' said Ferdia. 'Let's see you rip this joint, Ella.' His eyes as he handed over the instrument had that incredibly flattering interest in them again, but there was a challenge there too. She felt that small animal in the pit of her stomach curl up again: but this time it curled up even tighter.

Ella took the fiddle. It was an old one – she could tell from the scars on the rosewood – but a little beaut, with a tiny flower wrought in mother-of-pearl on the tailpiece. She ran expert eyes over the board and then raised the body of the violin to her face, pressing the patinated wood against her cheek for an instant, checking it out like a cat before tucking it under her left arm. Then she took a couple of steps backwards, distancing herself a little from the rest of the group. She wanted to hold back for the first couple of bars until she felt comfortable with the other musicians' form.

One. Two. Three. Ferdia's bow swept over the strings, and the music surged out. Whistle and bodhrán were in like Flynn, and then it was the piper's turn to elbow out the melody. *One* two three, *four* five six; *one* two three, *four* five six . . .

Ella started to move. It was impossible not to. She began by swaying almost imperceptibly, but as the tune got livelier and the rhythm became more and more insistent, she found herself swaying with more abandon. Then the fiddle was tucked under her chin, her left hand was supporting the fingerboard and her right hand was poised at an elegant angle, ready to let the bow hit the strings. Still she waited. When the next opportunity to jump in – in between phrases – presented itself, she grabbed it with both hands.

Ferdia turned round. For a split second he appeared a bit fazed at seeing her there, and then a smile spread over his face as he watched her settle into the swing of things. She smiled back. It was a smile of pure delight, but there was complicity in

337

there too. They were smiling the kind of smile that is shared between two strangers who have suddenly discovered that they speak the same language.

Her head was held proudly as she wielded the bow to and fro, back and forth across the strings, and she felt possessed by a wonderful sense of power. This was the power of music: this was the power exerted by the tradition that had been handed down from generation to generation of Irish. Once upon a time, every household in the country would have had a fiddle, house sessions would have been commonplace, and the people would have played and danced – jigs and reels and hornpipes – till dawn. This was the finest, fastest, sexiest music in the world!

Ella shut her eyes and felt the notes she was creating flowing out of her, diving under the carved wooden bridge into the belly of the instrument, bouncing in a wave off the back, and flooding out through the carved arabesques. She smiled to herself as the music took hold of her and transported her effortlessly into the realm of embellishment. This was where you strutted your stuff and displayed your virtuosity! This was where you improvised and cut notes with deft fingers and showed off with triplets! She could tell by the vibe emanating from the other musicians that they were all having a blast; her smile grew broader and behind her closed lids her eyes grew dreamier as she lost herself in the magical maze of the music.

And when she returned, minutes later, Ferdia

was still watching her, with something new in his eyes that she had never seen there before. There was respect there, the respect that one peer feels for another. But there was more. There was also a gleam that was unmistakable, and it was the gleam of very, very strong sexual attraction. Oh God! Yes! She had hooked him! And she had done it without recourse to any wiles, any pretence, any stupid game-playing. She had done it all by herself! She bit her lip to stop her smile becoming any broader, and looked back at Ferdia with challenge in her eyes as she treated him to a sample of ornamentation that sounded effortless, but was actually breathtakingly elaborate. He responded by moving nearer, echoing the notes she'd just played to prove to her that he could match her. She tried something else. A whole sexy galaxy of starry notes fluttered out of the instrument. Again he answered her, with an extra dollop of embellishment to ice the musical cake.

But the next few phrases, the ones that anticipated the climax, were all hers. She outclassed him, playing without thinking. Now it was *she* who was in charge! The laughter and naked admiration in Ferdia's eyes told her that, and he stepped back and surrendered centre stage to her. Ella swayed, every fibre of her being responding to each note she teased out of the instrument she was holding in her arms like a lover, feeling every pulse of the bodhrán's beat, still looking at him, and still smiling. She felt as if the animal inside her – the one that had been wound taut as the G-string on her violin – had uncurled, stretched like a panther, and found its voice at last. The final exultant phrase came. And then the last drawn-out shuddering note as Ella drew her bow down over the singing strings and let her right arm drop to her side.

Again there was that electric moment of silence before the crowd rose to their feet and roared their appreciation. Ella stood there breathing hard, her face slicked with sweat, her hair sticking to her forehead. There were damp patches on her tight cotton T-shirt, and she was still wearing that blissed-out smile. She looked positively post-coital. As she lifted her jaw off the hard edge of the chin-rest and shook her hair back over her shoulders, she became aware of Ferdia advancing towards her. He stood for a moment, looking down at her, and then he bowed his head until it was on a level with hers. The crowd went even wilder, thinking he was going to kiss her. But his mouth went to her ear, not to her lips. For a second she was bewildered by the warm sound of his voice in her ear. She, too, had been preparing herself yet again for a kiss from him – a kiss that was simply the inevitable finale to what had just gone down on the makeshift stage in the dingy pub. And then she registered what he was saying.

His voice was trickling into her ear like the sweetest honey. Acacia blossom honey. Or dripping clover. 'I am going to make you come,' he was saying. 'And come. And come. I am going to make you come like you have never come before in your life, and I am going to do it now. Get your coat.'

Ella thought she was going to swoon. In a daze, she made her way through the crowd, too muzzy with sexual arousal to be able to acknowledge the compliments that came her way. She reached the chair where she'd left her suede jacket and slung it over her shoulders, not bothering with the sleeves.

Just as she and Ferdia reached the door of the pub, it swung open violently. A white-faced garda pushed his way into the room. 'Jesus, Ferdia – thank Christ you and the boys are here. Can you get kitted up ASAP? A car's gone off the road into the Salt Lake. We need divers down there now.'

Chapter Fourteen

Ella went back to the hotel room on her own. She sat wretchedly on her bed for a while, doing nothing, not even twisting her hair. She could think of nothing but Ferdia. It felt as if her mind had been vacuumed clean of everything and everyone else. Hell's bells – how could it be otherwise, after what had happened between them? How to *describe* what had happened between them? It had quite simply been the mother and father of a *coup de foudre*.

She sat and she sat, sneaking frequent looks at her watch and wondering how long it would take to locate the car that had gone into the lake – and the unfortunate individuals who might have gone in with it. She hoped they were OK, and this filled her with self-loathing, because she knew that the principal reason she wanted them to be OK was a supremely selfish one. She figured it was more likely that Ferdia would get away sooner if no-one was injured, and the sooner he got away, the sooner he would come looking for her . . .

Oh God – what a let-down this evening had turned out to be! What a total, utter bummer! If someone had written a recipe for disappointment, it couldn't come much more *haute cuisine* than this. She consulted her watch again. It had been one minute and thirty-five seconds since she'd last looked at it. It reminded her of how she felt in the gym every time she used the treadmill. She would program the machine for a twenty-minute run, and after running for what felt like at least eighteen of those minutes, she would access the timer. It would tell her she'd been running for nine, and that she had eleven more excruciating minutes to run. She *hated* that timer, and now she hated her watch even more.

She heard movement in the corridor outside and tensed, suddenly alert as an Indian scout. But the footsteps went on by, and her shoulders slumped again. Then she became aware of rowdy noises coming from the car park outside. She ran to the window and peered round the curtains. A bunch of divers returning from the pub.

She wondered how many divers had been enlisted for the search, and how long it was likely to take. It was a pointless exercise. She knew nothing about the conditions that would affect the dive and dictate its duration. They might be diving in shallow water, or deep. They might or might not have spare tanks and facilities for refilling them.

The only thing to do to take her mind off Ferdia was sleep, and she knew sleep was impossible because her mind was too full of him. It was Catch 22.

But hey! she thought. If he was to come to her tonight, she needed to be ready! Immediately she sprang into action, taking off all her clothes and spraying herself very, very sparingly with Chanel 19. She didn't want to overwhelm all those sex pheromones that her body had gone to such trouble to manufacture earlier. Then she got into bed, turned the light out, and lay there staring at the shadows on the ceiling.

She focused in on a particularly interesting shadow. It looked a bit like the shape of Ferdia's thigh with his dive-knife strapped on. Dear God, she was a sad bitch! Try and think of something else, Ella, she told herself. Something terminally boring that you know you really have to concentrate on, and it ends up making you fall asleep whether you want to or not. Like her dive manual. Maybe she should turn the light on again and re-read the Search and Recovery chapter? No. She'd been subjected to enough punishment tonight. Something scientific, then. That would be good and boring. Pheromones? What was the scientific theory behind them, for instance? The pheromones in our sweat activate our base animal instinct for . . . No. Pheromones were synonymous with sex, and she'd just end up re-running that outrageously sexy mental video of her and Ferdia playing 'Toss the Feathers' together, and fantasizing about what might have been.

Oh *God* this was awful! What had she done to deserve this torture? *When* would he come? And how should she behave when he did? Should she be brazen? Coy? Cool? Flirtatious?

There was a creaking noise in the corridor outside her room and she stiffened again – but it was just the ancient fabric of the hotel shifting in its sleep. Then she remembered how someone had once told her that if you shut your eyes, it makes your sense of hearing more acute. Maybe she should try it? Then she'd be able to hear him when he finally arrived back.

As soon as Ella shut her eyes, all the physical activity that had taken its toll on her body that day kicked in. Within seconds, she was fast asleep.

* * *

She was woken by the sound of knocking at the door. She sat up in bed instantly, hair cascading over her bare shoulders, trying to ignore the hammering of her heart. Then she drew the sheet up over her breasts, pushed her hair back from her face and quickly smoothed a forefinger over her eyebrows. 'Come in,' she said, breathlessly.

'Ella. Hi.'

Richie came through the door and she felt sick with disappointment. 'Richie! Hi!' she said, trying not to look too let down. 'What time is it?'

'Nine o'clock. I thought it was about time to wake you. We should be ready to rock and roll in half an hour, and I thought you'd want to get some breakfast first.'

'Oh. Oh – sure. I'll be down in ten minutes.'

As soon as the door closed behind him she raced to the bathroom, had the most perfunctory of showers and flung on her clothes. Why hadn't she set the alarm? She was so *stupid*! What had possessed her to think that Ferdia would steal into her room some time before dawn to wake her with a kiss? He would have been too knackered after trailing around doing underwater search and recovery half the night to even think about sex. She gave herself a quick spray with Chanel 19, and then flew down the stairs to the dining room.

She surveyed the room with eyes that hadn't completely woken up yet. There was no sign of Ferdia. Ella made her way over to where Richie was sitting in front of a plate of bacon and eggs. She was glad there was no-one else at the table.

'Well, Ms Nesbit. You are some mean fiddler. That was a splendid display of virtuosity last night.'

'Thanks,' she said briefly. She didn't mean to sound ungrateful, but her fiddle playing of the previous evening was the last thing on her mind. What *was* on her mind was the whereabouts of Richie's cousin. 'Um – what happened about the accident?'

'What accident?'

'You know – the car that went into the lake?'

'Oh – that was a complete disaster.'

'Oh God – was it?' Ella clamped her hand to her mouth, flooded with remorse and guilt. She'd only asked the question as a preamble to the detective

346

work she needed to do. 'Anyone – anyone dead?' I will hate myself for the rest of my life if there is, she thought.

'No. No-one dead, no-one injured.' Thank God for that. 'In fact, the whole exercise was a complete waste of time.'

Ella thought she didn't want to be hearing this. 'What do you mean, a waste of time?'

'The car belonged to a local man. He was exceedingly drunk. So drunk that he was beyond panic – and very lucky indeed that his window was rolled down. When he hit the water he simply opened the car door, made it to the surface and walked the rest of the way home.'

'*What?*' Ella was aghast. 'Well – why didn't someone tell the police that?'

'The person who'd witnessed the car going into the water didn't know the driver had got himself out. They were already on the phone to the police, apparently, when the drunk calmly emerged from the lake without a scratch on him. Some story, eh?'

Ella felt like asking for the drunk's address. She wanted to run off to his house and give him a good kick up the arse. 'So everyone got kitted up and spent a load of time doing search and recovery for nothing?'

'Yeah. Ferdia and PJ were at it for ages. The search and recovery garda divers were halfway down from Dublin before they got the word to turn round and go back home.'

'Would you like a cooked breakfast?' The waitress was at her side, pen poised over pad.

Ella's appetite had vanished into the ether. 'Um, no thanks. I'll just have toast and coffee, please.' She turned back to Richie. 'When did they hear that the driver was OK?'

'When he eventually reeled through the door of his house soaked to the skin. His wife put two and two together, and rang the Guards. She was in agonies of mortification, apparently. It's the second time he's gone into that lake.'

The wife might have been in agonies of mortification, but it could be nothing compared to what she'd been put through. She, Ella Nesbit, had been in agonies of sexual frustration all night because of the drunken bloody driver's deficiency in the IQ department.

'What a fucking fiasco!' she thundered.

Richie gave her a curious look, and she realized that her reaction had been totally out of proportion to the incident. She tried to look as if it had merely offended her civic-mindedness.

'I mean, just imagine dragging out the Dublin search and recovery team! What an irresponsible thing to do!'

'Yeah. It's also messed up the dive schedule, bigtime.'

'What do you mean?'

'Well, neither PJ nor Ferdia can dive today. Too big a build-up of residual nitrogen. I know Ferdia was disappearing anyway, but PJ was to supervise the trainees. He's re-jigging the buddy teams now.'

'Oh.' There was one last question Ella needed to ask before her entire world collapsed around her. 'Is Ferdia still around?' She made her voice as careless as she could.

'No. He needed to get back to Dublin and his pooch. Perdita has him wrapped round her little claw. Had you heard she's not well?'

'Yeah.'

'He'd planned to head off first thing this morning, but he hung around until he got a phone call telling him that the dog had taken another downturn. I think he'd have liked to have stayed here and chilled for a while. That dive last night must have been pretty gruelling.'

'When did he leave?'

'Just before you came down. We had breakfast together.'

She looked across the table at Ferdia's unfinished breakfast. The waitress had arrived with her coffee. She set it down in front of Ella, then started to clear away the used dishes. Ella co-operated by mechanically handing the woman Ferdia's side plate and coffee cup. The cup was still warm! Oh God! She wanted to weep for her witlessness. Why oh *why* hadn't she set the alarm?

'Hi.' PJ sat down in the chair so recently vacated by Ferdia. Ella wondered if the chair was still warm, as well as the cup, and wished she'd sat there instead. 'I expect you've heard that we've had to review the buddy teams, Ella?'

She nodded, and then a warning bell went off in her head. This was a *déjà vu* from yesterday. What had Ferdia said then? *We can re-jig the buddy teams and make sure nobody's left out* . . . And she'd ended up with Julian. 'I'm still diving with Richie, aren't I?' she asked quickly.

'Yes.'

Thank you, God.

'But you'll be diving as a buddy team of three.' He consulted a list. 'Let's see – who have I down here with you? Ah yes, Julian Bollard.'

Julian chose that moment to walk past their table.

'Hey, Julian – you're diving with us today!' announced Richie.

Ella felt like the dame in *The Scream* by Edward Munch. She didn't know what to do, but she would do whatever it took to avoid diving with Julian Bollard. She knew she'd gone white. She knew she looked shellshocked. And then she had a brainwave. Slowly she got to her feet and stood there swaying a little, holding onto her chair.

'Are you OK, Ella?' asked Richie curiously. 'You look a bit weird.'

'No, I'm not OK,' she said in a whispery voice. 'I feel very strange, I think – I – I think I'm going to—'

And then she fell over.

'Oh, God – she's fainted!'

There was a sound of chairs being pushed back from tables and low excited murmurings in the room.

'OK – just keep back, will you?' It was PJ's voice.

350

Ella heard footsteps coming toward her, and then someone was uncurling her legs from under her. She felt herself being lifted and repositioned on her back. 'OK' – PJ again, taking control: 'will you all head on down to the dive shop? You may as well start getting kitted up.'

'Is she going to be OK?'

'Sure she is. She'll recover in a minute.'

Ella felt like a total fraud lying there listening to all those concerned people shuffling out of the room. But she had found herself stuck between the biggest rock and the hardest place she had ever been, and there had been no other way out. The prospect of diving with Julian – especially after the agonizing bodyblow she'd just been struck – was simply insupportable.

'Ella? Ella?' PJ's voice was low and in her ear now. 'Wake up. Come on, Ella, wake up.'

She wasn't sure how long to maintain this masquerade. One minute? Two? She'd never fainted before. She tried to think of a film where someone had fainted, so that she could get her timing right, but nothing came to her.

Then she heard Julian's voice. 'Shouldn't we loosen her clothing?'

That was her cue. She opened her eyes and fluttered the lashes briefly, then looked up at PJ. 'What happened?' she said, trying to look confused.

'You fainted,' said PJ.

'Oh. Oh, God – how weird. How did that happen?'

'Beats me,' said PJ. 'The only person who's ever fainted on me before is Ferdia. I have to hold his hand every time he goes to the doctor for his jabs. Did you get some kind of emotional shock, maybe?'

'No,' she lied. She sat up. 'Maybe it's just some kind of physiological girl thing.'

'How do you feel now?' asked Richie.

'A bit woolly.'

'Will you be able for the dive?' he asked dubiously.

'I don't think that's a good idea,' said PJ.

Ella tried to look disappointed.

'I'm sorry, Ella, but it would be irresponsible of me to let you go. I think you should take things easy.' He helped her to her feet.

'Here. Have a glass of water,' said Richie helpfully. He sloshed water into a glass for her and held out a chair. 'Sit down.'

She saw Julian look at his watch, and she knew he was getting antsy about being late for his dive.

'Please don't let me hold you up,' she said with alacrity. She wanted to be shot of him ASAP. She wanted to be shot of all of them. She just wanted to be on her own.

'Are you sure?' Richie looked uncertain. 'I feel awful abandoning you like this.'

'No, no, please don't worry. I'm fine – really and truly I am. I'd just like to get back to Dublin.'

'Will you be OK to drive?' asked PJ.

'Yes, yes, honestly I will.' A thought struck her. 'But what about you, Rich? *I'm* the one who's abandoning *you*! How will you get back?'

'I'll take him. No problem.' Some manly-chin acting from Julian. 'We can dive-talk all the way home.'

Oh, poor Richie! Her heart bled for him and she felt horribly guilty, but she just had to save her own skin.

'I'll see you – when, then?' Richie bent down and kissed her on the cheek.

'I'll ring you.'

'And I'll see you in work tomorrow, Ella.' Ugh! Oh, God! Julian was actually making the 'OK' sign with his thumb and forefinger. The pair of them shambled away backwards, and then turned and left the dining room.

'Hey,' she could hear Julian saying as their voices receded. 'Did I ever tell you the story about the time I went diving in Ko Phi Phi? I'd been using a double bladder BCD, you know the . . .' And then thankfully she could hear no more.

'Can I get you anything?' PJ was looking at her with concerned eyes.

'No, thanks.' She gave him a mournful look, which he misinterpreted.

'Don't worry about missing out on your dives, Ella,' he reassured her. 'We can either send you a refund for the ones you missed, or we can offset it against another dive weekend. Which would you prefer?'

'Another dive weekend, please,' she said automatically. She wanted to see Ferdia again.

PJ ran his eyes down the list of ActivMarine

activities on his clipboard. 'OK. Let's see. Where are we now? End of May, June, July . . . The next one's scheduled for the first weekend in August.'

'But that's ages away! I thought they were supposed to be every month!'

'Someone messed up the booking. We had to be flexible, and that's the earliest the hotel can accommodate us. Hey! I've just realized that that's the weekend after Ferdia's farewell party. He'll be on his way to the Caribbean, lucky sod.' PJ scribbled something on an A4 sheet, and Ella felt even more like the dame in the Munch painting. 'You're down in heavy pencil, Ella, and your timing's excellent. You got the last place.'

No, no, no, PJ. Her timing was not excellent. It was totally, devastatingly, derangingly awful.

* * *

She arrived at work the next day to find that she had no sessions booked at all. Everyone who'd booked studio time had wanted to use the new facilities out the back. She sat mooning over the tropical fish screensaver on her computer, trying to dream up excuses for phoning ActivMarine. Maybe she could pretend she'd left something behind in her room at Lissamore, and was wondering if it had been handed over to one of the ActivMarine staff? What could she have left behind her? A book. On an impulse she picked up the phone and punched in the number. An answering machine picked up.

Hell, hell, hell*fire*. 'Um. Hi. It's Ella Nesbit here,' she said, after the tone. 'I just wondered if any of you guys might have been given a book that I left in my room in Lissamore.' She was suddenly flooded with the most appalling confusion. 'It's – um – it's not *Passion's Monument*, by the way,' she found herself saying to her own incredulous horror. 'It's – um – it's –' As she cast around desperately, her eyes fell on a CD Rom that Jack liked to play on the computer during idle moments of the day. It was called *Monster Truck Madness*. 'It's called *Monster Truck Madness*. Thanks a bunch talk to you soon bye.'

She put down the phone and banged her forehead against the console. Oh God. What had she just *done*? What were they going to *think* when they got that message? As if she hadn't made enough of an idiot of herself at Lissamore, forgetting to lock doors, banging on walls in the middle of the night, pretending to faint . . . She was damn sure Ferdia'd been filled in on that. 'Ella Nesbit *fainted*? What a wimp . . .'

Oh God, oh God. She wished someone would call 'cut' on this disaster movie that was her life. Could anything else happen to make it worse?

It could, and it did. The door opened and Julian walked in.

'Hey!' he said, throwing a brochure onto the console. It was folded over at a page featuring a blue sky resort in Belize. Happy-looking scuba divers were pictured larking about on a dive boat. 'I'm booking this today. Want to come?' he asked.

Ella lifted her head from the console. She looked down at the glossy images and almost said 'yes'. Instead she tried to look unimpressed. 'Ha, ha, Julian,' she said. Then she looked a bit closer and added: 'It's not one of the ActivMarine packages, is it?'

'No. Kuoni. I'm having to fork out a lot of money for it.'

Kuoni on his Nesbit & Noonan salary? Unlikely. Ella suspected that Julian's daddy was more likely to be financing this little junket.

'So? Are you interested?'

'What? Get real, Julian. Even if I had the money I wouldn't be allowed the time off. I've had my holiday, remember?'

'We've not been busy. And it doesn't look like we're going to be, to judge by the Nesbit & Noonan agenda. I'm sure Patrick could let his favourite niece spend ten days in dive heaven with his favourite sound engineer.'

He *was* joking. What a jolly little japer Julian was! What a killing sense of humour he had!

She looked up at him and raised an unimpressed eyebrow, but there was nothing jokey about the expression on his face. Oh my God, thought Ella. This was for real. Julian Bollard was asking her to go away on holiday with him! In an attempt to disguise the look of gobsmacked incredulity that she was sure was contorting her features, Ella looked back down at the brochure and turned the page.

'I know it's expensive.' Julian's voice drawled on.

She realized abruptly that she was looking at the price list, and in a panic she turned back to the previous page. Oh hell – she was putting out all the wrong signals! She must look as if she were genuinely considering going along. This was so awful it couldn't really be happening to her.

'I'd be prepared to subsidize you, Ella,' he continued. She looked up, aghast. Julian was smiling down at her. He reached out a hand and cocked a finger under her chin. 'I've always fancied you, gorgeous. You know that. I get off on our little bouts of sparring just as much as I know you do. And when I suspected that Ferdia MacDiarmada was trying to muscle in, I decided to pre-empt him.' He picked up the brochure and gazed at the glossy photographs of the luxury resort. 'Just picture it,' he said. 'You and me in Dive Holiday Heaven. What do you say, toots? Sorry,' he gave her a complicitous smile. 'I mean, buddy.'

Ella didn't know whether to laugh or cry. Instead she shook her head dumbly. 'No, Julian,' she said. 'I wouldn't dream of going with you. I can't think for a minute how you thought I would ever say yes.'

He looked perplexed, as if she was speaking a language he couldn't understand. 'But why not?' he said. 'Where's the problem?'

She could see she was going to have to be brutal. 'Because I don't *like* you enough to go away on holiday with you, Julian. That's why not.'

Julian looked perplexed for another moment or

two, and then his eyes went all narrow and his mouth set like a trap. 'Ah. *OK*, Ella,' he said with contrived nonchalance. 'That's your lookout. Ab-so-*lute*-ly. I'm glad we know where we stand now.' He rolled the holiday brochure into a kind of truncheon and slapped the palm of his left hand with it twice. Then he looked down at the console. 'You do realize your gains are set very high there, don't you?' He gave her an ominous look, before turning and striding out of the room.

Ella knew she should have laughed, but she didn't. She felt horrible, and it was all bloody Julian's fault. *He* had made her feel horrible. God! As if their relationship wasn't bad enough without him adding a new dimension of the grotesque to it. And it wasn't *just* horrible he'd made her feel, she realized, as she returned her attention to the exotic fish swimming across her computer screen. He'd made her feel uneasy.

*　　*　　*

Over the course of the day she had even more cause to feel uneasy. Her uncle was antsy about something, she could tell, and even easygoing Jack looked grim.

'What's wrong with you two?' she asked after work in the pub. 'You've both been really uptight for the past while.'

'Business worries, Ella,' said Patrick, pulling hard

on his Marlboro Light. 'Count yourself lucky you don't have 'em.'

'What's the problem?' asked Julian. 'Or is it confidential?'

'There's no point in keeping it confidential any more,' said Jack, sounding uncharacteristically fatalistic. 'It's staring us all in the face at this stage. We've overstretched ourselves.'

'What do you mean?' Ella leaned forward in her chair.

'The new studio. It's not making money back fast enough. You must have noticed that there's been a falling off in bookings lately. And the building work next door has messed us up bigtime.'

Uh-oh, thought Ella, casting her mind back over the past few weeks. Everyone in the business knew that recording studios often had lean times when bookings weren't coming fast and furious. It was usually written off as a seasonal thing. But this lull had gone on longer than usual. Things should have started to liven up a little at this time of the year. Agencies needed to grab studio time before everyone disappeared on summer holidays.

'But why should there be a fall-off?' she asked. 'That new studio's so *sexy*! Everyone who uses it says how hi-tech and gorgeous it is.'

'It's not hi-tech enough, unfortunately,' said Patrick darkly. 'We just missed the boat. On Line Studios is having a shit-hot digital desk installed. It's the one facility everyone's raring to use. Our regular clients are starting to defect, and I suspect that they may not come back, even when the construction work next door's finally finished.'

'Oh.' Ella's brow furrowed as she tried to think of some solution to the problem. 'Well – couldn't we just install a digital desk of our own? And the building work's due to finish soon. The agencies are bound to come back then.'

Her uncle gave her a pitying look. 'Come on, Ella. We already pushed the boat out with that new Audiofile. We're in no position to crawl to the bank looking for extra money for more equipment. We're going to be crawling to them soon enough anyway. Crawling major league,' he added, gloomily.

She felt a sudden rush of alarm. 'Oh, God, Patrick. Are things really that bad?'

'Fraid so. We need someone to bail us out fast if we're not going to go under. I'm sorry to have to tell you this, sweetheart, but your job's on the line. And yours, too, Julian.' Patrick ground out the stub of his cigarette and immediately lit up another. Things must be really bad, thought Ella. Her uncle usually smoked a maximum of ten cigarettes a day. 'However,' he continued – and Ella knew he was trying to inject his voice with a reassuring note – 'you're both so good at what you do that I can't see you having any problems finding work elsewhere. You two babies will land on your feet.'

Ella felt awful. 'Hell, Patrick,' she said. 'I might be able to get work elsewhere, but what about you? It's your *business*!'

He shrugged. 'I've always wanted to downshift, you know that. And the kids are nearly grown, so I won't have them to worry about soon. It's going to be tougher on Jack.'

'Oh? Why's that?' Ella turned to her other boss and noticed for the first time how exhausted he looked. There were lines she hadn't noticed before etched around his mouth and eyes. She felt even more wretched that she hadn't sussed the situation ages ago. 'Oh, God – I don't mean to sound unsympathetic, Jack, believe me, but at least you've no family depending on you.'

'I will have soon,' he returned, giving her a tired smile. 'Angie's pregnant.'

'What?' Ella was taken aback for a split second before copping herself on. 'I mean – that's wonderful! Congratulations – you clever man!' She threw her arms around him, and as she did so she realized that once upon a time she wouldn't have been able to make the slightest physical contact with him without feeling a sexual *frisson*. Now here she was, clutched in his embrace, feeling – well, *happy* for him. If he'd made this announcement last week she would have been completely gutted by this revelation that he was now lost to her for ever.

'Cleverness didn't have a lot to do with it, sweetheart,' he replied, giving her a wry smile.

'Oh – you know what I mean,' she said, kissing his cheek and then sitting back. 'Tell me – how does Angie feel? Is she doing all right?'

'She's sick as a parrot every morning. But pleased as – well – punch.'

'Parrot. Punch. Parrot's punch,' she said, bemusedly. 'That rings a bell somewhere.'

'It's actually Pirate's Punch,' said Patrick. 'They paid for your junket in the Caribbean, remember?'

'And you'll be amused to learn that Angie's become addicted to it since she got pregnant.' Jack gave another tired smile. 'That punch is what she craves most after marshmallows.'

'Pirate's *Punch*! Oh – gross! She never used to be able to stomach the stuff.'

'It's strange but true. I spend my Saturdays trailing around the supermarket pushing a trolley piled high with crates of Pirate's Punch and giant-sized packets of marshmallows.'

'When do you have to let the bank know?'

It was Julian's Dun Laoghaire drawl, and it was the first time he'd spoken for ages. Everyone turned to look at him. He was sitting back in his chair, outwardly relaxed, but with a strangely intense, watchful glitter in his eyes.

'You mean about our financial problems?' queried Patrick.

'Yes.'

'I've a suspicion they already know that everything in the Nesbit & Noonan garden is far from rosy.' Patrick sighed heavily and reached for his pack of cigarettes. 'Shit. I'm out of them. Be a doll and run up to the bar for change for the machine, Ella. And order another round while you're at it.

I'm out to get slaughtered tonight.' He handed her a crumpled twenty.

Ella got to her feet and started to negotiate her way towards the counter, but before she'd gone two paces something made her stop dead.

'What if the name of the garden changed?' Julian was asking the question. Ella turned around. There was something smugly suggestive about his tone that she didn't like.

'What do you mean?' Patrick was rubbing a bleary eye with a forefinger.

'What if the garden known as Nesbit & Noonan became known as Nesbit, Noonan & Bollard? That might make the bank look on it as a rosier prospect.'

A silence fell. Patrick's finger froze mid-rub. Then he leaned forward and automatically reached for a cigarette, forgetting that he was out of them. 'I'm not quite with you, Julian,' he said. 'You're suggesting, are you, that – er – that we take you on board as a business partner?'

'Well, not me, strictly speaking. I mean my father. He's been looking around for a new business to invest money in. And he knows I'm keen on setting up on my own one day. What better experience for me than to be involved more directly in the day to day running of a recording studio?'

Oh God. Ella was gazing at Julian with an expression of sick dismay. She transferred her gaze to her uncle's face and started to send him urgent messages by thought transmission. No, Patrick. Please say no. Oh, God – say no! Things can't be so bad that you'd consider taking Julian *Bollard* on as a business partner! No, no, no, no, no, no, *no* . . .

Patrick was tapping his empty cigarette packet on the table. He was looking ominously thoughtful. 'Well, Julian. That's a very interesting proposition.' He stopped tapping and looked directly across the table at his prospective new partner. 'When do you think you could sound your father out as to whether he'd be interested?'

'Tonight,' said Julian without hesitation. 'And if you can come up with an attractive package for him tomorrow I'd be prepared to bet that he could give you a definite answer by the end of the week.' He leaned forward and put his elbows on the table. 'I'll help sell you as hard as I can, Patrick. It's in my interest to do so. I'll back you to the hilt.'

Patrick drew in a deep breath. 'Hell,' he said. Then he exhaled loudly, and with evident relief. 'Sure. Fire ahead and run it by him. If he agrees, then we're off the hook.' Patrick was smiling for the first time that evening. 'I really appreciate this, Julian. I owe you.'

Julian's expression was horrifically smug as he nodded acknowledgement that, yes, Patrick owed him. Then he looked up at Ella and did something even more horrific. He actually winked at her and *smirked.*

Ella turned and reeled towards the bar, still howling *Nooooooo!* inwardly. Oh God – how fucking, *fucking* awful. Her life was not going to be worth living if Julian Bollard's name was added to the Nesbit & Noonan sign above the studio door. And to the logo on the letterhead. And to the cards that she slid into those dinky little DAT boxes every day. He would make her life unbearable. He'd call her 'toots' and she wouldn't even be able to tell him to fuck off because, to all intents and purposes, he'd be her boss. She leaned her elbows on the bar and then she leaned her chin in her hands, wanting to cry.

'Evening, Ella,' said the barman amiably. 'Another round for the corner table?' He looked at her a little closer. 'Hey – what's the matter with you? You look white as a sheet.'

'Oh. I just need a drink. Badly.' She caught a glimpse of her reflection in the mirror behind the bar. She looked utterly shell-shocked. 'Um. Let's see. Three pints of Guinness please. And a Coors Light. Oh – and change for the cigarette machine.'

The barman looked puzzled as he handed over the change. 'Didn't know you smoked, Ella,' he remarked.

'I don't,' she answered. 'But I'm thinking of starting.'

* * *

When she got home there were two messages on her answering machine. One was just spooky heavy breathing. Could it be Julian? The unwelcome thought skittered through her head, and she erased the 'message' immediately. The second one was delivered in Ferdia's Galway accent. He sounded amused. 'Hello, Ella Nesbit. Sorry to disappoint you, but no book called *Monster Truck Madness* was handed over to anyone here. I suggest you phone the hotel and ask them to post it on to you. You never know – if you ask nicely, they might even throw in *Passion's Monument*. Hope to see you on a dive some time soon.'

Oh God, oh God, oh God. She would never have the nerve to book a dive now, not after making such a prize eejit of herself. She wanted to laugh out loud – very hollowly indeed – when she thought about how she'd planned to pull the wool over Ferdia's eyes and pass herself off as a classy dame. *Passion's Monument* had been bad enough, but *Monster Truck Madness*? *Ow!* Ella cursed herself for not having hit on something by Proust instead. She was just about to erase the message when something made her press 'play' again, just in case she'd missed something.

'Hope to see you on a dive some time soon . . .' No. That was definitely the end of the message. There was no reference to the musical foreplay they'd indulged in on Saturday night, no suggestion that they might take up where they'd left off, no reiteration of his promise to make her come like she'd never come before . . .

She hit the 'off' button and slumped back in the sofa. Hell's bells – what was she going to *do* with her life? She and Ferdia would never get it together before he went off round the world in July. And if

Julian's father came to the rescue and hauled Nesbit & Noonan out of their financial quagmire she might as well resign. She would not be able to bear having Julian Bollard lord it over her.

She went to bed that night thinking that her life sucked.

* * *

Julian's father did come to the rescue. He did it very quickly and very efficiently. The sign above the studio door was changed to Nesbit, Noonan & Bollard. Alphabetically speaking it should have read Bollard, Nesbit & Noonan, but Julian was careful to defer to his new partners' seniority. He still needed Patrick and Jack enough to brown-nose them. His attitude to Ella, by contrast, became one of total condescension whenever the other two weren't around. He made disparaging comments about her work, and needled her constantly. He poached some of her favourite clients by taking them out to restaurants that she could never afford in a million years, and he made sure he was booked in on any of the recording sessions that involved film stars. He hogged the new studio and made sure that most of Ella's work was confined to the old studio in the basement, which had definitely reached its best-before date compared to the gleaming new joint out the back.

Business picked up again once the heavy work in the building next door had been completed, and

Ella was kept busy. A series of half-hour television documentaries had been booked in to be dubbed, and Ella spent a week in July mixing sound effects, voice-overs and music. By the end of the stint she was seriously knackered. For some reason she hadn't been sleeping well, and her concentration was dodgy. At around nine o'clock on the evening she finished work on the series, her first priority was to get to the pub. She'd arranged to meet some of the staff from a nearby studio there. Their receptionist was getting married, and a serious hen night had been organized, kicking off at eight o'clock in Daly's. Ella had brought her party dress into work – the same little slip dress she'd worn to Jack's fortieth. As she struggled into it in the Nesbit & Noonan loo (Uh-oh. Of course she meant the Nesbit, Noonan & *Bollard* loo, as everyone was very careful to call it these days), she suddenly remembered that, in her hurry to get out of the studio, she'd forgotten to back up the project on the Audiofile. *Shit*, she thought, banging her forehead with a fist. She was going to be seriously late for her hen night. Quickly she tied the thongs on her sandals and ran into reception to retrieve the keys to her studio. Julian was there, scribbling something down in the diary.

'Very nice,' he said, when he got a load of what she was wearing. She hated the way his eyes roamed over her body. 'Off clubbing, are we?'

'Yeah,' she said. 'But I've to back up the project first. I bloody forgot.'

'I'll do it for you,' he offered. Ella almost did a double-take at his uncharacteristic helpfulness. 'I've to hang around here for a while. I arranged to meet someone in the pub at nine-thirty, so I've half an hour to spare.'

'Oh – would you, Julian? I'd really appreciate that. I'm running late.'

'It's no problem.'

'You're a star!' Desperation made her effusive. 'I'll buy you a drink later.' She flashed him the best smile she could muster and swung through the door.

Two hours later she was feeling no pain. Her tiredness was forgotten as she merrily drained another pint of Guinness in the pub. It was to be their last drink before they hit the Kitchen. As she slid her arms into her shrug, she spotted Julian making his way towards the bar. 'Hi!' she called, shimmying over to him. 'Did you back that up for me?'

'Yeah. It's sorted.'

'Brilliant. Thanks, Julian.' She signalled to the barman. 'A Coors Light for this man, please.' She hopped up on a barstool that someone had just vacated and started to rummage in her bag for money. When she finally located her purse and looked up again, Julian's gaze was focused on the expanse of her thigh that had been revealed when she'd climbed onto the barstool. She pulled the hem of her dress back down over her lace-top.

Julian gave her an unpleasant smile and ran his

tongue over his lips. 'I love the stockings,' he said.

Ugh! Ella quickly handed money over to the bartender. She didn't bother waiting for the small amount of change that was due – she just wanted to get out of there.

'See you on Monday, Ella,' Julian threw at her departing back. It sounded like a threat, and the bubble of Ella's buoyancy was punctured, suddenly. Fuck him, she thought, feeling tired again. Yes, she would see him on Monday. And on Tuesday, and on Wednesday, Thursday and Friday. She'd see him every bloody day of her working life until he buggered off and set up somewhere on his own, and they could take the hateful Bollard name off the logo at last. She fought her way through the crowded pub towards where her gaggle of girlfriends were getting ready to leave.

'Ella! Hi!' It was Angie, looking radiant and only just discernibly pregnant. Jack had a protective arm around her shoulder. 'Off clubbing?'

'Yeah,' said Ella.

'You don't sound very keen.' Jack raised an eyebrow at her.

'I was until five minutes ago. I was full of endorphins then.'

'What happened to them?' asked Angie.

'He –' Ella nodded her head in the direction of the bar where Julian was lounging, boring yet another sound engineer – 'hijacked them.'

'Not fair. You shouldn't allow anyone to hijack

your endorphins, Ella,' reprimanded Jack. 'That's one of the first rules of having fun.'

'He's always doing it,' returned Ella gloomily.

Angie smiled at her. 'I know a good way of getting them back,' she said.

'Oh? How?'

'Listening to someone showering you with compliments.'

Ella gave her a sceptical look. 'Convince me, then, why don't you?'

'OK. Here goes.' Angie took a deep breath and launched into laudatory mode. 'Wow – Ella! You are looking totally amazing! Look at your hair, all glossy and gorgeous like something out of a shampoo commercial! And where did you get that lipstick? The colour really suits you!' Angie leaned forward and inhaled. 'Let me guess. Chanel 19? How did the copy for that use to go? Witty, confident, *devastatingly* feminine . . . Come on, Jack – join in!'

'Witty, confident, devastatingly feminine?' he echoed. 'You to a T, Ella Nesbit.'

He reached for her hand and kissed it, and Ella found herself smiling.

'See? It's working! More, Jack!' urged Angie.

'Wow! That dress! It's *incredibly* sexy, Ella . . .' Jack let his eyes wander down her body, but this time she didn't feel icky. 'Mm-hm. Those heels – they make your legs look *so* elegant! And hey! Something tells me you're wearing lace-tops. Show me!'

371

Laughing, Ella pulled up the hem of her dress and gave him a provocative flash of stocking top. She was rewarded with an appreciative leer, and the endorphins started to kick back in. Life was weird, really, she thought. How come a man like Jack could make her feel good by ogling her legs, and a man like Julian just made her feel cheap and nasty?

'Oh, Ella!' Jack was panegyric. 'I *love* the stockings!'

The line Julian had used earlier. But someone else had once come out with that line, she remembered. *I love the stockings* . . . It had been Ferdia.

For some time now she had been mentally counting down the weeks until his departure date. Now she was counting down the days.

* * *

On Monday morning she sat down in front of the computer with a big mug of coffee and a doughnut and logged on. Friday's work would be backed up on exabyte tape number 247, she was told. She accessed the exabyte. It took ten minutes to perform the search. There was nothing on the tape. She bit her lip. OK. This had happened before. The stuff had to be on *one* of the exabytes that had been backed up on Friday. It must be on 246. She accessed 246. Ten minutes later it found a commercial for Esat Digifone. 245. It had to be on 245. She was panicking now. Her coffee had gone cold; her doughnut was only half eaten. She felt sweat break out under her armpits. There was a corporate narrative for a multinational conglomerate on tape 245. Oh fuck. She started to trawl through more of Friday's stuff, and then the phone went.

It was Georgia, the receptionist. 'There's a courier here for the Irish flora and fauna documentaries,' she said cheerfully. 'Can you drop in the DAT?'

Ella cleared her throat, but the voice that came out still sounded croaky. 'I'm afraid there's been a problem. I can't locate the tape that Friday's stuff should be on. Could you ask Patrick to come down here?'

He came down with a face like thunder. 'What the fuck has happened?' he asked.

'There's nothing on the exabyte,' she said piteously. 'Julian must have punched in the wrong number.'

'What do you mean *Julian* punched in the wrong number?'

'I was in a hurry to get out of here on Friday night. Julian volunteered to back up my stuff for me. He obviously screwed up.'

Patrick crossed his arms and stood looking down at her. She felt as small as a flea. 'Julian did not screw up,' he said. '*You* screwed up, Ella. You can't go passing the buck here. It was your responsibility to back up that tape and nobody else's. You have dropped me in the shit. Tell me what you're going to do.'

'Go back through the tapes?'

'Ella, if Julian punched in a wrong number as you suggested, you could have to go back through 247 tapes. At ten minutes minimum per tape, that's going to take – how long? Do some mental arithmetic for me.'

'Two thousand four hundred and seventy minutes,' she said in a very small voice.

'OK. How many hours is that?'

'About forty?' she said, in an even smaller voice.

'Forty, minimum,' said Patrick. She had never seen her uncle look so angry. 'I suggest that it would be quicker starting Friday's job from scratch.' He looked at his watch. 'You can't start now because you've a client due in at ten. You're going to have to work through lunch, and you're going to have to stay on working this evening until you drop. And you're going to have to work lunchtimes and evenings every day this week until the stuff's restored.' Patrick turned and walked away. At the door he turned. 'It goes without saying that you won't be getting overtime.'

Ella put her head in her hands. She wanted to weep. She wanted to scream. If she thought last week was tough, this week was going to be a killer. And it was all fucking Julian's fault. She was filled with blinding rage. She reached for the phone and punched in his extension number with furious fingers. 'Julian?' she said when he picked up. 'Do you know what you are? You are a fucking, fucking bastard.'

'Oh, hello, Ella,' came the smooth rejoinder.

'What a pleasant salutation to start the week with.'

'Tell me what exabyte number you punched my job in on Friday.'

'Mmm. Let's see. 247, wasn't it?'

'No, Julian. It's not on 247. And it's not on 246 or 245 or 244.'

'Oh dearie me,' said Julian.

'You did it deliberately, didn't you?'

'Did what deliberately?' His tone was suavely disingenuous.

'You deliberately punched in the wrong exabyte number, didn't you?'

'Ella, you may recall that you reeled exhausted out of the studio on Friday night, leaving me to finish your work for you. Did you ever stop to think that I might be as knackered as you? It's very easy to make a mistake at the end of a busy working week.'

'You don't fool me, Julian. I know you did it deliberately.'

'El-*la*,' he drawled, elongating the syllables of her name. 'Why would I do such an unprofessional thing?'

'To get your own back.'

'To get my own back for what?'

'For me telling you I didn't like you enough to go away on holiday with you.'

He gave an unpleasant laugh down the line. 'Don't flatter yourself, Ella Nesbit. There are hundreds of girls a lot better looking and more charming than you who would love to come away on holiday with me. I only asked you because I needed a dive buddy.'

'D'you know something, Julian? You are a fucking bastard. You have landed me in the deepest shit I've ever been in.'

'If I'm a fucking bastard, Ella,' he hissed, 'you are a fucking bitch. And I'll tell you something else for nothing. It never pays to speak to the boss like a fishwife.'

She put the phone down, white-faced and shaking with anger. The man was making her life intolerable.

'Ella? Are you all right?'

She turned to see Angie standing in the doorway.

'Oh – Angie! What am I going to do? Everything's going wrong in my life! I *hate* Julian Bollard!'

Angie shut the door and moved swiftly to an adjacent chair. 'What's happened?'

Almost inarticulate with rage, Ella filled her in on what had just gone down.

'Oh, Ella,' said Angie when she'd finished her stream of invective. 'You mustn't allow him to do this to you. You mustn't allow him to best you. You know that at the end of the day you're an infinitely more gifted sound engineer than he is. That's why I always book my sessions with you. You're a *creative*, Ella. Julian's a mere technician.' She invested the word 'technician' with utter contempt.

Ella managed a weak smile. 'Thanks, Angie. You're a total doll. Sorry for letting rip like that. It's just that the bastard really got to me this time.'

'Don't let him.' Angie gave her a catlike smile. 'Shall I tell you the best way to get back at him?'

'Oh yes! Please do!'

'Be happy.'

'Be *happy*?'

'Yes. Pretend he hasn't fazed you in the slightest. Act as if you haven't a care in the world. Smile, laugh, sing. He won't be able to handle that. But if you go around glowering the whole time, Ella, he'll know he's won.'

Ella contemplated this tactic. 'Oh, God, Angie. It'll be tough . . .'

'It'll be worth it. Believe me.'

*   *   *

It *was* worth it. The more she behaved like some sunny heroine in an old Disney movie, the less Julian liked it, and the blacker his mood became. But, as she had predicted, it *was* tough. Smiling at Julian Bollard was the most difficult thing she'd ever had to do. It made that aborted dive in Sheep's Head Bay seem like a halcyon day.

377

Chapter Fifteen

Around nine o'clock one evening later in the week, her phone rang. She allowed the answering machine to pick up. She'd been doing this a lot lately, because she'd been getting more and more of those unsettling messages with just breathing on the tape. She was convinced that Julian was behind them.

'Begin With Review And Friend,' she heard, and she picked up immediately.

'Hi, Rich!'

'Ella! How's it going? Have you recovered from your fainting fit?' he asked.

She looked blankly at the receiver. 'What fainting fit?'

'The last time I saw you, you'd fainted clean away on the floor of O'Neill's hotel.'

She'd forgotten about the swoon she'd staged to get out of diving with Julian. 'Oh, yeah. Yeah – I'm fine now.'

'You said you'd ring,' he said, in a mock-accusatory tone.

'Oh, God. I'm sorry, Richie. I've been up to my eyes at work.'

'No problem.' There was a pause, and then he took a deep breath and said – all in a rush – 'I was just wondering if you fancied doing something this weekend?'

'Oh. This weekend's bad, Rich. I'm busy Saturday and Sunday.' Dieter was due, and Leonie had booked special enclosure tickets for the racing at Leopardstown on Saturday, and dinner in the Merrion Hotel on Sunday.

'How about Monday, then? It's Ferdia's farewell bash in the Trident in Howth.'

Farewell! Oh God, how that word hurt! 'I haven't been invited,' she said, resisting the impulse to beg him for news about her dive god. Such as: *Has he sold his horse yet? Is Black Jack a racehorse? And if it is, will it be running at Leopardstown on Saturday?*

'You don't need an invite. Loads of people from ActivMarine are going.'

Hell. What was the point? He'd just look at her as if she was pond life. 'Can I take a raincheck, Rich? Maybe we could do a movie or something the following weekend? I could do with some cheering up by then, probably. And you're the man to do it.'

'Why will you need cheering up?'

She didn't want to say: *Well, because I'm cracked over your cousin and come next week I'll never see him again* . . . Instead she said: 'Oh. I'm just going through a tough time at work.'

'So am I.'

'What's up?'

'One of the people I was selling insurance to over the phone insulted me.'

'I imagine you get a lot of that in telesales. What did he say?'

'He thought I was that eejit radio presenter who makes hoax phone calls.'

'The one on the breakfast show?'

'Yeah. He kept saying things like, "Aaah – ye're a gas ticket. Aren't ye a great man for the crack." In the end I politely got rid of him by telling him I'd play a request for him.'

'What did he ask for?'

'Mr Blobby's song.'

When Ella finally put the phone down to Richie, she was laughing her ass off.

*　　　*　　　*

On Saturday she got dolled up in a brand-new tight red leather jacket, an embroidered white petticoat, white lace-trimmed stay-ups and a pair of red leather boots. As well as tickets for the enclosure, Leonie had booked a limo to take them there, and a table for lunch. It had been cloudy all week and drizzling sporadically – dismal weather for July and dismal weather for racing, but Ella was looking forward to it. She was dying to see Dieter and Leonie together again for the first time since Jamaica.

The first race was at two o'clock. At ten minutes to they were sitting at the restaurant bar sipping champagne and consulting the form. Ella leafed through the pages, looking vainly for Ferdia's horse, but there was no Black Jack running in any of the scheduled races.

Dieter had suggested that they hire the services of a tipster, but Leonie insisted that it was more fun to pick horses by their names. Her grandmother was wearing a silk frock that had a discreet – but undeniably provocative – slit on one side. She positively radiated happiness and looked at least a decade younger than her sixty-two years. So that's the effect love had on women! thought Ella. Endorphins were just such extraordinary things!

'Red leather and lace? A bit anomalous, isn't it, darling?' said Leonie, assessing Ella's outfit.

'It's kind of meant to be. I think the leather cuts across the girliness of the petticoat.'

'Oh – I see,' said Leonie with a nod of recognition. 'Is this what they mean by "attitude"?'

Ella smiled at her and shrugged. 'If you like,' she said. 'Although I'm not altogether certain what my attitude to anything is these days.'

'Whatever it is, it suits you, darling. It's actually a very sexy combination. I don't think I've ever seen you with a cleavage before – all that tight buttoned-up leather certainly gives you a boost. Now,' she said, returning her attention to the form, and underlining a name. 'That's an obvious choice for me. There's a filly here called Fleeter.'

Ella looked puzzled. 'Why is that an obvious choice?' she asked.

'Because it rhymes with Dieter of course.' Leonie flashed a smile across the table at her fiancé.

'She's daft as a broom, isn't she?' remarked Dieter to Patrick with a fond smile.

'You mean daft as a brush,' replied Patrick. 'But at least you know what you're letting yourself in for.'

'They're getting along like a house on fire, aren't they?' whispered Leonie in Ella's ear. 'I always knew Patrick would make a good son-in-law. Or is it stepson?' She took a swig of champagne. 'What a pity the odds on this Fleeter are so shockingly bad. Who are you going for, darling?'

'Um,' said Ella, scanning the print. There was a horse called Darling Julian running in the first race. 'Well not that one, anyway. I think I'll go for Big Blue.'

'Why?'

'Reminds me of diving.'

'Oh – of course. Your new passion.' Leonie turned the page. 'Camptown Racer!' she growled triumphantly. 'That's who I'm going for in the second race.'

'Explain?' said Patrick.

'Because Camptown is the capital of Jamaica, of course.'

'No, it's not, Leonie. Kingston is.'

'Oh. Well, then I'll go for Mister Punch, because that stinking punch won us our Caribbean holiday. That's got to be lucky. Who are you going for in race two, darling?'

382

It was staring her in the face. 'One Love,' said Ella.

One Love came last.

* * *

Because the weather was so bleak, they spent most of the afternoon in the restaurant, watching the races on television monitors. When the sixth and last race was announced, Dieter got to his feet. 'Come now,' he said. 'It is time to brave the wind and the cold. I cannot go to the races in Ireland and watch every single one on a television screen! We must go out onto the terrace for the final one.'

'Who are you backing in this one, Ella?' Leonie asked her.

'A horse called the Dark Horse,' she said. She'd stuck a fiver on it.

'Why the Dark Horse?'

'Because I met one recently.'

'A real dark horse?'

'A real dark horse.'

'Tell me all about him at once.'

'How did you know it was a he, Leonie?' asked Ella.

'Don't be silly, darling. All dark horses are men. Have you ever heard of a dark mare?'

'Nightmares are dark. I should know. I've been through a living one at work recently.'

'Hush hush.' Leonie narrowed her eyes in warning at Ella, and then she took her arm and drew her away from Patrick. 'Forget about work. I can tell Patrick's not madly happy with the current set-up either. We're here to have fun today. Now. Tell me more about this dark horse.'

Ella didn't need to be persuaded. 'He's this amazing guy I met at scuba, Granny. He's a master dive instructor, but he's also a demon fiddle player, *and* he's loaded. That was the real dark horse bit.'

'Goodness. What an amazing package. He sounds like a terrestrial god!'

'He is,' said Ella glumly.

Leonie registered Ella's tone. 'So where's the catch?'

'I'll never see him again. He's going off round the world.'

'When?'

'Next week. He's throwing a big farewell party soon.'

'So you'll see him then, won't you?'

'No. I haven't been invited.'

'Pshaw.' Leonie was the only person Ella knew who could get away with saying 'pshaw'. 'Gatecrash, darling, for heaven's sake. I did it all the time when I was your age.'

'Oh, Leonie, no. I wouldn't dare.'

Leonie looked surprised. 'What happened to that intrepid streak you were supposed to have inherited from me?'

'Well, it's not that I wouldn't dare to gatecrash a party. It's just that I don't think I could look *him* in the eye again. He thinks I'm a totally sad eejit.'

'Why's that?'

'He thinks I read books with titles like *Passion's Monument* and *Monster Truck Madness*.'

'What's wrong with that? *Monster Truck Madness* sounds very exciting, if you ask me.' Leonie lowered her voice. 'You know, I could really do with some easy reading. Dieter sent me a load of Kafka, and I'm finding wading through all that *Weltschmerz* very tough going. Maybe you'd lend me this *Monster Truck Madness*, darling, for light relief?'

Ella laughed. 'Oh, Leonie! It's difficult to explain, but I actually *don't* read books with daft titles like that.' Announcements were starting to come over the PA system, and people were drifting towards the doors. She checked out her watch. 'Come on – we'd better make tracks. They'll be starting any minute.'

Dieter and Leonie and Patrick and Ella finally joined the crowd of racegoers milling onto the terrace. There was an intense sense of anticipation in the air – not unlike the anticipation that had preceded the session in Sweeney's the night she'd ended up joining in the fiddle playing. The party moved to the far left-hand corner of the terrace, which adjoined the balcony reserved for owners and trainers. These superior beings were filing out of the members' bar, armed with binocular cases all bristling with enclosure tickets, and looking steely.

'I actually saw Menuhin play that piece in the Albert Hall,' came a strident, squirm-makingly posh voice from the adjacent balcony. 'It was an extraordinary experience. I'd go so far as to call it an epiphany, you know.'

'Mm?' A male voice.

'Absolutely. A personal epiphany for me.' The woman indulged in a sigh which she managed to imbue with a kind of nostalgic vibrato. 'Ah! The unabashed rubato of the Maestro! And the exquisite, haunting timbre of that Strad! Sheer heaven! The strains still linger in my mind, all these years later.'

This observation provoked a laconic 'Really?' from the person to whom the remark had been addressed. Ella sensed that the listener was trying to stifle a yawn. She couldn't blame him. This woman was ghastly.

'We met him backstage afterwards. Charming, *charming* individual. You could tell from his aura that he was simply saturated with genius. *Saturated* with it. As incandescent as – as – a *firework*!'

'Sounds like a bit of a damp squib to me,' came the rejoinder in a laid-back Galway accent.

Ella's ears flattened back against her skull in the manner of a cat that has just heard sudden birdsong. Surely that was Ferdia's voice!

'Ferdia!' The woman was playfully indignant. 'You are *so* irreverent!'

Hellfire! It *was* Ferdia! Ella swallowed hard, resisting with mindboggling difficulty the temptation to swing round and confront him. What on earth was *he* doing here? Her mind floundered around like a scuba novice for a second or two before re-establishing neutral buoyancy. His horse – of course. That was it. His horse *must* be running this evening! But she'd scanned the racing form from cover to cover and had seen no Black Jack listed. Maybe she'd got it wrong? Maybe the horse wasn't called Black Jack? It had been so difficult to hear Richie that night of the session when he'd filled her in on Ferdia's turf credentials. Maybe Black Jack was the famous sire or something? Richie could have been making some reference to blood-stock or breeding or whatever that horsy pedigree stuff called itself. The Dark Horse sounded like it could easily be related to a horse called Black Jack . . . Didn't it? Ohmigod, ohmigod – none of these logistics really *mattered* right now. What really *did* matter was – what was she going to do?

'Anyway, the Maestro himself told me that night that that particular Stradivarius—' resumed Mistress Posh in her droney voice, and then suddenly exclaimed: 'Oh! I'll finish the story later, darling. They're about to start. Hello! Isn't this marvellous!' The stalls opened and the horses burst out and started their thunderous procession down the track. 'Come on, come on, the Dark Horse!' exhorted Mistress Posh, in an even more strident tone. 'Well! Not a bad start, Ferdia! Maybe your gamble will pay off after all.'

As inconspicuously as she could, Ella edged nearer the railings that separated the terrace from the owners' and trainers' balcony. The track took the horses from right to left in her field of vision, and as the race progressed, she was able to slide her eyes sideways. She registered first an elegant behatted woman somewhere in her forties, and then Ferdia came into focus. He was decked out in what looked suspiciously like Paul Smith, his dreadlocks were ponytailed, and he was surveying the racecourse through field glasses. He was the most gorgeous sight Ella had ever seen in her life.

A symphony of gasps and groans erupted from the crowd, and Ella tore her eyes away from Ferdia. There'd been a pile-up at the fourth fence. Three of the front runners were down. 'You're OK,' observed Patrick. 'Your horse is still running. But the favourite's down.'

'The Dark Horse!' yelled Ferdia's posh companion, and Ella's attention swung back to the owners' and trainers' balcony. She saw his jaw muscles tense and his lips move in a barely audible, murmured echo. So! It *was* his horse! All around her people were seething with mounting excitement, waving their arms and shouting encouragement as the sweating beasts rounded the curve in the track and came sweeping up the home stretch. Over the PA system the commentator's voice was so frantic it was impossible to distinguish what he was saying. Suddenly a black horse broke away from the main body of the half-dozen front runners that were tearing towards the finishing line. It was as if it had taken wing, suddenly, like a dark Pegasus.

'The Dark Horse! Yes!' shrieked Mistress Posh.

'He's going to do it! How marvellous! He's won, Ferdia! He's won, won, won!' Ella returned her attention to the action on the next-door balcony, where the beaming female was throwing her arms around Ferdia's neck. Somewhere in the distance she could hear Leonie's voice excitedly congratulating her granddaughter for backing the winner, but she wasn't listening. Over Mistress Posh's shoulder she was suddenly looking directly into Ferdia's sea-green eyes. He smiled at her – a perilously sexy smile – and then politely disengaged himself from his companion, who immediately launched herself at the next available male, continuing her air-kissing ritual without missing a beat. Ella's heart missed at least half a dozen as Ferdia strolled over to the rail that divided them.

'Hello, Ella Nesbit,' he said, looking down at her in a way that made her want to faint at his feet. They looked at each other in silence for a long moment. Neither of them could deny the sexual vibe that was practically shimmering between them. Her eyes went to his mouth and the lust crescendoed. She had never wanted to kiss a man's mouth so badly in her life – not even Jack's. And then Ferdia spoke. He said: 'I hope you don't mind if I come straight to the point? I have a question for you. Do you remember what was the last thing I ever said to you?'

'You said that *Monster Truck Madness* hadn't been handed in at the hotel,' she found herself stammering. *Nooooo!* her internal voice yelled at her. *Ella, you klutz! Get it right for once, can't you?*

The amused look in his eyes intensified. 'No,' he corrected her. 'I'm referring to what I last said to you in person. I made a promise, I seem to recall. A promise motivated by extreme, unapologetic horniness. Shall I remind you?'

She nodded. She couldn't trust herself to speak.

He leaned in to her and the sensation of his voice in her ear was warm and liquid. The silken water of the Blue Lagoon came to mind. 'I told you I was going to make you come. In fact, if my memory serves me correctly, I told you that I was going to make you come like you've never come before in your life. I just hope I wasn't jumping the gun,' he added in a tone that smacked of a kind of amused afterthought. 'I hate hubris. Now.' Ferdia straightened up and looked directly into her eyes again. 'Will you leave here with me right now and let me take you somewhere breathtakingly romantic?'

She nodded again.

'Then get your coat,' he said to her for the second time ever. 'And meet me outside the owners' and trainers' bar in five minutes. Do you know where it is?'

She did. She'd passed it on the way in.

'Five minutes long enough for you to make your excuses?'

She nodded yet again. She couldn't manage to force a smile, let alone articulate a sentence. The muscles around her mouth felt atrophied.

Ferdia turned away without another word, smilingly negotiating his way around the ladies in oversized hats who fluttered on the balcony before disappearing through the door that led into the members' bar. Leonie was at her side in a flash. 'Who was *that*?' she demanded.

Ella was wearing a completely dazed expression. 'That,' she said, 'was the Dark Horse I was telling you about.'

'*The* Dark Horse? The diving Dark Horse?'

'Yes.'

'Wow.' Leonie's mouth dropped open. 'What a dude.'

'He's asked me to go off somewhere with him.' She spoke the words without conviction, like a bad actor, still unable to believe what had just happened.

'What? Where?'

'He didn't say. He just said somewhere breathtakingly romantic.'

'Oh, Ella! Go! Go at once!'

Ella turned beseeching eyes on her grandmother, desperate for advice. 'Should I? But what will I do when he finds out I'm an impostor, Leonie?'

'What do you mean, darling?'

'He thinks I'm some kind of groovy socialite.'

'But you said earlier that he thought you were a sad eejit who reads pulp fiction?'

'He thinks I'm that too.'

'Well, there you go. He obviously finds you

intriguing. Like a riddle wrapped in a mystery inside an enigma. Who said that?'

'Winston Churchill.'

'There you are, you see. You're not an eejit. You're an intelligent girl who knows these kind of things, and you're also a hugely accomplished musician and a respected professional sound engineer.'

'Oh.' Ella considered, winding a strand of coppery hair around her index finger. 'I suppose when you put it like that it gives me *some* credibility . . .'

'It's nothing but the truth. Look at you, Ella! You're gorgeous!'

'I get that from you. Thanks, Leonie.'

'Don't discount your mother. Entire orchestras were in love with her. Now run along while you're buoyed up with self-esteem. It's amazing what it can do for a girl.'

It was true. Angie had been right about compliments. They really *did* make you feel better. But still Ella remained unconvinced that she was worthy of the *Überdude* who had promised to transport her to hitherto uncharted realms of sexual delight. What would he expect of her in return? What if she was crap? She was seriously out of practice, for starters. And there was something about Ferdia, something about the way he looked at her, that made her self-confidence evaporate into the ether and turned her into a gibbering idiot.

Dieter was moving towards her, brandishing a bottle of champagne. Ella dithered a little more, and then made a last-ditch attempt at extricating herself from her imminent, nerve-racking tryst with Ferdia. 'Oh – I really can't do this, Leonie. I can't walk out on your celebrations . . .'

'Pshaw and phooey. Run! I'll make your excuses to Dieter. He'll understand. And if things pan out, don't worry about dinner in the Merrion tomorrow night. We'll simply toast your success if you don't turn up!'

Ella didn't say another word. She gave her grandmother a big hug and a kiss on the cheek, and then she turned and skittered back through the restaurant and down the stairs.

Outside, horses were just coming into the parade ring. She wondered which one was Ferdia's. She hadn't had a chance to get a decent look at it while it was running, and anyway, all dark horses looked the same to her. Ella reached the owners' and trainers' bar and peeked through the window. At the opposite end of the room she could see him. He was leaning with one hand against the wall, talking on a mobile. Half his face was in shadow, half was illuminated by the watery sunlight that filtered in through the plate glass. There was something businesslike about him, which was at odds with his relaxed physical stance – something *authoritative*. She'd seen the film *Tango* on video recently, and had found the dominant male stuff gobsmackingly sexy. Her politically correct persona had opened its mouth in a little momentary Oh! of indignation, and then, to her secret relief, it had turned its face to the wall and thoroughly connived at the thrill engendered by illicit concupiscence.

Across the room Ferdia shifted his stance, angling his body so that his broad shoulders were supported by the wall and stretching out one long, lazy leg to rest it on the rung of a barstool opposite. He was in three-quarters profile to her. The contours of his face were more than usually accessible, unobscured by his trademark dreadlocks and undisguised by his dive mask. In fact, his face looked so indecently exposed that Ella felt obliged to examine it in lingering detail. It wasn't a classical profile, or a handsome one. There was really very little that was symmetrical about it . . . but . . . But *that's* what made it sexy! OK – so his nose was broken – in fact, it had probably been broken more than once, by the look of it – but the other bones in his face looked as indestructible as Achilles'. His eyes were downcast and heavily hooded, his mouth was curved and gutwrenchingly sensual, and his skin was the dark gold-bronze of a weathered Adonis. Well, of course it was, Ella Nesbit you eejit! He hadn't been tagged with the moniker 'Dive God' for no good reason!

She watched as his right hand snaked into his trouser pocket, delved there for a tantalizing moment, and then emerged hefting a handful of small change. With his thumb he flicked over the coins, obviously checking their denomination. Then he turned and, still holding the phone to his left ear, disappeared in the direction of the Gents.

Ella visualized him sliding the coins into the slot of the vending machine (which would he opt for? she wondered. Ribbed for extra pleasure, satin finished for sensitivity, or heavy-duty for added protection?), and then pulling open the little drawer and extracting the packet. Or packets.

Suddenly he was in the bar again, moving towards her, looking directly at her through the window, still talking on the mobile. Ella turned away immediately, hoping to God that her face was well concealed by the curtain of her hair. She knew the expression of naked desire scrawled all over it made her look way too vulnerable, and she suspected she was going to need all her defensive wits about her. Be cool, she warned herself. Be grown-up. Be worldly.

When she next dared to look up, she saw that he had finished his phone call. Mistress Posh had joined him. He talked to her for a minute or two, then handed her the phone. As she tucked it away in the dinky little Vuitton purse that dangled from her wrist, he leaned towards her, disappearing momentarily under the giant, ostrich-feather-trimmed pagoda of her hat. Mistress Posh laughingly threw back her head, and laid what looked like a restraining hand on his arm. Ferdia shrugged, removed her hand with a smile, kissed her lightly on both cheeks, and turned away from her. Then he was moving towards Ella once more. He swung through the door, reached her, scooped her right hand into his left and started to pull her through the crowd. For Ella it was like being in a slow-motion action replay of the night in Sweeney's. She felt weak as water.

'Where's your car?' he asked.

'I don't have it.'

'In that case we'll have to get a cab. I'm not driving today either.'

'How did you get here?' She didn't care how he'd got there. He'd probably just swooped down from heaven. But she craved the convention of small talk the way an addict craves a fix.

'Helicopter.' Of course he did! 'You?'

'Limo.'

'Of course you did.' He threw her an amused look.

'Where are we going?' She was practically having to trot to keep up with him.

'I've booked a hotel room.'

She felt a rush of pure lust. It started in her groin, surged upwards through her stomach, and then gushed into her brain and erupted with the force of a geyser. She was drenched with it.

'Oh? Where?'

What? Who had said that? Oh, God – it had been her. She was speaking on automatic pilot, now.

'The Clarence Hotel.'

Holy fucking shomoly! 'Ah. Was the penthouse available?' A little joke. Oh, *God*! Her automatic pilot was obviously totally challenged in the humour department.

'Sorry. We're out of luck. There must be rock

stars in town tonight. But I've been assured that the room they've booked us into is the next best thing.'

Wow! she thought. Hip hip hooray! Shazam and pow! Yes yes yes!

'Cool,' said her automatic pilot.

'Ella! Hi!' said somebody else. They had reached the private Pavilion, and were obliged to stand back as a flurry of racegoers emerged. Oh no, thought Ella, stapling a reluctant smile onto her face before turning in slow motion, and thinking these thoughts as she did so: I don't want to run into anyone right now. I just want to be spirited straight into a bedroom in the Clarence Hotel. I just want to shag Ferdia MacDiarmada senseless. I just want to be shagged senseless by Ferdia MacDiarmada. This is hell. And, as she braced herself to face her interlocuter, the last thought that went through her head was: Well, at least it was a woman's voice that greeted me, so it's not Julian. At least I've been spared the worst nightmare scenario ever projected onto the life of Ella Nesbit. If it had been Julian I'd have ended up in Mountjoy prison on a murder charge (no, make that manslaughter. No judge in his right mind wouldn't sympathize with me) and I'd never have got near to shagging Ferdia senseless in the hippest hotel in the world.

'Well. Hi . . .' said Ella's automatic pilot voice. It was even more lacking in conviction than her bad actor voice. 'It's nice to see you again – Sophie.'

Sophie Burke was standing there, looking just like she did in the shampoo commercial she was currently starring in. Her chignoned blond hair was a skein of silver silk, her complexion was flawless, her smile was pearly, her lips were prettily plump with collagen. She was wearing a skirt that was too tight for her and a tart's blouse that exposed practically all of her bosom, noticed Ella. (Actually, Sophie was wearing a beautifully cut, discreetly sexy skirt and an expensive little tailored shirt that showed an inviting inch of cleavage.)

'Nice to see you, likewise,' fluted Sophie, air-kissing expertly. Behind the dark glasses Ella saw the actress slide a look of assessment at Ferdia. He must have passed the test, because: 'Come and join us for Pimm's, why don't you?' she trilled, indicating the group of unsmiling cool Calvin Klein clad sunglasses-wearing individuals who flanked her like bodyguards. Ella couldn't see Ben among them. 'It's my last day in Ireland – I've spent a whole week visiting family – and we're celebrating.'

Ella didn't ask. Sophie could have been celebrating a birthday or a film deal or an Oscar nomination or the successful housetraining of a pet poodle for all she cared. In fact, Sophie really *was* celebrating her last day in Ireland. She couldn't wait to get back to her *pied-à-terre* in South Ken and leave behind the more embarrassing of her Irish connections. The north Mayo contingent had descended on Dublin when they'd heard that their movie star relation was granting Mummy and Daddy Burke a flying visitation, and Sophie had spent a lot of time in her childhood bedroom clutching her childhood soft toys and bravely battling a migraine.

'Oh. Thanks for the offer, Sophie, but I'm afraid we can't. We're just on our way out.'

'Shame!' Sophie slid off her sunglasses and looked up at Ferdia with startlingly blue eyes. Hang on, thought Ella. *Blue* eyes? They'd been green the last time she'd seen her . . . Coloured contacts. Of course. 'Hi,' Sophie said to Ferdia in her best husky little-girl voice. 'I'm Sophie Burke,' she added with a coy little bite down on the lower collagen-packed lip, as if she knew the introduction was just a formality to be got through. After all, of course he knew – of course *everyone* knew – who she was.

'Loved you on the cover of *GQ*.'

'Thanks,' simpered Sophie.

'Very taste . . . ful.' Ella shot Ferdia a look. For a split second she had wondered if he'd been going to say 'tasty', but there was nothing salacious about the urbane smile he was bestowing on the film star.

'I thought so too. They eventually convinced me that the nude shots were a good idea, and I must say I was pretty pleased with them. I wasn't sure about the interview, though. I'd just split up from Ben – my husband – and I was feeling very vulnerable. You don't think I came across as someone who'd been too irreparably wounded, did you?'

'I didn't read the interview,' said Ferdia. 'I only looked at the photographs.'

'Oh.' Sophie tried hard not to look put out, but didn't succeed very well.

'I'm sorry to hear you've split up from Ben,' Ella interjected quickly. 'When did that happen?'

'Not long after I got back from Jamaica. Actually, I'm surprised our relationship lasted as long as it did.' So was Ella. 'I'd tried for years and years to make a go of it, but I should have listened to my father when I first told him we were getting married.'

This was so patently a cue for Ella to say: Oh? What did your father say to you? that she found herself saying it.

'He said that Ben wasn't good enough for me.'

'He wasn't, Soph,' said one of the Calvin Klein clones stalwartly.

'Thanks, Tarquin.' Sophie smiled at the clone, but there was a becoming tinge of sorrow in her beautiful blue eyes. She turned back to Ferdia, reassessed briefly and expertly, and obviously thought he was worth another try. 'Are you sure we can't persuade you to join us for Pimm's?' What man in his right mind could turn down the invitation implicit in those twelve words? Sophie wasn't asking Ferdia if he wanted to join her in a sickly beverage of lemonade laced with alcohol. She was asking him if he'd like to fuck a hot-shit movie star until she begged for mercy.

Ella was in like Flynn. 'We're sure, thank you, Sophie,' she said firmly. What she was actually saying was: *Back off, bitch. He's fucking* me *this evening, OK?*

'Shame,' said Sophie again. 'We could have

400

shared memories of Jamaica. Remember the day we went to Navy Island with that Rasta? It was quite extraordinary – I'm sorry – I don't know your name?'

'Ferdia.'

'Ferdia. Anyway, this Rastafarian took Ella and my friend Eva – you know Eva Lavery, the film star? – to a place called Navy Island, off the northeast coast of Jamaica. It was a deeply spiritual experience just to walk through the rain forest and be at one with nature. Not to have to fend off fans – well, for me and Eva, of course. It's not as if Ella has her own web site!' And Sophie went off into an enchanting little peal of laughter.

If Ella didn't get out of there *now* she ran yet another serious risk of being hauled up for manslaughter. But what to do? If she suggested they make tracks it would only make her look as if she was dead keen to get Ferdia into bed. Which she was, of course. But she didn't want *him* to know that . . .

'Oh, look,' said Ferdia. 'Serious VIPs having their photographs taken.'

'What? Where?' Sophie spun through 360 degrees to locate the VIPs, and, more importantly, the photographer.

Ferdia indicated with a casual hand the parade ring, where a triumphant owner – a prominent ex-government minister – was posing with his wife. 'Why do most of the women here go out of their way to disguise themselves as giant mushrooms?'

he asked no-one in particular. 'Those hats are insane.'

'Oh – it must be for the Society page of *Individual*,' Sophie declared. 'There's Oliver – he always does their photos. Olly! Hi! Long time no see!' And for the second time in Ella Nesbit's life, Sophie Burke turned away and shimmied towards the main event, abandoning her without a backward glance.

Ferdia watched her go, sycophants stumbling in her wake in their attempts to keep up with her.

'It girls rule,' he said.

'Do they?' countered Ella.

'Well, darling. You should know.' He reclaimed her hand, raised it to his lips and kissed the palm, rendering her speechless. Then he strolled through the gate and down the long curving driveway towards a taxi that was disgorging more dames in hats. 'I hope he had the nous to charge them double,' he said. 'One of those hats takes up as much room as a paying passenger. Come on – let's grab it.' He quickened his pace, striding towards the taxi with Ella's heart accelerating at the same rate as her feet. He held the rear door open for her, and slid in beside her.

'Where to, guv?' said the driver, and Ella's heart decelerated instantly. She could tell at once that this driver was in chatty mode, by the self-referential irony with which he'd invested the word 'guv'.

'We're going to the Clarence,' said Ferdia.

'Bono's gaff! Ha ha ha! No better man. No – I

mean it. Gave him a ride once. He was late for an interview on RTE. I think it was around the time they were doing the Zoo tour. There's a funny story about that, too. My sister had tickets for one of their gigs – Lansdowne Stadium, I think it was. Anyway, for some reason she was really on edge on the day of the concert – "on edge" hahaha, d'you get it? And the friend she was going with didn't turn up so my sister rang me and said . . .'

Oh sweet Jesus, thought Ella.

'Ah – ye're a right bastard!' The taxi driver blared his horn at a BMW that had shot in front of him without indicating. 'Bastard Beamer drivers think they own the road.' He swerved angrily around the Bastard Beamer, and Ella was slammed against Ferdia. He looked down at her and smiled, and Ella couldn't stop herself from focusing on his mouth and wondering just when he was going to kiss her and just what it was going to be like when he did. His eyes slid away from hers, downwards. They travelled to her mouth and lingered there, and then they travelled to her breasts and lingered even longer. Finally, they moved down to her thighs. If he'd touched her there she couldn't have felt sexier.

And then he did touch her there and actually Jesus Christ it *did* feel sexier. The touch was so light it was barely perceptible. An index finger grazed her knee, and then he was lifting her skirt slowly – *agonizingly* slowly. Millimetre by millimetre, until the tops of her stockings came into view. She was aware that her thighs had parted automatically, and some circumspect voice miles away down some corridor in her head was telling her to put her legs back together at once because nice girls don't do things like that, but she just told the voice to shut up. Then she steeled herself to look up at him, this man who made her want to be the most wanton, abandoned creature on the planet. He traced the lace top of her stocking with his thumb and his full lips curved, and his eyelids looked heavier than ever. Then his eyes travelled back up her body until they met hers. 'What a very clever girl you are,' he said in a very low voice. 'To have worn stockings.'

'Anyway,' resumed the cab driver, back on form after having taken out the Bastard Beamer. 'My sister rings me at about seven o'clock in a tizzy and says to me "Kevin," she says, "I can't find the tickets! And Dolores has gone AWOL" – Dolores was the friend. And I said to her . . . Jesus! Aren't Beamer drivers the pits! Did you ever see driving the cut of that? Well, did you? You can't deny that that's the worst piece of driving you've seen in a year. In a decade! Now can you?'

'If you ask me,' said Ferdia, tearing his eyes away from Ella's stocking tops and pulling the hem of her skirt over them. 'It's the worst piece of driving I've ever seen in my life. It's a tough job you have, mate.'

'Tell me about it!'

Oh, no! thought Ella. Why did you have to go and call him 'mate', Ferdia! She could tell that the word had established camaraderie beyond the shadow of a doubt in the mind of the driver. 'You wouldn't believe some of the stuff I've seen, mate! Let me tell you about the time . . .'

There was nothing else for it. Ferdia and Ella sat back and let him tell them about 'the time'. In mind-numbing, freeze-frame detail.

Chapter Sixteen

In the Clarence, Ella sat in the study just off the main lobby while Ferdia did all the bureaucratic stuff at the reception desk. She sat with her legs crossed, one 'relaxed' arm draped over the leather back of a chaise-longue, pretending to read the *Irish Times* and feeling like someone in a Terence Rattigan play. Beneath the carapace of insouciance she was limp, soft as kapok, and thrumming with lust. Ferdia had not made physical contact with her since he'd pulled her skirt back down over her stocking tops in the taxi, and she ached for his touch so badly that she wanted to scream. Hell! Everything seemed to be taking so *long*! The taxi driver hadn't had change for the £50 note that was the smallest denomination that Ferdia had on him, and then Ferdia had finally lost patience with his matey dithering and told him to keep the change. And now there were computers to be accessed and forms to be filled out and plastic to be swiped.

Ella snuck a look at her dive god over the top of the paper as he filled in the registration card and signed 'just there, please, sir', and flirted with the girl behind the desk. God, was he cool! He looked so in *control*, as if he booked into smart hotel rooms every day of the week! And then a nasty little niggle of a thought struck her. He'd done this before. Loads of times. He was a smooth operator, and she was handing herself to him on a plate . . . She found herself thinking about all the opportunities Ferdia must have had to screw the kind of women for whom the price of a dive holiday would be small change. He probably had a serious track record in seduction. Hell – he probably had a logbook for recreational sex as well as one for recreational diving. Did Ella really want to add her name to the logbook? How would he log her if she did? *Ella Nesbit. A complete walkover, but not a bad shag.*

She felt utterly miffed suddenly, like a spoilt child who'd just found out that everyone else in the class had got the latest, most desirable Barbie for Christmas, too. Oh, God. Had he done this with Philippa, the woman at the hotel in Lissamore? Or with the dame in the pagoda-sized hat who'd been so reluctant to let him go at the races earlier?

She didn't care. It was none of her business and as she looked at him she realized it never would be. He'd be gone in a week, and she might never, ever see him again.

So what was she doing here? Was this really what she wanted? Was she destined to spend the rest of her life meeting the wrong guy? She should stop this now. She was getting in too deep, and if she went to bed with this man she might never extricate herself from the morass of emotions that were swilling around inside her. And then Ferdia turned to her and smiled (oh, God! That smile!) and held out his hand . . . and she found herself getting up and trotting over to him like a puppy to its master.

They were shown up to the room by the manageress, who was professionally friendly (a huge relief after the relentless mateyness of the taxi driver), and who was totally unfazed by their deficiency in the baggage department. She showed them round – the balcony, the sound system, the champagne ready in an ice-bucket – and then she slid back out through the door and shut it softly behind her.

Ferdia and Ella stood on either side of the conker-brown leather chaise, looking at each other. It seemed to her that his look was one of unsmiling assessment. He narrowed his eyes and then indicated her jacket with a brief nod of his head. 'Take it off,' he said.

She hesitated, then she raised a hand and started to undo the buttons with shaky fingers. Because the leather was so new, unbuttoning was no easy task. It seemed to take for ever. Ferdia watched as she fumbled, but he made no move to help her. He just stood there with his right hand on his hip, his thumb hooked through the strap of his belt. Ella's fumbling became even more ineffectual, and she knew she was blushing. God, how uncool she was! Did his other women do this for him? Did his other women perform expert stripteases like Demi Moore in that awful film? Did they do all that stuff men were

meant to find such a turn-on – shaking back manes
of lustrous hair, slipping lacy straps off perfect
shoulders, sliding tongue tips suggestively along
parted lips? She felt like a rank amateur.

She'd reached the last button. Her red leather
jacket hung open, exposing her small breasts in
their broderie anglaise bra. Ella resisted the impulse
to cover herself with her arms. She had never felt
so vulnerable. With an eloquent gesture of his hand,
Ferdia indicated to her that she should lose the
jacket. She shrugged it from her shoulders and let it
crumple to the floor.

'Your skirt.'

This was easier. Two buttons and a zip. For one
blindingly awful instant she thought the zip was
going to get caught in a bit of loose embroidery, but
it came away with a not-too-indiscreet tug. Ella bit
her lip as the white cotton of her petticoat joined her
jacket on the indigo-blue rug, and then she stepped
out of the lacy circle it had formed around her boots
with the delicate precision of a circus pony.

Still Ferdia stood looking at her without moving.
She wasn't sure what to do next. If he instructed her
to lose more of her clothing at this stage she'd feel
– well, naked. Uncomfortably so. But he said
nothing. Finally he took in a deep breath and let it
out again in a long sigh. 'Jesus,' he said. And then
he started to move towards her.

She knew her chest was rising and falling visibly,
she knew he could hear her breathing, she knew
before she dropped her eyes that he had seen the

glimmer of arousal in them. When he reached her he lifted his left hand, and she stood immobile as he cupped his palm hard against the back of her head and let his fingers explore the contours of her skull. Then he entangled his fingers in her hair and dragged his hand down through it, down across the side of her neck, down over her collarbone, until he made contact with the lace trim of her bra. He rubbed the broderie anglaise between thumb and forefinger, and she felt his knuckle dig into the soft flesh directly above her nipple. She could not lift her eyes. His other hand was on her buttocks now, and he exerted a little pressure, moving her closer into him, so that his thigh was between hers.

An image flashed across her mind's eye of that time in the pool, when she had felt the over-whelming impulse to grind herself against him, and now this impulse was driving her again, only a thousand times more urgently. She shut her eyes, and when she opened them again a minute later, his head was bent over her breast. She felt his warm breath on her skin, and then she felt his tongue – and his hand. Oh! His hand was between her thighs now, and he was doing something so persuasive with his fingers that Ella felt compelled to strain against his palm. She snaked an arm around his neck and pulled herself into him, letting out a long, shuddering sigh . . . And suddenly she was coming. Oh, God! She was coming so hard she thought she would never stop . . . She could feel his fingers moving inside her, his rhythm matching her urgency, and then she tensed, eyes closed, breath bated, frozen for an infinite, ecstatic moment before winding both her arms round his neck and clinging to him desperately as her legs gave way beneath her and they dropped together to the floor.

She lay motionless, eyes still closed, lips parted, chest lifting and falling with exertion. She could feel him move beside her as he extricated his limbs from hers. She couldn't look at him. She knew her chest, her neck, her face would be slippery with sweat and scarlet from her orgasm. She felt his hand slide away, and then his mouth was on her there. Ella sucked in her breath and flinched. She was so tender she almost couldn't bear it. But his tongue was so gentle! It was so soft it soothed, and so languorous in its unhurried exploration of all the folds and whorls and intricate, velvety furls of her flesh and – oh *God* don't do that! she thought as she reached out and clutched his head . . . Oh! Jesus Christ, that's too much! (as she pulled him harder against her) . . . Oh, God, stop! And then she was coming again. And again. And again. Ella Nesbit was coming like she'd never come before in her life.

When Ferdia finally raised his head from her she found she could not move. She half opened her eyes, but when she saw him looking down at her she couldn't meet his gaze and so she shut them again. She tried to say something (What? 'Thank you, Ferdia?' How cringemakingly inadequate!) but she could manage nothing more articulate than a kind of croak. Then she cleared her throat and tried again. 'Well,' she said, in the kind of voice an alien might use. 'You certainly keep your promises.'

'Meaning?'

'You made me come. And come. You made me come like I have never come before in my life.'

'My pleasure, ma'am.'

Ella finally opened her eyes and looked at him. 'D'you think I should have a go at returning the favour?'

'I think that's a stunningly good idea, Ella Nesbit.'

Ella blinked and cleared her throat again. Then she started trying to rearrange her arms and legs into a sitting-up position before discovering that her limbs weren't being particularly co-operative.

'Um. I don't think my muscles are functioning properly. I don't seem to be able to—'

'Allow me,' Ferdia leaned over her and suddenly she was being airlifted onto the bed, and her bra and pants were dematerializing.

'You've still got all your clothes on,' she observed unnecessarily.

'Not for long,' he said, losing shoes and socks, jacket and shirt.

'Paul Smith?' she asked.

'All that coming has obviously affected your brain, Ella Nesbit. I'm Ferdia MacDiarmada, remember?'

'No. I meant your threads. Are they Paul Smith?'

'I haven't a clue. Who's he?'

'A designer.'

'Well, if he did design these trousers he obviously never bothered to find out how they'd feel if the wearer got a load of a broad sprawled on the floor wearing nothing but red leather boots and scanty lace underwear. Jesus! Relief at last!' He unzipped his fly – extracting the condom packet from his hip pocket before kicking his trousers onto the floor – and then he shucked off his underpants.

Ella's mouth fell open. 'Oh,' she said, in a kind of whisper. She raised her eyes to his. 'How may I accommodate you?' she asked, sending him a disingenuous smile.

'I'm sure you'll come up with something,' he said, expertly rolling on a condom.

Ella lay back against the bank of pillows and parted her legs.

'That looks good,' he approved. 'For starters.'

And then Ferdia MacDiarmada spread her legs further still, took his cock in his hand, and sank very, very slowly into her.

*   *   *

They left the bed twice that evening. Once to admit room service because all that sex had rendered them ravenous, and once to have a shower together.

'Why have you got "The Birdie Song" tattooed on your shoulder blade?' asked Ferdia, as he massaged shower gel over her back.

'It's not meant to be "The Birdie Song",' said Ella,

feeling foolish. 'It was supposed to be the first bar of the slow movement of Beethoven's Seventh. The tattooist got it wrong.'

'What an intolerable cross to bear – going through life with the naffest song ever composed branded indelibly on your flesh.'

'You're the first person who's looked at it closely enough to find out. I tend to keep it under wraps when I'm around people who know the score.' She leaned back and rubbed her cheekbone against his chest. 'Why have you no tattoos, Ferdia? I thought they were *de rigueur* for all you diver types.'

'I think I told you once – I hate needles. They make me faint. I anaesthetize myself with Jack Daniel's before getting injections. If I didn't suffer from such overwhelming wanderlust I'd never travel anywhere where vaccinations are necessary.'

'That kind of makes nonsense of that Dive Deep, Dive Hard, Fear Nothing ethic, doesn't it?'

'Yup,' he said, squeezing more shower gel between her shoulder blades and letting it drizzle down her spine. 'But it all pans out when you get hit by the rapture of the deep, don't you reckon?'

'The rapture of the deep?' she repeated. 'You mean nitrogen narcosis? I've never had it. How deep do you have to go to get narked?'

'You obviously haven't studied your manual for a while.'

'Remind me.'

'Well. In order for me to experience narcosis, it really depends on how deep you want me to

414

go.' He sucked her earlobe, and she smiled.

'You can forget your decompression limits, for starters.'

'But remember – the deeper I dive, the more pronounced the narcotic effect.'

'On you? Or on me?'

'On both of us.' His tongue slid from her earlobe to her collarbone, and his hands trailed across her belly. Ella let out a long shuddery sigh. 'All right, Ms Nesbit,' said Ferdia with decision. 'You're obviously in no mood to concentrate on the academic side of things, so let's get down to the practical stuff. D'you know something? You have the most intriguing belly button I have ever seen. Or felt.' He inserted a finger and she spooned herself against him, revelling in the sensation of his erection nudging against her spine.

'Ow! That tickles!' she said, not wanting him to stop. He probed a little deeper, and she returned the pressure, straining her hips against him, feeling him harden correspondingly. *Dive deep, dive hard . . .* It was like a refrain in her head now. *Fear nothing . . .* 'Oh! What else are you afraid of, Ferdia? Apart from needles? Sharks?'

'No. I've done a lot of shark dives. I'm seriously freaked by bristleworms, though.'

'Bristleworms? They sound benign enough.'

'Not when they sting your balls, they're not. One crawled out of a conch shell that I'd stuffed down my swimming trunks when I was snorkelling in St Lucia once. I was just twelve, and I've lived in fear

415

of those little bastards ever since. I suspect that experience was what triggered my antipathy for needles. Arms up, sweetheart.' He started to rub gel around her armpits.

'No-one's said that to me since my mother bathed me when I was a little girl,' said Ella. The feel of his fingertips as they circled the contour of her armpit was incredibly erotic. She eased her arms into a luxurious stretch, allowing him even more access.

'You still are a little girl,' he said, letting his hands travel to her breasts. 'You have the most delectably small breasts it's ever been my privilege to fondle.'

'*Delectably* small? I thought most men liked big boobs? I've often wondered whether I should investigate having implants.'

'Don't you dare! I've fondled a lot of implanted breasts in my time. It's like fondling a life-sized Barbie doll. Anyway, I have this theory that small breasts are more sensitive.' He circled the nipple of her left breast with his ring finger, so lightly his touch was barely perceptible. Her nipple sprang to attention instantly. 'See what I mean?' he said, with a lazy laugh.

She leaned back into him, aware that his cock was stiffer than ever where it rubbed against the small of her back. He cupped her left breast in his hand and trailed his other hand back over her shoulder, returning his attention to her tattoo. She felt him trace a finger along the treble clef and then run it down the stave, as he followed the notes. 'He certainly did get it wrong. It bears no resemblance to the Beethoven piece,' Ferdia said.

'It was my fault. I was pissed when I had it done, and I obviously didn't give explicit enough directions.'

Ferdia whistled the first couple of bars of the allegretto very softly between his teeth.

'You know it?' She knew he knew it. She'd heard him whistle it once before.

'I played it with the college orchestra.'

'Oh? Where did you study?'

'Trinity. You?'

'College of Music.'

'Did you want to play professionally?' He pushed the damp mass of her hair to one side and kissed the nape of her neck.

'Yes. More than anything. But I couldn't get work. I still fantasize about it.' She ground her buttocks harder against him, inviting him to enter her again. The pressure of his hand on her breast increased. Oh God! Playing professional violin wouldn't be the only thing she'd be fantasizing about in future. 'What about you?' she resumed, trying hard to sound normal.

'I never took my degree. I got bitten by the diving bug and dropped out of college halfway through my first year. Anyway, I could never have hacked it as a professional. I lacked application, according to my tutors.'

'But you still play, obviously.'

'Only the occasional session. I was always more into trad than classical. What about you?'

'A bit of both. They're both in my genes.' She felt sticky as honey and sweeter than syrup. This shower was doing nothing to freshen her up.

'And what beautiful, beautiful genes they are,' he murmured in her ear, sliding his hands down over her belly. The honey inside her started to drip. 'Your parents are musicians?'

'My mother was first violinist in the – um – National Symphony Orchestra for a few years. And my father's in a – in a – band . . .' She was having difficulty getting her words out. And when they eventually did come out they were so breathy she could hardly hear herself.

'Which one?'

'Celtic – oh! – Celtic Note.'

Ferdia gave a low whistle, and turned her to face him. 'Your old man is Declan Nesbit?'

She nodded.

'Well. I am impressed. No wonder you strutted your stuff with such chutzpah that night in Sweeney's, Ms Nesbit.' He pulled her closer to him. 'Come here. I've always wanted to fuck a real live princess.'

'What do you mean?' It was the smallest voice in the world, and it was coming from somewhere very far away.

'You're directly descended from the king of Irish fiddle players, aren't you?' His hand was between her legs now.

'But I'm a classicist at heart,' she managed, valiantly.

418

'That's cool, too,' he said. 'You might help me brush up on my vibrato. I'm sure I've lost the knack since I dropped out of college.' He was rubbing her clitoris with gentle, insistent fingers.

'Oh no you haven't,' said Ella, taking his face in her hands and smiling up at him. 'You are quite simply a *maestro*, Ferdia MacDiarmada. Your fingering is perfect.'

Those were her last articulate words for a very long time.

* * *

Much later, back in bed, Ella lay on her tummy, scoffing the last of the smoked salmon sandwiches they'd had sent up.

'Mm. Excellent, excellent grub,' she remarked. Ferdia was refilling her glass with champagne. 'This has to be the most welcome supper I've ever eaten.'

'It's more like breakfast,' said Ferdia.

'Oh? What time is it?' she asked, cursing herself the moment the words were out of her mouth. She didn't want to know what time it was. She wanted this rapturous idyll to go on for ever.

'I dunno,' he said, handing her the champagne flute and then wandering out through the glass doors that opened onto the balcony. 'But the sun's about to come up. Look over there.'

She joined him by the railing of the massive private balcony. The horizon of the untidy cityscape that lay stretched all around them was smudged with the rosy glow of imminent dawn. To their right were the roofs of Temple Bar, to their left, five storeys below, the River Liffey slid through the city on its way to the Irish Sea. Ferdia slung his arm around Ella's shoulders and she leaned into him. It felt wonderfully liberating to be standing stark naked on the balcony of this quintessentially charismatic hotel, watching the slow ascent of the sun over Dublin. How right he had been earlier when he'd told her he was going to take her somewhere breathtakingly romantic! She couldn't imagine that a more blissfully romantic scenario existed right now anywhere on the face of the planet. It was as if they were the only two lovers awake in the world. She took a sip of champagne, and then held her face up to be kissed. They transferred the wine between their mouths, letting some spill as the kiss became more passionate. Finally, Ferdia broke away from her mouth and lapped up the little pool that had accumulated in the hollow of her collarbone.

'I don't want to waste it,' he said, as he licked her clean. 'That's the last drop of vintage stuff I'll be indulging in for some time.'

'There's a half-bottle of Veuve Cliquot in the minibar,' said Ella. 'We could crack that.'

'No, no, my sexy little princess. I'm diving today. I'll need my wits about me.'

'You're diving today?' repeated Ella stupidly.

'It's Sunday now. I've to be in Portdelvin at half-past eight to get kitted up.'

'Oh.' Ella didn't want to be hearing this. She thought she might burst into tears. *Go away, real life! You suck!*

'But I think I'd like to see you come again before I go.' Suddenly Ferdia was swinging her up in his arms again. Dear God, he was strong! He made her feel as eensy and petite as the woman on the cover of *Passion's Monument* . . . He carried her back into the bedroom, deposited her on the bed, and looked down at her with a wicked smile. 'Before dawn he took her again,' he said, in an actor-ish sort of voice.

'What?'

'*Dashiel flung her roughly on the bed. "I see I am unable to tame your fiery temper by force, vixen", he said, "Let's see if this will help you to submit to me of your own free will." He licked a finger –*' Ferdia did just that – '*and before she realized what he was doing, he was touching her pleasure kernel.*'

He slid his hand between her legs. Ella burst out laughing.

'*"You dare to laugh, vixen?"* said Ferdia. '*"Damn your impertinence to hell! I will soon have you sobbing with desire and begging me for more!" Dashiel roughly parted her thighs with his other hand*'

'Yes!' thought Ella. She laughed again, and then she gave a little, theatrical gasp. '*Victoria gasped,*' she said. '*"Stop!" she pleaded, as she felt his finger explore her moist, most secret place. Despite herself, she could feel her pleasure kernel swell with shameful lust.*'

'*"Hah! You want me to stop?"*' barked Ferdia.

'*"Yes, yes" she panted. "Please stop!"*'

421

Ferdia took his hand away. '*He took his hand away. "Very well. I will desist if you insist."*'

Ella almost couldn't speak, she was laughing so much. '*"Yes! No! I mean—"*'

'*"What do you mean, you inarticulate bimbo? You mean you want me to touch you, do you not?"*'

'*"Yes," she said, lowering her eyes with shame.*' Ella lowered her eyes and was delighted to see that Ferdia was clearly aroused again.

'*"Where do you want me to touch you? Tell me," he demanded roughly, flipping her over.*'

'*"On my – my p-pleasure kernel," she faltered.*' It was too much. Ella doubled up with laughter as Ferdia, laughing, too, turned her over and entered her from behind.

'Roughly?' he asked.

'Yes, please,' said Ella. Then: 'Ow!' she said. And then she said: 'Oh, God . . .' And finally: 'Thank you . . .'

*   *   *

Some time later she awoke from a dozy half-sleep to see him standing by the side of the bed, looking down at her. She blinked, and smiled up at him.

'Look at you,' he said. 'All beautiful and aslumber.'

Oh, God, she thought. He even uses words like 'aslumber'! How divine! I couldn't have dreamt this man, could I? Ella stretched luxuriously, and then winced. 'Ow,' she said.

'What's wrong?'

'I'm stiff. I used muscles last night that haven't been used for a while.'

'And most captivating muscles they are, too,' he said, leaning over her and kissing her bare shoulder.

'Look who's talking.' Ferdia had the muscles of a sleek beast. She reached out and ran a hand down his chest and over the tanned skin of his stomach. 'Do you work out?'

'I wouldn't dream of it,' he said. 'That stuff's for blokes who sit on their backsides all day. I get enough exercise in my line of work.'

With her index finger she traced the line of a scar on his chest. 'How did that happen?' she asked.

'I had a close encounter with a Moray eel.'

'Ow!'

'Those bastards don't let go in a hurry,' he said. 'I had some difficulty tearing myself away. Literally.' He flashed her a pained smile, and then reached for his underpants.

'Where are you going?' she asked, sitting up in a sudden panic.

'I'm going to work,' he said.

'Oh, God. Is it that time already? It can't be.' She looked at her discarded watch. 'No, Ferdia – it's far too early. Look – it's only half-past seven. We needn't order a cab for at least another half-hour.' She felt like Juliet when Romeo gets up to leave after their first night together. 'And you'll need some breakfast. You can't dive on an empty stomach.'

'Don't teach your grandmother to suck eggs, new girl. I've dived on far less sustenance than smoked salmon and vintage champagne. Anyway, I can pick up a sandwich on the way to the DART.'

'The DART? Aren't you getting a taxi?'

'What? After forking out fifty quid for that cab yesterday? Are you out of your mind?'

She'd thought that money would have been no object. He was buttoning his shirt now. Ella jumped out of bed.

'Don't get up, princess,' he said. 'Stay on in bed. Phone down for breakfast and the papers and have a bath. Treat yourself. And don't forget to grab the freebies from the bathroom. I'll settle up on the way out.'

'No.' Ella stood naked and uncertain in the middle of the room. The balloon of her idyll had been pricked suddenly, and a slow puncture was setting in. She didn't want to stay on here without Ferdia. She didn't care that the joint was the height of sybaritism – she wouldn't be able to enjoy it. It would be like trying to play an out-of-tune instrument. She started to wander around the room, picking up items of her clothing as she went.

A horrible silence had descended and an atmosphere of grim inevitability prevailed.

'When are you leaving?' Ella had sat down on the chaise longue with her clothes piled in her arms. Her voice was croaky again.

'For Jamaica?'

She nodded.

'Next week.' Another silence fell, and all the colour drained from her world. She felt as if she was sitting in a picture in some small child's colouring book, but no-one had provided said child with crayons. Ferdia made an effort to sound conversational. 'Did I tell you I'd been offered a job in Salamander Cove? That Desirée's a persistent broad.'

He hadn't told her, and she didn't care. 'So this is your last week with ActivMarine?'

'Yeah.'

Oh God. 'Will I see you again! Before you go?' She couldn't help herself. She was pathetic with love. In a vain attempt to cover up her sudden painful deficiency in self-esteem, she started slowly pulling on her stay-ups. After some moments, when Ferdia still hadn't answered, she looked up. There was something curious about the way he was looking back at her.

'Do you mean . . . will we make love again before I go?' he asked.

'Yes,' she said. There was no point in being coy. They simply hadn't enough time to indulge in game-playing.

There was another long pause before he answered. 'That might be difficult.'

She'd known he was going to say that! Why had she been so stupid as to ask? But it didn't prevent her from carrying on. 'Why?' she said, wanting to slap herself across the face. As she rolled satiny white lycra up her calf she felt a hangnail snag it, and didn't care.

'The lease is up on my apartment. I've had to move out. I'm staying with Richie until I leave. Him and two others. I'm on the couch.'

She opened her mouth to say 'You could stay with me', and then shut it again. Ferdia would take one look at her *pied-à-terre* and hightail it out of there. She loved the dinky little artisan dwelling she rented, but it wasn't exactly what you could describe as *des res*, and because she'd been working till all hours last week, the place was in a total mess. An entire week's worth of dishes were stacked unwashed in the sink, no laundry had been done, and her bed looked a bit like the one that had been nominated for the Turner prize.

Oh, God – so *what*? So what if she was exposed as an impostor? Maybe she should just throw caution to the winds and tell him who she really was. An ordinary girl with an ordinary job and an ordinary lifestyle. If he couldn't live with that, then – well, then he wasn't worth wasting her tears on, was he? She knew it made sense. But then another thought infiltrated her brain. He'd be gone in a week. She would never see him again. Wasn't it better – if he ever did think of her again – for her to occupy a place in his mind where she'd be remembered as a contender, an equal? Someone with a touch of class . . .

'Will you come to my farewell party?'

She shook her mind clear of the thoughts that had been preoccupying her. 'Tomorrow evening?'

'Yes. It's in the Trident hotel. Do you know it?'

'Yes.' The Trident hotel was a vaguely seedy joint not far from ActivMarine in Portdelvin. Bit of a comedown from the Clarence, she thought. And then she thought: I can't go to Ferdia's party. I'd just get drunk and cry and make a total idiot of myself, and that would be his abiding memory of me. No. Let him remember me as the girl with the Merc, the girl who gets chauffeured to the races, the girl who fraternizes with film stars, the girl with designer labels, the girl who wears antique silk kimonos. Let him remember me as a princess – not some pathetic lovesick klutz. She looked up at him and shook her head. 'I can't come,' she said.

He moved to the window and stood motionless for a while, looking down at the river. 'I'll never forget you the way you were that morning when I ran into you in the corridor of O'Neill's hotel in Lissamore,' he said out of the blue. 'You were all sleepy and tousled and pouting and you were wearing something beautiful in silk. You were the sexiest thing I ever saw.'

That settled it. That was how he'd remember her for ever!

'Until now.' Ferdia turned and looked at her where she sat on the leather chaise in nothing but her lace-trimmed stay-ups. They gazed at each other for a while, Ella superhumanly resisting the impulse to reach out and draw him down to her. Somewhere a church bell chimed the hour. Ferdia shook his head and finished buttoning up his shirt. 'Gotta go,' he said.

Chapter Seventeen

After she and Ferdia parted company outside the Clarence she stumbled back to her little house feeling like the toad who'd kissed the handsome prince and lived the life of a princess for a day. She spent most of the rest of the day in bed listening to Portishead over and over, crying a lot, knocking back a bottle of rather nasty wine and repeating *Life sucks!* to herself like a mantra. They had actually been the last words she'd uttered before she fell into a sleep flooded with dreams of Ferdia. Ferdia floating over a reef, Ferdia on horseback (where did *that* come from?), Ferdia on the balcony of their hotel room, stark naked . . .

On Monday morning she woke to the sound of the phone ringing. She picked up to hear Julian Bollard's awful Dun Laoghaire accent at its most righteously indignant.

'Ella? You get your fucking ass in here right now. Do you realize what time it is? It's ten o-fucking-clock, and you had a session booked with AL&D at nine-fucking-thirty.'

Ella suddenly felt so weary she wanted to die. 'Oh, go *away*, Julian,' she said.

'What?'

Ella thought for a second before answering. 'Actually – make that "don't go away",' she said. 'Stay right there, Julian. Stay there and do the fucking session yourself.'

'*What?*' He sounded apoplectic. She would have laughed if she'd had the energy. 'What did you say?'

'You heard me.'

There was an outraged intake of breath, and then he said: 'Do you realize I could have you fired for this, bitch?'

'You can't fire me, Julian.'

'Why? Just because your uncle wouldn't let me?'

'My uncle's got nothing to do with this, Julian. You can't fire me because I'm a loose cannon and I'm firing myself.' She'd heard someone say it before in a film, and she'd thought *Yes!* when the actress who'd delivered the line had turned on her heel and walked out the door with her head held high. But she didn't feel any buzz now as she put the phone down. There was no sweet taste of revenge on her tongue, no little voice hissing *Hah! Take that, you gobshite!* in her head. No endorphins.

The phone rang again almost immediately. 'I thought I just told you to go away, Julian?' she said.

But it wasn't Julian's voice that answered her. It was Patrick's.

'What's the problem, Ella?'

'I hate him, Patrick. I can't take him any more. I'm sorry. Will you cope?'

'We'll cope. Just about.' She could hear his heavy

sigh over the phone. 'Look. Meet me after work, OK? Daly's, at seven. We need to talk about this.'

'OK. I really am sorry, Patrick. But if I went in there today I'd stick something sharp in him, I know I would.'

'I know, I know. I saw it coming. But you need to do some serious thinking, Ella. Daly's. Seven o'clock.'

'Julian won't be there, will he?'

'Not a chance. I'll have him working overtime on a hot Audiofile.'

'I'll be there.'

She put the phone down, slung on her old towelling robe, and shambled into the kitchen, opening the window to let in some fresh air. Then she sat down at the kitchen table with her head in her hands and did as Patrick had advised her. She thought. And she thought. She thought about her past and she thought about her future. She thought as rationally as she could, weighing pros against cons. She had no job and no income: but she did have prospects. Picking up a job wouldn't be a problem, she knew that. She was too good a sound engineer, and head-hunting went on all the time in her line of work. She could lift the phone to virtually any studio in town right now and be offered work.

But another voice inside her head kept challenging the rational one. Come *on*, Ella! it said. Think harder. Is that what you *really* want? So she thought harder. She cast her mind back to what the grim-faced careers guidance person had said to her in her final year at school. *Being a professional musician will be tough. You should get some training behind you to fall back on.* It had been good advice, and she'd taken it in the end. But then she remembered what her violin teacher had said to her one evening when they'd been to see Anne-Sophie Mutter perform in the National Concert Hall. *What a way to earn a living, Ella – doing the thing you love most in the world! Wouldn't you kill to be able to do that!* Ella knew a handful of people who were lucky enough to do just that – to earn a decent income doing something they were passionate about. Her father was one of them. Ferdia was another. And so was—

Something made her look up. A breeze from the open window had blown something off her notice-board. She bent down and picked it up from where it had fluttered to the floor. It was the photograph of Raphael that Eva Lavery had taken the day they'd visited Navy Island. She'd stuck it onto her noticeboard along with a handful of her other favourite photographs – including one of Ferdia that she'd taken on the Lissamore dive weekend.

As she looked at it, she remembered the story Eva had told her – of how Raphael had had to turn his life around after he'd been struck down by the bends. *When you have a gift you are grateful and full of praise. Jah gave me my gift. But Jah has the right to take away that gift also. Be grateful for what you have, Ella. Be grateful, and full of praise* . . . And then she thought of what Desirée had written on her underwater slate the day she'd got through her training dive. *I can tell you are a fighter . . .* And then she thought of what Patrick had said to her at Christmas. *Dreams can come true, Ella, if you pursue them hard enough and want them badly enough.*

She knew what she wanted right now. She wanted Ferdia MacDiarmada. She wanted him more than she'd ever wanted anyone – more than she'd ever wanted Jack Noonan. She wanted him so badly it was like a physical ache, deep inside her. And if she didn't do something about it today she'd spend the rest of her life regretting a missed opportunity.

She got to her feet and pinned the photograph of Raphael firmly back on the noticeboard beside the one of Ferdia. He was looking at her with challenging eyes. Ella narrowed her eyes back at him, and then she scooted into the bathroom and rooted out the Chanel 19 soap and body lotion that she kept for very special occasions. She'd done enough thinking. She'd thought hard enough to make a really difficult decision, and now it was time for action.

She would go to his party tonight. She would confess that she was an impostor and a fraud, and that she wasn't the groovy socialite type she'd led him into believing she was. She would tell him that she felt she had to get things straight between them before he left for Jamaica, and she would be completely candid about the fact that she fancied him rotten; after all, she reasoned, if you put all your cards on the table there was very little point in being coy about it.

Oh God – what if he laughed at her! What if he *sneered*? Ella turned on the shower and dived under the spray, shampooing her hair vigorously, as if trying to scrub the scary thoughts out of her head. She wouldn't think about the outcome: she couldn't let herself be spooked at this stage of the campaign. It might all go pear-shaped – of course it might – but Ferdia was worth fighting for, and fighting was something she was very good at. Positive thoughts – that's what she needed. *Feel the fear* and all that shit. She fought hard to conjure a positive vibe. Hey! Maybe they could meet up again in a couple of months' time! She'd be flying over in the autumn for Leonie's wedding – and – and – Well. They could take it from there. That's as far into her future as she dared to project.

*   *   *

At around six o'clock she left the house. She wanted to walk in Stephen's Green before meeting her uncle. A walk would help to clear her head, maybe help her to work out some temporary *modus operandi* for Patrick. She felt like a total shit for letting him down. Maybe he could let her and Julian work separate shifts or something, until he got himself a new engineer? Maybe they could have strict demarcation lines between the studios, so that she and Julian never had to cross paths? One thing was certain – she had done the right thing. She had meant it earlier when she'd said that she'd stick something sharp in Julian slimeball Bollard if she ever had to set eyes on him again.

She was standing at the pedestrian crossing on the corner of the Green when she felt someone touch her elbow.

'Ella?' It was Richie. He kissed her on the cheek. 'Hi!' he said. 'You look great.'

'Thanks!' Ella had toyed with the idea of wearing a party frock to the do in the Trident, and then decided against it and stuck on a pair of jeans and a plain white shirt. She didn't really think she looked great, but – hell. What you see is what you get. Her new philosophy. There would be no more game-playing, no more cases of mistaken identity.

'Have you time for a coffee?' asked Richie.

She looked at her watch. 'Sure.' It would mean she'd have to forgo her walk, but suddenly that wasn't important any more. If she went for a coffee with Richie she could pick his brains about Ferdia. Find out what her chances with him were, now that she was about to come clean about who she really was. The thought of her pathetic masquerade as an 'It' girl still had the power to make her cringe. It had been so *stupid* of her to pretend to be someone she wasn't! She ought to have known that it could only end in tears. And there had been plenty of those last night, she thought, casting her mind back to the mad bitch who'd wept and wailed under the duvet accompanied by Portishead. It was about time she started laughing again. 'You always managed to make me laugh, Richie,' she said, linking his arm. 'Let's see if you can do it today.'

'Make you laugh?'

'Mm-hm.'

'Oo-er. Are things really that bad?'

She laughed. 'Nobody ever says oo-er except in comics.'

He shrugged his shoulders at her and gave her his lop-sided grin. 'Well, at least it raised a smile. Come on. Let's go in here.'

He indicated a nondescript café. They sat down on plastic chairs at a plastic table and exchanged glances as a pretty, overly made-up waitress radiating indifference shambled towards them. 'Not much chance of a grande skinny decaff almond latte here, methinks,' observed Richie. 'Cappuccino do you, Ella?'

'Cappuccino's fine, thanks.'

'Bella Donna!' pronounced Richie in theatrical tones. 'I would feast my eyes a little longer on your pulchritude, but – alas! – it is not to be, for we have come a long and weary way and require refreshment most grievously. What beverages have you to offer for our delectation today?'

The girl looked at him suspiciously. 'Wha'?' she said.

'Might you have some arabica of which we might partake, for instance? Or are the beans which I am certain you grind with your own fair hands of a less exotic provenance?'

'A joker, righ'?' said the girl brusquely, and with great contempt. 'Tell us what yiz want in plain English.'

'Two cappuccinos, please.'

'The cappuccino machine's broken.'

'In that case, make that two ordinary coffees, please.'

The girl slouched away with a venomous backward look, and Richie turned to Ella. 'You just can't get the staff these days,' he remarked equably.

Oh yes, you can, thought Ella, her mind conjuring up recent images of starched linen napkins, and champagne flutes, and plates of smoked salmon sandwiches on a tray set down by a discreet porter. If you can afford them.

'So. What's new?'

'Loads.' She flashed him a big smile. 'I quit my job.'

'Well, knock me sideways with a cocked hat. When?'

'Today.'

'What? Why?'

'Because of Julian Scumbag Bollard.'

'Well, now. I can't say I blame you. He's a bit of a Tartar that Julian bloke, isn't he?'

'How do you know?'

He looked sideways at her. 'I had the pleasure of diving with him, remember?'

'Oh, God – yeah! That time in Lissamore! How did that go?'

'It was bloody awful. He whizzed around under

436

water like someone in a James Bond film. And I wished I hadn't taken him up on his offer of a lift. He talked about himself non-stop. By the time we got back to Dublin I wanted to jump out at the first traffic light we hit.'

'Oh, Jesus, Richie – I'm so glad you found that out for yourself. He's a total fuckwit, and I hate his guts.' A wave of pure relief flooded through her suddenly. 'Hallelujah and Praise the Lord! I will never have to work with Julian Bollard ever again. Oh. Thanks.' This to the waitress, who had set two cups of watery-looking coffee-coloured liquid in front of them.

'Here's to you, then, brave girl. Life's too short to work for an asshole like that.' Richie raised his cup at her. 'But what are you going to do when *real* life comes calling? Will it be easy enough for you to find another job?'

'I haven't a clue. I don't want to think about real life just yet.' She stirred her coffee pensively and then laughed. 'Oh, God! I wish I could have seen his face! I should have done it in person instead of over the phone.'

'Well,' said Richie. 'At least you're laughing.' He took a sip of his coffee and then made a face. 'Jesus. This coffee is shite. Let's go and grab a pint some-where instead. I'll get this.' He put a hand over hers to discourage her from paying, and hailed the surly waitress, who pretended not to see.

'I can't go for a pint with you, Rich,' said Ella, looking at her watch. 'I have to go and do some confrontational stuff with my uncle. He's not going to be crazy about the fact that I've dumped him in it. But I'll see you later.'

'Later? Where?'

'Ferdia's farewell party.'

'I thought you weren't going.'

She gave him an enigmatic smile. 'I changed my mind.'

'Cool! Although it's not going to be much of a party if fucking Ferdia carries on being such a prize jerk.'

Ella's ears pricked up instantly. 'What do you mean?'

'He won a shitload of money at the races recently, but it hasn't made him a happy man. He's been mooning around getting drunk and maudlin and droning on about some dame he met.'

'What dame?' Ella was in like Flynn. Richie glanced at her, registering her sudden interest. She gave a little cough and swiftly changed her approach. 'I mean, it's kind of out of character for him, isn't it? He's such a cool dude, normally.'

'Well, I've certainly never seen him behave like this before. You'd think he was in some sick romantic movie starring Meg Ryan. He's effing and blinding and saying things like: "Why didn't I realize it sooner? Why did I leave it so late? I should have known that weekend in Lissamore..."' Richie put on a lugubrious Galway accent. Then: 'Why is that serving wench ignoring me?' he said in his normal voice, looking across at the counter.

438

Ella didn't answer. She hoped the serving wench would continue to ignore Richie for as long as it took for her to siphon off the information she wanted.

'So, who's the dame?' she asked, as casually as she could.

'Haven't a clue,' he said. 'All I know is he came home drunk late yesterday afternoon and was a pain in the arse all evening. It's no fun living in a flat with three other men and have one of them in a black humour over some tart. Oops. Sorry for the politically incorrect speak.'

'That's OK,' said Ella. She was slowly filling up with endorphins, like an inflating balloon. 'So Ferdia's staying with you, is he?' she asked disingenuously. She already knew the answer, but she was desperate to prolong this conversation, even if it meant that Patrick was kept waiting for her in Daly's.

'Yeah. The lease was up on his flat.'

'It must be a bit crowded. Four blokes in a flat. Yeuch!'

'We're not all smelly Neanderthal apes, you know. Ferdia even showers occasionally.'

She remembered the smell of his soap. Longing washed over her.

'I don't,' remarked Richie.

'You don't *shower*?' She shook herself free of the memory of the scent of his cousin's skin against hers. 'I never took you for a pig, Rich.'

'I prefer baths. That is, when I can get into the

bloody bathroom. There always seems to be someone taking a dump when I want to take a bath.'

'Thank you for sharing the lavatorial habits of your room mates with me, Richie.' Then something struck her. 'Why didn't Ferdia just move into a hotel?' she asked.

'A hotel?'

'Yeah.'

'He couldn't afford to stay in a hotel.'

'But – but you said he won a shitload of money?'

'Yeah. He's a mad bastard. He took all that money that he made from selling his share of that racehorse and stuck it right on its nose. And whaddyaknow, the horse performed, and Ferdia won a fortune.'

'The Dark Horse?'

'Yeah. How did you know that?'

She wasn't going to elaborate. Instead she said: 'I thought you said his horse was called Black Jack?'

'What? No. He *won* it in a game of blackjack.'

Things were moving too fast for her now. She needed time to digest this information. 'Hang about, Richie,' she said, after a long pause. 'You told me that Ferdia had sold a horse—'

Richie laughed. 'Ferdia deal in bloodstock! Jesus, Ella. Cop yourself on. I told you he won a *share* in a horse in a poker game from someone with more money than sense, and then he sold it. He got around ten grand for it – can you believe that?'

'Jesus! What kind of stakes were they playing for?'

'The stakes weren't a consideration. It makes sense to call some booby's bluff when you're holding a royal flush. What was *really* insane was to stick that kind of money on the nose of a dodgy runner.'

'I didn't think bookies accepted bets that big?'

'They don't. He spread the money around a bit. *He's a rambler, he's a gambler . . .*' Richie swigged back some coffee, and then sent the cup skeetering across the table. '*Shit!*' he spat.

Ella did some quick calculations. 'He must have collected around ninety thousand,' she said.

'Yeah, 90 K's about right. He's being understandably coy about the exact amount – he doesn't want ten zillion people hitting him for a loan – but he says it's enough for him to buy into his own dive outfit.'

Her heart did a somersault. 'He's decided to stay on in Dublin?'

'No, no. He agreed to work the outfit in Jamaica for a minimum of six months, and he's a man of his word. He wouldn't let them down. But once he's through there he wants to try and invest in a joint of his own.'

'In Jamaica?'

'He's not sure. He'd be keen on Australia, but the visa thing might be a problem. In the Caribbean they apparently have ways of cutting through red tape if you have enough influence. And money is influence.' He raised a hand at the waitress and was studiously ignored. 'If that bitch doesn't bring me the bill soon I'm going to do a runner. You're looking very pensive all of a sudden.'

'Am I?' She took a sip of disgusting coffee. And another one. And another. And finally she said: 'So. Ferdia's not rich.'

Richie scoffed. 'Damn right he is.'

'No, no, what I mean is—' she took another sip of coffee – 'he wasn't rich till now.'

'No. Jesus, Ella! How can you touch that stuff! In fact, he was even poorer than me.'

'But you're *really* poor, Richie.' She hoped she didn't sound rude. She was just having considerable difficulty in processing all this new information.

'You forget that I have morphed into a whiz-kid telesalesperson.'

'Oh, yeah.' She *had* forgotten.

A silence fell. There was something funny about the way Richie was looking at her. 'Maybe you'd consider me as a serious suitor now that my dive god cousin is no longer going to be hanging around as a contender for your affections?' he blurted.

Ella turned crimson. 'What? How did you find out about us? Did he tell you?' she blurted back.

'What?'

Oh God. What had she said? Backtrack, Ella, backtrack.

'Did he tell me *what*?' insisted Richie.

'Um.' Ella was trying like mad to work out how she could backtrack, but it was no use.

She went redder and redder, and then realization dawned on Richie's face. 'Oh. Shit! It was *you*! It's *you* that's got him all messed up and emotional!'

She didn't say anything.

Richie shook his head in amazement. 'Jesus, Ella, I knew you fancied him, and I suspected it was reciprocated, but I didn't know it had got real. How did it happen? *When* did it happen?'

She relented. 'I met him at the races on Saturday.'

'And took him back to your place?'

Ella demurred.

'Oh, come on, girl! Don't go all coy on me now! Not now I've discovered you're Ferdia's nemesis. Shit. Trust my dive god cousin to rob me of my one and only true love.' He'd said it in a jokey voice, but Ella sensed that there was real regret somewhere under the clown face. She felt a little flash of guilt, and then she shook it off and answered him.

'No. We didn't go back to my place. He took me to a hotel –'

'Jesus Christ! Not the Trident!'

'No.' She permitted herself a small smile. 'Not the Trident. And not my gaff . . .'

She remembered how she hadn't invited him to stay at her gaff because she didn't want him to see how she really lived. What a joke! What a total, total klutz she'd been! How could she ever have thought that it would have made any difference to a man like him? Ferdia MacDiarmada wouldn't ever be taken in by stupid superficial trappings like posh cars and designer clothes and an 'It' girl lifestyle and all that – all that *materialistic* shit. He didn't belong to some horsy set who sat around on exclusive balconies at the races talking about Yehudi bloody Menuhin. She could see that now, and it absolutely made sense. He was suddenly revealed to her in a brand new light, and she liked what she saw. She really, *really* liked it. He hadn't taken her to the Clarence in some smooth display of his wealth and taste – he'd taken her there because he was celebrating the fact that his spectacular gamble earlier that day had paid off! Who *wouldn't* be tempted to cut some swank in a posh hotel if they'd just won a fortune?

This new knowledge was having a strange effect on her. Now that she knew Ferdia *wasn't* rich he was even *more* desirable. She was actually *relieved* he wasn't rich. She wanted to curse herself over and over. Why oh why had she been so foolish as to go around posing as something she wasn't? Why hadn't she picked up the phone to him weeks ago? Why hadn't he picked up the phone to *her*? But there was a reason for that, she figured. Relationships between instructors and trainees wouldn't exactly be encouraged by ActivMarine.

'Well, Ella?' Richie was still waiting for her to answer his question. 'Spill the beans. I want to know how to impress the next girl I fall for. By the sickeningly moony look on your face he obviously took you somewhere pretty special.'

'He took me to the Clarence.'

'The *Clarence!* No shit. You stayed overnight?'

She bit her lip and nodded. She knew she was still

a bit pink. 'In Room 508. It's the next best thing to the penthouse.'

'Wow! My cousin is *such* a smooth operator! Did he do the champagne thing?'

'Yeah.' She gave that dreamy smile again. She just couldn't help it. Then she jumped out of her reverie. 'Why? Does he do that with all the girls?'

Richie shook his head. 'Not that I know of. But it's kind of mandatory behaviour when you're staying in a joint as classy as the Clarence, isn't it?' He slumped back in his chair with a bewildered smile on his face. 'Well. Ferdia MacDiarmada really is a dark horse isn't he?'

Ella smiled back. 'You took the words right out of my mouth,' she said.

* * *

Patrick was looking pretty pissed off when Ella finally showed up in Daly's.

'Please don't be cross with me, Patrick!' she begged, as she threw her arms round his neck. 'I'm sorry I'm so late.'

Her uncle held her at arm's length and gave her a curious look. 'How could I be cross with someone who looks so radiant?' he said. 'What has happened in your life that suddenly makes it worth living again? I thought you'd trail in here looking like the Little Match Girl.'

'Who?'

'Didn't your mother ever read you fairy stories when you were a kid?'

'Um. No, actually.'

'Ask a stupid question . . .'

She sat down beside him and sent sign language to the barman to bring over two pints. Then she turned to her uncle. 'Now,' she said in a businesslike voice. 'Listen to me, Patrick. I did what you told me. I did a lot of thinking today, and I made a lot of decisions about my life. But the first thing I want to say is that I'm really, really sorry about the resigning thing. I'd just reached the end of my tether with Julian and there's no way I could—'

Patrick raised a hand to stop her in her tracks. 'It's cool, Ella. It's all sorted. I've done a bit of under-hand stuff.'

'What do you mean?'

'I've poached Dave Leary from On Line,' he said.

'*Dave?* Wow.' Ella was impressed. Dave Leary was a top-notch sound engineer. 'How on earth did you manage that?'

'I'd approached him ages ago, before Julian came on board. He said he'd think about it, and then he said no, but that I wasn't to be put off asking again in a year's time. So that's exactly what I did. And hey presto – the timing was perfect. He's ready to move on.'

'Right now?'

'No. He'll give them a month's notice and in the meantime we'll take a freelance on board.'

Ella made a rueful face. 'Shit, Patrick. This is going to cost you money, and it's all my fault.'

'It certainly is. Freelancers, pay increases – yes –' this in response to her slightly indignant look – 'Dave's looking for more than you ever got, but he'll be worth it.' He lit up a cigarette and leaned back in his seat. 'So *I'm* sorted. How about you? What are you going to do with your windfall?'

'Windfall?'

'Didn't you get the e-mail I sent you on Saturday?'

Accessing e-mail had been the last thing on her mind yesterday as she'd swigged back wine and droned along to Portishead. 'No.'

'Well, then, you're in for some surprise, toots. To the tune of £900.'

'*What?*'

'That horse you backed was a nice little earner for you.'

Ella was perplexed. 'But I only stuck a fiver on it.'

'I know you did. Dieter stuck ninety-five more on, though.'

'What do you mean?'

'He was doing it all afternoon, apparently. Upping the ante behind everyone's back. He must have lost a fortune, but at least you won one.'

Ella prinked. 'Hey! Cool! That'll take the sting out of being unemployed for a while! Good old Dieter.' She gave Patrick a radiant smile, which she turned on the barman as their pints arrived.

'Hello, Ella,' said the barman. 'You're looking very pleased with yourself this evening. What has you in such good form?'

'I'm in love,' she said with a candour so disarming that the barman said: 'Well. That's something to celebrate. These are on the house, so.' He ignored her proffered tenner, and returned to his zone behind the counter.

'In love?' queried Patrick. 'Has this anything to do with your hasty exit from the racecourse on Saturday evening?'

'Yes.'

'I thought as much. Leonie hinted to me that there was some man involved. Is it reciprocated?'

She gave him that radiant look again. 'Absolutely.'

'So tell me about it.'

And Ella proceeded to fill her uncle in on the events of the past couple of days. 'But the most brilliant thing of all, Patrick,' she said breathlessly as she came to the end of her story, 'is that he's not who I thought he was!'

'Translate.'

'He's not rich.'

'And this is a *good* thing?'

'Yes, yes! Oh – it's too complicated to explain –' she shot a quick look at her watch – 'and I'm in one hell of a hurry. He's throwing a farewell party out in Portdelvin tonight, and I need to get out there. He needs to know that I'm not rich either.'

'You're *not* rich.'

448

'I know, I know! I *told* you it was complicated. But it all has a lot to do with something Dad said to me at Christmas. He said that dreams can come true if you pursue them hard enough.'

Patrick was looking sceptical. 'Darling – it's your dad you're talking about, not the Dalai Lama.'

'Don't be cynical, Patrick – please? I have to try – can't you see that?'

There was a long pause. Then Patrick said: 'So. What's going to happen when this dive god goes away?'

'I've been thinking about that too.' Ella gave a little frown of concentration. 'I could go and visit him in Jamaica. I'll be going there in November, anyway, for Leonie's wedding. And then when he sets up his dive outfit in the Caribbean I could work for him. Help out in his shop or something.'

'He's setting up his own dive outfit?'

'Yes, and—'

'I thought you said he was poor. How can he afford it?'

'Well, he's really loaded, but that's far too complicated to go into right now—'

'Ella, Ella.' Her uncle was looking at her with concern. 'I know your dad encouraged you to chase a dream, but is this it? You're a talented musician. You're a highly respected sound engineer. You're seriously considering giving everything up to go and work in some dive outfit in the Caribbean?'

'Well – it might be Australia. It depends on the visa situation.' She reached for his hand and leaned

449

towards him. 'Look. I've felt *pinioned* for so long, Patrick. D'you know what I mean? I've got to do some flying. I've *got* to take some risks in my life.' She thought of the extraordinary risk that Ferdia had taken. That uncompromising bet he'd put on the Dark Horse. If it hadn't come in first, he'd have lost everything. 'I can't walk on the woolly side for ever.'

'The woolly side?'

'You know. Cotton-woolly. As opposed to the wild side. I've played it safe for too long.'

Patrick still looked dubious. 'Jesus, Ella. First you pack in your job, and now you're running off to the Caribbean with some geezer you hardly know. Don't you think you should take things a bit slower?'

'No.'

Patrick looked at her with thoughtful eyes. Then he laughed and gave a resigned shrug. 'There's no arguing with that "no". I know by the mutinous way you set your chin.'

Ella laughed. 'Thank you. I love you, Patrick,' she said. Then, just as she leaned over to kiss her uncle, the door of the pub opened and Julian Bollard slid through like slime. 'Aagh – look – I'm out of here! There's Julian coming in. I thought you said he'd be toiling over a hot Audiofile?'

'He's obviously finished. Have you any idea what time it is?' Patrick stretched out his arm and showed her his wristwatch.

Ella's hand flew to her mouth. 'Oh, no! My watch

is running slow! Hell's teeth – that party will be kicking by now! I gotta run, Patrick.' She dropped another kiss on her uncle's cheek, then jumped up and slung her backpack over her shoulder.

'Ella?'

She turned round. Her face was flushed with excitement, her eyes were bright with love.

'Take care. I don't want to have to start scraping you off the ceiling if things don't work out.'

'They *will* work out, Patrick. All I have to do is hold onto what Dad said. Remember? Dreams can come true if you pursue them hard enough! I'll talk to you tomorrow!'

And then she was weaving her way through the crowded pub, running late for her date with destiny.

Chapter Eighteen

The DART took her to Portdelvin. It was much later than she'd have liked by the time she arrived at the Trident hotel. The receptionist in the lobby told her that the function rooms were on the first floor. Ella ran up the steps with a hammering heart and a mouth drier than 007's martini, abstractedly registering a horrible oil painting of Neptune on the landing. The sea god was standing on a chariot waving his trident, wearing such a ferocious expression that he looked more like a devil than a deity.

The music spilling out through the open door of one of the rooms told her where the party was. The place was jammed. Ferdia was obviously a popular bloke. Ella paused on the threshold and scanned the crowd, looking for him. What would she say when she saw him? As far as he was concerned, she'd said her final farewell to him yesterday morning. She'd told him quite categorically that she wouldn't be able to make his party – how to explain the sudden change of heart? But they'd been lovers, after all! Lovers didn't need words to communicate with each other. Maybe they'd just look at each other and *know*.

'Hey! There you are!' Richie was swinging his way towards her through the crowd.

'Hello again,' said Ella, glad to see her unlikely Cupid. He'd remarked – as he'd finally managed to settle the bill for the disgusting coffee earlier – on the irony of the situation. How bloody, bloody unfair it was that he should be acting as a go-between for his cousin and the object of his own desire!

He dropped a kiss on her cheek. 'I saw you come in. You looked like a frightened doe.'

'Oh, God, did I? I was trying hard to look cool.' She snuck a surreptitious look over his shoulder, but it wasn't surreptitious enough, because Richie copped on at once.

'Don't worry – he's here,' he said. 'Last time I looked he was out on the balcony swigging back Jack Daniel's and gazing at the moon in a sickeningly soulful way. How's that for reassurance?'

She felt a rush of something. Whether it was adrenalin or endorphins she wasn't sure. 'Did you tell him you'd run into me?'

'No. I want to see the expression on his face when he gets a load of you. You look great.'

'You're sweet. That's the second time you've said that to me today.'

'I'll say it again if you like. Hell, Ella – you'd look great to me even if you were wearing Fergie's cast-offs. My cousin is a lucky dog, and I hate his guts.' He took her by the hand and started threading his way through the crowd. 'I should be charging him

453

a fee for this. Maybe I should set up a dating agency. I could call it Richie's Rides.'

She gave him a dig with her elbow. 'Jesus, Richie. You are incorrigible.'

He smiled down at her. 'Although, having said that, I wouldn't have thought you were an obvious match for Ferdia.'

'Thanks.'

'No offence meant. It's just that he has a thing for older women, usually.'

For some reason this produced an unpleasant flutter in the pit of her stomach.

'So I suppose you're the exception that proves the rule,' he added.

The French windows that led onto the balcony were open. Ella was dying for some air. It was hot and muggy in the function room, and her face had flared up and the palms of her hands were slithery with nervous sweat.

'I'll let you go first,' Richie whispered in her ear. She could tell by his voice he was smiling. 'Hell, is he in for a surprise!'

Ella took a deep breath, and then she stepped out onto the balcony.

Ferdia was leaning against the wall to her right. Except he wasn't on his own. He had a woman in his arms and they were indulging in a seriously sexy kiss. Ella froze for a fraction of a second, then spun round and barged straight into Richie, who let out a yelp as she stood on his toe. In her peripheral vision she saw Ferdia glance up, and the woman in his arms turn around. She was svelte, Italianate, forty-ish. It was the woman he'd bonked all night that weekend at Lissamore. It was posh Philippa.

Ella made an inarticulate noise and shouldered her way back into the party, aware that Richie was hot on her heels. Gyrating bodies and unfamiliar faces swam into focus and then receded. She had to get away from this *danse macabre*; she needed air. She wove her way across the floor as slowly as if she was wading through water. She was a drowning woman, a diver who'd gone too deep and whose gauge had hit empty. At last she reached the door. She bolted through it and clattered down the stairs, practically hyperventilating, with Richie still behind her. Satan waved his trident at her from the wall, banishing her to hell.

Richie caught up with her on the front steps. 'Stop, Ella! Stop!' He stretched out a hand and grabbed her sleeve, but she shrugged him off. 'Please stop.' This time he reached for her arm with both his hands and succeeded in physically restraining her. 'Stop.' They were both breathless. Ella's face was crimson, and she was weeping tears of humiliation so hot they scalded her cheeks. 'Oh God, Ella. I'm sorry. I am so, so sorry. I had no idea.' Richie's voice was hoarse with pain for her. She tried to break free again, but he took her in his arms and clasped her against his chest until she slumped like a rag doll, and let herself be held. She sobbed and sobbed, inhaling raggedly. Oh

God! He smelt like Ferdia! That same clean, soapy smell . . . Ella sobbed even more shamelessly. 'There, now. There,' murmured Richie. 'Get it all out. It's OK. Shh, shh.'

He led her to the steps of the hotel, and they sat down, Ella leaning her head against Richie's shoulder. She wept like a child while he rocked and soothed her. 'There, there,' he crooned, over and over into her ear. 'Shh. There now. Good girl. It's OK. Everything's going to be all right.'

It was amazing the effect the clichéd words of comfort produced in her. Gradually, gradually she calmed, until her flood of tears had dried up into a trickle of gulps and hiccups. She felt as she had done once when she was a little girl, when her uncle had comforted her after a bad fall.

When he could see that she had cried herself out, Richie produced a rather grubby tissue from his pocket and wiped her cheeks, and then he held it up to her nose and instructed her to blow. 'Whoa,' he said. 'How could such a pretty little nose produce so much snot?'

Ella managed the wannest smile of her life, and then she stood up.

'Thanks, Rich,' she said. 'You are a chum. I mean that.' There was nothing more to be said. 'I'll see you.' She turned away and started walking down the footpath.

Richie stood and watched her. 'Are you going home?' he asked.

'No,' she said, turning back to him. He looked

quite bereft. 'I'm going to do what stupid girls always do when they make fools of themselves.'

'What's that?' he asked.

'I'm going for a long walk. And I'm going to lick my wounds.'

She started walking towards the pier.

'Ella?' He sounded uncertain. 'Ella – you're not going to do anything – well – *daft*, are you?'

She gave a hollow laugh. '"Men have died from time to time," Rich,' she lobbed back over her shoulder. '"And worms have eaten them, but not for love." Shakespeare.' She walked on.

The people she passed on the promenade were all bad-tempered and ratty looking, and suddenly Ella felt flooded with misanthropy, riddled with nihilism, and swamped with self-loathing. She remembered something her mother had used to chant, in the days before she'd fled to the arms of her lover in Tuscany: *Oh how I hate the human race. Oh how I hate its ugly face . . .*

She heard running feet behind her. In a movie, this would be Ferdia, come to rescue her from hideous reality. But her life wasn't a movie, and of course it wasn't Ferdia. It was Richie. 'Look. Do you want me to come with you?' he said.

'No, no, Richie. Thanks for the offer. I just need to be on my own for a while. Try and shake off these black dogs.'

'OK. I understand.' He hung back, and she advanced a couple more paces. Then: 'Can I follow you down after a decent interval?' he asked. 'I owe you a drink after what happened back there. And you probably need one.'

She stopped again. He was silhouetted against the marine blue spotlight that illuminated the front of the hotel, looking very tall and very authoritative and very reassuring. She smiled at him. 'You are such a nice man, Rich,' she said. 'You are the nicest man I know, and – yeah. I really would like a drink.' She took in a great, shuddering sigh. 'You'll give me about half an hour to exorcize my demons though, won't you?'

'Sure.' He stood and watched her go, and then he turned and went back up the steps of the Trident hotel.

Ella walked fast to the end of the long pier, with her head down and her hands in her jeans pockets. It had been a hot day, but now it was muggy, and the darkening sky was even darker where storm clouds were gathering on the horizon.

Her internal voice was vociferous as it berated her. 'You stupid, stupid bitch,' it said. 'You first-class klutz. What were you *thinking* of? What pooka got into your brain and persuaded you that Ferdia MacDiarmada would be interested in a girl like you? You'd witnessed at first *hand* the kind of women he's into. Why couldn't you have taken on board the evidence of what you'd seen with your own two short-sighted eyes?' Even Julian had pointed it out to her! *I've seen some very classy broads indeed make idiots of themselves over Ferdia* . . . 'Why couldn't you have *recognized* that

458

the only thing the two of you had in common was sex? Common being the operative word. After all, it's pretty *common* behaviour to let yourself be smooth-talked into a one-night stand, isn't it? *Isn't it?* No girl with an ounce of self-esteem, an ounce of self-respect would have been the walkover you were.' What contempt Ferdia MacDiarmada must have felt for her as he got on the DART on Sunday morning: trading an acquiescent bitch on heat for a class piece of ass like posh Philippa – a dame so besotted with him that she'd travelled all the way across Ireland for his farewell party!

Oh God. She was inflicting such pain upon herself that she started to weep again, awash with self-hatred and despair. She slumped against the pier wall, and stopped her ears with her fists, but the voice was merciless.

'"I could go and visit him in Jamaica!"' it mocked her. '"And then when he sets up his dive outfit in the Caribbean I could work for him! Help out in his shop or something!"' Oh, *Jesus.* How could she have been so *naïve*? '"I can tell you are a fighter!"' continued the voice in its relentless mimicry. It sounded like the voice of a ventriloquist's dummy. '"You can make a dream come true if you pursue it long enough!"'

Oh God! Where had she been *living* for the past few hours? She'd taken a first-class ticket to Cloud Cuckoo Land, on a flying visit. But at least it had been a return ticket. She, Ella Nesbit, had been shuttled unceremoniously back to Real Life, for a crash landing with no survivors.

And now the image of Ferdia on the balcony shimmered before her mind's eye, devastating in its lucidity. In his arms, posh Philippa. Everything that she could never be. It was *she* who had lured Ferdia into the emotional rough patch that Richie had told her about. It was staring her in the face now. Ferdia hadn't been referring to *Ella* when he'd mentioned the Lissamore dive weekend to his cousin. He'd been referring to Philippa. Ferdia MacDiarmada was obviously just a bastard who thought with his cock.

She sat there, staring out to sea with unseeing eyes. Were all men like that? No. Of course they weren't. She remembered – she remembered – Raphael. Was he staring out to sea, too, right now, on that green island on the other side of the world? Her gorgeous, gorgeous, gentle Rastafarian. The most soulful, beautiful man she'd ever met. She remembered the altruism that had radiated from his eyes with a lustre that she had never seen in any man's eyes before or since. Until . . . until . . . Tonight. That look had been in Richie's eyes tonight. How concerned he had been for her when he'd registered the enormity of her anguish! How good he'd smelt when he'd held her close, letting her tears soak into the fabric of his shirt! He'd even had a tissue! How reassuring he'd been, how *there* for her, how *caring* . . .

She heard her own shaky intake of breath. Had

her Mr Right been under her nose all along? She'd always thought of Richie as a pal, a mate, someone to lark around with. She'd never thought of him in a sexual way at all. He was just a boy friend. But he wasn't a boy. He was an attractive man . . .

She glanced over her shoulder, and saw him now, a dark shape lounging against the wall at the other end of the pier, watching her. She looked out to sea again, and when she looked back she saw that he had started to make his way along the pier towards her, not hurrying, taking his time, obviously wanting to allow her all the headspace she needed. Ella turned and focused on the horizon. A breeze ruffled the water and the salty, tangy smell of sea came to her, drying the salt tears on her face. And then she became aware of another scent mingling with the sea smells. Clean, musky, masculine – with a top note of vanilla . . .

'Hi, Rich,' she said, in a very small, subdued voice. 'Thanks for looking out for me.' She got to her feet and turned to him. But it wasn't Richie who was standing there. It was Ferdia.

For the second time that evening she froze. He stood quite still, too, looking down at her. Oh, God! Had he taken pity on her? Had Richie told him that she deserved, at the very least, an *explanation* after what he'd put her through? Had Richie ignited the spark of guilt that had prompted him to come down onto the pier and explain, gently, exactly why he wasn't interested in more than just a casual fling? Men had done that to her before in the past, and she'd always had a sneaking suspicion that there was an element of *schadenfreude* in their admissions. They'd dipped their barbs in treacle before they'd shot her down, watching her plummet back to earth with a mildly sadistic pleasure. Was that how Ferdia would do it? Smile as he twisted the knife?

'What do you want?' she asked, dreading the answer.

'You,' he said. And he took her face between his hands and kissed her and kissed her and kissed her.

*   *   *

They went back to the Trident hotel, but they didn't go back to the party.

It was like a re-enactment of the evening in the Clarence, with Ella loitering in reception while Ferdia booked a room for them. And even though the Trident was vastly inferior to U2's joint, for Ella it was the most beautiful place on earth. She bestowed beaming smiles on the indifferent receptionist, she thought the fabric flowers in the lobby were lovelier than the real thing, and their room – when the key was finally located – was like something out of a fairy tale, with a Gauguin painting on the wall, a charming old-fashioned blue candlewick bedspread on the bed, and a view over the sea. She was in heaven, and there was a god. Her very own beautiful Dive God.

They went straight to bed. And after their first fuck they said, simultaneously: 'We need to talk.'

And then they fell upon each other and fucked each other silly all over again.

Finally, around midnight, they lay exhausted on the bed, not touching, just looking into each other's eyes. From the street below came the usual drunken post-party sounds.

'You missed your farewell party,' said Ella.

'I didn't miss it at all. I was having a horrible time at that party. I had a much better time here with you. Thank you very much.'

She gave him a sceptical look. 'You didn't look as if you were having a horrible time when I walked in on you.'

'I had a *seriously* horrible time trying to extricate myself from Philippa's tender embrace, I can tell you. That took some diplomacy.'

Ella remembered the tearful row that had gone on in the bedroom next door to hers in Lissamore. 'Was she very upset?'

'You could say that. The minute I got away I cornered Richie at the bar and asked him where you'd gone. I needed to clear things up with you before heading off to Jamaica.' She wished he hadn't brought up the subject of Jamaica. She couldn't ask the question that begged to be asked. *Will you miss me?* It hung unspoken on her lips for a long moment before Ferdia said, 'I'll miss you, you know.'

Oh God. 'Really?' She gave a too-casual shrug. A little dismissive laugh that sounded unconvincing even to her own ears. 'But you hardly know me.'

He smiled. 'I've a hunch I know you better than you think.'

'What do you mean?'

'I enjoyed observing you. You were pretending for ages, weren't you? To be somebody you weren't.'

She coloured. 'What do you mean?' she asked again. She knew she was stalling. The expression in his eyes told her he'd seen through her so easily she might have been plate glass.

'You seemed to put on an act. Not all the time; but sometimes I got the impression that you were trying very hard to be – what's the word I'm looking for?'

There was no point in dissembling. He'd got her spot on. 'Sophisticated?'

'That's almost right, but there's a better word. *Urbane.* That's it. It seemed to me that you'd constructed some kind of elaborate defence mechanism. It kept me off your case for ages.' Oh, *God*! What a bad joke her life was! 'I used to find it funny,' he added.

'Funny? Funny as in intriguing?' She remembered what Leonie had said about her being like a riddle wrapped in a mystery inside an enigma.

'No. Funny as in amusing. Especially when the urbane veneer kept slipping, and I'd catch you doing a pratfall. Like that time you turned up hungover for your first dive and flashed your stocking tops at me. That wasn't a terribly urbane thing to do, but it was fantastically sexy.'

OK. So her attempts at being urbane had been

pathetic. But she was starting to like what she was hearing. 'You fancied me then?'

'God, yes.' He leaned on his elbow and looked down at her gravely. 'You'd started stealing into my thoughts like a little cat burglar, Ella Nesbit. At first I tried to ignore you, but then you started visiting me more and more often. Especially at night. You were responsible for some of the sweetest dreams I've ever had.' His head dropped back onto the pillow. She reached for one of the dreadlocks that spilled over the pillowcase and started to twist it round her finger. 'Hell – remember that time you performed your safety stop in Lissamore? I almost couldn't maintain eye contact with you my erection was bothering me so much.'

'Oh!' The endorphin rush she experienced on hearing this was so intense she tingled.

'And then, that time you wandered out of the bedroom next to mine—'

'I heard you bonking in there all night. I hardly got any sleep that time!'

'Sorry about that. When I realized you'd been listening I got seriously turned on.'

'Pervert.'

'Absolutely.' He gave her a smile that made her want to melt. 'But the most apocalyptic moment had to be when you played your fiddle at me. That was the best foreplay I ever had.' She leaned over and kissed him. 'However, some small, smart-arsed voice of reason was warning me off at the same time.'

'Oh? Why?'

'I didn't think my life needed any more complications before I left for Jamaica. And now look what you've gone and done.'

'Complicated things?'

'You, my funny, sexy little violin-playing princess, have complicated things more effectively than a kitten with a ball of twine.'

They exchanged rueful smiles. Then, simultaneously, their smiles faded as lust flared up again. But this time her orgasm, ecstatic as it was, was marred for Ella by one tiny little niggling thought that gnawed at the back of her mind like a miniature terrier. We *really* need to talk, she thought.

And eventually, some time in the early hours of the morning, they did talk. They talked for a long, long time. He told her about his plans for setting up his own dive outfit, and Ella told him about having quit her job. He told her about how his co-shareholders in the Dark Horse had been responsible for the private suite and the helicopter that had transported him to Leopardstown, and she told him how Dieter had been responsible for the champagne and the limo that had transported her there. They talked about loads of things. They filled each other in on their childhoods, and Ella told him how she had spent most of hers rigid with mortification at the antics of her family. She even told him about how she had used to try and disguise her violin case by wrapping it in her coat and carrying it vertically against her chest, because she was sick of being teased about it at school.

'The violin wasn't sexy in those days,' she explained. 'I really resented having to study it. I always wanted to be the girl drummer in some cool band. How did you cope?'

'It never bothered me. People used to make remarks about it being namby-pamby, but I didn't care. I was doing it because I wanted to.' He turned his face to hers on the pillow and smiled. 'Being physically big helped. People didn't make remarks more than once. Your ex-colleague Julian tried to be withering about it on a couple of occasions, but when I warned him to back off he just reverted to bullying the juniors.'

'He mentioned that he'd been to school with you.'

'He was a gobshite even then.' He laughed. 'You should have seen the horrified expression on his face the first time he turned up at ActivMarine and realized that not only was his namby-pamby violin-playing old classmate a master instructor, but that he also had the bad luck to be allocated to my training group. He hasn't stopped bum-sucking me since.'

'And you thought he was my *friend*? How *could* you, Ferdia?'

'Well, he acted very pally with you. It was an easy enough mistake to make. I have to say you went down a bit in my estimation when I thought you were mates.'

467

'Jesus! He's the reason I am now unemployed.'

'Poor Ella.' He spoke the words lightly, but she read concern in his eyes. 'Any idea as to what you might do?'

'Maybe I could work for you when you have your own joint in the Caribbean,' she said in a jokey voice, hoping he'd say, Hey! What a great idea!

But of course he didn't. He just laughed. 'I'd love to get a load of you lugging tanks about all day, princess.' Then he looked thoughtful. 'Are you going to look for work in another studio, or are you still dreaming about playing professionally?'

'Still dreaming,' she said. 'But reality bites, I suppose. I'll have to start phoning around. See if anyone's looking for a sound engineer.'

'But if someone offered you work as a professional violinist, you'd take it?'

'Like a shot.'

'Anywhere in the world?'

'Except Jury's cabaret,' she said.

'OK.' He was looking at her very strangely. 'I have an idea coming on. Have a look at this.' He reached for his jacket where it lay on the floor, and pulled a sheet of fax paper from the pocket.

'What is it?'

'Read it.'

She scanned the page and found her mouth curving into a slow smile. 'Is she serious?' she asked.

'It's worth a try. Give her a ring.'

'At this hour of the night?'

He looked at his watch. 'It's only ten o'clock in the evening over there.'

Ella picked up the phone and dialled 9 for an outside line. Then she consulted the fax sheet and punched in a lot of numbers. 'Is this completely bonkers?' she asked, as she waited for the connection to be made.

'She liked you, didn't she?'

'Yes. I think so.'

He narrowed his eyes at her, assessing her. 'Did you get a cocktail named after you?'

'Yes.'

'Then she liked you. What did she call it?'

'The cocktail?' She gave him a smug smile, feeling very pleased with herself indeed for having earned such a groovy moniker. 'She called it a Siamese Fighter.'

'Really?' he said, lounging back against the pillows. 'I would have thought Sea Horse would have been more appropriate, myself.'

She looked puzzled. 'Why?'

'Because you're such an astonishingly good ride, of course.' Ferdia grinned at her, but before she could aim a kick at him, she heard the phone on the other end ringing.

In Jamaica, Desirée picked up.

Ella braced herself. She could hardly believe she was doing this. 'Desirée?' she said in as bright a tone as she could muster. 'You probably don't remember me. It's Ella Nesbit here, calling from Ireland. I certified with you last—'

'Ella! My Siamese Fighter! Of course I remember you! Hey! What's this about! Why are you calling me from halfway across the world?'

'You sent a fax today, Desirée – to Ferdia MacDiarmada?'

'That's right, honey! How is that bad boy?'

Ella glanced over to where Ferdia was reclining like a naked pasha against a bank of pillows, yawning expansively and looking sexier than any man had a right to look. The rush of lust she felt made her smile. 'He's bad, all right. And as a matter of fact, he's here with me now. We're in a hotel in a place called Portdelvin.'

Desirée laughed down the phone. 'Raphael done got it right again, as usual! He said you two should get it together! You give that Ferdia a big kiss from me, girl!'

Ella felt shy, suddenly. She was almost too embarrassed to ask what she wanted to ask. It was such a long shot . . . She took a deep breath. 'The thing is, Desirée – you put a kind of jokey PS on that fax. Suggesting that Ferdia bring his violin with him?'

Another laugh from Desirée. 'I was only half joking, honey chile. That Diandra done run off with a wealthy Mexican gentleman, and there's no-one around Salamander Cove to serenade those diners at night.'

'Desirée?' Another deep breath. 'Would I do?'

There was a beat, and then another, during which

Ella's heart plummeted. What a wuss she was to have made this phone call!

'Would you *do*!' Desirée's voice was on the line again, sounding nearly an octave higher. 'As a serenader? Honey – are you serious?'

'Yes. I know it's not your brief, but you're the only person there who will remember me. I'm good—'

'I *know* that, honey. I remember. You had some gentleman from New York offer you a job. And not only are you good, but you're damn easy on the eye. Dem tourists like to look at a pretty girl while they eat.' Desirée's voice slid into a more confidential tone. 'You and Ferdia have hooked up good and proper, yeah?'

'Well – yes. We're – um.' She didn't want to be too expansive while he was lounging there listening. 'We're . . .'

'You happy, honey?' crooned Desirée.

'Oh, *God* – yes I am!'

'Then I cannot have my Leopard Shark unhappy without you, can I? I cannot have him work my outfit, pining all the time for his woman back in Ireland. I know how bad my man Raphael would feel without his Desirée to keep him warm at night.'

'So?' Oh, God. Ella was beginning to allow herself to hope. 'Do you think you could run it by management for me?'

'Well, honey, this strikes me as being something so fortuitous that we will have to *make* it happen! Put me on to that bad boy.'

'OK.' She felt weak with anticipation. 'Desirée – if this pans out, I owe you. Bigtime.'

'If you want something badly enough in this life honey, you can get it. That's what I always say.'

'That's funny.' Ella smiled down the phone. 'That's what my dad says, too. Here's your Leopard Shark.' She handed the phone to Ferdia and sat down on the bed.

'Desirée! Darlin'! How's it going?'

Ella heard an indistinct burble coming over the receiver.

'Yeah, yeah,' said Ferdia, with a broad smile. 'Yeah. I'm looking forward to it, too.'

More burble.

Then: 'She plays a real mean fiddle, Desirée. *Much* meaner than me. It would be kind of nice if we could wangle it so we worked the same joint. I am kind of fond of her, yeah.'

Ella was staring at him, her mouth a little O of anticipation. He smiled down at her, and slid his thumb into it.

'Yeah. Will you do that for me? You are a star. Her? She is a princess. But you know that already. I will hear from you later? Excellent. If this works out, then she's going to have to start packing her bags fast. Oh, you know me. I always travel light. Yeah. Just my dive bag and my backpack. And a bottle of duty-free Jack Daniel's for my favourite dive mistress. You, of course.'

A laugh over the receiver, and then a laconic burble.

'Take care yourself, honey chile. See you next week.' And Ferdia put the phone down.

'It looks like you might have a job,' he said, sliding his thumb out of Ella's mouth.

Her hands flew to her face. 'Oh, God! What did she say?'

'She said yes. She said she would have no problem persuading them. Apparently the staff still talk about the night you played in the Pagoda restaurant.'

'Oh God!' Endorphins surged and bubbled out of her and exploded all around them like glittering angel dust. 'Oh, my God! Are you serious? Are you really, really serious, Ferdia?' She knelt up on the bed and flung her arms around him. 'I cannot believe this! This is like a dream come true!' She sat back on her hunkers suddenly, eyes wide, hands clamped over her mouth. '*Am* I dreaming?' she asked.

Ferdia reached over and pinched her nipple. 'Did you feel that?' he asked.

'Yes.' She gazed up at him, moony with love. 'It felt lovely.'

'Then you're not dreaming,' he said.

* * *

She packed all her belongings into boxes and Ferdia delivered them in the dive van to her uncle's garage. All she needed was her violin case and a backpack and a plane ticket – which was more than

473

adequately covered by the £900 the Dark Horse had won for her. She didn't even need her jabs. She'd had them the last time she'd been to Salamander Cove. Ferdia went white when she told him how the needle had slipped, and she filed that little observation away under: 'Things I Know About Ferdia', resolving to take it out and torture him with it the next time he annoyed her. She e-mailed the manager of the resort, and made another phone call to Desirée to sing her praises for fixing things for her.

Leonie phoned Ella on the evening of her arrival at Salamander Cove, to wish her happy birthday. Arriving in the resort on the day of her birthday was the best present she could have had. Apart from what Ferdia had given her, of course.

'How are things?' asked Leonie. 'Is it as gorgeous as ever?'

'Oh – it's even better!' replied Ella happily, curling up on the bed. She was wearing her favourite sarong and a hibiscus blossom in her hair and absolutely nothing else. 'You know the way there always seemed to be a kind of pink glow in the air?'

'Yes?'

'Well, it was even pinker today.'

'That's what love does to a place,' observed Leonie sagely. 'Unless your sunglasses are rose-tinted. What's your room like?'

'Smaller than ours was, but with the same amazing view.' It was getting dark outside. The sky was like inky blue velvet. On the headland that jutted into the bay, she could just make out the shape of a man sitting, contemplating the ocean. A tiny pinprick of red flared, and she knew it was a joint. Raphael? The figure rose suddenly, and raised a hand high in the air, as in a gesture of benediction. Her guardian angel! She blinked, and he was gone.

Leonie sighed. 'I can't wait to see it again. The sooner Dieter finishes all his wheeling and dealing and wraps up the business the better.'

'Have you finally fixed a date?'

'The last week in November. Around the same time as we went out there last year. Heavens above and eat my socks! A whole year will have gone by!'

'Yup. Just like in *A Tale of Two Cities*.'

'What on earth are you rambling on about, Ella? I suppose you've been doing nothing but smoke ganja since you got there.'

'*A Tale of Two Cities*. "It was the best of times. It was the worst of times." Remember? Famous opening lines. Anyway, that's what last year was like.'

'Ronan!' Leonie spoke crossly to her cat. 'Yeuch! He's just spat a furball out onto my Turkish runner. Bastard. Now – what was I going to ask you? Oh, yes – will you serenade Dieter and me every time we dine in that restaurant? What was it called? The Pavilion?'

'Nice try, Leonie. It was the Pagoda.'

'Oh. Right. When are you starting work?'

'Day after tomorrow. They've allowed us some time to get over our jet lag.'

'How will you spend it?'

Ella looked at the balcony where Ferdia, naked but for a white towel slung round his hips, was looking out over the deep blue Caribbean sea. He turned round to her and smiled. He was wreathed in blue smoke, and his blond dreadlocks were haloed around his head, and she thought she might swoon with love for him. Her dive god!

'Oh. How do you think, Leonie?'

'Aqua diving?'

'Except we divers don't call it aqua diving.'

'Oh? What do you call it?'

'We call it "Going Down,"' said Ella, as Ferdia MacDiarmada took a last toke, tossed away the roach, and walked towards the bed. 'I have to go now, Leonie,' she said. 'I'll e-mail you soon, all right? Goodbye.'

'You don't mean "goodbye", Ella. You mean "one love".'

'Yes,' said Ella. 'Yes. I do. One love.'

THE END

IT MEANS MISCHIEF
by Kate Thompson

'More than enough colour to enliven even the dreariest day'
Irish Independent

Young Dublin actress Deirdre O'Dare has just landed her first big role and desperately wants to shine – and to impress David, the director she has fallen madly in love with.

But while Deirdre loves David, David loves leading lady Eva. Meanwhile, Sebastian and Rory wait in the wings . . .

A funny, entertaining and sexy backstage tale set in Dublin's theatre world, *It Means Mischief* details the romantic adventures of a young woman who – during one long, hot summer – discovers the difference between infatuation, lust and love.

'A terrific, gossipy tale of lovey-dovey Dublin theatre folk . . . Unputdownable'
Irish Post

A Bantam Paperback
0553 81245 9

MORE MISCHIEF
by Kate Thompson

'A funny, romantic and gloriously escapist read'
MARIAN KEYES

Life is sweet for rising stage and TV soap star Deirdre O'Dare. But jealous fears, spawned by arch-rival Sophie, that roguish boyfriend Rory is having a Hollywood fling threaten to ruin her happiness. Retreating from Dublin to the hauntingly beautiful West of Ireland to work on a screenplay and lick her wounds, she meets gorgeous Gabriel – straight out of the Diet Coke ad and squire of the local manor. How could a girl possibly refuse?

In this moving and wickedly funny tale by the bestselling author of *It Means Mischief,* Deirdre O'Dare learns some painful, enlightening and hilarious lessons about the art of life and love as she comes face to face with the most difficult decision she's ever had to make.

A Bantam Paperback
0553 81246 7

A SELECTION OF FINE NOVELS
AVAILABLE FROM BANTAM BOOKS

THE PRICES SHOWN BELOW WERE CORRECT AT THE TIME OF GOING TO PRESS.
HOWEVER TRANSWORLD PUBLISHERS RESERVE THE RIGHT TO SHOW NEW
RETAIL PRICES ON COVERS WHICH MAY DIFFER FROM THOSE PREVIOUSLY
ADVERTISED IN THE TEXT OR ELSEWHERE.

50329 4	DANGER ZONES	*Sally Beauman*	£5.99
50630 7	DARK ANGEL	*Sally Beauman*	£6.99
50631 5	DESTINY	*Sally Beauman*	£6.99
40727 9	LOVERS AND LIARS	*Sally Beauman*	£5.99
50326 X	SEXTET	*Sally Beauman*	£5.99
40497 0	CHANGE OF HEART	*Charlotte Bingham*	£5.99
40890 9	DEBUTANTES	*Charlotte Bingham*	£5.99
40895 X	THE NIGHTINGALE SINGS	*Charlotte Bingham*	£5.99
17635 8	TO HEAR A NIGHTINGALE	*Charlotte Bingham*	£5.99
50500 9	GRAND AFFAIR	*Charlotte Bingham*	£5.99
40296 X	IN SUNSHINE OR IN SHADOW	*Charlotte Bingham*	£5.99
40496 2	NANNY	*Charlotte Bingham*	£5.99
40117 8	STARDUST	*Charlotte Bingham*	£5.99
50717 6	THE KISSING GARDEN	*Charlotte Bingham*	£5.99
50501 7	LOVE SONG	*Charlotte Bingham*	£5.99
50718 4	THE LOVE KNOT	*Charlotte Bingham*	£5.99
81274 2	THE BLUE NOTE	*Charlotte Bingham*	£5.99
40973 5	A CRACK IN FOREVER	*Jeannie Brewer*	£5.99
17504 1	DAZZLE	*Judith Krantz*	£5.99
17242 5	I'LL TAKE MANHATTAN	*Judith Krantz*	£5.99
40730 9	LOVERS	*Judith Krantz*	£5.99
17174 7	MISTRAL'S DAUGHTER	*Judith Krantz*	£5.99
17389 8	PRINCESS DAISY	*Judith Krantz*	£5.99
40731 7	SPRING COLLECTION	*Judith Krantz*	£5.99
17503 3	TILL WE MEET AGAIN	*Judith Krantz*	£5.99
17505 X	SCRUPLES TWO	*Judith Krantz*	£5.99
40732 5	THE JEWELS OF TESSA KENT	*Judith Krantz*	£5.99
81287 4	APARTMENT 3B	*Patricia Scanlan*	£5.99
81290 4	FINISHING TOUCHES	*Patricia Scanlan*	£5.99
81286 6	FOREIGN AFFAIRS	*Patricia Scanlan*	£5.99
81288 2	PROMISES, PROMISES	*Patricia Scanlan*	£5.99
40941 7	MIRROR, MIRROR	*Patricia Scanlan*	£5.99
40943 3	CITY GIRL	*Patricia Scanlan*	£5.99
40946 8	CITY WOMAN	*Patricia Scanlan*	£5.99
81291 2	CITY LIVES	*Patricia Scanlan*	£5.99
81245 9	IT MEANS MISCHIEF	*Kate Thompson*	£5.99
81246 7	MORE MISCHIEF	*Kate Thompson*	£5.99

All Transworld titles are available by post from:

Bookpost, PO Box 29, Douglas, Isle of Man, IM99 1BQ

Credit cards accepted. Please telephone 01624 836000,
fax 01624 837033, Internet http://www.bookpost.co.uk
or e-mail: bookshop@enterprise.net for details

Free postage and packing in the UK. Overseas customers:
allow £1 per book (paperbacks) and £3 per book (hardbacks)